Pioneers of Ethnomusicology

To Alan P. Merriam (1923–1980), who foresaw the need for such a book

Pioneers of Ethnomusicology

Mervyn McLean

Llumina Press

*Cover photos (L–R): Alexander Ellis (1814–1890), Carl Stumpf (1848–1936),
Jaap Kunst (1891–1960), George Herzog (1901–1983)*

© 2006 Mervyn McLean

All rights reserved. Apart frin fair dealing for the puposes of private study, research, criticism or review, no part of this publication may be reproduced or transmitted in any form or by any means electronic or mechanical, including photocopy, recording, or any information storage and retrieval system, without permission in writing from both the copyright owner and the publisher.

Requests for permission to make copies of any part of this work should be mailed to Permissions Department, Llumina Press, PO Box 772246, Coral Springs, FL 33077-2246

ISBN: 1-59526-596-1

Printed in the United States of America by Llumina Press

Library of Congress Control Number: 2006922126

CONTENTS

Introduction	9
The role of history	10
What is ethnomusicology?	12
Part I: The growth of the discipline	17
Philosophical underpinnings	19
World view	19
Nationalism	20
The rise of science	21
Evolution	25
The idea of progress	29
Antecedents	30
Françoise Joseph Fétis (1784–1871)	31
Organology	32
Schools of music	33
The "seminal eighties"	37
The Austro-German schools	39
Development of the Berlin Phonogram-Archiv	39
Dispersal of Hornbostel's Berlin group	41
The Vienna school	42
Methods of the Austro-German schools	43
From simple to complex	43
The stone in the pond	43
The quest for origins	45
The Darwinian hypothesis	47
Darwin on natural selection	47
Other theories of origin	49
The contemporary ancestor	50
The genesis of the idea	51
The American school	52
The earliest pioneers	52
George Herzog (1901–1983)	54
Curt Sachs (1881–1959)	56
Charles Seeger (1886–1979)	56
International societies	59
The middle years in America (1960–80)	61
Jaap Kunst (1891–1960)	61
The waning influence of Europe	62
The UCLA/Indiana divide	63
Mantle Hood (1918–2005)	63
Bi-musicalility	63
Alan P. Merriam (1923–1980)	65
Music in culture	65
New directions (1980–2000)	67
Writings on the wall	67

Remodelling Ethnomusicology?	68
Earlier work	69
Analysis	70
Product and process	70
Theory-building	70
Other disciplines	71
Comparison	71
The "crisis of representation"	71
John Blacking (1928–1990)	72
The "holistic" approach	72
Whither ethnomusicology?	75
Paradigms past and present	76
Part II: The subject divisions	79
Introduction	81
Folk music	81
Definition	81
European folk song	81
Anglo-American folk song	82
Early collectors of English folk song	82
Cecil Sharp (1859–1924)	84
Frank Kidson (1855–1926)	85
Later collectors	85
A.L. Lloyd (1908–1982)	86
Scholarship in America	87
Oriental music	88
Tribal music	89
The Americas	89
Africa	89
Oceania	90
Part III: The biographies (A–Z)	91
Introductory note	92
The role of the individual	92
Personal qualities	93
Disciplinary background	94
Part IV: Intellectual ancestry charts	247
Introduction	248
Chart 1: Berlin School	249
Chart 2: Vienna School	250
Chart 3: American School	251
Part V: Issues	253
Introductory note	254
Field work	255
Insider/outsider relations	255
Authenticity	258
The role of the observer	260

Instruction	261
Bi-musicality	262
Archiving and documentation	264
Archiving	264
Cataloguing	265
Classification	265
Armchair ethnomusicology	266
Bibliography	267
Transcription	268
Prescriptive v. descriptive notation	270
The question of detail	271
Conceptual notation	273
The case for literacy	275
Composite transcription	277
Intonation	278
Machine transcription	283
The limits of perception	287
Reliability of transcription	289
Analysis	290
Aesthetics	292
Methods of analysis	292
Standard analysis	292
Cantometrics	293
Kolinski	294
Linguistic approaches	297
Text/music relationships	297
Statistics	299
Music and communication	299
Music structure v. social structure	302
Perspectives from Oceania	304
Feld and the *muni* bird	305
Structural terminology	306
The case for independence	307
Music system analysis	310
Comparison	314
Music areas	317
Diffusion	319
Cantometrics	321
Universals	321
Product and process	322
Repertoire	323
Mechanisms of change	324
The role of the subliminal	327
Merriam's feedback model	328
Anthropology v. music	329
Aftermath	332
UCLA v. Indiana	332
Popular music	332

Models	333
Leaps of logic	333
Split brains	334
Postlude	335
Chronology	339
References	357
Appendix: A Field Questionnaire	405
Acknowledgements	411
Illustration credits	412
Index of subjects	416
Index of persons	419

INTRODUCTION

In my treatment of the ethnomusicologists who feature in this book, it may seem at times that I have assumed the role of "Jack the giant killer". My intention, however, is to give credit where it is due, and equally to avoid lip service when I think praise is unwarranted. It should be unnecessary to add that my purpose is not to criticise people, but to evaluate ideas. There are no absolutes in ethnomusicology. Most of those who were and are involved in it have been right some of the time and wrong in others. There has been vigorous resulting debate over the years on many issues, by and large without rancour on the part of the participants. Long may it continue.

In his book *Theory and Method in Ethnomusicology*, published in 1964, Bruno Nettl comments that the time was not then right for a history of the contribution of ethnomusicologists because most were still living.[1] Of late, particularly in the 1980s and 1990s, there have been numerous deaths of the people of whom he wrote, so some evaluation of their work is now appropriate. The word most frequently used in biographies, obituaries, and "In Memoriam" articles concerning them is "pioneer", hence the title of the present book. All but a few of the persons featured in it belong to the discipline now known as ethnomusicology, and formerly called vergleichende musikwissenschaft, or comparative musicology.

Traditionally, ethnomusicologists have studied what is now increasingly known as "world music". It embraces folk and tribal music and the music of non-Western high cultures such as those of the Orient and the Middle East. Its scope has steadily expanded to include all forms of world music except Western classical music, which is left to musicologists without the "ethno-" prefix.

The inclusion of non-Western art musics under the rubric of ethnomusicology has led to a curious anomaly. Oriental and Islamic "high" cultures have a long history of indigenous scholarship, and a large body of indigenous music theory. Such music has as much right to be called "classical" as our own. So why reserve this term to Western art music? And, if it is inappropriate to do this, isn't an Indian scholar who studies his own classical music a "musicologist" rather than an ethnomusicologist? Moreover, if this is agreed, isn't a Westerner who studies the same music also a musicologist? The best-known Western authority on Chinese music, Laurence Picken (1909–), for example, prefers to be so regarded. In the end, it is probably a matter of emphasis. The main thrust of Picken's work is historical, which allies him with historical musicologists who apply similar techniques to Western music. On the other hand, scholars such as the Indonesian specialist Mantle Hood (1918–2005), and William P. Malm (1928–), the best-known Western interpreter of Japanese music, are more broadly based and would never have considered calling themselves anything other than ethnomusicologists. Hood, indeed, wrote a book based on his personal experiences and packed with methodology called "*The Ethnomusicologist*".[2]

Choice of persons for inclusion in the book is highly selective, as well as constrained at times by lack of biographical information, and apologies are offered in advance for inadvertent omissions. To keep content within bounds, the first criterion for selection has been impact upon the field of ethnomusicology at large. First and foremost must be those who appear in the standard

---

[1] Nettl 1964:12-13.
[2] Hood 1971.

histories of ethnomusicology and whose contribution to the development of the discipline is acknowledged by all. Individuals whose scholarly output has been slight are mostly excluded, except in cases where such contributions are acknowledged by others to be seminal. Collectors and authors of editions have also generally been omitted unless they also wrote about music. Also left out are a large number of scholars who have worked in the field of European folk music, often as historical musicologists rather than ethnomusicologists, who have published mostly in European languages other than English. Only the best known of these, such as Bartók and Kodály have been included. The same is true of most indigenous scholars, unless they have been prominent in the international arena. The list of scholars judged marginal to the objectives of the book is extremely long,[3] and it must be left to others to provide the necessary evaluations of their work and contributions.

To qualify as pioneers, most persons who are featured belong to what I would call the first and second generation of ethnomusicologists, many of whom were active before the term itself was coined. Living ethnomusicologists are mostly excluded, however eminent they may be. Scholars born after 1930 whose contribution has mainly been to "new directions" that became prominent in the 1980s have also been omitted. To widen the scope would vastly have overburdened the book, which in any case is concerned more with the past than the present. But there is no strictly chronological cut-off point, and where anomalies would have occurred, the exclusion rules have been broken on occasion. It would have been invidious, for example, to exclude the renowned Latin American music scholar Isabel Aretz, while including her eminent but not more famous deceased husband, Luis Felipe Ramón y Rivera (1913–1993).[4] An exception has also been made for Trevor Jones (1932–) of Australia whose work on Arnhem Land music initiated ethnomusicology studies there. Also, the American ethnomusicologist Bruno Nettl (1930–) has been included because of his special significance. Through his text books, his bibliographies, his editing, his exemplary monographs, his wide-ranging interests, and his prodigious output of scholarly books and articles, he has contributed profoundly to the discipline, and for this reason must be regarded as a contemporary pioneer.

THE ROLE OF HISTORY

The philosopher Jeremy Bentham (1748–1832), was a believer in the power of circumstance: if Shakespeare had not been caught poaching, he would have been a wool merchant.[5] Nothing as dramatic has happened in the history of ethnomusicology, but chance does undoubtedly impact upon lives. History is made up of chains of events, and willy-nilly we are all caught up in them, as I believe I can demonstrate from personal experience.

In 1959, I was in London, with no thought of becoming an ethnomusicologist, when an event occurred that changed my life. I received a letter from Maud Karpeles, secretary of the International Folk Music Council (IFMC), inviting me to visit her. In the course of the visit, she suggested that I submit a proposal for a paper to be read at the next conference of the IFMC in 1960, and in doing so set in train the events that led step by step to my own career.

---

[3] See Blum 1991:4-9 for charts containing the names of many more scholars.
[4] Afer the present book went to press, the writer learned with regret that Isobel Aretz has since died.
[5] Cited by Russell 1946:749.

At the time of my visit, Miss Karpeles was in the midst of the final proofs of her definitive edition of the monumental *English Folk-songs from the Southern Appalations*,[6] jointly collected by her and Cecil Sharp in the Appalachian Mountains area of America during World War I. Readers may have seen the 2001 movie "Song Catcher" about Sharp's predecessor in the area, Mrs Olive Dame Campbell, who gave Sharp the idea for the trip and, with her husband, helped him to plan it. The sequence that led to Sharp's own involvement and that of Maud Karpeles went like this:

- In 1905, Cecil Sharp became interested in English folk dances and sought to record them.

- Maud Karpeles, then 20 years old, was deeply involved in folk dance revival and, as a dancer herself, became caught up with Sharp's enthusiasms.

- Sharp gathered about him a group of young people who shared his ideals, among them Maud Karpeles.

- In 1914, upon the outbreak of World War I, the young male members of Sharp's group were called up for military service, and the group dispersed.

- In 1916, when Sharp began collecting in the Appalachians, he needed an assistant who would write down the song texts while he notated the tunes. As males from his group were no longer available, and Mrs Campbell was also unable to accompany him, he chose Karpeles.

- Were it not for the foregoing, and Karpeles proving such a loyal and devoted follower of Sharp, the International Folk Music Council in which she was the prime mover might never have been founded.

- If the IFMC had not been founded, I would not have met Maud Karpeles, would not have been invited to read the paper that became my first publication, and I would almost certainly not have continued the study of Maori music, which occupied me for most of the rest of my life.

- If I had not collected Maori music, much of the Maori cultural heritage would have been lost, the Archive of Maori and Pacific Music would not have been founded at the University of Auckland, ethnomusicology would have developed differently in New Zealand, and a revival of waiata singing which the archive assisted would have taken a different form.

And so it goes . . . consequence upon consequence. Were it not for Cecil Sharp in the first place, or indeed for the subject of the Song Catcher film, none of the subsequent events would have happened in the same way.

In the above series of events, I was just one small cog in a very big wheel. What were the events that led to the emergence of ethnomusicology itself? Who were the prime movers? What motivated them? What influences were brought to bear on them, and what were the consequences? This book will try to find out.

---

[6] Karpeles 1966.

WHAT IS ETHNOMUSICOLOGY?

Questions of definition have commanded much attention on the part of ethnomusicologists and considerable space in the journals, even before the discipline as such was launched in the early 1950s. In Europe, under the guidance of Maud Karpeles, Cecil Sharp's definition of folk song was debated and ultimately adopted formally by members of the International Folk Music Council,[7] though not without later objection from persons, especially in America, whose view of folk song was broader. As well, after the term ethno-musicology became established in the United States (initially with a hyphen), debate began about the precise connotation of this term.[8]

After coining his famous definition of ethnomusicology as "the study of music in culture", it is an issue that occupied much time and attention from Alan P. Merriam. During a university leave to Australia in 1976, he thought about it long and hard, to the despair of some of his colleagues and audiences at his lectures, when he raised the subject again and again. He did so with me on his way to Australia. I replied that I had recently attempted to write a Bulletin for Schools on the subject of ethnomusicology (which in the end I chose not to publish). I tried it out on ethnomusicologists around the world to obtain their reactions. Their replies about the nature of ethnomusicology all cancelled each other out. I told Alan that if they were all correct there was no such thing as ethnomusicology. After finishing his deliberations in Australia, Alan wrote a paper about it and, having examined over 40 definitions, came to essentially the same conclusion.[9]

Today, after the lapse of a quarter of a century, there is an even greater lack of unanimity. Topics considered by professional ethnomusicologists, as evident from their papers in standard journals, have proliferated to a degree that rules out Merriam's dream, and that of John Blacking (1928–1990), who felt the same way, of ethnomusicology as a united discipline.

In terms of what ethnomusicologists do, rather than what they say they do, or ought to do, a definition by Helen Myers is worth quoting:

> Ethnomusicology includes the study of folk and traditional music, Eastern art music, contemporary music in oral tradition as well as conceptual issues such as the origins of music, musical change, composition and improvisation, music as symbol, universals in music, the function of music in society, the comparison of musical systems and the biological basis of music and dance... In general, music in oral tradition and living musical systems are the realms that have most appealed to scholars in this field. Nevertheless most ethnomusicological research also involves history, and for many studies history is the focus. Often ethnomusiclologists study cultures other than their own, a situation that distinguishes this field from most historical musicology. As a consequence of its broad scope, definitions of ethnomusicology abound...[10]

If this sounds like a discipline without agreement on where it is going, or perhaps even where it has been, it is hard to disagree. Far from seeking unity, ethnomusicology appears now to be

---

[7] Karpeles 1973:3.
[8] See Nettl 1983:1-11 for a discussion of issues up to this date.
[9] Merriam 1977.
[10] Myers 1993:3.

making a virtue of its diversity. A 2003 web page [11] showing member affiliations of the Society for Ethnomusicology lists no fewer than 30 subject areas running the gamut from A to W as follows:

> Acoustics, Aesthetics, Anthropology, Archeomusicology, Archives and Museums, Area Studies, Art and Art History, Composition, Cultural Studies, Dance, Diaspora Studies, Folklore, Gender, Linguistics, Literature, Music Education, Music Journalism, Musicology, Organology, Performing Arts, Physics, Popular Music, Psychology, Public Culture, Public Sector, Sociology, Technoculture, Theatre, Theory, World Music and World Beat.

The problem with this not even complete list is that publications and research relating to any one such subject area is likely to be of little or no interest to students of the others. So the end result is a huge melange of articles on disparate subjects that hardly anyone reads.

To encompass all such shades of practice and opinion, the best solution might well seem to be "go with the flow" and redefine the subject as: "The scholarly study of world music", namely the application of scholarship of any kind to music of any kind. As a definition this may seem impossibly broad but it at least corresponds to the current reality, with historical musicology, which still applies mostly to Western art music, remaining the sole field as yet outside of its orbit.

But is such a broad or scatter-gun approach acceptable? I personally do not believe so. To begin with, the term "world music" has been adopted by the recording industry as a "catch-all" marketing device for the promotion of international or third-world popular music. This would bring the entire far from scholarly fringe of world music within the range of ethnomusicology. It does the same for the whole field of popular music in general, which may be handy for ethnomusicologists who are already studying it, but invites intellectualising on matters perhaps best left to disc jockeys, pushing the boundaries ever further outwards.

Consider the following single month's offerings at the time of writing of World Music CDs:

> Jewish music of Uganda
> Rita Marley, "The Queen Of Reggae"
> Irish accordion playing
> "Korean-style" instrumental music
> An "Afro-Portuguese Odyssey"
> "Educational multicultural activities for children"
> Classic Blues by various artists
> Peggy Seeger: "Traditional folk songs"
> Ugandan flautist and vocalist Samite
> Blues singer Charlie Patton
> Mexican fiddler Juan Reynoso
> Tex-Mex "Legend of the Conjunto!", Raul 'El Ruco' Martínez
> Senegalese song-writer Ismael Lo
> Singer and guitarist Boubacar Traore (Mali)
> Women of Mali: "The Wassoulou Sound"

---

[11] Society for Ethnomusicology 2003.

"Paris supergroup" 4 Etoilesase ever."
AfroCuban singer Tshala Muana
Baaba Maal (Senegal)
Tulear (Madagascar)

If we are to embrace the world music label, tell me what these have in common, other than being both popular and in some sense folk or "ethnic", and I will tell you what ethnomusicology is. Alternatively, ask anyone but an ethnomusicologist!

As if the above were not enough, another problem with accepting "world music" as the subject of our investigations, is that it is embroiled in an ethical wrangle which will sound very familiar to ethnomusicologists who agonised over the same issues a decade and more ago. In a 1999 *New York Times* article by David Byrne entitled "I hate world music", some of these issues are raised. While evincing admiration for innovative music now emerging in third world countries, the burden of his complaint is that rather than recognising such music in its own terms, it ghettoises it. What Byrne really hates, in other words, is not the music but the World Music label and implications that surround it. On this basis alone, rather than reopen old wounds, it would be well for ethnomusicologists not to join the fray.

Meanwhile, confusion obviously reigns, and it may not be an accident that on a Television New Zealand news programme a few years ago, the well-known composer of New Zealand Maori popular music, Dalvanius Prime, who was responsible for the 1983 Patea Maori Club top of the charts hit song "Poi e!", was referred to not as a popular recording artist, but as an "ethnomusicologist".

On the problem of definition, then, I really have no answer. In terms, however, of historical rather than current or possible future perspectives, there is still reason to think of ethnomusicology in terms of its internal sub-divisions as set out by Nettl and others more than 40 years ago. At that time, and still to a large degree, there was a three-way split, albeit with much overlap, between folk music, tribal music, and the art music of Oriental high cultures such as China, Japan, India, Indonesia and the Middle East.

Other ways of delineating the subject areas are also relevant. A commonly applied two-way East–West split, encompassing all but tribal music is Oriental–Occidental. Within both can be found folk, classical and popular music. Folk music originated as oral tradition within rural non-literate areas, while classical and popular music thrive on the resources of urban areas. Geographically, one could think of the several subject divisions in terms of distance from centres of urban art and popular music, with urban music at the core, rural music surrounding it, and tribal music on the periphery. Because of the proximity of rural areas to the cities, folk music shares some of its characteristics with city music, and historical interchange can be demonstrated. Until very recently, tribal music developed along its own lines, isolated by continental and other barriers, often for millennia, allowing for the emergence of numerous unique and distinctive forms of music in areas such as North America, sub-Saharan Africa, Australia, and Oceania.

Ethnomusicology now encompasses all of these subject divisions except Western classical, though even this may change. There is some argument that the methods of ethnomusicology could be applied equally to Western classical music, in which case ethnomusicology would become the study of all music and the problems of definition would move to method.

In terms of Western scholarship, folk music has the longest pedigree and has tended to be the domain of European scholars. Still largely unexploited, and representing a huge reservoir for future study, is the folk music of the Orient, which has been largely ignored in favour of Oriental classical traditions. At a Beijing conference I attended in the 1980s, examples were played of different styles of Chinese folk music from isolated areas of that vast country, in diverse styles, utterly different from Chinese classical forms. These, I am sure, are the tip of the proverbial iceberg. A massive collecting effort within China, which began in 1979 by the Chinese Ministry of Culture and the Chinese Musicians' Association in Beijing, has resulted in the publication of an immense anthology, called *Zhongguo minzu minjian vinyue jicheng* (Anthology of Folk Music of the Chinese Peoples). Now nearing completion in some 300 volumes, it contains c.9,000 pages of texts, contextual information and cypher notations of folk song, opera, narrative-singing, instrumental music and dance music from each of 30 provinces and regions within the Chinese People's Republic. Even so, this vast resource encompasses only about ten percent of the materials so far collected.[12] Ethnomusicologists need have no fear they will run out of interesting forms of music to study.

Tribal music of North America, Africa and Oceania has tended to attract scholars with an anthropological background. Oriental art music became the province of scholars whose training was principally in music rather than anthropology, whose background was composition, and who were drawn to the study of art musics other than their own largely because of the exotic, to them, nature of the sounds. Particularly after the publication of Alan P. Merriam's *The Anthropology of Music* in 1964, it should have been the case that the most fully-rounded ethnomusicologists would have expertise in both of the principal parent disciplines of music and anthropology. Some have had such training, of whom David McAllester (1916–), Bruno Nettl (1930–), and John Blacking (1928– 1990) are outstanding examples. Many have not, and it is mostly these who have taken ethnomusicology along its present disparate paths. Meanwhile, popular music has emerged as a major focus to inflate the subject matter further, and the desired end of a united discipline recedes ever further into the middle or far distance. The answer, in part, could well be a call for "back to basics." Some of what went before we are well rid of, but other once central issues have never been resolved, remain in contention, are full of interest, and are worthy of resurrection. Principal among them is the study of music systems as such – which never had much of an airing – and ultimately, by way of comparison, neglected and maligned as this may now be, an understanding of what music really is.

Definition is one of those topics now evidently seen as "old hat" and no longer of much interest. Lest, regardless of the foregoing, it should be thought that I agree with this, and the problem has gone away, let me make it clear, that in one respect at least, I believe it is now more of an issue than ever. Along with their inability to define what they mean by ethnomusicology, many practitioners are now muddying the waters with terminology that plainly means different things to different people. In such circumstances, intelligible discourse cannot take place. Without agreement on the precise meaning of the terms they use, ethnomusicologists are in danger of literally not knowing what they are talking about. To the old and thorny issue of "what is ethnomusicology?", then, should be added a more careful use of terminology and, in some cases, a good clearout of the terminological cupboard would not go amiss.

---

[12] For a review see S. Jones 2003.

Part I: The Growth of the Discipline

Pioneers of Ethnomusicology: Part I

Hernándo Cortés (1460–1521)   Franciso Pizarro (c.1471–1541)

Sir Francis Drake   James Cook   Louis de Bougainville
(1540–1596)   (1728–1779)   (1729–1811)

Philosophical underpinnings

WORLD VIEW

In medieval times, Latin was the lingua franca of scholarship, facilitating exchange of information within Europe, and providing students with a choice of the great universities such as Oxford (founded 1190) and Cambridge (1209) in England, and their equivalents elsewhere, such as Bologna (1088), Paris (1150), Salamanca (1218), Padua (1222), Toulouse (1229), Sienna (1246), Pisa (1343), Cracow (1364), Vienna (1365), Heidelberg (1386), and Cologne (1388), to mention only a few.[13] The earliest students or "wandering scholars", known as vagantes or goliards, performed songs with Latin verses, doubtless leaving their mark on European folk song. They were bands of young men who were particularly active in England, France, and Germany. They reached their zenith in the 12th and early 13th centuries, achieving considerable notoriety as a result of their dissolute behaviour, and songs which included drinking and love songs as well as satires against the Church. Around 1225, their influence waned as the great medieval universities grew, and wandering students were replaced by resident ones.[14] Peripatetic and cosmopolitan as such students may have been, however, their horizons, and those of their teachers and immediate successors, did not extend much beyond the European continent.

In 1295, world horizons expanded when Marco Polo (1251–1324) returned from the court of Kublai Khan, with tales of his long journey, having established an overland trade route to China. The account of his travels was translated into many languages and appeared in many editions over the next several hundred years.

The 14th century was a period of protracted war, death, and famine, during which the population of Europe shrank to little more than half of its former state. The Hundred Years War began in 1338, and the Black Death decimated Europe after 1347.

In the 15th and 16th centuries, Portuguese and Spanish navigators opened up sea routes to Africa, the Far East and the New World. In the Americas, Hernándo Cortés (1460–1521) and Francisco Pizarro (c.1471–1541) conquered and plundered the ancient Aztec and Inca civilisations of Mexico and Peru. In pursuit of treasure, Elizabethan privateers began to roam the Spanish Main, and during 1577–80 Sir Francis Drake (1540–1596) circumnavigated the globe, beginning a long tradition of British sea supremacy.

At the beginning of the 17th century, the establishment of the East India Company led to a huge British-dominated trade empire, centred upon India, marked also by a protracted but ultimately unsuccessful attempt by the French to gain a foothold. At the same time the Dutch, by means of the Dutch East India company, gained ascendancy in Indonesia.

Eighteenth century voyages of discovery and exploration by British, French, Dutch, Spanish and other navigators completed the map of the world and led to the establishment of colonies in every continent. Perhaps the most famous seafarer during this period was England's Captain James Cook (1728–1779), whose ships circumnavigated the world three times between 1768

---

[13] Mikael 2002.
[14] Reese 1949:200.

and 1780. When they returned to Europe, they brought back with them artefacts which now grace the museums of the world and, in the journals that Cook and his associates wrote, recorded invaluable scientific, ethnographic and casual information, including observations on music. Meanwhile, the return of Louis de Bougainville (1729–1811) from the South Seas in 1769 created a sensation in France, stimulating the popular imagination much as moon shots were to do 200 years later.[15]

The 19th century was a period of unprecedented colonial expansion by European powers, with Britain in the lead, and France, Russia, Germany, Belgium, Italy and other nations all expanding their borders or competing for territories in remote places throughout the world. By the end of the century most of the world was in the hands of colonial powers.

From about half way through the 19th century, as knowledge of the world's peoples grew, anthropology emerged as a recognised discipline, and museums of ethnology dedicated to comparative study began to be established.

> In 1850, the Museum of Ethnology was established in Hamburg, Germany, and in 1866 the Peabody Museum of Archaeology and Ethnology came into being at Harvard University for the purpose of collecting and analysing cultural materials. In 1851, A.H. Pitt-Rivers, working at the University Museum of Oxford, arranged the tools and weapons of contemporary peoples . . . in an attempt to illustrate how man had evolved or progressed in his technical abilities.[16]

The stage was now set for a similar attempt at classifying music.

NATIONALISM

Almost too obvious to require comment is the phenomenon of national pride, which has been an outcome of coalitions against common enemies, trade collectives, and the emergence of supra-social units of population world-wide. One has only to think of the empires of antiquity such as Greece and Rome to realise how powerful and far-reaching such sentiment can be. At its worst it has been a justification throughout history for war, conquest, and subjugation of others. At its best, it confers benefits in terms of knowledge gained and of collective achievement. In 19th century Europe it was a driving force behind the collection of folk song and, from about mid-century, the emergence of composers who made deliberate and conscious use of folk song. Thus, when the English composer Ralph Vaughan Williams (1872–1958) wrote a book about folk song, he chose as his title "*National Music*".[17] In his opening chapter, he is in no doubt there is such a thing as a national idiom. Just as nobody could mistake Wagner for Verdi or Debussy for Richard Strauss, so too, after several pages of digression, he reaches the conclusion that "the greatest artist belongs inevitably to his country as much as the humblest singer in a remote village".[18]

---

[15] Hammond 1970:3..
[16] Holmes 1965:43.
[17] Vaughan Williams 1963.
[18] Vaughan Williams 1963:1, 7.

Vaughan Williams, as is well known, incorporated English folk tunes and folk idiom into his own compositions which, in consequence, are accepted as quintessentially English; Bartók and Kodály did the same in Hungary; so did Smetana and Dvorák in Bohemia; Grieg in Norway; Borodin, Moussorgsky and Rimsky-Korsakov in Russia; and a host of others elsewhere. All incorporated elements of the folk song of their countries into their compositions.

THE RISE OF SCIENCE

As a discipline, ethnomusicology is more concerned with science than with art. Appreciation of exotic forms of music, their intrinsic worth, and even a desire to promote them may play a small part, but it is not essential. The necessary frame of mind for scholarship belongs to the modern period of Western philosophy from the Age of Enlightenment onwards. In his *History of Western Philosophy*, Bertrand Russell observes:

> Almost everything that distinguishes the modern world from earlier centuries is attributable to science, which achieved its most spectacular triumphs in the seventeenth century. The Italian Renaissance, though not medieval, is not modern; it is more akin to the best age of Greece. The sixteenth century, with its absorption in theology is more medieval then the world of Machiavelli. The modern world, so far as mental outlook is concerned, begins in the seventeenth century.[19]

Sir Isaac Newton (1642–1727)

Russell goes on to outline the achievement of astronomers in proving the true nature of the solar system. The final proof that the earth rotates around the sun and not the other way round was provided by Isaac Newton (1642–1727), building upon the work of his predecessors Copernicus, Kepler, and Galileo, thereby ushering in what may be called the Scientific Age.

"The seventeenth century was remarkable, not only in astronomy and dynamics, but in many other ways connected with science . . . The compound microscope was invented, just before the seventeenth century, about 1590.[20] The telescope was invented in 1608 . . . Guericke (1602–88) invented the air pump. . . Clocks . . . were greatly improved [and] scientific observations became immensely more exact and extensive than it had been at any former time."[21]

---

[19] Russell 1946:547.
[20] Claimed by some writers but disputed by others to have been invented by Dutch spectacle-makers Hans Janssen and his son Zacharias. The honour may instead belong to Galileo Galilei, who developed an occhiolino or compound microscope in 1609.
[21] Russell 1946:556.

There were equally momentous advances in other sciences: Gilbert (1540–1603) on magnetism, Harvey (1578–1657) on the circulation of the blood, discovery by Leeuwenhoek (1632–1723) of spermatazoa and protozoa, "Boyle's law" of gases, Napier's invention of logarithms in 1614, the development of differential and integral calculus by Newton and Leibniz, the publication of Newton's *Principia* in 1687, and multiple others. By the year 1700, as Russell points out, the mental outlook of educated men was completely modern; in 1600, except for a very few, it was still largely medieval.[22]

Philosophically, these advances were responsible for profound changes in attitude. In medieval times to be humble before God was prudent, because God could punish the sin of pride with pestilence, floods, earthquakes, Turks, and Tartars, and signal them with the appearance of comets. But it was impossible to remain humble in the face of such triumphs as those listed above.

> Nature and Nature's laws lay hid in night.
> God said "Let Newton be," and all was light.[23]

The 19th century belief in progress, of which more will be said later, was one of the outcomes. Along with the shrinking of the earth in cosmic terms as a result of scientific advance came an expansion and consolidation of horizons geographically. The earth, in a sense, was no longer God's domain, but man's. At the height of its power, Britain, which won the race for world dominion, had an unsurpassed naval presence, a thriving global trade and, despite the loss of its American colonies, an empire stretching through Africa, India, Malaysia, Australia, the Pacific islands, and Canada, upon which, according to the proud boast of the time, the sun never set.

But all of this came later. Philosophies of music history took a long time to come to terms with the new realities.

In the 17th century, while science was making its heady advances, music history was still dominated by theology. Orpheus charmed the birds below, while Gabriel blew his trumpet above.[24]

During the 18th century "Age of Enlightenment", historians' views of music became increasingly secularised but were dominated by ultimately sterile debates on the merits of the "modern" music of the time compared with that of the "Ancients" of Greece and Rome which, for some, was regarded as a golden age from which music had thenceforth declined. Warren Dwight Allen's assessment of 18th century histories is that they were on the whole

> objective studies which attempted rational classification into neat divisions or stages. They contained very little of the mysticism that was to color nineteenth-century works, but laid down emphatic dogma as to what was 'natural and simple and graceful'.[25]

---

[22] Russell 1946:558.
[23] Pope *Epitaphs*: Russell 1946:560.
[24] Frontispiece to Printz: *Historische Beschreibung der Edelen Sing- und Klingkunst* (1690), cited by Allen 1962:71.
[25] Allen 1962:85.

The Growth of the Discipline

Sir John Hawkins (1719–1789)   Charles Burney (1726–1814)

The pre-eminent music historians of the 18th century were Sir John Hawkins (1719–1789), who published a history of music in 1776 and, especially, his rival Charles Burney (1726–1814), who published the first volume of his multi-volume *A General History of Music* shortly before Hawkins, in the same year. These two so dominated music scholarship in England that, according to Warren Dwight Allen, the history of music seemed at the beginning of the 19th century "to he a subject that had been exhausted," and no further work of any significance was carried out in it until another 30 or more years had elapsed, "roughly equivalent to the period of Beethoven's creative life." [26]

Neither Hawkins nor Burney, however, are of much relevance to ethnomusicology, except for their neglect of the subject. In approach the two were chalk and cheese to each other. Hawkins looked back and Burney looked forward. Both, in their way were intolerant of differences. Hawkins disliked the fashionable opera and instrumental music of his own time. Burney espoused them. Hawkins praised the music of 16th and 17th century composers. Burney dismissed or rejected them. Burney can be said to have won the dispute, partly because of a scurrilous campaign which he waged against Hawkins in the press, partly because he was a better writer, and partly because his view of music as continuous development fitted better with the tenor of the times.

The cultural conservatism of the two, however, was to be enduring. With few exceptions, it was not until well into the 19th century that European writers about music began seriously to take account of non-Western music.

---

[26] Allen 1962:103.

Meanwhile, advances in science had gathered pace to a degree that must have seemed astonishing to educated persons who lived through these times. New discoveries in astronomy, biology, chemistry, geology, physics and other sciences were legion, and technology was altering the lives of everyone in the Western world. Developments such as the locomotive, railroads, the phonograph, electric light and the automobile would have been hard to miss, not to mention the spectacular Crystal Palace and Great Exhibition of London in 1851, that brought many industrial innovations to popular attention.

Not least of all the advances was the publication, in the same decade as the Exhibtion, of Charles Darwin's *On the Origin of Species*, introducing a concept that was to revolutionise Western thought. Darwin's other major publication *The Descent of Man* in 1871 was equally significant, and evolution not only of species but also of institutions was henceforth to be part of the ideal of progress that became a hallmark of the century.

Charles Darwin (1809–1882)

EVOLUTION

The publication of Darwin's *On the Origin of Species* (1859) and especially his *The Descent of Man* (1871) must rank as among the literary successes of all time. The first edition of *Origin of Species* is said to have sold out on the day of publication, and a reprint of 3000 copies was issued only two months later. The publisher had badly under-estimated demand. But what was the reason for such large initial sales? The first printing was of an already respectable 1250 copies. The answer was surely not a snappy title: the full title was *On the Origin of Species by Means of Natural Selection, or the Preservation of Favoured Races in the Struggle for Life*. Nor on the basis of the title alone would anyone know that the book was packed with information about plant and other species of possible appeal to amateur naturalists such as beetle and butterfly collectors. One can only suppose that pre-publication publicity was extraordinarily effective. After its release, however, the book excited controversy, and sales would have gained momentum because of it. Theologians labelled Charles Darwin the most dangerous man in England and, as reported by the *Saturday Review*, the uproar over the book quickly "passed beyond the bounds of the study and lecture-room into the drawing-room and the public street."

Contrary to popular belief, Darwin was not the originator of the idea of evolution, and nor was he the only proponent of it in the 19th century. Charles Darwin's own grandfather, Erasmus Darwin (1731–1802), wrote on the subject in 1794;[27] Jean-Baptiste Lamarck (1744–1829) published a rival theory of evolution half a century before Darwin's work;[28] and in Darwin's own time the philosopher Herbert Spencer (1820–1903) was at least as influential, and it was he, not Darwin, who originated the phrase "survival of the fittest." It was Darwin, however, who captured most of the attention in the eyes of posterity, and it is Darwin, above all, whose ideas have endured.

Darwin, who suffered severe ill-health during the latter part of his life, was too ill to defend his own ideas publicly but his cause was taken up by the biologist Thomas Henry Huxley (1825–1895), who became known on this account as "Darwin's bulldog". The German biologist Ernst Haeckel (1834–1919), called "Darwin's apostle in Germany", likewise took up the cause in that country, and the name Darwin was well on the way to becoming a household word. Darwin, who in his early education began as an unsuccessful student of classics, and dropped out of medical school without graduating, ended his life laden with honours, and was buried in Westminster Abbey.

---

[27] Darwin, E., 1794-96.
[28] Lamarck 1801.

L. Erasmus Darwin
(1731–1802)

R. Jean-Baptiste Lamarck
(1744–1829)

L. Thomas Henry Huxley
(1825–1895)

R. Ernst Haeckel
(1834–1919)

Bertrand Russell explains Darwin as follows:

> What Galileo and Newton were to the seventeenth century, Darwin was to the nineteenth. Darwin's theory had two parts. On the one hand, there was the doctrine of evolution, which maintained that the different forms of life had developed gradually from a common ancestry... Darwin supplied an immense mass of evidence for the doctrine, and in the second part of his theory believed himself to have discovered the cause of evolution. He thus gave to the doctrine a popularity and a scientific force which it had not previously possessed...
>
> The second part of Darwin's theory was the struggle for existence and the survival of the fittest. All animals and plants multiply faster than nature can provide for them; therefore in each generation many perish before the age for reproducing themselves. What determines which will survive? To some extent, ill luck, but there is another cause of more importance. Animals and plants are, as a rule, not exactly like their parents, but differ slightly by excess or defect in every measurable characteristic. In a given environment, members of the same species compete for survival, and those best adapted to the environment have the best chance. Therefore among chance variations those that are favourable will predominate among adults in each generation. Thus from age to age deer run more swiftly, cats stalk their prey more silently, and giraffes' necks become longer. Given enough time, this mechanism, so Darwin contended, could account for the whole long development from the protozoa to homo sapiens.[29]

The crucial difference between Darwin's idea of evolution and that of his main predecessor Lamarck, was the concept of chance variation as the prime determinant. Lamarck believed that species adapted according to need and, having learned a response, the acquired characteristic was inherited by their offspring. Darwin's contrary theory of "natural selection" was the one that came to be endorsed by modern genetics, and was eventually adopted by biologists, relegating Lamarkianism to the ranks of discredited theories.

But it was Spencer, who was a follower of Lamarck, rather than Darwin, who captured the spirit of the age by allying evolution with the idea of progress, and extending the concept to include social institutions as well as biological adaptation.

Spencer was a prolific author and was immensely influential. He wrote books and articles not only on biology, but on subjects as diverse as education, ethics, politics, psychology, and sociology, bringing to them all his conviction that human progress occurs spontaneously so long as people are free.[30] Within his lifetime, some one million copies of his books were sold, and his work was translated into French, German, Spanish, Italian, and Russian.[31]

> When he died he was the most famous and most popular philosopher of his age and was seen by many as a 'second Newton'. His ideas were esteemed in Russia, China, Mexico and Brazil, and in Japan his influence was greater than any other foreign thinker.[32]

---

[29] Russell 1946:752.
[30] Powell 1995.
[31] Sweet 2001.
[32] Young 1967.

Herbert Spencer (1820–1903)

Spencer's theories were by no means accepted by everyone. Darwin's admirer T.H. Huxley is reported to have said that "Spencer's idea of a tragedy was a deduction slain by a fact." A worse tragedy is that he became a victim of his own success, with his ideas appropriated, exaggerated beyond recognition, and misapplied by a movement known as "social Darwinism" which, in its most extreme form, supported abuses and evils to which Spencer himself was opposed, and which he repudiated.

In the context of present-day globalisation and market economics, Spencer could well be poised for a come-back. He was an early advocate of laissez faire and non-intervention by governments, and was a passionate defender of individual liberties. His views were especially consonant with American establishment ideals of the time, albeit subverted by later robber barons, and the American entrepreneur and philanthropist, Andrew Carnegie (1835–1919) was an especial admirer. Following Spencer, he adopted as his own motto: "All is well since all grows better."

Despite the adulation that came Spencer's way during his lifetime, his eclipse after his death was almost total. One reason may be that we no longer live in an optimistic age. Another is the undeserved opprobrium that descended upon him as a result of the excesses of Social Darwinism. There may be some justification also for the following judgement by Spencer's biographer, J.D.Y. Peel, who said:

> Posterity is cruellest to those who sum up for their contemporaries in an all-embracing synthesis the accumulated knowledge of their age. This is what Spencer did for the Victorians.[33]

The most likely reason for 20th century rejection of Spencer, however, was his choice of the wrong side in the evolutionary debate over inheritance of acquired characteristics, which Darwin won and Spencer, who followed Lamarck, lost. But even upon this issue Spencer may yet be vindicated, at least in terms of social progress, for which biological backing is not a requirement. In this respect, at least, it may be hoped that humankind can learn collectively from past mistakes, and in the written and oral record the learned behaviour of one generation can indeed be inherited by the next.

---

[33] Cited by Young 1967.

THE IDEA OF PROGRESS

Although, like evolution, the concept of progress was far from exclusive to the 19th century, there is no doubt that this period of history was strongly imbued with it, as well as a prevailing spirit of optimism. There were many reasons for this. Chief among them was the rise of science and technology and the benefits conferred by the Industrial Revolution. The benefits were offset by ensuing social ills: filthy towns, crowded tenements, child labour, deplorable working conditions, and more, but the good outweighed the bad. Life was harsh and poverty was no less rife before the Industrial Revolution, but reforms gradually occurred, conditions steadily improved, and self-advancement was possible. In most ways, people were now better off.

Evolution both of species and institutions was also seen as an inevitable progression to ever higher and better-adapted forms, just as the earth itself had evolved from primordial gas to its present state. After all, modern man, it was now revealed, had evolved from the amoeba, through fish, and a succession of mammals, to early hominids and *homo sapiens*. In England, pride could be taken in national achievement: Britannia ruled the waves; trade was good; the empire spanned the globe; standards of living were by and large increasing; and except for minor skirmishes in foreign places, all seemed to be well with the world at large. In America, the war of independence had been won, and the entrepreneurial spirit loomed perhaps even larger. Progress was a simple fact of life; and humankind was seen inevitably to triumph over whatever might come its way.

The power of the press also played a substantial part. In numerous books and articles, besides proselytising evolution, Herbert Spencer was a leading articulator of such sentiments. In an essay on "Progress: Its Law and Causes", first published in 1857, he expanded the concept of "organic progress" or evolution, into a universal law of progress which was all-embracing:

> Now, we propose in the first place to show, that this law of organic progress is the law of all progress. Whether it be in the development of the Earth, in the development of Life upon its surface, in the development of Society, of Government, of Manufactures, of Commerce, of Language, Literature, Science, Art, this same evolution of the simple into the complex, through successive differentiations, holds throughout. From the earliest traceable cosmical changes down to the latest results of civilization, we shall find that the transformation of the homogeneous into the heterogeneous, is that in which Progress essentially consists.[34]

In his first book, published six years earlier, he declared that

> progress . . . is not an accident, but a necessity. Instead of civilisation being artificial, it is part of nature; all of a piece with the development of the embryo or the unfolding of a flower. The modifications mankind have undergone, and are still undergoing, result from a law underlying the whole organic creation; and provided the human race continues, and the constitution of things remains the same, those modifications must end in

---

[34] Spencer 1911:154.

completeness. As surely as the tree becomes bulky when it stands alone, and slender if one of a group. . . so surely must things be called evil and immoral disappear; so surely must man become perfect.[35]

Such unbounded optimism today looks simply foolish, and Spencer himself somewhat modified his views later in life, but he was not to know of the terrible events that lay ahead in the following century,[36] which would help to drive his philosophy into oblivion. His ideas nevertheless prevailed for a long time. In 1933, indeed, in the midst of the Great Depression, and in the very year that Hitler became chancellor of Germany, the Chicago World's Fair was proclaiming "A Century of Progress".

Antecedents

From at least the 18th century onwards, missionaries, travellers, and ethnographers wrote, often extensively, about the music they observed in foreign lands. Many also collected and documented musical instruments which are now available for study in European and other museums. The historical perspective provided by their collections and written accounts, interpreted with due care, remains indispensable to the present day. Frank Harrison reproduces many of the written accounts, with English translations, in his book *Time, Place and Music*.[37] An early compilation of writings about China, for example, by a French Jesuit, Jean-Baptiste Du Halde (1674–1743), appeared under the title *Description géograpique, historique . . . de l'empire de la Chine et de la Tartarie chinoise* in 1735,[38] drawing upon reports and memoirs of Jesuit missionaries to China from the 16th century onwards. Among the materials is an article about music with a clear statement " . . . the beauty of their concerts does not consist in the Variety of Voices, or the Difference of Parts, but all sing the same Air, as is the practice throughout Asia".[39] The learned 18th century music historian Charles Burney was probably familiar with it because, when Captain James Cook's last expedition (1776–80) returned from the South Seas after the death of Cook, Burney, through Lord Sandwich, who was patron of the expedition, forced Captain King of the *Discovery* to deny the evidence of his own ears and cast doubt upon his statement that Tongans sang in parts, on the grounds that if the Greeks, Romans and Chinese had never learned to sing in parts, then neither could the Tongans![40] According to Harrison, Du Halde's compilation became the main source of information about China until late in the 18th century.[41]

In his first text book, *Music in Primitive Culture*, Bruno Nettl points out that interest in non-Western music can be traced back as far as the Renaissance, with Orlando de Lasso (1532–1594) interesting himself in the music of Neapolitan negroes; two centuries later, Jean Jacque Rousseau's dictionary of music (1767) contains examples of folk, Chinese and American Indian

---

[35] Spencer 1851, cited in Young 1967.
[36] Even Winwood Reade, an American social Darwinist who ended his best-selling world history *The Martyrdom of Man* (1876) with a defence of war, slavery, forced labour and exploitation, would surely have thought differently if he had been able to foresee the future.
[37] Harrison 1973.
[38] Halde 1735.
[39] Harrison 1973:162.
[40] McLean 1999:142.
[41] Harrison 1973:161.

music; in 1779, a monograph on Chinese music by Father Jean Joseph Amiot was published; and in 1792 there appeared "On the Musical Modes of the Hindoos", by Sir William Jones.[42] These and other early works are more than curiosities, and have probably been much more influential than often supposed. Moreover, there are other notable works as well that ought to be added to the list. Towards the end of the 18th century, a fashion seems to have emerged for "universal" histories of music that would take account of the growing knowledge of non-Western music that was beginning to accumulate. Five volumes under the title *Geschichte der Musik*, published over the course of 20 years (1862-82) by August Wilhelm Ambros, featured in volume 1 the music of China, India, Arabia and Greece. In a valuable paper, Joep Bor draws attention to several others:[43]

- J.B. de La Borde: *Essai sur la Musique Ancienne et Moderne* (1780) discussed not only music of the ancient Jews, Chaldeans, Egyptians, Greeks and Romans, but also Chinese, Hungarian, Persian, Turkish, Arabic, African, Russian and Siamese music.

- William C. Stafford: *A History of Music* (1830) devotes almost a third of its space to ancient and non-Western music from multiple areas.

- J. Adrien de La Fage: *Histoire générale de la musique et de la danse* (1844). Included in this work was material drawn from J.M. Amiot (1779). W. Jones (1792), G-A. Villoteau (1809), N.A. Willard (1834) and others. In his first volume he deals with Chinese and Indian music and dance, and in his second with Egyptian, Coptic and Hebrew.

FRANÇOISE JOSEPH FÉTIS (1784–1871)

Françoise Joseph Fétis's publication *Histoire génerale de la musique* (1869–76) is again devoted very substantially to non-Western music, with 150 pages on Indian music alone in volume 1. Although Fétis has been criticised as wrong in much of what he wrote as a result of the inadequate information at his disposal, in one respect at least he was salutary. He saw the value of examining the differences between music systems and did not believe in the progressive model that had prevailed hitherto: "art does not progress, it simply changes."[44] Fétis also earned a place in the annals of ethnomusicology by collecting musical instruments that formed the nucleus of the Musée Instrumental du Conservatoire Royal de Musique, Brussels, later to be catalogued by the Belgian organologist Victor-Charles Mahillon (1841–1924).

Fétis's magnum opus, in common with that of his contemporary, Ambros, was unfinished, and by this time it had probably become impracticable to compile a history of all the world's music at the hands of a single author, however voluminous the work. What may have been the last of

---

[42] Nettl 1956:26-7.
[43] Bor 1988.
[44] Bor 1988:59-62.

such universal histories was compiled not by a European but by the Indian scholar, Raja Sir Sourindro Mohun Tagore (1840–1914), under the title *Universal History of Music* (1896).[45]

I will refrain from reproducing a list here of other, mostly German, works relating to non-Western music that were published throughout the 19th century. Most were concerned with what Warren Dwight Allen perceptively calls "The Quest for Origins,"[46] a topic to be taken up in another section. Enough has been said, however, to contradict any notion that the study of non-Western music did not begin until the emergence of "comparative musicology" at the beginning of the 20th century. In all that was undertaken, there were very clear continuities with the past.

Organology

The somewhat strangely named science of organology owes its name to an early 17th century treatise by Michael Praetorius (c.1570–1621), entitled *De organographia*,[47] from the Greek word *organon*, denoting a "tool or instrument." The *Shorter Oxford English Dictionary* admits "organography" in its meaning of "A description of instruments" as entering English in 1674,[48] but makes no mention of organology, which was presumably coined by analogy with ethnology (as distinguished from ethnography) to denote the comparison of musical instruments. In current usage, it is anomalous that the term carries such an implication, as organologists typically concern themselves with description perhaps more than comparison, especially as comparison of any kind is currently out of favour with ethnomusicologists. Were it not that "organology" as an overall name is now too well entrenched to be withdrawn, one might agree with Mantle Hood, who suggested reviving "organography" as a more accurate term for the description of musical instruments.[49]

As objects brought back to Europe by missionaries, travellers, explorers and (later) ethnographers began to accumulate, museums were established to house them, and means were devised of displaying, cataloguing and describing them. To name just four of the more famous European museums with musical instrument collections: in England there is the British Museum, London, founded in 1753 and opened to the public in 1759, with many thousands of instruments; the Pitt-Rivers Museum, Oxford, founded in 1884, currently has c.6000 instruments; in Germany there is the Museum für Völkerkunde, Berlin, founded in 1873, with c.6,500 instruments; and in Austria there is another Museum für Völkerkunde, Vienna, founded in 1928, with c.4000 instruments.

In England, the pre-eminent early collector of musical instruments was Francis William Galpin (1858–1945), whose name is commemorated by the Galpin Society, which was formed in 1946 in order to continue his work "by the publication of original research into the history, construction, development and use of musical instruments." Also worthy of note is Henry Balfour (1863–1939), author of *The Natural History of the Musical Bow* (1899), and first curator of the Pitt-Rivers Museum, who remained in the post for 48 years. Although not ethnomusicologists as

---

[45] Bor 1988:62.
[46] Allen 1962:Ch.9.
[47] Praetorius 1619.
[48] Onions 1959.
[49] Hood 1971:123-4.

such, their work as collectors and authors of descriptive studies, analogous as it is to that of collectors and authors of editions of folk music, has contributed to the advance of the discipline.

Perhaps the most famous continental name associated with musical instrument research is that of Victor-Charles Mahillon (1841–1924), who published a monumental 5-volume catalogue (1880–1922) of the instruments in the Brussels Conservatoire museum, of which he became the curator in 1879. His classification of musical instruments into four main categories of autophones (later termed idiophones), membranophones (drums), chordophones (string instruments) and aerophones (wind instruments) became the foundation for a more elaborate and widely adopted system devised by Curt Sachs and Erich von Hornbostel in Germany.

As tangible objects, readily describable, and with performance contexts providing insight into music practice, musical instruments provided materials for some of the earliest studies bearing upon ethnomusicology. Perusal of early treatises, together with examination of ethnographic collections, instruments recovered in archaeological context, and depictions of instruments in graphic art, enabled studies to be carried out of ancient music cultures that would otherwise hardly have been possible. Among the more outstanding examples are works by Sendrey on *Music in Ancient Israel* (1969), including information on the music of the early neighbouring civilisations of Sumeria, Babylonia, Phoenicia and Greece; Izikowitz on *Musical Instruments of the South American Indians* (1934), based on the collection of the Göteborg Ethnographic Museum in Sweden; and Kunst on *Hindu-Javanese Musical Instruments* (1968), with its extensive use of temple reliefs. Nor should it be forgotten that Curt Sachs's interest in ethnomusicology began with his work on musical instruments, culminating with publications such as his *Reallexikon der Musikinstrumente* (1913), *Handbuch der Musikinstrumentenkunde* (1920), and *The History of Musical Instruments* (1940). More recent compendiums of information are those of Marcuse (1964 & 1975), and the *New Grove Dictionary of Musical Instruments*.[50]

Schools of music

Without schools of music able to offer professional instruction, it is doubtful whether musicology, and ultimately ethnomusicology, would ever have come about. As with so much else of significance, the critical developments took place in the 19th century. The famous Paris Conservatoire was founded in 1784 under the name École royale de chant et de déclamation, then renamed in 1795 as the Conservatoire national de musique et de déclamation, serving as a model for similar institutions elsewhere. Among its many emulators were the conservatories of Prague (1811), Brussels (1813), Vienna (1817), Geneva (1835), Leipzig (1843), Cologne (1845), Munich (1846), and Berlin (1850), followed by many others during the remainder of the century, including a relatively late start in England, where Trinity College of London was established in 1872, and the Royal College of Music in 1873. In America, conservatories and similar institutions likewise appeared in the second half of the century, among them Oberlin, Ohio (1865); Boston, Cincinnati, and Chicago (all in 1867); and the Peabody Conservatory, Baltimore, in 1868.[51]

---

[50] Sadie 1984.
[51] Scholes 1972a:930.

The different conservatories tended to specialise in different areas of music study. By the 1830s, Paris became focused on opera; Vienna specialised in training oratorio singers; and Prague concentrated upon orchestral players. Most offered instruction in harmony and counterpoint, and some in music theory, but composition, and especially music history, had to wait until the end of the century.[52]

By mid-century, the piano, which had been invented in 1709 by Bartolomeo Cristofori in Italy, was now centre stage. Over the course of a century-and-a-half, there had been many improvements to the mechanism; composers of both classical and romantic idiom had produced numerous piano works; virtuoso pianists were among the elite of the concert platform; firms such as Broadwood in England were mass-producing pianos, and the ideal had grown among the middle classes of "a piano in every home." Renowned teachers such as Anton Rubinstein (1829–1894) in St Petersburg, Franz Liszt (1811–1886) in Geneva and Weimar, and Clara Schumann (1819–1896) in Frankfurt had emerged; and music schools responded to the demand, both in the curricula they offered and by opening their doors to greater numbers of students.

Of the various music schools, that of Leipzig was perhaps especially significant in terms of later influence on ethnomusicology. Even before the time of J.S. Bach, who was cantor at Leipzig from 1723 until his death in 1750, Leipzig had a reputation as a city of music. It had the benefit of its long-established Thomasschule with its famous choir; its reputation grew throughout the 19th century after the establishment of "Gewandhaus" concerts organised by the composer Felix Mendelssohn, and the presence there to this very day of the world-renowned Gewandhaus Orchestra. The conservatory there thrived under the leadership of Mendelssohn, who himself taught piano and composition, and the city soon became a mecca for aspiring musicians. Among the many who flocked to Leipzig, were two American pioneers of ethnomusicology, John Comfort Fillmore (1843–1898), who studied organ at the conservatory in 1866–67, and Theodore Baker (1851–1934) who began studies at Leipzig university in 1874. Famous teachers in Leipzig included Moritz Hauptmann (1792–1868), who taught theory and composition at the conservatory from its inception in 1843; his pupil Oscar Paul (1836–1898), who was Baker's supervisor at the university; and Hugo Riemann (1849–1919) who began teaching at Leipzig university in1895, and is regarded as one of the founders of modern musicology in Germany.

Hugo Riemann (1849–1919)

---

[52] Scholes 1972a:929-30; Weber 2003.

An especially important graduate just two years earlier than Riemann's advent was Johannes Wolf (1869–1947), who took his doctorate at Leipzig in 1893 and later taught an entire generation of comparative musicologists, including Curt Sachs. Nor did the impact of Leipzig cease with Wolf and his students. Associated scholars of later years included Abraham Idelsohn (1882–1938) and Werner Danckert (1900–1970), who both studied there; Heinrich Husmann (1908–1983) who taught there; and Alfred Sendrey (1884–1976), Edith Gerson-Kiwi (1908–1992), and Kurt Reinhard (1914–1979), all of whom studied there.

As training institutions for musicians, universities were later on the scene than music schools, with those of Austria and Germany taking the lead in the 19th and early 20th centuries, though still lagging behind other disciplines. Of the 19th century German luminaries, even Riemann, who was among the greatest of them, with a phenomenal scholarly output, never achieved the rank of ordinarius or full professor at Leipzig university, even though his presence there helped to maintain Leipzig as a world-renowned training centre for music. Little wonder, then, that the same proved true of comparative musicology and ethnomusicology, when these emerged as independent disciplines.

The advent of music as an academic subject has more than a little to do with university degree structures. Nowadays, when a PhD is a standard entry-level qualification for most university appointments, including those in ethnomusicology, it tends to be forgotten that this was not always so.

In Europe, where musicology began, the PhD had been standard since the 19th century. In America, where ethnomusicology as such had its origins, Cornell became the first university to establish a chair in musicology, in 1930, and here too, the PhD was standard. But in Britain, until very recently, the usual higher music degree was a MusD, which was reserved to composition. It may not be a coincidence, then, that as late as the 1960s there was still no institutional support for ethnomusicology in England, where the foremost authorities in the subject, Henry George Farmer (1882–1965), Arnold Bake (1899–1963), and Laurence Picken (1909–) all earned their living in other fields. Meanwhile, in New Zealand, which followed the English system until the 1960s, the present writer benefited from a change of regulations to become only the third person in New Zealand to gain a PhD in music, and the first to do so in ethnomusicology.

Thomas Alva Edison
(1847–1931)

Friedrich Chrysander
(1826–1901)

Philipp Spitta
(1841–1894)

Guido Adler
(1855–1941)

The "seminal eighties"

It is in this decade of the 19th century that Bruno Nettl sees the beginnings of a later ethnomusicology emerging in Europe:

> ... it is difficult to relegate the beginnings of ethnomusicology to a decade other than the 1880s. It is in this decade that landmark publications and other events heralding the principal issues and paradigms of later ethnomusicology first appeared. Intercultural studies, field work, the study of music in culture, comparative organology, analytical problems, all of these surfaced in a way almost simultaneously.[53]

Specifically, Nettl cites the first issue of the German journal *Vierteljahrschrift für Musikwissenschaft* (1885), exactly half way through the decade, as an illustration of an emerging view of musicology at the hands of its editors Friedrich Chrysander (1826–1901), Philipp Spitta (1841–1894), and Guido Adler (1855–1941). In this volume appears an article by Adler, seminal to musicology, in which he sets out subject divisions for the discipline, including in it a place for comparative musicology, thereby laying the groundwork for what was later to become known as ethnomusicology. Also in this significant first issue of the journal were articles by Chrysander on Vedic chants; by Spitta on an 18th century collection of popular or vernacular music; an article by Mathis Lussy (1828–1910) on the correlation between metre and rhythm; and a large study by Carl Stumpf on the psychology of music in England, dealing with origin theories, comparing contributions by Herbert Spencer, James Sully, Charles Darwin and Edmund Gurney. In summary, with its inclusion of articles on methodology, theory, psychology of music, popular music, and non-Western music among others, Nettl sees this journal issue as "often properly regarded as the centrepiece of a period in which musicology as a discipline began."

Adler defined comparative musicology in his article as

> the comparison of the musical works, especially the folk songs of the various peoples of the earth for ethnographic purposes, and the classification of them according to their various forms.[54]

It was an exceptionally clear statement both of a goal and a method, soon to be followed up by Stumpf and others in what was to become known as the "Berlin School" of comparative musicology.

But Adler's ideas did not emerge in isolation. Nettl goes on to describe other events of the 1880s, some seemingly trivial or irrelevant, like the invention of the fountain pen, some clearly formative, like the division of Africa among European colonial powers, and four in particular that, along with Adler's definition of comparative musicology, were truly seminal for ethnomusicology.

The first of the four was a contribution by the American inventor Thomas Alva Edison (1847–1931) which had its beginnings towards the end of the 1870s. Before this time, Edison had al-

---

[53] Nettl 1995a.
[54] Adler 1885:14.

ready developed a vote recorder (1868), a printing telegraph (1869), the stock ticker (1869), an automatic telegraph (1872), an electric pen (1876), and the carbon telephone transmitter or microphone (1877).

Edison's epoch-making new device was signalled by a nursery rhyme. In the same year that Edison invented his carbon telephone transmitter, he spoke the following words into his newly invented phonograph, and heard them played back:

> Mary had a little lamb
> Its fleece was white as snow
> And everywhere that Mary went
> The lamb was sure to go

The heart of the original device was a cylinder wrapped with tinfoil, far too fragile to be a practicable recording medium, but within the next decade the first commercial phonographs were in production, and wax cylinder recordings, which replaced the initial tinfoil, became familiar world wide.

Edison himself predicted use of his machine for dictation, talking books and speaking clocks, the teaching of elocution, recording lectures and family memorabilia, telephone answering machines, the reproduction of music, and the "preservation of languages by exact reproduction of the manner of pronouncing".[55] It was the latter use, extended to the recording of songs, that was to prove crucial in the history of ethnomusicology.

Four years after Edison's invention of the phonograph, occurred a further significant event, too early to have had the benefit of the new recording machine, this time in the form of a PhD dissertation. In 1881, another American, Theodore Baker (1851–1934), who had gone to Leipzig to study music in 1871, took his degree there with a thesis entitled "Ueber die Musik der nordamerikanischen Wilden". Published the following year, and based upon Baker's own personal investigations among Seneca Indians of New York State, it was the first general work on American Indian music.

Two years after the publication of Baker's thesis came a another landmark publication, this time by an English mathematician, philologist, and acoustician, Alexander John Ellis (1814–1890) who, on account of his work, was regarded by Hornbostel and Lach of the emergent Austro-German school of comparative musicology as the founder of the new discipline,[56] a view later to be echoed by Jaap Kunst (1891–1960),[57] and others.

Kunst, who has himself been called "the father of ethnomusicology", attached great importance to the precise measurement of musical intervals, and it was Alexander Ellis who made this possible, besides helping to pioneer the comparative approach to music. In 1884, he published a ground-breaking paper, "Tonometrical Observations on Some Existing Non-harmonic Scales", which he revised and re-issued a year later under the title "On the Musical Scales of Various Nations." In this work he measured the pitch of notes produced on non-Western musical instru-

---

[55] Anon 2003.
[56] Haydon 1941:216.
[57] Kunst 1959a:2.

ments, demonstrated the existence of tonal systems different from those of the West, and introduced the cents system of measuring musical intervals in hundredths of a semitone, which became an indispensable tool of ethnomusicologists.

As indicated above, Ellis's work appears to have had immediate impact in Germany, where it is said to have influenced Carl Stumpf, who wrote a review of it.[58] Be this as it may, in 1886, in the same second issue of Adler's journal as his review of Ellis's revised paper, Stumpf published a long article in which he provided transcriptions and analyses of the singing of a Bella Coola Indian named Nutsiliska,[59] and in so doing helped to get the new discipline of comparative musicology firmly under way.

In the USA, sound recording started its long association with ethnomusicology when Jesse Walter Fewkes (1850–1930), an ethnologist, began recording North American Indian music with the Edison phonograph. In 1890 he recorded songs of the Passamaquoddy Indians in Maine, followed by Zuñi (1890) and Hopi Pueblo (1891) recordings, some of which were transcribed and analysed by Benjamin Ives Gilman (1852–1933).[60]

Soon, other individuals were recording in the field and, to house the growing collections, the first of the great sound archives of the world, the Phonogrammarchiv der Österreichischen Akademie der Wissenschaften, was established in Vienna in 1899. The world-famous Berlin Phonogram-Archiv (established 1900) was not far behind, and the stage was set for Stumpf's Berlin school of comparative musicology.

The Austro-German schools

DEVELOPMENT OF THE BERLIN PHONOGRAM-ARCHIV

There were three key figures in the early history of comparative musicology. The subject had its beginnings in Berlin with the establishment of the Berlin Phonogram-Archiv by Carl Stumpf (1848–1936), and work carried out there by his students Otto Abraham (1872–1926) and Erich von Hornbostel (1877–1935).

Two contemporaries of Hornbostel, who are also sometimes counted as members of his "Berlin School" were Johannes Wolf (1869–1947) and Georg Schünemann (1884–1945). Wolf was prominent rather as the teacher of several later comparative musicologists, including Curt Sachs. He was a musicologist who, as mentioned earlier, took his doctorate at Leipzig in 1893. He was a specialist in medieval and early music. Schünemann was a specialist in music education, who studied musicology under both Wolf and Stumpf, and neither he nor Wolf appear to have had any professional involvement with ethnomusicology in terms of personal research. However, although not an ethnomusicologist, Wolf helped to publicise and promote the study of non-Western music, and was a co-founder of the Zeitschrift für vergleichende Musikwissenschaft in 1933.[61]

---

[58] Stumpf 1886b.
[59] Stumpf 1886a.
[60] Gilman 1891.
[61] Hoffman-Erbrecht & Potter 2003.

Johannes Wolf (1869–1947)
teacher of many early comparative musicologists

Stumpf was a German philosopher and theoretical psychologist noted for his research on the psychology of music, who took his DPhil at the University of Göttingen in 1870.[62] Abraham was a German physician and psychologist. He graduated in medicine at Berlin University in 1894, and thereafter dedicated himself primarily to psychoacoustics and the physiology of music,[63] serving from 1896 to 1905 as assistant to Stumpf at the Psychological Institute of Berlin.[64] Hornbostel was an Austrian musicologist and ethnologist whose PhD, at Heidelberg in 1900, was in chemistry, after which he moved to Berlin where, influenced by Stumpf, he combined musicological studies with experimental psychology.[65]

In 1900, Stumpf instituted the collection that later became the Berlin Phonogram-Archiv, as a section within the Psychological Institute of which he was the founder director, using as a nucleus wax cylinders of a Siamese theatre group of dancers and musicians who visited Berlin in September of the same year, which he recorded in association with Abraham,[66] In 1906, Hornbostel was named as first director of the archive, retaining the post until 1933, when he was dismissed by the Nazi regime because his mother was a jew.[67]

The archive was a brilliant concept, and Hornbostel was the driving force within it. Around him he gathered students and colleagues who later spread his methods around the world; in association with Curt Sachs he developed the Sachs/Hornbostel method of classifying musical instruments which, with some modification, has since become standard; and he actively solicited recordings from ethnographers and others who by now were recording on wax cylinder all over the world, besides later undertaking field work of his own. And this was far from all. Hornbostel made conspicuous use of the resulting collections. With Stumpf and Abraham, he developed and publicised still-used methods of transcription and analysis, and was soon publishing the first of a string of papers, over 80 in all, on Japanese, Turkish, Indian, Amerindian and other musics. In the 1970s, in recognition of the value of Hornbostel's writings, an initiative was launched to reissue his publications in English translation as a *Hornbostel Opera Omnia*, but the project lapsed after the publication of a single volume.[68]

DISPERSAL OF HORNBOSTEL'S BERLIN GROUP

George Herzog (1901–1983), Mieczyslaw Kolinski (1901–1981), Marius Schneider (1903–1982), and Fritz Bose (1906–1975) were all students or colleagues of Hornbostel,[69] together with Curt Sachs (1881–1959), who was later to become the most famous of them all. Herzog, Kolinski and Sachs (of whom more will be said later), as well as Hornbostel himself for a time, all ended up in the United States, after Hornbostel's dismissal and the subsequent breakup of the group.

- Bose, who studied under Stumpf, Hornbostel and Sachs, worked after Hornbostel's dismissal on developing an approach for relating music and race, thereafter concentrating mostly on European folk music.

---

[62] E-Brit "Stumpf, Carl"; Wellek 2003.
[63] Katz 2003a.
[64] Katz 2003a.
[65] E.Brit.: "Hornbostel, Erich Moritz von.".
[66] Lotz 2003.
[67] E.Brit. "Hornbostel, Erich Moritz von."
[68] Wachmann et al. 1976.
[69] Blum 1992:170.

- Robert Lachmann (1892–1939), who obtained his doctorate in 1922 under Stumpf, was another member of the group who had the misfortune to be Jewish and, like Hornbostel, lost his living in Berlin as a result of Nazi intervention. He eventually moved to Israel, and pioneered the introduction of comparative musicology there.

Apart from Bose, the most prominent of those who remained in Berlin was Schneider, who succeeded Hornbostel as director of the Berlin Phonogram-Archiv and continued in the post until the end of the war in 1945.[70] His next ten years were spent in Spain, and from 1955 until his retirement in 1968 he taught comparative musicology at the University of Cologne.

Three other members of Hornbostel's so-called Berlin School are worthy of mention:

- Hans Hickmann (1908–1968) studied under Sachs and Hornbostel in Berlin, taking his PhD in 1934. He settled in Cairo in 1933, where he became an expert on Egyptian music, not returning to Germany until 1957, when he took up the chair of ethnomusicology at the University of Hamburg.

- Heinrich Husmann (1908–1983) was another student of Hornbostel in Berlin, gaining his doctorate in 1932. In 1933 he began teaching at the University of Leipzig, remaining there until 1944, when he moved to Hamburg.

- Walter Wiora (1906–1997) studied in Berlin under Hornbostel and Sachs, taking his doctorate in 1937, afterwards holding various posts until his final appointment as professor of musicology at Saarbrücken (1964–72).

Also sometimes regarded as a member of the Berlin School was Walter Kaufmann (1907–1984), because he studied under Sachs at the Staatlich Hochschule für Musik in Berlin, from which he graduated in 1930.

THE VIENNA SCHOOL

Beginning at about the same time as the Berlin School, a number of German-speaking scholars became established in what has become known as the Vienna School of comparative musicology in Austria, where the Phonogrammarchiv der Österreichischen Akademie der Wissenschaften had been established, with similar aims to that of Berlin. Scholars in Vienna included Richard Wallaschek (1860–1917), Robert Lach (1874–1958), Siegfried Nadel (1903–1956), and Walter Graf (1903–1982). Among early recordings in the Vienna archive was a collection by Rudolf Pöch (1870–1921), made in the north coast of New Guinea from 1904–06, that later became the subject of a study by Graf.[71]

According to Ida Halpern (1910–1987), who was a pupil of Lach, whereas the Berlin School emphasised psychology, acoustics and the origins of music, the Vienna School focused mainly on "evolution of world culture, searching for stages of development".[72]

---

[70] Successors to Schneider as director have been Kurt Reinhard (1952–68), Dieter Christensen (1968–72), and Artur Simon (1972–)..
[71] Graf 1950. The recordings themselves are now also available on CD (Schüller et al. 2000).
[72] Halpern 1976.

METHODS OF THE AUSTRO-GERMAN SCHOOLS

Early comparative musicolgists in Austria and Germany concerned themselves mainly with analysis of the structure of non-Western music, and with theories about the origins of music. Theories were built in terms of social evolution, and a belief in invariant stages of culture progressing from savagery through barbarism to civilisation. This evolutionary theory of music has long since been abandoned by most ethnomusicologists, but lingered longest in Europe, where echoes of it are still to be found.

From simple to complex

Fundamental to the idea is evolution from simple to complex, as in Herbert Spencer's "law of organic progress", where the very phrase occurs. Music was considered to have developed in the same manner as living organisms, ever upward and onward "to the latest results of civilization". But the idea had serious flaws:

First, it was highly ethnocentric, taking for granted an unwarranted superiority of Western culture in its comparison with others. From such a viewpoint our own culture is the best and everyone else is at various stages of arrested development in their progress towards the pinnacle of achievement we believe ourselves to represent. It was a point of view that could be sustained only in ignorance of the many sophisticated music systems other than our own which are still coming to light. A hundred years ago there may have been some excuse for being unaware of them, but no longer.

Second, and again redolent of Herbert Spencer, is what Alan P. Merriam has called the "simple-old syndrome",[73]. Here the assumption is made that the simplest music is the oldest, and complex music the most recent. Simple is defined in terms of small range, few notes, simple forms and simple rhythms, but there are difficulties:

> (a) What is simple and what is complex? Two-note music, for example, though melodically apparently simple can be complex rhythmically and in other ways.

> (b) No music style has been studied for long enough to determine whether simple styles do become complex and, except for musical instruments recovered in archaeological context, music, unlike material culture, does not leave evidence.

> (c) Most telling of all, simple-but-new and complex-but-old styles are known: for example, as Nettl has pointed out, the change from complex counterpoint to homophony in 18th century Europe.[74]

The stone in the pond

Also fundamental to the Austro-German approach to comparative musicology was the idea that "widespread equals old". The classic illustration is of a stone flung into the middle of a pond. As the stone hits the water, ripples begin to spread from the point of impact in wider and wider

---

[73] Merriam 1964a:285.
[74] Nettl 1964:198.

concentric circles until they reach the edge of the pond. The most recent ripples are the ones of smallest circumference in the middle. The oldest are the ones that have reached the edge. In just this way, it was believed, elements of culture begin life in a centre from which they then spread out. If one wishes to know what the ripples used to be like, one looks at the oldest ones that have spread furthest. In cultural anthropology it was a theory that became known as "diffusionism". The Germans called it "Kulturkreise", or "cultural circles".

Again there is evidence that this may sometimes or even often be true of music, but is not necessarily true. If it were, rock music would be older than the Charleston because it is more widespread. The best-known musicological application of Kulturkreise theory or diffusionism is Curt Sachs's classification of musical instruments into cultural strata, another idea that stems from evolutionary theory and was taken up by comparative musicologists. Hornbostel isolated eleven strata, and Sachs, before he simplified his theory, recognised twenty-three.[75]

The deficiencies of the method are well known, and there is no need to review them in detail. The interested reader will find a full discussion in Merriam's book *The Anthropology of Music*.[76]

Sachs, though himself well aware of some of the pitfalls, noted as his chief axioms:

> 1) An object or idea found in scattered regions of a certain district is older than an object frond everywhere in the same area.
> 2) Objects preserved only in remote valleys and islands are older than those used in open plains.
> 3) The more widely an object is spread over the world, the more primitive it is.[77]

On the basis both of these ideas and upon recovery of musical instruments from archaeological sites, Sachs goes on to classify instruments into three broad "strata":

> An *early stratum* comprising instruments found in Palaeolithic excavations and geographically scattered throughout the world.
>
> A *middle stratum* of instruments from Neolithic excavations and geographically present in several continents.
>
> A *late stratum* of instruments from more recent Neolithic sites and confined geographically to limited areas.[78]

According to Sachs, there are no drums, stringed instruments or "flutes with holes" in the earliest stratum. But Sachs chooses to disregard the possibility that drums and chordophones were present in early times but failed to survive archeologically because they were made from perishable materials. Recently also, a fragment of an alleged Neanderthal flute with apparent fingerholes has been found in Slovenia,[79] which, if validated, belongs well within Sachs's Palaeolithic stratum.

---

[75] Sachs 1940:63.
[76] Merriam 1964a:287-90.
[77] Sachs 1940:62.
[78] Sachs 1940:63-4.
[79] Turk 2003.

Merriam goes to the heart of the matter, and reserves his major criticism for the three premises upon which the entire scheme is based, observing that "if we cannot accept them on the scale proposed by Sachs then the theory must fall."[80] His final judgement is that diffusion studies can be valid if their limitations are realised and cautions first put forward by Herskovits are taken into account, namely that historical unity can be assumed in the areas concerned, and that the aim is to establish a probability rather than absolute proof of a connection.[81]

Associated with lingering evolutionism in Europe is a continuing preoccupation with problems about the origins of music. The long-standing fascination with the subject could well have occurred because no consensus on it can possibly be reached, investing the topic with the same degree of allure as problems of metaphysics for which science has not yet found an answer.

THE QUEST FOR ORIGINS

Theories of the origins of music are legion. In some cultures it is attributed to the supernatural. According to Merriam, the Basongye people of the Congo say that music came from Efile Makulu (God); the Flathead Indians of Montana relate it to be the Vision Quest in which songs are sought from supernatural entities; and the Asaba of Nigeria attribute it to forest gods.[82] Musical instruments can similarly be attributed to supernatural sources. The Lau people of the Solomon Islands, for example, impute the origin of panpipes to the Gosile, legendary creatures who are the offspring of women who have died in childbirth.[83]

Western ideas of the origin of music have not entirely neglected the supernatural. Music was long supposed to be of divine origin, and this is not far removed from the ideas of such persons as Johann Scheibe (1708–1776),, a German kapellmeister writing in 1754 who thought that Adam and Eve must have "lifted their voices in grateful song on the day of their creation," and so vocal music was discovered by the first human beings in paradise.[84] A non-human origin for music is also implicit in the ancient Greek and medieval concept of "music of the spheres" which supposed that the planets in their orbits were accompanied by celestial music.

There have been numerous attempts to summarise theories of musical origins: Kunst,[85] Nadel,[86] Nettl,[87] Sachs,[88] and Schneider,[89] together with Allen,[90] who provides the most detailed exposition, have all tried their hand at it. Most, however, fall into the trap of proposing their own equally untenable theories after rebutting all the others.

It is tempting to agree at the outset with Merriam that "while the ultimate origin of music may provide material for interesting and even logical speculation, theories can only remain theo-

---

[80] Merriam 1964a:290.
[81] Merriam 1964a:295.
[82] Merriam 1964a:74-7.
[83] Ivens 1930:214-5.
[84] Allen 1962:51.
[85] Kunst 1959a:46-55.
[86] Nadel 1930 and in McAllester 1971:277-89.
[87] Nettl 1956:134-7.
[88] Sachs 1943:Ch.1 & 1962:Ch.4.
[89] Scneider 1957:5-7, 20-2.
[90] Allen 1962:Ch.9.

ries."[91] My own view, indeed, has long been that speculation of the kind is a monumental waste of time and effort, and the subject could profitably be abandoned, if not relegated to the same status as theories of perpetual motion in physics, except insofar as it is appropriate for ethnomusicologists to document myths of origin. Recently, however, there has been a revival of interest: an entire conference has been held on the subject, and a book of the resulting papers has been published.[92]

The conference, which was held in Florence in 1997, was organised by a group of Swedish "biomusicologists" who hope to establish a new sub-discipline of musicology devoted to the subject. Those taking part were mostly scientists of various kinds, including biologists, animal communications experts, brain specialists, and others. Bruno Nettl, who was one of only two ethnomusicologists present, and who himself presented a paper on the related conference theme of "universals", while fascinated with what he had learned about animal communication, found himself acting mainly in the role of a "nay-sayer",[93] largely, one supposes, because the lessons already learned by ethnomusicologists are not yet fully appreciated by the scientists.

Perhaps the most fundamental unresolved question that must be answered before the question either of origins of music or of the related subject of music universals can be considered is: "What is music?" Much ink has flowed on this topic, but ethnomusicologists have been unable to come to an agreed conclusion.

In popular parlance, kettles sing; ones ears may sing; only slightly more credibly, birds sing; and one of the papers at the above conference was about the "songs" of hump-backed whales. Darwin, who is said not to have had a good musical ear, took an even broader view in his *Descent of Man*, using "music" to refer to anything he did not think of as speech, including bird song, cricket stridulation (produced by rubbing legs together), animal cries of various kinds, and reports of singing apes. The Basongye, who evidently did not confuse literal truth with analogy, may yet be proved right when they said to Merriam: "Birds don't sing, and the wind doesn't sing in the trees. Only humans sing."[94]

This question aside, however, if any progress is to be made on the venerable and so far unproductive search for origins of music, it is perhaps more likely to emerge from brain physiology than any of the approaches of the past. The latter nevertheless can still serve in the role of warnings to be heeded and blind alleys to be avoided, and perhaps also have some merit as entertainment. The topic must be considered in the present work because it is part of the history of ideas. It was a major preoccupation of European diffusionists and their predecessors, bound closely as it was with their evolutionary approach to music, and their ordering of music into cultural strata. For them, to discover the ultimate origin of all music would have been something of a holy grail.

The cultural strata idea probably came from palaeontology rather than evolutionary theory as such, but physical fossils were certainly a key component of searches for the "missing link" in the evolution of man, and musical fossils in supposed cultural strata were an outcome. Darwin was not a

---

[91] Merriam 1964a:285.
[92] Wallin et al. 2000.
[93] Pers.com. 2003.
[94] Alluded to in Merriam 1964a:64-5.

musician, beginning his career, in fact, with a strong interest in geology, which occupied much of the work he did during his voyage on the *Beagle*. But his influence upon comparative musicologists resulted primarily from his 3,500 words on the origin of music in his *The Descent of Man*,[95] which set comparative musicologists on an ultimately unrewarding 100-year-long journey, looking for ways to prove him right or wrong. He was not the first to consider the subject. Rousseau and Spencer both preceded him, and their theories were part of the debate. Darwin's theory, however, has probably commanded more attention than the others, and was recently resurrected at the Florence conference referred to above, in a paper by Geoffrey Miller.[96]

1. The Darwinian hypothesis

According to Darwin, the origin of singing is sexual. Under the stress of sexual excitation man is supposed to have become a singer, and the beginnings of music is thus allied to bird calls and the mating calls of animals. Nadel, Sachs and Nettl all take the trouble to solemnly refute this by pointing out that birds are biologically unlike men, that they often sing outside the mating season, and there is an absence of music-like mating calls among apes.

If, rather than relying on latter-day interpretations, one examines Darwin's actual arguments, in his *Descent of Man*, they are not so easily dismissed.

In the course of information throughout his book, and his extensive additional argument and comment on the specific issue, he shows in case after case that birds, insects, fish, and mammals other than man all utter quasi-musical sounds that do not qualify as speech but perhaps legitimately could be called music, in order to attract the opposite sex. His reasonable conclusion is that it would fly in the face of all known facts about evolution to suppose that man was any different.

Darwin on natural selection

The questions which Darwin asked himself during his five-year voyage on the *Beagle* have parallels in the world of music. Throughout the voyage, as the *Beagle* progressed from one place to another and Darwin observed the manifold forms of plant and animal life that came to his attention, he was confronted with similarities and differences that in either case were seemingly inexplicable. The prevailing theist view was that the various forms of life remained as they had always been, without change from the time they were created, and their present distribution resulted from the migration of their ancestors from the region in which the Ark stranded them after the biblical deluge. There appeared to be only two alternatives: either "spontaneous generation", or "descent with modification" as propounded by Lamarck but rejected by Darwin. In looking at the only certain cases of descent with modification, namely domestic animals and cultivated plants, Darwin came to the conclusion that the principle at work in both cases was "selection". But this left him with the problem of how selection could be applied to undomesticated organisms living in a "state of nature". A reading of an essay on population by Thomas Malthus (1766–1834)[97] set him on the path towards the answer he sought, namely, competition of varieties and the selection of those best adapted to the conditions. This was his principle of "natural selection".[98]

---

[95] Darwin 1871.
[96] Miller 2000.
[97] Malthus 1798.
[98] Huxley 1893.

The doctrine of "favourable variations by natural causes" explained the diversity of living forms in terms of a long series of competitive adaptations and survivals of the "fittest", as Spencer expressed it, or in Darwin's own words, the "best adapted", accounting for even the most complicated adaptations.[99]

A final step concerned the manner in which such individual adaptations to environment were passed from the generation in which they first occurred to the next. Again there were only two choices. Either inheritance of acquired characteristics took place, or chance genetic variations perpetuated themselves by natural selection if they happened to be favourable to the organism. As is well known, it was the latter view that Darwin adopted.

The parallels with music are quite striking. Just as happens with living species, as well as with languages, with which there is yet another parallel, there is great diversity of different forms of music, and at the same time family resemblances among some of them. Can the principles of evolution espoused by Darwin be brought to bear to explain them?

Cecil Sharp's principles of historical continuity, individual variation and community selection [100] spring to mind as making use of some of the same terminology. But there is no direct connection. Sharp's "variation" occurs at the whim of the singer and confers no advantage or disadvantage; Darwin's variation results from an adaptation to environment which confers a competitive advantage. Sharp's selection results from preferential choices made by successive generations of singers in the oral chain; Darwin's selection is biological and has nothing to do with choice. All Sharp and Darwin have in common, then, is that both living organisms and music can be said to evolve.

The feature most standing in the way of applying Darwin's theory of natural selection to music is that in the latter case the element of competitive advantage is absent. No form of musical variation can confer a benefit which advantages one individual more than another, especially with regard to winning a mate. It would be stretching facts unduly to regard individual love songs as the pre-eminent form of music, and the idea is even less applicable to whole communities.

There remains the question of whether environment (food, climate etc.) can have any effect on music independent of natural selection. This is the question asked by Alan Lomax, John Blacking and others on the subject of whether there is a relationship, and in particular a causal one, between music structure and social structure. The answer here as well (see later) appears to be no.

---

[99] Huxley loc.cit.
[100] Set forth in Sharp 1909.

Other theories of origin

2. Imitation of bird song

According to this theory, humans began to sing when, for no particular reason, they copied birds. Kunst objects reasonably enough that nowhere in the world do we find people singing like birds.[101] The Kaluli of Papua New Guinea might disagree (see "Feld and the *muni* bird" later), but the association of their music with birds is mythical rather than real.

Karl Bücher

3. The "rhythm" theory

A theory proposed by Karl Bücher (1847–1930)[102] is that music arose from group work.[103] Bücher discovered that the Western folk repertory as well as some primitive ones contains a number of work songs, and he proposed that this must have been the first type of song. Against this the objection has been raised that many primitive people do not have work songs.[104]

4. The "call" theory

This theory was advanced by Carl Stumpf, and at about the same time (c.1910) by one of the architects of diffusionism, Father Wilhelm Schmidt (1868–1954). Jaap Kunst says he is "fully inclined to agree with this" as he himself made the same suggestion in 1922.[105] Stumpf maintained that when one wishes to make oneself heard over a long distance the voice is raised spontaneously and the discovery is made that the voice can be heard further away if it is intoned on one pitch. Moreover, if the cry is uttered simultaneously by men and women so that it sounded on two different pitches at once, octaves, then fifths, fourths and other intervals will result, after which the discovery will be made that these can be uttered consecutively.[106] Nettl objects that there is no evidence of primitive peoples making use of sustained signals on a single pitch.[107]

5. Music from speech theories

(a) Impassioned speech. The view that music originated from emotional or impassioned speech was held by J.J. Rouseau, Herbert Spencer, and the composer Richard Wagner. They noticed that when a speaker becomes emotional his speech automatically acquires some musical characteristics,[108] and in this they saw the origin of all music.

---

[101] Kunst 1059a:47.
[102] Bücher was an eminent historical and anthropological economist and a founder of journalism as an academic discipline in Europe. Between 1882 and 1883 he held the Chair of Geography, Ethnography, and Statistics at the Imperial University of Dorpat (now Tartu) (Drechsler & Kattel 1997).
[103] Bücher 1909.
[104] Nettl 1956:63.
[105] Kunst 1959a:58.
[106] Schneider 1957:6.
[107] Nettl 1956:135.
[108] Nettl 1956:135.

The idea seems plausible enough when one considers quasi-musical utterances such as those of auctioneers or race commentators. And throughout the world can be found sprechgesang or recitative styles of music which sound as though they may have derived from speech. Recent examples in the field of popular music are "rap" songs and "hiphop". In his *The Descent of Man*, however, Darwin argues that "it would be altogether opposed to the principle of evolution, if we were to admit that man's musical capacity has been developed from the tones used in impassioned speech", because this would require speech to have preceded music.

(b) Tone language. This theory was argued by Schneider in the *New Oxford History of Music*.[109] It proposes that music developed from proto-languages that used pitch to convey meaning, but has met with the objection that lexical differentiation according to pitch is a recent innovation in the speech of most regions where it is found such as China.[110]

(c) To the impassioned speech and tone language theories may be added a further speech theory by Siegfried Nadel in his article about the origins of music,[111] prompted by the observation that in most primitive cultures there is a special and close relation between music and religion. This led Nadel to suppose that music came into existence from the desire of primitive peoples to have a special language other than ordinary speech for communication with the supernatural.

Finally, to the above theories can be added numerous not necessarily exclusive others such as origins in alliteration, competition, dancing, excessive nervous energy, or fear.

There is no point in detailed commentary or discussion of the merits or otherwise of any of the above theories. All can be demolished at a single blow by attacking their premises or assumptions. Aside from other objections that may leap to mind, it is probably safe to say that all or most of these theories, *in common with their refutations*, depend upon one or both of two unfounded and unwarranted assumptions. The first is that it is feasible to talk at all about *the* origin of music. As Sachs says: "origin theories took it for granted that so complicated a thing as music had grown from one root, which is of itself more than improbable."[112]

The contemporary ancestor

The second untenable assumption behind origin theories of music is a matter of method. It is the modus operandi upon which most of the theories depend for their evidence: namely, the notion that in order to find out what the so-called "developed" forms of music such as our own used to be like, we must look at survivals in "primitive" music of today, which is supposed to have been in some kind of stasis for millennia. Curt Sachs departed somewhat from this position in his later writing. But it is nevertheless implicit in most of his work. In his *Short History of World Music*, he states the idea in the following terms:

> ... the prehistory of music is after all referred to the anthropological method to look for primeval tribes which having retreated to far away isles, secluded valleys, or inaccessible jungles have in their growth been arrested in the level of stone age civilisations, in practically unadulterated conditions.[113]

---

[109] Schneider 1957:6-7.
[110] Nettl 1956:136.
[111] Nadel 1930.
[112] Sachs 1943:19.
[113] Sachs 1956:1-2.

He points out that the method is not without its dangers but goes on to assert: "This then is the inevitable fact; whoever wants to know the origins and early rise of music must read them from fossil remains of primitive life of today." [114]

This idea that present day "savages" are the equivalent of our own primitive forebears was a fundamental tool of the Austro-German school of comparative musicology in its search for origins, and its systematic ordering of different forms of music into evolutionary layers or strata following the methods of Kulturkreise.

Of course, it was deluded. To begin with, there are far too many such cultures and far too many differences between them for all to have been ancestral. Nor was it sensible to suppose that they had all reached their present state unaltered in any way from primordial times, without either developmental histories of their own, or without influence from others. The search for "pure" cultures was a search for phantoms. It was also redolent of then contemporary Germanic ideas of race and racial superiority, leading in the end to the Nazi myth of pure Aryan Germans, and the witch-hunts and exterminations that followed. In terms of ethnomusicology, perhaps the one good thing that came of it was the reaction it created, and the impetus it gave to the next stage in the history of the discipline.

The genesis of the idea

Though commonly attributed to the Austro-German comparativists, the idea of the contemporary ancestor, like many others, was in the wind long before it became prominent in Germany. In 1763, an English clergyman and amateur musician, John Brown (1715–1766), published his book *A Dissertation on the Rise, Union, and Power . . . of Poetry and Music*,[115] in which, heavily influenced by Père Lafitau,[116] who was himself anticipated by still earlier scholars, he advanced the idea that whatever was common to the origins and progress of man could most effectively be investigated "by viewing Man in his savage or uncultivated state." [117] A German translation of this work appeared in 1769, and could well have influenced the comparative musicologists. Thirty-six stages of melody, dance and poetry were proposed by Brown, from an early unity with one person, through "perfection" in ancient Greek society, and then downward by degeneration to the separation of the three at the present day.[118] Under the stimulus of evolution, this idea was stood on its head by latter-day comparativists, to produce their stages of culture in the opposite direction from savagery, through barbarism, to the pinnacle of perfection supposedly represented by our own music of the West.

---

[114] Sachs 1956:2.
[115] Brown 1763.
[116] Lafitau 1724.
[117] Allen 1962:82.
[118] Allen loc.cit.

The American school

THE EARLIEST PIONEERS

Three crucial events mark the beginnings of ethnomusicology in the United States, as indicated earlier. All of them related to the study of American Indian tribal music (rather than exotic art musics which interested earlier scholars), and necessarily involved both field work and an anthropological approach to the work. They were Thomas Alva Edison's invention of the phonograph in 1877, which made field recordings of actual sound possible; Theodore Baker's 1881 thesis on Seneca Indian music resulting from his own field work; and the first field recordings of North American Indian music, made by Jesse Walter Fewkes in 1890.

Baker's training as a musicologist was in Leipzig, Germany, and except for early keyboard tuition, owed nothing to America. Baker prepared as a young man for a career in business, but preferred instead to study music, and went to Germany in 1874 to do so.[119] The thesis he wrote in Leipzig was far ahead of its time, dealing with elements of performance style, including the treatment of consonants and vowels in the song texts, melodic range, general quality of voice, and aspects of singing style, such as slide, growl, portamento, and ornamentation, that did not become prominent again in analysis until they were resurrected a century later by Alan Lomax.[120]

Theodore Baker's supervisor at Leipzig was Oscar Paul (1836–1898), whose background was in both music and philology, and whose influence doubtless accounted for Baker's emphasis upon vowels, consonants and manner of singing in his dissertation. Paul's own teachers were Ernst Friedrich Richter (1808–1879) and Moritz Hauptmann (1792–1868) whose specialties were music history and theory of music. Paul's willingness to accept a student dissertation on a topic as unusual as American Indian music, and perhaps Baker's analytic approach, could well have resulted from the influence of Hauptmann, whose belief it was that the principles underlying music must be universally true of human thought. For Hauptmann, the concepts of unity, opposition and reunion underlay all musical elements, including harmony, scales, metre and rhythm.[121]

Jesse Walter Fewkes's contribution to ethnomusicology was as a collector. He trained and qualified first as a marine zoologist, and later as an archaeologist. There is no evidence that he had any musical training, and indeed this seems unlikely as he chose to have his recordings transcribed and analysed by Benjamin Ives Gilman (1852–1933).

Later important early scholars in America – perhaps we can call them first generation ethnomusicologists – included Alice Cunningham Fletcher (1838–1923), recognised as one of the first woman anthropologists in America; Frances Densmore (1867–1957), an indefatigable collector and transcriber of American Indian music, many of whose publications have since been reissued in facsimile; Helen Heffron Roberts (1888–1985), the first writer to delineate North American

---

[119] E-Brit.
[120] Nettl 1995a.
[121] New Grove article on Hauptmann.

Indian music areas,[122] though perhaps better known still for her book *Ancient Hawaiian Music*;[123] and George Herzog (1901–1983), who introduced Hornbostel's analytic methods into the United States.[124]

By the end of her life, Alice Fletcher had achieved immense prestige as an expert in the field of American Indian studies, especially as a result of work begun in 1881, when she had her first experience of Indian music and custom by living for a time among Omaha Indians in Nebraska. She nevertheless had no formal training in either anthropology or music; except in an endowed museum fellowship she never held an academic position; and, although she published extensively in the latter part of her life, she made no theoretical contributions to either subject. Much of her work was done in collaboration with a young mission-educated Omaha man, Francis La Flesche (1857–1932), whom she had informally adopted as a son, and with John Comfort Fillmore (1843–1898), who undertook transcription and analysis of her recordings between 1893 and 1896. La Flesche's involvement was crucial, and he went on to do significant work of his own, especially on Osage tribal ceremonies, which he documented in immense detail.[125] Fillmore worked with both Fletcher and La Flesche and was relied upon by them for musical expertise. His work was marred by peculiar ideas about "incipient harmony" in American Indian unison songs, and by furnishing his transcriptions of them with harmonisations.[126]

Frances Densmore worked on her own and was completely self-sufficient. Her early training was exclusively in music, and in all else she was self taught. Under the auspices of the Bureau of American Ethnology she travelled year after year to reservation after Indian reservation recording music, transcribed and analysed it, and had the results of her labour published by the Bureau before beginning the cycle all over again. Between 1901 and 1940, she studied the music of 76 tribes, recorded more than 2,500 songs, and published at least 22 monographs and 175 articles.[127]

Less well known than Fletcher and Densmore, though contemporary with them, was Natalie Curtis (1875–1921). Also known under her married name of Burlin, Curtis has gained reputation principally for her publication *The India's' Book*,[128] containing hand notations of more than 200 native American songs which she personally collected. Like Fletcher and Densmore, she never taught or held an academic position, but worked on her own. Trained as a pianist and composer, she became interested in native American culture while on a visit to Arizona in 1900, and subsequently visited more than 18 tribes in order to obtain examples of their music. She was killed in 1921, when she was only 46 years old, in a motor-vehicle accident while in Paris.[129]

Like Fletcher, Densmore and Curtis, Helen Roberts never taught. She also never followed up on an extremely promising and productive start as a scholar. Her ethnomuicological work came to an abrupt end in 1936, when Rockefeller Foundation funding that kept her employed ran out. As she had independent means she chose to retire, and stayed in retirement throughout the remain-

---

[122] Roberts 1936.
[123] Roberts 1926.
[124] In his paper "The Yuman Musical Style" (1928).
[125] La Flesche 1921–30.
[126] Lee et al. 1985.
[127] Rahkonen 2003.
[128] Curtis 1907.
[129] Rahkonen 1998.

ing almost 50 years of her life, growing orchids, travelling for recreation, and engaging in good deeds, but eschewing ethnomusicology as a career.[130] She had plenty of reason for disaffection. Apart from losing her job, she was treated shamefully by Seeger and Herzog, and cannot be blamed for quitting the scene.[131]

GEORGE HERZOG (1901–1983)

Herzog was born in Budapest, Hungary. He trained in comparative musicology under Hornbostel at the Berlin Phonogram-Archiv, emigrated to the United States in 1925, studied anthropology at Columbia University under Franz Boas (1858–1942) and Ruth Benedict (1887–1948), and gained a PhD in anthropology at Columbia in 1931.

It is Herzog who is credited with beginning the American School of comparative musicology by combining the methods of Hornbostel with those of American cultural anthropology. Herzog retained Hornbostel's analytic methods but abandoned the trappings of evolutionism and invariant stages of culture that continued to dominate in Europe. It is extremely fortunate that Herzog began his activities in the United States when he did, because it was Boas above all who was responsible for the ideas that Herzog put into practice. Nor was Boas's influence limited to Herzog. He taught Ruth Benedict, who was another of Herzog's tutors, as well as Helen Roberts, who was later to make her own contribution to American ethnomusicology, and Melville Herskovits (1895–1963), who taught Alan P. Merriam. Were it not for Boas, then, American ethnomusicology, and indeed anthropology itself, might have continued along some of the same unproductive paths followed by comparative musicologists in Europe and by Boas's predecessors in America.

Boas's methods developed as a reaction against evolutionism and the notion of stages of culture. Key ideas contributed by him to later anthropology were:

- In depth study. Every component of a culture is regarded as important, and data on all of them should be collected. Boas, indeed, himself recorded Kwakiutl music of British Columbia,[132] during a North Pacific Expedition he directed between 1897 and 1902, as well as earlier at the 1893 Columbian Exposition at Chicago.[133]

- Cultural relativism. Each culture has its own frame of reference and should be interpreted on its own terms.

- Historical particularism. Each culture has its own unique history, and universal laws of culture cannot be assumed.

---

[130] Rahkonen 2003; Frisbie 1989:104.
[131] Seeger left her without support, and probably at her own expense, as secretary of a defunct organisation, the American Society for Comparative Musicology, for which he had taken responsibility, and Herzog lost an important manuscript of an entire book, obliging her, despite failing eyesight, to start over with the writing (Frisbie 1991:250).
[132] Myers 1993:21.
[133] Myers 1993:22.

In the course of his professional life, Herzog set the scene for a number of important long-term trends in ethnomusicology:

The first, following Boas, was to affirm the importance of personal field experience, conducting expeditions to almost a dozen North American Indian tribes.

Another important contribution, which emerged out of his Berlin experience, was to promote archiving of recorded materials.

Herzog was also a superb researcher. A sampling of especially significant papers written by him, as assessed by Nettl,[134] is as follows:

- "Speech-Melody and Primitive Music" (1934) took up the special relationship between music and tone languages.

- "Plains Ghost Dance and Great Basin Music" (1935a) may be the first properly ethnohistorical study in ethnomusicology.

- "Special Song Types in North American Indian Music" (1935b) establishes an archaic stratum of styles overlapping musical area boundaries.

- "A Comparison of Pueblo and Pima Musical Styles" (1936) is a major model of comparative study.

- "Music in the Thinking of the American Indian" (1938) is one of the first writings explicitly discussing the ideas about music held by a tribal society.

- "Song", in Funk and Wagnall's *Standard Dictionary of Folklore* (1950) provides the most comprehensive, if brief, discussion of folk music yet published in English.

The last of these is demonstrative of Herzog's wide-ranging expertise not only as a specialist in North American Indian music, but also in the area of folk song, inspired, perhaps, by the work of his Hungarian compatriot, Béla Bartók, whom he admired and was instrumental in bringing to the United States. In Herzog, then, three streams can be said to have converged. As Nettl expresses it:

> ... the hand of Hornhostel, the comparativist and the archive-builder, of Bartók the careful processor and analyst concerned with authenticity, of Boas the methodical fieldworker, of the confluence of folkloristics, linguistics, and ethnography.[135]

In the late 1940s, tragically, Herzog began to succumb to mental illness, and after about 1951 there were no further papers or insights from him as the illness took its toll, and the final two decades of his life had to be spent in institutional care, retired from academia.

---

[134] Nettl 1981; Nettl 1991..
[135] Nettl 1991:271.

Thanks mostly to Herzog and his teacher Boas, the American School of ethnomusicology diverged from European comparative musicology largely because it focused upon uses and functions of music as well as music structure. The approach, in other words, began to be anthropological as well as musicological. It has been suggested with some justification that Americans were more empiricists and less theoreticians at this time because in the USA, with scores of North American Indian tribes right on the doorstep, theories could be taken easily into the field, whereas in Europe, comparative musicologists were mostly dependent on materials collected by others. Eventually, both in Europe and in the USA, the term comparative musicology lost favour as a name for the discipline, principally because it was regarded as no more comparative than any other branch of knowledge, and was supplanted by the term ethnomusicology around 1950.

CURT SACHS (1881–1959)

Although immensely influential and a dominant figure, even posthumously with the publication of his book *The Wellsprings of Music*,[136] Curt Sachs represented a side-stream of ethnomusicology. Senior to Herzog by exactly 20 years, he never shook off the evolutionary approaches of his European contemporaries and forebears. In the 1950s, in the eyes of the musical establishment he was *the* ethnomusicologist. Today his eclipse is almost total.

Herzog left Germany early and did so voluntarily. Sachs, who was German-born, followed only when forced to do so, after the rise of the Nazi regime and the breakup of Hornbostel's Berlin School in 1933. He did not engage in field work, and was not remotely interested in American Indians, but remained a comparativist pure and simple, building large-scale theories of stylistic origins through developmental stages, with the entire world as his domain.

CHARLES SEEGER (1886–1979)

Contemporary with Sachs, though he lived for 20 years longer, was the American musicologist, Charles Seeger. Like Sachs, he remained aloof from personal field work and the anthropological approach, but was not a comparativist either, though he accepted the post of president in 1933 of a soon to be defunct Society for Comparative Musicology, which assumed the mantle of its German predecessor after National Socialism brought such activities to an end in Germany. By training he was a composer, conductor for a time, and critic, who turned to musicology before there was any such established discipline in America, and by the end of his life had become a revered theorist and had earned a reputation as a philosopher of music.

Seeger's status as a theorist appears to have been established very early as a result of an article he wrote in 1930 on the subject of "Dissonant counterpoint",[137] in which he gave advice to then modernist composers on how to avoid consonance. His friend and fellow composer Henry Cowell (1887–1965), who had been a student of Seeger's during World War I, wrote ecstatically of Seeger in 1932:

> Charles Seeger is the greatest musical explorer in intellectual fields which America has produced, the greatest experimental musicologist. Ever fascinated by intricacies, he has solved more problems of modern musical theory, and suggested more fruitful pathways for musical

---

[136] Sachs 1961.
[137] Seeger 1930.

composition (some of which have proved of great general import), than any other three men.[138]

It was a reputation that stayed with Seeger throughout his career, which extended over most of the next half century. Recently, at least three books have been published about him, a biography,[139] and two that set out to interpret his thought: *A Question of Balance* by Taylor Aitken Greer, and *Understanding Charles Seeger*, by Bell Yung and Helen Rees.[140]

The publisher's blurb for Greer's book describes Seeger as "One of this century's most influential musical intellects". The Yung and Rees blurb represents him as:

> A giant in the development of American musicology . . . His ideas about music and musicology, incorporating perspectives as wide-ranging as physics, philosophy, and anthropology, set the stage for the rise of modern ethnomusicology.

How justified are the accolades? It has to be said that Seeger indeed enjoyed immense prestige and acclaim. But it is hard to know why. His credentials were slender; compared with others such as Herzog, he wrote very little that was specific to ethnomusicology; and, except at the beginning of his career and later taking part in seminars at UCLA, was not active as a teacher.

Among thinkers who are said to have influenced Seeger was the British philosopher Bertrand Russell (1872–1970). One must doubt, however, whether Seeger absorbed the essentials of Russell. Certainly he did not even try to emulate Russell's incisive and crystal-clear style of writing. Russell had a rare ability to convey complex ideas intelligibly, but the same cannot be said for Seeger. Bruno Nettl (charitably) speaks of Seeger's "occasional incomprehensibility" and "tendency to say simple things in complex ways."[141] Tongue in cheek, as an in-joke directed towards those who have struggled with Seeger's prose, Gilbert Chase entitled a review of Seeger's collected essays "An Exagmination Round His Factification for Incamination".[142]

Above all, it would seem to have been Seeger's charisma rather than the content of his writing that has contributed most to perceptions of him. All who have written about him are unanimous in praise of his personal qualities. In a review of Pescatello's biography of Seeger, Vivian Perlis, who herself had experience of interviewing him, comments:

> For the most part it is difficult to be critical of Seeger: his personality was so attractive that those who knew him would forgive him almost anything . . . It remains for those in the respective fields to know if Seeger's ideas are as brilliant as he made them seem. It was the pleasure of hearing Seeger that made the impact. His talk was mesmerising, although often too long, and his delight in himself was contagious: audiences, whether individual interviewers or crowds of students and colleagues found him irresistible.[143]

---

[138] Nicholls 1990.
[139] Pescatello 1992.
[140] Greer 1998; Yung & Rees 1999.
[141] Nettl 1988:22,
[142] Chase 1979.
[143] Perlis 1995:291.

In a comparison of the work of Seeger with that of Herzog,[144] Bruno Nettl seems hard pressed to name a single idea of Seeger's that has had any lasting influence upon ethnomusicology except for his development of the melograph (a machine for graphical display of music), which itself has ceased to be significant. Rather, Seeger emerges as an revered leader whose theoretical writings have provided ethnomusicology with intellectual status and philosophical standing.

Seeger lived into his nineties, his reputation as an elder statesman of music growing all the while. He kept himself to the fore and became extremely well known. In the course of his life he involved himself with numerous musical organisations, as member, as office-holder, and in his later years in an honorary capacity. In the latter role and even earlier, he was useful for his mere presence. Just as organisations of various kinds like to have a person of eminence as a "patron", honorary president, or titular head, who is not expected to do anything, so too Seeger was recruited because of his standing. When the Society for Ethnomusicology was formed, Frances Densmore, who was too elderly for an active role, gave permission for her "name" to be used, and she was duly appointed to the Executive Board, though she never attended any meetings.[145] Similarly, Seeger was approached in 1952, after the initial informal meeting of scholars that agreed upon setting up an organisation, but it was Merriam and the other founders who did all of the work. Seeger's appointment a few years later at UCLA was also of this nature. As a research associate he had no formal responsibilities,[146] but was retained year after year because his presence conferred status on Mantle Hood's fledgling Institute of Ethnomusicology.

What then of Seeger's actual work? Most of it took the form of highly abstruse writings that hardly anyone has ever read, which few profess to understand, which in fact often mean very little if one takes the trouble to unravel them, and which have had no discernible impact beyond appearing impressive. It is hard to avoid the conclusion that Seeger's reputation as an influential thinker has been over-inflated, though no one seems willing to say so. The prevailing image of Seeger is of the great man, akin to Einstein, whose theories took years to be fully understood, but ultimately transformed our understanding of the universe. The title of one of Seeger's papers, "Toward a Unitary Field Theory for Musicology",[147] redolent of Einstein as it is, suggests indeed that Seeger envisaged such a role for himself. So does the title *Principia Musicologica*,[148] which he chose for a proposed book that was never actually written and perhaps not even started, that just as clearly derived its title from Isaac Newton and the philosophers Alfred Whitehead and Bertrand Russell, who in both cases produced genuinely revolutionary and influential books with the title *Principia*.[149]

But no such future status for Seeger is likely. As memory of him fades, he will be judged for what he did rather than the perceptions of him that are still current. In my view, far from being beneficial, Seeger's influence upon ethnomusicology has been pernicious in at least three ways:

---

[144] Nettl 1991.
[145] Frisbie 1991:249.
[146] Seegers role at UCLA appears to have been limited largely to volunntary attendance at seminars, where he took part in discussions. His position at UCLA in 1960 required no duties of him: "no responsibilities, no classes or seminars, no publications demanded." (Hood 1979:77).
[147] Seeger 1970.
[148] Hood 1979:77.
[149] Newton 1686; Whitehead & Russell 1910.

1. Because of his reputation as an intellectual giant, Seeger's long-standing presence as a senior figure at UCLA certainly aided that institution. However, the assumptions behind the development of the UCLA melograph, and the justifications offered for it by Seeger have undermined standard transcription to the point that it has now been virtually abandoned, and this in turn has helped to nudge ethnomusicology away from analysis and comparison. All of these developments are entrenched in current orthodoxy but, as will be argued later, are now in need of reconsideration.

2. Difficult and seemingly profound as they are, Seeger's writings have convinced too many academics that the road to success is to follow his example and write impenetrable theoretical prose. Herzog, on the other hand, who is the better model, pragmatically combined the best of what was available to him at the time, while rejecting the worst, got on with the task of actually doing something rather than explaining why it could or should not be done, and produced a string of works and insights that have been genuinely useful. One hopes that it is Herzog's methodology rather than Seeger's that will prevail.

3. Finally, Seeger's eclecticism has also become standard practice and has reached a point where this too is creating problems. Ethnomusicology has always benefited from ideas and concepts first developed in other disciplines. Not every such idea, however, is truly applicable to music. Seeger read widely and applied what the read to his own thought about music, using such ideas principally as a trigger rather than applying them rigorously. Some of the resulting connections were tenuous at best. Allying him with Einstein and modern physics on the basis of a paper title is particularly absurd, raising the possibility that others of his ideas were also of such a nature.

International societies

When I first entered the field of ethnomusicology in the late 1950s, there was a fairly clear-cut division between the two main international societies that still serve the discipline. America was the home of the Society for Ethnomusicology (SEM), which emerged in the early 1950s from initiatives of Alan P. Merriam, David P. McAllester, Willard Rhodes, Charles Seeger, and others. In Europe there was the International Folk Music Council (IFMC), founded somewhat earlier than the SEM, under the aegis of Maud Karpeles (1885–1976) as its secretary.

International travel in those days was not as readily accomplished as it is now. Each organisation held its own meetings on opposite sides of the Atlantic; they published their own separate journals, and their memberships tended to be different. IFMC meetings were held in Europe, necessarily with three official languages of English, French and German, while the SEM, which met in the United States, could afford to be monolingual. The IFMC meetings, though international in scope tended to place more weight on folk song, particularly from Europe.

The IFMC nevertheless can be regarded in a sense as a parent of the SEM. In 1950, on the initiative of Stith Thompson (1885–1976), a distinguished American folklorist and faculty member at Indiana University, the IFMC departed from its usual rule and held its third meeting not in Europe, but at Indiana University, USA. Among scholars who attended the meeting were a number who later became prominent in the SEM and/or American ethnomusicology, including Marius Barbeau (1883–1969), Samuel Bayard (1908–1997), Bertrand Bronson (1902–1986),

George Herzog (1901–1983), Barbara Krader (1922–), Gertrude Kurath (1903–1993), Alan Lomax (1915–2002), Charles Seeger (1886–1979), Richard Waterman (1914–1971) and others. Significantly, too, it was at this meeting that Bruno Nettl (1930–), then a graduate student, decided to become an ethnomusicologist.[150]

Successive IFMC presidents included folk music stalwarts such as Ralph Vaughan Williams (1872–1958) and Zoltán Kodály (1882–1967). The earliest presidents of the SEM included all four of its co-founders, Willard Rhodes (1956–57), Charles Seeger (1960–62), Alan Merriam (1962–64), and David McAllester (1964–66), with Mieczyslaw Kolinski (1958–59) as the next president after Rhodes. A photo of the founders was taken by William P. Malm at the 1971 meeting of the SEM, held at Duke University, Durham, North Carolina.

Founders of the SEM: L-R, Charles Seeger, Alan Merriam,
Willard Rhodes, David McAllester. Photo; William P. Malm

SEM meetings had greater emphasis on tribal musics, particularly North American Indian and African, reflecting the interests of most of its members. Another difference between the two organisations was in the average age of members. The SEM was led by younger more forward-thinking people than the IFMC. The latter tended to be dominated by respected older scholars, many of them espousing views and interests no longer in the mainstream of American ethnomusicology. In Europe, debate still took place on subjects such as the origin of music, long after it was abandoned in America, and the echoes of diffusionism and the earlier comparative musicology of the Austro-German school were still to be heard. Much of the debate, indeed, circulated around theoretical positions of one kind and another upon which the protagonists had staked their reputations, and were defended with vigour.

As international travel became more usual, and academics were able to secure funding for it, American members became more numerous in the IFMC, and eventually came to dominate this

---

[150] Nettl 2002:82-3.

organisation also. It changed its name to ICTM (International Council for Traditional Music), expanded its scope increasingly away from Europe, and its secretariat moved eventually to America, where it remained for the next 35 years.[151]

Whereas formerly its meetings were held annually in different European venues, now they moved from country to country, unlike the SEM which continued to hold meetings exclusively in America. This, indeed, became the main difference between the two organisations, as both were now effectively American.

Meanwhile, filling the gap left by the departure of the ICTM, John Blacking (1928–1990) founded the European Seminar in Ethnomusicology (ESEM) in 1981. Although nowhere nearly as large as the two older organisations, it has a respectable membership of about 400, is international in scope like the other two organisations, and on the model of the old IFMC has been holding annual meetings in different European centres since 1983. It does not, however, publish a journal, and as yet no new directions have emerged that can be said to have influenced ethnomusicology as a whole. The journals of the ICTM and SEM, on the other hand, are highly influential because these are now the main publishing outlets for ethnomusicologists at large, and the papers their editors choose to publish receive more exposure than those published in less well known or accessible quarters.

An additional, relatively new, publishing outlet is *Ethnomusicology Forum* (formerly *British Journal of Ethnomusicology*), established in 1992, with objectives and content similar to the other international journals and, perhaps even more in line with current trends than they are, with ethnomusicology defined broadly as "the study of 'people making music', and encompassing the study of all musics, including Western art music and popular musics."

The middle years in America (1960–80)

It may be that were it not for the Dutch East India Company, ethnomusicology would not have got its name, and there would be no gamelans in North America.

The beginnings of both developments lie with the establishment of the company in 1602, the Dutch trade empire which resulted, and the employment from 1920–34 of a former Amsterdam bank clerk named Jaap Kunst as a colonial civil servant in Indonesia.

JAAP KUNST (1891–1960)

Kunst's interest in Indonesia began a year earlier than his employment there, when he toured the country as the violinist of a string trio. During this tour he heard for the first time the Indonesian gong ensemble known as gamelan, and became fascinated with it. His decision to stay on in Indonesia was prompted by his desire to learn more about the music. On weekends and during his

---

[151] After its break from Europe, the IFMC/ICTM secretariat moved first to Queen's University, Kingston, Ontario, Canada (with Graham George as Secretary-General, 1969–80), then to Columbia University, New York (where Dieter Christensen served as Secretary-General, 1981–2001), and finally to UCLA (with Anthony Seeger as Secretary-General, 2001– 05).

annual vacations he took advantage of unlimited free train travel that his employment offered to pursue his interest, spending most of the remainder of his free time in writing up the results.[152]

Kunst returned to the Netherlands in 1936, where he became successively curator at the Colonial Institute (later Royal Tropical Institute), Amsterdam, and lecturer, then reader, at the University of Amsterdam.

Kunst is remembered for three main contributions to ethnomusicology, all of which were to have long-standing consequences. The first was his coining, in 1950, of the te-rm ethnomusicology itself, as a replacement for the former name "comparative musicology". It is questionable whether this was a beneficial move. The end result, though this was not Kunst's intention, was the virtual abandonment of comparison as one of the objectives of the discipline. Kunst's second commonly acknowledged contribution was the publication of his bibliographic survey, entitled *Ethnomusicology*,[153] which inaugurated an entirely beneficial emphasis on bibliography which has characterised the discipline ever since. Finally, his reputation has remained high because of his many writings on Indonesian music, and the status he achieved for it in the West.

Kunst's influence, however, is by no means limited to the above. A prominent theme in his writings is the importance he placed upon the work of Alexander Ellis (1814–1890) in providing a precise means of measuring tonal intervals, a concern that places Kunst squarely with the comparativists of the Berlin School, and in his case was an essential component of his work relating to Indonesian tuning systems.

Kunst's most distinguished student at Amsterdam was Mantle Hood (1918–2005), an American who was later to establish an Institute of Ethnomusicology at the University of California, Los Angeles (UCLA), where he applied and elaborated the lessons he had learned from Kunst.

THE WANING INFLUENCE OF EUROPE

Even in the early 1950s, when Hood was studying with Kunst in Amsterdam, it was an unusual arrangement. In Britain, ethnomusicology had no institutional base but was dependent upon the individual efforts of a handful of scholars such as Arnold Bake (1899–1963) and Laurence Picken (1909–), whose living was earned in other disciplines. In the rest of Europe, ethnomusicology was still largely concerned with folk music and what was left of comparative musicology after the departure of its most productive advocates such as Curt Sachs for the United States. It was in the latter country that ethnomusicology was to be nurtured and developed during its most formative years, and the flow of potential students was almost exclusively one way. Throughout the 1960s and 1970s, ethnomusicology was established as an option within music and anthropology departments at universities throughout the country until, today, it has a presence in nearly all of them.

The death of Kunst in 1960 severed one of the remaining ties with Europe, and coincides with the beginnings of new concepts in ethnomusicology, in the shape of a dualism that dominated the discipline throughout the 1960s and 1970s, and is still not fully resolved.

---

[152] Heins 1994:14.
[153] Kunst 1959a.

On the one side was Kunst's former student Mantle Hood and his Institute of Ethnomusicology, promoting the musicological approaches exemplified by Kunst. On the other was Alan P. Merriam (1923–1980) at Indiana University, who challenged the primacy of exclusive preoccupation with music sound, and championed the application of approaches derived from anthropology.

THE UCLA/INDIANA DIVIDE

Mantle Hood (1918–2005)

Unlike Merriam, Hood's professional training was exclusively in music. He began by studying composition, gained an AB in music (1951), and MA in music (1952) at UCLA, and went on to compose works in later years such as Implosion (1982) for percussion quartet, and Udan Bostan (1996) for gamelan.[154] During this period, also, he turned to writing novels. His primary focus, however, was on ethnomusicology: in particular, gamelan music of Java and Bali, and theoretical writings derived from his experience with this genre after graduating PhD under the tutelage of his Indonesianist mentor Jaap Kunst at the University of Amsterdam in 1954.

Hood's most recent contribution to ethnomusicology was a theory he began developing in 1989,[155] called a "quantum theory of music." At one of his presentations, attended by scientists, he was asked if he would mind writing the formula on the chalkboard. He replied that he was not yet ready to do so.[156] Like his colleague Seeger before him, it is evident he used modern physics not in any scientific way, but as a vehicle for ideas which he hoped might ultimately develop beyond analogy. Hood's ideas on the topic have evident appeal outside of ethnomusicology. As perusal of the world wide web will confirm, they have attracted New Age fellow-travellers among whom Hood's quantum theory has achieved almost cult status. It is nevertheless as an Indonesianist and proponent of performance studies, especially in gamelan, that Hood remains best known and has exerted greatest influence.

Not long after beginning to teach at UCLA, Hood introduced America's first Indonesian gamelan group as an instructional aid, in 1958, and provided theoretical justification for it with writings on a concept which he called "bi-musicality".

Bi-musicality

Hood introduced the term in a paper entitled "The Challenge of Bi-Musicality",[157] written out of his experience with performance groups at UCLA, which by 1960 had expanded to include Javanese gamelan, Balinese gamelan, Balinese gendèr wajang, Japanese gagaku, Japanese nagauta, Persian music and South Indian music.[158] Most of the paper is concerned with the practical difficulties faced by students in comprehending an unfamiliar idiom, and no extravagant claims for the method are made. Only in the last few sentences does Hood allude to the term "bi-musicality", which is the subject of his article. He refers to several graduate students

---

[154] Giuriati 2003.
[155] For Hood's own explanation of the progress of his theory see Hood 2000:368-9.
[156] Hood 1998.
[157] Hood 1960.
[158] Hood 1960:56.

who managed themselves "quite capably" in several different musical cultures. Rather than refer to these students in terms of "bi-", "tri-", or "quadra-musicality" he preferred to retitle the paper simply to read "The Challenge of Musicality".[159] So why did he allow the original title to stand? Left hanging is the question of whether "bi-musicality", in the sense of equal competence in more than one music system, as implied by analogy with bilingualism, is attainable. The term, however, was now firmly to the fore by virtue of the title, and as such has become part of the vocabulary of ethnomusicology without need for definition.

Three years after writing his initial paper, Hood set the parameters for extended debate in a famous and highly influential book chapter entitled "Music the Unknown".[160] After an historical survey similar to those offered earlier by Kunst and Nettl, Hood goes on to raise issues that became extremely important in later years, mostly resulting in outcomes that favoured Hood's own perceptions of them.

One was to throw doubt on the efficacy of Western notation as a means of transcribing non-Western music. His solution later in the article was to proselytise on behalf of Seeger's melograph, which offered an "objective" form of machine transcription, free of perceived biases and faulty perceptions of human transcribers.

A second departure from common practice was to discredit comparison as "premature", on the grounds that not enough was yet known to permit conclusions to be drawn.

A third and related concern was to emphasise the importance of obtaining a performing knowledge of the music under study before attempting to pronounce upon it.

Hood's conclusion was to reject nearly everything that had been published pre-Hood, in the following terms:

> All of these considerations force me to conclude that almost all of the so-called standard references in ethnomusicology, aside from some descriptive value, must be largely discounted in their analytical and comparative conclusions, based as they are on over-simplifications, generalities, compounded inaccuracies and primitive methodology.[161]

Although no reference to "bi-musicality" as such appears in Hood's essay, there is strong emphasis throughout about the value and primacy of live performance, along with further favourable reference to performance groups at UCLA, and there is overwhelming attention to Oriental art music, especially Hood's own specialty area of Indonesia.

Merriam was not favourably impressed. In a review of Hood's paper he offered three main criticisms of it. He chided Hood for conveying the impression that ethnomusicology is almost exclusively concerned with the music of the Near and Far East; that little was happening in ethnomusicology except at Hood's own institution of UCLA; and especially he questioned the efficacy of performance groups as a teaching aid.[162]

---

[159] Hood 1960:59.
[160] Hood 1963.
[161] Hood 1963:234.
[162] Merriam 1964b.

Hood's emphasis on music performance and his concept of bi-musicality as a means of gaining insight into musical styles has nevertheless become a staple of ethnomusicology classes taught in university music departments throughout the world. Largely it is taken for granted and has ceased to be debated, though it was at the core of a schism between the methods of Merriam and Hood and their respective students in the 1960s.

The issue, however, ran much deeper than performance groups or whether too much emphasis was being placed upon activities at UCLA. A phrase from Hood's essay that was bandied about constantly at the time by his supporters was "music in terms of itself". Merriam's followers were by no means certain that music could or should be studied in this way.

Alan P. Merriam (1923–1980)

Merriam began his academic career in a somewhat similar fashion to Hood. Like Hood, his earliest degrees, in his case a BA at Montana State University and an MM at Northwestern University, were in music. Thereafter, and even before, the paths taken by the two diverged.

Merriam had the good fortune to be born into a family within which both music and learning mattered. His father was a professor of English at Montana State University, and his mother was both an accomplished cellist and the holder of a degree in library science.[163] Little wonder that Merriam became an ardent proponent of bibliography as an essential tool for ethnomusicology.

At an early age, Merriam began both piano lessons and learned to play the clarinet. During his high school years and at university he played clarinet in jazz bands. At Northwestern, while studying for his master's degree in music, be came into contact with Richard Waterman (1914–1971), an Africanist in the anthropology department who shared his enthusiasm for jazz. Waterman introduced Merriam to anthropology, and Merriam then switched tracks to this subject, studying under Waterman and Melville Herskovits (1895–1963) who had been a student of Franz Boas, and graduating PhD in 1951 with a dissertation on Afro-Bahian cult songs.

Already, Merriam was applying anthropology to music, and went on to do so in ever more rigorous ways. It is significant that his interests were in tribal music, having followed jazz to its origins in Africa, whereas Hood had gravitated from one form of art music, namely Western, to another, Indonesian. Hood continued along the path of Oriental art music and Merriam of tribal music, the one under the aegis of a music department, the other as an anthropologist, and therein lay the seeds of the division in approach between the two men.

Music in culture

These days, most people think they know what is meant by "culture", but when the term was introduced it had more specific connotations than is perhaps now the case, although even then in its scientific sense it lacked a fully agreed definition.[164] Central to American anthropology of the 1960s, in its most common form of "cultural anthropology", is what has become known as the "culture concept". Merriam's own working definition of "culture", which he ascribed in lectures to his teacher Herskovits, was "man's cumulative learned behavior", from which it follows that

---

[163] Card et al. 1981:ix.
[164] Herskovits (1953:305) refers to over 160 different formal definitions of the term.

"cultures" can be regarded as the shared or collective learned behaviour of particular groups. This, at any rate, apposite as it obviously is to ethnomusicology, is the term as accepted by Merriam,[165] and if the meaning has since changed, this was not part of Merriam's thinking and should not be attributed to him.

In a lead article in the journal *Ethnomusicology*, in the same year that Hood published his paper on "bi-musicality", Alan P. Merriam introduced his now famous definition of ethnomusicology as "music in culture". So common has the phrase since become, and so many more implications have been attached to it than intended by Merriam, it may be worth revisiting what it was he actually said.

Merriam begins his article by pointing out that early emphasis in ethnomusicology had been on elements of music structure such as scales and tonal systems, but this approach had been joined in America by increasing awareness of the relationship of music to culture. In recognition of this, he proposed to define ethnomusicology as "the study of music in culture".[166]

It was a new idea and it was to have an immense impact, but as important as the definition itself was what Merriam did *not* say. He did not suggest that the study of music structure should be abandoned. Neither did he claim that music structure is unimportant. On the contrary, he clearly set out a threefold strategy for investigation with no implication that any one part of it should have primacy over the others, namely: 1) the gathering of materials in the field; 2) transcription and analysis; 3) application to relevant problems.[167]

Far from being sidelined, the second or laboratory phase of investigation is referred to later in the article as "of course, basic" in establishing an essential taxonomy.[168] As an anthropologist, however, Merriam's primary concern in the article was the first and last of the three components of study, and he goes on to consider aspects of music in culture that were currently being neglected and needed to be addressed, among them uses and functions of music, text-melody relationships, the role and status of musicians, ownership of music, processes of composition, learning and instruction, and others.[169]

It can be assumed that Merriam was already working on the manuscript of his monumental book, *The Anthropology of Music*,[170] which he published four years later. It was by no means the kind of book that could be tossed off in a year or two, and all of the topics raised in the paper

---

[165] Merriam 1964b:21.
[166] Merriam 1960:109.
[167] Merriam 1960:109.
[168] Merriam 1960:111.
[169] Music in culture remained Merriam's primary concern for the rest of his life. But he continued to accept the value of analysis and comparison of music structures as well. Lest there should be any doubt about this, one need only refer to his own very clear statement on the matter, published two years after his death in 1980:

> I wish to state that my basic position has not changed: I am still interested in the study of music as culture, and the study of music sound structure is a means to a more limited end than that which I usually wish to undertake. My purpose, then, is to remind us that structural studies clearly do have their place in ethnomusicology, that such studies lead naturally and inevitably to comparisons of structures, and that such comparisons can, under specific circumstances, lead to new and broadened knowledge of music (Merriam 1982;175).

[170] Merriam 1964a.

of 1960 resurface in it as chapter and section headings and as the subject of extended discussion. It is hard to overestimate the importance to ethnomusicology of this book. It is not an exaggeration to say that in the writing of it Merriam transformed the discipline.

In 1971, Mantle Hood published his awaited answer to Merriam in a book he called *The Ethnomusicologist*.[171] It dealt exclusively with organology and matters relating to music structure, and there were no concessions either to Merriam or to anthropology.

If any further evidence was needed of the fundamental differences of outlook and approach of the two men, this book supplied it. It was a case of "north is north and south is south and never the twain shall meet", and this was mirrored by the teaching offered in the respective departments. Hood's students were instructed in systematic musicology and Merriam's in anthropology. Hood's performance groups continued to proliferate at UCLA, and there was none at Indiana. Neither programme could be said to offer a full training in all of the many skills that by now were required of a practising ethnomusicologist. Meanwhile, in other institutions, regard was had to the teachings of both men, and attempts were made to integrate them.

The intellectual history leading step by step to the Hood/Merriam standoff is clear. The path followed by Hood begins with Alexander Ellis and his tonometrical analysis, reaching Hood himself through his Indonesianist teacher Jaap Kunst. Merriam's intellectual forebear was Franz Boas, with his emphasis upon studying every element of a culture, reaching Merriam though his teacher Melville Herskovits, who shared the same convictions.

In 1980, Merriam was killed in an air crash, and his programme within the anthropology department at Indiana University came to an end. His mantle fell upon John Blacking (1928–1990), a British-born ethnomusicologist whose story, together with what became of the Hood/Merriam dichotomy will be taken up later.

New directions (1980–2000)

WRITINGS ON THE WALL

In 1976, during his sabbatical year in Australia, just four years before his untimely death, Alan P. Merriam delivered a series of lectures at the University of Sydney, some of whose content has been reported by Stephen Wild.[172]

In his Sydney lectures, Merriam was critical of trends he saw emerging in ethnomusicology, which have since been amply confirmed by events.

First he was concerned about a dearth of comparison in ethnomusicology, and praised Lomax as one of the few scholars still to espouse it.[173] Secondly, he worried about a move towards cognitive anthropology and an obsession with minutiae amounting to learning more and more about less and less. In his view, ethnomusicology was becoming too concerned with theory-building.

---

[171] Hood 1971.
[172] Wild et al. 1982.
[173] Lomax's work is discussed in a later section on Cantometrics.

In terms of what should be done he saw a fusion of musicology and anthropology, which he regarded as the two main contributing disciplines to ethnomusicology, as essential if a true discipline of ethnomusicology were to emerge, and ethnomusicology should be concerned equally with product and process. He also pointed to a need for ethnomusicology to be more open to influence from disciplines such as psychology, sociology, acoustics, aesthetics and human biology. In all such matters he was prophetic and his fears and expectations, though not all of the expected benefits he foresaw, have been amply realised. Rather than dismiss Merriam's ideas of 30 years ago as "old-fashioned" or, worse, forget about them altogether, present-day ethnomusicologists would do well to heed them.

Some of the trends that worried Merriam, and which indeed now dominate the discipline, began earlier with two attacks on the then establishment that were mounted in the 1970s, both published in the journal *Ethnomusicology*.

Except for a mild initial flurry of attention, neither had much influence until recently. Both, however, are now regarded as significant. The first was a paper by Marcia Herndon (c.1941–1997) entitled "Analysis: Herding Sacred Cows?".[174] The other was a paper by Kenneth Gourlay (d. 1994).[175]

In her paper, Herndon queries the value of musical analysis, especially using methods espoused by Mieczyslaw Kolinski (1901–1981), who had invented a number of supposedly universal methods for analysing elements of music structure. Kolinski was an easy target because hardly anyone in ethnomusicology saw merit in his methods in any case, and few researchers made use of them except Kolinski himself. A series of exchanges between Herndon and Kolinski ensued, and then the topic appeared to subside.

Gourlay's paper was more broad-based than that of Herndon. Its principal argument was that the presence of an observer, namely the ethnomusicologist, affects the situation under observation and renders "scientific" description difficult or impossible. Rejecting the approaches of Nettl, Merriam, and Blacking on these grounds, he proposed an alternative "model" based on ideas attributed to Seeger, Chase, Herndon, Fogelson, Blum and Wachsmann. It is a problem to which Gourlay offers no real solution except perhaps, by implication, to abandon objectivity in favour of sufficient immersion in a music culture to be able to afford a "subjective" approach.

The idea itself was far from new, and most ethnomusicologists, including those criticised by Gourlay, were well aware of the dangers of influencing events or imposing inappropriate biases upon observation, and took care to avoid them in their work. Although Gourlay's paper had little impact at the time, however, it marks the beginnings of a major thrust away from the older verities and, as will be seen, an ultimate reshaping of the discipline.

REMODELLING ETHNOMUSICOLOGY?

Three papers bear upon the subject, all post-Merriam, and all from affiliates of UCLA,, whose ethnomusicology programmes have continued to build upon the work of Mantle Hood and

---

[174] Herndon 1974.
[175] Gourlay 1978.

Charles Seeger. Timothy Rice is a current professor of ethnomusicology at UCLA; James Porter is a former UCLA professor; and Peter Manuel, the youngest of the three, underwent all of his training at UCLA.

The first of the three papers, though far the longest, and despite its seemingly auspicious title "Toward a Remodeling of Ethnomusicology",[176] is the least germane. Ironically in view of Merriam's worries about too much theory-building, it concerns Merriam's own three-part feedback model of concept–behaviour–sound (see Part V) which by this time had served the discipline for more than two decades, and it elaborates the theoretical implications of a more intricate model by the author, Timothy Rice, which he hoped would provide a unified approach for ethnomusicologists and be productive of further advances of the discipline. Two of four respondents who had been invited to comment on the paper criticised Rice's model as not doing justice to Merriam, and one of the two strongly questioned the need for such a model at all. Curiously, neither the author nor any of the respondents noticed resemblances between Rice's exposition of his model and ideas first articulated by Cecil Sharp at the turn of the 20th century, and strongly endorsed by the International Folk Music Council in the early years of its existence under Maud Karpeles. Essentially, though he did not say so, Rice was directing attention to the process of oral transmission about which Sharp's famous concept of historical continuity, individual variation and community selection (see later) was a far better formulation of the process than Rice's.

The second and third papers, by Porter and Manuel, published simultaneously in the same issue of *Transcultural Music Review*, survey new perspectives in ethnomusicology up to the year 1995.[177] As they cover similar ground, I shall consider them together,[178] doing so where possible in terms of Merriam's assessment of trends. Discussion of the issues raised in these papers will be taken up in Part V.

Earlier work

Porter makes the valid point that part of the legitimacy ethnomusicology has won for itself results from "a distinguished body of literature over the past century." Manuel makes it clear, however, that ethnomusicology has turned its back on much of this literature, dismissing its subject matter and methods as old-fashioned and irrelevant to current concerns. According to Manuel, most of the seminal important writings of the 1950s and 1960s are now regarded as outdated.

Porter is nevertheless in agreement with Manuel. His soothing words about the legitimacy of earlier work are belied by statements later in his article. Merriam's approach, now labelled "neo-functionalism" and Mantle Hood's "bi-musicality" (strangely in view of the still current proliferation of performing groups whose rationale depends upon this concept) are represented as having influence only until 1980.

In the 1960s and 1970s, younger North American scholars are said to have replaced European-derived "comparative musicology" with its perceived evolutionary assumptions, with enthusiasm for the "pure", "the aboriginal", the "native", the "noble savage" and "societies without history".

---

[176] Rice 1987.
[177] Porter 1995; Manuel 1995.
[178] Page numbers cannot be cited because they are missing from the web versions of the papers that were consulted.

This, I have to say, is an outrageous overstatement and misrepresentation of what actually took place. I was there, so I can vouch for the facts on these issues. In my own case, I had certainly rejected Sachsonian evolutionism by 1958, despite (or perhaps because of) being brought up on it, but I did not forego comparison, and neither I nor anyone I know believed in pure cultures without history. Quite the reverse, in fact, was true as I recall the situation. It would seem that the legitimate effort to recover and document disappearing styles by means of extensive field work and recording before they died out has been misinterpreted. The assumption behind this point of view appears to be that as change is inevitable, such efforts are wasted. But matters such as rate of change, or what factors result in change, or indeed any insights whatsoever into change as a process, cannot be gained without base studies upon which to judge them, and these the field workers of the past have provided.

Analysis

Manuel, who it must be remembered comes from a background of performance-oriented instruction, concedes that an understanding of such matters as Indonesian modes is essential for performance purposes. However, according to him:

> Other sorts of analysis that were undertaken have been seen to have little lasting value; for example, the interval counts conducted by scholars like Merriam, Kolinski, and others are regarded by modern scholars as quite useless; in Merriam's case (e.g., 1967), such analyses are particularly odd, since they are so irrelevant to, and indeed contradictory to the sort of holistic analysis he so adamantly advocated.

This sounds like vintage Herndon. Interval counting is obviously ridiculous as an end in itself, but is essential as a means to an end, and it is clear that this is not understood. My own work involving interval counts was done in association with melodic interval diagrams in order to determine the actual path of a melody in relation to the tonal centre and other parameters.[179] Applied to Maori and Tikopia tonal systems this enabled identification of modes no less important than those of Indonesian music, and in the absence of indigenous music theory were capable of determination in no other way.

There appears also to be a misconception of what is meant by holistic analysis. All it should mean is to take everything (including music structure) into account, which is what Merriam did. Neglecting structure is not holistic.

Product and process

Merriam's ideal of a fusion of musicology and anthropology, with equal emphasis on product and process, is plainly not even on the horizon. In what seems to be an understatement, Manuel refers to musicological analysis as overshadowed by ethnological studies, drawing more from anthropology than from musicology.

---

[179] McLean 1966.

Theory-building

Numerous theoretical models are described by Porter in terms of their application to ethnomusicology, in each case by one or more ethnomusicologists. The overall impression is conveyed that every description of music must somehow be fitted into a theoretical framework, an impression confirmed by Manuel, who believes that while earlier descriptive studies served their purpose, "the important works in recent ethnomusicology have been those which are animated by a more specific theoretical focus." Merriam's concern that ethnomusicology was becoming too preoccupied with theory-building is amply confirmed.

Other disciplines

Manuel refers to current diversity within ethnomusicology, including approaches derived from acoustics, folklore, history, linguistics, media studies, sociology, and others. Porter points to additional importations from perception and cognition (as foreshadowed by Merriam), together with aesthetics, culture studies generally, philology, psychology, semiotics, and sociology of music. On top of this, the two authors point to a variety of approaches within ethnomusicology focusing on specific study topics or areas of study such as gender, politics, popular music, and urban ethnomusicology.

It will be recalled that Merriam saw a need for ethnomusicology to be more open to influence from other disciplines. This, at least, has come to pass, though at cost of more theory-building. By and large, the idea-gathering from other disciplines seems to me a strange and eclectic mix, not necessarily "scientific" as represented, and hardly the stuff of a new direction in ethnomusicology. Certainly, it is a long way distant from the united discipline which Merriam hoped for.

Comparison

A quarter of a century ago, Merriam was already lamenting a lack of comparison in ethnomusicology. Beyond a claim that it was already gone by the 1960s and 1970s, Porter and Manuel make no mention of it at all. It never did quite disappear, however, and some, indeed, is still taking place, as witness my own book about Polynesian music, *Weavers of Song*,[180] which is unabashedly comparative. In later pages I shall be arguing that work of this kind is still worth doing.

The "crisis of representation"

Here is a topic that was not even thought of in Merriam's time, but has since loomed large, especially among ethnomusicologists who choose to work in "high culture" areas of the world with their own long-standing traditions of indigenous scholarship. At the heart of it is a notion that it is impossible for persons of any culture to interpret another without introducing unacceptable biases. The attempt to do so leads, in Manuel's words, to accusations of "arrogant, authoritarian condescension, particularly by scholars from the imperialist West." Such concerns have led at best to a "crisis of confidence" on the part of ethnomusicologists who have been deterred from entering the field, and are now in process of reinventing their discipline. If it is any comfort to

---

[180] McLean 1999.

them, I suggest that the reverse of the cultural cringe may be the more appropriate stance, on the assumption that, with good will on all sides, interpreting someone else's culture is a less difficult, though demanding, task than penetrating ones own. I look forward to more analyses of Western music from third world scholars.

Apart from the universal tendency of each generation of scholars to question the last, and carve out new niches for themselves, what is the explanation for the above trends, and what is the common denominator? Most of the developments that have taken place are ostensibly "anthropological" and as such could well have resulted from the influence of John Blacking, who was the most outspoken and best-known advocate of the anthropology of music apart from Merriam.

JOHN BLACKING (1928–1990)

John Blacking was a British anthropologist and ethnomusicologist whose 23-month field experience, from 1956–58, with the Venda people of South Africa, provided him with materials for almost all of his subsequent writings. He catapulted into prominence with a best-selling book *How Musical Is Man?*,[181] based upon a series of public lectures, which established him as a thinker, and was translated into numerous languages. His influence was immense. Although he published many papers about the Venda, he wrote only one book about them, based upon his PhD thesis with the University of the Witwatersrand, South Africa, called *Venda Children's Songs*.[182] More will be said of this later.

Blacking's anthropological training was as an undergraduate at Cambridge University, England, under Meyer Fortes (1906–1983). Fortes was a "structural-functionalist" in the tradition of Bronislaw Malinowski (1884–1942) and Raymond Firth (1901–2002), who were his principal teachers. Originally trained in psychology, he was an Africanist with a primary interest in family and kinship.[183] Blacking's interest in Africa, his use of participant observation, and his neo-functionalist approach, can be attributed to this early training.

Like Charles Seeger, Blacking was a person of immense charisma, his forceful personality contributing as much to the acceptance of his views as his arguments themselves, especially as expressed in his book, *How Musical is Man?* This book, written as it was for a lay audience, has been charitably described as "capable of multiple interpretations".[184] Worse still, it is full of faulty logic of the kind sometimes described as "lateral thinking", and is bereft of evidence in support of the views expressed in it.

Only now, more than a decade after his death, are some of the better-known ideas Blacking advanced beginning to be questioned. Like Seeger, however, Blacking will ultimately be judged not only for the influence he undoubtedly exerted, but for the credibility of the statements he made, and the validity of the arguments he advanced.

---

[181] Blacking 1973.
[182] Blacking 1967.
[183] Anth.
[184] Baily 1990:xiv.

The "holistic" approach

In many ways, Blacking out-Merriamed Merriam, pushing Merriam's ideas to limits beyond those to which Merriam himself subscribed. A principal difference between the two lay in their treatment of music structure. Merriam's concern was to redress a balance and ensure equal treatment for music structure and music behaviour rather than a predominance of the former. Blacking moved the discipline, though almost certainly unintentionally, towards a predominance of the latter.

Whereas Merriam wanted equal attention to music structure and behaviour, Blacking wanted them integrated, and to the extent that this was impossible, structure as an object of study began first to be neglected, then avoided, and finally abandoned, along with its hand-maidens, transcription and analysis. It is not a result Blacking himself would have wished. Yet it became a latter-day outcome of Blacking's strongly affirmed view that music and its cultural context should be described not separately but as interrelated parts of a total system, following a method he called "cultural analysis".[185]

In a related development, the term "holistic", which in the Boas–Herskovits–Merriam tradition ought to mean simply to have regard to all aspects of music-making in its wider context, appears to have undergone a shift of meaning to signify an integrated "model" which, according to Porter,[186] combines approaches from semiotics and cognitive anthropology.

The problem with this is that there are some aspects of music structure that cannot be integrated with behaviour. Let me illustrate from Maori music:

In one of my early papers, I discussed Maori song types.[187] They are clearly differentiated by Maori themselves into named categories such as waiata, pao, poi, oriori and others. Each can be distinguished, and are so treated in the paper, in terms of song function, performance practice, and music structure, and each is distinctive in each such respect. Blacking was faced with a similar situation in South Africa, where the Venda people also had named song types serving different functions, performance practice appropriate for each, and a music system capable of transcription into Western notation and analysis using standard methods.

How can this be handled in terms of a "holistic" approach in the new sense of the word? It can't, because these are all separate categories. All one can do is to draw attention to the relationships of the several components insofar as these apply, and as best one can. I chose to present my Maori information under song type headings, systematically describing the three elements of function, performance and structure for each. There are interconnections of what I would call an obvious kind. The role of the song leader, for example, varies according to the nature of the song type and the circumstances in which it is performed, and this is accommodated by the musical form, which is one of the elements of song structure. Thus, in waiata performance, leader solos mark off textual lines, which are coincident with musical strophes, whereas in oriori, which have a different structure, leader solos are confined to the beginnings of stanzas. On the other hand, there are aspects of song structure such as melody and rhythm which are merely

---

[185] Baily 1990:xiv.
[186] Porter 1995.
[187] McLean 1969.

conventional to the song type, for which Maori have no terminology, and are not related in any noticeable way either to function or to performance. Finally, there are aspects of singing style such as voice timbre that are common to more than one song type. It would be a grave error to assume some kind of causal relationship simply on grounds of association, yet this, I believe, is what proponents of the new "holistic" approach are seeking. Moreover, unless components of a system are first isolated, they cannot be compared, and understanding of any relationships between them is impeded.

Although Blacking's stance of "cultural analysis" whereby analysis of music sound was supposed not to be considered in isolation from its cultural context is indissolubly associated with him, it is worth noting that he was himself not totally committed to it. He resiled from it in his later teaching, arguing the necessity of distinguishing the non-musical from the purely musical,[188] and had already begun to have second thoughts as early as 1970, when he wrote:

> Although I call this kind of analysis a Cultural Analysis,[189] it is no less a formal analysis of music sound. Similarities of tonal and rhythmic patterns *within* the body of songs discussed are essential data in discovering rules that are applicable to Venda music but their similarity is always considered in the context of Venda culture and not as sound *per se*.[190]

Blacking, indeed, followed this very approach in his *Venda Children's Songs*, where his concept of cultural analysis was introduced. First he presented a body of transcription and analysis of the music, which occupied most of the book, and *then* attempted to relate it to cultural context. Blacking complained in later years that too few people had actually read this book, which is probably true as otherwise the idea that he had proved a connection between social structure and music structure would not have become so prevalent.

In the Preface to his *Venda Children's Songs*, Blacking explains his purpose in the following terms:

> This study sets out to provide a documentary record of the traditional children's songs of the Venda of the Northern Transvaal, and an analysis of their music which relates its structure to their cultural background. Alan Merriam's important book, *The Anthropology of Music* emphasises the need to study music in culture. It follows that if music is regarded as human action, music sound can no longer be analysed independently, but must be studied as sound in culture. . .[191] This study reveals some of the non-musical sources of the sound of the Venda children's songs. . . Underlying my analysis is the assumption that music can only be fully understood as humanly organised sound. . . In my analysis of Venda children's songs, I have attempted to explain their structure in the context of Venda culture, for it is in this context only that their essential meaning is to be found.[192]

---

[188] Baily 1990:xiv.
[189] Blacking 1967:191-8.
[190] Blacking 1970:2.
[191] Of course this does not "follow" at all. This kind of argument is typical of Blacking, whereby an "if" is commonly followed by a "therefore" with hardly any intervening steps.
[192] Blacking 1967:5-6.

How far did Blacking succeed? Sadly, no specific connections are demonstrated except to show that different genres of Venda music share some characteristics.

In his final chapter "The Cultural Analysis of Music", Blacking begins with a claim that his analysis of 56 songs "shows how musical structures grow out of the cultural patterns of which they are a part." [193]

- Melodic intervals and speech-tone of the song texts are found to interact but neither follows the other absolutely.

- Rhythmically and melodically, most of the children's songs are found to be "compressed, and sometimes simplified, versions of adult music." [194] As one would expect if this is true, children are confirmed to have opportunity for listening to adult music and become familiar with it. Also, and again predictably, as children speak the same language as the adults, speech-tone is found to affect their music in the same way. Blacking concludes: "At every level of analysis, therefore, the forms of the music are related to the forms of the culture from which they are derived." [195]

The two genres to which most children's songs are related are the national dance, and reed-pipe music of boys' dances. Particular to the children's songs are their choice of words for the song texts, and restriction of the vocal range to suit immature voices. This too Blacking invests with cultural significance, saying: "Thus there are many non-musical factors which regulate the structure of the music, and any analysis of the music is as much an analysis of these as it is of the musical sounds that emerge." [196]

Blacking himself must have realised that his results fall short of expectations aroused in his Preface. He accordingly promises to provide more evidence "in another publication" where he will "develop the idea that thematic relationships express the relationships of the social groups who make the music . . ." [197] Regrettably, he never did so in a satisfactory way. His credo that social structure and music sound are related was one to which he was to return again and again in the course of his future writings. Invariably he did so in the form of assertion,[198] never offering proof. Sometimes, as in *Venda Children's Songs* he promised to supply the evidence at some future date; sometimes he simply rang the changes on his earlier statements; and at others he referred readers back to *Venda Children's Songs*.

Blacking's biography throws considerable light both upon his success and his failings. He was intensely musical, having learned the piano from an early age, becoming competent enough to consider a career as a concert pianist. He was passionately egalitarian, perhaps as a reaction against the excesses of the English class system into which he was born. He was deeply religious, having been educated at a cathedral choir school and brought up as an Anglican "churchman", at one stage giving thought to ordination. Finally, he served in the military in Malaysia, where he not only gained an interest in Malaysian music but also, as an officer, was exposed to

---

[193] Blacking 1967:191.
[194] Blacking 1967:193.
[195] Blacking 1967:193.
[196] Blacking 1967:195.
[197] Blacking 1967:196.
[198] Several of Blacking's statements on the issue are quoted (with sources) in Agawu 1997.

the constraints of military discipline. These combined experiences perhaps account for his authoritarian nature in matters concerning music, as well as his strong sense of mission and promotion of ideas on "faith" rather than feeling obliged to offer evidence for them.

WHITHER ETHNOMUSICOLOGY?

In the wake of John Blacking, the hunt has continued for the elusive social correlates of music, without conspicuous success, despite some claims to the contrary. Meanwhile, no other issues have emerged to cause as much debate; no one can be said to have replaced Blacking as a leader, as he had succeeded Merriam; and no champion has emerged to promote yet other approaches to the subject. Ethnomusicology remains a divided and directionless discipline, though a highly active one. Until the next compelling issue emerges, should it ever do so, the question of what happens next is unanswerable.

Paradigms past and present

In light of the preceding sections, three periods in the history of ethnomusicology can be distinguished, namely: Early (–1960), Middle (1960–80), and Late (1980–2000). The first culminated with the comparative musicology of the Austro-German Schools; the second was characterised by the rise and rapid development of ethnomusicology as such in the United States; and the most recent has been a theory-dominated period of American ethnomusicology during which earlier methodologies and concerns have been either under challenge or abandoned. Although within each of these periods there have been multiple approaches and cross-currents at work, it may not be too unrealistic to suggest that the first was philosophically dominated by evolutionism, the second by functionalism, and the last by a heavy dose of post-modernism.

There is a widespread unstated assumption that each new paradigm necessarily supersedes the preceding one. Radical change of this kind is not, however, inevitable. Different approaches can lead to different perspectives of the same data and can co-exist. If this can be agreed, then approaches espoused by earlier ethnomusicologists who are identified with one or other of the now unfashionable or seen to be outmoded paradigms, need not be rejected as "old hat" or "out of date" or mistaken. From the early period of ethnomusicology, a case in point can be made for Charles Darwin. In terms of present-day renewed interest in the "biology of music" as exemplified especially by John Blacking, Darwin needs to be rescued from the oblivion into which he has been cast because of rejection of evolutionary ideas of music as espoused by earlier scholars of comparative musicology. His 3,500 words on origins of music in his *Descent of Man* have again become relevant, but more importantly his ideas about evolution have shaped modern thought in ways far more profound than the earlier misguided application of them by the comparative musicologists might suggest, and may yet do so again.

Closer to our own time is the work of Alan P. Merriam, who is commonly identified with "functionalism" and in consequence of this is currently out of favour. Some reappraisal is necessary here as well.

Although I believe excessive theory-building is one of the problems now besetting ethnomusicology, and would like to see less of it, the problem of mind-set in terms of theory is far from new. From the very beginnings of the discipline, ethnomusicologists have been influenced by the prevailing currents of thought in each period of its history. As has been seen, the early comparative ethnomusicologists were committed to approaches arising out of evolutionism. The next generation of American ethnomusicologists came from an anthropological background of functionalism, which had emerged as a reaction to evolutionism, and this in its turn began to be displaced by other approaches. Since the 1970s there has been an increasingly eclectic mix of approaches which have included Lévi-Strauss structuralism, Chomskyan linguistics, Marxist analysis and, most recently, as suggested above, a strong infusion of post-modernism. As a perhaps not irrelevant aside, I note that according to the internet encyclopedia, Wikipedia, critics of post-modernism tend to spell it with a hyphen, while supporters prefer one word. Could the successful campaign to omit the hyphen from ethno-musicology have had similar significance? Be this as it may, I suggest that the now prevailing post-modern cast of ethnomusicology has gone too far, and there are still insights to be salvaged from past approaches, particularly from the era of the immediate past which, in my view, has been too hastily abandoned.

Part II: The Subject Divisions

UL: Davies Gilbert (1767–1839)
UR: Sabine Baring Gould (1834–1924)
LL: J.A. Fuller-Maitland (1856–1936)
LC: Ralph Vaughan Williams (1872–1958)
LR: Percy Grainger (1882–1961)

Introduction

Most ethnomusicologists, regardless of theoretical or other contributions they may have made, have carried out field work in one or more areas and are known for their expertise in the music of those areas. Of ethnomusicologists already considered, for example, Jaap Kunst and Mantle Hood were primarily Indonesianists, while Alan P. Merriam and John Blacking were Africanists.

For convenience, most of the remaining pioneers of ethnomusicology considered in this book will be introduced under area headings. The pages following do not purport to be a history of ethnomusicology in the particular areas. Historical surveys of each area, including consideration of indigenous and still living scholars left out of the present work are available in Helen Myers's book *Ethnomusicology: Historical and Regional.* [199]

Folk music

DEFINITION

In Part I, I typified folk song as having originated as oral tradition within rural formerly non-literate areas, both in Europe and in the Orient, in places where there is also a tradition of urban art music and/or church music that may or may not have influenced the folk music. Characteristically, such songs were sung by artisans and country agricultural workers who, in England, where large numbers of such songs were collected, belonged to what used to be called the "unlettered classes".

On the evidence of the collectors themselves, this is certainly true of the bulk of what has generally been accepted as folk music. More ink has probably been spilt, however, on the nature of folk song and questions surrounding it, even than upon the equally vexed problem of defining ethnomusicology. Once we all thought we knew what folk song was, but as time has gone by the boundaries distinguishing it from other forms of music have become ever more diffuse, and, in light of current concerns that have moved away from hierarchical classifications, some scholars would even argue that there is no such thing.

An early definition of folk song, which may have been the first in English, was published in the America *Century Dictionary* in 1889. It read:

> A song of the people; a song based on a legendary or historical event, or some incident of common life, the works and generally the music of which have originated among the common people, and are extensively used by them.[200]

EUROPEAN FOLK SONG

Although scholars from continental Europe were the main participants in early meetings of the International Folk Music Council, and were predominantly folk music specialists, their concerns

---

[199] Myers 1993.
[200] Sharp 1965:3.

were primarily historical and did not impact greatly upon ethnomusicology as it was later to develop. The two main exceptions were Béla Bartók (1881–1945) and, Zoltán Kodály (1882–1967), whose methods in Hungarian folk music research, by directing attention towards classifying large bodies of folk song, and particularly the acclaimed transcription methods of Bartók, were to enter the mainstream of American ethnomusicology.

ANGLO-AMERICAN FOLK SONG

In both England and America, most early scholarly folk song activity was by collectors who wrote little or nothing about the songs they collected and cannot be said to have had much influence on ethnomusicology. On this account, and because there were so many of them, their biographies have been left out of the present book. Their contribution must, however, be acknowledged.

Early collectors of English folk song

In her book *A Guide to English Folk Song Collections*, Margaret Dean-Smith lists no fewer than 58 collections of English folk song published from 1822–1952, "made wholly, or in their greater part, from oral communications."[201]

If carols are admitted as folk songs, the very first published collection of English folk songs was that of Davies Gilbert (formerly Giddy) (1767–1839), High Sheriff of Cornwall (1792–93), a member of parliament for Helston (1804) and Bodmin (1806–32) in Cornwall, president of the Royal Society (1827–30), and the recipient of an honorary DCL degree from Oxford University (1832).[202] His book was published in 1822 under the title of *Some Ancient Christmas Carols with the Tunes to Which they were Formerly Sung*. The same collector published an expanded collection under the same title in the following year.[203]

The first collection to be made of folk song airs for their own sake is generally credited to be that of the Rev John Broadwood (1798–1864), squire of Lynn near Dorking, south of London, in Sussex, whose book, containing just 16 songs, was published anonymously in 1843.[204] The title page, which was printed in an amazing variety of type is unusually explicit as to the contents of the book (see opposite).

Broadwood's niece, Lucy Broadwood (1858–1929), who later became a well-known collector in her own right, describes, in a family story,[205] her uncle's insistence that the songs should be noted exactly as sung:

> When Mr Dusart, the Worthing organist was asked to harmonise Mr Broadwood's collection, he made great outcries over intervals which shocked his musical standards. A flat seventh never was and never could be. And so forth. To which it is recorded that Mr

---

[201] Dean-Smith 1954:25-39.
[202] Anderson 1996–2003.
[203] Dean-Smith 1954:25.
[204] Broadwood 1843.
[205] Lucy was not even born when her uncle's book was published, so the story was hearsay from others in the family.

Broadwood confirming his intervals by vehement blasts on his flute, replied "<u>musically</u> it may be wrong, but I <u>will</u> have it exactly as my singers sang it." [206]

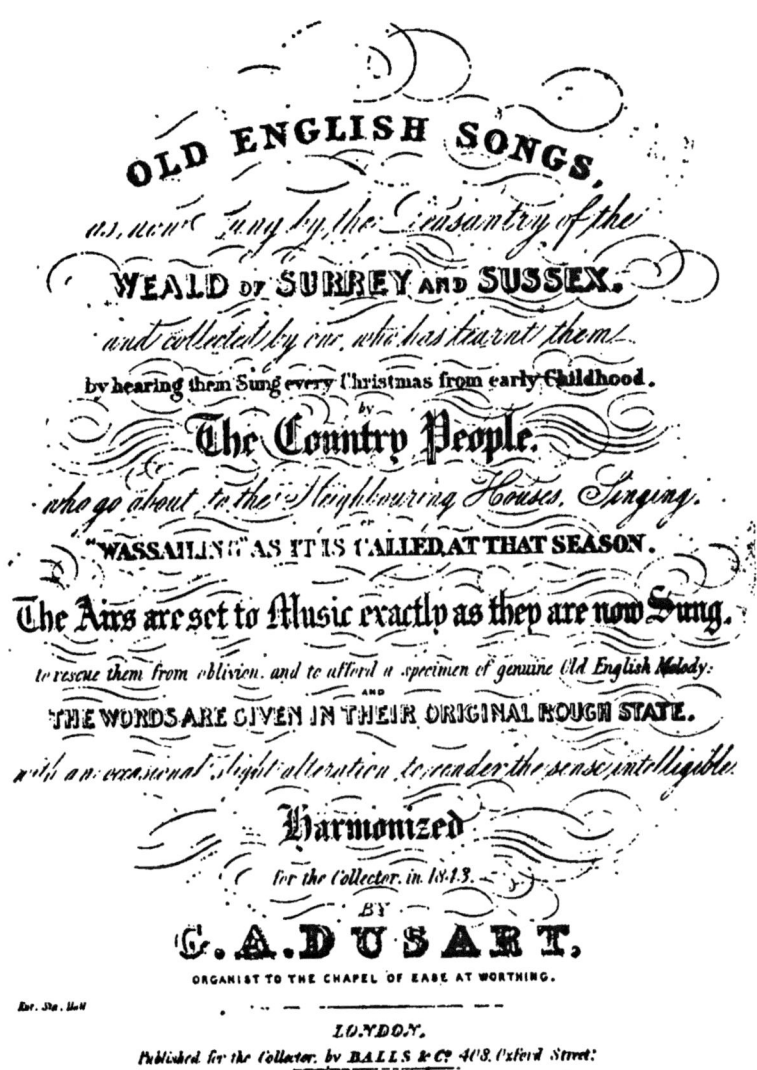

Broadwood's title page

Broadwood was a remarkable pioneer who was very much ahead of his time. It was to be someyears before other collections with both texts and tunes were taken "from the mouths of the people", and systematic folk song collecting did not begin for more than another 40 years when another cleric, the Rev Sabine Baring Gould (1834–1924), after a chance remark at a dinner table, began in 1889 to collect the folk songs of Cornwall and Devon.

---

[206] Karpeles 1973:79-80.

Born at Exeter in 1834, educated at Cambridge University (MA 1856), ordained in 1864, squire and parson of the parish of Lewtrenchard in West Devon from 1881–1924, Baring Gould not only collected and published folk songs on his own account but also collaborated with other well-known collectors in joint publications. Besides collecting folk songs and writing voluminously on other subjects, he wrote the words of many hymns, including "Onward Christian Soldiers". Besides this, he was a notable eccentric, said to have taught at Hurstpierpoint with a pet bat perched on his shoulder![207] His *Songs and Ballads of the West Country*, of which he himself took most pride, were published in four volumes between 1889 and 1892, with the airs published "precisely as noted." Altogether he published 110 songs.

Other notable collectors who published in the same decade were William Alexander Barrett (1834–1891), who published his *English Folk Songs* in 1891; Frank Kidson (1855–1926), with his *Traditional Tunes*, also in 1891; and Lucy Broadwood (1858–1929) and J.A. Fuller-Maitland (1856–1936), with their *English Country Songs* in 1893. Barrett was another ecclesiastic, an organist and vicar of St Paul's Cathedral in London, holder of a BMus degree from Oxford University (1870), and a music critic for the *Morning Post*.[208]

From this time onwards, the collection and publishing of folk songs began to gather pace. Landmark occasions were the establishment of the English Folk Song Society in 1898, and the publication of Cecil Sharp's first collection of *Folk Songs from Somerset*, in 1904. The primary objective of the Folk Song Society was the collection and preservation of folk songs, ballads and tunes, and the publication of such of these as may be deemed advisable. Its main activities were to publish an annual journal containing songs collected by its members, and from the beginning emphasis was laid upon the music.[209]

Cecil Sharp (1859–1924)

Of those who contributed to the journal, Cecil Sharp is universally acknowledged to be the greatest. He did not begin collecting until he was over 40 years old, but thereafter devoted the last 21 years of his life to the task.[210] In all he is credited with the collection of an astounding 4977 tunes of which 501 were provided with accompaniments, 1118 were published without accompaniments, and 3358 remain unpublished. All of this was accomplished without benefit of recording machines, entirely by means of hand notation from living performances. Besides collecting, he was tireless in making the songs known, not only to scholars but to people in all walks of life. He gave illustrated lectures up and down the country, campaigned in the public press, and was influential in getting folk songs introduced into schools. More than anyone else he was responsible for the folk song movement in England.

In his book *English Folk Song: Some Conclusions* (1907), he expressed strong views about the nature of folk song which, because of their later adoption by the International Folk Music Council, placed an indelible stamp on the conduct of folk song research for the rest of the century. Crucial to Sharp and his followers in England was the means of transmission of folk song, which was seen to be exclusively through oral tradition, as a result of which songs gradually be-

---

[207] Rainbow 2003; Graebe 2000, which contains more biography.
[208] Howes 1969:104, who mis-spells the name as Barratt.
[209] Karpeles 1973:83-4.
[210] Karpeles 1973:92.

came modified over the course of many generations until they conformed to the taste of the singers at large, becoming a true form of what has also been called "national song". Although Sharp's ideas were to become entrenched within English folk song scholarship, there were some dissenting voices.

Frank Kidson (1855–1926)

Just as a later dichotomy resulted from the different approaches of Hood and Merriam to ethnomusicology in the United States, so too in England there is a methodological opposition in folk song study between the views of Cecil Sharp and those of his contemporary Frank Kidson. Kidson was perhaps unwise to dismiss Sharp's ideas as "conjectures", because as Sharp's reputation grew, and ultimately prevailed, Kidson's went into decline, and when he died it was as a scholar once regarded as a foremost authority but now on the way to being forgotten.[211] Yet there need not have been a conflict. Sharp was an apostle of the transmogrifying influence of oral tradition upon songs which entered the folk idiom. Kidson was an antiquarian, skilled at tracking tunes back to their origins in printed sources, who claimed that folk songs were nothing more nor less than old popular music. Both protagonists were credited with attitudes they did not possess. As a pre-eminent collector himself, Kidson accepted the validity of oral tradition; and Sharp never denied that folk songs could have their origin in written sources.

Later collectors

Next to Sharp, the composer Ralph Vaughan Williams (1872–1958) probably did more than anyone to bring folk song to the notice of the public, not least by his beautiful arrangements and by the incorporation of folk song into his own works. Those who know of Vaughan Williams only as one of England's greatest composers may be surprised to learn that he was also an assiduous collector who notated over 800 tunes (including variants).[212] Besides collecting, he also wrote essays about folk song that have been brought together in his book *National Music* (1963).

Other composer collectors were George Butterworth (1885–1916), who was killed in action during World War I, and Percy Grainger (1882–1961), well known not only as a folk song collector, primarily in Lincolnshire, but also as a concert pianist and for his folkish compositions "Country Gardens" and "Molly on the Shore". Grainger is the subject of John Blacking's last book, in which Blacking portrays Grainger as a neglected figure in terms of ideas relevant to ethnomusicology.[213] The book is really a vehicle for a further airing of Blacking's own ideas, and Grainger's contribution to it is slight. As an ideas man, a much better case could have been made for Grainger's senior contemporary Ralph Vaughan Williams.

Of other folk song collectors in England, the most notable after Cecil Sharp were two maiden ladies of independent means: one, who has already been mentioned, was Lucy Broadwood (1838–1929), the niece of John Broadwood, and the other was Anne Geddes Gilchrist (1863–1954). Miss Gilchrist was a formidable scholar with an encyclopaedic knowledge of folk tunes

---

[211] Francmanis 1999.
[212] Karpeles 1973:85.
[213] Blacking 1987.

and their variants. Reportedly, scholars from both sides of the Atlantic would write to her asking her to identify tunes and she seldom failed them.

According to Maud Karpeles, after Cecil Sharp's death in 1924 there was little further collecting of folk song in England until 1952 when the British Broadcasting Corporation organised a systematic recording campaign.[214] Few entirely new songs were discovered, but many variants were uncovered and in all some 1600 items were recorded which considerably enriched the store of traditional material.[215]

In the eyes of Maud Karpeles, this ranked as a final flurry of activity. She begins the last chapter of her book *An Introduction to English Folk Song* with a positive statement that "The corpus of English folk song has now been collected, though stray songs, mostly variants, still turn up and will continue to do so." [216] With the advent of notated collections and, above all, gramophone records by means of which a song can always be referred back to an original, she believed it hardly possible for a newly composed song now to become a folk song. And for the same reason the slow former evolution of genuine traditional folk songs was seen to have been checked to a large extent. She ends with the thought that we must now distinguish between the "making" and the "practice" of folk song, though in the past both processes were indispensable. In other words, although folk songs may no longer be in the making, we can still enjoy singing them and, thanks to the collectors of the past, there is a large and beautiful repertoire from which to choose.

A.L. Lloyd (1908–1982)

Inevitably, the Sharp orthodoxy has been challenged by later scholars. For A.L. Lloyd, who was one of the architects of the post-World War II British folk song revival, the crucial element in folk song was not the means of transmission but the working-class origin of the composers. Thus, while Sharp and his associates rejected 18th–19th century industrial songs as folk song because there had been insufficient time for the transforming power of oral tradition to have worked upon them, Lloyd accepted them and lobbied in their favour.

---

[214] Karpeles 1973:99.
[215] An edited series of these recordings was issued in a classic set of "source singer" LPs, "Folk Songs of Britain," vols. 1-10, initially under the Caedmon label, and reissued later by Topic, as follows:
"Folk Songs of Britain, Vol. I: Songs of Courtship," Caedmon TC1142 (1961); Topic 12T157 (1968).
"Folk Songs of Britain, Vol. II: Songs of Seduction," Caedmon TC1143 (1961); Topic 12T158 (1968).
"Folk Songs of Britain, Vol. III: Jack of All Trades," Caedmon TC1144 (1961); Topic 12T159 (1968).
"Folk Songs of Britain, Vol. IV: The Child Ballads, Vol. 1," Caedmon TC1145 (1961); Topic 12T160 (1969).
"Folk Songs of Britain, Vol. V: The Child Ballads, Vol. 2," Caedmon TC1146 (1961); Topic 12T161 (1969).
"Folk Songs of Britain, Vol. VI: Sailormen and Servingmaids," Caedmon TC1162; Topic 12T194 (c. 1970).
"Folk Songs of Britain, Vol. VII: Fair Game and Foul," Caedmon TC1163; Topic 12T195 (c. 1970).
"Folk Songs of Britain, Vol. VIII: A Soldier's Life for Me," Caedmon TC1164; Topic 12T196 (c. 1971).
"Folk Songs of Britain, Vol. IX: Songs of Christmas," Caedmon TC1224; Topic 12T197 (as "Songs of Ceremony," c. 1971).
"Folk Songs of Britain, Vol. X: Animal Songs," Caedmon TC1225; Topic 12T198 (as "Songs of Animals and Other Marvels," c. 1971).
[216] Karpeles 1973:101.

Scholarship in America

Most folk song scholarship relevant to mainstream ethnomusicology in the United States has taken place on Anglo-American folk song. In Canada, where there is a large French-Canadian tradition, the work of Helen Creighton (1899–1989) and Marius Barbeau (1883–1969) as collectors is especially important. In South America, the folk song idiom is predominantly of Iberian origin. The best-known pioneer scholars of Latin American folk music are Carlos Vega (1898–1956), Isabel Aretz (1913–2005) and her husband Luis Felipe Ramón y Rivera (1913–1993).

Unlike Great Britain, where the study of folk song remained exclusively in the hands of non-professionals, in the United States of America it gained an institutional base, mostly in university departments of English, though departments of folklore were also later set up There was an even greater army of amateur collectors than in Britain, but often they were encouraged by and worked in co-operation with professional folklorists. As in Britain, the emphasis to begin with was primarily on texts, and only later did tunes become a subject for study.

Two scholars whose names are indelibly associated with folk song research in the USA are Francis James Child (1825–1896) and George Lyman Kittredge (1860–1941). Child's great work was his 5-volume *The English and Scottish Popular Ballads* (1883-98), considered the definitive edition of what have become known as the "big ballads", each of which is now commonly referred to by means of a Child number. Thus, from Volume 1, the "The False Knight on the Road", for example, is Child no.3, and "Lord Randal" is Child no.12. Though neither Child nor Kittredge, who was his successor as Professor of English at Harvard University, was concerned with tunes, and worked from print and manuscript rather than oral tradition, their work in identifying and documenting ballad texts was seminal, and their biographies are accordingly included in the present work. Later American folk song scholars whose biographies appear are Phillips Barry (1880–1937); Bertrand Bronson (1902–1986), whose life's work was upon the tunes of the Child ballads; and Samuel Bayard (1908–1997).

After World War II, a new phenomenon resulted from the folk song revival, when folk song was embraced as a genre by the popular music industry. Especially in America, groups such as the Kingston Trio became popular, along with solo recording artists such as Burl Ives (1909–1995), and newly composed songs in folk idiom began to appear and were accepted by many people as genuine.[217] Elsewhere as well, as in New Zealand, which was colonised too late to develop a folk song tradition of its own, entire repertories of newly composed "folk song" emerged, and have similarly won acceptance.[218] In the USA, primarily as a result of the egalitarian efforts of Alan Lomax (1915–2002), who began as a collector but was also profoundly influential in winning acceptance under the folk umbrella for artists such as Woody Guthrie (1912–1967), the boundaries of what could be regarded as "folk music" gradually expanded to the point that ear-

---

[217] After a detailed account of the development of commercial folk music by the popular music industry in the United States, and the multiple problems this has caused, Bronson (1969b:256) concludes that for any serious study of traditional folk-song "we must return to our older anthologies, or to collections made, if not actually published or issued, before the Second World War.
[218] The best known collection of putative Zealand folk songs, compiled by Rona Bailey and Herbert Roth (1967) includes numerous "original musical settings" by Neil Colquhoun.

lier views of it were sidelined as "purist" and irrelevant to the real world. For the purposes of the present book, such problems need not concern us. Unlike us, the pioneers of folk music research had reason to believe they knew what they were dealing with.

Oriental music

The Orient is conventionally considered under headings of Near, Middle and Far East, looking at it from the viewpoint of Great Britain, but with boundaries that are by no means uniform or agreed. In the first edition of the *Harvard Dictionary of Music*, for example,[219] Polynesia was regarded as Oriental! More recently, the tendency has been to classify in terms of geographical divisions of Asia, with China, Japan and Korea, for example considered under the heading of East Asia; Mongolia and Tibet under eastern central Asia; India and Pakistan under South Asia; Burma, Cambodia, Indonesia, Laos, Malaysia, Singapore, the Philippines, Thailand, and Vietnam under South-east Asia; and Arab states of the Middle East, the Arabian peninsula and the Gulf States, as well as nations such as Israel, Turkey and Iran all subsumed under West Asia. Only those countries whose music was studied by scholars featured in the present book are considered below. In alphabetical order of area:

Arabic music generally was the subject of study by Henry George Farmer (1882–1965) and Robert Lachmann (1892–1939).

Chinese music was described very early by Jean Joseph Marie Amiot (1718–1793) and later by a now little known but important Dutch writer, J.A. Van Aalst (1858–?).

Egypt became the specialty of Hans Hickmann (1908–1968).

India has a long history of early studies by Western scholars, beginning with Sir William Jones (1746–1794). Others included Charles Russell Day (1860–1900), A.H. Fox Strangways, (1859–1948), Arnold Bake (1899–1963), Walter Kaufmann (1907–1984), and Alain Danielou (1907–1994). An Indian scholar who strongly influenced Western perceptions of Indian music was Raja Sir Sourindro Mohun Tagore (1840–1914).

Indonesian studies have been the province of Jaap Kunst (1891–1960), Colin McPhee (1900–1964), and Mantle Hood (1918–2005).

Notable scholars of Japanese music have included Sir Francis Taylor Piggott (1852–1925), Eta Harich-Schneider (1907–1986), and Shigeo Kishibe (1912–2005).

Jewish studies were carried out by Alfred Sendrey (1884–1976), Abraham Idelsohn (1882–1938), Eric Werner (1901–1988), and Edith Gerson-Kiwi (1908–1992).

Mongolian music has been described most notably by the Swedish ethnomusicologist Ernst Emsheimer (1904–1989).

---

[219] Apel 1956.

Philippines music studies owe most to the work of José Maceda (1917–2004).

The music of Tibet became better known than it used to be in the West as a result of recordings issued and described by Peter Crossley-Holland (1916–2001).

Turkey had the benefit of work by the post-war head of the Berlin Phongramm-Archiv, Kurt Reinhard (1914–1979).

Tribal music

Tribal music refers to the traditional music of peoples formerly known as "primitive" or "pre-literate", i.e. people whose social organisation is mostly tribal; who live in small non-urban, relatively isolated, communities; who lack advanced technology; who have relatively simple life-styles; and who had no form of writing until this was introduced as a result of European contact. Because of the absence of writing, their music is or was passed from one generation to another exclusively by means of oral transmission. Most such peoples whose music has been studied by ethnomusicologists live in North or South America, sub-Saharan Africa, or Oceania.

THE AMERICAS

The earliest scholars associated with the study of North American Indian (now known as Native American) music have already been considered. Others include Zygmunt Estreicher (1917–1993), a specialist in Eskimo music; Marius Barbeau (1883–1969) and Ida Halpern (1910–1987), both of whom collected Canadian Indian music; and Willard Rhodes (1901–1992), a founding member of the Society for Ethnomusicology who published a notable series of LP recordings of American Indian music with the Library of Congress.

Amer-Indian styles of Central and South America are a special case because of the admixture of folk music resulting from early Spanish and Portuguese contact; and Caribbean music tends to be treated as Afro-American because of the early infusion there of African culture. Much of the work done on both ancient [220] and contemporary music of this vast area is relatively recent, from scholars who are not considered in the present book.

AFRICA

Africa became an early subject of attention by American anthropologists, partly because of the presence in North America of a large component of African culture resulting from the slave trade, and a desire to track traits associated with this immigrant population back to its roots in Africa. Ethnomusicologists trained by such anthropologists soon extended this concern to music. Most notable among them were Melville Herskovits (1895–1963) and Richard Waterman (1914–1971), who have already been mentioned as teachers of Alan P. Merriam (1923–1980), and Merriam himself, much of whose field work was in Africa. Other important Africanists included John Blacking (1928–1990), Percival Kirby (1887–1970), André Schaeffner (1895–1980), and Klaus Wachsmann (1907–1984).

OCEANIA

---

[220] Notably Stevenson's *Music in Aztec and Inca Territories* (1968).

Oceania is the huge area of the world embracing all of the islands of the Pacific Ocean, together with New Guinea, Australia and New Zealand. Except for the latter two places, it is seriously understudied, with most of its many peoples still awaiting scrutiny of their music. Pioneers of ethnomusicology who have worked in Oceania include Helen Roberts (1888–1985) for Hawai'i; Trevor Jones (1932–), Alice Moyle (1908–2005), and Catherine Ellis (1935–1996) for Australia; Charles Myers (1873–1946) for the Torres Straits Islands between Australia and New Guinea; Jaap Kunst (1891–1960) for Irian Jaya; and Edwin Burrows (1891–1958) for Polynesia and the island of Ifaluk in Micronesia.

Part III: The Biographies (A–Z)

Pioneers of Ethnomusicology: Part III

Introductory note

The biographies, and the intellectual history charts that follow them, are not intended for consecutive reading. Their purpose is to provide essential information, in a readily accessible form, about the individuals featured in them, to assist future research or simply satisfy readers' curiosity about them, and to provide further information about those who are featured elsewhere in the present book. The biographies form a reference dictionary, in alphabetical order of surname, of pioneers whose work has formed an essential part of the history of ethnomusicology in its formative years. The intellectual history charts set out their relationships to each other and to their teachers in each of the major schools of ethnomusicology. Discussion of issues arising out of the work of the pioneers is taken up in Part V.

In the biographies, where different sources cite different dates for the same events, an effort has been made at reconciliation, though possibly not always successfully. On occasion, there is a margin of error of a year or two on either side of the stated dates.

The role of the individual

Bruno Nettl has pointed out that the emergence of individual scholars has occasionally wrought sudden changes, because the field, in its beginnings, was so sparsely populated.[221] This is profoundly true, and more could be made of it. Until very recently, ethnomusicology has been bound up less with institutions and organisations than individual scholars who have given the discipline life, and have added lustre to the institutions in which they happened to work. Every advance in ethnomusicology has, indeed, begun with an individual. But the old adage is also true that "no man is an island". The founders of the discipline did not live in social isolation: they were themselves influenced by events, by their teachers and others who impacted upon their lives, and in some cases by sheer happenstance. An outstanding case in point is provided by Alexander Ellis (1814–1890) who, because of his invention of the cents system for measuring musical intervals, and his demonstration of "non-harmonic" scales in fixed pitch exotic musical instruments, is often called the "father of ethnomusicology". Less well known than Ellis's own role is the influence of two notable predecessors. One was the famous German acoustician Hermann Helmholtz (1821–1894), whose work Ellis began to study in 1863. The other was Professor John Donaldson (1789–1865) of the University of Edinburgh, a specialist in acoustics and an early collector of musical instruments, under whom Ellis studied theory of music.[222] This must have been during the period 1853–56, when Ellis was enrolled as a student of literature and arts at the university.[223] Lack of any mention of Ellis in the graduation records of Edinburgh university may indicate that his attendance was exclusively in music, as Donaldson's courses were without fee and were not examined. Significantly, in view of Ellis's later work in acoustics, an inventory of apparatus used by Donaldson for his lectures includes equipment for the precise measurement of pitch, including a 16-foot monochord which had a brass rod "divided with Mathematical exactness into 1260 equal parts".[224]

---

[221] Nettl 1964:12.
[222] Hipkins & Dent 1948.
[223] Irene Ferguson (pers.comm.)
[224] Field 1997:513.

Hermann Helmholtz
(1821–1894)

John Donaldson
(1789–1865)

Ellis ultimately published his own translation into English of a major book by Helmholtz. And it seems more than probable that Ellis owed his interest both in acoustics and its application to musical instruments, as well as the methods he used for the measurement of pitch, to Donaldson.

Contemporaries as they were, and sharing common interests as they did, many of the early ethnomusicologists knew each other, and were called upon in due course to write obituaries of those who had preceded them. Commonly, the persons who knew each celebrity best was a pupil, and such obituaries furnish insights into the influence exerted each upon the other. A revealing illustration is provided by Merriam's extensive obituary of Waterman,[225] who was one of his teachers. In the course of this, it is fascinating to see certain ideas, familiar from ones reading of Merriam's *Anthropology of Music*, appearing almost verbatim in Merriam's exposition of ideas first advanced by Waterman. Hence the growth of the discipline has been characterised not only by the sudden changes referred to by Nettl, but also by a steady advance of ideas as a result of successive scholars building upon the work of their predecessors. Among them all, however, were some truly remarkable individuals, all of whom can rightly be called pioneers.

Personal qualities

What do the greatest of the great have in common? To judge from their obituaries which, like funeral orations, may not be entirely reliable, many inspired great loyalty and even affection among their students and colleagues. Some, such as Seeger, Blacking and Merriam had extremely powerful personalities, and it is they, perhaps, who are most often seen to have exerted

---

[225] Merriam 1973.

influence. But the more than 90 others whose biographies appear in the present book are no less important. A combination of talent, hard work and determination was characteristic of nearly all of them, often in the face of considerable adversity. They were not, as a rule, people who were disposed to give up. Most took exceptional pains in their work, taking nothing for granted, labouring life-long to dot the 'i's and cross the 't's. Their work was also what they most liked doing, so many continued to make major contributions long after formal "retirement". Some may have been misled by preconceptions that coloured their perceptions, clouded their judgement, and led them up attractive but ultimately unrewarding garden paths. Some, such as the early diffusionists, followed such pathways hand in hand. But even they had their contribution to make, and ethnomusicology still has something to learn from them. If I may mix my metaphors, one lesson might well be that despite the attractions of whatever it is that lies over the garden wall, ones own garden is still worth the cultivation, and the time-honoured means of doing so should not be relegated to the garden shed. The pioneers of ethnomusicology followed the best traditions of scholarship, combining the methodologies of science and the humanities. Like their present-day counterparts, they were always willing to make use of ideas from other disciplines, and did so, often to brilliant effect. There were few among them, however, who did not undertake effective field work, did not archive their recordings, did not transcribe, did not analyse, and did not compare. The need to do so may be their greatest legacy.

Disciplinary background

PERFORMANCE

Most ethnomusicologists probably had music lessons in childhood, becoming in this way musically literate, and gaining some competence as instrumentalists, even if the fact is not specifically recorded in their biographies. Many came from musical families where music was encouraged. As one might expect from the presence in so many homes of a piano, this was the favoured instrument, with the violin and other instruments well behind in popularity. A few ethnomusicologists, of whom most were also composers, notably Bartók, Collaer, Harich-Schneider, Kolinski, Maceda, and McPhee, began their careers as concert pianists. Others, such as Blacking and Curtis, were good enough pianists to consider such a career. Still others, such as Densmore and Roberts began as teachers of piano. Other types of performance, however, were by no means negligible. Kunst toured as a violinist with a chamber music group, and Bake went on tour as a vocalist. Kunst's training as a violinist could well have sharpened his ear and accounted for his interest and ability in the study of tuning systems. And Waterman's participation as a double bass player in dance bands surely contributed to his later interest in jazz and ultimate specialisation in Afro-American music.

COMPOSITION

It is not a surprise to find composition figuring large in the training of many of the pioneer ethnomusicologists. The main avenues of higher learning in music were conservatories, many of which taught composition as well as performance. Composition also became a primary focus of university music departments when these began to be established, and there was simply no other way to become a professional musician.

Like performance, training in composition had its effect in terms of attitude. For some musicians, such as Bartók and Kodály, who were primarily composers, the motivation for study was the introduction of folk music into their own works as a mark of national or cultural identity. Others who were also composers, turned to ethnic music simply because they found it interesting. From Jairazbhoy's essay on Peter Crossley-Holland, for example,[226] it is clear that this scholar at least was first attracted to ethnic music, in his case that of Tibet, by a fascination with the exotic nature of the sound, and again the prospect of incorporating it into his own compositions.

MUSICOLOGY

Because musicology as a discipline did not become established until after Adler's systemisation of it in 1885, all those whose training was in musicology were post-Hornbostel. Earlier comparative musicologists came from a variety of disciplinary backgrounds. A surprising number had training in law, which might well have had some influence upon them.

OTHER DISCIPLINES

Some of the disciplines from which ethnomusicology is now drawing its latest and newest ideas seem almost to represent a lurch into the past. The early comparative musicologists, whose work developed into modern ethnomusicology, often had their primary (and/or sometimes subsidiary) training in disciplines other than music, notably aesthetics, philology, philosophy, physiology, and especially psychology, in which Abraham, Bose, Stumpf and Wallaschek among others all had training.

Adler, who can be said to have launched musicology as a discipline, did his best to steer it away from aesthetics, which was a preoccupation of his predecessor, Hanslick,[227] towards a more scientific approach, and it is notable that many of his followers had backgrounds in natural and/or social sciences, whose approaches, along with those of philology, became a hallmark of comparative musicology. Abraham was a physician; Hornbostel's PhD was in chemistry; and Adler, Lach and Wallaschek were all graduates in law. So, later, was Kunst, and both Adler and Kunst practised law for a time. Not surprisingly, in view of the recency of ethnomusicology as a discipline, the trend continued well into modern times. Kunst's English contemporary, Charles Myers, who made a pioneering study of Torres Straits music,[228] earned his reputation not as a musician but as a psychologist; the foremost English expert on Indian music, Arnold Bake, was Reader of Sanskrit at the University of London; and the eminent specialist in Chinese music, Laurence Picken, is a biologist.

The following is a summary of the backgrounds of some of those whose biographies follow:

PERFORMANCE
Bassoon: C. Ellis, T. Jones.
Cello: Kodály, Moyle, Stumpf
Clarinet: Farmer, Galpin, Merriam, Sachs, Werner

---

[226] Jairazbhoy 1983.
[227] Eduard Hanslick (1825–1904), noted Austrian music critic, aesthetician, and historian.
[228] Myers 1912.

Double bass: Waterman
Flute: Kirby, Van Aalst
Guitar: Vega
Harpsichord: Gerson-Kiwi, Harich-Schneider, T. Jones
Horn: Farmer
Oboe: Fox Strangways, T. Jones
Organ: Baker, Densmore, Fillmore, Fox Strangways, Galpin, Hickmann, Sharp
Piano: Aretz, Barbeau, Bartók, Blacking, Boas, Collaer, Curtis, Daniélou, Danckert, Densmore, C. Ellis, Emsheimer, Fillmore, Fox Strangways, Gerson-Kiwi, Harich-Schneider, Herzog, Hickmann, Hipkins, Hornbostel, Karpeles, Kodály, Kolinski, Maceda, McPhee, Marcel-Dubois, Merriam, Moyle, Nadel, Rhodes, Roberts, Sachs, Schaeffner, Schneider, Seeger, Sharp, T. Jones, Waterman, Werner
Trombone: Waterman
Tuba: Waterman
Viola: Kodály, Ramón y Rivera
Violin: Farmer, Herskovits, Kodály, Kunst, Myers, Ramón y Rivera, Sharp, Stumpf, Van Aalst, Vega
Voice: Bake, Daniélou, Idelsohn

COMPOSITION
Aretz, Bartók, Brailoiu, Crossley-Holland, Curtis, Danckert, Emsheimer, Gilchrist, Hickmann, Hood, T. Jones, Kodály, Kolinski, Lach, Maceda, McPhee, Merriam, Nadel, Ramón y Rivera, Reinhard, Rhodes, Sachs, Schaeffner, Seeger, Sendrey, Vega, Werner

MUSICOLOGY
Aretz, Bose, Danckert, Emsheimer, Estreicher, Gerson-Kiwi, Graf, Halpern, Harich-Schneider, Husmann, T. Jones, Kaufmann, Kirby, Kolinski, Lach, Lachmann, Maceda, Nadel, Nettl, Ramón y Rivera, Reinhard, Schneider, Sendrey, Vega. Wachsmann, Werner, Wiora

OTHER
Acoustics: A.J. Ellis
Aesthetics: Bose, Stumpf, Wallaschek, Werner
Anthropology: Aretz, Barbeau, Blacking, Burrows, Herskovits, Herzog, Kolinski, Lomax, Maceda, Merriam, Nadel, Roberts, Waterman
Archaeology: Fewkes, Fletcher, Schaeffner
Art history: Sachs
Biology: Fewkes, Myers
Business: Baker
Chemistry: Collaer, Hornbostel, Myers
Classics: Amiot, Balfour, A.J. Ellis, Fox Strangways, Galpin, Myers
Conducting: T. Jones
Dance: Daniélou
Divinity: Barry, Galpin
English: Bayard, Bronson, Kittredge
Ethics: Gilman
Ethnology: Bose, Fewkes, Marcel-Dubois, Reinhard, Schaeffner
Folklore: Aretz, Barry, Ramón y Rivera

Geography: Boas
History: Child, Farmer, Herskovits, Marcel-Dubois
Languages: Bake, Farmer, W. Jones, Kodály, Lachmann, Wachsmann
Law: Adler, Barbeau, W. Jones, Kunst, La Flesche, Lach, Piggott, Sharp, Wachsmann, Wallaschek
Librarianship: Gerson-Kiwi, Lachmann, Nettl
Literature: Barry, A.J. Ellis
Mathematics: Boas, Child, A.J. Ellis, Gilman, Sharp, Werner
Medicine: Abraham, Myers
Natural sciences: Abraham, Balfour, Danckert, Myers, Stumpf
Philology: Baker, Bose, Child, A.J. Ellis, Marcel-Dubois, Schneider, Stumpf, Wallaschek
Philosophy: Bose, Gilman, Hornbostel, Lach, Lomax, Nadel, Sendrey, Stumpf, Wallaschek, Werner
Psychology: Abraham, Bose, Gilman, Kolinski, Myers, Nadel, Stumpf, Wallaschek
Physics: Boas, Myers
Physiology: Crossley-Holland
Religious studies: Schaeffner
Sociology: Harich-Schneider
Theory of music: Fillmore, Gilchrist, Ramón y Rivera
Theology: Amiot, Barry, A.M. Jones, Stumpf
Zoology: Balfour, Fewkes

Biographies

(SOLOMON) OTTO ABRAHAM (1872–1926)
German psychologist and comparative musicologist

Born: Berlin, Germany, 31 May 1872
Died: Berlin, Germany, 24 Jan 1926

Education:
Studied medicine and natural sciences, Berlin University,? –1894

Qualifications:
DrMed, Berlin University, 1894

Appointments:
Assistant to Carl Stumpf (q.v.), Psychologisches Institut, Berlin University, 1896–1905
Assistant to Erich von Hornbostel (q.v.), Berlin Phonogram-Archiv, 1905–26

Writings:
Papers co-published with Hornbostel included studies of Japanese music (1902–03), Indian music (1903–04), Turkish music (1904) and Canadian Indian music (1906). The pair also provided joint guidelines for future workers by suggesting methods for transcription of exotic music (1909–10). For other writings, see Katz 2003a.

****

Abraham evidently spent his entire academic life in Berlin, successively working for Stumpf, whom he joined only two years after Stumpf established his psychological institute in Berlin, and with Hornbostel after Stumpf established the Berlin Phonogram-Archiv.

Abraham's significance to ethnomusicology is two-fold. He was responsible, with Stumpf, for recording a visiting Siamese theatre group to Berlin in 1900, resulting in wax cylinder recordings which became the nucleus of the Berlin Phonogram-Archiv; and he had a long and productive association with Erich von Hornbostel, whose assistant he became when the latter was appointed as first director of the archive in 1905. Together they published a number of papers in which Abraham's name appears as the principal author, perhaps only because it happens to be first in the alphabet. Another possibility, however, is that Hornbostel may have had little to do with the writing, appearing as co-author only in accordance with custom of the time which gave the senior figure of an institution this privilege. Most of the work involved transcription and analysis of recorded music.

Refs.: Katz 2003a; NDB; Schmidl 1926–38.

JEAN JOSEPH MARIE AMIOT (1718–1793)
French Jesuit missionary writer on music

Born: Toulon, France, 8 Feb 1718
Died: Beijing (Peking), China, 8 Oct 1793

****

After a classical education, Amiot entered the Society of Jesus as a novice in 1737, taught in Jesuit colleges for ten years, then, on being ordained, requested assignment to the China mission. He arrived in Beijing in 1751 and remained there until his death.[229]

During his 50-year residence in China, Amiot mastered not only the Chinese language but also Tartar. Having earned the confidence of the Chinese emperor Kien-Long (Ch'ien Lung), he was able to remain in Beijing and continue his life's work there even after the French government suppression of the Jesuits in 1773. With the publication in 1779 of his book *Mémoire sur la musique des Chinois*, he provided the Western world with the first extensive study of Chinese music that, although marred by inappropriate editing, was much quoted throughout the 19th century. Lieberman notes that important manuscripts by Amiot remain unpublished, including a study of 18th century Chinese music practice and a notebook containing 54 tunes transcribed into staff notation.[230]

Refs.: Fred Lieberman (pers.comm.); Jesuit Family Album 2003; Lieberman 2003.

---

[229] Lieberman 2003. In a pers. comm. Lieberman adds that the commitment to permanent residence was a requirement of the Chinese government.
[230] Lieberman 2003.

ISABEL ARETZ (1913– 2005)
Argentine/Venezuelan ethnomusicologist, folklorist, and composer

Born: Buenos Aires, Argentina, 13 Apr 1913
Died: Buenos Aires, Argentina, 1 Jun 2005

Education:
Studied piano, Buenos Aires National Conservatory of Music, 1923–31
Studied composition, Buenos Aires National Conservatory of Music,1928–33
Studied instrumentation with Villa-Lobos in Brazil,1937
Studied anthropology, Museo de Ciencias Naturales de Buenos Aires 1938–40
Studied folklore and musicology with Carlos Vega (q.v.), Museo de Ciencias Naturales de Buenos Aires, 1938–44

Qualifications:
Doctorate in music, Universidad Católica Argentina (Argentine Catholic University), 1967
Topic: . Argentine folk music

Appointments:
Professor of ethnomusicology, Escuela Nacional de Danzas de Argentina, 1950–52
Research fellow in folklore and ethnomusicology, Instituto Nacional de Folklore de Venezuela, Caracas, 1953–65
Head, folklore department, Instituto Nacional de Cultura y Bellas Artes, Caracas, 1965–70
Founder/director, Instituto Interamericano de Etnomusicología y Folklore, Caracas, 1971–85
Director, Centro para las Culturas Populares y Tradicionales (CCPYT), Caracas, 1989–90
Director, Fundacíon de Etnomusicologíá y Folklore (FUNDEF), Caracas, 1991–95
Director, Fundación Internacional de Etnomusicología y Folklore de Argentina in Buenos Aires, 1996–?

Offices:
President, Fundación Internacional de Etnomusicología y Folklore (FINIDEF), Caracas, 1986

Honours:
Numerous scholarships, fellowships, and awards for both composition and scholarship.

Field work:
With her husband Luis Felipe Ramón y Rivera (q.v.) extensive travel throughout hispanic America, collecting the folk music of Venezuela, Argentina, Chile, Bolivia, Peru, Uruguay, Paraguay, Colombia, Ecuador, Panama and Mexico.

Writings and compositions
See Béhague 2004a.

Refs.: Béhague 2004a; Stevenson 2006.

ARNOLD ADRIAAN BAKE (pronounced BAH-kuh)
(1899–1963)
Dutch scholar of Sanskrit and Indian music

Born: Hilversum, Netherlands, 19 May 1899
Died: London, England, 8 Oct 1963

Education:
Haarlem Gymnasium, Netherlands, c.1913–16
Studied Oriental languages, including Javanese, Malay, Arabic and Sanskrit, University of Leiden, Netherlands, 1918–23
Studied at Utrecht University, Netherlands, working on Sanskrit treatises on the theory of music, 1924–25
Studied music and language under Rabindranath Tagore, at Santiniketan, West Bengal, 1925–29

Qualifications:
DLitt, Utrecht University, 1930
Topic: Translation of a Sanskrit musical treatise *Sangita darpana*

Appointments:
Senior Research Fellow, Brasenose College, Oxford, 1934
Music Adviser, All-India Radio, Delhi, war years–1946
Lecturer in Sanskrit and Indian music, School of Oriental and African Studies, London, 1948
Reader, in Sanskrit and Indian music, School of Oriental and African Studies, London, 1949–63

Field work:
India and Nepal, 1931–34, 1937–46
India and Nepal, 1955–56

Writings:
Among Bake's publications are encyclopaedia articles on the music of India for *Die Musik in Geschichte und Gegenwart* ,[231] *Allgemoine Enzyklopadie der Musik* (Barenreiter), the *Grove Dictionary of Music and Musicians,*[232] and the *New Oxford History of Music* .[233] See also Kunst 1959a:#170-98 and Jairazbhoy 2003.

---

[231] 5th edition, edited by Blume 1949–68.
[232] Blom 1954.
[233] Bake 1957.

* * * *

Early in life Bake trained as a singer, and at one time considered becoming professional. During the war years in India, he gave a number of concerts and recitals when "it was his wont to include songs from well-nigh every part of the world ".[234]

From 1934 onwards, when he embarked on a lecture tour of the United States, Bake was pre-eminent as the leading authority in the West on Indian music, and was a stalwart of the International Folk Music Council from its inception in 1947 and as a member of its Executive Board for a decade preceding his death.

In 1958, Bake and his wife were involved in a street accident in Leiden, from which he never fully recovered. When I knew him in 1959–60, he was still walking with a stick, and had difficulty negotiating some of London's pavements.

In his Grove article on Bake, Nazir Jairazbhoy, who was Bake's assistant at SOAS, reports him as:

> a tireless scholar, continually discovering new material and recasting his lectures, which ranged far beyond the usual discussions of north and south Indian classical music and its theory. They included such diverse elements as Vedic chant, ancient music theory, the philosophical and aesthetic basis of Indian music, folk and tribal music and dance of India, music of the devotional and mystic groups, and the music of Tagore.

Refs.: Jairazbhoy 1991; Jairazbhoy 2003; Marr & Karpeles 1964; UCLA Ethnomusicology Archive 2003a; University of London Library 2003a.

---

[234] Marr & Karpeles 1964:110.

THEODORE BAKER (1851–1934)
American music scholar and lexicographer

Born: New York, USA, 3 Jun 1851
Died: Dresden, Germany, 13 Oct 1934

Education:
Trained as a young man for a business career
Went to Germany to study music, where he became a pupil of Oscar Paul at the University of Leipzig, 1874

Qualifications:
PhD, University of Leipzig, 1882
Topic: Seneca Indian music [235]

Career:
Organist in Concord, Massachusetts, USA, bef. 1874
Literary editor and translator for American music publishing firm of Schirmer Inc., 1892–1926

Field work:
Seneca Indian, New York State

Writings:
See below.

****

Baker's PhD thesis on Seneca music ranks as the first serious study of Native American music. In the course of his work for Schirmer Inc., he made many translations into English of books, librettos and articles. In 1900, he published the work for which he is best known: *Baker's Biographical Dictionary of Musicians*, which has since gone through many editions. He is also well known for his translations from the German of three hymns: "How Great Our Joy", "How a Rose E'er Blooming", and, especially, "We Gather Together".

Refs.: Cyber Hymnal; E-Brit ; Hitchcock 2003.

---

[235] Published as Baker 1882.

HENRY BALFOUR (1863–1939)
English museum curator and organologist

Born: Croydon, England, 11 Apr 1863
Died: Hedington, Oxford, England, 19 Feb 1939

Education:
Charterhouse School, and Trinity College, University of Oxford, 1881–?

Qualifications:
BA in natural science (biology), Trinity College, University of Oxford, 1885
MA, Trinity College, University of Oxford, 1888

Career:
Curator, Pitt-Rivers Museum, Oxford, 1891–1939

Offices:
Corresponding member, anthropological societies of Paris, Rome, Florence, Washington, Upsala and Vienna
President, Anthropological Institute of Great Britain and Ireland, 1903–04
President, Anthropological Section of British Association, 1904 & 1929
President, Museum Association, 1909
President, Folklore Society, 1923–24
President, Oxford Ornithological Society, 1924–35
President, Royal Geographical Society, 1936–38
Other presidencies: Oxford Anthropological Society; Prehistory Society of E. Anglia; and Somersetshire Archaeological and Natural History Society.

Fellowships:
Fellow of Exeter College, Oxford, 1903
Fellow of the Royal Society, 1924
Also FSA, FRAI, FZS, FRGS

Honours:
Awarded the honorary title of Professor by University of Oxford

Field work:
Travelled widely in search of artefacts to Scandinavia and elsewhere in Europe, SE and W Africa, and as far afield as Assam and Australia.

Writings:
Author of many publications on ethnological and archaeological subjects. Kunst 1959a lists a dozen publications of relevance to ethnomusicology (#208-19) of which the most significant is his *The Natural History of the Musical Bow* (1899).

****

Though not an ethnomusicologist or even, so far as his biographical information reveals, a musician, Balfour is significant for his work as an organologist.

Refs.: Mark R. Dickerson (pers.comm); Haddon 1940; La Rue 2004; Royal Society 2003; WWW v.III.

MARIUS BARBEAU (1883–1969)
Canadian anthropologist, ethnologist and folklorist

Born: Ste Marie-de-la-Beauce, PQ, Canada, 5 Mar 1883
Died: Ottawa, Canada, 27 Feb 1969

Education:
Studied humanities, Collège de Ste Anne de la Procatière, 1897–1903
Studied law, Laval University, ?–1907

Qualifications:
BA, Collège de Ste-Anne-de-la-Procatière, 1903
LL L, Laval, University, 1907
Admitted to Canadian bar, 1907
BSc in anthropology, and Diploma in Anthropology, Oriel College, University of Oxford, 1910
Topic: The Totemic System of the North-Western Tribes of North America

Appointments:
Ethnologist and later Director, Department of Anthropology, National Museum, Canada, 1911–48
Lecturer, University of Ottawa, 1942
Lecturer, Laval University, 1942–45
Professor agrégé, Laval University, 1945–?

Offices:
President, American Folklore Society, 1918
President. French Division, Royal Society of Canada, 1933
Co-founder, Folklore Archives, Laval University, 1946
Founder/President, Canadian Folk Music Society, 1957–63

Honours and awards:
Rhodes scholar at Oriel College, University of Oxford, 1908–10
Fellow, Royal Society of Canada, 1916
Doctor, Honoris Causa, University of Montreal, 1938
Honorary Fellow, Oriel College, University of Oxford, 1941
Parizeau Medal, 1946
Lorne Pierce medal for literature, 1950
Honorary DLitt, Laval University, 1952
Honorary doctorate, University of Oxford, 1953
Canada Council Medal, 1961
University of Alberta gold medal National Award, 1965
Companion of the Order of Canada, 1967
Centennial medal, 1967

Diplome d'Honneur, Canadian Conference of the Arts, 1968

Field work:
Huron, Salish, Wyandote, Iroquois and Tsimshian Indian, Canada, 1911–12
NW Coast Indian, 1914–?
French-Canadian folk, 1916–?

Writings:
Barbeau's literary output was extraordinary, comprising about 100 books and almost 600 articles, on a range of subjects in both French and English. For a bibliography of writings relevant to ethnomusicology, see *Ethnomusicology* 14(1):132-42 (1970).

****

Barbeau's mother, Marie Virginie Morency, was an educated woman who introduced him to folk songs through her love of music. His father, Charles Barbeau, a farmer and horseman, told folk stories, and also performed a vast repertoire of old-time fiddle tunes. Barbeau received piano lessons from his mother until the age of 12, but apart from this appears to have had no formal training in music. He is said to have been shown how to "set down folk tunes in musical notation" by the Canadian musician Sir Ernest MacMillan (1893–1973), and the linguist Edward Sapir (1884–1939), who among his other accomplishments composed music. Barbeau's relevance to ethnomusicology is principally as an early recordist of Canadian Indian music and as a prolific collector and recordist of French Canadian folk songs. Altogether, he left 13,000 original texts and variants of Indian and French songs, 8000 with tunes.

Refs.: BRC-(D); Katz 1970; Katz 2003b; Landry &Ménard 2001.

PHILLIPS BARRY (1880–1937)
American folk song scholar

Born: Boston, MA, USA, 18 Jul 1880
Died: Framingham, MA, USA, 29 Aug 1937

Education:
Barry was home schooled until the age of 13, then prepared for Harvard University by tutors, entering Harvard at the age of 16. There followed:

Undergraduate studies, Harvard University, 1896–1900
Graduate studies, Harvard University, 1900–04
Divinity School, Harvard University, 1910–13

After gaining his AB degree, Barry, who was tone deaf at the time and had no music instruction, spent the summer of the year 1900 preparing for graduate school by studying theory and practice of music and in training his ear. This enabled him in the fall semester "to attend profitably courses in the Division of Music." [236]

At graduate school, Barry studied classical and medieval literature and folklore under George Kittredge (q.v.), Leo Wiener (1862–1939), professor of Slavic languages and literature, and Kuno Franke (1855–1931), a specialist in medieval literature and poetry. Barry was particularly impressed by lectures he heard from Franke during 1903–04 on the history of the German romantic movement, prompting him soon afterwards to begin successful collecting on his own account of ballads in New England, despite a prevailing belief that these did not exist.

Qualifications:
AB, Harvard University, 1900
AM, Harvard University, 1901
STB (Bachelor of Sacred Theology), Harvard University, 1913

Appointments:
Instructor in English, languages and ancient history, Ebert Tutoring School, Croton, Mass., 1921–26

Field work:
Collected folk songs mainly in New England, and collaborated with other scholars in Vermont and Maine, 1904–14

Writings:
See Herzog 1938b:440-1 and Porter 2003a for lists, and Alvey 1973 for a full discussion. The as yet uncatalogued Barry collection of MS materials is held by the Houghton Library, Harvard University, under accession numbers MS Storage 118 in 26 boxes, and MS Storage 154 in 3 boxes.[237]

---

[236] Harvard University 1940.
[237] Houghton Library (pers.comm.).

****

Barry was an independent scholar of private means who never taught at a university. Nor, although he had a degree in theology and is said to have been ordained, did he become a church minister. Evidently he was subject to ill-health during much of his life. While still a student at Harvard he suffered "penetrating headaches" and an "unrecognised heart ailment";[238] an acute physical breakdown occurred in 1905, resulting in a decision that his condition precluded any permanent teaching position;[239] and he died when he was only 57 years old.

Barry is best known for his theory of "communal recreation", a similar idea to principles of "historical continuity, individual variation and community selection" advanced in 1907 by Cecil Sharp (q.v.).[240] He founded the Folk-Song Society of the North-East and edited its Bulletin from 1930 until his death, doing most of the writing for it and using it as a vehicle for the publication of his own ideas.[241] One of his accomplishments, using the methods of Kittredge, was to track cowboy songs to their origin in written literature. Bertrand Bronson says of him:

> Barry was a man of ranging interests which he did not manage to bring under perfect control; but there was little question that what commanded his deepest sympathy was the music of the ballads, and he devoted much of his very considerable energy to it. Barry was probably self-taught in music, and his theory outran his expert knowledge; but he insisted on the essential importance of the ballad tunes, on the fact that it was song that must be captured, not just a text, and that traditional lines of transmission were also a significant factor in the entity to be studied. The soundness of these precepts would be seen when in due time *British Ballads from Maine* appeared (1929), edited by Barry and collectors Fannie Eckstorm and Mary W. Smyth, with the tunes accurately noted by George Herzog, a musical anthropologist in the Hornbostel tradition and friend of Béla Bartók. This was the first American collection in which critical attention was paid to the individual ballads as folk-songs existing in a socio-historical milieu, a family tradition, words and music combined. Barry was also a pioneer in the use of a dictaphone in collecting, though he does not seem to have relied heavily upon it, nor to have transcribed many of the songs he recorded on wax cylinders – perhaps because of the clumsiness of the apparatus and the risk of destroying the records by repeated playing.[242]

Refs.: Alvey 1973; Harvard Archives 2005; Harvard University 1925 & 1940; Herzog 1938b; Porter 2003a.

---

[238] Harvard University 1940.
[239] Op.cit..
[240] There can be little doubt that Barry, in fact, gained this idea from Sharp. Alvey (1973:82) points out that Sharp's 1907 book *Some Conclusions* "is cited, significantly, in the very article with which Barry first introduced the term 'individual invention plus communal recreation '. "
[241] Both the Bulletin and the society itself became defunct when Barry died.
[242] Bronson 1969a:246.

BÉLA BARTÓK (1881–1945)
Hungarian composer, pianist, folk song collector, and scholar

Born: Nagyszentmiklós, Hungary (now Sînnicolau Mare, Romania), 25 Mar 1881
Died: New York, USA, 26 Sep 1945

Education:
Learned piano initially from his mother, Paula Voit (1857–1939)
Studied piano and composition, Royal Hungarian Academy of Music, Budapest, 1899–1903

Appointments:
Professor of pianoforte, Royal Hungarian Academy of Music, Budapest, 1907–34

Freed from teaching by the Academy in order to work on his collection of Hungarian folk music for publication by the Hungarian Academy of Sciences, 1934–40

Honours:
Member, Hungarian Academy of Sciences, 1934
Honorary doctorate, Columbia University, 1940

Field work:
See below

Writings:
For a list of some of Bartók's writings see Kunst 1959a:#256-283a. For collected essays by Bartók see Suchoff 1992 and Suchoff 1997. See also below.

****

Like his friend an compatriot, Zoltán Kodály (q.v.), Bartók, though notable also as a concert pianist, is renowned both as a composer and as a pre-eminent collector and transcriber of Hungarian folk song. Again like Kodály, he is also recognised for his effective use of Hungarian folk idiom in his own compositions. Bartók became aware of genuine Hungarian folk music in 1904 while staying at the northern Hungarian resort of Gerlice Puszta (now Ratkó, Slovakia), where he heard a Transylvanian-born maid, Lidi Dósa, singing in an adjacent room, and noted down her songs. Afterwards, he wrote to his sister saying: "Now I have a new plan: to collect the finest Hungarian folksongs and to raise them, adding the best possible piano accompaniments, to the level of art-song." The following year, in March, he met Kodály, who was already active in folk song scholarship, and they began their long and productive association which resulted in the collection of thousands of folk songs.

Except for Arab folk music collected in the Biskra District of Algeria in 1913 and a field trip to Turkey in 1936, Bartók worked exclusively within the borders of what was then Hungary where, together with Kodály, he collected not only Hungarian folk music as such, but also large numbers of Romanian and Slovak folk songs on his own. The amount of work he accomplished was prodigious. Though careful to say he is quoting from memory, László Vikárius of the Bartók Archives in Hungary (pers.comm.) estimates that

> Bartók might have collected around 3,000 Romanian, 2,500 Hungarian and 2,500 Slovak melodies as well as Arab, Turkish, Ruthenian, Serbian, and a very few Bulgarian ones. But he also classified some 10,000 more Hungarian melodies when he was appointed to the Hungarian Academy of Sciences.

In 1940, Bartók emigrated to the United States, and during 1941–42, was commissioned by Columbia University to transcribe a Harvard University collection by Milman Parry of Serbo-Croatian folk songs. In collaboration with Albert B. Lord, this resulted in the publication, a decade later, of their *Serbo-Croatian Folk Songs* (1951), containing texts and transcriptions of 75 songs. This work is also valuable for its introduction in which Bartók comments on his method of transcription and explains the signs and symbols he adopted.

Refs.: Blom 1948a; Gillies 2003; László Vikárius (pers.comm.).

SAMUEL PRESTON BAYARD (1908–1997)
American folk song scholar

Born: Pittsburgh, PA, USA, 10 Apr 1908
Died: Pittsburgh, PA, USA, 10 Jan 1997

Education:
After prior study at Pennsylvania State College, studied folklore and comparative literature with George Lyman Kittredge (q.v.) at Harvard University

Qualifications:
BA in English, Pennsylvania State College, 1934
MA in English, Harvard University, 1936

Appointments:
Instructor, Pennsylvania State University, 1945–?
Professor of English and comparative literature, Pennsylvania State University, ?–1973

Offices:
President, American Folklore Society, 1965–66

Field work:
Collected folk songs, SW Pennsylvania and NW Virginia, mostly in the summer months, 1928–63

Writings:
See Kunst 1959a:#302-304a, Porter 2003a, and below.

****

Besides documenting Pennsylvania fiddle and fife melodies in two books, *Hill Country Tunes* (1944) and his monumental 628pp. *Dance to the Fiddle, March to the Fife* (1982), Bayard made important contributions to the theory of tune relationships, including identification of "tune families". He was renowned as a "tune detective", with an encyclopaedic knowledge of Anglo-American folk music repertory, and as a collector was a true pioneer. According to his own testimony, the music of the items he collected was recorded "by hand and by ear, sometimes on a recording machine", making him, as Blaustein comments, "the first and one of the very few academically trained U.S. scholars to combine the interests and concerns of a folklorist with the technical skills of a musicologist."

Refs.: Blaustein 1997; Pennsylvania State University 1997; Porter 2003b.

JOHN ANTHONY RANDALL BLACKING (1928–1990)
English ethnomusicologist

Born: Guildford, England, 22 Oct 1928
Died: Belfast, Northern Ireland, 24 Jan 1990

Education:
Attended Salisbury Cathedral Choir School, 1934–42
Attended Sherborne School, Dorset, 1942–47
Learned piano from an early age; became proficient enough to consider a career as a concert pianist
Studied anthropology, King's College, Cambridge University, 1949–52

Qualifications:
BA in archaeology and anthropology, Cambridge University, 1953
MA, Cambridge University, 1957
PhD, University of the Witwatersrand, 1965
Topic: Venda children's songs

Appointments:
Commissioned officer, Coldstream Guards, 1947–49, including service in Malaya, 1947–49
Assistant to André Schaeffner (q.v.), Musée de I'Homme, Paris, 1952
Archive assistant, International Library of African Music, Johannesburg, 1954–58
Lecturer in social anthropology and African government, University of the Witwatersrand, 1959–64
Professor of anthropology, University of the Witwatersrand, 1965–69
Professor of social anthropology, Queen's University, Belfast, 1970–90
Visiting professor, University of Washington, 1971
Visiting professor, University of Pittsburgh, 1980
Visiting professor, University of Western Australia, 1983
Visiting professor, University California, Berkeley, 1986

Offices:
President, Society for Ethnomusicology, 1982–83
Founder, European Seminar in Ethnomusicology, 1981

Honours:
Honorary DLitt, University of the Witwatersrand, 1972
Rivers memorial medal, Royal Anthropological Institute, 1986
Koizumi Fumio Prize, Tokyo, 1989

Field work:
Recording expeditions with Hugh Tracey (q.v.), Mozambique and Zululand, c.1954
Venda, Northern Transvaal, South Africa, 1956–58

Writings:
Full lists of writings are in Baily 1990:xvi-xxi and in Byron 1995:247-52. Blacking's most influential book was his highly acclaimed *How Musical Is Man?* (1972).

****

There is extensive discussion of Blacking's contribution to ethnomusicology elsewhere in the present book.

Refs.: Baily 1990; Baily 2003; Ryron 1995; Byron 2004; Cambridge University Archives (pers.comm.).

FRANZ BOAS (1858–1942)
German/American cultural anthropologist

Born: Minden, Westphalia, Germany, 9 Jul 1858
Died: New York, NY, USA, 22 Dec 1942

Education:
Studied sciences, mathematics, languages, and humanities at universities of Heidelberg and Bonn, 1877–9
Doctoral student in physics and geography, University of Kiel, 1879–81
After a year of military service (1881-2) prepared in Berlin for his first field expedition, a geographical study in the arctic (begun in 1883)

Qualifications:
Baccalaureate, University of Heidelberg, 1881
PhD in physics, University of Kiel, 1881
Topic: Optical properties of sea-water

Appointments and career:
Assistant curator, Königliches Museum für Völkerkunde, Berlin, and Docent in geography, Berlin University, 1885–86
Assistant editor, *Science* magazine, New York, 1887–88
Docent in anthropology, Clark University, Worcester, 1888–92
Chief assistant, Chicago World's Fair and Collections manager, Field Museum of Natural History, 1892–94
Associate, American Museum of Natural History, as temporary employee, 1894–96, Assistant curator, 1896–1901, and Curator, 1901–05
Lecturer in physical anthropology, Columbia University, 1896–99
Professor of anthropology, Columbia University, 1899–1936

Offices:
President, American Anthropological Society, 1907–08
Editor, *Journal of American Folklore*, 1908–25
President, New York Academy of Sciences, 1910
Founder, *International Journal of American Linguistics*, 1917
President, International Congress of Americanists, 1928
President, American Association for the Advancement of Science, 1931

Honours:
Honorary degrees from several European universities, including Oxford

Field work included:
Baffin Island, 1883–84
13 field trips totalling 871 days among Kwakiutl and other tribes of British Columbia, 1886–1931

Writings:
Boas was the author of over 600 publications. His correspondence, manuscripts of talks, lectures and articles, together with diaries and field notes and photographs are held in a Franz Boas collection (B B61) by the American Philosophical Society. For writings relevant to music see Kunst 1959a:#378-89, and DeVale 2003a.

****

Although as a youth Boas was primarily attracted to the natural sciences, he was by no means bereft of musical talent, and music formed an important part of his life. He began to learn the piano early, and his appreciation of the classic composers increased as he grew older.[243] At Heidelberg, after he began university studies, he had a piano in his room.[244] And at Bonn he formed a trio, took part in the choir, and attended concerts of such famous performers as Sarasate, Joachim, and Clara Schumann.[245] Playing the piano remained also a source of pleasure in his later life. After settling at Clark University, for example, he hired a piano, upon which he played mostly 18th century music, especially Mozart, "whose sonatas he played from beginning to end."[246]

Boas became the acknowledged founder of American cultural anthropology, providing it with distinctive methodology, and guiding it away from unproductive evolutionary theories that continued to dominate in Europe and among some of his contemporaries. Although not an ethnomusicologist as such, he deserves to be counted as one, because of the profound influence he exerted upon the subject, both through his anthropological writings and the legacy he left as a teacher of the next generation of anthropologists, including such notable scholars as Ruth Benedict, Melville Herskovits (q.v.), Alfred Kroeber, Margaret Mead, and Edward Sapir. He was an early advocate of field work, phonographic recording, archiving, and the study of music as an integral element of culture, besides introducing key concepts (discussed in Part I) which have become hallmarks of the discipline.

Refs.: Alroy 2003; American Philosophical Society 2004; ANB; Andrews University 2004; Cole 1999; DeVale 2003a; E-Brit.; Everyman; Rohner 1969.

---

[243] Cole 1999:32.
[244] Cole 1999:40.
[245] Cole 1999:46.
[246] Cole 1999:141.

FRITZ BOSE (1906–1975)
German comparative musicologist

Born: Messenthin, Stettin, 26 Jul 1906
Died: Berlin, Germany, 16 Aug 1975

Education:
Studied musicology, ethnology, and psychology under Carl Stumpf (q.v.), Erich von Hornbostel (q.v.) and Curt Sachs (q.v.), Berlin University, 1925–33

Qualifications:
PhD, Berlin University, 1934
Topic: , Die Musik der Uitoto

Appointments:
Curator, Institut für Lautforschung, Berlin, 1934–45
Music consultant, Race and Resettlement Office of the SS, 1935
Assistant lecturer, Berlin University, 1941
Director, historical musicology, Institut für Musikforschung, Berlin, 1953–?
Director, folk music, Institut für Musikforschung, Berlin, 1966–?
Teacher, and from 1967 Hon. Professor, Technical University, Berlin, 1963–71

Offices:
Founder/Director research commission into song, music and dance, Deutsche Gesellschaft für Volksliedkunde, 1956–72
Editor, *Jahrbuch für musikalische Volks- und Völkerkunde*, 1963–?
Founder/Director, Gesellschaft für Musik des Orients, 1966–72

Field work:
Several field trips to Lorraine, Finland, and South Tyrol, 1934–40

Writings:
Bose's principal works appear to have been a paper derived from his PhD dissertation on music of the Uitoto of Colombia,[247] and a survey of world music using the methods of Hornbostel.[248] For other writings see Eggebrecht & Potter 2003, and Kunst 1059a:#415-438a.

****

As a non-Jewish product of Erich von Hornbostel's Berlin School of comparative musicology, Bose survived the enforced breakup of Hornbostel's group under the Nazi regime. His pre-war work for the SS attempted to find a scientific basis for relating music and race. Later he became a respected administrator and expert in organology, folk music, and ethnomusicology in general.

Refs.: Eth 6(3):253-4 (1962); Eggebrecht & Potter 2003; Jürgen-K. Mahrenholz (pers.comm).

---

[247] Bose 1934.
[248] Bose 1953.

CONSTANTIN BRAILOIU (1893–1958)
Romanian/French ethnomusicologist

Born: Bucharest, Romania, 13/25 Aug 1893
Died: Geneva, Switzerland, 20 Dec 1958

Education:
Studied composition, Paris Conservatoire, 1912–14

Appointments:
Professor of music history and aesthetics, Académie Royale de Musique, Paris, 1921
Secretary-general, Society of Romanian Composers, 1926–44
Taught at Académie de Musique Religieuse de la Sainte Patriarchie, 1929–35
Cultural adviser, Ministry of Foreign Affairs, Romania, 1938
Attaché, Romanian Legation, Berne, 1943–46
Co-founder, Archives Internationales de Musique Populaire (AIMP), Musée d'ethnographie, Geneva, 1944
Worked at the Musée d'ethnographie, Geneva, 1944–58
Worked in ethnomusicology department, Musée de l'Homme and Sorbonne Institute of Musicology, Paris, 1948

Field work:
Romania, 1929–32

Writings:
See Kunst 1959a:#458-467a, Rouget 2003, and below.

****

Brailoiu ranks as one of the most undeservedly neglected of the pioneer ethnomusicologists, possibly for no better reason than having written mostly in French or Romanian. He was one of the few ethnomusicologists who specialised in music systems analysis. Some of the most important of his writings have been translated into English and are available in a book edited and translated by A.L. Lloyd (q.v.) entitled *Problems of Ethnomusicology*.[249]

Refs.: Laurent Aubert (pers.comm.); Aubert 1985; Rouget 2003.

---

[249] Lloyd 1984. For a review see McLean 1985.

BERTRAND HARRIS BRONSON (1902–1986)
American folk song scholar

Born: Lawrenceville, NJ, USA, 22 Jun 1902
Died: Berkeley, CA, USA, 14 Mar 1986

Education:
Rhodes scholar, Oriel College, University of Oxford, 1922–25

Qualifications:
AB, University of Michigan, 1921
AM, Harvard University, 1922
PhD, Yale University, 1927
MA, University of Oxford, 1929

Appointments:
Instructor in English, University of Michigan, 1925–26
Instructor, University of California, Berkeley, 1927–29
Assistant professor, University of California, Berkeley, 1929–38
Associate professor, University of California, Berkeley, 1938–45
Visiting professor, Yale University, 1945
Professor of English, University of California, Berkeley, 1945–69
Alexander lecturer, University of Toronto, 1948-59
Berg professor, New York University, 1973

Honours:
Guggenheim fellowships, 1943, 1944, 1948
Humanities Award, American Council of Learned Societies, 1959
Honorary docteur des lettres, Laval University of Quebec, 1961
Medal of Honor, Rice University, 1962
Honorary LHD, University of Chicago, 1968
Wilbur Cross Medal, Yale University, 1970
Honorary LHD, University of Michigan, 1970
Honorary LLD, University of California, 1971

Writings:
Bronson's major work was his 4-volume *The Traditional Tunes of the Child Ballads* (1959–72). Additionally, his book *The Ballad As Song* (1969) brought together a number of his most important essays, written over a span of 30 years.

****

Following in the footsteps of Phillips Barry (q.v.), a major part of Bronson's achievement was to help persuade folk song scholars that a folk song is more than a poem, as it was commonly treated in collections, but an integral combination of words *and* music.

Bronson liked to say of himself that he had four quills in his quiver: Chaucer, Shakespeare, Johnson and his age, and the musicology of the ballad. It was the latter that established his reputation among ethnomusicologists, but the others were also relevant. He was able to bring his training as an English scholar to bear on the subject. In his book *The Ballad As Song* he raises issues such as the taxonomy and ordering of melodic variations, comparative analysis of Anglo-American folk tunes, the morphology of traditional variation and transmission, and the relationship of words and melody, many of which remain relevant today.

Refs.: BRC-(B); Eth 6(2):143 (1962); Porter 2003c; University of California 2003.

EDWIN GRANT BURROWS (1891–1958)
American ethnomusicologist

Born: Wyoming, OH, USA, 8 Oct 1891
Died: Storrs, CT, USA, 13 Jul 1958

Qualifications:
BA, Cornell University, 1913
MA in anthropology, Yale University, 1932
PhD in anthropology, Yale University, 1937
Topic: Cultural differentiation of Western Polynesia

Career and appointments:
Journalist, *Springfield Republican* and the *Boston Evening Transcript*, 1913
Lieutenant, US Army, 1917–19
Journalist, *Stars and Stripes* and other newspapers, 1918
Taught journalism, University of Michigan
Journalist, *Honolulu Advertiser*, 1926–30
Bishop Museum Fellow, 1931–32
Ethnologist, Bishop Museum, 1933–34
Instructor in anthropology, University of Connecticut, 1939
Assistant professor of anthropology, University of Connecticut, 1940–45
Associate professor of anthropology, University of Connecticut, 1946–49
Military intelligence specialist, South Pacific, US War Department, 1942–44
Investigator, Pacific Science Board, 1947–53
Professor of anthropology, University of Connecticut, 1950–58

Field work:
Uvea and Futuna, Western Polynesia, 1933–34
Ifaluk, Micronesia, 1947–48

Writings:
See below.

****

Burrows was among the few scholars to have specialised in Polynesian music. His first monograph, *Native Music of the Tuamotus* (1933), began life as a master's thesis at Yale University. It was an analysis of dictaphone cylinders brought back from a Tuamotu Survey, conducted by the B.P. Bishop Museum, Honolulu, from 1929–31,[250] while Burrows was working as a journalist with the *Honolulu Advertiser*. Burrows owed availability of the recordings to his appointment as a fellow, and later as an ethnologist, at the Bishop Museum, evidently beginning work on the cylinders around mid-1931. There is mention of him at this time in the correspondence of his colleague Peter Buck (Te Rangi Hiroa) (1877–1951), who later became director of the museum. On 24 July 1931, Buck wrote:

---

[250] Burrows 1933:3.

> Burrows our musical ethnologist has been working on Emory's Tuamotu recordings. He reduced one to music and sang it over to me with quite a pleasing pronunciation. I think he will make a good man as he is rather a nice fellow into the bargain.[251]

The presentation of the thesis at Yale resulted from a long-standing association between Yale and the Bishop Museum, dating back to the missionisation of Hawai'i by "men of Yale",[252] as a result of which the director of the Bishop Museum held office also as a professor at Yale. Burrows's associate, Peter Buck, was seconded as a visiting professor at Yale, from 1932–34, while Burrows continued working as an ethnologist at the Bishop Museum, using his position there to conduct field work of his own in Western Polynesia. Two ethnographic monographs ensued: *Ethnology of Futuna* (1936) and *Ethnology of Uvea* (1937), each with attention to musical instruments, together with a specifically musical monograph, *Songs of Uvea and Futuna* (1945), all published by the B.P. Bishop Museum. The relationship with Buck resumed with Burrows's doctoral dissertation, *Western Polynesia: A Study in Cultural Differentiation* (1938), supervised by Buck at Yale, which used musical instruments among other cultural elements in a distribution analysis which successfully distinguished Eastern and Western Polynesian culture areas. At Yale, Burrows also received anthropological training from Clark Wissler (1870–1947) and Edward Sapir (1884–1939), both of whom qualified under Franz Boas (1858–1942), the doyen of American anthropologists, who also taught George Herzog (q.v.), Melville Herskovits (q.v.), and Helen Roberts (q.v.). Of the two, Wissler, who was appointed as the first professor of anthropology at Yale in 1931, and introduced the concept of "culture areas" used by Burrows in his doctoral dissertation, must have been especially influential. For a complete list of Burrows's publications see McAllester 1959:16-17. For an annotated list of his Oceania writings, including manuscript materials, see McLean 1995.

Refs.: Barnett 1959; Burrows 1970:3-4; McAllester 1959.

---

[251] Sorrenson 1986-88 (2):187.
[252] Condliffe 1971:176-8.

FRANCIS JAMES CHILD (1825–1896)
American folk song scholar

Born: Boston, MA, USA, 1 Feb 1825
Died: Boston, MA, USA, 11 Sep 1896

Education:
Attended English High School, Boston, bef. 1840
Attended Public Latin School, Boston, 1840–41
Studied mathematics and other subjects, Harvard University, 1842–49
Studied Germanic philology, Berlin and Göttingen, 1849–51

Qualifications:
BA, first in his class, Harvard University, 1846
MA, Harvard University, 1849
PhD, University of Göttingen, 1854 [253]

Appointments:
Tutor in mathematics, Harvard University, 1846–48
Tutor in history and political economy, Harvard University, 1848–49
Boylston Professor of Rhetoric and Oratory, Harvard University, 1851–76
Inaugural professor of English, Harvard University, 1876–94

Honours:
Honorary doctorate of philosophy, University of Göttingen, c.1854
LLD, Harvard University, 1884
LHD, Columbia University, 1887

Writings:
See below.

****

Child's outstanding achievement, and the one with which his name will forever be associated, was his 5-volume anthology of British ballads, *The English and Scottish Popular Ballads* (1883–98).

Refs.: ANB; Bynum 1974; E-Brit; Harvard University 1930:244; Johnson & Malone 1946; Nelson 2003; Helene C. Williams (pers.comm.).

---

[253] Awarded despite not having written a dissertation.

PAUL COLLAER (1891–1989)
Belgian musicologist, pianist and conductor

Born: Boom, near Antwerp, Belgium, 8 Jun 1891
Died: Brussels, Belgium, 10 Dec 1989

Qualifications:
Prix de l'Piano et Harmonie, Conservatoire de Malines
DrSc in chemistry, Université Libre de Bruxelles, 1919

Appointments and career:
Gave concerts in Belgium and abroad as pianist and orchestral conductor, 1910–53
Professor, Mechelen Atheneum
Director, Flemish music service, Belgian National Radio, 1937–53

Offices:
Founder, Pro Arte concerts, Brussels, 1921
Founder, Colloques de Wégimont, 1954
President, Scientific Board, International Institute for Comparative Music Studies, Berlin

Honours:
Biannual International Prize for Music, Unesco, 1985

Writings:
See Spiessens & Janssens 2003, and Kunst 1959a:#719-728c.

****

Collaer's interest in non-Western music is said to have been aroused during World War I when the French and English armies had Berbers, Senegalese, and other non-European soldiers in their ranks, and Collaer "listened eagerly to their songs." After World War II, he obtained recordings from the BBC. London, with which he began the ethnic collection of Flemish Radio, along with recordings of Belgian folk music. In 1953 he organised, at a castle near Liege, the Colloques de Wegimont, a series of annual meetings which became an international forum for scholars such as Marius Schneider (q.v), Gilbert Rouget (1916–), Constantin Brailoiu (q.v.), Claudie Marcel-Dubois (q.v.), and others.

Refs.: De Hen 1980; Eth 5(3):244 (1961); Spiessens & Janssens 2003.

PETER CROSSLEY-HOLLAND (1916–2001)
English composer and ethnomusicologist

Born: London, England, 28 Jan 1916
Died: London, England, 27 Apr 2001

Education:
Abbotsholme School, Derbyshire
Studied physiology and music, St John's College, University of Oxford, 1933–36
Studied composition with John Ireland, Royal College of Music, 1937–39
Studied composition privately with Edmund Rubbra and others

Qualifications:
BA, University of Oxford, 1936
MA, University of Oxford, 1941
BMus, University of Oxford, 1943

Appointments:
Regional director, British Arts Council, 1943–45
Assistant, Music Division BBC, and later music organiser for the Third Programme, 1948–63
Assistant director, Institute of Comparative Music Studies and Documentation, Berlin, 1964–66
Visiting teacher, University of Illinois, 1966
Visiting professor, University of Hawai'i, 1968–69
Visiting teacher, UCLA, 1969–71
Professor of music, UCLA, 1972–83

Offices:
Editor, *Journal of the International Folk Music Council*, 1965–68

Honours:
Golden Disc Award, Japanese Ministry of Education, 1966
Gold Medal, Preis der Deutsche Schallplatten Kritik
Honorary Fellowship, University of Wales, Lampeter, 1986
Honorary Fellowship, University of Wales, Bangor, 1992

Field work:
India: Sikkim, Ladakh, Jawaharlal, and Tibetan refugees, 1962

Writings:
For a list of writings see *Selected Reports*, 4: xiii–xxv (1983)

****

Crossley-Holland was a "composer-ethnomusicologist" for whom composition was central, and his attitude to the music he studied was plainly that of an artist. Apart from composition, which he pursued throughout his life, his particular interests were Celtic music, Tibetan music, and pre-Columbian musical instruments. James Porter, who was a colleague of Crossley-Holland at UCLA, reveals he was not interested in anthropological approaches to music but stressed rather the "spiritual" nature and "transcendental affect" of the music he was dealing with. This "also colored his deep affinity with pre-Columbian and Celtic musics" about which, in his teaching and writings, he sought to communicate the "serene wisdom" of the music. As well, his "other worldliness" was legendary.[254]

Refs.: BRC-(A); Follows 2005; Jairazbhoy 1983; Morgan 2003; Porter 2001; Porter 2003.

---

[254] Porter 2001:324-5.

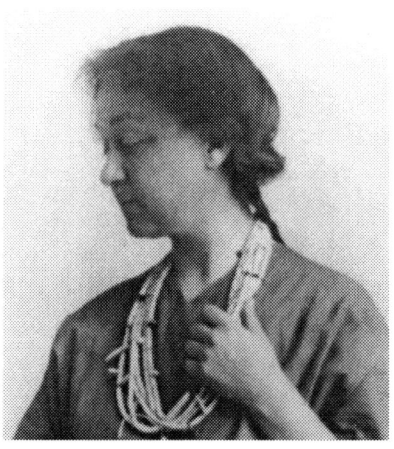

NATALIE CURTIS (1875–1921)
(Known also under her married name of Burlin)
American pianist, composer, and musical folklorist

Born: New York, NY, USA, 26 Apr 1875
Died: Paris, France, 23 Oct 1921

Education:
Studied music, National Conservatory, New York
Studied piano, Berlin, Paris, Bonn and Bayreuth

Field work:
Recorded and studied the music of at least 18 native American tribes, including Apache, Hopi, Navajo, Pima, Pueblo, Yuma and Zuñi in the Southwest, and Arapaho, Cheyenne, Dakota, Kiowa and Pawnee from the Great Plains, as well as others as far afield as Maine and British Columbia.

Writings:
The Indians' Book (1907), contains transcriptions of more than 200 Native American songs, and her Hampton research culminated with a 4-volume work, *Hampton Series Negro Folk-songs* (1918–19), and *Tales from the Dark Continent* (1920). A collection of her personal papers is housed at the University Archives of Hampton University. For a full list of her writings, see Rahkonen 1998.

****

There is reference to Curtis in Part I.

Refs.: ANB; -E-Brit; Rahkonen 1998.

WERNER DANCKERT (1900–1970)
German musicologist and ethnomusicologist

Born: Erfurt, Germany, 22 Jun 1900
Died: Krefeld, Germany, 5 Mar 1970

Education:
Studied natural sciences and mathematics, University of Jena; musicology, University of Leipzig; musicology, University of Erlangen; musicology, piano and composition, Leipzig Conservatory, 1919–24

Qualifications:
Doctorate, University of Erlangen, 1924
Topic: History of the gigue

Appointments:
Assistant to Gustav Becking (1894–1945),[255] University of Erlangen, 1924–25
Lecturer, University of Jena, 1927–37
Lecturer, University of Berlin, 1937–38
Professor, University of Berlin, 1938–39
Reader, University of Graz, 1939–42
Head, Department of Music, University of Graz, 1943–45
Professor, University of Rostock, 1950

Writings:
For lists, see Katz & Potter 2003, and Suppan 1971. His unpublished papers are held by the University of Freiburg library under accession number NL18.

****

As an ethnomusicologist, Danckert was notable for his writings on melodic style, and for his studies on European folk music. After World War II, for political reasons, Danckert lost his living, moving first to Rostock, East Germany in 1950, and finally in the same year to Krefeld, West Germany, where he spent the remainder of his life without an academic post. Another of his misfortunes was his adherence to "Kulturkreise" principles. For this reason, although Suppan rates Danckert as "among the giants of German musicology," Nettl describes his 1939 book on European folk song as "unorthodox and not widely accepted".[256]

Refs: BRC-(A); Katz & Potter 2003; Suppan 1971; Universitätsbibliothek Freiburg, 2001.

---

[255] Becking was a German musicologist who himself was at the beginning of his career when Danckert was his assistant, having taken his doctorate only four years previously and only just been appointed as a lecturer at Erlangen (New Grove 2004).
[256] Nettl 1961:13.

ALAIN DANIÉLOU (1907–1994)
French musicologist, artist and orientalist

Born: Neuilly-sur-Seine, France, 4 Oct 1907
Died: Lausanne, Switzerland, 27 Jan 1994

Education:
St John's College, Annapolis, Maryland, 1926–27
Studied piano, classical dancing, singing and composition, Paris, after 1927
Studied Sanskrit, philosophy and music in traditional schools, Benares, India, 1935–50

Qualifications:
Gained baccalaureate, Paris, 1925

Appointments:
Research professor of music, Hindu University of Benares, and associate director, School of Indian Music, Benares, 1949–53
Director, Adyar Library of Sanskrit Manuscripts, Madras, 1954
Director of Studies, Centre d'Etudes de Musique Orientale, Paris, after 1959
Founder/director, International Institute for Comparative Music Studies, Berlin and Venice, 1963–79

Honours and awards:
Legion d'honneur, chevalier, 1967
Chevalier des Arts et Lettres, 1970
Prix Broquette-Gonin, Academie Française, 1971
Officier, L'Ordre National du Mérite, 1974
Unesco/CIM prize for music, 1981
Commandeur des Arts et Lettres, 1985
Medaille Kathmandu de l'Unesco, 1987
Personnalite de l'Annee en France, 1987
Personnalite de l'Annee a titre international, 1989
Premio Cervo (Italy), 1991
Legion d'honneur, officier, 1993

Writings:
The Ragas of Northern Indian Music (1968) is his principal work. For other writings on music see Spieth-Weissenbacher and Gribenski 2003a.

****

In 1932, Daniélou travelled extensively, finally settling in Benares, India, where he remained for many years. In India, he learnt Hindi, became deeply committed to Indian culture, and held professional appointments in Benares and Madras. In 1959, he returned to Europe, where, under the aegis of his International Institute for Comparative Music Studies, which he established in Berlin and Venice, he publicised Indian and other traditional music by organising concerts and by issuing LP record anthologies through Unesco. As an advocate for Indian music and culture, his influence was immense, attracting the attention and support of artists such as Ravi Shankar and Yehudi Menuhin. His books on Indian art, sculpture, literature, religion, philosophy and music have been published in twelve countries and translated from the original French into languages which include English, German, Italian, Spanish, Portuguese and Japanese. However, his writings on Indian music, obsessed as they are with theoretical claims involving minute divisions of the octave, are by no means universally accepted. His work has also been criticised for inaccuracies and for misquoting the texts upon which he bases his theories. The key to Daniélou's character and thought lies with his personal commitment to Hinduism, about which, on his own evaluation, in a supplement to his memoirs, he has written:

> The only value I never question is that of the teachings I received from Shaivite Hinduism which rejects any kind of dogmatism, since I have found no other form of thought which goes so far, so clearly, which such depth and intelligence, in comprehending the divine and the world's structures.

Refs.: Anon 2003b; BRC-(B); Spieth-Weissenbacher &Gribenski 2003a.

CHARLES RUSSELL DAY (1860–1900)
English soldier and authority on Indian music

Born: Horstead, Norwich, England, 19 Apr 1860
Died: (of wounds) Paardeberg, South Africa, 18 Feb 1900

Education:
Cheam School, Eton College, and Oxford

Career:
Joined 3rd Royal Lancashire Militia, 1880
Lieutenant, Ist battalion Oxfordshire Light Infantry, 1882
Became interested in Indian music and musical instruments while with the 43rd regiment in India, 1882–87
Took part in suppression of Moplah Riots, Southern India, 1884–85
Promoted to Captain, 1889
Employed in musical department, Royal Military Exhibition, South Kensington, 1890
Member, English Committee, Vienna International Musical Exhibition, 1892
Adjutant of Volunteers, 1892–97
Promoted to Major, 1899
Assisted Paris Musical Exhibition, 1900
Served at Klip Kraal , Relief of Kimberley. and Paardeberg (where he was mortally wounded), Boer War, 1899–1900

Writings:
Author of *The Music and Musical Instruments of Southern India and the Deccan* (1891), and *A Descriptive Catalogue of Musical Instruments* (1891), from a royal military exhibition held at Chelsea, London, in 1890. His Indian MSS. and collection of Indian musical instruments are housed in the South Kensington Museum, London.

Refs.: British Light Infantry Regiments 2003; Fuller-Maitland 1948; Mockler-Ferryman 1901:293-6.

FRANCES THERESA DENSMORE (1867–1957)
American ethnomusicologist

Born: Red Wing, MN, USA, 21 May 1867
Died: Red Wing, MN, USA, 5 Jun 1957

Education:
Studied piano, organ and harmony, Oberlin Conservatory of Music, Ohio, 1884–86
Studied piano with Carl Baermann, Boston, and Leopold Godowsky, Chicago
Studied counterpoint with John K. Paine, Harvard University

Appointments and career:
Taught piano, St. Paul, Minnesota, 1887–89
  Collaborator, Bureau of American Ethnology, Smithsonian Institution, 1907–57
Consultant, National Archives, 1941–43

Honours:
Hon. AM, Oberlin College, 1924
National Association of American Composers and Conductors award, 1940–41
Doctor of Letters, Macalester College, St. Paul, 1950
Minnesota Historical Society citation for distinguished service, 1954

Field work:
White Earth Indian Reservation, Minnesota, 1905
Chippewa, Mandan, Hidatsa, and Sioux, Dakotas, 1910–15
Later recording expeditions included: Pawnee (Oklahoma), Papago (Arizona), Indians of Washington and British Columbia, Winnebago and Menominee (Wisconsin), Pueblo Indians of the Southwest, Tule (Panama), 1920–30

Writings:
See below.

****

In 1910 and 1913, Densmore published her 2-volume monograph *Chippewa Music*, the first of a long series of monographs to be published by the Bureau of American Ethnology, which began supporting her work in 1907, and continued to do so throughout the remainder of her life. In all, she published 21 books and over 200 articles. For a bibliography, see Merriam 1956-57 and for additions and corrections see Merriam 1958 and Gillis 1958. Merriam's bibliography is prefaced by the following statement about the contents:

> Based on material collected in the field, oftimes under adverse conditions, these studies range over a wide geographic and cultural area from British Columbia , through the Northern Woodlands, Northern and Southern Plains and the Pueblos, to the Gulf States (Florida to Texas). In addition to the notations and analysis of hundreds of songs, the mono-

graphs include excellent ethnographic reports, the fullness and accuracy of which bespeak not only the investigator's talent as a sensitive observer and student of culture, but also the felicitous human relations she enjoyed with her many informants. . .

The Smithsonian-Densmore collection [of 3591 cylinders],[257] now housed in the Archive of American Folk Song, Library of Congress, is an irreplaceable document of an aboriginal culture before it had suffered too extensively under the impact of modern civilization.[258]

Refs.: ANB: Anth; E-Brit; Frisbie 1991; Kurath 1958; Minnesota Historical Society 2002; Rhodes 2003.

---

[257] Korson 1959:(Pt 1) 1.
[258] Merriam 1956–57:14.

A(LEXANDER) J(OHN) ELLIS (1814–1890)
English mathematician, philologist, and acoustician

Born: Hoxton, London, England, 14 Jun 1814
Died: London, England, 28 Oct 1890

Education:
Early education at a private boarding school, Walthamstow, London
Shrewsbury, 1826–29
Eton College, 1830–32
Studied mathematics and classics, Trinity College, Cambridge University, 1833–37
Entered Middle Temple as a student, but without an intention of following the law
Enrolled as student of arts and literature, University of Edinburgh, 1853–57
Studied music and acoustics under Professor John Donaldson (1789–1865) during his time at the University of Edinburgh

Qualifications:
BA, Cambridge University, 1837

Offices:
President, Philological Society, 1873–74 & 1880–81
Life Governor, University College, London, 1886

Honours:
Fellow of the Cambridge Philosophical Society, 1837
Fellow of the Royal Society, 1864
Fellow of the London Mathematical Society, 1865
Fellow of the Society of Antiquaries, 1870
Fellow of the College of Preceptors, 1873
Silver medals from Society of Arts for each of several papers read 1877–85.
Honorary LLD, Cambridge University, 1890

Writings:
See below

****

Ellis began as a mathematician, turning to the study of phonetics in 1843 of which the chief resulting work was *Early English Pronunciation* (1869–89). As a proponent of spelling reform he was editor of weekly newspapers called *The Fonetic Frend* (1849) and *The Spelling Reformer* (1849–50), and also transformed many standard works into reformed orthography, including "Paradise Lost" (1840), "The Pentateuch", the "New Testament" (1849), and Shakespeare's plays "The Tempest" and "Macbeth" (also in 1849). As an acoustician, he published a series of papers from 1863 onwards, and an English translation of Helmholtz's *Die Lehre von den Ton-*

empfindungen (1863) under the title *On the Sensations of Tone* (1875). A second edition in 1885, with Helmholtz's approval, included an appendix containing reprints of many of Ellis's own papers.

Ellis changed his surname from Sharpe in 1825 because of a legacy which provided him with the means for a life of independent scholarship. His significance for ethnomusicology results from his study of extra-European scales, and his invention of the cents system of measuring musical intervals, expressed in units of hundredths of an equally tempered semitone. With the assistance of Alfred James Hipkins (q.v.), using a battery of tuning forks, he accurately determined the pitch of notes produced on fixed pitch non-European musical instruments, and calculated the intervals between them in cents. His most influential resulting paper, "On the Musical Scales of Various Nations", was published in 1885. For a full list of Ellis's musically relevant writings, see Kunst 1959a:#1070–82.

Refs.: Everyman 5:303; Irene Ferguson, University of Edinburgh (pers.comm); Hipkins & Dent 1948; MacMahon 2004; Stephens & Lee 1908-09: vol.XXII; Thomas & Rhodes 2003.

CATHERINE ELLIS (1935–1996)
Australian ethnomusicologist

Born: Birregurra, Victoria, Australia, 19 May 1935
Died: Adelaide, Australia, 30 May 1996

Qualifications:
MusBac (piano and bassoon), University of Melbourne, 1956
PhD, University of Glasgow, 1961
Topic: Strehlow's recordings of Aranda music from Central Australia

Appointments:
Research assistant to T.G.H. Strehlow, University of Adelaide, 1957–58 & 1962
Post-doctoral fellow, University of Adelaide, 1963
Research fellow, Elder Conservatorium of Music, University of Adelaide, 1964–69
Lecturer, Elder Conservatorium of Music, 1970–84
Reader, University of Adelaide, 1984
Professor of music, University of New England, 1985–95

Offices:
Founder, Centre for Aboriginal Studies in Music, University of Adelaide, 1975
President, Musicological Society of Australia, 1988–89

Honours:
Order of Australia, 1991
Honorary Doctorate of Letters, University of New England, 1995

Field work:
Pitjantjara, South Australia

Writings:
See Barwick 1995, Ryan 1997, and Gallusser 2003.

****

Ellis was one of just three acknowledged pioneers of ethnomusicology in Australia on the subject of Aboriginal music, of whom the others were Trevor Jones (q.v.) and Alice Moyle (q.v.). Besides engaging in active research, a major focus of Ellis's endeavour was the involvement of indigenous peoples in the study process. To this end she established an innovative Centre for Aboriginal Studies in Music at the University of Adelaide, and published regular newsletters about the Centre's activities.

Refs.: Barwick 1996; Eth 7(2):149 (1963); Gallusser 2003; Kartomi 1997.

ERNST EMSHEIMER (1904–1989)
German/Swedish ethnomusicologist

Born: Frankfurt-am-Main, Germany, 15 Jan 1904
Died: Stockholm, Sweden, 12 Jun 1989

Education:
Studied composition and piano, Frankfurt
Studied musicology with Adler, University of Vienna, 1924

Qualifications:
PhilDr, Freiburg University, under Wilibald Gurlitt (1889–1963), 1928
Topic: Johann Ulrich Steigleder (a 17th century German organist)

Appointments:
Fellow, Phonogram-Archives, Museum for Ethnology, Archaeology and Anthropology, Russian Academy of Sciences, Leningrad, 1932–36
Fellow, Ethnographical Museum of Sweden, Stockholm, 1937–38
Director, Musikhistoriska Museet, Stockholm, 1949–73

Honours:
Honorary doctorate, University of Uppsala, 1960
Honorary professorship, University of Uppsala, 1967

Field work:
Northern Caucasus, 1936
Albanians of Yugoslavia, 1959
Lapps in Sweden, 1961
Bergers of Morocco, 1973

Writings:
See below.

****

As a museum administrator, Emsheimer was an important advocate and supporter of early music. As an ethnomusicologist he is best known for his contribution to a multi-authored Sino-Swedish expedition report, *The Music of the Mongols*,[259] for which he supplied an analysis and many music transcriptions. For a full list of writings see Bergsagel & Karlsson 2003.

Refs.: Bergsagel & Karlsson 2003; Eth 7(2):149 (1963); Ling 1990.

---

[259] In Heden et al. 1943.

ZYGMUNT ESTREICHER (1917–1993)
Polish/Swiss ethnomusicologist

Born: Fribourg, Poland, 3 Dec 1917
Died: Geneva, Switzerland, 12 Sep 1993

Education:
Studied at Kraków conservatory and university, and at the University of Fribourg

Qualifications:
Doctorate, Fribourg University, 1946
Topic: Inuit dance-songs

Appointments:
Choirmaster, 1940–45
Library posts, Fribourg and Neuchâtel, 1946–47
Head, music section, Museum of Neuchâtel, 1948–50
Lecturer, University of Neuchâtel, 1951–54
Director, University of Neuchâtel Library, 1954–60
Reader in musicology, University of Geneva, 1961–68
Professor in musicology, University of Geneva, 1969–88

Writings:
For his writings, mostly on Eskimo music, see Kunst 1959a:#1124-33, and Darbellay & Baumann 2003.

Ref.: Darbellay & Baumann 2003.

HENRY GEORGE FARMER (1882–1965)
British musicologist, orientalist and conductor

Born: Birr, Ireland, 17 Jan 1882
Died: Law, Scotland, 30 Dec 1965

Qualifications:
MA, University of Glasgow, 1924
PhD, University of Glasgow, 1926

Appointments:
Principal horn player, Royal Artillery Band, 1902–10
Musical Director, Broadway Theatre, London, 1910–14
Musical Director, Empire Theatre, Glasgow, 1914–47
Founder/conductor of the Glasgow Symphony Orchestra, 1919–43
Editor, *Musicians' Journal*, 1929–33
Music librarian, Glasgow University Library, 1951–65

Awards:
Carnegie Research Fellowships, 1930–31, 1931–32
Leverhulme Research Fellowship, 1933–35

Honours:
Honorary DLitt, University of Glasgow, 1934
Honorary DMus, University of Edinburgh, 1949

Writings:
The most accessible of Farmer's works are chapters he contributed on ancient music of Mesopotamia and Egypt, and "The Music of Islam" in volume 1 of the *New Oxford History of Music* (1957). His papers are housed in a special collection at the Glasgow university library. For lists of his writings see Kunst 1959a:#1156-1210 and Katz 2003c, and for a full bibliography see Cowl & Craik 1999.

****

Farmer began his musical career as a violinist and clarinetist with the Royal Artillery Band, moving on after years of private study to become principal horn player in 1902. Forced after eight years to give up the horn because of ill-health, he then embarked upon a career of almost 40 years as a conductor. Meanwhile, he qualified as a scholar by enrolling as an external student at the University of Glasgow, winning prizes in Arabic and history, and obtaining both an MA degree (1924) and a PhD (1926). In this interest, he was following in the footsteps of his father, who served with the army in India and the Middle East and was fluent in both Hindustani and Arabic.

After Farmer's graduation, there followed a series of fellowships that enabled him to travel to European libraries to study Arabic manuscripts. Besides publishing on the subject of Arabic music, Farmer also wrote works on the history of Scottish and military music. It is as an orientalist, however, that he gained his principal reputation. His scholarly interests were exclusively historical, centring upon theory, instruments, treatises and other manuscript works, with no engagement either in field work or contemporary folk or classical traditions.

Refs.: BRC-(A); Glasgow University Library 2003; Katz 2003b.

JESSE WALTER FEWKES (1850–1930)
American ethnologist

Born: Newton, MA, USA, 14 Nov 1850
Died: Forest Glen, MD, USA, 31 May 1930

Education:
Studied natural history, Harvard University, c.1872–77
Studied zoology, University of Leipzig, 1878–80

Qualifications:
AB, biology, Harvard University, 1875
PhD, marine zoology, Harvard University, 1877

Appointments:
Curator, Museum of Comparative Zoology, Harvard University, 1880–87
Field director, Hemenway Southwestern Archaeological Expedition, 1889–94
Ethnologist, Bureau of American Ethnology, Washington, DC, 1895–1918
Chief, Bureau of American Ethnology, Washington, DC, 1918–28

Offices:
Editor, *Journal of Ethnology and Archaeology*, 1890–91
President, Anthropological Society of Washington, 1909–10
President, American Anthropological Association, 1911–12

Honours:
Among the Hopi, initiated into the Snake and Flute fraternities and given the name Naquapi, "Medicine Bowl", c.1891
Knight of the Royal Order of Isabella la Catholica, Madrid, 1892
Gold medal ""Literis et Artibus", Sweden, 1894
Fellow, American Academy of Arts and Sciences
LLD, University of Arizona, 1915

Field work:
Extensive field work in ethnology, archaeology and invertebrate zoology
Phonograph recordings, Passamaquoddy Indians, Maine, 1890
Phonograph recordings, Zuñi Indians, Arizona, 1890
Phonograph recordings, Hopi Pueblo Indians, Arizona, 1891

****

Fewkes's primary significance to ethnomusicology is as the first recordist on phonograph cylinders of American Indian music. Fewkes's Zuñi and Hopi recordings were analysed by Benjamin Ives Gilman (q.v.).

Refs.: BRC-(C); DeVale 2003b; Hough 1932; Nichols 1919; Smithsonian Institution 1998; WWWA.

JOHN COMFORT FILLMORE (1843–1898)
American writer on music

Born: near Franklin, CT, USA, 4 Feb 1843
Died: Taftville, CT, USA, 14 Aug 1898

Education:
Studied organ and piano, Oberlin College, Ohio, 1862–65
Studied theory of music and organ, Leipzig, 1866–67

Appointments:
Instructor, Oberlin College, Ohio, 1867–68
Professor of music, Ripon College, Wisconsin, 1868–78
Professor of music, Milwaukee College for Women, 1878–84
Founder/director, Milwaukee School of Music, 1884–95
Director of music, Pomona College, California, 1895–98

Honours:
Honorary AM, Oberlin College, 1870
Diploma and medal, International Exposition of Music, Bologna, 1888

Writings:
See below.

****

Fillmore's significance was principally as a collaborator with Alice Cunningham Fletcher (q.v.) and her co-worker Francis La Flesche (q.v.), both of whom relied upon him for technical advice on music. DeVale says research has not corroborated a claim by Fillmore to have transcribed recordings collected by Fletcher, Franz Boas and others for their publications, but there is, in fact, no doubt. Fillmore n.d. is a report on his Kwakiutl transcriptions for Boas; correspondence with Fletcher shows that he began work on the Boas Kwakiutl cylinders in 1893;[260] and in Fletcher's publications he appears as an acknowledged co-writer, although in the case of their Omaha book it appears he worked "almost exclusively" with field transcriptions made by Fletcher herself.[261] He and Fletcher shared a peculiar belief that American Indian music was in an undeveloped pre-harmonic stage and could be improved by adding harmony to it. Fillmore's ideas on this were published in two journal articles,[262] and provoked some controversy at the time.

Refs.: ANB; BRC-(C); Claremont libraries (pers.comm.); McNutt 1984; DeVale 2003c.

---

[260] Presumably these were Kwakiutl cylinders Boas is reported by Myers to have recorded at the Chicago. Columbian Expostion in the same year (Myers 1993:23, 24).
[261] Myers 1993:23. .
[262] Fillmore 1888; Fillmore 1895.

ALICE CUNNINGHAM FLETCHER (1838–1923)
American ethnologist

Born: Havana, Cuba, 15 Mar 1838
Died: Washington, DC, USA, 6 Apr 1923

Education:
Early education at Brooklyn Female Academy
Informal instruction in archaeology from Frederic Putnam (1839–1915), Curator/Director, Peabody Museum of Archaeology and Ethnology, 1879

Appointments:
Special Agent, Bureau of Indian Affairs, 1883–92
Mary Copley Thaw Fellow, Peabody Museum, Harvard University, 1891–1923

Offices:
Secretary, Association for the Advancement of Women, 1873–76
President, Women's Anthropological Society of America, 1890–99
Department of Interior consultant, World's Columbian Exposition, 1892–93
Vice-president, Section H, American Association for the Advancement of Science, 1896
Member, editorial board, *American Anthropologist*, 1899–1916
President, Anthropological Society of Washington, 1903
President, American Folklore Society, 1905
Hon. Vice-president, Section H, British Association for Advancement of Science, 1911

Field work:
Archaeological field work, Florida and Massachusetts, 1878
Music of Omaha Indians, Nebraska, 1881
Later field work as adjunct of activities concerning land allotment, including Nez Percé, Idaho, 1889

Writings:
Fletcher's major contribution is an 1893 monograph, *A Study of Omaha Indian Music*, in collaboration with Francis La Flesche (q.v.) and J.C. Fillmore (q.v.),[263] and a larger 1911 Omaha monograph, incorporating the results of her joint work with La Flesche on Omaha Indian culture.[264] For other writings, see DeVale 2003b and Kunst 1959a:#1261–7.

****

Fletcher's work is disscussed in Part I.

Refs.: Anth; DeVale 2003d; E-Brit; Hough 1923; Lee & La Vigna 1985; Rahkonen 2003; Rohde 2000.

---

[263] Fletcher et al. 1893.
[264] Fletcher & La Flesche 1911.

#

A(RTHUR) H(ENRY) FOX STRANGWAYS (1850–1948)
English musicologist, critic and editor

Born: Norwich, England, 14 Sep 1859
Died: Dinton, near Salisbury, England, 2 May 1948

Education:
Wellington College, and Balliol College, University of Oxford, where he studied classics
Studied music, especially piano, Berlin Hochschule für Musik, 1882–84

Qualifications:
MA, Balliol College, University of Oxford, 1882

Appointments:
Schoolmaster, Dulwich College, 1884–86
Form master/choir master and organist/House master (from 1901), Wellington College, 1887–1910
Music critic, *The Times*, London, 1911–25
Music critic, *The Observer*, London, 1925–39

Offices:
Unpaid literary agent for the Bengali song-writer, Rabindranath Tagore (1861–1941), 1912–14
Founder/editor, *Music and Letters*, 1920–37

Field work:
India, Indus and Ganges basins, 1910–11

Writings:
The Music of Hindostan (1914) is the work for which he is best known. He was an important contributor to the third edition of *Grove's Dictionary of Music and Musicians* (1927), and also collaborated with Maud Karpeles in a biography of Cecil Sharp (1933). For lists of writings, see Kunst 1959a:#1282-90 and Colles & Howes 2003.

****

Fox Strangways became interested in Indian music during a vacation to India in 1903, returning there in 1910 specifically to undertake field work. His resulting cylinder recordings are in the National Sound Archive, London. They incluce "tribal and folk songs, snake charmer's music, 'outdoor' *shannai* hand music, Vedic chant, *ghazal* and *tappa*, as well as North and /South Indian classical music." [265]

Refs.: BRC-(A); Colles 1948a; Colles & Howes 2003; Howes 1969b; Jairazbhoy 1993; Wilson 2004.

---

[265] Jairazbhoy 1993:279.

FRANCIS WILLIAM GALPIN (1858–1945)
English cleric, collector of musical instruments, organologist and botanist

Born: Dorchester, England, 25 Dec 1858
Died: , Richmond, Surrey, England 30 Dec 1945

Education:
King's School, Sherborne, 1872–77
Studied classics and divinity, Trinity College, Cambridge University, 1877–82
Studied organ with William Sterndale Bennett (1816–1875), and played the clarinet under Charles Stanford (1852–1924) in the Cambridge University Musical Society.

Qualifications:
BA, Cambridge University, 1882
Ordained, 1883
MA, Cambridge University, 1885

Appointments:
Curate, Redenhall with Harleston, Norfolk, 1883–87
Curate, St Giles-in-the-Fields, 1887–91
Vicar, Hatfield Regis (now Hatfield Broad Oak), 1891–1915
Vicar, Witham, 1915–21
Surrogate and rural Dean of Witham, 1915–33
Rector, Faulkbourn, 1921–33
Canon, Chelmsford Cathedral, 1917–31
Canon Emeritus, Chelmsford Cathedral, 1931–45

Offices:
President, Essex Archaeological Society, 1921–26
President, Musical Association (later Royal Musical Association), 1938–42

Honours:
Fellow, Linnean Society, 1877
Honorary freedom of the Worshipful Company of Musicians, 1905
DLitt, Cambridge University, 1936

Writings:
Galpin contributed some 60 articles on musical instruments to the 2nd, 3rd and 4th editions of *Grove's Dictionary of Music and Musicians* (1900, 1927 & 1940), for which he also supplied illustrations from his personal collection. For lists of other writings on musical instruments, see Kunst 1959a:#133-47 and Williamson 2003. See also below.

****

Galpin was a man of broad interests and accomplishments, including contributions to subjects as diverse as botany and archaeology, but it was as a musician that he most excelled. During his schooldays, an early interest in music was encouraged both at home and at King's School, Sherborne; he became an accomplished clarinettist; and at Cambridge university devoted most of his leisure time to music, including organising an 82-strong amateur orchestra, and as a librarian to the Cambridge University Musical Society. Later, during his tenure as a clergyman, he was active in encouraging community music-making, and organised concerts in which he himself performed on instruments from his own collection such as the viol, recorder, serpent, baryton, marimba, and nyastaranga.

While still at school at Sherborne, Galpin had begun to collect musical instruments, and eventually accumulated more than 500, which were purchased and transferred to the Museum of Fine Arts, Boston in 1916. Included in the collection are not only numerous fine European instruments, but also many Chinese, Japanese, African, Middle Eastern and Native American examples.[266] Among Galpin's writings are descriptive catalogues of collections, as well as publications on old English instruments, Native American instruments, and ancient, including Sumerian, instruments.

Refs.: Colles 1948b; Brian Galpin (pers.comm.); Myers 2004; Williamson 2003; WWW v.III.

---

[266] Museum of Fine Arts, 2003.

The Biographies A-Z

EDITH GERSON-KIWI (1908–1992)
German/Jewish (Israeli) musicologist

Born: Berlin, Germany, 13 May 1908
Died: Jerusalem, Palestine, 16 Jul 1992

Education:
Studied at Stern Conservatory, Berlin, 1918–25
Studied harpsichord with Wanda Landowska, Ecole de Musique Ancienne, 1931
Studied musicology, universities of Freiburg, Leipzig and Heidelberg

Qualifications:
Diploma in piano, Leipzig Musikhochchule, 1930
Doctorate, University of Heidelberg, 1933
Topic: 16th-century Italian frottola and canzonetta [267]
Diploma in library studies, Bologna University, 1934

Appointments:
Scientific assistant, Liceo Musicale, Bologna, 1934
Taught piano and music history at music academies in Jerusalem and Tel-Aviv, 1937–?
Assistant to Robert Lachmann, Jerusalem Archive for Oriental Music
Head, Archive for Oriental Music, Jerusalem, 1947
(Incorporated into School of Oriental Studies, Hebrew University, 1953)
Senior lecturer in musicology, Hebrew University and Tel Aviv University, c.1966–68
Professor, Tel Aviv University, 1969–?

Offices:
Founder, Museum of Musical Instruments, Rubin Academy of Music, Jerusalem, 1963
Chairman, Israeli Musicological Society, 1974

Writings:
For lists see Katz 2003d and Kunst 1959a:#1398-1402d. For selected writings and a bibliography see Gerson-Kiwi 1980.

****

With her recordings, publications, and teaching, Gerson-Kiwi is credited by Katz with laying the foundations of ethnomusicology in Israel.[268] Her recordings and field work materials are held by the National Sound Archives at Hebrew University, Jerusalem, and printed and manuscript materials by the Center for Jewish Music, Hanover, Germany.

The following information about her was supplied by Israel J. Katz:[269]

---

[267] Published as Gerson-Kiwi 1937.
[268] Katz 2003c.
[269] pers.comm.

Although she published about three book-sized monographs, she did contribute many important articles and encyclopedic entries on Oriental-Jewry (mainly in the Middle Eastern area)... Her transcribed examples are exemplary. Having worked closely with Lachmann [q.v.] in Palestine (mainly Jerusalem) up to the time of his death in 1939, she is probably the best authority on Lachmann's work (two of the monographs are devoted to it). In 1960, escorted by an Israeli Army convoy, she spent a fortnight on Mt. Scopus (where the Old Hebrew University was located). There was able to rescue documents and recordings made by Lachmann and Idelsohn [q.v.].

Refs.: Israel J. Katz (pers.comm.); Edwin Seroussi (pers.comm.); Katz 2003c; Thompson 1964.

ANNE GEDDES GILCHRIST (1863–1954)
English folk song scholar and authority on psalmody and hymnody

Born: Manchester, England, 8 Dec 1863
Died: Lancaster, England, 24 Jul 1954

Education:
Private instruction in theory of music and composition from Dr J.M. Bentley.[270] Reports that she trained at the Royal Academy of Music appear to be mistaken.[271]

Honours:
Fellow of the Society of Antiquaries, 1935
Gold Badge of the English Folk Dance and Song Society
OBE, 1945

Field collecting:
SE and N England, mostly from c.1895–1910 [272]

Writings:
Besides numberless annotations to work contributed by others, between 1906 and 1948 Gilchrist contributed some 40 articles to the *Journal of the Folk-Song Society*, as well as more than 30 articles and book reviews for *The Choir* magazine, together with articles in a variety of other periodicals. Her personal papers are deposited in the English Folk Dance and Song Society's Vaughan Williams Memorial Library. For a select list of her writings and comment on topics addressed in them see Wolz 2005.

****

Though Gilchrist was brought up as a child in Lancashire and resided there for most of her life, both of her parents were Scottish. The first folk song she notated was sung to her by her father, and he it was who insisted that she must notate it exactly as sung, rather than follow the dictates of her classical music training, an admonition she followed faithfully thenceforth, and which enabled her to uncover the modal nature of the tunes. Another major influence upon her was Frank Kidson (q.v.), to whom her first notation had been sent and who, at eight years her senior, was already an established folk song scholar. He had similar antiquarian interests to hers, and a growing reputation as a "tune sleuth". He became a friend and mentor with whom she corresponded regularly and exchanged information for the rest of his life. In later years, having assumed the mantle of Kidson, she herself became an expert on tracking tune origins, sharing her knowledge freely on behalf of others, with literally thousands of tunes said to have passed through her hands for identification. At Kidson's urging, Gilchrist joined the English Folk-Song

---

[270] Howes 1948:239. All the present writer has been able to find out about Bentley is that he was conductor of the Bolton Choral Union from its inception in 1887 until 1903 (Anon 2005). Bolton is 12 miles from Gilchrist's home town of Manchester.
[271] Wolz (2005:ftnt 5) reports that enquiries have revealed there is no record that Gilchrist was ever a student there.
[272] Unlike many other collectors, Gilchrist did not undertake formal field trips, but collected mostly from relatives, friends, and contacts arising during the course of her everyday life (Wolz 2005)

Society in 1905, and this too was a seminal event, both for Gilchrist and the society itself on whose editorial board she served from 1906 onwards, and whose journal was later to owe much of its lustre to her contributions.

Refs.: Boyes 2003b; Dean-Smith 1957-58; Howes 1948; Wolz 2005.

BENJAMIN IVES GILMAN (1852–1933)
American psychologist and music scholar

Born: New York, NY, USA, 19 Feb 1852
Died: Boston, MA, USA, 18 Mar 1933

Education:
Studied at Williams College, Massachusetts, bef. 1872
Graduate student in logic and mathematics, John Hopkins University, 1881–82
Studied philosophy and ethics, University of Berlin, 1882–83
Graduate student in psychology, Harvard University, 1883–85
Studied at University of Paris and in Italy, 1885–88

Qualifications:
AB, Williams College, 1872

Appointments:
Lecturer in psychology of music, Colorado College, Cornell, Princeton, and Harvard universities, 1890–92
Instructor in psychology, Clark University, 1892–93
Curator, Boston Museum of Fine Arts, 1893
Secretary, Boston Museum of Fine Arts, 1894–1925

Offices:
President, American Association of Museums, 1913–14

Honours:
Hon AM, 1901

Field work:
Recorded Javanese, Samoan, Syrian, Turkish and Kwakiutl Indian music at the Chicago World's Fair, 1893. These recordings were transferred from the Peabody Museum to the Library of Congress in 1970.[273]

Writings:
Published analyses of Zuñi and Hopi songs recorded 1890–91 by Jesse Walter Fewkes (q.v.).[274]

****

There is reference to Gilman's work in Part V.

Refs.: Boston Museum of Fine Arts (pers.comm.); DeVale 2003e; WWWA.

---

[273] Melville 1980.
[274] Gilman 1891; Gilman 1908.

WALTER GRAF (1903–1982)
Austrian musicologist

Born: St Pölten, Austria, 20 Jun 1903
Died: Vienna, Austria, 11 Apr 1982

Education:
Studied musicology, University of Vienna, under Adler, Lach and others, ? –1933

Qualifications:
PhD, University of Vienna, 1933
Topic: German influences on Estonian folk song

Appointments:
Head, Phonogrammarchiv, Österreichischen Akademie der Wissenschaften (Austrian Academy of Sciences), 1957–63
Lecturer, University of Vienna, 1958–61
Assistant Professor, University of Vienna, 1962
Associate Professor of comparative musicology, University of Vienna, 1963

Writings:
See New Grove and Kunst 1959a:#1484–96.

Refs.: BRC-(A); Eth 6(1):55 (1962); New Grove "Graf, Walter".

IDA HALPERN (1910–1987)
Austrian/Canadian ethnomusicologist

Born: Vienna, Austria, 17 Jul 1910
Died: Vancouver, Canada, 7 Feb 1987

Education:
Reform-Realgymnasium, Vienna, 1929
Studied musicology, University of Vienna

Qualifications:
PhD in musicology, University of Vienna, 1938

Appointments:
Lectured on music, University of Shanghai, 1938–39
Taught music appreciation, University of British Columbia, 1940–61
Part-time lecturer, University of British Columbia, 1960s & 1970s [275]

Offices:
Founder/president, Hon. president, Friends of Chamber Music, Vancouver, 1948–52
President, Vancouver Women's Musical Club, 1960–62

Honours:
Order of Canada, 1978
Hon LLD, Simon Fraser University, 1978
Hon DMus, University of Victoria, 1986

Field work:
Kwakiutl, Nootka, Haida, Bella Coola and Coast Salish Indians, northern coastal British Columbia, Canada

****

Born and educated in Austria, Halpern fled with her husband a year before the outbreak of World War II to Shanghai, where she lectured at the University of Shanghai before emigrating to Canada in 1939. The following year she began a long involvement with the University of British Columbia where, although not formally affiliated as an academic, she gave the first courses in music appreciation. In 1944 she became a naturalised Canadian citizen.

Halpern's main activity and interest as an ethnomusicologist was documenting and preserving the Canadian Indian music of northern coastal British Columbia. Her field recordings of more than 500 songs are deposited with the Provincial Archives of British Columbia at Victoria, Canada, and eight LPs from her collection, including booklets containing notes and transcriptions, were published with Ethnic Folkways.

---

[275] Pers.comm. Alan Thrasher.

Although Halpern was revered and honoured for her activities in support of the musical life of Vancouver, as an ethnomusicologist she was distinguished primarily as a collector. A 1976 paper she wrote about ethnomusicology reveals long-outdated personal views of the subject, unchanged from her student days in Vienna in the early 1930s, when she studied comparative musicology under Robert Lach (q.v.). A similar approach is true of a Centennial Workshop on Ethnomusicology she organised at the University of British Columbia in 1967, when discussions were held comparing completely unrelated musics such as Eskimo, Polynesian, Tibetan and Australian Aborigine.[276]

Refs.: Borden 2001; Halpern 1976; Lieberman 1987; Prokop 2003.

---

[276] The proceedings of this conference, including the complete discussions, were later published in two volumes under the editorship of Peter Crossley Holland (1968 & 1976).

ETA MARGARETE HARICH-SCHNEIDER (1897–1986)
German harpsichordist, pianist and musicologist

Born: Oranienburg, Berlin, Germany, 16 Nov 1897
Died: Vienna, Austria, 16 Oct 1986

Education:
Studied piano and musicology, Berlin
Studied harpsichord with Landowska, 1929–35

Qualifications:
MA in sociology, New School for Social Research, New York, 1955

The photograph of Harich-Schneider is from a no longer extant 1927 portrait.

Career:
Début as pianist, Berlin, 1924
Début as harpsichordist, Berlin, 1931
Professor, Hochschule für Musik, Berlin, 1933–39
Director, music department, US Army College, Tokyo, 1945
Taught Western music to musicians of imperial court, Tokyo, 1947–49
Professor of harpsichord, Vienna Musikakademie, 1955–61

Honours and wards:
City of Frankfurt Kulturpreis, 1925
Research fellowship, Guggenheim Foundation, 1955–57
Research fellowship, Bollingen Foundation, 1962–66

Writings:
Harich-Schneider's *A History of Japanese Music* was published in 1973. For other writings see Kunst 1959a:#1612-1618a and Salter 2003.

****

In 1940, Harich-Schneider was dismissed from her professorial post in Berlin after refusing to join the Nazi party. She fled to Tokyo, where she lived from 1941–49, becoming increasingly interested in Japanese music. In 1949, she moved to New York, remaining there until 1955, when she moved to Vienna to take up a post as professor of harpsichord. As an authority on Japanese music, she delivered guest lectures at the universities of Chicago, London, Paris, Utrecht, Amsterdam and Leiden.

Refs.: BRC-(A); Harich-Schneider 1978; Salter 2003; Thompson 1964.

MELVILLE HERSKOVITS (1895–1963)
American cultural anthropologist

Born: Bellefontaine, OH, USA, 1 Sep 1895
Died: Evanston, IL, USA, 25 Feb 1963

Education:
As a young man played the violin, and a principal interest was music
Graduated from high school, Erie, Pennsylvania, 1912
Enrolled at University of Cincinnati and in theological studies, Hebrew Union College, 1915–?
Studied at University of Chicago, ?–1920
Studied anthropology under Franz Boas, Columbia University, 1920–23

Qualifications:
PhB in history, University of Chicago, 1920
AM in anthropology, Columbia University, 1921
PhD in anthropology, Columbia University, 1923
Topic: The Cattle Complex in East Africa

Appointments and career:
Early in his career reviewed concerts for newspapers, New York
During World War I served with the US Army Medical Corps in France
Lecturer in anthropology, Columbia University, 1924–27
Assistant professor of anthropology, Howard University, 1925–26
Assistant professor of sociology, Northwestern University, 1927–30
Associate professor of sociology, Northwestern University, 1931–34
Professor of sociology, Northwestern University, 1935–37
Professor of anthropology and first chairman, Northwestern University, 1938–63

Offices:
Editor, *American Anthropologist*, 1949–52
President, American Folklore Society, 1945
President, African Studies Association, 1957–58

Honours:
Guggenheim Memorial Fellow, 1937–38
Viking Fund Medalist, 1953

Field work:
Suriname (South America),1928 & 1929; Dahomey, Ghana, Nigeria (West Africa), 1931; Haiti and Trinidad (Caribbean), 1934; Brazil, Dutch Guiana (South America), 1941–42; Africa, 1953, 1954, 1955, 1957, & 1962.

Writings: See next page

****

Although not an ethnomusicologist, Herskovits deserves honorary status as one because of his field recordings, of which those of Suriname were analysed by Kolinski;[277] his insistence that music should be considered on equal terms with other cultural elements; and his influence upon Alan P. Merriam (q.v.), who was one of his students. He is significant also as an exponent of cultural relativism, maintaining in his book *Man and His Works* (1948) that all standards of judgement are culture-bound. For a list of his musical writings, see Merriam 1963. For a detailed account of the content of Herskovits's field recordings, and his findings concerning them, see Simpson 1973:51-5.

Refs.: ANB: Anth; Herskovits Library 2001; Merriam 1963; Simpson 1973.

---

[277] Kolinski 1935.

GEORGE HERZOG (1901–1983)
Hungarian/American ethnomusicologist

Born: Budapest, Hungary, 11 Dec 1901
Died: Indianapolis, IN, USA, 4 Nov 1983

Education:
Royal Hungarian Academy of Music, Budapest, 1917–19
Berlin Hochschule für Musik, 1920–22
Studied piano with Egon Petri, 1921
Kaiser Friedrich Wilhelms University, Berlin, 1922–24
After emigration to the United States in 1925, studied anthropology under Franz Boas (q.v.) and others, Columbia University, USA

Qualifications:
PhD in anthropology, Columbia University, 1938
Topic: Musical styles of Pueblo and Pima Indians

Appointments:
Assistant to Erich von Hornbostel (q.v.), Berlin Phonogram-Archiv, 1923–25
Research associate in anthropology, University of Chicago, 1929–31
Research associate, Institute of Human Relations, Yale University, 1932–35
Visiting lecturer, Columbia University, 1936–37
Visiting assistant professor, Columbia University, 1937–38
Assistant professor of anthropology, Columbia University, 1939–48
Professor of anthropology, Indiana University, 1948–1961

Awards:
Guggenheim Fellow, 1935–36, 1947

Field work:
Participant, University of Chicago Anthropological Expedition to Liberia, 1930–31
Apache, Comanche, Dakota, Maricopa, Navaho, Pima, Pueblo, Yuma and Zuñi Indian

Writings:
For an almost complete bibliography see Krader 1956. Two minor further items are listed in *Ethnomusicology*, 8(3):321 (1964).

****

Hungarian-born George Herzog is generally acknowledged as the true father of ethnomusicology in the United States. When he emigrated from Germany in 1925, he brought with him the analytic methods of Béla Bartók (q.v.) and Zoltán Kodály (q.v.) from Hungary, together with those of Erich von Hornbostel (q.v.) at the Berlin Phonogram-Archiv in Germany, where he had worked as an assistant to Hornbostel.

In the United States, Herzog qualified himself as an anthropologist by studying under Franz Boas at Columbia University, graduating PhD in 1938 with a dissertation that ranks as possibly the first truly comparative study of the music of two North American Indian tribes. Thenceforth he combined the methods of his earlier mentors with those of Boas, producing a unique blend that combined the best of the musical approaches from Europe with the anthropological ones then emerging in the United States.

Archiving activities:
On the model of the Berlin Phonogram-Archiv, and with the support of Boas, Herzog established an Archives of Folk and Primitive Music at Columbia University in 1936, transferring this to Indiana University when he took up his professorship there in 1948. At Indiana this collection became the nucleus of the present Archives of Traditional Music, of which George List (1911–) took over the directorship in 1954, and was succeeded in 1976 by Frank Gillis (1914–1999).[278]

As a scholar, Herzog produced a seminal string of publications that charted the course of ethnomusicology for decades. As a teacher and a colleague, he influenced many of the next generation of ethnomusicologists. David McAllester (1916–), who was one of his students, recalls him as follows:

> Small, intense, with a bristling black moustache and a sometimes mordent wit, he taught in an informal, in fact rambling way. He rarely brought notes to class and followed his lively intellect wherever it led, much of the time reporting his own research or that of his colleagues in related fields. He was fascinated by regularities in human behavior and we learned to analyze the oral arts in melody, song texts, folklore, proverbs, phonology, grammar, and the symmetry of kinship systems. He taught linguistics as well as "primitive music" and, though his Hungarian accent never diminished, he corrected our English grammar and our musical transcriptions, alike, with meticulous rightness. . . . George Herzog could be terrifying in the cause of scientific integrity at scholarly meetings, but he was admired and loved as a genius and a delight by his intimates.[279]

Refs.: BRC-(A); Christensen 1983; Eth 4(2):99 (1960); Katz 2003e; McAllester 1985; Nettl 1981.

---

[278] Indiana University 2000.
[279] McAllester 1985:86-7.

HANS ROBERT HICKMANN (1908–1968)
German composer and comparative musicologist

Born: Rosslau bei Dessau, Germany, 19 May 1908
Died: Blandford Forum, Dorset, England, 4 Sep 1968

Education:
As a student was a talented pianist, organist, and conductor
Studied at the Rumpf'sche Konservatorium and the University of Halle, 1928–34
Studied music education, Staatliche Akademie für Kirchen und Schulmusik, Berlin–Charlottenburg
Studied at the University of Berlin under Erich von Hornbostel (q,v,), Curt Sachs (q.v.) and others

Qualifications:
PhD, University of Berlin, 1934
Topic: "Das Portativ" [280]

Appointments and career:
Settled in Cairo, Egypt, 1935
Worked in Cairo as an organist, conductor, teacher and broadcaster, and composed music for films, chorus, chamber groups, voice and piano
Lectured on Egyptian music at numerous places throughout Europe and at international conferences, 1949–52
Director, German Cultural Institute, Cairo, 1957
Returned to West Germany, 1957
Privatdozent in ethnomusicology, University of Hamburg, 1957–63
Professor of Ethnomusicology, University of Hamburg, 1964–?
Director, Musikhistorisches Studio (Archiv–Produktion), Deutsche Grammophon Gesellschaft, Hamburg, 1958–?

Offices:
Inaugural President, Deutsche Gesellschaft für Musik des Orients, 1959

Honours:
Palmes Academiques, French Academie
Bundesverdienstkreuz, First Class

Field work:
Siwa oasis, Egypt, 1932–33

****

Hickmann was a specialist in Egyptian music, interested in demonstrating its relationships to musical traditions of Europe and Asia. For a bibliography of writings 1934–64 see Neumann

---

[280] Published, Kassel: Bärenreiter, 1936.

1965. For an obituary and supplementary bibliography of writings 1965–69 see Gillis et al. 1969.

Refs.: BRC-(A); Anderson 2003; Eth 7(1):67 (1963); Gillis et al. 1969;. Peter Petersen (pers.comm.).

ALFRED JAMES HIPKINS (1826–1903)
English piano tuner, acoustician, and writer on musical instruments

Born: Westminster, London, England, 17 Jun 1826
Died: London, England, 3 Jun 1903

Career:
Apprenticed as a piano tuner to J. Broadwood & Sons in 1840, when he was 14 years old, Hipkins continued to work for the firm for the rest of his life. He became renowned as a piano-tuner, with Chopin reportedly preferring him above all others as tuner on his visits to England.[281]

Writings:
In addition to scientific writings on acoustics and musical instruments, Hipkins contributed substantially to the 1st edition of the *Grove Dictionary of Music* (1878–89), and to the 9th edition of *Encyclopaedia Britamnica* (1875–89). His illustrated *Musical Instruments Historical Rare and Unique* (1888) included examples from India, China, Japan and South Africa. For some of his other writings see Kunst 1959a:#1841-4.

****

Evidently essentially self-educated in music, Hipkins began to study piano-playing the year he started work at Broadwoods, and added organ-playing the following year. As a keyboard musician he became highly competent, also pioneering a revival of early keyboard instruments (harpsichord and clavichord). In 1851 he gave more than 40 recitals on Broadwood pianos at the Great Exhibition of London, and in a demonstration of period instruments performed Bach's Chromatic Fantasia and Fugue on the clavichord, and some of the Goldberg Variations on the harpsichord before the Musical Association, in 1886.

As an authority on musical instruments, he took part in the planning for international exhibitions in London (1885), Vienna (1892) and Paris (1900); delivered lectures on musical instruments (from 1883), including Cantor Lectures to the Society of Arts (1891); was Honorary curator of the Royal College of Music; and was a Fellow of the Society of Antiquarians (1886). His primary significance for ethnomusicology was as an associate of Alexander Ellis (q.v.).

Refs.: Baker 2004; Ehrlich 2003; Thompson 1964; University of London Library 2003b; WWW v.1.

---

[281] Fuller-Maitland 1932:110.

KI MANTLE HOOD (1918–2005)
American composer and ethnomusicologist

Born: Springfield, IL, USA, 24 Jun 1918
Died: Ellicott City, MD, USA, 31 Jul 2005

Education:
Studied composition privately with Ernst Toch, 1945–50
Studied at UCLA and with Jaap Kunst at the University of Amsterdam

Qualifications:
AB in music, UCLA, 1951
MA in composition, UCLA, 1952
PhD, University of Amsterdam, 1954
Topic: The Nuclear Theme as a Determinant of Patet in Javanese Music

Appointments:
Instructor, UCLA, 1954
Assistant professor, UCLA, 1956–58
Associate professor, UCLA, 1959–61
Professor, UCLA, 1962–74
Adjunct Professor, University of Maryland, 1976
Professor, University of Maryland, 1980–96
Professor, University of West Virginia, 1996–?
Visiting professor, University of Ghana, 1963–64
Visiting professor, Yale University and Wesleyan University, 1977
Visiting professor, University of Beijing, 1983
Visiting professor, Queen's University, Belfast, 1985
Visiting professor, Schola Tinggi Seni, Indonesia, 1998

Offices:
President, Society for Ethnomusicology, 1966–67

Honours and awards:
Fulbright Fellowship for study in the Netherlands, 1951–53
Ford Foundation Fellowship for study in Indonesia, 1956-58
Fulbright Fellowship for study in India, 1976
Honorary life member, European Seminar in Ethnomusicology, 1985
Title 'Ki' (lit. "the venerable") conferred by Indonesian Government, 1986
Elected to Indonesian Dharma kusuma (Society of National Heroes), 1992
USINO (United States-Indonesia Society) Award, 2002 [282]
Honorary doctorate, University of Cologne, 2003 [283]

Field work:
Indonesia, 1956–58

---

[282] UCLA news release.
[283] *SEM Newsletter* 38(2):6.

Writings:
See Giuriati 2005.

****

In 1958, Hood established the first performance groups at UCLA as a means of imparting "bi-musicality" to students, and imported the first Indonesian gamelan into the United States for the purpose. In 1960, he established an Institute of Ethnomusicology at UCLA, which continued under this name until Hood's departure from UCLA in 1974, when it was disestablished and re-convened under the umbrella of the music department. Hood's initiative of performance groups, however, caught on and they are now standard in ethnomusicology programmes throughout the United States, with a total of more than 100 gamelan groups now said to be in operation there.[284]

There is extensive reference to Hood throughout the present book.

Refs.: BRC-(A); Eth 5(3):244 (1961); Giuriati 2005.

---

[284] UCLA Asia Institute 2002.

ERICH VON HORNBOSTEL (1877–1935)
Austrian comparative musicologist

Born: Vienna, Austria, 25 Feb 1877
Died: Cambridge, England, 28 Nov 1935

Education:
Von Hornbostel came from a highly musical family. His mother was a well-known singer; in early youth he studied harmony and counterpoint; and he was an accomplished pianist and composer by the time he reached his late teens. His higher education, however, was in the natural sciences and philosophy at the universities of Heidelberg and Vienna, 1895–99.

Qualifications:
Doctorate in chemistry, University of Vienna, 1900

Appointments:
Assistant to Carl Stumpf (q.v.), Psychologisches Institut, Berlin University, 1905–06
Director, Phonogram-Archiv, Berlin, 1906–33
Privat-Dozent (Associate Professor), Berlin University, 1923–33

Writings:
For a full bibliography see Merriam 1954b.

****

More than any other person, Hornbostel was responsible both for the beginnings of comparative musicology in Germany and the direction it took. With his assistant, Otto Abraham (q.v.), he published a number of joint papers analysing recordings of non-Western music deposited in the Berlin Phonogram-Archiv, of which he was director. He also collaborated with Abraham on systematic methods of transcription and analysis. His other work, following precedents set by Carl Stumpf (q.v.) and the English phonetician Alexander Ellis (q.v.), was concerned primarily with psycho-acoustics, and with precise measurement and tonometrical analysis of exotic scales and tuning systems, gaining for comparative musicology a reputation for exact and quantifiable scientific study of music. This was substantially eroded when a controversial theory of "blown fifths" ("Blasquinte") developed by Hornbostel to explain scales of non-tempered intervals was later discredited. A major contribution by Hornbostel was his collaboration with Curt Sachs (q.v.) on the Sachs/Hornbostel system of classifying musical instruments.

Besides Abraham and Sachs, Hornbostel had a number of students and assistants who later became prominent and helped spread his methods both in Europe and around the world (q.v. Bose, Herzog, Hickmann, Husmann, Kolinski, Lachmann, Schneider, Wachsmann and Wiora).

Refs.: Christensen 1991; Katz 2003f.

FRANK STEWART HOWES (1891–1974)
English music critic, editor, and writer

Born: Oxford, England, 2 Apr 1891
Died: Standlake, Oxfordshire, England, 28 Sep 1974

Education:
Oxford High School
St John's College, University of Oxford, 1910–14
Royal College of Music, London, 1920–22

Appointments:
Staff member, *The Times*, London, 1925–42
Chief music critic, *The Times*, London, 1943–60
Lecturer in music history and appreciation, Royal College of Music, London, 1938–70
Lecturer, University of Glasgow, 1947 & 1952

Offices:
Editor, *Folk Song Journal* and *Journal of the English Folk Dance and Song Society*, 1927–45
President, Royal Musical Association, 1947–58
Chairman, Musicians' Benevolent Fund, 1936–55

Honours:
FRCM
Hon RAM
CBE, 1954

Writings:
Howes's main contribution to folk music studies is his *Folk Music of Britain – and Beyond* (1969a), described by Maud Karpeles in her obituary of him as gathering together the knowledge of a lifetime and presenting it "in a most masterly and readable way."

Refs.: BRC-(B); Cooper 2003; Karpeles 1974; McVeagh 2004.

HEINRICH HUSMANN (1908–1983)
German musicologist

Born: Cologne, Germany, 16 Dec 1908
Died: Brussels, Belgium, 8 Nov 1983

Education:
Attended Realgymnasium in Deutz, near Cologne
Studied musicology at Göttingen University and University of Berlin, where his teachers included Johannes Wolf and Erich von Hornbostel (q.v.), 1927–32

Qualifications:
Doctorate, University of Berlin, 1932
Topic: Organa tripla of the Notre Dame school

Career and appointments:
Assistant lecturer in musicology, University of Leipzig, 1933–41
Lecturer in musicology, University of Leipzig, 1941
Lost livelihood under Soviet occupation after the World War II, and fled to Hamburg
Supernumerary professor, Musicological Institute, Hamburg, 1949–55
Reader, Musicological Institute, Hamburg, 1955–57
Professor, Musicological Institute, Hamburg, 1958–59
Professor of musicology, University of Göttingen, 1960–77
Visiting professor, Princeton University, 1962, 1966
Visiting professor, University of Wisconsin, 1967–68

Offices:
Editor, *Schriftenreihe des Musikwissenschaftlichen Instituts der Universität Hamburg*, 1956–66

Writings:
Two important studies by Husmann concern the relationships between the musical cultures of the orient and antiquity and those of Europe.[285] For other papers of ethnomusicological significance, see Kunst 1959a:#2000-2008c. For fuller bibliographies of his writings, see Eggebrecht et al. 2003 and Becker & Gerlach 1970:325-35.

Refs.: BRC-(A); DBE; Eggebrecht et al. 2003.

---

[285] Husmann 1956, 1961.

ABRAHAM ZEVI IDELSOHN (1882–1938)
Latvian-born Jewish cantor and musicologist

Born: Pfilzburg (Phoelixburg), Latvia, 11 Jun 1882
Died: Johannesburg, South Africa, 15 Aug 1938 [286]

Education:
Trained as a cantor in Libau and Königsberg
Studied at Stern Conservatory, Berlin, and at the conservatory and university, Leipzig

Career:
Cantor, Adat Jeshurun congregation, Leipzig, 1902
Cantor, Regensburg, 1903–05
Lecturer in Jewish music and liturgy, Hebrew Union College, Cincinnati, 1924–30

Honours:
Honorary doctorate, Hebrew Union College, 1933

Writings:
See Katz 1975–76 for a full bibliography.

****

In 1906, Idelsohn migrated to Jerusalem and lived there until 1921. In 1921 he left Jerusalem and, after an extended lecture tour, settled in Cincinnati (1922–30).

> Idelsohn was the first to apply the methods of comparative musicology to the study of Jewish music, and was also first to record music on wax cylinders in Palestine . . . He discovered relationships between ancient Hebrew (mainly Yemenite) and early Christian (Byzantine, Jacobite and Gregorian) chant that had hitherto remained undetected. His magnum opus, the *Hebräisch-orientalischer Melodienschatz*, summarizes his work in Palestine (vols.i–v) and Cincinnati (vols.vi–x). Although he was largely self-taught as a musicologist, his writings represent an impressive contribution to the study of Jewish music.[287]

Refs.: BRC-(B); Gerson-Kiwi 1973–74; Gerson-Kiwi & Katz 2003.

---

[286] Gerson-Kiwi (1973–74) gives different dates of 14 July for his birth and 14 August for his death.
[287] Gerson-kiwi & Katz 2003.

KARL-GUSTAV IZIKOWITZ (1903–1985)
Swedish anthropologist

Appointments:
Professor of ethnography and social anthropology, Göteborg University, 1955–70
Head, Göteborg Museum of Ethnography, 1955–67 [288]

Field work:
Central America and SE Asia
Lamet hill peasants, Laos, 1935

Writings
Izikowitz is known to ethnomusicologists principally for his noteworthy book *Musical and Other Sound Instruments of the South American Indians* (1935). See also Kunst 1959a-:#2044-6a & 1960:#4740.

Ref.: Karin Pettersson, Göteborg University Library (pers.comm.), transl. from Swedish National Encyclopedia.

---

[288] The Ethnographic Museum which Izikowitz directed is now defunct and its collections transferred (2005) to a new Museum of World Culture.

FATHER A(RTHUR) M(ORRIS) JONES (1899–1980)
English cleric, teacher and ethnomusicologist

Born: London, England, 4 Jun 1899
Died: 12 Apr 1980

Education:
Keble College, University of Oxford, 1919–21
Wells Theological College, 1921–22
London Day Training College, 1928–29

Qualifications:
BA, University of Oxford, Hons. Theology with distinction, 1921
MA, University of Oxford, Hons. Theology with distinction, 1928
DipEd, University of London, 1929

Career and appointments:
Military service, British Army, 1917-19
Assistant Priest, Church of England, Ashford, Kent, 1922–24
Assistant Priest, Church of England, Maidstone, Kent, 1924–29
Warden, St Mark's College, Mapanza, Northern Rhodesia (now Zambia), 1929–51
Lecturer in African music, School of Oriental and African Studies, University of London, 1952–66

Honours:
DLitt, University of Oxford (awarded through the Board of the Faculty of Music at Oxford for African music research), 1961

Writings:
See below.

****

Father Jones is best known for two books. The first is his 2–volume *Studies in African Music* (1959), volume 2 of which contains detailed music transcriptions in landscape format of multi-part music. The other is his *Africa and Indonesia* (1964) in which he attempts to prove Indonesian colonisation of West Africa on the basis of xylophone tunings and other evidence. In a dual review,[289] Hood rejects Jones's methodology and findings, while Fleming, in a largely favourable review, suggests that if a connection exists it would most likely have resulted from known Indonesian colonisation of Madagascar (Malagasy) in East Africa, and would have gone overland from there rather than direct. For other writings see Kunst 1959a:#2091-2105.

Refs.: BRC-(B); Jane Waller, SOAS, London (pers.comm).

---

[289] Hood and Fleming 1966.

TREVOR A(LAN) JONES (1932–)
Australian composer and musicologist

Born: Sydney, Australia, 18 Dec 1932

Education:
Studied piano, oboe, bassoon, and composition, New South Wales Conservatorium, 1947–52
Studied music, University of Sydney, 1950–53
Studied musicology and composition, Harvard University, 1955–56
Studied musicology with Thurston Dart (1921–1971), Kings College, Cambridge University, 1956–58
Studied composition and harpsichord-continuo with Herbert Howells (1892–1983), Royal College of Music, London, 1957–58
Studied conducting privately with Sir Eugene Goossens (1893–1962), London, 1958–59

Qualifications:
BA (1st class honours), University of Sydney, 1954
MA (1st class honours), University of Sydney, 1959

Appointments:
Teaching fellow, Department of Music, University of Sydney, 1954
Temporary lecturer, Department of Music, University of Sydney, 1959–60
Senior lecturer, University of Western Australia, 1960–65
Foundation professor and chairman, Department of Music, Monash University, Melbourne, 1965–88

Honours and awards:
Frank Albert Prizes, University of Sydney
Busby and Sydney Moss Scholarships, University of Sydney
Fulbright Travel Award and Suttonstall Fellowship, Harvard University, USA

Field work:
In association with anthropologists Ronald and Catherine Berndt, recorded and studied secret, secular and sacred music of the Yalngu clans, NE Arnhemland, Northern Territory, Australia, 1964

Writings:
See Gallusser 2004 and below.

****

Jones's compositions have been mainly for choir. He has also written instrumental chamber works and incidental music for a documentary film. His Fugue in Jazz Rhythms won joint first prize in the Recorder Society of NSW's Composers Competition in 1963.

Jones's ethnomusicology research took place mostly in the early years of his career. His interest began with recordings of Arnhem Land music from Northern Australia, collected by Professor A.P. Elkin (1891–1979) during field expeditions he carried out from 1949–52. Jones transcribed and analysed the music, and collaborated with Elkin in a joint book, *Arnhem Land Music*.[290] At the same time Jones became interested in the quintessential Aboriginal musical instrument, the didjeridu, taught himself to play it, devised a notation system for it, and has written extensively about it. He also pioneered ethnomusioclogy courses at the University of Western Australia and Monash University.

Refs.: Australian Music Centre 2005; Gallusser 2004; Trevor Jones (pers.comm.).

---

[290] Elkin & Jones c.1957.

SIR WILLIAM JONES (1746–1794)
English lawyer, orientalist and Sanskrit scholar

Born: Westminster, London, England, 28 Sep 1746
Died: Calcutta, India, 27 Apr 1794

Education:
Harrow School, London, 1753–63
University College, University of Oxford, 1764–70

Qualification:
Masters degree, University of Oxford, 1770

Appointments:
Tutor to son of 1st Earl Spencer, 1766–70
Admitted to Middle Temple, 1770
Called to bar, 1774
High Court judge, Calcutta, 1783–94

Offices:
Founder/President, Asiatick Society of Bengal, 1784–94

Honours:
Elected Fellow of the Royal Society, 1772
Knighted, 1783

Writings:
"On the Musical Modes of the Hindoos." (1792).

****

Jones was one of the foremost intellectuals of his day, with an extraordinary gift for languages, including Sanskrit, which he learned after taking up his appointment as High Court judge in Calcutta. He is said to have been expert in 13 languages, with acquaintance of 28 others.[291] His one paper on Indian music was translated into German and reprinted at least eight times, exerting correspondingly great influence in Europe. For all of his gifts, however, Jones's paper was detrimental to understanding of Indian music because of his conviction that "although the Sanskrit books have preserved the theory of their musical composition, the practice seems almost wholly lost." Rather than provide a realistic view of a living practice, it conveyed a false impression that Indian music had undergone a lengthy devolution from a former "golden age."[292]

Refs.: Bor 1988; Platt & Woodfield 2003; Sundaram 1986.

---

[291] *Encyclopaedia Britannica*, 11th edition, 1910–22.
[292] Bor 1988:58.

MAUD PAULINE KARPELES (1885–1976)
English folk song collector, editor and administrator

Born: London, England, 12 Nov 1885
Died: London, England, 1 Oct 1976

Education:
Hamilton House School, Tunbridge Wells, 1900–05
Studied piano for six months, Berlin, 1906

Offices:
Co-founder, International Folk Music Council, 1947
Hon. Secretary, International Folk Music Council, 1947–63

Honours:
OBE, 1960
Honorary doctorate, Laval University, Canada, 1961
Honorary doctorate, Memorial University of Newfoundland, 1970
Honorary President, International 'Folk Music Council, 1964–76

Field work:
Appalachian mountains, USA, with Cecil Sharp, 1916–18
Newfoundland, 1929–30
Return visit to Appalachians, 1950 & 1955

Writings:
Karpeles 1966 is her definitive edition of the Appalachian folk songs jointly collected by her and Cecil Sharp during World War I, and finally issued after many years of devoted effort, when she was 81 years old; Karpeles 1967 is her biography of Cecil Sharp; and Karpeles 1973 is her own highly readable account of English folk song. Other writings are listed in Boyes 2003. Her papers are held by the Vaughan Williams Memorial Library.[293]

****

As a writer and editor, and as an assistant and long-time advocate of Cecil Sharp (q.v.), Maud Karpeles was significant, but it is in her role as the guiding hand behind the International Folk Music Council throughout its early life that she will perhaps be best remembered.

Her association with Sharp began in 1909 when she and her sister witnessed a Morris dance demonstration at a Stratford-on-Avon summer school organised by Sharp. She joined Sharp's first school of Morris dancing in London, and in 1910 formed a Folk Dance Club which became the nucleus of the English Folk Dance Society, founded by Sharp the following year. Karpeles became a key member of the new organisation, serving on its committee, taking part in folk dance demonstrations organised by Sharp and, from 1913 onwards, increasingly taking over administration duties from him.

---

[293] See Atkinson 2001 for an account.

After the outbreak of World War I in 1914, Sharp went to America, where Karpeles later joined him, and from 1916–18 they conducted an historic 46-week field trip in remote areas of the Appalachian mountains of North Carolina, Tennessee, Virginia and Kentucky, where they found English folk songs still extant after some 200 years that had meantime been lost in England. Sharp notated the tunes while Karpeles transcribed the texts. Altogether, they collected an astonishing 1612 tunes with texts, representing some 500 different songs, from 281 singers.[294]

After Sharp's death in 1924, Karpeles's association with him did not end. She devoted the rest of her life to promoting his work and ideals, initially through the English Folk Dance and Song Society, later as his literary executor and by editing editions of his works, and latterly through the International Folk Music Council.

In 1935, Karpeles organised a highly successful international folk dance festival in London, in which 18 different nations took part. The experience may well have convinced her of the feasibility of establishing a permanent international society devoted to folk music.

Nothing could be done during World War II and the events leading up to it, but within two years of cessation of hostilities, in September 1947, Karpeles assembled delegates from 28 countries for a meeting at which the International Folk Music Council (IFMC) was formed, with Dr Ralph Vaughan Williams as president and Karpeles as executive secretary. She remained in this role until her retirement in 1963, when she became Honorary President, steering the IFMC through its early years of annual conferences and scholarly activity, including 15 years during which she edited its journal.

Refs.: Atkinson 2001; Boyes 2003a; Heaney 2004a; Rhodes 1977; Wachsmann 1976.

---

[294] Karpeles 1966:xii.

WALTER KAUFMANN (1907–1984)
Austro-Hungarian/American conductor, composer and musicologist

Born: Karlsbad (now Karlovy Vary), Bohemia, Czech Republic, 1 Apr 1907
Died: Bloomington, IN, USA, 9 Sep 1984

Education:
Attended Staatsrealgymnasium, Karlsbad, 1918–26
Studied composition under Franz Schreker and musicology under Curt Sachs (q.v.), Staatlich Hochschule für Musik, Berlin, 1926–30
Studied musicology, German University of Prague under Paul Paul Nettl and others, 1930–34

Qualifications:
Although he completed the requirements for a PhD in musicology at Prague university, as a political statement he refused to accept the degree because the Ordinarius (Becking) was the leader of the Nazi youth group in Prague.

Appointments:
Conducted opera, Berlin, Karlsbad, and Eger (Cheb), Bohemia, 1927–33
Director of European music, All-India Radio, Bombay, 1935–46
Guest conductor, BBC, London, 1946–47
Professor of piano and composition, Conservatory of Halifax, Nova Scotia, 1947–48
Conductor, Winnipeg Symphony Orchestra, 1948–57
Professor of musicology, Indiana University, 1957–77

Field work:
Extensive travel in India, Tibet and China during tenure with All India Radio at Bombay, 1935–46

Writings:
See below.

****

Kaufmann is best known to ethnomusicologists for his two books *The Ragas of North India* (1968) and *The Ragas of South India* (1976), and for his book *Musical Notations of the Orient* (1967). For a complete list of his compositions and writings see Noblitt 1981:381-6. Kaufmann's papers are held by the Cook Music Library at Indiana University.

Refs.: BRC-(A); New Grove "Kaufmann, Walter."; Rahkonen 1985; William and Gayle Cook Music Library 1997–98.

FRANK KIDSON (1855–1926)
English folk song collector, antiquary, and writer

Born: Leeds, England, 15 Nov 1855
Died: Leeds, England, 7 Nov 1926

Offices:
Founder member, English Folk Song Society, 1898

Honours:
Honorary MA, University of Leeds, 1923

Writings:
Kidson was a pioneer collector of English folk song whose Yorkshire and north country collection, *Traditional Tunes* (1891) won praise and established his reputation. For the second edition of *Grove's Dictionary of Music and Musicians* (1904–10), edited by J.A. Fuller-Maitland, Kidson contributed no fewer than 365 entries, most relating (to cite only from the first few volumes) to persons (many of them obscure), such as "William Barley"; song titles such as "Campbells are Coming" or "Hail Columbia"; song or dance genres such as "Catch", "Hornpipe", "Minuet" or "Morris dance"; publishing firms such as " Chappell & Co"; institutions such as "Folk Song Society"; and folk music instruments such as "Guitar" or "Hurdy Gurdy". For a list of his other writings see Thompson et al. 2003.

****

In scholarly terms, Kidson is something of a mystery man, whose work has gone undeservedly into eclipse as a result of the prominence of his contemporary, Cecil Sharp (q.v.). The *New Grove* article about him says "the extent of his contribution to folksong scholarship has yet to be evaluated." In his first collection, *Traditional Tunes* (1891), he matched materials collected in oral tradition with texts published in early broadsides, thus relating oral tradition to printed sources. He had extraordinary expertise as a bibliographer and tune sleuth, gaining a reputation from antiquarian associates as "the musical Sherlock Holmes". He amassed a large private library of 9000 folk song and other volumes, and compiled an immense unpublished index of English folk songs, amounting to 100,000 entries. The index, together with the bulk of his personal library, is now available for use in the Mitchell Library, Glasgow.

Refs.: Francmanis 1999; Francmanis (pers.comm.); Thompson et al. 2003.

PERCIVAL ROBSON KIRBY (1887–1970)
Scottish/South African musicologist

Born: Aberdeen, Scotland, 17 Apr 1887
Died: Grahamstown, South Africa, 7 Feb 1970

Education:
Studied music under Charles Sanford Terry (1864–1936), University of Aberdeen

Qualifications:
MA, University of Aberdeen, 1910

Appointments:
Organiser, Natal Education Department, 1914–21
Professor of music, University of the Witwatersrand, 1921–52

Honours:
FRCM, 1924
Honorary doctorate, University of the Witwatersrand, 1931
Honorary doctorate, Rhodes University, Grahamstown, 1965

Field work:
Transvaal, Bechuanaland (Botswana), Swaziland, Vendaland and Ovamboland, 1930–34
Kalahari Desert, 1936

Writings:
For a bibliography of his works, see Bryer 1965.

****

In 1914 Kirby emigrated to South Africa, where he spent his first eight years in a non-academic post as a music organiser for the Natal Education Department. Thereafter, for the rest of his working life, he served as professor of music at University College, Johannesburg (later the University of the Witwatersrand). His reputation was gained substantially as a result of his large field collection of South African musical instruments, now housed at the University of Capetown, and a substantial book on the subject, first published in 1934. The collection contains more than 600 instruments, including some that are no longer being made. His photos, slides and field notes are housed separately in the manuscripts and archives division of the University of Capetown library.

Refs.: BRC-(A); Michael Nixon (pers.comm.); Tyrrell 2003; University of Capetown 2003.

SHIGEO KISHIBE (1912–2005)
Japanese ethnomusicologist

Born: Tokyo, Japan, 16 Jun 1912
Died: Tokyo, Japan, 4 Jan 2005

Education:
Studied oriental history, Tokyo Imperial University, 1933–36

Qualifications:
Bachelor's degree, Tokyo Imperial University, 1936
Doctorate in literature, University of Tokyo, 1960

Appointments and career:
Associate Professor, University of Tokyo, 1949–60
Professor, University of Tokyo, 1961–73
Professor, Teikyô University, 1973–94
Research fellow, Tokyo National Institute of Cultural Properties, 1952–58
Visiting associate professor, UCLA, Harvard University and University of Hawai'i, 1957–58
Visiting professor, University of Washington and Stanford University, 1962–63
Visiting professor, University of Hawai'i, 1973–74

Offices:
Director, Japan Society of Musicology
Director, Japan Society of Theatre Science
President, Society for Research in Asiatic Music (Tôyô Ongaku Gakkai), 1978–80 & 1984–93
Member of Honour, International Music Council, 1986
Member, Executive Board, International Folk Music Council & International Musicological Society

Honours:
Japan Academy Prize, 1961
Japanese Order of the Rising Sun, Third Class, 1982
Tanabe Hisao Prize, 2000

Field work:
China, India, Iran, Korea, Japan, and the Philippines. His first field trips were to Korea (1941), and China (1943).

Writings:
Kishibe's best known and most accessible work in English is his book *The Traditional Music of Japan* (1984). Another notable work was his [*A Historical Study of the Music of the Tang Dynasty*] (1960), published in Japanese, for which he received the Japan Academy Award, the most prestigious prize for scholarship in Japan. The work was reprinted in 2005. For a list of

Kishibe's publications, mostly in Japanese, see Kanazawa 2003. See also Nelson 2003 for an annotated bibliography of 100 of Kishibe's major works, and synopses in English of many of them, as supplied originally by Kishibe and edited by Nelson.

****

Kishibe was a specialist in the history of Asian music, particularly Chinese and Japanese. Long before "bi-musicality" was promoted as a concept in the West, he became a proficient player of numerous Japanese and other musical instruments. Unlike most of his compatriots, he was well known in the West, not only for his book but also because of his visiting appointments in the USA, his executive role in the IFMC and IMS, and his attendance at international meetings.

Refs.: Eth 6(1):55-6 (1962); Kanazawa 2003; Steven G. Nelson (pers.comm.);Tsukada 2005.

GEORGE LYMAN KITTREDGE (1860–1941)
American scholar of English literature and folk song

Born: Boston, MA, USA, 28 Feb 1860
Died: Barnstable, MA, USA, 23 Jul 1941

Education:
Attended Roxbury Latin School, 1875–77
Studied classics, Harvard University, 1878–82
Studied in Germany, 1886–87

Qualifications:
AB, Harvard University, 1882

Appointments:
Taught Latin, Phillips Exeter Academy, New Hampshire, 1883–88
Instructor in English, Harvard University, 1888–90
Assistant Professor in English, Harvard University, 1890–93
Professor of English literature, Harvard University, 1894–1936

Offices:
President, Colonial Society of Massachusetts,1900–07
President, Modern Language Association of America, 1904–05
President, American Folklore Society, 1904–05

Honours:
Honorary LLD, University of Chicago, 1901; John Hopkins, 1915; McGill, 1921; Brown, 1925
Honorary LittD, Harvard University,1907; Yale, 1924
Honorary DLitt, Oxford University, 1932
Honorary DCL, Union College, 1935

****

Kittredge succeeded Francis Child (q.v.) in the chair of English at Harvard University. Known familiarly to his students as "Kitty", he was a noted authority on Shakespeare, Chaucer, and Sir Thomas Malory. After the death of Child, he completed and edited the final volume of Child's 5-volume anthology of British ballads, *The English and Scottish Popular Ballads* (1883–98) and saw it through to publication. He also spent many hundreds of hours organising Child's accumulated papers in 33 folio volumes, now in the Houghton Library of the Harvard College Lib-rary.

Refs.: ANB: BRC-(C); Bynum 1974; E-Brit: WWWA.

ZOLTÁN KODÁLY (1882–1967)
Hungarian composer, folk song collector, scholar, and educator

Born: Kecskemét, Hungary, 16 Dec 1882
Died: Budapest, Hungary, 6 Mar 1967

Education:
While attending Archiepiscopal Grammar School in Nagyszombat, learnt to play the piano, violin, viola and cello, and taught himself the elements of composition.
Studied composition, Royal Hungarian Academy of Music, Budapest, 1900–05
Studied German and Hungarian, University of Budapest, 1900–06

Qualifications:
Diploma in composition, Royal Hungarian Academy of Music, Budapest, 1904
Diploma in teaching, Royal Hungarian Academy of Music, Budapest, 1905
DPhil in modern languages, University of Budapest, 1906
Topic: Strophic Construction of Hungarian Folksong

Appointments:
Teacher of music theory and composition, Budapest Music Academy, 1907–?
Music critic for the magazine Nyugat and daily paper Pesti napló, 1917–19
Deputy director, Budapest Music Academy, 1918–19

Offices and honours:
President, Royal Hungarian Academy of Music, Budapest, the Hungarian Council of Arts, and the Hungarian Academy of Sciences, 1946–49
Received government decorations, 1947, 1952, 1962
Awarded three Kossuth Prizes, 1948, 1952, 1957
Honorary doctorate, Budapest, 1957
Honorary doctorate, University of Oxford, 1960
Honorary President, International Society for Music Education, 1964
Honorary doctorate, East Berlin, 1964
Herder Prize, 1965
Honorary doctorate, University of Toronto, 1966
President, International Folk Music Council, 1961–66
Order of the Hungarian People's Republic, 1962

Field work:
Extensive folk song collecting in Hungary, both in association with Béla Bartók (q.v.) from 1905 onwards and independently. He is estimated to have personally collected between 3000 and 4000 traditional melodies, most of which are still in MS.

Writings:

Kodály's best known scholarly work is his *Folk Music of Hungary* (1960). For an extensive list of his writings, including correspondence, books, and articles, see Eösze et al. 2003.

****

It is as an internationally acclaimed composer that Kodály is best known, but in common with his friend and fellow composer Béla Bartók (q.v.), he was also a prolific collector and scholar of Hungarian folk music. Kodály was the more academic of the two and, having been exposed to folk song from childhood, he was already familiar with it and had begun studying it before Bartók's interest was also aroused. Together they brought Hungarian folk music to international attention, as well as incorporating it into their own compositions.

Refs.: Blom 1948b; Eösze et al. 2003; Howes 1967; Krader 1967; Tallián 2003.

MIECZYSLAW KOLINSKI (1901–1981)
Polish/Canadian composer and ethnomusicologist

Born: Warsaw, Poland, 5 Sep 1901
Died: Toronto, Canada, 8 May 1981

Education:
Early education was in Hamburg
Studied piano and composition, Hochschule für Musik, Berlin, 1923–26
Studied musicology, psychology and anthropology, Berlin University, where his teachers included Erich von Hornbostel (q.v.) and Curt Sachs (q.v.), ?–1930

Qualifications:
PhD, Berlin University, 1930
Topic: Comparison of Malaccan and Samoan polyphony

Appointments:
Assistant to Erich von Hornbostel, Berlin Phonogram-Archiv, 1926–33
Lecturer, University of Toronto, 1966–79

Offices:
President, Society for Ethnomusicology, 1958–59

Writings:
For a complete bibliography and a list of compositions see Falck & Rice 1982:xx-xxiv.

****

Kolinski was a highly skilled transcriber of music, beginning as part of his doctoral work and continuing under Hornbostel at the Berlin Phonogram-Archiv. After 1933, when forced to move from Germany because of Nazi prohibitions upon jews, he moved to Prague, where he transcribed Surinamese, Dahomeyan, Togonese, Ashanti, Haitian, and Kwakiutl Indian music for the anthropologists Melville Herskovits (q.v.) and Franz Boas (q.v.) of Northwestern University and Columbia University. Obliged to move again because of the Nazi advance, he went in 1938 to Belgium, where he remained in hiding throughout the German occupation. In 1951 he emigrated to New York, and became an American citizen, subsisting by undertaking music editing and as a music therapist at St. Albans National Hospital and Goldwater Memorial Hospital, New York.

In 1966 he moved to Canada to take up a position as lecturer in music at the University of Toronto, continuing to teach there even after his retirement in 1976. In 1974 he became a Canadian citizen, and in 1979 was awarded the title of Scholar Emeritus by the University of Toronto Faculty of Music.

As a pianist, he made a debut in Hamburg at the age of 18 with a performance of Tchaikovski's Piano Concerto no.1 with the Oldenburg Symphony Orchestra. His compositions include three ballets, Symphonic Fantasy, Prelude for Orchestra, Dahomey Suite, American Suite (based on Negro spirituals (for voice and string quartet)), together with numerous chamber pieces and piano works.

As an ethnomusicologist he was noted principally for his elaborate systems of describing contour and other elements of musical analysis (Kolinski 1961, 1965a, 1965b).

Refs.: BRC-(A); Beckwith & Averill 2003; Cavanagh 1981; Diamond Cavanagh 2001; Eth 3(3):132 (1959): Falck & Rice 1982.

JAAP KUNST (1891–1960)
Dutch ethnomusicologist

Born: Groningen, Netherlands, 12 Aug 1891
Died: Amsterdam, Netherlands, 7 Dec 1960

Education:
Studied law, University of Groningen, 1911–17

Qualifications:
LLM, University of Groningen, 1917

Appointments:
Colonial civil servant, Indonesia, 1920–34
Curator, Royal Tropical Institute,[295] Amsterdam, 1936–56
Privaat-docent (unsalaried lecturer), University of Amsterdam, 1942–52
Lector (reader) in ethnomusicology, University of Amsterdam, 1953–60

Offices:
Honorary President, Society for Ethnomusicology, 1959
President, International Folk Music Council, 1959–60

Honours:
French Legion of Honour
Officier in de Ore van Oranje Nassau, 1954
Member, Royal Netherlands Academy of Sciences, 1958

Field work:
Netherlands
Indonesia, including Sumatra, Sulawesi, Flores, Timor, Moluccas and Irian Jaya.

Writings:
Standard works resulting from Kunst's time in Indonesia include monographs on music of Nias,[296] Flores,[297] and Java,[298] together with a volume on Hindu-Javanese musical instruments.[299] Comprehensive lists of Kunst's writings can be found in Kunst 1959a #2358-2418, and Kunst 1973. Kunst's writings on New Guinea music have been brought together in a posthumous English translation from the Dutch.[300] Heins et al. 1994 contains English translations of many of his other articles and lectures originally written or delivered in Dutch.

---

[295] Known until 1950 as the Colonial Institute.
[296] Kunst 1939.
[297] Kunst 1942.
[298] Kunst 1973.
[299] Kunst 1968.
[300] Kunst 1966.

* * * *

Kunst came from a highly musical household, as both his parents were pianists, educated at the conservatories of Leipzig and Dresden respectively. Kunst himself began to learn the violin at the age of five, and became a dedicated chamber music violinist, remaining so throughout his life, besides playing with symphony orchestras in Groningen and Amsterdam.

While studying law at the University of Groningen, he spent summer vacations on the island of Terschelling, Friesia, Netherlands, crediting this with influencing the future course of his life as a result of the folk music he heard and collected there.

After his graduation, Kunst worked for a while first as a bank clerk and then as an administrative assistant at the Amsterdam City Hall, giving this up in 1919 to go on tour in the Dutch East Indies, with a string trio of which he was the violinist, performing at numerous clubs in Java, Sumatra, Sulawesi and Borneo. During this time he heard the Javanese gamelan for the first time, and became fascinated with it.

Kunst stayed on in Indonesia having found employment there and, with his wife, collected, studied, and published extensively on the music.

In 1921, he began a correspondence with the director of the Berlin Phonogram-Archiv, Erich non Hornbostel (q.v.), as a result of which he adopted Hornbostel's methods, as well as depositing his wax cylinder recordings with the archive in exchange for supplies of blank cylinders.

In 1934, Kunst's employment in Indonesia ended and he spent the next two years supporting his family by means of lecture tours in Europe and elsewhere, ceasing this when he became curator of the Royal Tropical Institute, Amsterdam, in 1936.

By the time Kunst began teaching in 1942, he already had a considerable following because of his many writings during the years he spent in Indonesia, and as a result of his later lecture tours of the Netherlands. Kunst is credited with the coining of the term ethnomusicology in 1950 and, especially as a result of his bibliographic survey *Ethnomusicology*,[301] is accepted as one of the main persons responsible for the subject as a discipline. As an Indonesianist his impact has been especially strong at UCLA, through Mantle Hood (q.v.), who introduced gamelan studies there and was a pupil of Kunst.

Refs.: Ton Bruins (pers.comm.); Eth 4(2):99; E-Brit; Heins et al. 1994; Hood 2003.

---

[301] Kunst 1959a & 1960.

FRANCIS LA FLESCHE (1857–1932)
American ethnologist

Born: Omaha Indian Reservation, near Macy, NE, USA, 25 Dec 1857
Died: Omaha Indian Reservation, near Macy, NE, USA, 5 Sep 1932

Education:
Presbyterian mission school, Omaha Indian Reservation
Studied law, National University Law School Washington while working as clerk for the Bureau of Indian Affairs

Qualifications:
LLB, National University Law School Washington, 1892
LLM, National University Law School, Washington, 1893

Appointments:
Interpreter, Speaking tour of E. USA by Chief Standing Bear and Thomas H. Tibbles, 1879–80
Interpreter, Senate Committee on Indian Affairs, 1881
Clerk, Bureau of Indian Affairs, 1881–1910
Ethnologist, Smithsonian Bureau of American Ethnology, 1910–29

Offices:
President, Anthropological Society of Washington, 1922–23

Honours:
Fellow, American Association for the Advancement of Science
Honorary Doctor of Letters, University of Nebraska, 1926

Field work:
Collaboration on Omaha ethnography with Alice Cunningham Fletcher (q.v.), 1880–1910.
 Work on his own, especially on Osage language, music and rituals, followed the association with Fletcher. In contrast with Fletcher, who recorded representative songs from different ceremonies, La Flesche concentrated upon recording entire ceremonies in as much detail as possible. He also pioneered the technique of continuous recording, making use of two machines with overlap to avoid breaks. La Flesche's 254 Osage cylinders have been reprocessed by the Federal Cylinder Project of the Library of Congress, complementing his own extraordinarily detailed documentation (see below).

Writings:
La Flesch published the results of his Osage studies in four large volumes over a period of nine years from 1921–30, the last of them just two years before his death in 1932.

****

For more about La Flesche see Part I.

Refs.: BRC-(B) & (D); Alexander 1933; Lee & La Vigna 1985; Rohde 2000; Walcott 1981.

ROBERT LACH (1874–1958)
Austrian comparative musicologist and composer

Born: Vienna, Austria, 29 Jan 1874
Died: Salzburg, Austria, 11 Sep 1958

Education:
Studied law, University of Vienna, 1893
Studied composition, Gesellschaft der Musikfreunde Conservatory, Vienna, 1893–99
Studied philosophy and musicology, University of Vienna, 1896–99

Qualifications:
DrPhil, German University, Prague, 1902
Topic: The development of ornamented melody

Appointments:
Austrian provincial administration, 1894–1904
Director, music collection, Imperial and Royal Court Library, Vienna, 1912–20
Habilitation, University of Vienna, 1915
Reader, University of Vienna, 1920–26
Professor of music history, philosophy and music aesthetics, Vienna State Academy, 1924–?
Professor of musicology, University of Vienna, 1927–39

Offices:
Editor, *Denkmäler der Tonkunst in Österreich*, 1954

Field work:
Recorded Russian prisoners of war, 1916–17

Writings:
For selected works see Potter 2003, and for a complete listing see Graf 1954.

****

Lach's teachers in musicology included Wallaschek (q.v.) and Adler, both of whom he eventually succeeded at the University of Vienna. His compositions included 13 works for the stage, 10 symphonies, nearly 80 works of chamber music, 8 masses, a requiem, and about 450 songs and choral works. As a comparative musicologist his approach to music history was evolutionist.

Refs.: BRC-(A); DBE; Graf 1958; NDB; Potter 2003.

ROBERT LACHMANN (1892–1939)
German/Jewish comparative musicologist

Born: Berlin, Germany, 28 Nov 1892
Died: Jerusalem, Israel, 8 May 1939

Education:
Studied English, French and Arabic at universities of Berlin and London
Studied Semitic languages under Eugen Mittwoch and musicology under Johannes Wolf and Carl Stumpf (q.v.), Berlin University, after 1918
Studied librarianship, Berlin Staatsbibliothek, 1924

Qualifications:
Doctorate, Berlin University, 1922
Topic: Urban music in Tunisia, based on his own field recordings

Appointments:
Interpreter, Wünsdorf POW camp, during World War I
Librarian, Berlin Staatsbibliothek music department under Johannes Wolf, 1927–33
Head, Phonogram Commission, Congress of Arab Music, Cairo, 1932
Founder/head, Phonogram Archive for Oriental Music, Hebrew University, Jerusalem, 1935–39

Offices:
Editor, *Zeitschrift für vergleichende Musikwissenschaft*, 1933–35

Field work:
Collected folklore and music from African and Indian prisoners. Wünsdorf POW camp during World War I
Tunisia, bef.1922, 1926–27 & 1929
Tripoli, 1925; Kabylia, 1927; Tunis & Morocco, 1930
Samaritan and other Jewish communities, Jerusalem, 1935–39

Writings:
Gerson-Kiwi 1974 includes an inventory of the Lachmann Archive and a complete list of his published writings. See also Gerson-Kiwi 2003 for a select bibliography. A book by Ruth Katz (2003) includes letters and lectures of Lachmann.

****

Lachmann was a specialist in Arab music. After being ousted from his employment in Germany by the Nazi regime, an invitation to found a phonogram archive at Hebrew University in 1935, and his work in Jerusalem during the last four years of his life, marks the beginning of ethnomusicology in Israel. Gerson-Kiwi ranks him as "one of the finest exponents of the early European school of comparative musicology."

Refs.: BRC-(A); Gerson-Kiwi 1973–74; Gerson-Kiwi 2003.

A(LBERT) L(ANCASTER) LLOYD (1908–1982)
English folk-singer, broadcaster, and writer

Born: London, England, 29 Feb 1908
Died: London, England, 29 Sep 1982

Writings:
For a bibliography see Arthur 1993.

****

Self-educated and of English working class origin, A.L. Lloyd was the epitome of a scholar who can be said to have pulled himself up by his bootstraps.

Australia: c.1924–33

Orphaned at the age of 15, he was shipped off to Australia as an assisted migrant, where he worked on sheep stations for nine years. In the evenings he educated himself with the aid of books on art and music, obtained by means of a distance learning service from the Sydney public library. During this period also he learned Australian "bush songs" from station hands, shearers and drovers, writing the words down in exercise books, and memorising the tunes as best he could.

London: c.1934–37

After a spell of work looking after merino sheep in South Africa, Lloyd moved on to London where he became an associate of a Marxist historian of about his own age, Leslie Morton (1903–1987), and as a result of this influence joined the communist party. While unemployed in 1936, Lloyd continued his self-education by obtaining a ticket (as Marx had done before him) for the British Library Reading Room, where he familiarised himself with the work of all the leading British folk song collectors, at the same time himself beginning to collect songs from singers he met.

Antarctic: 1937–38

In 1937, Lloyd went to Liverpool and signed on for a 7-month trip to the Antarctic as a worker on the whaler *Southern Empress*. At foc'sle sing-songs he sang popular songs with his shipmates, perhaps honing his skills as a singer, besides picking up "a number of fine sea songs."

BBC: 1938–39

After his return from the Antarctic, Lloyd's real career began when he had his first radio script accepted by the BBC, in 1938. Drawing upon his whaling experiences, it was entitled "The Voice of the Seamen," and proved such a success that the BBC offered him permanent employment. He had now entered the middle class, with this own office, secretary and unlimited access to the BBC collection of folk recordings.

War years and later

In 1940, Lloyd found journalism work with the *Picture Post*, beginning a long association that continued intermittently for ten years, and included visits to South America and the Middle East. In 1941 he enlisted in the army and was seconded as a writer to the Ministry of Information, a job which provided enough free time to enable him to continue his studies and writings on folk music. A major result was his book *The Singing Englishman* (1944), a polemic, written from a Marxist standpoint, that was severely criticised for a number of inaccuracies and misstatements by Maud Karpeles in a review.[302] Lloyd took the criticisms to heart, choosing later not to issue a second edition, when he was asked to do so, but instead to write an entirely new book, his *Folk Song in England* (1967). This did not escape criticism either, but is notable for its accessible writing style, its convincing arguments relating folk songs to social events at the time of their composition, and a strongly argued case for admitting late-period industrial songs to the hallowed ranks of folk song.

> Capitalism killed the folk song, we are told: enclosure starved it, the steam-engine put paid to it, the miseries of nineteenth century industrialisation blighted the culture of the working people. A gloomy picture: is it just? [303]

These are the opening words of Lloyd's chapter on the topic, ushering in a fresh perspective on folk song which was to prove both influential and productive. His impact, however, was by no means limited to his books. He was a polyglot linguist who is said to have picked up languages after only a few weeks exposure as others might collect postage stamps, an ability he put to good use with visits to Romania, Bulgaria and Albania, in Eastern Europe, where he recorded folk songs.

In the 1950s and 1960s, he was a prime mover of the post-war British folk song revival, assisting it with his own performances of folk songs at clubs and other venues, broadcast talks on BBC Radio 3, issue of gramophone records under the Topic label, and publications such as the *Penguin Book of English Folk Songs*, written jointly with Ralph Vaughan Williams.[304] From 1971 onwards, he also taught regularly at London University.

Refs.: Arthur 2003; Duran 1982; Gregory 1970; Gregory 1997.

---

[302] Carpools 1944.
[303] Lloyd 1967:316.
[304] Vaughan Williams & Lloyd 1959.

ALAN LOMAX (1915–2002)
American folk song collector and scholar

Born: Austin, TX, USA, 15 Jan 1915
Died: Holiday, FL, USA, 19 Jul 2002

Education:
University of Texas, 1931 and ?1934–36
Harvard University, 1932–33
Columbia University, graduate work in anthropology, 1939

Qualifications:
BA in philosophy, University of Texas, 1936

Appointments:
Archive of American Folksong, Library of Congress, 1937–42
Office of War Information and US Army Special Services, during World War II
Director of Folk Music, Decca Records, 1946–49
Research Associate, Department of Anthropology and Center for the Social Sciences, Columbia University, 1962–89
Director, Association for Cultural Equity, and Research Associate in Anthropology, Hunter College, 1989–95

Honours:
Especially during his latter years, Lomax was the recipient of numerous awards including:
National Medal of Arts, 1986
National Book Critics Circle Award for Nonfiction, 1993
Folk Alliance Lifetime Achievement Award, 1995
Honorary Doctorate, Tulane University, 2000
National Academy of Recording Arts & Sciences Trustees' Award, 2003

Field work:
Southern United States, New England, Michigan, Wisconsin, New York, Ohio, Haiti, and the Bahamas, 1933–42
Prison songs at Parchman and Lambert penitentiaries, Mississippi, 1947–48
Southern Baptist churches, True Light Baptist Church in Dallas, Texas, and the Rose Hill Baptist Church in Greenville, Mississippi, 1948
England, Scotland, and Ireland, 1950–58
Spain, 1952–53
Italy, 1954–55
Virginia, Kentucky, Alabama, Mississippi, Tennessee, Arkansas, and the Georgia Sea Islands, 1959–60
Eastern Caribbean, 1962
Soviet Union, 1964
Dominican Republic, Morrocco, 1967
Louisiana, Alabama, Pennsylvania, Arizona, North Carolina, Virginia, Georgia, and Mississippi, 1978–85

From time to time, Lomax also recorded at his home bases of the Library of Congress, Washington, DC (1933–42), and from 1948 onwards in New York city.

Writings:

Lomax's most important book was his *Folk Song Style and Culture* (1968), reporting the results of his Cantometrics project (see below). For a select list and comments on his other writings, see Thieme 2003. For a bibliography see Lonergan 1994. For selected writings and a complete bibliography, see Cohen 2003.

****

Alan Lomax worked outside the purview of conventional ethnomusicology, although serving as guest lecturer from time to time at universities, including Chicago, Columbia, Indiana, and New York. He was an outstanding collector of American and European folk music, with an egalitarian view that changed perceptions of folk song in America and abroad. His collecting activities began when he was still a teenager, in association with his father John Avery Lomax (1867–1948), whom he accompanied on field trips after his father became curator of the Archive of American Folksong at the Library of Congress in 1933. Their joint book *American Ballads and Folk Songs* (1934) was acclaimed as the largest single collection of American folk song to that date. Later, he continued recording on his own both in America and the Caribbean, and from 1950–58 in Great Britain, Italy and Spain. Publication of his huge collection of field recordings began on Rounder Records in 1997, and is projected to run to 100 CDs.

During the course of his working life as a broadcaster and populariser of folk song, Lomax produced many recordings, documentaries and radio series including a 26-week series American Folk Songs for CBS, 1939–40; another 26-week series, Wellsprings of Music (CBS), the following year; On Top of Old Smokey for Mutual Broadcasting (1948); and numerous radio and television broadcasts of folk music for the BBC (1950–58).

From 1963–89, with the support of foundation grants, his time was spent mostly as director of a Columbia University project of his own devising called Cantometrics, which sought to compare samples of music world wide in an attempt to chart social correlates of music and track the origins of styles. Few ethnomusicologists believed his results, but Lomax was respected for his efforts, and methods he formulated for quantifying hitherto neglected elements of singing style have since been adopted and emulated.

From 1989–94, his Cantometrics project now concluded, he developed his Global Jukebox, an "intelligent museum" software project for studying music and dance of the world, into which he incorporated Cantometrics together with related coding systems called Choreometrics and Parlametrics for study of dance and speech respectively.

Refs.: BRC-(B); E-Brit; Don Fleming (pers.comm.); Rounder Records 2003; Thieme 2003.

JOSÉ MACEDA (1917–2004)
Filipino composer, pianist and ethnomusicologist

Born: Manila, Philippines, 31 Jan 1917
Died: Quezon City, Philippines, 5 May 2004

Education:
Studied piano, Manila Academy of Music, ?–1935
Studied piano with Alfred Cortot (1877–1962), École Normale de Musique, Paris, 1937–41
Studied piano with Robert Schmitz, San Francisco, 1946–49
Studied musicology with Lowinsky, Queens College, New York, and Lang at Columbia University,1950–52
Studied anthropology, University of Chicago and ethnomusicology, Indiana University, 1957–58
Studied ethnomusicology, UCLA, 1961–63

Qualifications:
Diploma of music, Manila Academy of Music, 1935
PhD in ethnomusicology, UCLA, 1963
Topic: Music of the Maginadanao in the Philippines.
(Because Maceda gained his PhD relatively late in life, he is the sole person to have qualified formally in ethnomusicology among the pioneers who are featured in the present book.)

Appointments and career:
Piano soloist, France, USA and Philippines, 1935–57
Professor of piano and, later, ethnomusicology, University of the Philippines, 1952–90

Honours:
Ordre des Palmes Academiques, France, 1978
University of The Philippines Outstanding Research Award, 1985
John D. Rockefeller Award, Asian Cultural Council, New York, 1987
Philippine National Science Society Achievement Award, 1988
Tanglaw ng Lahi award, Ateneo University de Manila, 1988
Gawad ng Lahi award, Cultural Center of The Philippines, 1989
Fumio Koizumi Prize, Tokyo, 1992
National Research Council Award, 1993
Araw ng Maynila award, 1996
Nikkei Award, Tokyo, 1997
Fondazione Civitella Ranieri award, Italy, 1997
National Artist for Music, Philippines, 1997
Civitella Ranieri Award, Italy, 1997
Officier dans l'Ordre National du Mérite, France, 1997
Chevalier de la Légion d'Honneur, France, 2001

Field work:
Philippines, E. & W. Africa, Brazil, China, Indonesia, Malaysia, Myanmar, Thailand, and Vietnam. Recordings made by him in these areas are among more than 2,500 hours of field recordings in 51 language groups held by the University of The Philippines Ethnomusicology Center archives. Also in the archive are musical instruments, photographs, text transcriptions, and translations. Additionally, 64 tape reels of Mindanao music recorded by Maceda in 1954 and 1961 are held by UCLA Archives. His field work methods are set out in his publication *A Manual of a Music Field Research* (1981).

Writings:
For a select list of compositions and writings, see Kasilag 2003. For another list of publications, see also Trimillos 2005.

****

Maceda was the pre-eminent ethnomusicologist of the Philippines, famous both there and abroad as much for his work as a composer, educator, and earlier as a concert pianist, as for his scholarly activities. His compositions combine avant-garde techniques with influences from his field work. When he was proclaimed as National Artist for Music in 1997, the citation referred to him as ". . . an unstinting beacon in the formation and reaffirmation of a national ethos that embraces Filipino, as well as Asian, worldview."

Refs.: BRC-(A); Kasilag 2003; Manila Times 2004; 'The Living Composers Project, 2004; Trimillos 2005; UCLA Ethnomusicology Archive 2004.

VICTOR-CHARLES MAHILLON (1841–1924)
Belgian organologist, acoustician and wind instrument maker

Born: Brussels, Belgium, 10 Mar 1841
Died: St Jean-Cap Ferrat, Belgium, 17 Jun 1924

Career:
Entered the instrument-manufacturing firm established by his father, Charles Mahillon, 1865
Curator, Musée Instrumental du Conservatoire Royal de Musique, Brussels, 1877–1924 [305]

Offices:
Founder editor, *L'Écho musical*, 1869–86

Honours:
Silver medal, Paris, 1878
Gold medal, Inventions Exhibition, London, 1885
Cross of the Legion of Honour, 1889

Writings:
See below.

****

As a musical instrument manufacturer, Mahillon pioneered the early music movement by making copies of rare instruments such as the Bach trumpet, and by organising concerts of music played on old instruments.

After his appointment as curator of the Brussels conservatory musical instruments collection in 1877, he expanded upon a nucleus of 78 instruments collected by the Belgian music historian Françoise Joseph Fétis (1784–1871), together with Indian instruments given to King Leopold II of Belgium by Sourindro Mohun Tagore (1840–1914),[306] ultimately, over the course of half a century, building up one of the largest collections in Europe, of some 3300 items. These he dedicated himself to cataloguing and describing. As a writer, Mahillon contributed articles on wind instruments to the 9th edition of the *Encyclopaedia Britannica*, as well as articles in the journal he established in 1869. His crowning achievement, however, was his monumental 5-volume analytical catalogue of the conservatory collection, published between 1880 and 1922. For a list of writings see Waterhouse 2003.

Refs.: E-Brit; Hipkins 1948; Waterhouse 2003.

---

[305] Myers (1993:118) says Mahillon was succeeded in 1924 by Ernest Glosson (1870–1950).
[306] Myers 1993:117-8. Along with the instruments, Tagore also contributed a number of books about Indian music, which Jairazbhoy (1990:68-72) suggests provided Mahillon with an unacknowledged basis for his classification system.

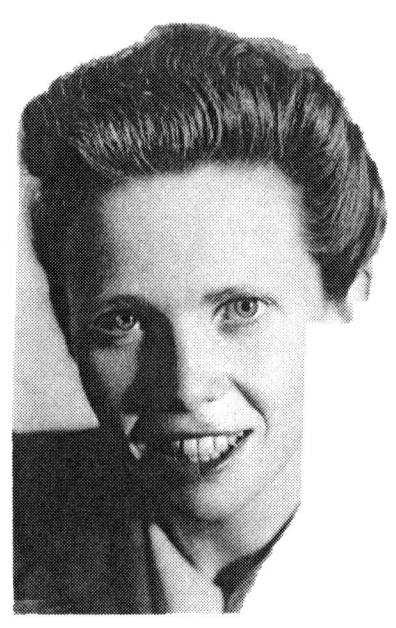

CLAUDIE MARCEL-DUBOIS (1913–1989)
French ethnomusicologist

Born: Tours, France, 19 Jan 1913
Died: Paris, France, 1 Feb 1989

Education:
Studied piano, Paris Conservatoire, 1926–28
Studied history, philology and ethnology, Institut d'Art et d'Archéologie, Paris, 1931–33
Studied, Institut d'Ethnologie, Paris, 1934–35
Studied, Ecole Pratique des Hautes Etudes, Paris, 1937–39

Qualifications:
Diploma, Ecole Pratique des Hautes Etudes, 1939

Appointments
Worked with Curt Sachs (q.v.) and André Schaeffner (q.v.), Department of ethnomusicology, Musée de l'Homme, 1934–40
Chargée de Mission des Musées de France, 1941
Founder/director, Department of ethnomusicology, Musée National des Arts et Traditions Populaires, 1945
Maître de recherche, Centre National de la Recherche Scientifique, Paris, 1957
Taught ethnomusicology, Ecole des Hautes Etudes en Sciences Sociales, Paris, 1961–?
Director, Centre National de la Recherche Scientifique, Paris, 1966–?

Honours:
Hon. doctorate, Laval University, Quebec, 1961

Writings:
See below.

****

Marcel-Dubois's work centred chiefly on the evolution of folk instruments and classification of folk music, especially French. For lists of her weritings see Kunst 1959a:#2732-2738 and Spieth-Weissenbacher 2003. For a full bibliography see Cheyronnaud 1990:-80-5.

Refs.: Cheyronnaud 1990; Spieth-Weissenbacher 2003.

SIBYL MARCUSE (1911–2003)
German/American scholar

Born: Frankfurt am Maine, Germany, 13 Feb 1911
Died: Berkeley, CA, USA, 3 May 2003

The photograph shows Marcuse tuning a harpsichord

Education and career:
Early education in a variety of European schools and languages
Studied at several European universities
Lived in China, 1932–35
Migrated to the USA after the outbreak of World War I in 1939
Worked for relief organisations in New York
Became a naturalised American citizen, 1945
Studied at a school for piano technicians, New York
Worked for harpsichord makers John Challis, Detroit, and Hugh Gough, London
Set up own business as a harpsichord and piano technician, New York
Curator, Yale University Collection of Musical Instruments, 1953–60

Honours:
Curt Sachs Award, American Musical Instrument Society, 1984 [307]

Writings:
See below.

****

Sibyl Marcuse is another person who was not nominally an ethnomusicologist, but deserves to be regarded as one because of her contribution to the discipline. Her expertise was in organology on a world-wide scale. Her dictionary of musical instruments (1964) remains a valuable standard work, despite the appearance of the multi-volume *New Grove Dictionary of Musical Instruments* two decades later.[308] As the cover description of Marcuse's dictionary indicates, it provides a comprehensive record of instruments from all round the world, "telling when, where, how and by whom thousands of musical instruments have been used." Her subsequent volume *A Survey of Musical Instruments* (1975) systematically traces the history of musical instruments in each of the major categories of the Sachs/Hornbostel classification system. Both volumes were a product of extensive travel and use of library resources both at Yale, and abroad, putting to use her ability to read scholarly literature in many languages.

Refs.: BRC-(A); Anon 2004; Schott 2003a & 2003b.

---

[307] Web page: http://www.amis.org/awards/sachs_marcuse.htm
[308] Sadie 1984.

COLIN McPHEE (1900–1964)
Canadian/American composer and ethnomusicologist

Born: Montreal, Canada, 15 Mar 1900
Died: Los Angeles, CA, USA, 7 Jan 1964

Education:
Studied piano and composition, Hambourg Conservatory, Toronto, c.1913–c.18
Studied piano and composition, Peabody Conservatory, Baltimore, 1918–21
Studied piano with Arthur Friedheim (1859–1932), Canadian Academy of Music, Toronto, 1921–24
Studied piano and composition, Paris Conservatoire and Schola Cantorum, 1924–26

Qualifications:
Teacher's certificate in piano, Peabody Conservatory, Baltimore, 1919
Diploma in composition, Peabody Conservatory, Baltimore, 1921

Appointments:
Musical adviser, Radio Program Bureau, Office of War Information, 1945–47
Faculty member, Institute of Ethnomusicology, UCLA, 1960–64

Honours:
National Institute of Arts and Letters Award, 1954

Field work:
Bali, Indonesia, 1931–38
UCLA Ethnomusicology Archives have eight sound tape reels of material collected by McPhee in Bali, 1961

Writings:
McPhee was principally a composer whose numerous works included orchestral, choral and other scores, including dozens of transcriptions, mostly for piano, of Indonesian gamelan music, which established him as a scholar relevant to ethnomusicology. His written legacy is primarily in two books: *A House in Bali* (1946) recounts his 1930s field experiences, and his magnum opus, *Music in Bali* (1966), reports the results of his research.

****

After completing his student years in Paris, McPhee spent five years as a professional musician in New York (1926–31), becoming involved there with "new music" activities in association with composer friends such as Aaron Copland (1900–90) and Henry Cowell (1897–1965). In 1931, after hearing recordings of gamelan music, he moved to Bali, where he spent most of the remainder of the decade enjoying an affluent life-style as a "gentleman scholar", supported financially by his wife, who had independent means. His creative energies as a composer waned during this period, and indeed ceased altogether [309] as his attention turned increasingly towards study of the gamelan. From 1939–52, his marriage at an end, McPhee was back in New York, subsisting – except for a spell of work with the war office – mostly on the proceeds of sporadic writing assignments and occasional speaking engagements. In 1952, McPhee's fortunes changed briefly with the arrival in New York of a Balinese concert group which played to full houses and received rave reviews. As a resident expert, McPhee was called upon to write previews, and a year later his Balinese-inspired composition, *Tabuh-Tabuban*, which became his best-known work, received an American premiere performance in New York. Its success was immediate, and resulted in a number of commissions for further works. For the last four years of his life, from 1960 onwards, McPhee taught at Mantle Hood's Institute of Ethnomusicology at UCLA. His book, *Music in Bali*, upon which he had been working for much of his life, was published posthumously in 1966. For a full biography of McPhee's life and work, see Carol Oja's book *Colin McPhee: Composer in Two Worlds* (2004).

Refs.: Escoffier 2002; Eth 8(2):iv (1964); Oja 2003; Oja 2004; UCLA Ethnomusicology Archive 2003b.

---

[309] Oja 2004:82.

ALAN P(ARKHURST) MERRIAM (1923–1980)
American ethnomusicologist

Born: Missoula, MT, USA, 1 Nov 1923
Died: near Warsaw, Poland, 14 Mar 1980

Qualifications:
BA in music theory and composition, Montana State University, 1947
MM Northwestern University, 1948
PhD in anthropology, Northwestern University, 1951
Topic: Songs of the Afro-Bahian Cults: An Ethnomusicological Analysis

Appointments and career:
Military Service, US Army Air Force; served in Italy, 1943-45
Instructor, Northwestern University, 1953–54
Assistant professor of sociology and anthropology, University of Wisconsin, 1954–56
Assistant professor of anthropology, Northwestern University, 1956–58
Associate professor of anthropology, Northwestern University, 1958–62
Professor of anthropology, Indiana University, 1962–80
Distinguished visiting professor, University of Montana, 1965
Fulbright visiting professor, University of Sydney, 1976
Visiting scholar, University of California, 1978

Offices:
Co-founder, Society for Ethnomusicology, 1953
Editor, *Ethnomusicology Newsletter*, 1952–57
Review Editor, *Journal of American Folklore*, 1957–58
President, Central States Anthropological Society, 1960–61
Chairman, American Council of Learned Societies, 1962–65
President, Society for Ethnomusicology, 1962–64
Editor, *Ethnomusicology*, 1975–78

Field work:
Flathead Indian, Western Montana, 1950, 1958
Basongye & Bashi, Zaïre, and Burundi, 1951–52, 1959–60, 1973

Writings:
For a full bibliography of Merriam's more than 300 publications, see Card & Rahkonen 1981b and Card & Rahkonen 1982. The latter is a reprint of the former, less an index of subjects and books reviewed.

* * * *

Merriam's impact upon ethnomusicology, and indeed his role in the very establishment of the discipline, was profound.

Merriam was one of the founders of the Society for Ethnomusicology in America, working hard both to create an organisation and as editor of the newsletter which helped to get the new discipline under way, transforming after a few issues into the *Journal of the Society for Ethnomusicology*. Trained in both music and anthropology, it was in the application of anthropology to music that Merriam was to make his mark. Single-handedly, he created a new sub-discipline with the publication of his book *The Anthropology of Music* in 1964. It appeared just in time to influence the present writer in the preparation of his doctoral thesis on Maori music,[310] for which Merriam was one of the examiners.

Alan Merriam's life was cut tragically short at the peak of his career by the well-known Polish air crash of 1980. On television, not knowing he had been a victim, we saw horrifying images of body-bags at the crash scene. Shortly before, Alan had written to me, somewhat bemused at being invited to Warsaw, where he was to address a conference, saying ironically: "As you know, Mervyn, I'm the world's greatest authority on Polish music!" When the plane went down, the news of Alan's death was broken to stunned international friends and colleagues by his closest friend, Frank Gillis. The Silver Jubilee of the Society for Ethnomusicology, held at his home campus of Indiana University not long afterwards, became a valedictory of a kind for him. He had obtained funding for me to attend the conference, where I chaired one of the sessions, took part in a panel discussion, and delivered a paper, but Alan's death cast a pall over the proceedings. Everyone who knew him had the same reaction. The Alan we all knew was "larger than life", a big man, both physically and in spirit, and it was hard to believe he was really dead. Many of us took years to come to terms with the event.

Refs.: BRC-(B);Eth 6(2):143-4 (1962); Gillis 1980; Morgan & Nettl 2003.

---

[310] McLean 1965a.

ALICE MARSHALL MOYLE (1908–2005)
South African-born Australian ethnomusicologist

Born: Bloemfontein, South Africa, 25 Dec 1908
Died: Sydney, Australia, 10 Apr 2005
Migrated to Australia with her parents as a child, c.1912

Qualifications:
BMus, piano and cello, University of Melbourne , 1930
BA (Hons), University of Sydney, 1954
MA, University of Sydney, 1957
Topic: Intervallic structure of Australian aborigine singing
PhD, Monash University, 1975
Topic: Styles and genres of Northern and Central Australian aborigine music

Appointments and career:
Private piano teacher, 1930–33
Music critic, *Wireless Weekly*, Sydney, 1939–43
Part-time teaching fellow, Music Department, University of Sydney, 1960–63
Research officer, Australian Institute of Aboriginal Studies, 1964–65 & 1974
Research fellow, Australian Institute of Aboriginal Studies, 1966–73

Offices:
President, Musicological Society of Australia, 1982–83

Honours:
Member of the Order of Australia, 1977
Honorary Fellow, Australian Academy of the Humanities, 1994
Doctor of Music (honoris causa), University of Sydney, 1989
Honorary doctorate, University of Melbourne, 1995

Field work:
Extensive field work among Australian aborigines, especially in the Northern Territory, under the auspices of the Australian Institute of Aboriginal Studies (now Australian Institute of Aboriginal and Torres Strait Islander Studies), of which she was a founding member.

Writings:
For a numbered list of Moyle's writings, discs and films, see Stubington 1984:372-81. Her papers are lodged with the Australian Institute of Aboriginal and Torres Strait Islander Studies in Canberra.

****

Already over 50 years old when she first became interested in Aborigine music, Alice Moyle dedicated most of the next 40 years of what proved to be a very long life to the study. By coincidence, her first field trip was in 1958, the same year that the present writer began field work among the New Zealand Maori and, compounding the coincidence, the supervisor for her MA thesis, the musicologist Peter Platt (1924–2000), who was then a Senior Lecturer at Sydney university, moved not long afterwards to New Zealand as Professor of Music at Otago University, where he supervised the present writer's MA thesis in 1958, and later his PhD.

Refs.: AIATSIS 2005; Stubington 1984.

CHARLES SAMUEL MYERS (1873–1946)
English psychologist

Born: London, England, 13 Mar 1873
Died: Winsford Glebe, near Minehead, Somerset, England, 12 Oct 1946

Education:
Studied mainly classics, City of London School, from age of 11, c.1884–90
Studied biology, chemistry and physics, St Bartholemew's Hospital, London, 1890–91
Studied natural sciences, Gonville and Caius College, Cambridge University, as foundation scholar, 1891–95

Qualifications:
1st class Natural Sciences Tripos, Cambridge University, 1893–95
BA, Cambridge University, 1895
MB, St Bartholomew's Hospital, London, 1898
MA, Cambridge University, 1901
MD, Cambridge University, 1902
ScD, Cambridge University, 1909

Appointments:
House physician, St Bartholomew's Hospital, 1899–1900
Demonstrator in experimental psychology, Cambridge University, 1904–05
Professor of psychology, King's College, London, 1906–09
Lecturer in experimental psychology, Cambridge University, 1909–11
Director, Laboratory for Experimental Psychology, Cambridge University, 1912–14
Consulting psychologist, British Armies in France, 1915–19
Reader in experimental psychology, University of Cambridge, 1919–27

Offices:
Editor, *British Journal of Psychology*, 1911–24
First president, British Psychological Society, 1920
Co-founder, National Institute of Industrial Psychology (NIIP), 1921
President, International Congress of Psychology, 1923
President, Section 1, British Association, 1922 & 1931

Honours:
FRS, 1915
CBE, 1919
Honorary DSc, University of Manchester, 1927
Honorary LLD, University of Calcutta
Honorary DSc, University of Pennsylvania

Field work:
Member, Cambridge Anthropological Expedition to Torres Straits and Sarawak, 1898–99

Writings:
See Kunst 1959a:#2943-51 for his contributions on music, all published within the single decade 1904–14. The most important of them are a chapter on music of the Veddas of Ceylon (1911), and two studies resulting from field work with the Cambridge Ethnological Expedition of 1898–99, on Torres Straits music (1912), and Sarawak music (1913–14).

****

Myers was a multi-talented individual who excelled in classics during his school days. He had aptitude also in languages, as well as a precocious ability in science. His love of music, he attributed to his mother, who "had exceptional powers of musical expression and pianoforte technique." [311] He himself played the violin, doing so in the hospital orchestra at St Bartholomew's Hospital, London, when he was a medical student there, and playing also in the Royal Amateur Orchestral Society, London. Later, when he began studies in Natural Sciences at Cambridge University, he reorganised the University Musical Club into amateur performance of chamber music in which, as a violinist, he "took a prominent part." [312]

In 1898, Myers accepted an invitation from Dr Alfred Cort Haddon (1855–1940) to take part in the Cambridge Ethnological Expedition of that year to Torres Strait and Sarawak. One of his tasks was to assist Haddon in anthropological investigation of native rites and customs. But his main work, in co-operation with the expedition psychologist, Dr William Halse Rivers (1864–1922), was a study of the hearing, smell, taste, reaction times, rhythm, and music of the peoples of the two regions. Myers's later publications on the music were significant contributions to ethnomusicology.

During 1912–14, Myers became director of a newly established Laboratory for Experimental Psychology at Cambridge University, for which he himself contributed much of the money for equipment. There, his research related mostly to "primitive music, synaesthesia, the influence of timbre and loudness on auditory localization, individual differences in the attitudes of listeners to musical sounds, and visual contrast." [313] At this time, Myers's work was strikingly similar to that of the Berlin Phonogram-Archiv under Stumpf (who was also a specialist in psycho-acoustics) and Hornbostel. As part of the work of his laboratory, it seems that Myers was assembling his own equivalent of the Berlin institution. "When the Great War came in August, 1914", Myers recalls, " I tried vainly to continue the work in which I was then engaged of studying the unique recordings of Australian music which the late Professor Baldwin Spencer had presented to the large collection of phonographic musical records which I had gathered together from all parts of the uncivilized world." [314]

Walter Baldwin Spencer (1860–1929) was an Australian anthropologist who conducted field work in central and northern Australia between 1894 and 1926. Myers was fully capable of ana-

---

[311] Myers 1936:217.
[312] Myers 1936:217.
[313] Myers 1936:222.
[314] Myers 1936:222.

lysing Baldwin Spencer's recordings at a standard comparable with that of Hornbostel and his Berlin associates. A British school of ethnomusicology could have ensued. But it was not to be. Although he was then 41 years old, Myers felt it his duty to help with the war effort. Rejected for service because of his age, he went to France where he was able to get himself appointed as hospital registrar at Le Touquet, later gaining a commission in the Royal Army Medical Corps in France, where he served for the remainder of the war, pioneering recognition of "shell-shock" as a medical condition, as an alternative to shooting soldiers for cowardice or sparing them only if regarded as "certifiably insane".

When the war ended, Myers returned to Cambridge for a single year, before giving up academia forever in reaction to lack of recognition for his work in applied psychology, and in favour of setting up an academically independent, though unendowed, National Institute of Industrial Psychology (NIIP), which he co-founded in 1921, thereafter devoting the rest of his working life to it. In so doing, he had lost his institutional base, and doubtless the collection of recordings he had assembled at Cambridge. It was the end of the line for his musical studies, and after 1914 there were no further music publications from him during the remaining more than 30 years of his life.

Refs.: Bartlett 2004; Cambridge University Archives (pers.comm.);[315] Myers 1936; Royal Society 2003; WWW v.4.

---

[315] Information concerning degrees. Source: UA Graduati 12/169.

S(IEGFRIED) F(ERDINAND) NADEL (1903–1956)
Austrian/British anthropologist

Born: Lemberg, Austria, 24 Apr 1903
Died: Canberra, Australia, 14 Jan 1956

Education:
Secondary schooling, Vienna
Studied piano and composition, Musik Akademie, Vienna, 1920
Studied musicology, psychology and philosophy, University of Vienna, where his teachers included Guido Adler and Robert Lach (q.v.), 1921–25
Postgraduate study in anthropology, London School of Economics under Bronislaw Malinowski and Charles G. Seligman, 1932–35

Qualifications:
DrPhil in psychology and philosophy, University of Vienna, 1925
Topic: Zur Psychologie des Konsonanzerlebens
PhD in anthropology, University of London, 1935
Topic: Political and religious structure of Nupe society

Appointments and career:
Assistant conductor, Dusseldörf Opera House, 1925
Led a student opera company on a tour of Czechoslovakia, 1927
Assistant, Psychologisches Institut, Vienna, 1927–c.31
Government anthropologist, Sudan, to investigate the Nuba tribes, 1938–41
Served in British Military Administration, Eritrea, with rank of Major and later Lieutenant-Colonel, 1942–45
Secretary for Native Affairs, British Military Administration, Tripolitania, 1945–46
Senior lecturer in anthropology, London School of Economics, 1946–47
Reader in anthropology, King's College, University of Durham, 1948–49
Foundation professor of anthropology and sociology, Research School of Pacific Studies, Australian National University, 1950–56

Honours:
Rivers Memorial Medal of the Royal Anthropological Institute, 1950

Field work:
Nupe and other groups, northern Nigeria, 1933–35

Writings:
See below.

****

Nadel's early life was devoted to the study and pursuit of music. At 17 years of age it was his ambition to become an orchestral conductor, or perhaps a composer. To this end he enrolled in the Musik Academie of Vienna, and soon afterwards began advanced instruction in pianoforte. A year afterwards he became a student at the Musikhistorisches Institut of the University of Vienna. Later, in 1923, he enrolled at the Psychologisches Institut at the same university, becoming interested thereafter mainly in the psychology of music. After his graduation from the university he nevertheless realised the first of his early ambitions by conducting opera, and working as a accompanist and conductor at the conservatorium of music. Evidence of a growing interest in music ethnography came with a series of programmes he compiled for Radio Vienna, which included illustrated surveys of African, Javanese, Caucasian and American Negro music, as well as exotic instruments such as the nose flute and marimba.

Two years after his graduation from the Psychologisches Institut, Nadel was hired as an assistant there, but continued to occupy himself also with music. Around 1931 he moved to Berlin to work on a biography of the composer Busoni, and there became an associate of Erich von Hornbostel (q.v), beginning work with him a year later, and also pursuing a study of African languages. This was a major turning point.

Because of his earlier residence in Vienna, Nadel is commonly regarded as a member of the Vienna school of comparative musicology, despite his subsequent move to Berlin and association with Hornbostel. Neither association, however, was to endure. Nadel's biography of Busoni, published in 1931, was the last of his writings on music. He continued to compose for a few years subsequently but, sadly, the fruits of these endeavours, which included MS scores of songs, string quartets, and a sketch for a piano concerto, were destroyed during a bombing raid on London in 1940. During the bulk of his career, Nadel chose to make a clean break with music. In 1932 he was granted a Rockefeller fellowship in association with the International Institute of African Languages and Culture, and travelled to London to undertake postgraduate studies in anthropology. During the rest of his career, which occupied him entirely from about the age of 30 until his death at the age of only 52, he became a renowned anthropologist, and an eminent specialist in the ethnography of the Nupe of Nigeria. For his writings relating to ethnomusicology see Kunst 1959a:#2954-60. A strange anomaly in the first entry on Kunst's list represents Nadel (could there have been more than one Siegfried Nadel?) as publishing it when he was only about 11 years old. His best-known ethnomusicology paper, representative of the Vienna school, and considered important enough for republication in McAllester's *Readings in Ethnomusicology* (1971), is his study of "The Origin of Music" (1930).

Refs.: Anth; LSE; NDB; Salat 2004; Stanner 1956.

BRUNO NETTL (1930–)
Czech born American ethnomusicologist

Born: Prague, Czechoslovakia, 14 Mar 1930

Qualifications:
AB, Indiana University, 1950
MA, Indiana University, 1951
PhD in musicology, Indiana University, 1953
MA in library science, University of Michigan, 1960

Appointments:
Visiting lecturer, University of Kiel, 1956–58
Librarian, Wayne State University, 1958–61
Associate professor of music, University of Illinois, 1962–66
Professor of music and anthropology, University of Illinois, 1967–92
Visiting professor, Washington, 1985, 1988, 1990; Louisville, 1983; Colorado College, 1992, 1998; Harvard, 1990; Carleton College, 1996

Offices:
President, Society for Ethnomusicology, 1970–71
Editor, *Yearbook for Traditional Music*, 1974–76
Editor, *Ethnomusicology*, 1961–65 and 1998–2002

Honours:
Distinguished Alumni Award, Indiana University, 1986
Fumio Koizumi Prize, Tokyo, 1993
Honorary doctorate, University of Chicago, 1993
Honorary doctorate, University of Illinois, 1996
Honorary doctorate of Humane Letters, Carleton College, 2000
Honorary doctorate, Kenyon College

Field work:
Native American, especially Blackfoot, 1960s, 1980s
Iran, 1966, 1968–69, 1972
Southern India, 1981–82

Writings:
There is scarcely a topic in ethnomusicology upon which Nettl has not at some time written, either in books or in papers for scholarly journals. See Bohlman 2003 for a select list of publications. See also the following for titles of some of Nettl's books.

****

Nettl's father was the well-known musicologist Paul Nettl (1889–1972), and his mother was a piano teacher and recitalist.[316] Nettl came to the United States at the age of about 9, in 1939, when his father left Czechoslovakia for America as a result of anti-semitism.

The following is Nettl's own self-evaluation of interests from his web page at the University of Illinois, including reference to some of his most recent publications:[317]

Research Interests

Principal interests: ethnomusicology; musical cultures of Native American peoples, Iran, and South India; theory and methodology of ethnomusicology; ethnomusicological study of Western classical music culture.

Selected Publications

Author of several books, including:

Theory and Method In Ethnomusicology (1964)
The Study of Ethnomusicology (1983)
Eight Urban Musical Cultures (1978)
Blackfoot Musical Thought (1989)
Heartland Excursions: Ethnomusicological Reflections on Schools of Music (1995)
The Radif of Persian Music (2nd ed. 1992)

A noteworthy recent book is his semi-autobiographical *Encounters in Ethnomusicology* (2002). For comments on Nettl's role in ethnomusicology, and some of his other writings, see elsewhere in the present book.

Refs.: BRC-(B); Bohlman 2003; Eth 4(1):45 (1960); Nettl 2002.

---

[316] Nettl 2002:16.
[317] Nettl 1998.

SIR FRANCIS TAYLOR PIGGOTT (1852–1925)
English judge and legal authority

Born: London, England, 25 Apr 1852
Died: London, England, 12 Mar 1925

Education:
Paris, Worthing College, and Trinity College, Cambridge University

Qualifications:
BA in law, Cambridge University, 1876
MA & LLM, Cambridge University, 1879

Career:
Called to Bar, 1874
Special mission to Italy, 1887
Legal adviser to British Minister of Japan, 1887–91
Secretary to the attorney-general, Sir Charles Russell, for the Bering Sea arbitration, 1893
Procureur and Advocate-General, Mauritius, 1894–1905
Acting Chief Judge, Mauritius, 1895–97
Secretary to the Attorney-General Sir CharlesRussell, MP, on the Behring Sea Arbitration, 1898
Chief Justice, Supreme Court, Hong Kong, 1905–12

Honours:
Knighted 1905

Field work:
Japan, 1887–91

Writings:
See below.

****

Piggott wrote a large number of legal works as well as a single work on music, *The Music and Musical Instruments of Japan* (1893), materials for which must have been gathered during his tenure as legal adviser to the British Minister of Japan. There is no information on what he was doing in 1892, when the book may have been written.

Refs: Cambridge University Archives (pers.comm.); Wesley-Smith 2004; WWW v.II

LUIS FELIPE RAMÓN Y RIVERA (1913–1993)
Venezuelan ethnomusicologist and composer

Born: San Cristóbal, Venezuela, 23 Aug 1913
Died: Caracas, Venezuela, 21 Oct 1993

Education:
Studied violin, viola, harmony, and theory of music, Escuela Superior de Música, Caracas, 1928–34
Studied folklore and musicology, under Carlos Vega (q.v.), Institute of Musicology, Buenos Aires, and Isabel Aretz (q.v.), whom he later married, Colegio Libre de Estudios Superiores, Buenos Aires, 1945–47

Qualifications:
Diploma as viola teacher, Escuela Superior de Música, Caracas, 1934

Appointments:
First violist, Orquesta Sinfónica Venezuela, 1934–38
Head, music section, Escuela de Artes y Oficios, San Cristóbal, 1939
Founder/director, Escuela de Música de Táchira, 1940–45
Chief of musicology, Servicio de Investigaciones Folklóricas Nacionales, Caracas, 1947–48
Director, Americana Orchestra, Buenos Aires, 1948–52
Director, National Institute of Folklore of Venezuela, Caracas, 1953–76

Offices:
President, Venezuelan Society of Authors and Composers, 1972–73
Co-founder, Fundación Internacional de Etnomusicología y Folklore, 1986.

Field work:
Extensive collection in Latin America, 1950s and 1960s

Writings:
See Béhague 2003.

****

Ramón y Rivera's main fields of study were Venezuelan folk and traditional music, and comparative study of Latin American music in general. As a composer his work was closely associated with the popular music of his home state of Táchira.

Refs.: Béhague 2003; Caroni Music 2004; Stevenson 1994.

KURT (AUGUST GEORG) REINHARD (1914–1979)
German ethnomusicologist and composer

Born: Giessen, Germany, 27 Aug 1914
Died: Wetzlar, Germany, 18 Jul 1979

Education:
Studied musicology and composition, University of Cologne, 1933–35
Studied musicology and ethnology, University of Leipzig, under Husmann (q.v.), and musicology, University of Munich, 1935–38

Qualifications:
Doctorate, University of Munich, 1938
Topic: Burmese music

Appointments:
Worked for Staatliche Musikinstrumentensammlung, Berlin, 1939–45
Head, Department of private music teaching, Petersen Conservatory, 1947–52
Director, Berlin Phonogram-Archiv, 1948–68
Privatdozent, Free University, Berlin, 1948
Professor of comparative musicology, Free University, Berlin, 1957–68

Field work:
Turkey, 1955

Writings:
See Eggebrecht 2003a and Kunst 1959a:#3370-88b.

****

Reinhard's chief scholarly interests were organology, the traditional music of China and Turkey, and ethnomusicology in music education. He also composed songs, chamber music, and orchestral music under the pseudonym Georg Beydemüller. His outstanding achievement was to rebuild the once-great Berlin Phonogram-Archiv after World War II, which had left it a shattered institution with dilapidated equipment and only 250 Edison cylinders, the remainder of the collection either destroyed or dispersed for safe-keeping to other institutions. Beginning work in an almost unsalaried capacity, Reinhard dedicated 20 years of his life to resurrecting the archive. By the time he retired in 1968, he left to his successors a collection that had grown more than a hundred times, to well over 25,000 recordings.

Refs.: BRC-(A); Christensen 1980; DBE; Eggebrecht 2003a.

WILLARD RHODES (1901–1992)
American ethnomusicologist

Born: Dashler, OH, USA, 12 May 1901
Died: Sun City, AZ, USA, 15 May 1992

Education:
Studied at Wittenberg College, Springfield, Ohio, 1922
Studied at Mannes School of Music, New York, 1923–25
Studied piano and composition from Alfred Cortot (1877–1962) and Nadia Boulanger (1887–1979), École Normale de Musique, Paris, 1925–27

Qualifications:
AB, BMus, Heidelberg College, Tiffin, Ohio, 1922
MA, Columbia University, 1925

Appointments:
Conductor and chorus master, American Opera Company, 1927–30
Assistant conductor, Cincinnati Summer Opera Company, 1928–33
Director of music, public schools of Bronxville, New York, 1935–37
Education specialist, Bureau of Indian Affairs, 1938–51
Associate in music, Columbia University, 1937–53
Professor of music, Columbia University, 1954–69

Offices:
Co-founder, Society for Ethnomusicology, 1953
President, Society for Ethnomusicology, 1956–58
President, Society for Asian Music, 1961
President, International Folk Music Council, 1968–73

Field work:
North American Indian, 1939–43, 1947, 1949–52
Zimbabwe and Zaire, 1958–59, 1961–62
South India, 1966
Nigeria, 1974

Writings:
For writings up to the date of Rhodes's retirement see Gillis 1969. See McAllester 1993 for a comprehensive list, with commentary.

****

Like so many ethnomusicologists, Rhodes was brought up in a family background of music. His father was a United Brethren pastor who led hymns and enjoyed singing in male quartets; his mother was a piano teacher and organist from whom Rhodes had his first piano lessons.

Rhodes is notable principally for his extensive field recordings, especially of North American Indian music, recorded from 1940 onwards while working for the Bureau of Indian Affairs, with equipment supplied in part by the Library of Congress. The original recordings are held by the Folksong Archive, Library of Congress, with duplicates at UCLA Archives, which also houses his later recordings. Altogether, Rhodes recorded more than 50 American Indian tribes, from 14 states, besides issuing LPs of selected items from his collection (ten with the Library of Congress, and another two under the Folkways label).

Tribes recorded during his North American field trips included Apache, Arapaho, Arikara, Assiniboine, Blackfeet, Caddo, Cheehallis, Cherokee, Cheyenne, Choctaw, Clayoquot, Comanche, Creek, Crow, Dakota/Sioux, Delaware, Havasupai, Hopi, Jemez, Kiowa, Kiowaa-Apache, Klallam, Klamath, Kwaakiutl, Laguna, Makah, Mandan, Navajo, Nez Perce, Nitinat, Paiute, Pawnee, Pima, Potowatomi, Quileute, Quinault, San Ildefonso, San Juan, Santa Clara, Shawnee, Shoshone/Bannock, Shoshone, Sioux (Lakota and Dakota), Skokomish/Twana, Snuqualmie, Taos, Tlingit, Ute, Walapai, WarmSprings, Washo, Wichita, Winnebago, Ykima, Zia, and Zuñi.[318]

Later, after becoming full professor at Columbia University, he undertook field trips to Africa, where he recorded 95 tapes, and to India, where he recorded 31 tapes. The famous and distinctive beard that became Rhodes's hallmark, was a product of a trip to the Kalahari Desert from which he also returned with a broken leg.

Refs.: Eth 7(1):66 (1967); Korson & Hickerson 1969; Library of Congress 1996; McAllester 1993; UCLA Ethnomusicology Archive 2003c.

---

[318] For an article about the collection, including field dates and locations, see Korson & Hickerson 1969.

HELEN HEFFRON ROBERTS (1888–1985)
American ethnomusicologist

Born: Chicago, IL, USA, 12 Jun 1888
Died: North Haven, CT, USA, 26 Mar 1985

Education:
Studied piano, Chicago Musical College, 1907–09
Studied piano, American Conservatory of Music, Chicago, 1910–11
Postgraduate piano studies, American Conservatory of Music, Chicago, 1913 & 1914
Studied anthropology, Columbia University, under Franz Boas (q.v.), 1916–19

Qualifications:
MA in anthropology, Columbia University, 1919
Topic: "Coiled Basketry in British Columbia and Surrounding Region."

Appointments:
Research assistant in anthropology and instructor, Institute of Human Relations (Institute of Psychology until 1929), Yale University, 1924–36

Offices:
Co-founder, American Society for Comparative Musicology, 1933
Co-founder, American Musicological Society, 1934
Treasurer/Secretary, American Society for Comparative Musicology, 1934–35
Secretary, American Society for Comparative Musicology, 1935–37
Member, Board of Directors, New Haven Symphony Orchestra, 1952–?
Secretary, New Haven Symphony Orchestra, 1969–?

Field work:
Jamaica, winter 1920–21
California, summer 1922
Hawaii, 1923–24
California, including Karuk, 1926–28
Rio Grande Pueblos, including Acoma, Cochita, Isleata and Taos, 1929–30

Writings:
For a bibliography of Roberts writings and unpublished manuscripts see Roberts 1967. See also Frisbie 1989 for an update.

****

Throughout the latter part of her long life, Helen Roberts was an enigmatic figure to most ethnomusicologists. It was rumoured she had gone blind shortly after publishing her 1926 book on Hawaiian music, in the preface of which she refers to "troublesome eyesight", which made it impossible for her to read the music proofs.[319] Her condition, however, was evidently successfully treated as, although she had to give up piano playing, she was still driving in her 80s. The main reason for the sudden cessation of a highly promising and productive career was loss of her job in 1936 when funding ran out for the Yale University Institute of Human Relations at which she worked. At this point in her life, Roberts, who had independent family means, chose to retire. She lived for another 49 years, travelled extensively for pleasure, cultivated her garden, and undertook philanthropic work but, except for acceding to a request to compile her bibliography, and informal help to students and colleagues, she was never again active in ethnomusicology.

Apart from her writings, which are exemplary, Roberts was an outstanding transcriber of music who has left a large such legacy for future scholars. After her graduation from Columbia University in 1919, she made transcriptions of Pawnee Indian music for Jesse Walter Fewkes (q.v.) and of California Indian and Nootka music for the linguist Edward Sapir (1884–1939).[320] In all, before retiring in 1936, she completed an astonishing total of almost 3000 transcriptions, of which about half were from her own field recordings.[321]

Refs.: Charlotte J. Frisbie (pers.comm.); Frisbie 1989; Krader 2003.

---

[319] Rpberts 1926:5.
[320] Frisbie 1989:99.
[321] Frisbie 1989:107.

CURT SACHS (1881–1959)
German/American musicologist and ethnomusicologist

Born: Berlin, Germany, 29 Jun 1881
Died: New York, NY, USA, 5 Feb 1959

Education:
As a youth, Sachs attended the Französisches Gymnasium in Berlin and at the same time took lessons in piano, music theory, composition, and clarinet. At the University of Berlin he studied music history and the history of art, taking his doctorate in the latter subject.

Qualifications:
PhilD, in history of art, Berlin, 1904
Topic: Plastic Art in the Italian Renaissance

Appointments:
Director, Staatliche Instrumentensammlung, Berlin, 1919
Lecturer , University of Berlin, 1919–20
Reader , University of Berlin, 1921–27
Professor , University of Berlin, 1928–33
Worked with André Schaeffner (q.v.), Musée du Trocadero, Paris, 1933–37
Visiting Professor, Sorbonne, Paris, 1933
Professor of music, New York University, 1937–53
Adjunct Professor of music, Columbia University, New York, 1953–59

By 1933, having trained primarily as an art historian, Sachs had long since turned to music and was by now well established as a successful curator of the state collection of musical instruments in Berlin, which he completely reorganised, and at the same time held office as a full professor at the University of Berlin. In that year, however, in common with other Jewish intellectuals, Sachs was deprived of all his appointments by the Nazi regime and forced to leave Germany. After a sojourn in Paris from 1933–37, during which he worked at the Musée de l'Homme with André Schaeffner (q.v.), he made his way to the United States and spent the rest of his professional life there.

Offices:
President, American Musicological Society, 1948–52
Honorary President, Society for Ethnomusicology, 1957–59

Honours:
Honorary doctorate, Hebrew Union College
Honorary doctorate, Free University of Berlin
Ordinarius emeritus, West German Government

Writings:
See following.

****

Sachs's most enduring work was as an organologist. An early outcome was his *Reallexikon der Musikinstrumente* (1913), taking the form for the first time of an alphabetical listing of instruments from "all times and nations." The following year he and Erich von Hornbostel (q.v.) published their "Systemtik der Musikinstrumente" in which they set out the principles of their jointly devised, and later to become standard, Sachs-Hornbostel system for classifying musical instruments. Also noteworthy from Sachs's time in Berlin is his *Handbuch der Musikinstrumentenkunde* (1920).

It is as a comparativist and populariser of world music, however, that Sachs is best known. Though his scholarship is flawed by a now discredited evolutionary approach to music history, he is described in the New Grove dictionary as "a giant among musicologists, as much because of his astounding mastery of a number of subjects as because of his ability to present a comprehensive view of a vast panorama." His books include *World History of the Dance* (1937), *The History of Musical Instruments* (1940), *The Rise of Music in the Ancient World* (1943), *Rhythm and Tempo* (1953), *A Short History of World Music* (1956), and his posthumous *The Wellsprings of Music* (1963). See also Kunst 1959a:#3526-79, and Brown 2003.

Refs.: BRC-(A); Brown 2003; E-Brit; Geiringer 1948; Kunst 1959b.

ANDRÉ SCHAEFFNER (1895–1980)
French musicologist and ethnomusicologist

Born: Paris, France, 7 Feb 1895
Died: Paris, France, 11 Aug 1980

Education:
Studied piano, harmony and composition, Schola Cantorum, Paris, 1921–24
Studied ethnology, Institut d'Ethnologie, Paris, 1932–33
Studied ethnology, Ecole Pratique des Hautes Etudes, Paris, 1934–37

Qualifications:
Diploma in religious science and archaeology, Ecole du Louvre, Paris, 1940

Appointments and career:
Founder/director, music department, Musée d'Ethnographie du Trocadéro (later Musée de l'Homme), Paris, 1929–65
Cataloguer, Paris Conservatoire Library, 1932–41
Cataloguer, Centre National de la Recherche Scientifique, 1941–65
Artistic secretary, Orchestre symphonique de Paris, 1929–31
Artistic secretary, Concerts de la Pléiade, 1943–47
Teacher, Institut d'Ethnologie, Paris, 1936–43

Offices:
President, Société Française de Musicologie, 1958–61

Field work:
Six expeditions to West Africa, 1931–58

Writings:
For a bibliography see Krader 1958.

****

Schaeffner's principal significance to ethnomusicology was as an organologist and founder/administrator of the musical instruments section of the Musée de l'Homme in Paris. Ethnomusicologists who worked with the collection during Schaeffner's tenure included Curt Sachs (q.v.) from 1933–37, Claudie Marcel-Dubois (q.v.) from 1934–40, Constantin Brailoiu (q.v.) from 1948–53, and John Blacking (q.v.) in 1952.

Refs.: BRC-(A); Rouget 1981; Spieth-Weissenbacher & Gribenski 2003b.

MARIUS SCHNEIDER (1903–1982)
German comparative musicologist

Born: Hagenau, Alsace, 1 Jul 1903
Died: Marquartstein, Germany, 10 Jul 1982

Education:
Studied philology and musicology at the universities of Strasbourg and Paris
Studied piano with Alfred Cortot (1877–1962), at the Paris Conservatoire, bef. 1923

Qualifications:
Doctorate under Johannes Wolf, Berlin University, 1930
Topic: 14th century European Ars Nova

Appointments:
Assistant to Erich von Hornbostel (q.v.), Berlin Phonogram-Archiv, 1932–34
Director, Berlin Phonogram-Archiv, 1935–44
Founder/Director, Department for Ethnomusicology, Instituto Español de Musicología, Barcelona, 1944
Lecturer, Consejo Superior de Investigaciones Cientificas, Barcelona University, 1947–55
Taught at University of Cologne, 1955–68
Taught at University of Amsterdam, 1968–70

Writings:
See below.

****

Schneider's most long-standing interest was in the history and world-wide distribution of polyphony; he published a book on the subject in 1934, just four years after gaining his doctorate, and reissued it with additional material the year after his retirement from the University of Cologne.[322] He is best known for his adherence to the methods of the Berlin School of comparative musicology, of which he remained a leading exponent after his elevation to director of the Berlin Phonogram-Archiv, when Hornbostel, followed by Sachs and others, was dismissed by the Nazi regime. Although most of his writings were in German, Schneider's approach became familiar to speakers of English as a result of his long article on primitive music in volume 1 of the *New Oxford History of Music* (1957), at a time when such methods and assumptions had already been superseded in the United States of America.[323] For a full list of Schneider's writings, see Günther 1969.

Refs.: BRC(A); Günther 2003.

---

[322] Schneider 1969.
[323] The choice of Schneider for this task would have that of the editor of the volumes, Egon Wellesz (1885-1974), who was Austrian and would have been familiar with Schneider's work.

CHARLES (LOUIS) SEEGER (1886–1979)
American composer and musicologist

Born: Mexico City, Mexico, 14 Dec 1886
Died: Bridgewater, CT, USA, 7 Feb 1979

Education:
Early education by tutor in Mexico
Attended Hackley School, Terrytown, New York, before entering Harvard University

Qualifications:
BA in music, Harvard University, 1908

Appointments:
Volunteer conductor, Cologne Opera, Germany, 1910–11
Professor of music, University of California, Berkeley, 1912–19
Lecturer, Institute of Musical Arts, New York, 1921–33
Lecturer, New School for Social Research, New York, 1931–35
Technical adviser on music, Roosevelt Resettlement Administration, Washington DC, 1935–37
Assistant to director, Federal Music Project, Washington DC, 1937–41
Chief, Music division of the Pan-American Union, 1941–53
Visiting professor, Yale University, 1949–50
Research associate in folklore, University of California, Los Angeles, 1957–70
Research associate, Institute of Ethnomusicology, University of California, Los Angeles, 1961–71
Lecturer, Harvard University, 1972

Offices and affiliations
Founder/chairman, New York Musicological Society, 1930–34 [324]
Member, Composers' Collective, New York, 1931–35 [325]
Vice-president, Gesellschaft für Vergleichende Musikwissenschaft, 1935–36
President, American Society for Comparative Musicology, 1933–36
Chairman, American Library of Musicology, 1933–36
President, American Musicological Society, 1945–46
Co-founder, Society for Ethnomusicology, 1953
President, Society for Ethnomusicology, 1960–61
Honorary president, Society for Ethnomusicology, 1972–79

Honours:
D Fine Arts, University of California at Berkeley, 1968
Comendador, Orden al Merito, Chile

---

[324] When this started it had only five people in it (Dunaway 1980:162).
[325] Dunaway 1980:159.

Writings:
"Charles Seeger: Selective Bibliography, 1923–1966," in *Anuario interamericano de investigación musical/Yearbook for Inter-American Musical Research/Anuario interamericano de pesquisa musical*, 2:37–42 (1966). For a select list of about 40 publications, see *Yearbook of the International Folk Music Council*, 11:79-82 (1979). For a complete bibliography of Seeger's writings and a list of his compositions, see Peacatello 1992:317-28. For the full text of 18 selected essays of Seeger's own choice, see Seeger 1977.

****

Seeger is renowned for his theoretical ideas on music. For a biography see Pescatello 1992. For books which seek to explain his thought, see Greer 1998 and Yung & Rees 1999. For an assessment of his influence on ethnomusicology, see elsewhere in the present book.

Refs.: ANB; BRC-(B); Eth 4(2):99 (1960); Hood 1979; Pescatello 2003; Rhodes 1979.

ALFRED SENDREY (1884–1976)
Hungarian/American conductor, composer and musicologist

Born: Budapest, Hungary, 29 Feb 1884
Died: Los Angeles, CA, USA, 3 Mar 1976

Education:
Studied philosophy and composition at the university and Royal Hungarian Academy of Music, Budapest, 1901–05
Studied musicology, University of Leipzig, 1930–32

Qualifications:
PhD, University of Leipzig, ?1932

Career:
Opera conductor, Cologne (1905–7), Mülhausen (1907–9), Brno (1908–11), Philadelphia and Chicago (1911–12), Hamburg (1912–13), New York (1913–14), Berlin-Charlottenburg (1914–16), Vienna (1916–18), and Leipzig (1918–24)
Conductor, Leipzig Symphony Orchestra, 1924–32
Music director, Central German Radio, Berlin, 1932
Teacher, Klindworth-Scharwenka Conservatory, 1932
Radio programme director, Radiodiffusion National, Paris, 1933–40
Teacher, 92nd Street Young Men's Hebrew Association, 1941–45
Teacher of composition and conducting, Westlake College of Music, Los Angeles, 1945–52
Music director, Fairfax Synagogue, Virginia, 1952–56
Music director, Sinai Temple, Springfield, Massachusetts, 1956–64
Professor of Jewish music, University of Judaism, Los Angeles, 1962–72

Honours:
Honorary doctorate, University of Judaism, 1967

Writings:
Sendrey's classic *Bibliography of Jewish Music* (1951), containing thousands of entries, formed the basis both for his own future scholarly work, and that of many others. His best known studies are *Music in Ancient Israel* (1969), *The Music of the Jews in the Diaspora* (1970), and *Music in the Social and Religious Life of Antiquity* (1974). For other writings see Katz 2003f.

****

As can be seen from the list of his appointments above, Sendrey spent most of his career as a conductor of opera, teacher, and music director, turning to scholarship principally in the last decades of his life.

Refs.: Israel J. Katz (pers.comm.); Katz 2003g.

CECIL SHARP (1859–1924)
English folk song collector, editor and writer

Born: London, England, 22 Nov 1859
Died: London, England, 23 Jun 1924

Education:
Miss Bennett's private school, Lansdowne House, Brighton, c.1866–68
Uppingham Public School, 1869–74
George Heppel coaching school, Highfield, Weston-super-Mare, 1874–?
Private coaching from Rev J.T. Sanderson, Royston, ? –?
Clare College, Cambridge University, 1879–82

Qualifications:
Passed the first examinations for BMus at Cambridge University but did not complete the degree
BA in mathematics, Cambridge University, 1883

Career:
Clerk of Arraigns, South Australia, 1884–87
Assistant organist and choir master, Adelaide Cathedral, Australia, 1884–89
Partner and co-director, Adelaide College of Music, Australia, 1889–91
Conductor, Finsbury Choral Association, 1892-96
Staff member, Metropolitan College, Holloway, 1893–97
Music master, Ludgrove Preparatory School, England, 1893–1910
Principal, Hampstead Conservatoire of Music, England, 1896–1905

Honours:
Honorary MusM, Cambridge University, 1923

Field work:
Somerset and other English counties, 1903 onwards
Appalachian mountain area, USA, with Maud Karpeles, 1916–18

Writings:
Sharp's first publication was *Folk Songs from Somerset*, issued in five parts between 1904 and 1909. *English Folk Song: Some Conclusions*, the first serious comprehensive study of the subject, followed in 1907, and remained in print through several editions for more than 60 years. His first publication on dance was *The Morris Book* (1907–13). For a full listing of writings see Karpeles 1967, pp.201-8.

Pioneers of Ethnomusicology: Part III

****

In 1882, Sharp emigrated to Australia, where, after obtaining elementary legal instruction, he became Clerk of Arraigns and an associate to the chief justice of South Australia. In 1889 he switched careers to music and became assistant organist at Adelaide Cathedral and co-director of the Adelaide College of Music, besides taking an active part in Adelaide musical life, acting as honorary director of a string quartet club, and conducting choirs. After gaining many private pupils in piano, singing, composition and music theory, in 1889 he entered into a partnership to become joint director of the Adelaide College of Music for young women,[326] soon doubling its attendance to 60 pupils. In 1892, he returned to England, becoming a music master at Ludgrove Preparatory School and principal of the Hampstead Conservatoire of Music. Sharp's musical activities were all the more remarkable as, except for piano lessons taking part in singing classes as a schoolboy at Uppingham Public School, and taking some examinations towards a BMus while at Clare College, Cambridge, he was self-taught in music and had no formal qualifications in the subject.

Two events are said to have interested Sharp in English folk song and dance. In 1899 he saw folk dancing at Oxford, and in 1903 at Hambridge, Somerset, he heard a gardener sing "The Seeds of Love."

In 1905, he founded the English Folk Dance Society, and, in a campaign of lectures and publications, initiated the teaching of folk song and folk dance in English schools, beginning a movement that led to an English folk song revival and the use of folk song by composers such as Ralph Vaughan Williams (1872–1958), Gustav Holst (1874–1934), and others. In 1910 he resigned his position as music master at Ludgrove Preparatory School, where he had taught for 18 years, and thereafter subsisted entirely on lecture fees and royalties.[327]

As a collector of folk song, Sharp's most noteworthy effort took place during World War I when, with Maud Karpeles (q.v.) as his assistant, he made a celebrated 46-week field trip to the Southern Appalachian mountain area of the United States, when English folk songs, some long extinct in the home country, were collected.

In his book *English Folk Song: Some Conclusions* (1909) he enunciated his famous principles of historical continuity, individual variation and community selection that became the cornerstone of the International Folk Music Council, as promoted by his long-term supporter and advocate Maud Karpeles.

Refs.: Anon 1912; Cambridge University Archives (pers.comm.); E-Brit; Fox Strangways 1933; Heaney 2004b; Howes 2003; Karpeles 1967.

---

[326] Later, in 1898, it became the Elder Conservatorium of Music.
[327] Karpeles 1967"78.

JOSHUA STEELE (1700–1796)
?Irish engineer, speech and music theorist, and writer

Born: ?Ireland, c.1700
Died: Barbados, Caribbean islands, 27 Oct, 1796

****

Steele lived for many years in London where, in 1756, he was elected a member, and in 1779 vice-president, of the Society of Arts, Manufactures and Commerce. His correspondence with the Society relates mostly to practical matters such as ship tonnage, an engine for sugar mills, flax growing, silk grass, salt works, and the like. In 1780 he removed from London to estates he owned in Barbados, where he was active in attempting to secure more liberal treatment for slaves.

Steele is remembered principally as a pioneer of speech analysis, but he deserves recognition also for his extremely early work on musical instruments. Soon after the return to London of Captain James Cook's second voyage around the world in 1772, Steele published the results of his examination of two Tongan panpipes and a Tahitian nose flute supplied to him from the expedition by Furneaux and Banks.[328] His notation of the pitches of one of the Furneaux panpipes has been verified by a later almost identical independent notation by Richard Moyle, which is a testament to the accuracy of Steele's work.[329]

Refs.: Cragg 2004; Kassler 2003; RSA Archive; Stephen & Lee 1908–09: vol. XVII.

---

[328] Steele 1775a & 1775b.
[329] McLean 1999:132.

(FRIEDRICH) CARL STUMPF (1848–1936)
German psychologist, acoustician and musicologist

Born: Wiesentheid, Franconia, Germany, 21 Apr 1848
Died: Berlin, Germany, 25 Dec 1936

Education:
Latin school, Kitzingen, 1858
Gymnasium, Bamburg, 1859–63
Gymnasium, Aschaffenburg, 1864–65
Studied philosophy and theology, University of Würzburg, 1865–68
Studied briefly for priesthood, Eclesiastical seminary, Würzburg, 1869
Studied philosophy and natural sciences, University of Göttingen, ?–1870

Qualifications:
Graduated University of Würzburg, 1868
DrPhil, University of Göttingen, 1870

Appointments:
Privatdozent, University of Göttingen, 1870–73
Professor of philosophy, University of Würzburg, 1873–79
Professor of philosophy, University of Prague, 1879–84
Professor of philosophy, University of Halle, 1884–89
Professor of philosophy, University of Munich, 1889–94
Professor of philosophy, Friedrich-Wilhelm University, Berlin, 1894–1921
Founder/director, Psychologisches Institut, Berlin, 1894

Honours:
Doctor Honoris, Berlin University, 1910

Writings:
Stumpf's first important work bearing upon music was a 2-volume work on tone psychology, the first systematic treatment of this subject.[330]

His first publication of an ethnomusicological nature was a paper in 1886 of the songs of Bella Coola Indians from British Columbia, who had visited Berlin.[331] It appeared in the second issue of the journal in which Adler defined comparative musicology (vergleichende Musikwissenschaft), and on this account, though not quite accurately, is often regarded as initiating the new science.[332]

---

[330] Stumpf 1883-90.
[331] Stumpf 1886a.
[332] Papers in the first issue of this journal the previous year have a possibly better claim.

Later in the same journal is a review by Stumpf of A.J. Ellis's "On the Musical Scales of Various Nations", a publication which influenced Stumpf's own subsequent work.

In the following year, Stumpf signalled his continuing interest in non-Western music with another contribution to Adler's journal, this time on Mongolian song.[333]

In 1892, again in Adler's journal, Stumpf published an evaluation of methods used by Benjamin Ives Gilman (q.v.) the previous year to transcribe cylinder recordings of North American Indian music by Jesse Walter Fewkes (q.v.), who was the first to make field recordings in North America. Both the recordings and Gilman's analysis of them were highly significant developments, and Stumpf immediately saw the potential for further such work, advocating in this article the formation of sound archives which would gather together such recordings and make them available for analysis. It was advice that Stumpf himself was later to follow with his foundation of the Berlin Phonogram-Archiv.

For further publications by Stumpf, see Kunst 1959a: #3984-99 and Weller 2003.

****

Stumpf's especial talent was to combine science with music. It was his good fortune to be born into a highly educated and accomplished family. His father was a physician, and his two uncles on his father's side were both active in science. His paternal grandfather was a noted historian, and his maternal grandfather a court physician who came to live with the Stumpfs after his retirement, and taught young Carl the rudiments of Latin. Also on this side of the family were "remarkably many doctors", and no fewer than three university professors, all of whom Stumpf knew personally. With such a background, Stumpf comments in his autobiography that the love of medicine and natural sciences was in his blood. His love of music, which at first was even greater, he attributes to his father, who was an excellent singer, and his mother, who was a good pianist. His own account of his early musical development is worth quoting in full:

> Even in Kitzingen from singing in the massbooks, I had learned the old-fashioned notes of the four-line system, and could soon sing at sight in any key.
>
> At Bamberg we had a complete orchestra which met regularly at the free-standing Aula-building for practice under the direction of the excellent conductor Dietz. One could learn to play any instrument, free of charge. At the age of seven, I had commenced to study the violin, and during my student years had several opportunities to play in public. Besides this, I had learned without instruction to play five other instruments with more or less success. When we played or sang together at home, the leadership was left to me, and I formed the habit of hearing music analytically, i.e., by following the single voices or parts. Quite objectively speaking, I cannot understand how, without this ability, one can really appreciate in polyphonic music the beauty of the pattern, the weaving in and out of the individual voices, composition in the true sense. The copying of notes, which for reasons of economy I practiced assiduously also aided me to gain an insight into the trade secrets of music, as it served Rousseau in a similar manner. In my tenth year I began to compose (my very first work was an oratorio, "The Walk to Emmaus," for three

---

[333] Stumpf 1887.

> male voices), and during the last years of my course this developed into a dominating passion while I was studying the theory of harmony and counterpoint in the manuals of Silcher, Lobe, and Gottfried Weber. I composed quartets for strings and other pieces, but unfortunately inspiration did not always keep step with labored reflection. The only product of any originality was a scherzo in complete 5/4 time. Thus, at the age of seventeen, I entered the university with more love of music than of erudition.[334]

Stumpf's early interest in music turned to philosophy, at the university of Würzburg and later, interrupted by an abortive year studying for the priesthood, to psychology, at Göttingen. At Würzburg and Göttingen he successively came under the influence of Franz Brentano (1838–1917), founder of "act psychology", or "internationalism", and Rudolf Lotze (1817–1881), a perceptual theorist under whom he completed his doctorate. In his social life music continued to be important to him. During his student years with Lotze, he played cello for quartets during musical evenings at Lotze's house. And later at Würzburg a mutual admiration for Beethoven's Trio in B Major brought him together with his future wife. Increasingly, however, music and science became conjoined in his professional life also. As a result, Stumpf became noted principally for his contributions to psycho-acoustics and problems of sound perception. In a series of papers he introduced and elaborated his own theory of consonance, which he called "sound fusion" ('Verschmelzungstheorie'), prompting attention to this subject by his later followers, especially Mieczyslaw Kolinski (q.v.). His role as a founder of comparative musicology began as a result of his establishment of the Psychological Institute of Berlin in 1894, and the incorporation into it, in 1900, of a sound archive that later became the Berlin Phonogram-Archiv under the direction of his student, Erich von Hornbostel (q.v.).

Refs.: BRC-(A); E-Brit; Stumpf 1930; Vir.Lab; Weller 2003.

---

[334] Stumpf 1930:390-1.

RAJA SIR SOURINDRO MOHUN TAGORE (1840–1914)
Indian scholar and patron of Indian music

Born: Calcutta, India, 1840
Died: Calcutta, India, 5 Jun 1914

Education:
Studied Sanskrit, Hindu College, Calcutta, c.1849–58
Studied sitar from Indian master musicians, c.1847–58
Received private instruction in Western music from Anglo-Indian tutors

Offices:
Sponsor and founder Bengali Music School, 1871
Founder Bengal Music Academy, 1882

Honours:
Commander in the Order of Leopold
Commander in the Order of Albert of Sax
Chevalier of the Imperial Order of Medjedieh
Officer of the Academy of the Institute of France
Honorary member of the Royal Academy of St Cecilia of Rome
Doctor of Music, University of Philadelphia
Honorary doctorate, University of Oxford, 1896
Many honorary memberships and awards from c.30 countries in Asia and Europe.

Writings:
See Kunst 1959a:#4022-32, and references in the publications cited below. A particularly important publication was his *Hindu Music from Various Authors* (1882), which brought together writings in English from a number of earlier scholars.

****

A member of one of the richest and most influential families in 19th century Calcutta, Tagore devoted himself to the promotion of Hindu music both at home and abroad, becoming extremely well known as a result. Though not an ethnomusicologist, he is important for his influence upon the nascent discipline in Europe, as a result both of his writings and of his gifts of books and musical instruments to prominent individuals, schools, and museums. Victor Mahillon's classification of musical instruments into four classes, which became the foundation of the Sachs-/Hornbostel system, mirrored that of Tagore, set out half a decade earlier (1875), with which Mahillon must have been familiar; research on Indian scales, by Alexander Ellis in England, and by Abraham and Hornbostel in Germany, was based upon Tagore's prior publication *The Musical Scales of the Hindus* (1884); and descriptions by various writers of Indian musical instruments, based on European museum collections, beginning with Mahillon (1880), and including Sachs (1914), all made use of instruments donated by Tagore and manufactured according to his specifications.[335]

Refs.: Bor 1988; Capwell 1991; Jairazbhoy 1990; Trasoff 2003.

---

[335] Bor 1988:64.

HUGH TRAVERS TRACEY (1903–1977)
English/South African farmer and ethnomusicologist

Born: Willand, Devon, England, 29 Jan 1903
Died: Krugersdorp, Transvaal, South Africa, 23 Oct 1977

Education:
Educated in Bath, England.

Appointments:
Regional director for Natal, South African Broadcasting Corporation, 1935–47

Offices:
Co-founder, African Music Society, 1947
Secretary, African Music Society, 1948–53
Founder, International Library of African Music, Roodepoort, 1954
Editor, *African Music*, 1955–71

Honours:
Honorary DMus, University of Capetown, 1965

Field work:
Extensive recording in Zimbabwe and elsewhere in sub-Saharan Africa from 1929 onwards, at first on acetate discs using clockwork apparatus, and later using magnetic tape.

Writings:
Although Tracey acknowledged he was "not a musician", and was also not an anthropologist, he was able to write useful general works as well as an authoritative book focusing on musical instruments, *Chopi Musicians* (1970) in which he analysed the structure of Chopi xylophone orchestras.[336] For his other writings see Duran 2003 and Kunst 1059a:#4115-36j.

****

Hugh Tracey migrated from Devon, England to Southern Rhodesia (now Zimbabwe) in 1921, establishing himself as a tobacco farmer. In 1929, having become interested in the singing of his plantation workers, he began recording their music, thereafter recording ever more extensively throughout sub-Saharan Africa, and ultimately establishing his International Library of African Music in order to disseminate the results. In all, he edited and issued over 200 LP recordings besides numerous 78 rpm recordings. As well, he publicised the music by means of radio broadcasts and lectures delivered at some 50 universities in the USA, Britain and Africa.

Refs.: Duran 2003; Jones 1977; Andrew Tracey (pers.comm.).

---

[336] Tracey 1948/1970.

J.A. VAN AALST (1858–?)
Belgian writer on Chinese music

Born: Narnur, Belgium, 14 Oct 1858

Career:
Postal clerk, Guandong Province, China, 1881–82
Postal clerk, Customs Service, Beijing, 1883–95
Deputy Commissioner and Acting Audit Secretary, Customs Service, Beijing, 1896–98
Commissioner and Postal Secretary, Beijing, 1899–1901
Commissioner, Chinese Revenue Department, Samshut, Amoy, and Wuchow, 1902–14

Honours:
Order of the Double Dragon, 2nd Division, 3rd Class
Chevalier and Officer of the Order of Leopold, Belgium
Chevalier of the Order of Orange, Nassau, Holland
Laureat of the Conservatory of Ghent (Composition and Harmony), 1875

Writings:
Chinese Music (1884)

****

Van Aalst's book on Chinese music (1884) was evidently written for distribution at an International Health Exhibition held in London in 1884, when lectures on Chinese music were delivered by Van Aalst, most likely as an adjunct of Chinese performances which probably took place. Nothing is known of Van Aalst's musical background except that he played the flute, violin and hautboy at amateur performances in Beijing, arranged by the Inspector General there, Sir Robert Hart (1835–1911), who is credited with introducing one of the first Western brass bands into China.

Ref.: Kuo-Huang 1988.

CARLOS VEGA (1898–1966)
Argentine musicologist and folklorist

Born: Cañuelas, near Buenos Aires, Argentina, 14 Apr 1898
Died: Buenos Aires, Argentina, 10 Feb 1966

Education:
Attended High School, Cañuelas
Studied violin at age 17, and guitar later in Buenos Aires
Studied ethnography, Argentine Museum of Natural Sciences, Buenos Aires
Taught himself musicology and folklore

Appointments:
Head of musicology, Museo de Ciencias Naturales de Buenos Aires (Argentine Museum of Natural Sciences), 1926–?
Founder/director, Instituto de Musicología, Buenos Aires, 1931–?
Taught musicology, Universidad Católica Argentina, Buenos Aires

Honours:
National History and Folklore Prize, 1947
Honorary member of many institutions at home and abroad

Field work:
Numerous field trips throughout Argentina and other South American countries, collecting several thousand items of folk music and dance, 1931–c.50

Writings:
See Aretz 1966a:320-1, Aretz 1966b:82, and Béhague 2004b.

Refs.: Aretz 1966a; Aretz 1966b; Béhague 2004b.

KLAUS P(HILIPP) WACHSMANN (1907–1984)
German/British ethnomusicologist

Born: Berlin, Germany, 8 Mar 1907
Died: Tisbury, Wiltshire, England, 17 Jul 1984

Education:
High school education at Arndt-Gymnasium, Dahlem, Berlin, ?–1926
Studied law, Berlin, c.1927–30
Studied musicology and comparative musicology with Hornbostel (q.v.), Sachs (q.v.) and others, Berlin University, c.1930–33
Continued music studies, University of Fribourg, Switzerland, 1933–35
Postgraduate studies in Bantu languages and phonetics, School of Oriental and African Studies, London, 1936

Qualifications:
PhD, University of Fribourg, Switzerland, 1935
Topic: Pre-Gregorian chant

Appointments:
Assistant and Acting Educational Secretary-General, Protestant Mussions, Uganda, 1944–47
Curator, Uganda Museum, Kampala. 1948–57
Scientific officer (ethnology), Wellcome Foundation, London, 1958–63
Professor of music, Institute of Ethnomusicology, UCLA, 1963–68
Professor of music and linguistics, Northwestern University,1968–75
Visiting professor of music, University of Texas, 1976–77
Visiting professor, University of Edinburgh, 1978
Visiting professor, Queen's University, Belfast, 1978
Richard Merton Gast Professor, Institute of Ethnomusicology, University of Cologne, 1978–79

Offices:
President, Society for Ethnomusicology, 1967–69
President, International Folk Music Council, 1973–77

Honours:
Bronze medal, Royal African Society, 1958
Order of Merit, Federal Republic of Germany, 1984

Field work:
Uganda 1949, 1950 & 1954

Writings:
For a complete listing see Seeger & Wade 1977:390-3.

****

Wachsmann was another, like Sachs and Hornbostel, who was forced to leave Germany after 1933 because of the Nazi regime, which in his case prohibited him from studying in Germany. As an ethnomusicologist he was principally an Africanist, with emphasis on the music of Uganda, and with a strong focus also on organology. He was also prominent as a leading member of the International Folk Music Council. His field recordings, comprising 75 tapes made in Uganda (and a small number in Tanzania) are held by the National Sound Archive in London, with copies at the Uganda Museum and at UCLA.

Refs.: Christensen 1984; DeVale 1985; Morgan & DeVale 2003; Seeger &Wade 1977:xv-xvi; UCLA Ethnomusicology Archive 2003d.

RICHARD WALLASCHEK (1860–1917)
Czech/Austrian aesthetician and writer on music

Born: Brno, Czechoslovakia, 16 Nov 1860
Died: Vienna, Austria, 24 Apr 1917

Education:
Studied law and philosophy Vienna, Heidelberg and Tübingen, 1878–85
Studied law, Berne, 1886
Studied at the British Museum, London, 1890–95

Wallaschek's book *Primitive Music* (1893) was published in London during this period and was presumably compiled using the resources of the British Museum library, whose reading room would already have been famous as a result of Karl Marx's celebrated use of it decades earlier. Wallaschek's London sojourn must also have brought him into contact with the University of London, as two persons from there are acknowledged in the Preface of the book for their assistance. They were James Sully (1842–1923), Professor of Philosophy of Mind and Logic at the University of London, 1892–1903, who was a writer on psychological subjects with emphasis on Wallaschek's own later speciality, the psychology of music; and Thomas Rhys Davids (1843–1922), Professor of Pali and Buddhist Literature at University College, London, 1882–1904. Sully, especially, can be credited with influencing Wallaschek, and it may be that Wallaschek was his pupil.

Qualifications:
Graduated in philosophy, Tübingen, 1885
Graduated in law, Berne, 1886

Appointments:
Lecturer in philosophy, Freiburg, c.1887–c.90
Lecturer in psychology and aesthetics of music, University of Vienna, 1896–?
Music critic, *Die Zeit*, 1896–1904
Lecturer, aesthetics of music, Conservatory of the Gesellschaft der Musikfreunde, Vienna, 1900–03
Professor (unsalaried), University of Vienna, 1908–10
Professor (salaried), University of Vienna, 1911–17

Writings:
See below.

****

Wallaschek is credited with beginning the so-called Vienna School of comparative musicology with his appointment in 1896 at the University of Vienna, where he was succeeded by Robert Lach (q.v.). He is best known for his book *Primitive Music* (1893), which seems to have established his reputation, and was even reprinted in a beautifully-bound facsimile edition by Da Capo Press in 1970. Although praised by Anthony Seeger for early insights into the nature of music performance,[337] it has been overtaken by later scholarship. It is laden with evolutionism and speculation about the origins of music. It is also compiled substantially from unreliable secondary sources and is full of mistakes and misinterpretations.

For other writings by Wallaschek see Kunst 1959a:#4271-9, and Fuller-Maitland et al. 2003.

Refs.: DBE; Fuller-Maitland et al. 2003.

---

[337] Seeger 1992:96.

RICHARD A(LAN) WATERMAN (1914–1971)
American ethnomusicologist

Born: Solvang, CA, USA, 10 Jul 1914
Died: Tampa, FL, USA, 8 Nov 1971

Education:
Primary and secondary education, Santa Barbara, USA
Attended Santa Barbara State College, 1930–32 and 1935–37
Attended UCLA, 1932–34
Attended Claremont College, 1939–41
Attended Northwestern University, 1941–43

Qualifications:
AB, Santa Barbara State College, 1937
MA in anthropology, Claremont State College, 1941
Topic: Functionalism of Bronislaw Malinowski
PhD in anthropology, Northwestern University, 1943
Topic: African Patterns in Trinidad Negro Music

Appointments:
Teacher and counsellor, Santa Ynez Valley Union High School, California, 1937–40
Instructor, Northwestern University, 1943–45
Assistant professor, Northwestern University, 1945–51
Associate professor, Northwestern University, 1951–56
Visiting associate professor, University of Washington, 1953–54
Associate professor, Wayne State University, 1956–61
Professor, Wayne State University, 1961–68
Professor, University of South Florida, Tampa, 1968–71

Field work:
Puerto Rico and Cuba, 1946
Cuba, 1948
Yirkalla, northern Australia, 1952

Writings:
Nettl's assessment is that Waterman's "greatest contributions were the interpretation of black American music using the concept of syncretism, the introduction of research in urban American subcultures and the assembling of major bibliographies."[338] Waterman's contribution to bibliography was a lengthy series of instalments on Asian music published in *Notes*.[339] His work on syncretic change, as exemplified by an analysis of the characteristics of West-African sub-

---

[338] Nettl 2003.
[339] Waterman 1947-51.

Saharan music and their retention in New World Negro music,[340] was a breakthrough, albeit now so well understood as to be taken for granted. For a full list of publications and a discography see Gillis & Merriam 1973.

****

Waterman had an early interest in music, evidently without benefit of formal instruction, learning to play trombone and tuba in a boy scout band, and teaching himself piano and double bass in his high school years. During his years at Santa Barbara State College, he played in dance bands and began a life-long association with jazz as a double-bass player.

As an anthropologist and ethnomusicologist, Waterman is significant not only for his own seminal work on Afro-American music, but also for the influence he had upon Alan P. Merriam (q.v.), whom he taught from 1948–51, in association with his colleague at Northwestern University, Melville Herskovits (q.v.). The two together provided Merriam with many of the tools and insights he so brilliantly employed in later years.

Refs.: Bascom 1972; Eth 4(1):45 (1960); Merriam 1973: Nettl 2003.

---

[340] Waterman 1952.

ERIC WERNER (1901–1988)
Austrian/American musicologist

Born: Ludenberg, near Vienna, Austria, 1 Aug 1901
Died: New York, NY, USA, 28 Jul 1988

Education:
Berlin Hochschule für Musik, ? –1924
Studied at universities of Berlin, Graz, Göttingen, Prague, Strasbourg, and Vienna

Qualifications:
Doctorate in musicology, University of Strasbourg, 1928
Topic: Comparison of synagogue music and early Christian chant

Appointments:
Saarbrücken Conservatory, 1926–33
Jewish Theological Seminary in Breslau, 1935–38
Professor of liturgical music, Hebrew Union College, Cincinnati, 1939–67
Professor of musicology and comparative liturgy, Department of Music, Tel-Aviv University, 1967–72

Writings:
Werner is considered the most prolific scholar of Jewish music during the latter-half of the 20th century. His best known publications are his chapter on the music of post-biblical Judaism in the *New Oxford History of Music* (1957) and, expanding upon the subject of his dissertation, his book *The Sacred Bridge* (1970). For a full bibliography of his writings, see Katz 1988.

****

Werner was another scholar who fled Nazi persecution by emigrating to the United States, where he gained an appointment in succession to Idelsohn (q.v.) at Hebrew Union College, Cincinnati. Before entering university he became proficient both as a clarinettist and a pianist. His early professional training was in both composition (with Busoni and others) and musicology at different universities under the tutelage of such scholars as Adler, Lach (q.v.), Sachs (q.v.), and Wolf.

> Werner's pioneering research into Jewish music . . . encompassed such diverse subjects as comparative Jewish and Christian chant, synagogue liturgy and chant, the Dead Sea Scrolls, medieval Jewish music and the traditional music of Ashkenazi Jewry.[341]

Refs.: BRC(B); Katz 1989; Katz 2003h.

---

[341] Katz 2003h.

WALTER WIORA (1906–1997)
Polish/German musicologist

Born: Kattowitz (now Katowice), Poland, 30 Dec 1906
Died: Tutzing, Germany, 9 Feb 1997

Education:
Hochschule für Musik, Berlin, 1925–27
Studied musicology, Berlin, under Hornbostel (q.v.), Sachs (q.v.), and others, and at Freiburg, 1927–36

Qualifications:
PhD, Freiburg, 1937
Topic: Development of folksong

Appointments:
Assistant, Deutsches Volksliedarchiv, Freiburg, 1936–41
Reader in musicology, Posen, 1942
Served in German army, 1942–45
Archivist, Deutsches Volksliedarchiv, Freiburg, 1946–58
Professor of musicology, Kiel, 1958–64
Visiting professor, Columbia University NY, 1962–63
Professor of musicology, University of Saarbrücken, 1964–72

Writings:
See below.

****

Wiora is best known to ethnomusicologists for his book *The Four Ages of Music* (1967) which, in Sachsonian tradition, attempts a universal history of music in terms of cultural epochs. For other writings see Eggebrecht 2003 and Kunst 1959a:#4394-4420a.

Refs.: Baker 1984; Bartlett 2004; Bull ICTM 90:3 (1997); Eggebrecht 2003b.

Part IV: Intellectual Ancestry Charts

Introduction

For those scholars whose training was exclusively in composition or performance, the names of their teachers are omitted because the charts are intended only to show lines of influence in terms of ideas.

As well as the links shown, which are mainly of teacher/pupil relationships, it can be assumed that contemporaries all influenced each other to one degree or another.

Mostly not shown in the charts are links which span more than one generation. Thus, in the case of the Berlin School (Chart 1), Husmann was taught by both Wolf and Hornbostel, and Bose was a student of both Stumpf and Hornbostel as well as Sachs. Additionally, and also not shown, Lachmann, who was a student of Wolf, was also taught by Stumpf.

Intellectual Ancestry Charts

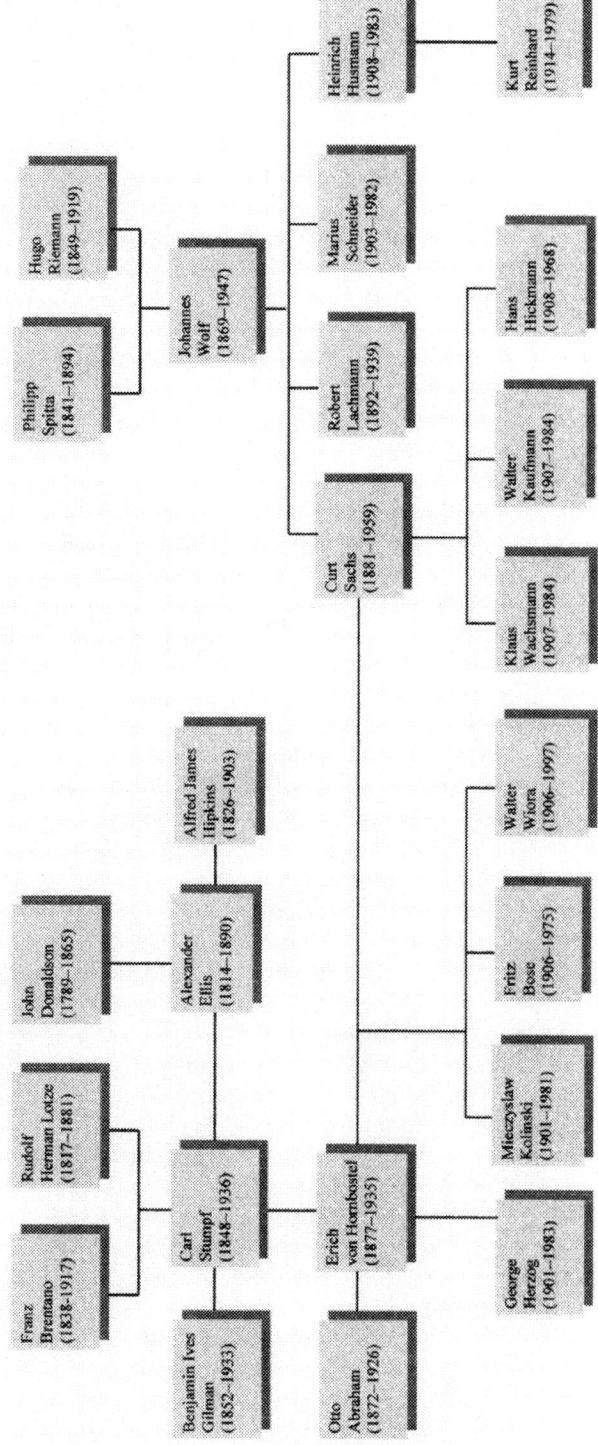

Chart 1: Berlin School

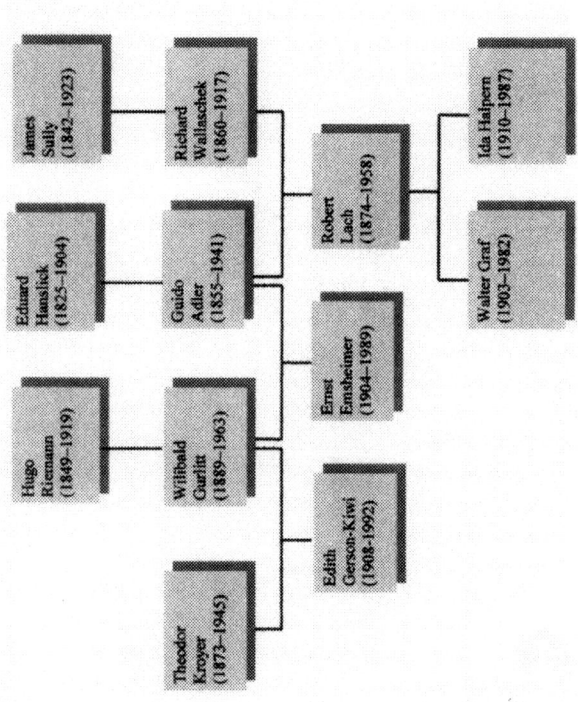

Chart 2: Vienna School

Intellectual Ancestry Charts

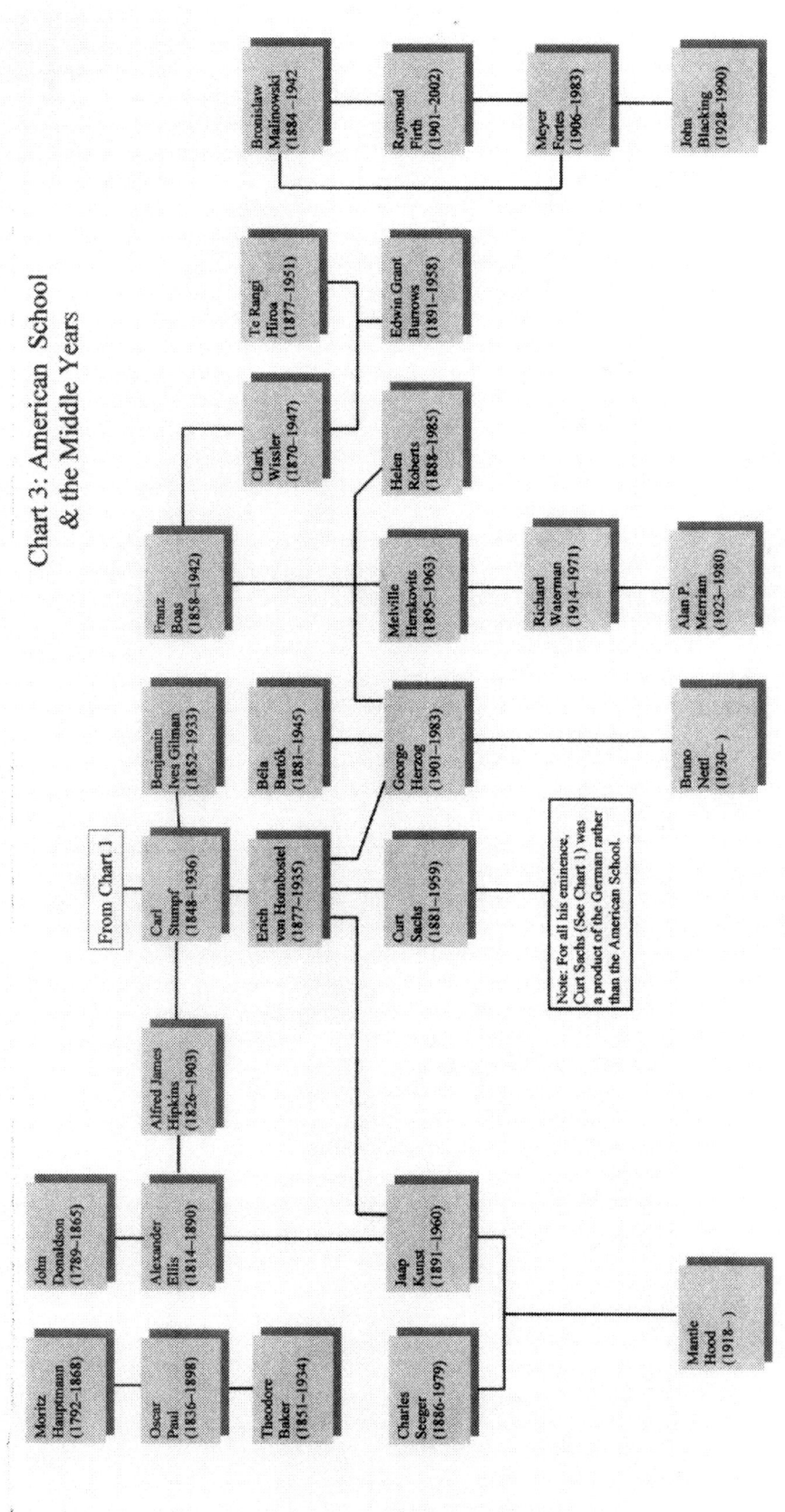

Part V: Issues

Introductory note

Part V deals with issues arising from the work of the pioneers, grouped under headings of Field Work, Archiving and documentation, Transcription, Analysis, Comparison, Product and process, and Aftermath.

Field work

Most ethnomusicological studies begin with field work. Comprehensive information on field work is readily available in standard text books, including some devoted wholly to the subject, and no purpose would be served by reiterating any of it here.[342] Some of my own approaches are touched upon in my memoir about field work in New Zealand: *To Tatau waka: In Search of Maori Music*,[343] and a field questionnaire which proved useful both for my own work and that of my students is reproduced as an appendix in the present book.

Although there is substantial agreement among most ethnomusicologists on how to go about field work, there is still controversy arising out of the ethics debates of the 1980s and later about whether it is appropriate or even possible to undertake it at all.

INSIDER/OUTSIDER RELATIONS

For a number of years from the 1980s onwards, there was vigorous debate and whole conference sessions devoted to the topic of insider/outsider relations. It was fuelled, perhaps, by several ongoing trends. For the acknowledged "high cultures" there is a long and honourable tradition of outsiders essentially apprenticing themselves to a recognised master of the particular tradition, taking lessons in the tradition, just as one would do when learning violin or piano in a Western music conservatory, and afterwards, when sufficient knowledge has been gained, interpreting this tradition to persons unfamiliar with it. In the early decades of the 20th century, anthropologists began almost universally to follow the methods of Bronislaw Malinowski (1884–1942), who popularised "participant observation" as a method for gathering field data. This too was taken on board by ethnomusicologists. During the early development of the discipline, scholars, such as Hornbostel and others of the Berlin School, had little choice but to study collections of recordings gathered by others, often with inadequate contextual information, and invariably without the insights that living among the practitioners can provide. In America, where there was greater institutional support for field work than in Europe, and American Indian tribes were "on the doorstep", such "armchair ethnomusicology" fell out of favour. Particularly in the case of tribal cultures, the standard method followed by most ethnomusicologists was to begin with a period of field work during which recordings would be made and documented, and interviews carried out on matters of interest to the ethnomusicologist. A further stage was reached when "insiders" who had been trained in the West began to study their own music, enriching and informing ethnomusicology as a result of the further insights they were uniquely able to provide. Nor did they necessarily remain exclusively garrisoned in their own areas. Some, especially after the introduction of performance-based studies by Mantle Hood at UCLA, were recruited by music departments in Western institutions and became professors there. Musicians in this category who spring to mind include J.H. Kwabena Nketia (1921–) for Africa and Trân Van Khê (1921–) for Vietnam. A final development was a deliberate effort spearheaded by Barry Brook (1918–1997) to involve "insiders" in the compilation of what Brook hoped would be a world history of music. Beginning with the title "Music in the Life of Man" (MLM),

---

[342] Among such sources are Goldstein 1964; Herndon & McLeod 1983; Hood 1971,Ch.4; Karpeles 1958; Maceda 1981; Myers 1992, Chapters 2-3; Nettl 1964, Chapter 3; Post et al. 1994; Royal Anthropological Institute 1951; Tracey 1969; and Vansina 1973.

[343] McLean 2004.

and evolving eventually to a more high-sounding and less gender-specific "The Universe of Music: A History" (UMH), conferences were held throughout the world, and there was a flurry of activity as senior ethnomusicologists joined the effort, if only to make sure it would develop along sensible lines. Sadly, the effort disintegrated. Too much grant money was spent on conferences, some issues were never resolved, even in terms of tables of contents for proposed volumes, long delays ensued, and eventually Barry Brook died without seeing his project to fruition. Meanwhile a new commercial initiative emerged with similar objectives, and this proceeded rapidly, often subsuming materials compiled in the first instance for its predecessor. All volumes of the resulting *Garland Encyclopaedia of World Music* have now been published, if not always to critical acclaim.

The above may be counted as gains, but the insider debate has had one highly unfortunate outcome. Ethnomusicologists have become wary of passing judgement on matters about which insiders may disagree. The tendency is to accept the insider view, or at any rate defer to it, and regard any challenge to it as presumptuous or even necessarily wrong. And at the most extreme end of the spectrum, outsiders are condemned as "colonialists" or "academic imperialists" who are exploiting the "intellectual property" of the insider. While perhaps useful as a platform for debate, views of this kind are accepted neither by most ethnomusicologists nor most insiders. But they have nevertheless had damaging results. Rather than ignore them in the hope that they will go away or, as some ethnomusicologists have done, or worse still accept them and retreat to safe ground, such extreme views should be confronted and resisted. No field of human endeavour should be denied to researchers on grounds of ethnicity, whether European or non-European. The sensible point of view is that insiders and outsiders have complementary skills and both viewpoints are needed to advance knowledge. The legitimate outcomes of the insider/outsider debate can be met by increased collaboration and greater attention to the needs of insiders, without necessity to abandon field work or neglect the non-Western music systems of the world. There are indeed lessons to be learnt from the debate, but not at the expense of destroying a discipline. For some of us, and for some of the early pioneers of ethnomusicology, the paths ahead were already being laid down decades before the present crisis of confidence erupted. One thing has always been clear, and perhaps it accounts for the neglect of insider concerns that prevailed for so long. By and large the peoples whose music ethnomusicologists choose to study are not remotely interested in scholarship. They have co-operated until now not in order to provide visiting scholars with a living or with sufficient samples of music for their purposes, but because they saw their own music as vulnerable to loss or under threat of extinction, and the visiting ethnomusicologist's equipment and expertise as a means of helping to preserve it. For a long time rank and file ethnomusicologists ignored this imperative, regarding preservation as neither an essential or even legitimate part of their discipline, and certainly in no sense an obligation. For many, after their work was finished, sending back a copy of the resulting dissertation or a few tape duplicates was considered a sufficient quid pro quo. Such researchers were not merely insensitive but can be regarded with some justification as indeed exploiters, and the dragons' teeth they sowed have grown armies to oppose us. The greatest of the pioneers had no such attitude. Along with the subjects of their research, they too saw the need for "preservation". They recorded far beyond their own immediate research needs; they proselytised; they disseminated; and they established archives and record collections. Above all, they listened to the people among whom they worked, and heeded their concerns. It is unfortunate that their example was too often not followed by others.

The problem of what I have called "song loss" [344] is now much greater than it used to be, and is correspondingly of increasing concern to indigenous peoples. Just as some 15,000 animals and plants throughout the world are now on the United Nations world endangered species list as a result of the impact of introduced European species, so too unique forms of music are under threat for the same reason. Like the plants and animals, whole music systems have disappeared, while others are on the verge of extinction and in need of conservation. In New Zealand, there is a government Department of Conservation (DOC) whose work it is to intervene in the natural world by breeding and releasing back into the wild endangered species that in some cases have declined down to the last few breeding pairs. Ethnomusicologists are uniquely equipped to do a similar job for music. Part of the problem, however, is that "preservation" is still not seen as a need by ethnomusicologists at large. The discipline itself has become a "gestalt" or system with components that inter-react. Other elements of this system play their part. If preservation is to be a legitimate aim, there must be something worth preserving. But if a disappearing style or genre is no "better" than whatever has replaced it, or has no intrinsic value in its own right, why bother? The answer, simply, is that ethnomusicologists do not have to pick up sides on what is better or best. Any discrete style is worth preserving from a study point of view, and if it is valued by its practitioners then the ethnomusicologist has an obligation to assist them in their efforts to maintain it. That is what reciprocity is about. How can an ethnomusicologist do this? In the "old days" there was less of a problem. The visiting outsider had a monopoly of suitable equipment and expertise, or even of enough money to purchase recording materials. Nowadays almost any Third World person can aspire to own a cassette recorder, can obtain blank tape for a few cents, is perfectly capable of making his or her own recordings, and many do so. Many Third World countries have established their own sound archives and have vigorous collecting programmes of their own. So the visitor would seem to have nothing to offer. Again, however, the ethnomusicology "gestalt" becomes relevant. Ethnomusicologists are not mere technicians, and by representing themselves as such they are selling themselves short. Analysis of music systems has currently gone out of fashion along with other former verities of ethnomusicology. Welcome back. It is, in fact, the only hope for real "preservation". Let me explain why:

When a music system goes into decline, aspiring learners run into difficulty if they are unfamiliar with the system. Especially in today's environment, with globalisation going on apace, learners are often more familiar with the norms of European, especially popular, music than they are with their own indigenous styles. As a result, they introduce unconscious changes into their music when they attempt to learn it, and a different product emerges. Their seniors criticise them for inability to learn, and either the new product displaces the old, or the erstwhile learners become discouraged, give up, and the tradition itself dies or moves further into decline. For most present-day ethnomusicologists this is not a concern except insofar as the process of change itself may be of interest. But for the practitioners it is a disaster. They don't want their heritage to disappear. Can the ethnomusicologist help to reverse this process? Yes. The answer lies with one of the very earlier planks of the discipline from which ethnomusicology is currently retreating. There is an analogy with the acquisition of spoken language. A child learns a language at his or her mother's knee. An adult learner, who no longer possesses the sponge-like learning capabilities of a child, must do so by recourse to grammar books and instruction. The same is true of music. To be successful in learning an unfamiliar music system, an adult learner must gain some understanding of its rules. An adequately trained ethnomusicologist can provide

---

[344] McLean 1965b.

music transcriptions, can analyse the system and, having done so, can write the rules. As an example, when the rules are understood it should ultimately be as practicable for a latter-day Maori to compose a waiata in the style of the 1960s as it is for a music student in a Western academy to write a 3-part invention in the style of Bach. Is this a sufficient quid-pro quo? Realistically, not at the moment. But I plead for an eye to the future. Ultimately, followers of the Maori Ringatu Church, who currently sing wholly from memory, may be performing their liturgy from a hymn book with the tunes written down as they are in the West and, if this should come to pass, some of the effort involved in defining the Maori music system will have had practical benefit. Beyond this, however, I would argue that any advance in human knowledge is worthwhile, again regardless of the ethnicity of the investigator, and benefits can accrue in unforseen ways. My own recent book with Margaret Orbell, *Songs of a Kaumatua* ,[345] containing music transcriptions which most Maori people at the moment cannot read, has been received as a sacred taonga (treasure) within Maoridom. And therein lies at least part of its justification. The book elevates the status of the songs in it, and reveals something of their beauty and cultural value to the outside world. Even if it does no more than this it will have been worth the writing.

Two successful initiatives emanating from Auckland university's Archive of Maori and Pacific Music, which I founded in 1970, may also be cited as precedents to be followed elsewhere. The first was the institution of a free dubbing service which, over the years, has provided many hundreds of Maori groups and individuals with the means to assist maintenance of their own living tradition. The other was an exercise in insider/outsider co-operation called a Territorial Survey of Oceanic Music (TSOM), which I initiated in the 1980s. Funded jointly by Unesco and the Polynesian Cultural Center, Hawai'i, this secured the co-operation of governments all around the Pacific for field work involving both a qualified outsider ethnomusicologist and a locally nominated co-worker who would be trained by the visitor in field techniques that would enable further collection to be done when the project finished. Eleven field trips in all were mounted, yielding large amounts of professionally recorded and thoroughly documented music, together with subsequent publications. Both are initiatives that could well be emulated elsewhere.

My advice to ethnomusicologists is simply to get on with the job. Leave the soul-searching to others, and have some confidence in your own ability to work effectively on behalf of both ethnomusicology and the people among whom we are privileged to work.

AUTHENTICITY

One of the reasons ethnomusicologists are reluctant to take part in music conservation is scepticism about whether such efforts are justified. Central to the debate are questions about authenticity.

"Authenticity" was a concern and preoccupation of many members of the old European-based International Folk Music Council as adjudicated and articulated by Maud Karpeles.

In his editorial to the new-look *Yearbook of the International Folk Music Council* which supplanted the former IFMC *Journal* soon after Karpeles's retirement, and subsequent shift of the IFMC secretariat to North America, Alexander Ringer (1921–2002), with his new editorial

---

[345] Orbell & McLean 2002.

broom, began sweeping out the old premises in no uncertain terms. He refers to what he describes as "so-called acculturation" as by this time seeming to occupy a "catalytic" position in all forms of cultural creativity, and goes on to conclude:

> If so, then the fashionable concept of 'authenticity' has no more validity as a basic postulate in the philosophy of folk music research than 'purity', its nineteenth century counterpart. Both are essentially romantic myths that occupy legitimate position in the realm of ideology but are basically irrelevant, if not dangerous to scholarly investigation.[346]

This is a very strong statement, and is undoubtedly representative of a very widely held view that by now is possibly close to universal. But it is an over-reaction. It's a pity the scholarly pendulum swings so violently from extreme to extreme. The truth in this case, as in so many issues, lies somewhere close to the middle of the two views, and there is still, indeed, much to be said for the views espoused by Karpeles.

She herself was far too sensible to make foolish mistakes in the matter. In an early paper on the subject,[347] she considers authenticity to be a comparative rather than an absolute quality. Next, without being doctrinaire, she adopts as a working definition Cecil Sharp's famous dictum that folk song is a product of oral tradition, as such is a collective product that is shaped over the generations by many people, and in this respect differs from "popular" music. Another outcome of the oral tradition process is that so long as this continues to operate, folk music "never attains final form",[348] so no claim is made by Karpeles that authenticity in folk music is dependent on stability. Another point of acknowledgement is that mutual borrowings and influences from art music have always taken place, so "purity" is not part of Karpeles's concept either.

Having laid the groundwork, she moves on to a practical example. What about hillbilly songs, she asks, and what about guitar accompaniment which had become common in folk song performance only within the previous 30 or so years? Can these be regarded as authentic? Her answer at the outset of her paper is no, because they do not conform to all three of Cecil Sharp's criteria of individual variation, continuity, and community selection: "continuity which preserves the tradition; variation which springs from individual creative impulse; and selection which pronounces the verdict of the community".[349]

What then, Karpeles, now asks, should the test of authenticity be? Her answer owes nothing to analysis, but is simply that this judgement should be based on artistic grounds, paying respect to folk music which has stood Sharp's test of time, while also accepting modern elements if these merge with the older ones sufficiently to make a satisfying whole. It is hard to know why Ringer should consider this so "dangerous", but some explanation for its rejection can be offered.

The current preoccupation with abstract theory derived mostly from outside disciplines puts ethnomusicology at a remove from its own primary subject matter, with music "sound" as such now regarded as by and large no longer important, interesting, or even relevant. The current

---

[346] Ringer 1969:4.
[347] Karpeles 1951.
[348] Karpeles 1951:11.
[349] Karpeles 1951:12.

concerns of "process" rather than "product" form a package within which past scholarship is either ignored or rejected as "old fashioned", with ideas about "authenticity" by no means the only casualty. Present-day scholars of this persuasion can afford to be dismissive of earlier work because of their distancing from transcription, analysis and comparison, which ensures that they will not be impeded in their views by evidence from these quarters. Were Sharp, Bartók and Kodály and other collectors totally wrong in their views on authenticity? Were the latter two scholars deluded to suppose that the Romanian and Slovak music they collected differed in real and fundamental ways from the Magyar music that had previously been accepted as genuine folk? Was Sharp wrong to see a difference between "Searching for lambs" and "There's a tavern in the town"? For that matter, was I wrong in my work on Maori music to distinguish traditional waiata musically as well as conceptually and in terms of song function and performance practice from modern products such as European-derived action song? And was I wrong to spend a large portion of 20 years of my life salvaging disappearing classic waiata that were being displaced by action song? I think not. The last word has not been said on the authenticity debate, and before assuming there is no such thing as authenticity there is room for middle ground.

In the new politically correct environment, "authenticity" has become a proscribed word and, as so often happens, the baby has gone out with the bathwater. At its most extreme, the new orthodoxy regards change as not only inevitable, which no one would dispute, but inimical of any kind of stability. The notion, though I have not seen it expressed so baldly, is almost as if no such thing as a style can exist, because by the time it is studied and defined it will have changed to something else. So, from this standpoint, it is useless to make the effort. Matters such as rate of change or distinguishing one form of change from another, or establishing base-lines from which change can be measured, are no longer concerns.

An observation by Nettl about authenticity, written more than 40 years ago, obvious as his point may seem, is worth reiterating. Nettl pointed out that within the American Indian repertoire there is a great difference between a song sung in a style uninfluenced by Western traditions and one learned from 'Europeans. "Both," he added, "are certainly worthy of study, but the difference between them must be realized.[350] Anyone who has worked in tribal areas elsewhere will be as aware as Nettl of the truth of this observation. Certainly there are degrees of cross-fertilisation, depending on the nature of the systems involved, the degree of contact between them, and the attitude of the receiving culture both to externally imposed change and to innovation within its own system. Such matters are better understood now than they were in the 1960s, but the essential point remains that differences exist, and while no one believes in pristine "pure" styles with no history either of their own or of culture contact to be considered, it is not useful to abandon work on the topic just because a term has become entangled with inappropriate methodologies and mythologies and for this reason has fallen out of favour.

THE ROLE OF THE OBSERVER

Another not yet resolved issue is the problem of the observer, raised so many years ago by Kenneth Gourlay.[351] I have made it clear I do not agree with him that objectivity is an unattainable goal. Nor do I believe it to be so far out of reach that one may as well abandon the effort. I do

---

[350] Nettl 1951:5.
[351] Gourlay 1978.

maintain, however, that the effect of the observer has to be minimised in a conventional field situation. Traditionally this was accomplished by taking great care not to influence results by anything the observer might say or do, and especially by never asking leading questions. During my own field work in the Cook Islands in 1967, for example, I was obliged at times seemingly to go round and round in circles in an effort to avoid putting a direct question, but at last getting the wanted information without compromising results by suggesting an answer in the form taken by the question.

In his work with the Kaluli of Papua New Guinea, Steven Feld broke these rules, and has been praised for doing so. His method was the very reverse of the standard one that earlier ethnographers took such pains to follow, and his results, indeed, could have been obtained in no other way. Revealing himself and his objectives to his informants in a manner consistent with the post-modernist approach of "reflexivity", he engaged in discussion about aesthetics with Kaluli intellectuals, effectively on the basis of "I'll show you my music if you'll show me yours".[352] The end result, inevitably, has as much of Feld in it as it does of Kaluli. Feld entered the field with the already formed intention of writing, in his own words, "an ethnography of sound as a symbol system." [353] Not surprisingly, this is exactly what he did and what his methods were best adapted to achieve.

It is apparent there can be no agreed rules on how observation should be carried out if both types of study are equally legitimate. Attempts to gather systematic information on the one hand, and limited goal studies such as Feld's on the other, require different methods.

INSTRUCTION

What then of the alternative approach of placing oneself as a pupil wholly in the hands of an acknowledged master musician, and simply doing what one is told? In India, the convention of visiting scholars learning in situ by means of this method began very early. Sir William Jones (1746–1794), A.H. Fox Strangways (1859–1948), Charles Russell Day (1860–1900), Arnold Bake (1899–1963) and Alain Daniélou (1907–1994) all studied extensively in this way before writing about the music. Undoubtedly this contributed to the universal uncritical acceptance of Indian theories about intonation which prevailed in all quarters until Nazir Jairazbhoy (1927–), himself of Indian parentage, mounted a challenge to it in the 1960s (discussed in a later section). The tendency of ethnomusicologists is still to accept whatever practitioners may say about their music, without confirming the statements by using Western methods of analysis. If practitioners are always right, what would be the harm? If they are sometimes wrong, as generally conceded for our own culture, interesting avenues open up in terms of contrasting the one set of views with the other. Unless it should be thought that practitioners are never in error, one only has to look at the controversy about piano "touch" in the West that was rife when I was a student. Many pianists were convinced they could affect a note, without benefit of pedal, after it was struck, despite assurances from physicists that this simply could not happen, because the hammer at this point has left the string and the key has no contact with it.

---

[352] The method is revealed in a section of Feld's book *Sound and Sentiment* entitled "Participation and Reflection" (Feld 1982:230ff).
[353] Feld 1994.

Percy Scholes (1877–1958) was inclined to accept the possibility of piano "touch" in such a sense, on the grounds that so great a musician as Bülow,[354] who goes so far in his edition of Beethoven's piano sonatas as to mark passages "Quasi Clarinet" and "Quasi Horn", could not have been completely mistaken about it. Bülow, however, also advised his piano students to imitate in their piano playing the violin tone of Joachim rather than that of Sarasate.[355] Perhaps there was some difference in the playing of these two violinists that was reproducible on the piano, but the alternative explanation may be preferred that this was no more than a "mad illusion" on Bülow's part. Suppose, however, an Indian ethnomusicologist had sat at the feet of von Bülow. Would piano "touch" in such an extreme sense now be as much a part of Indian belief as extreme precision of Indian intonation is in ours? Instruction from acknowledged masters is indeed a powerful and , in some circumstances, even essential method of learning, but let's not get sanctimonious about it.

Finally, this is yet another issue that applies mostly to "high art" cultures such as those of India and Indonesia, and in any case usually limited to instrumental traditions, where music is learned in this way. In most folk and tribal cultures music is learned by informal participation, without benefit of master musicians.

BI-MUSICALITY

Mantle Hood is perhaps most celebrated for his concept of bi-musicality, and performance-based teaching designed to achieve it. As a method, it is an extension of indigenous teaching, but on a vastly increased scale, rather like Western music centres which provide elementary group instruction for school children. Most university departments of music, and all conservatories, attach importance to performance as a means of communicating knowledge about music. When I was a student in the Otago university music department in the 1950s, for example, practical music-making such as membership of the university choir, madrigal singing group, or chamber orchestra was expected of all students. Mantle Hood extended this principle to non-Western music. As an Indonesianist, a primary interest, and the subject of his doctoral dissertation, was the music of the Indonesian ensemble of metallophones known as gamelan. He was the first in the USA to import a gamelan from Java, and the performances of his students at UCLA became something of a sensation, sparking a desire on the part of other music departments to acquire their own gamelans, until today there are said to be more than 100 of them in the USA. It is now indeed standard practice there for music departments to add non-Western performance to the student curriculum, and some students have reportedly reached high levels of competence. So far, so good, but the concept of bi-musicality as such deserves more scrutiny than it commonly gets. It seems to make sense that the best way to penetrate an unfamiliar form of music is to learn to perform it. Most ethnomusicologists practice this up to a point. It was not unknown for folk song collectors such as Cecil Sharp, having learnt songs, to "trade" them with

---

[354] Hans (Guido) Freiherr von Bülow (1830–1894), German operatic conductor and pianist, renowned for conducting without a score. He is described in the New Grove as "a musician of formidable ability, with absolute self-command and an acute intellectual power of interpretation," but also "quarrelsome, nervous, passionate and given to extremes of mood." (Fifield 2003).
[355] Scholes 1972.

their informants in order to obtain more.[356] In his lectures on African music, Alan Merriam was able to perform two different metres simultaneously, one from each hand, in order to demonstrate African polymetre. As part and parcel of my own work on Maori music, I learnt to sing songs, and could lead a waiata on occasion without complaint from other singers. But this is a far cry from fully understanding the music system, or being fully functional within a music system, and most ethnomusicologists are probably realistic enough not to aspire to such heights. John Blacking, for example, in an interview with Keith Howard,[357] explained the value to him of learning to sing Venda children's songs and participating in Venda drum ensembles, but added that he never attempted to become an expert performer because he didn't view this as his task and had neither the time nor the inclination for it.

The truth is that a student performer in a gamelan ensemble is no more equipped as a result of this experience to understand the intricacies of Indonesian music than a beginning piano student is to understand the complexities of the Western keyboard repertoire. Such an accomplishment is commonly left to the final stages of conservatory training, after years of prior study; and such students, unlike those in a gamelan group, have had the benefit of study within their own music system. Speaking of my own experience, I doubt if I learned a lot about Elizabethan or Italian madrigals by being able to read my part and sing along in the Otago university madrigal group. All this did for me, as I am sure must be true of most of the students in a gamelan group, was to familiarise me to some degree with the sound of the music, as well as providing a performance experience.

More than 40 years ago, when Hood's gamelan classes were still in their infancy, and Hood was still in process of promotin them, Alan Merriam put the matter into perspective. He cautioned that performance classes were even then in danger of becoming ends in themselves and, as such, more concerned with imparting aesthetic pleasure than studying music. He also raised doubts about the extent to which one could become a participant in a culture through playing its music. Performance, he considered, could give limited insight into a culture

> but there is a world of difference between the ethnomusicologist learning *in situ* and the student learning at an American university. The former has the added incalculable advantage of participation to whatever extent he is allowed in another culture. The latter participates only in a portion of its fragile and imported shell.[358]

My own experience with Maori students at Auckland university bears out Merriam's caveats. It might be argued that I simply wasn't a very good teacher, or didn't know enough about the style, but, against this, precisely the same results emerged when Maori teachers, skilled in the tradition, attempted the same task. One of my duties, when associated with the Maori Studies programme at Auckland university was to help teach a course on Maori Poetry and Song to undergraduate Maori students. Each year, with varying success, a waiata was taught as part of the class instruction. The students were highly motivated to learn and were by no means lacking in musical ability but, although ethnically Maori, and in some cases native speakers of Maori as

---

[356] A somewhat dangerous practice, it is true. The New Zealand ethnographer, Johannes Andersen (1873–1962), for example, is reputed to have gone up the Wanganui River teaching string games, and down the Wanganui collecting them again!
[357] Howard 1991:61.
[358] Merriam 1964b:183.

well, they by and large had no more experience of waiata singing than students of European descent. The music system with which they were most familiar was the European one, and non-metrical, limited range, non-diatonic waiata were initially foreign to them, even though they had a head start with speaking and understanding the texts. Invariably they had difficulty even in hearing the unfamiliar melodies and rhythms and took the best part of a year to begin to master them. Even at the end of the process, their hold on a song was often tenuous, and they were all too prone to revert to more familiar ways of singing when they tried to sing independently.

If the New Zealand experience is typical, bi-musicality in the fullest sense may be an elusive performance goal.

Archiving and documentation

ARCHIVING

Reference has already been made to the vital role of archiving in the history of ethnomusicology. Comparative musicology as such began with sound archiving when Carl Stumpf established the Berlin Phonogram-Archiv in 1900, and he and his successors actively solicited wax cylinder field recordings from anthropologists and others, and subjected the recordings to detailed analysis.

A useful series of articles in *The Folklore and Folk Music Archivist*, published by the Archives of Folk and Traditional Music at Indiana University when George List (1911–) was director, provides information on some of the earliest established archives. The history of the Berlin Phonogram-Archiv is outlined by Kurt Reinhard;[359] the Vienna PhonogrammArchiv by Walter Graf;[360] the Archive of Folksong at the American Library of Congress by Rae Korson;[361] the International Library of African Music by Hugh Tracey;[362] and the BBC Folk Music Collection by Marie Slocombe.[363]

Numerous other archives could be named, all faced with the problem of how best to conserve recordings in a variety of now obsolete and obsolescent formats such as cylinder, disc, wire, and tape. Most are now progressively digitising their collections. Ultimately, sound archives throughout the world could be offering their holdings "on-line" in the same manner as libraries which are increasingly making books, journals and digital images available in this way.

Besides safeguarding the collections by ensuring they are stored in more than one site in a form indistinguishable from the original, digitising them will assist archives to meet other equally important goals. Ideally, sound archives should be active institutions engaged not only in the collection, conservation, documentation and dissemination of recorded materials for study but also as agents for repatriation of wanted early recordings to indigenous communities. In the United States, the Library of Congress and the Smithsonian Institution have taken a lead in do-

---

[359] Reinhard 1962.
[360] Graf 1962.
[361] Korson 1959.
[362] Tracey 1961.
[363] Slocombe 1964.

ing this. For Oceania, a model is provided by the Archive of Maori and Pacific Music at the University of Auckland.[364]

CATALOGUING

In his book *Anglo-American Folksong Scholarship* (1959), D.K. Wilgus observes that folk song scholarship "must collect, catalogue, and study its materials, roughly in that order," but regrettably the second step at this time was barely under way.[365] In the field of folk song study, there is a long tradition of collecting which mostly antedated the latter activities. In the scholarly study of Oriental art music and tribal music, cataloguing is usually neglected altogether. Why should this be? In the case of folk song, there was understanding at the outset that the materials to be dealt with were discrete items or "pieces", sung much the same way each time they were performed, and identifiable either by a formal title or by the first words of the texts. No one is in any doubt about what is meant when a scholar speaks of "Greensleeves" or "The Seeds of Love". Items of sung repertoire other than folk song are not generally so regarded, but not always justifiably. For example, Polynesian traditional repertoire, including Maori, is made up of named items, identifiable by their first lines or sometimes titles and in this respect is similar to folk song. Unlike most folk songs, however, the composers are often known, and their names and the circumstances of composition are handed down orally from generation to generation of singers, along with the tunes and the words. As the product of known composers, they are more like art songs in the West than folk songs, and, because of this and the value attached to them by the singers, perhaps should rank as "classical" repertoire. As such, of course, they ought to be catalogued and published in "editions" containing both words and music as is customary with folk songs. To my knowledge, few catalogues or editions of such materials have been undertaken, and in this respect my own catalogues and anthologies of traditional Maori songs could again perhaps be taken as a model.[366]

CLASSIFICATION

This topic has been a particular concern of European archivists who have large collections of notated folk song which they would like to file in such a way that variants appear together and genetic relationships emerge. Most of the systems that have been developed take advantage of regularities of one kind or another that appear in folk song but not as a rule in tribal and other repertories, and therefore have limited application outside of European traditions.Best known is a method developed by Béla Bartók (1881–1945) for classifying Hungarian folk song.[367] This and other methods are outlined by Erdely,[368] and are discussed in detail by him in his book *Methods and Principles of Hungarian Ethnomusicology*.[369] In a review of volume 1 of Bartók's monumental collection of Slovakian folk songs, Fritz Bose gives a good summary of Bartók's method and offers criticisms. In Bartók's earliest work, classification was by number of lines, line or phrase finals, number of syllables per line and melodic range. In his 1959 collection of

---

[364] q.v. McLean 1977b; McLean 1978; & McLean 1990a.
[365] Wilgus 1959:241.
[366] McLean 1983; McLean 1991b; McLean & Curnow 1992a; McLean & Curnow 1992b; McLean & Orbell 1990; Orbell & McLean 2002.
[367] Bartók 1931.
[368] Erdely 1962.
[369] Erdely 1965:43-73.

Slovakian folk songs, rhythm is used as a further criterion, with dotted rhythm tunes separated from those of even rhythm.[370] Bose's criticisms of this scheme are that it uses certain striking traits as its only criteria while neglecting others that are equally important. Especially, it fails to show thematically related tunes, while separating variants and throwing together unrelated melodies. European ethnomusicologists have devised many other schemes of classification since Bartók, and their task in indeed daunting, as collections run to many thousands of tunes. More than a dozen papers on the subject were published in an issue of *Studia Musicologica* which contains papers read at a Budapest conference of the IFMC in 1964,[371] and work has continued to be published in the IFMC journal and elsewhere since that date. Outside of Europe the subject still has some relevance, though again confined so far to folk song, as a result of work on "tune families" begun by Samuel Bayard.[372]

ARMCHAIR ETHNOMUSICOLOGY

Some present-day ethnomusicologists, like those of Hornbostel's Berlin School, either started their activities or worked at times on recordings collected by others. All three of Australia's pioneer ethnomusicologists began their work in this way. Ethnomusicology had its beginnings in Australia when Trevor Jones (1932–), analysed field recordings made by the anthropologist A.P. Elkin (1891–1979), with whom Jones collaborated on a joint book, *Arnhem Land Music* (195-). The doyen of Australian ethnomusicologists, Alice M. Moyle (1908–2005) also began with a study of Elkin's recordings before going on to independent work of her own. And soon afterwards Catherine Ellis (1935–1996) began her career by working as a research assistant to another anthropologist, T.G.H. Strehlow, completing her doctoral thesis, published in 1964, with an analysis of his recorded materials from Central Australia. Norma McLeod likewise began with a Master of Arts thesis at the University of London in which she analysed field recordings made by the British anthropologist Raymond Firth (1901–2002) and others on the Polynesian Outlier island of Tikopia.[373] Another Oceanic example is provided by Dieter Christensen (1932–) who, before he moved to the United States, worked closely with the anthro-pologist Gerd Koch in Berlin both before and after Koch conducted field work in Tuvalu, Western Polynesia. In an ensuing book, Koch supplied song texts, translations and ethnographic information, while Christensen provided transcriptions and musical analyses of songs recorded by Koch.[374] This precedent was later followed by Gesine Haase, whose doctoral dissertation from the same institution is an analysis of recordings made by Koch in the Santa Cruz islands of Melanesia.[375] The present writer provides another example with his transcriptions and analysis of Tikopia recordings [376] from the augmented collection of Raymond Firth, in this case working with the advantage of my own high-quality recordings of one of Firth's informants, Ishmael Tuki, together with prior personal field work in related areas, and a voluminous correspondence with Firth, who acted as informant and supplied ethnographic information in response to my questions to him.

---

[370] Bose 1961:63.
[371] *Studia Musicologica* volume 7, 1965.
[372] Bayard 1950.
[373] McLeod 1957.
[374] Christensen & Koch 1964.
[375] Haase 1977.
[376] McLean 1990b & McLean 1991.

Of course, work with archive collections needs to be carried out with due regard for cultural and performance context, ideally with a background of prior familiarity with the material as, for example, when Béla Bartók worked on someone else's collection of Serbo-Croatian folk song in 1941–42, and later published his results in association with Albert Lord.[377] Disregard of the principle of prior familiarity can lead to strange results. At Indiana University's Archives of Traditional Music, for example, whose collections I studied in the 1960s, I was amused at a graduate student assessment in the files of a Maori haka, which referred to a "drum-beat" allegedly audible on tape — strange indeed as the Maori do not use drums. In fact, the putative drum sounds were the product of bare feet stamping on a wooden concert stage. With care, however, such blunders can be avoided, and, although a field work baptism is now rightly regarded as necessary for a practising ethnomusicologist, it need not exclude work on archival collections of related musics. Although currently little used by ethnomusicologists, archival collections will, indeed, someday come into their own again for comparative analysis of styles, should this return to favour. Additionally, as the collections grow, they will be invaluable for analysis of historical change within particular cultures. In New Zealand, for example, the collections of the Archive of Maori and Pacific music now provide an almost continuous profile of traditional Maori music from the earliest known recordings, dubbed by Percy Grainger in 1909, through to the present day, and in the United States, thanks to the early field work and archiving of recordings by workers such as Fewkes, Fletcher and Densmore, even greater time depth is available.

Archive collections will also become useful for another and related reason. After a long discussion of scholarly activity in delineating music areas and plotting geographical distribution of music styles, Nettl rather pessimistically observes that if musical map-making was ever close to being a "hard science", it is no longer so if one uses contemporary data, because of the coming of mass media to the world, together with an increase in travel, publication, and emigration.[378] The remedy will be increased use of archival collections made by the pioneers of ethnomusicology in the years before such radical changes became a problem.

BIBLIOGRAPHY

Bibliography is alive and well in ethnomusicology, and has always been recognised as essential. Kunst, Merriam, Nettl and other key figures all espoused it and, from the beginnings of the discipline, bibliography has played a vital role. A worthy early contribution is a bibliography of Asian musics compiled by Richard Waterman and published in *Notes*.[379] For a period of 10 years, the International Folk Music Council published an *Annual Bibliography of European Ethnomusicology* (1966–75). From its inception, the journal *Ethnomusicology* published a classified "Current Bibliography" section, together with discography and filmography, in each of its three annual issues, and encouraged its members to contribute, besides publishing bibliographies of individual scholars from time to time, and area and other bibliographies such as Australia and New Guinea,[380] Afro-American,[381] Indian,[382] Canadian Indian,[383] and Eskimo music.[384] In the

---

[377] Bartók & Lord 1951.
[378] Nettl 1983:232.
[379] Waterman 1947-51.
[380] Alice Moyle 1971.
[381] Maultsby 1975.
[382] Barnett 1970..
[383] Guédon 1972.

year 2000, Current Bibliography disappeared from the journal and moved to the SEM web site,[385] where a search engine enhances its usefulness.

A start with book-length bibliographies for the entire then new field was made with the publication of Kunst's general bibliography, called *Ethnomusicology*, in 1959, with a supplement in 1960.[386] Substantial book-length annotated supplements have since been published by Schursma covering the next three decades,[387] and by Post for the period of the 1990s.[388] Nettl's small book *Reference Materials in Ethnomusicology*,[389] with its subject divisions, remains a useful guide to earlier work. As well, there have been major regional and other bibliographies of Africa,[390] Black music,[391] China,[392] dissertations,[393] jazz,[394] Japan,[395] Jewish music,[396] Korea,[397] Latin America,[398] North America,[399] and Oceania,[400] together with others too numerous to list.

There has been even more attention to discography, with numerous titles relating to world music now available. The need for abstracts has been met for music publications in general by *RILM Abstracts* (ongoing), which includes ethnomusicological titles though, like all such enterprises, because of the huge volume of eligible publications, has trouble keeping up-to-date The most pressing current need is to update some of he above works, for further regional bibliographies, and for bibliographies of specialised subject divisions within ethnomusicology.

Within the present book, it is not practicable to supply extensive bibliography for the persons whose biographies are included in it, because this in itself would stretch to book length. Instead, attention is drawn in each biography to the most important works of the person concerned, and reference is added for published bibliographies. Where not already specified, information can often be found in Kunst's *Ethnomusicology*,[401] and/or select bibliography is available in the on-line *New Grove Dictionary of Music and Musicians*.

Transcription

"Transcription", as ethnomusicologists use the word, is the process of notating music performance on paper. As defined by the *Harvard Dictionary of Music*, it is "the reduction of music

---

[384] Cavanagh 1972..
[385] http://webdb.iu.edu/sem/scripts/publications/ographies/cb/cb.cfm
[386] Kunst 1959a & 1960.
[387] Schuursma 1992.
[388] Post 2004.
[389] Nettl 1967.
[390] Aning 1967, Gaskin 1965, Gray 1991, Lems-Dworkin 1991, Thieme 1964, Varley 1970.
[391] De Lerma 1981.
[392] Lieberman 1979.
[393] Gillis & Merriam 1966.
[394] Merriam 1954a.
[395] Tsuge 1986.
[396] Sendrey 1951.
[397] Song 1971.
[398] Chase 1962.
[399] Haywood 1961.
[400] McLean 1995.
[401] Kunst 1959a & 1960.

from live or recorded sound to written notation".[402] But at this point one must depart from the dictionary, which goes on to represent ethnomusicologists as transcribing solely in "descriptive" terms, contrasting this with the use of "prescriptive" notation by composers as a means of directing performers. As will be explained later, however, ethnomusicologists as well as com-posers can make effective use of prescriptive notation.

Aside from indigenous systems of notation that have been developed particularly in the Orient, and are preferred to Western notation by some specialists in these cultures, just three methods of notation are commonly employed by ethnomusicologists. The first is Western staff notation, with or without additional symbols; the second makes use of manually produced graphs and diagrams; and the third is electronic or machine transcription. Other systems such as sol-fa, number or cypher, and "shape note" notation are less often used.

The use of staff notation "for the transcription of exotic melodies" was first systematised by Abraham and Hornbostel,[403] whose method also later formed the basis for recommendations issued by the International Music Council.[404]

Using staff notation, some of the most productive early ethnomusicologists such as Hornbostel, Kolinski, Roberts and others transcribed thousands of songs. There was good reason for this. A large corpus of transcribed songs was an essential preliminary to analysis, and remains so. My own case is not atypical. Before tackling a commission from Raymond Firth to provide a structural analysis of his Tikopia collection, I spent all my research time for two years transcribing in full some 60 songs. Only then did I begin detailed analysis. The results justified the effort because out of the data emerged both rhythmic and other rules, and a system of Tikopia modes that hitherto was unsuspected, and without the transcription and analysis could not have been discovered. Nowadays, however, both large-scale transcription and analysis are eschewed by most ethnomusicologists. Whole books are published with neither in evidence. Why has this happened?

It would seem that the current flight from transcription has taken place for multiple reasons:

One profoundly influential cause was evidently a judgement at UCLA that, for performance purposes, Javanese gamelan music was best notated not in Western notation, but by means of the indigenous Javanese number notation system. As attention at UCLA was predominantly directed towards non-Western art musics with long-standing such notation systems of their own, the perception appears to have taken root that Western notation is inappropriate in all circumstances. Mantle Hood, indeed, who was a powerful advocate for machine transcription, went so far as to brand standard notation as an "ethnocentric crutch".[405]

A second reason, also emanating from Mantle Hood's Institute of Ethnomusicology at UCLA, was the move there to apply machine transcription, using what Hood calls the "Seeger solution" to problems of transcription, on the grounds that this is more "objective" as well as less culturally biased. Although machine transcription using the Seeger melograph never did live up to

---
[402] Randel 2003:902.
[403] Abraham & Hornbostel 1909-10 & 1994.
[404] International Music Council 1952.
[405] Hood 1971:90.

early expectations of it, ethnomusicologists at large may well have become concerned that future developments in machine transcription would show up their own hand notation efforts as deficient or, at worst, render them redundant. This concern, at least, can now be laid to rest, arising, as it does, and will be explained later, from lack of understanding about the transcription process itself. A machine can provide a highly detailed "descriptive" transcription, but never a "prescriptive" one. Except as a transcription aid and for analysis of intonation and micro-data (such as attack, decay and vibrato), machine transcription cannot, in fact, substitute for the judgement of a human transcriber.

A third reason for neglect of standard transcription is that it is hard to do, and fewer people than in the past now have the skill to undertake it or, in the face of current attitudes, are willing to invest time to learn it.

In a long 1992 article on transcription, Ter Ellingson treats the subject throughout as a now irrelevant and outmoded historical process. In these views, Ellingson is evidently representative of the current orthodoxy. If, however, as this orthodoxy suggests, objective transcription is impossible using Western notation and invariably gives misleading results, stylistic and areal uniformities elucidated in the past by analysis of transcriptions could never have emerged. The so-called defective hand transcription methods of Cecil Sharp, and others, for example, would never have revealed the English modal system, or my own transcriptions of Tikopia songs the Tikopia modes, which were unsuspected until after the transcriptions were done and analysis carried out. The same is true of the Maori "rule-of-eight" system of numerical metre, which in this case emerged when the transcriptions were examined by a third party who happened to be a trained linguist. Such transcriptions prove the validity of the process, as do the multitude of transcriptions at the hand of other scholars that over many years have increased our knowledge of music systems world wide. Ellingson's criticisms are over-generalisations based on too few particulars and a narrow view of world music confined largely to Oriental and other systems with which he is most familiar and which evidently present special problems. Most of the objections he voices about transcription simply do not apply to the many music systems for which analysis has proved them to be suited.

The current research emphasis away from "product" towards "process" and a shift to topics such as cognition, symbolism, metaphor, gender studies and a host of others is represented by Ellingson as an alternative to now outmoded transcription and analysis which focused, inappropriately according to him, on music sound. Of course it is not a substitute and there is no reason why the two approaches cannot be continued in parallel.

PRESCRIPTIVE v. DESCRIPTIVE NOTATION

In a 1958 paper, Charles Seeger made an important and fundamental distinction between two methods of music notation he called "prescriptive and descriptive." To use his own words, the one is "a blue-print of how a specific piece of music shall be made to sound" and the other "a report of how a specific performance of it actually did sound." [406] After this admirable start, Seeger somewhat obfuscates the issue. To put it in its simplest terms, however, the distinction itself could be illustrated, perhaps, by comparing a published standard notation of the New Zea-

---

[406] Seeger 1958:1.

land national song, "God Defend New Zealand", with an exact transcription of a football club's rendition of it, complete with all the deviations introduced, intentionally or otherwise, by the quite possibly inebriated singers. Which is the "correct" version? Plainly in this case the published one, which was written and approved by the composer, and serves as a referent for future performances, offsetting the possibility that the football club versions would be learned and passed on orally with all their imperfections to the next generation of singers, ultimately, perhaps, producing a not even recognisable variant.

Seeger goes on to express his belief that Western notation is really only suitable for the writing of Western music, because as a prescriptive device it was developed for this purpose, and carries with it "between the notes" implications that are inappropriate for other forms of music. To overcome this disability, new symbols can be added to the existing ones; hand graphing may be substituted; or a machine can be developed to draw the graphs automatically. Only in this way, Seeger goes on to demonstrate, can subtle elements of style like crescendo and decrescendo, attack, decay and vibrato be represented. In this, Seeger is setting up a case for the melograph machine he later commissioned to be built, and "descriptive" music writing is stated by him to be essential if musicology is ever to become a descriptive science.

In this, however, while happy to adopt Seeger's useful terms "descriptive" and "prescriptive", I beg to differ. No practising musician in the West would be content to perform either from a "descriptive" notation, whether or not laden with extra symbols, or from the graphical product of a machine. Why should a performer from another culture be any different? The assumption implicit in Seeger's rejection of prescriptive music writing is either that non-Western musicians don't read such notation and have no use for it, or that their music is so much more complex than ours that a prescription of it is impossible. Neither presumption is necessarily true, and in my view a Maori waiata is as deserving of a prescriptive notation as a European hymn, an English folk song or a Beethoven sonata. Fortunately there are ways to produce such notations once the music system has been worked out. The solution is to include in the notation only those elements that are essential to the performance, as demonstrated by the performers themselves. Matters such as attack, decay, and vibrato are peripheral even in European music and can safely be left out unless shown to be intrinsic to the style.

Also left out of a prescriptive notation are the "between the notes" elements of style, referred to by Seeger. These are not, as supposed by Seeger, implied by the notation, but are merely absent from it. The Western musician becomes familiar with these as a result both of instruction and familiarity with the idiom. A piano student, for example, spends long hours mastering the art of legato playing which enables the notes on paper to be connected in an aesthetically acceptable manner. But the notation system itself provides no guidance on this except to make a distinction if staccato is required instead. Similarly, a transcription of a Maori recited composition, notated without indication of pitch, leaves it to the performer to execute drops of pitch which occur naturally at the ends of phrases, in practice could be performed in no other way, and accordingly do not need to be indicated in the notation.

The question of detail

It must be emphasised that the difference between a descriptive and a prescriptive notation is not, as often assumed, the mere presence of "detail" in the one and absence of it in the other.

Simply leaving out detail results not in a prescriptive notation but a skeletal or pared down one which, like descriptive notation itself, may have its uses for analysis, but is not prescriptive. A prescriptive notation is one that is intended to convey to a performer the essentials for a culturally acceptable performance of the music, and to convey also to an analyst the culturally relevant aspects of the music necessary for a full understanding of it. What matters in a prescriptive transcription, in other words, is not absence of detail as such, but the presence of significant detail. The details to be left out have to be those whose omission will make no difference to the correctness of the performance as judged not by the transcriber but by the performer or practitioner of the style.

The debate about how much detail to include in a transcription is a long-standing one, centring largely on the merits or otherwise of machine transcription (see later). The difference between the significant and the non-significant in notation, however, is something that John Blacking for one understood and applied to his work. In discussing his Venda transcriptions he writes:

> During twenty-two months' intimate contact with Venda music, I learnt to distinguish what is musically significant: I have therefore omitted the notation of coughs, sneezes, shouts, wrong notes and faulty entries, which some musicologists seem to regard as the hallmark of good transcription.[407]

The contrary idea that detail is paramount can probably be laid at the door of the great transcriber of Hungarian folk music, Béla Bartók. He has always been admired for his acute ear and the wealth of minute detail in his transcriptions, and for this reason his work has probably been seen as a standard to be emulated. I am unaware of whether there was ever a revival of folk song in Hungary resulting from Bartók's work. But if Cecil Sharp and others had included extraneous performance detail in their transcriptions of English folk music, the later folk music revival in England, aided as it was by their published transcriptions, might never have happened. What mattered here were the magnificent modal tunes, later to be so effectively made use of by nationalist composers such as Ralph Vaughan Williams (1872–1958) and now accepted as icons of English identity.

The one demerit for a transcriber of attempting prescriptive notations of non-Western music is that they depend heavily on the familiarity of the transcriber with the style, are inevitably to this degree "subjective", and can be startlingly different from the sound as heard on a recording of the music in question. The danger to the transcriber in such cases is that the transcription will be rejected as "inaccurate" because of its lack of conformity to particular performances of the item transcribed.

The necessary familiarity with the style can obviously come only after considerable exposure to it. John Blacking gained confidence in his ability to judge unfamiliar Venda music after not quite two years in the field; Cecil Sharp had a much longer experience of English folk song to guide him, extending over some 20 years; and Jaap Kunst gained familiarity with Netherlands folk music as a result of repeated summer vacations on the Friesian island of Terschelling, where he conducted his earliest field work. None hesitated to depart from a literal transcription

---

[407] Blacking 1970:4.

of a performance if this seemed appropriate. A nice story about Kunst, which has been quoted unjustly to his detriment, illustrates the point:

During the transcription of one of his Terschelling songs, Kunst is said to have remarked: " 'He sings it now like this, but he probably means this!', and he wrote down the latter".[408] Far from being cavalier with his informants, Kunst had become aware very early in his career of the prescriptive/descriptive distinction (albeit as yet unnamed) and chose not to represent what, in his judgement, was a mistake on the part of the singer.

When I began my own transcriptions of Maori music, as the requisite familiarity was then lacking, my transcriptions were necessarily largely "descriptive". If I was uncertain of a singer's intention, I transcribed the passage concerned as nearly as possible exactly as heard and as sung. On occasion this required the devising of special symbols to indicate practice for which standard notation was unavailable. One such symbol, applied to a single song by a single singer recorded during my first field trip, involved an upward microtonal inflection that occurred on a particular note at each repetition of the strophe. As the song progressed, this turned eventually into an unequivocal major second, showing that the earlier inflections were merely gropings or incipient rises towards the intended note. In a published or final transcription of this song, persisting with the inflected notes rather than substituting the intended one would give a misleading impression of the song.

One highly noticeable feature of Maori singing, which would be entirely inappropriate to show in a prescriptive (or, indeed, any) transcription, is a tendency to "flat". It is barely discernible when each repeating strophe is compared with the one before or after, but if the first strophe of the song is compared with the last, after multiple repetitions and a performance that may have lasted for three or more minutes, the pitch will be found to have dropped by upwards of a minor third. Analysis shows that the drooping frequently takes place on just one note in the repeating strophe. All of the other notes then adjust to the new one, pulling down the pitch of the tonal centre, until the offending note is again reached and the process repeats. Should this note be indicated in the transcription as flat? Plainly not because, if it were meant to be flat, the succeeding notes would not adjust to it. An incautious or too literally-minded transcriber might interpret this process as microtonal downward "modulation" in a succession of quarter-tone or smaller shifts of "key". Of course, it is no such thing. It is simply flatting, no different in principle from that to be heard in the singing of almost any untrained Western choir. As such, it is not a process intrinsic to the Maori music system, even though it commonly occurs.

Conceptual notation

In his survey of transcription for Helen Myers's book *Ethnomusicology: An Introduction*,[409] Ter Ellingson comes close to rejecting transcription in Western notation as a still viable alternative to other methods.

Early in the article, he reports the late 20th-century trend as "neither strictly prescriptive nor descriptive, but rather cognitive or 'conceptual' ", which "seeks to portray musical sound as an

---

[408] Heins 1994:18.
[409] Myers 1992.

embodiment of musical concepts held by a culture." This he sees as reflecting a general move "away from objectivist intercultural discovery procedures towards problems of conceptualization seen from within a culture . . ."[410] So described, it is a little hard to know what is meant by this as an alternative to prescriptive notation, but it plainly cannot apply if the culture concerned has no concepts of music relevant to notation which can guide the transcriber. It would appear to be a product of study bias towards so-called "high cultures" with notation systems and/or a body of written music theory of their own. As will be seen, however, there is no reason why prescriptive notation, as defined above, cannot be universally applied or meet the same criteria.

Later in his article, Ellingson elaborates upon his earlier statement and mounts arguments for a different approach to transcription. Part of the problem has nothing to do with the merits or otherwise of transcription as such but is simply a shift away from problems that require its use. Thus Ellingson identifies a move in research focus from "product" to "process", and a concurrent shift from earlier concerns and areal emphases for which transcription was necessary and appropriate towards "social, political, economic and symbolic factors in musical systems."

Scales and intervals are represented by Ellingson as "transcriptional artefacts" as if they are somehow not real. And the "greatest upheaval" is seen to reside in the discovery of equiheptatonic scales in SE Asia (and later Africa and Oceania), which cannot easily be represented in standard notation, as well as the revelation of Indonesian scales whose interval structures vary from octave to octave, throwing doubt on scales as a series of "fixed discrete tone steps."

Long-standing difficulties involving complex problems of rhythm and polyphony in African music have evidently also played their part, and numerous innovative and non-standard ways of dealing with these, as developed by researchers on African music, are cited.

Finally, examples of Tibetan melodies are quoted from Ellingson's own area of expertise for which no form of transcription is deemed to be appropriate.

Taken together, the inference is drawn that European notation is defective and a "crucial question" must be asked as to whether it leads to "misconceptions, violations of musical logic and distortions of objective and acoustic fact".[411] All of the time and in all cultures, one can reasonably ask, or only some of the time and in some cultures? If the latter is true then the above difficulties are not a valid argument against transcription.

Ellingson's solution is a departure from both descriptive and prescriptive notation to a machine-aided graphical alternative he calls "conceptual transcription". Standard notation is conceded as having worked "quite well" in the past, and it is only in "special cases and wider perspectives" that they fail. Nevertheless, the trend, he believes, is towards the new paradigm. Explaining this in his own words:

> In classical Hornhostelian transcription, musical features are presumed to be unknown and awaiting discovery in the objective representation of musical sound; and the transcriber is responsible for precisely and exhaustively notating all objective features of musical sound

---

[410] Ellingson 1992:110-1.
[411] Ellingson 1992:137-40.

that might lead to any significant discovery whatsoever. In a conceptual transcription, essential features are presumed to be already known through fieldwork, performance lessons, study of traditional written and aural notations and learning and leadership processes. The transcription then becomes a means not of discovering, but of defining and exemplifying the acoustical embodiment of musical concepts essential to the culture and music.[412]

But is this a good idea, and are the criticisms mounted against standard notation convincing? I believe not. The term "prescriptive" remains the most useful if the object is to convey the intention of a performer, and standard notation remains the best way of accomplishing it. The bottom line of Ellingson's description of "conceptual transcription" is that it is useless for discovering anything new, and serves only to reinforce and illustrate the transcriber's own preconceptions. Moreover, it is not even needed. If, as Ellingson concedes, standard notation remains appropriate for most applications, then there is no reason to abandon it, especially as it has performed until now not merely "quite well", as he represents it, but superlatively well, resulting in numerous insights which no alternative system could possibly match. Few ethnomusicologists would claim that it is perfect, or that it is appropriate for every form of world music. But transcribers have always made use of technical aids, whether tuning forks, monochords, wax cylinder dictaphones, acetate discs, wire and tape recorders, oscilloscopes, sonographs, frequency analysers or melographs to assist transcription, and today's technical aids and alternative representational systems are no different in principle. They can be used as substitutes for transcription if necessary, but otherwise as useful supplementary devices to aid the transcription process, with a transcription in standard notation still emerging as an end product that encapsulates most of the information sought, and remains most readily comprehensible to a majority of trained ethnomusicologists.

The case for literacy

What of the claim that European notation necessarily misrepresents the non-European and should no longer be undertaken at all? Crucial to this is the concept of literacy itself. The historian H. Stuart Hughes advances the interesting idea that the 17th through 19th centuries in Europe were centuries dominated by literary languages, during which rationalism, individualism, capitalism and the nation state all emerged to begin the "classic" era of European world domination; language was "fixed in the dead print of grammars and dictionaries"; and sight predominated over hearing.[413] Just as spoken language is given fixed form in the written word, so too does music become fixed when it is notated, and literacy in music becomes as much of a requirement as literacy in language. This, indeed, is commonly advanced by musicologists as the great leap forward that enabled the intention of individual composers to be conveyed to the future and faithfully reproduced in performance, however long the lapse of time after the creation of the music. But this is not all. Once music has been written down, it becomes possible to examine the notation in order to compile the equivalent of the grammars and dictionaries of spoken language.

---

[412] Ellingson 1992:141-2.
[413] Hughes 1964:38ff, cited by Hopkins 1977:250.

In all of this there is a familiar constellation of ideas that goes some way towards explaining the latter-day backlash against transcription as a legitimate means of representing non-Western music. Rationalism dominated scholarship in the 18th century Age of Reason, tempered by British empiricism; the individual and individual expression reigned supreme in 19th century Western art; the value ascribed to literacy in the West led to 20th century classification of cultures as literate or non-literate; and the rise of the nation state, especially that of the United Kingdom, led ultimately to colonialism and the imposition of Western values on the rest of the world. With the collapse of colonialism, recognition of alternative cultural values, and many of the earlier verities falling out of favour or being called to question, little wonder that transcription should join the list.

Understandable as it may be, however, guilt by association is not an acceptable basis for judgement; nor are the merits or influence of one philosophy as opposed to another. In the end, such matters as 17th century rationalism and empiricism are irrelevant. In practical terms, transcription in standard notation remains as useful for non-Western music as it is for the Western system for which it was first devised. By good fortune, it is close to "universal" in the sense that it makes possible the representation of pitch, duration and most other elements of music structure, as found in music systems everywhere, and not just those of the West.

No one supposes that we should abandon reading, writing and world literature in favour of the unsupported spoken word. Nor does anyone suggest it was not a good idea to devise orthographies for spoken languages which hitherto had never been written down. As soon as Maori people learned to read and write in the 1830s, after an orthography had been devised for Maori by European missionaries, they themselves enthusiastically began to compile waiata books containing the texts of their own traditional songs, making efforts to be as faithful to the oral originals as possible in doing so. Many of these manuscript books are now preserved in New Zealand libraries, others will doubtless be added to them as time goes on, and future scholarship by Maori people themselves will be aided. What's so different about writing down the music as well? When *Traditional Songs of the Maori*, containing both texts and music transcriptions of 50 traditional Maori songs was reprinted in 1990,[414] one reviewer thought it was a waste of effort because Maori do not learn songs from music notation. He was wrong, and will become increasingly so in future as more Maori people become literate in reading music. An opposite point of view was expressed by a Maori academic before the publication of *Songs of a Kaumātua*, containing transcriptions of a further 60 songs.[415] He was well aware of the effect of "fixing" the texts and music in such a publication, fearing that this would hinder alternative interpretations of the songs. He too was mistaken, in part by ignoring the deep conservatism of his own people and the expressed intent of all of the singers to be accurate in their renditions. Moreover, the recordings themselves from which the transcriptions were made also serve to fix the particular performances as a standard to be followed. These were supplied on CD both with *Songs of a Kaumātua* and a third edition of *Traditional Songs of the Maori*,[416] where they can be used by learners in association with the transcriptions. By this time, Maori people had begun to sing the songs differently, not from any intention or desire to do so, but because by then the mostly young learners had lost the necessary familiarity with traditional style to be capable of

---

[414] McLean & Orbell 1990.
[415] Orbell & McLean 2002.
[416] McLean & Orbell 2004.

reproducing earlier models, and were unwittingly changing them to conform to the rules of European music which by now was their first musical language. With both notations and recordings as a guide, they will now have the opportunity to assess whether they wish to persist with the new versions or would rather modify them to bring them into closer conformity with the old.

Composite transcription

How can one make a successful prescriptive transcription? And having made the attempt, how can one be sure it is correct? If there is a discrepancy between a transcription and a recorded performance, there are just two possibilities: either the performer made a mistake which the transcriber chose to ignore, or the transcriber is wrong. To avoid error, the transcriber should ideally be as familiar with the system as the performer. But there is another way.

Maori waiata take the form of repeating melodic strophes, coincident with textual lines, in which the same melody is repeated over and over, with different words line by line. The principle, in other words, is much the same as in European strophic songs where a single melody serves for each verse of a song. In a waiata, the "basic melody" is, or ought to be, the same at each presentation, varying only in the manner in which text is accommodated to the tune. Comparison of strophes provides a simple way of identifying occasional unintended departures from the tune during performance.

A related technique I have used for Maori waiata whenever there are sufficient recordings with which to work, is to compare different renditions of the same song, either by the same or different singers, and include in the transcription only those aspects of the performances that are common to all or most of the several recordings. In this way a consensus can be arrived at of the essential features of the song, as demonstrated by the singers. Obviously this is a technique that can be used only if the song has an identifiable culturally agreed tune that is meant to be performed the same way on each occasion, and is performed by groups whose members are in conformity with each other (i.e. in what Lomax would call a "cohesive" performance). These desiderata all apply to Maori waiata. Another sine qua non is to make sure that the performances used for the composite transcription really do have the same melody and are not variants. Plainly, one would not attempt to merge variants.[417]

I hope it does not have to be emphasised that this process is not done haphazardly or at the whim of the transcriber and, although Western notation is employed, is in no sense imposing "Western" prescriptive conventions on the music transcribed. The object always is to determine the intention of the singer in terms of the singer's own music system, while taking account of performance variability.

An illustrative use of this technique was my transcription of the waiata "Ka eke ki Wairaka" as published in *Traditional Songs of the Maori*.[418] The first recording I obtained of this song was in somewhat Europeanised style and was sung throughout in a uniform 3/4 time. Later re-

---

[417] For an example of variant versions of a song from different districts, see transciptions 15 and 15A in McLean and Orbell 1990.
[418] McLean & Orbell 1990, Song 6.

cordings all contained sections in 7/8 time, applied to different passages of the song in each case, though with some overlap. The 7/8 resulted from a lengthening by one quaver of a particular long note in the song but not in all of the strophes. On this evidence, I thought it justifiable to notate the entire song in 7/8, applying the lengthening in every strophe, and thereby producing a "prescriptive" notation that reflected the perceived intentions of the singers. Years later, I found a superb recording of the same song in the collection of the New Zealand Broadcasting Service, recorded on acetate disc from a group of Ngati Tuwharetoa singers in the years before I began my own field work. The entire performance was in 7/8 time, vindicating my transcription. And when I led the song myself at Maori meetings, I always did so in 7/8, which was matched by the other singers when they joined in, drawing praise from one notable singer on the last occasion I did so: "You pretty good!"

Having recounted one success, let me also reveal a failure, resulting this time from lack of recordings from which to make a composite transcription. It concerns one transcription of mine I am sure will ultimately come home to haunt me and will doubtless be cited to my detriment. In *Songs of a Kaumātua*,[419] written jointly with Margaret Orbell, who provided the song translations, there is a pao sung by Kino Hughes for which no other recording exists and which it was not practicable to transcribe as sung. Kino sang it in a highly idiosyncratic variable sprechgesang stereotypic style which he occasionally used for pao known to no one else, and which could not be represented in music notation, except perhaps as a series of contours of no fixed pitch, varying throughout the song. The particular song broke all the rules enunciated above in terms of suitability for transcription. Margaret, however, wanted to include the song in the book, because of the text, so I agreed to attempt a transcription of the music. After playing the song many times, and being reminded in doing so of other similar performances by Kino, it seemed to me that hidden among Kino's contours was the shadow of a tune it may once have resembled (a kind of enigma variation or "hidden theme" like the tunes buried in jazz improvisations), so I attempted a reconstruction. It was highly speculative; it was not truly prescriptive unless I happened to be right in my conjectures; I was extremely doubtful about it; and I wish now I had not included it. Let me say, however, that with this exception the prescriptive transcriptions in this book are closer to the intentions of the singers than some of the recordings from which the transcriptions were made, and this is the rationale for the method.

INTONATION

Early in the history of ethnomusicology there was arguably an over-emphasis on matters bearing upon intonation, arising from presuppositions about its importance within music systems. It would take a person with a very blunt ear indeed not to notice the apparent "out of tuneness" of a Scottish bagpipe, a Solomon Islands equiheptatonic panpipe ensemble, or a Balinese gamelan. And it would have been equally obvious to early scholars that the tonal systems of exotic styles did not always accord with the system of equal temperament that is now usual in the West. There had, indeed, been argument among musicologists since time immemorial about the exact nature of the ancient Greek tonal system (though no one for millennia had first-hand experience of it), resulting in numerous publications about it. Early attention became focused on exotic tonal systems with the publication of A.J. Ellis's " On the Musical Scales of Various Nations",[420]

---

[419] McLean & Orbell 2002.
[420] Ellis 1885.

which made use of the cents system of precise pitch measurement introduced by him. Also, as knowledge of the Indian 22-sruti tonal system as expounded by indigenous Indian theorists from about the 2nd century AD onwards added its impact, this too would have contributed to an expectation that exotic tonal systems involved perception of fine tonal gradations of incredible precision, and careful measurement of intervals was necessary in order to elucidate them. Thus Jaap Kunst, whose primary research interest was the music of Indonesia, emphasised the importance of pitch measurement, not only for unravelling the Indonesian tonal system but, by implication, for all music. In consequence he regarded Ellis's cents system of measuring intervals as one of the essential precursors leading to the development of ethnomusicology as a discipline. In arriving at this judgement, Kunst undoubtedly had in mind the Berlin School of comparative musicology, which was founded by Carl Stumpf, and greatly influenced later ethnomusicology. Stumpf reviewed Ellis's paper the year after it was published,[421] and thereafter he and his associates in Berlin made extensive use of its methods for "tonometrical" analysis of scales as part of their effort to place comparative musicology on a firm scientific footing by means of precise objective measurements.

The Berlin emphasis on precise tonometrical analysis was emulated also by one of the first American scholars to attempt analysis of North American Indian music, Benjamin Ives Gilman (1852–1933), who was likewise influenced by Ellis, and in turn impacted upon Stumpf.

In his article on Zuñi melodies,[422] Gilman documented minute deviations from the Western tempered scale which he believed to be characteristic, even though Stumpf pointed out technical flaws in the equipment that affected the recordings' reliability, and John Comfort Fillmore argued that the deviations from the Western scale were accidental and insignificant.[423] Gilman's approach nevertheless set an extremely unfortunate precedent that was to be followed by others.

Kunst devotes a considerable portion of his book *Ethnomusicology* to explaining various methods developed by Hornbostel and other Berlin School scholars of calculating the cent values of intervals.[424] One of Hornbostel's pupils, Husmann, published a set of tables to simplify the task,[425] and several later scholars did likewise.[426]

Kunst's views about the fundamental importance of Ellis's contribution have been echoed ever since by ethnomusicologists, but without examining them critically. A similar attitude to that of Kunst towards pitch measurement is implicit also in Seeger's wish to develop electronic transcription devices that would be more accurate than the human ear (albeit begging the question of why the human ear of the transcriber is unable to discriminate pitches intended for and produced by other humans). It seems to have been overlooked that the "exotic" tuning systems described hitherto were confined to instruments of fixed pitch. Ellis himself was careful to emphasise this in the titles of his papers. But, for one reason or another, the expectation that non-Western peoples conform to the pitch of their fixed pitch instruments in their vocal music, and sing with

---

[421] Stumpf 1886b.
[422] Gilman 1891.
[423] DeVale 2003.
[424] Kunst 1959a:2-9.
[425] Husmann 1951.
[426] All of these methods have now been overtaken by electronic instruments that provide a cents readout of any note.

amazing precision, seems to have become part of the thinking of Western musicologists, without need to test the assumption. Thus, even before Ellis published his papers, when the English scholar James A. Davies tried to notate the songs of Maori visitors to Cambridge, England, in the 1850s, he noticed the discrepancy between the intervals they sang and those of the European tempered scale, and notated them as precisely as he could, having assumed a use of quarter tones similar to the enharmonic genera of the ancient Greeks.[427] The notion of Maori quarter tones has persisted to the present day, on the part of Maori and Europeans alike, as an unshakeable article of New Zealand popular belief, despite evidence to the contrary. The truth is that Maori do not sing in quarter tones, though at times they may seem to do so. Careful analysis of the entire corpus of some 1300 traditional Maori songs recorded during my field work of the 1950s and 1960s demonstrates conclusively that quarter tones are not systematic in Maori music but, when they appear, are a product of performance variability.[428] Davies's work, however, has had repercussions much beyond its effect on the New Zealand popular psyche, having reached ethnomusicologists as well. Ellingson, in his recent survey of transcription practice,[429] speaks approvingly of Davies, stressing the accuracy of his method and its relevance to future work:

> James Davies went so far as to devise a graduated monochord for tonometric studies which convinced him that Maori scales were non-diatonic, and he devised special signs to show quarter-tone differences from European notes in his transcriptions. Behind this seemingly esoteric fixation on minute details lies a revolutionary development: Europeans were beginning to discover music as it existed in the real world of cultural diversity, rather than as imagined and misperceived through the constrictions of their own localized practices and theories. A solid scholarly tradition was forming that, towards the end of the 19th century, was developing a consensus that European concepts and methods, including transcription in European notation, gave an inadequate and misleading base for musical understanding.[430]

Accepting for the moment that my own view of Maori quarter tones is more realistic and reliable than that of Davies, who had access to only a few singers who were not necessarily expert, what does this tell us? If Davies was not after all dealing with the "real world" but was imposing a different and fictitious reality of his own, derived as it was from ideas about the music of the ancient Greeks and a notion that the Maori system was the same, the foundation for future studies, was far from "solid" but more like quicksand. Moreover, a number of subsequent scholars have managed to sink themselves in the same quagmire. For example, when Catherine Ellis began to study the scales of Aboriginal songs of Central Australia in the 1960s, much of her effort went into the precise calculation of intervals using the cents system.[431] And before this, intonation was a primary concern of Norma McLeod at the University of London, in her master's thesis on Tikopian songs from the Raymond Firth collection, using in her case an apparatus of vibrating resonant reeds to judge the pitches.[432] Such efforts were, in fact, largely wasted, be-

---

[427] Davies 1855.
[428] McLean 1996:245ff.
[429] Ellingson 1992.
[430] Ellingson 1992:116-7.
[431] Ellis 1964; Later, using a method of electronic measurement involving filters in steps of 2 cps, she claimed that Aborigines sang in "arithmetic" steps of the same 2 cps (Ellis 1965), but evidently failed to recognise that this result could have been a product of the measurement method rather than the singing.
[432] McLeod 1957.

cause they were carried out with insufficient understanding of performance variability. The demise of supposed Maori quarter tones was not the only casualty of improved understanding:

- Using the same apparatus as employed by McLeod at the University of London, Jairazbhoy demonstrated that Indians do not conform to the theoretical 22-sruti system, and showed that performance variability was, in fact, such that if tempered intervals were used instead of the theoretically prescribed ones, the performance would be accepted as authentic by Indian audiences.[433] There is even, indeed, a question as to whether the instruments measured by Ellis which "proved" the system were representative. A contemporary of Ellis, the Indian scholar Sourindro Mohun Tagore (1840–1914), whose writings in English were accepted in the West as authoritative, is reputed to have "Sanskritised" names of Indian instruments as well as "presented a number of highly questionable reconstructions of ancient instruments, together with hybrid forms which were possibly of his own invention." One of these, "a so-called sruti vina (i.e. a small sitar with fixed frets)", he sent to Ellis and asked for it to be tested to determine the pitches of the 22 sruti intervals.[434] Was it a prepared instrument?

- After extensive field work and analysis of hundreds of recordings from the Pintupi and Alyawarra tribes of central Australia, Richard Moyle has made convincing analyses of their music and the scales they employ without need for elaborate measures of intonation.[435]

- Finally, the same proved true of my own later analysis of the entire Firth collection of Tikopia songs first worked upon by McLeod, in this case revealing a system of standard modes governing all of the intervals used,[436] and proving that small deviations of pitch were non-significant.

It may be argued that Maori singers must once have used quarter tones but have lost them since 1855, perhaps under the impact of European music, or that Indian singers once conformed to the sruti system but have likewise and for the same reasons ceased to do so. This, however, is not tenable. Davies noted variability on the part of his singers at the time of notating them but chose to ignore it. Moreover, a study of Maori flute scales from museum specimens antedating Davies reveals scales whose steps are not microtonal and which conform to present-day vocal scales.[437] Finally, as early as 1792, the Orientalist Sir William Jones (1746–1794) was pointing out that Indian scales, as actually performed, did not conform to the sruti system but seemed closer to the European one.[438]

---

[433] Jairazbhoy's findings (Jairazbhoy & Stone 1963) have since been amply vindicated by Levy (1982) in a careful analysis which confirms that far from being invariable and precise, Indian performances deviate from all of the theoretical systems of tuning whether just, pythagorean or equally tempered. The pitches most consonant with the drone are found to be most stable, and the flat third, sixth and seventh most variable. As well, pitches tended to be sharpened when ascending and flattened when descending (for a review, see Row 1984). None of this should be a surprise. Much the same happens in Western music, which does not conform in performance to its theoretical norms either. To provide only two examples, violinists know to tune their A string slightly sharp to the piano in order to get the best fit between their playing and a piano accompaniment; and opera singers notoriously deviate in pitch.
[434] Bor 1988:64.
[435] Moyle 1979; Moyle 1986,
[436] McLean 1991.
[437] McLean 1996:op.cit.
[438] Jones 1772, cited by Ellingson 1992:114-5.

It may well be that even tonal systems whose intervals are known and acknowledged to be fundamentally different from those of the West, such as those of Indonesia and the Middle East, have emerged invariably as a product of instrumental music rather than unaccompanied vocal music, where there are no referents such as the fixed pitches of the gongs in a gamelan to guide the performers. One unquestionable example of this is the famous equiheptatonic system of the 'Are'are people of Malaita in the Solomon Islands, as demonstrated in publications and recordings by Hugo Zemp. This tuning system of seven equal intervals within the octave, occurs in some but not all of the 'Are'are panpipe ensembles, and, significantly, does not apply to the vocal music of the same people, which is non-equiheptatonic.[439]

It need not be a surprise that extremely precise intonation such as supposed Maori quarter tones and the intervals of the Indian sruti system are either non-existent or are not observed in practice. Close to 90 years ago, Stumpf and Hornbostel were aware that the object of a transcription should be to work out the "intention" of the singers,[440] and implicit in this was an understanding that performances are not always exact, but are subject to variability.

Performance variability is a fact of our own Western music system as well, and this has been known for the best part of 70 years as a result of pioneering work by the American psychologist Carl Seashore.

Carl E. Seashore (1866–1949), photographed in 1945

Seashore showed that even the famous Western violinists of his time, such as Elman, Kreisler, Menuhin, Slatkin and Szigeti, for whom exact intonation was a credo, deviated from exact pitch on an average of 0.1 of a tone, or 20 cents.[441] The standard Western tempered scale, the so-called natural scale, and the Pythagorean scale were all shown to be within the limits of violin-playing variability, with the latter closer than the others.[442] Discrepancies in the performance of vocal music are even greater, disguised in Western art-singing by the use of vibrato and other devices of artistic licence. "It is obvious", said Seashore, "that singers never remain for as much as a tenth of a second in true pitch as a physical fact."

Seashore's findings are vindicated by more recent understanding of what is going on to produce such deviations. An article in the *New Grove Dictionary of Musical Instruments* (1984) states:

> A singer or violinist will inflect certain intervals depending on their immediate context, but he does not produce thereby a specific temperament because at different moments he

---

[439] Zemp 1972.
[440] Ellingson 1992:120.
[441] Seashore 1938:212.
[442] Seashore 1938:224-5.

will represent each note of the scale by different shades of pitch within a fairly narrow band (about half as wide again, perhaps, as his vibrato).[443]

This being the case, why then should we expect performers of traditions other than our own to be any more exact? And except to demonstrate the imprecision of adherence to tonal systems, whatever is the point of ever greater accuracy of measurement?

Western concepts, methods, and transcription in European notation do not after all impede understanding. Quite the reverse is true, because it is only through empirical methods and analysis that knowledge of the true structure of a music system can emerge. The message must be not that transcription and analysis is useless, as some ethnomusicologists now suppose, but simply that they must have regard to performance reality.

MACHINE TRANSCRIPTION

The idea of registering folk music objectively with the aid of electronic apparatus appears to have had its origins with a method called "phonophotography" developed in the 1920s by Milton Metfessel.[444] By the use of this method in the 1930s, Carl Seashore was able to answer many of the fundamental questions about the nature and limits of musical perception fully two decades before these became an issue among ethnomusicologists.[445]

Machine transcription of music assumed prominence for ethnomusicologists in the 1950s with two parallel developments: the first was the announcement by Charles Seeger at UCLA of his "Instantaneous Music Notator", which became known as the Seeger Melograph Model A,[446] together with the publication by Seeger of some interim results from its use in 1958;[447] the other, also in 1958, was the publication of a monograph by Karl Dahlback, called *New Methods of Vocal Folk Music Research*, reporting the results from a machine that had been developed in Norway.[448] Other similar machines were later developed in Israel and Czechoslovakia.

Besides the model A melograph, which was capable of registering only whistling, two further melographs, models B and C, were built for UCLA, of which the last was the most ambitious. Papers resulting from work done with the Model C were published in *Selected Reports* in 1974.[449] The machine was eventually dismantled some time during the next five years and never replaced.[450] But no commitment followed for a return to standard hand transcription. On the contrary, according to Hood, as a result of the brief reign of the machine "we *knew* (italics Hood's) there can be no 'scientific' research in music without its equivalent or better." [451] This leap of faith on the part of Hood appears to have gone unchallenged, and has contributed to the

---

[443] Lindley 1984:540.
[444] Metfessel 1928.
[445] Seashore 1938.
[446] Seeger 1951.
[447] Seeger 1958.
[448] Dahlback 1958.
[449] *Selected Reports in Ethnomusicology*, 2(1).
[450] Hood 1979:78.
[451] Hood 1979:78.

demise of standard transcription as a tool in the arsenal of ethnomusicology, branding any subsequent reliance upon it as "unscientific".

Crucial questions arising from work with the melograph are: how accurate should a transcription be, and how far should the precision of the transcription be allowed to go?

Seeger was in no doubt. Only by the use of the melograph, he believed, could an adequate descriptive notation of the desired kind be made. Conventional notation could never suffice, as it is to oral tradition that the knowledge of what happens "between the notes" is customarily left, and it is this kind of detail that the machine can reveal. Moreover, in notating the music of other cultures by conventional methods, transcribers single out only structures that happen to be familiar to them, ignoring everything else for which they have no symbols.[452] In Seeger's est-imation, then, transcribers necessarily hear anything unfamiliar to them through a screen of ethnocentrism so dense that significant detail must always elude them. According to Seeger: "We do not hear what we think we hear".[453]

On the latter point, it must be conceded at once that Seeger indeed has a case. People at large do seem unable to perceive the unfamiliar, both visually and aurally. We know, for example, that the colour spectrum is continuous, yet we conceptualise only seven colours of the rainbow, seeing them in distinct bands that our conditioning has taught us to name. European radio and television announcers in New Zealand, after years of practice and instruction, are still unable to pronounce Maori names. And, as already explained, Maori young people who attempt to learn waiata are unable to hear the unfamiliar interval patterns, substituting for them the European ones they know best. Are ethnomusicologists like this too? I would suggest, on the contrary, that training and experience does count for something, otherwise we have all been wasting our time. The answer to overcoming ethnocentric bias is intensive listening, and immersion in the culture to be studied.

On the issue of detail, Jaap Kunst flatly rejected Seeger's ideas. "It is possible," he said, "by applying a mechanical visual method of sound registration . . . to carry the exactitude of a transcription to a point where we cannot see the wood for the trees, so that the structure of the piece being transcribed has got completely out of hand. In my own view", he added, "the transcription by ear, in European notation, as nearly exact as possible, combined with the measurement of actually used intervals is nearly always sufficient for ethnomusicological purposes."[454]

Battle lines were thereby drawn, with Hood predictably supporting Seeger. In his 1963 article "Music the Unknown" he maintained:

> Thus we may state categorically that a thorough stylistic analysis of music–whether Western or non-Western–must be founded on the most accurate and detailed information that the imagination of the investigator and the marvels of an electronic age can produce.[455]

---

[452] Seeger 1958:186.
[453] Seeger 1958:194.
[454] Kunst 1959a:38.
[455] Hood 1963:273.

In his review of Hood's article, Merriam raised a fundamental possible flaw of the machine approach, pointing out it was not yet known what is and what is not significant in determining a musical style. "Is it not at least conceivable," he went on to say, "that the grosser measurements may be accurate enough to serve our understanding and that the time spent in achieving these finer details may be time lost?" [456]

Merriam's warning, prescient as it turned out to be, was not heeded, and in his later book *The Ethnomusicologist*, Hood was still speaking of the need for "objective display that eliminates the personal prejudice and aural bias naturally accumulated in the old methods of manual transcription." [457] In this statement, Hood was echoing Seeger's second argument that transcribers are necessarily incapable of perceiving the significant detail that only a machine can reveal.

An irony of Hood's book is that elsewhere in it he recounts an early object lesson from Kunst, when Hood was Kunst's student, during which Kunst, consistent with his later caveats concerning too much exactitude, advocated an exactly opposite approach.[458] Kunst was teaching Hood the rudiments of transcription by setting as an exercise the transcription into Western notation of an Indonesian soloist. While Kunst played a 78 rpm record of the music, he and Hood were to transcribe it independently, and then compare the results. To Hood's chagrin, Kunst transcribed the whole piece in about 20 minutes while Hood managed only a few notes, becoming bogged down on each attempt at a point in the music where there was an extremely complex cluster of five notes. When the time came to compare the two transcriptions, Kunst drew a circle around Hood's note cluster over which he had taken such pains, and revealed his own version of a single symbol placed over a quarter note! "This," he said, pointing to Hood's attempt, "is much too detailed. Get the principal pitches down and don't worry about the ornamentation. Too many details obscure the flow of the melody. Your notation won't look the way it sounds." And, Kunst might have added, the way it was intended to be sung. Kunst, who, unlike Hood at this stage in his career, was familiar with the Indonesian music system, had written what Seeger was later to call a "prescriptive" rather than "descriptive" notation. Because of his familiarity with the style, Kunst's "subjective" judgement in this case was superior to Hood's attempt at a more detailed and "objective" transcription.

It seems, however, that Hood was disinclined even as a student to agree with Kunst, arguing with him that, far from being unnecessary, the detail left out by Kunst established the Javanese character of the piece. In his book, Hood argues that the significance of the incident was to illustrate how much detail there should be in a transcription. There is, however, a more fund-amental point to be drawn from Kunst's lesson. In the notation of Western music, conventions have long since been worked out to the point that "ornaments" such as mordents, appogiaturas and turns do not have to be written out in detail but can be indicated, like Kunst's Indonesian note cluster, with a single agreed symbol. Ornaments such as grace notes are also not written out in exact time values, but rob their time from the notes to which they are attached in the notation. No Western performer would dream of asking for grace notes of this kind to be written out in exact time values, because the performer is aware that such exactitude is not essential to the performance, and the performer knows, in any event, how to interpret the symbol. The real problem

---

[456] Merriam 1964b:182.
[457] Hood 1971:21.
[458] Hood 1971:50-4.

with the Indonesian transcription in question would not have been how much or how little "detail" it was appropriate to indicate but whether Kunst's symbol was satisfactory as a conventional representation of the Indonesian sound, the test of which would be whether it could be rendered in appropriately Indonesian fashion by an Indonesian singer. To answer this question it would be necessary to know the conventions governing such melodic devices and whether they were invariable in performance, improvised, or subject to performance variability.

It is a little unfortunate that the term "ornamentation" carries with it an implication that such passages are non-essential. There are plenty of styles in which "ornament" is intrinsic. But this does not rule out the use of conventional transcription symbols such as grace notes to represent it. The Maori pao, for example, which is frequently highly ornamented (or, in technical terms, full of rapidly performed transient notes), is as much an object lesson as the Indonesian example with which Kunst tested Hood. In the Maori case, the "ornamentation" is best indicated in transcription not in written out form, but as a cluster of grace notes before or after a principal note to which the grace notes are tied in the transcription, and from which they rob their time like those of Western music. The same could be done for current improvisatory pop singing in which singers almost routinely embellish principal notes in such ways. If a study were made of this type of ornamentation it would almost certainly be found that the singers were following conventional if unformulated rules of some kind, as otherwise a style as such could not emerge. For such an exercise, the melograph could indeed be useful, not as a substitute for conventional staff notation, but as an aid towards it.

Who then, was right, Seeger and Hood, or Kunst and Merriam? There are two questions to be considered. The first is the question of detail and how much or how little to include in a transcription. The second is the issue of perceptual limits and whether these are severe enough to rule out human transcription as a reliable method.

On the first issue, the bottom line is significance. As earlier indicated, what matters in a transcription is not detail as such, but significant detail, which depends upon human interpretation and which a machine is unable to distinguish from the non-significant.

On the second issue, it seems obvious that no music system can exploit parameters that are beyond the capabilities of humans to perceive. In a 1963 paper," The Musical Significance of Transcription", George List rejects the assumption that normally inaudible detail can ever be musically significant, maintaining in common-sense fashion that

> Since music is man made, what is musically significant must be phenomena which man can hear, not phenomena which he cannot hear.[459]

Hood, on the other hand, puts a case for the importance of this normally inaccessible detail by setting up a distinction between the macroscopic and microscopic:

> If 70 or 80 per cent of musical information is microscopic . . . we are attempting to speak scientifically about an invisible world. The critical measurement of tuning and scale may

---

[459] List 1963:196.

not assume musical significance until the far more challenging aspects of the tone quality, attack, release, decay and other musical sound phenomena are better understood.[460]

This too seems a valid stance, and one would not wish to minimise the importance of the microscopic in understanding the nature of musical sound. But it is the macroscopic elements that are of primary importance in transcription, along with a kind of halfway house of elements that lie just on the borderline of perception. Every ethnomusicologist attempting transcription has resorted to slowing down the recording to clarify an elusive rhythmic or other detail, and for these a melograph or other electronic device can be truly useful. This aside, the domains of macroscopic and microscopic are separate, and reasonably belong to different areas of study. Merriam offers a sensible compromise in the debate by observing it may be that conventional notation simply gives us one kind of information while the melograph provides another that is equally important.[461]

It remains, then, to assess just what human perceptual limits night be, because it is these that will determine what is or is not practical for transcription. Fortunately, there is no need for speculation, as acousticians have long since supplied the needed information.

The limits of perception

Perhaps it is necessary to state the obvious that the validity of transcription depends upon the ability of the transcriber. Some individuals, among whom one hopes ethnomusicologists are not numbered, have disabilities of perception that rule them out forever as potential transcribers. I knew one person, incredibly, who was unable to discriminate any pitches within the interval of a fourth, and smaller melodic steps were all the same to him. He became, I believe, a minister of religion and had no musical ambitions, though he must have had difficulty with hymn-singing. Unless one is (say) a violinist capable of playing in tune, a wise preliminary to transcription might well be to take a Seashore battery of tests to find out what ones limits might be.

In applying his tests, Seashore found a considerable range of ability for both pitch and time discrimination, though it seems even an average ear would be good enough to transcribe within limits set by Seeger of 1/10 of a second in duration and 1/10 of a tone (20 cents) in pitch discrimination as sufficient for practical purposes.[462]

Seashore found that for A=435 an average ear could hear a difference of about 3 cycles (Hz), which is 1/17 of a tone or about 12 cents. A very sensitive ear could hear 0.5 cycles or less, which is less than .01 of a tone or two cents. A study of the pitch discrimination of sixteen professional musicians of the Royal Opera in Vienna found thresholds for frequency ranging from 1/49th to 1/540th of a tone, i.e. from four cents to less than half a cent! [463] It would seem, then, that human limitation of pitch perception is not a problem for transcribers.

---

[460] Hood 1963b:191.
[461] Merriam 1964:59-60.
[462] Seeger 1958:33 (McAllester reprint).
[463] Seashore 1938:50.

But what about singers? Here again, tests carried out by early acousticians provide the answers, as well as an explanation of why it is that the standard five lines of the European musical staff suffice for most music, and provide no scope for any interval smaller than a semitone.

Seashore's findings for Western violinists and opera singers have already been alluded to, showing performers continually off the mark by an eighth of a tone or more. Metfessel reported similar results for American Negro singing, showing pitch deviations from all intervals of the same order. Most notes seem to have been within plus or minus 30 cents of the intended one.[464] In this context, Seeger's 20 cents again seems reasonable unless one is making a special study of intonation or unless one is particularly interested in the minutiae of performance at or below normal thresholds.

It is hard to avoid the conclusion that arguments in favour of the "objectivity" of melographic methods and substituting melographs for human transcription, have been mounted either in ignorance or in disregard of the findings of Metfessel and Seashore using phonophotography, which yielded graphs of melodic contour similar to those produced automatically by the melograph. Likening the results to those obtained when visually examining supposedly clean fingernails under a microscope, Seashore concluded:

> . . . we find that the unaided ear, like the unaided eye, has marked limits in sensitivity and, therefore, does not detect the countless deviations in tones which tone photography brings out in astonishing detail.[465]

It is detail, in other words, "that the musician never hears",[466] whether performing or transcribing. Performers, with their unaided ears hear and evaluate their own product, so why should the unaided ear of the transcriber not do likewise?

To return to Seashore's analogy, machine transcription of music can no more accomplish this than a microscope can reveal the significant visual detail of a painting.

The value of machine transcription, then, lies not in substituting for the macro data which conventional transcription can supply, but with micro data of a different order. Attack, decay, vibrato, and other elements of music which normally go unnoticed are not unimportant, but just different.

Having exanined the arguments mounted by Hood and Seeger against hand transcription and found them wanting, it remains only to consider how reliable this process might be in practice. Here too, available evidence is reassuring.

---

[464] Metfessel 1928:166 (composite graph).
[465] Seashore 1938:255.
[466] Seashore 1938:254.

RELIABILITY OF TRANSCRIPTION

In a 1963 article, Mantle Hood said he would rather attempt interplanetary flight in a Wright Brothers aeroplane than continue to doctor the five-line music staff with what he called "the mystical signs of diacritical annotation." [467]

As we have seen, however, he was attempting "descriptive" notations of a kind so complex that only a machine could, in fact, provide the wanted detail. What about transcriptions whose objectives are more modest than this: namely to reveal only as much descriptive detail as necessary to convey the "macro" elements of the style that are significant to a performer? Can a human transcriber produce sufficiently reliable such transcriptions for analytic, comparative and prescriptive purposes? Assuming a good enough ear, adequate training in transcription skills, and sufficient experience of the music to be transcribed, the answer to this is an unqualified yes.

In 1968, I taught a graduate class in transcription and analysis at the University of Hawai'i. Each week I set an assignment requiring each student to transcribe the same piece of music, chosen as exemplary of different problems, be it pitch, rhythm, or some other element of music structure. These I also transcribed myself, the class taking the form of comparison of the several efforts. Although differing on points of detail, which then became the subject of class discussion, the transcriptions were remarkably uniform. Except in the unlikely event that the members of the class shared common disabilities affecting the reliability of their work in exactly the same ways, the results amply vindicated the reliability of transcription, using Western notation, as a method.

A published experiment along the same lines was a 1964 "Symposium on Transcription and Analysis", published in the journal *Ethnomusicology*,[468] in which four prominent ethnomusicologists, Robert Garfias, Mieczyslaw Kolinski, George List and Willard Rhodes, each transcribed a Hukwe bow song without communicating with each other, and then compared the results. The experiment was a little marred as a result of each participant transcribing different portions of the bow song, and one (Garfias) abandoning standard notation for the voice part in favour of a graphical method. Again, however, the results were conclusive. There was more agreement than disagreement among the participants, and transcription was able to capture the essence of the bow song.

A decade later, List ran another experiment of his own, this time involving transcription both by ear by different transcribers and by machine of several different songs from diverse traditions. After comparing the results, List found only a handful of discrepancies, applying to a small number of individual notes, and amounting in no case to more than a quarter tone in terms of pitch or of a 16th note in terms of duration. In List's own words:

> The inescapable conclusion is that the capability of the unaided human ear should not be underestimated. The evidence indicates that transcriptions made by ear in notated form are sufficiently accurate, sufficiently reliable to provide a valid basis for analysis and comparative studies of . . . pitch and duration.[469]

---

[467] Hood 1963b:191,
[468] England et al. 1964.
[469] List 1974:375-6.

Pioneers of Ethnomusicology: Part V

Analysis

Ultimately everything is related to everything else, so to this extent those who insist on a "holistic" view of ethnomusicology are right. But "everything" is far too extensive a domain to comprehend or come to terms with, so some compartmentalisation is necessary. The answer might be thought to lie with the writing of computerised web documents that would allow "links" to be pursued at will, in all their labyrinthine complexity. But this would not reveal the nature of the relationships. Like it or not, if we wish to know the answers to most questions, analysis cannot be avoided. This is true not only in the general sense of the word, but also in its more circumscribed one of musical analysis, as applied to music structure. "Transcription and analysis", indeed, is treated in most music school curricula as a subject area in its own right, applying in both cases to music sound.

Little of any significance appears to have been published on analytic method in ethnomusicology in recent years. I cannot claim to be abreast of the entire field, but this impression is confirmed by a 1998 bibliography of transcription and analysis [470] compiled by Max Peter Baumann of Bamberg University who, as a still active teacher in the subject, can probably be relied upon not to have missed much. His bibliography contains 79 entries running the gamut of most of the standard sources. A breakdown by decade of entries yields the fol'owing table:

```
1880   1
1900   1
1910   1
1920   1
1930   111
1940   1
1950   11111 111
1960   11111 11111 11111 11111 11111 1
1970   11111 11111 11111   11111 11111
1980   111
1990   11111 1111
```

Allowing for the fact that all of the 1990s entries are either republications, were written by Europeans, or are in Helen Myers's retrospective survey of ethnomusicology,[471] it is apparent there has been little interest from American scholars in either transcription or analysis since their heyday in the 1960s and 1970s.

Why should this be? One answer could be that computerised systems of analysis such as Humdrum toolkit software,[472] might convey an impression that analysis is now so automated and routine that all relevant questions must already have been answered. After all, the thousands of scores now available in Humdrum format include examples of nearly 40 folk repertories from Acoma Indian to Zuñi, so surely these at least can now be analysed rather easily. Judging from the Humdrum list of typical research problems that can be answered in this way, however, this

---

[470] Baumann 1998.
[471] Myers 1992.
[472] http://www.music-cog.ohio-state.edu/Humdrum/

cannot be taken for granted. Typical questions that can be asked of the system seem largely of a specific or even trivial nature, such as: "Are German folk songs more likely to be in triple metre?" By and large, though at cost of an immense amount of tedious labour, I probably did better with my Paramount punch card system in the 1960s, used to assist analysis of Maori music, which at least had the merit of containing analytic fields of my own devising that were strictly relevant to the corpus at hand, and were not dependent on encoding from full transcriptions. Although I am not familiar with the new computerised analytic programmes, it seems to me that, while possibly useful as analytic aids, they would be unable to penetrate the essentials of non-Western music systems with features that are either not recognisable by the programme or require some degree of intuition on the part of the analyst.

A second reason for the demise of analysis might be that, after a lapse of a decade or more, notice had at last been taken of Herndon's article about "Sacred cows", written in 1974,[473] which is indeed now occasionally cited by opponents of analysis. This, however, is doubtful. Herndon may have thought she was breaking new ground, but for most of us at the time seemed more than a little ingenuous. Nothing she said was new, and much of it, such as her criticism of Kolinski's methods, was already taken for granted by most ethnomusicologists.

A third reason might be that, like transcription, analysis is hard to do, and for a lot of people hard to understand. Manuel, for example, refers to ethnological studies as inherently more readable and accessible than musicological ones such as Jairazbhoy's *Rags of North Indian Music*,[474] comparing this work with that of Steven Feld as follows:

> By contrast, Steven Feld's *Sound and Sentiment* which is a more anthropological study, contains little technical musicological analysis, and is accessible to a much wider audience; indeed, the book is considered to be required reading by most ethnomusicologists.[475]

I, on the other hand, found the lack of analysis in Feld's work to be a deficiency, and I was able to gain little idea of what Kaluli music was actually like until he issued recordings of it. Feld used only the minimal amount of analysis required to illustrate and reinforce his ideas about Kaluli aesthetics, and the nature of the Kaluli music system remains a subject for future study.

It is probably true that books containing analysis are less comprehensible than those that do not but, if so, this is a price worth paying, and both types of study have their place. The contrast in methodology between Feld and Jairazbhoy, however, does raise an interesting if marginally related side-issue. With his linguistic background, one of Feld's concerns was music as communication, a topic which will be taken up later. Feld's view, evidently, is that music communicates emotion, and it is this element of aesthetics that dominates throughout his book. Before going on, then, a few words about aesthetics, may not be out of place. Alan P. Merriam's view was that aesthetics as such is a topic of less relevance in tribal musics than it is in the West, and that the concept itself is essentially a Western one,[476] a conclusion that may be broadly true but,

---

[473] Herndon 1974.
[474] Jairazbhoy 1971.
[475] Manuel 1995.
[476] Merriam 1964a:Ch.13.

as Feld has shown, is not universal. The subject, however, is vast, and a lot more complicated than is commonly realised.

AESTHETICS

Once, more than 30 years ago, I rashly agreed to write a paper on the "aesthetics" of music in Oceania, for a conference to be held in Wellington, New Zealand. I had many references to performance standards throughout Oceania, and naïvely thought it would be easy to write about them. I spent an entire summer on preparatory reading and writing for the paper, ending with a small library of key books on aesthetics, and a stack of xerox and MS pages of commentary close to 3 feet high, some of which I hoped to assemble into a paper. All that ever reached the printed page was a short extract I incorporated into a paper written later for a conference at the University of Western Australia.[477] I had discovered that aesthetics is a huge and labyrinthine subject, with a history of more than 2000 years, not only spanning the fields of art, music and philosophy, but also impinging upon many others. As well, it was beset with multiple problems of terminology and interpretation, few of which had been resolved, even without adding a layer of cross-cultural perspective. At the end of my summer I thought I was close to getting to grips with it all and perhaps even of making some contribution of my own, which I proposed to title "Beauty and the Best". But I had to stop work on it to resume teaching, and never returned to it. Plainly, at the very least, aesthetics is a complex field in its own right, which means different things to different people, and considerable background is required in order to add meaningfully to its literature. At any rate, discussion of performance standards is not the same thing, and ethnomusicologists should beware of thinking so.

METHODS OF ANALYSIS

The present book is not a manual of methodology, so brief mention only will be made here of the three best-known systems of analysis.

Standard analysis

This is the method, already referred to, developed by Erich von Hornbostel and his associates in Berlin, introduced into the United States by Herzog, and popularised in textbooks by Nettl. It examines music componentially under the headings manner of singing, melody (including scales, range, contour and melodic intervals), rhythm and metre, tempo, form and polyphony. It is simple, relatively easy to apply, and, although improved ways of looking at each of the components and their relationships with each other may be needed, it has served its purpose well.

Even without training in the method, ability to analyse musical style in such terms is already, to a considerable degree, second nature to most listeners and is a testimony to the power of human perception. If, as the advocates of machine transcription suppose, the human ear is so incapable of judging musical parameters, how is it that in as little as half a second of exposure to a piece of music in familiar idiom, it is possible to correctly identify so much of what is going on? Instantly one knows whether one is listening to a solo voice, choir or an instrument or instrumental ensemble; in the former case whether male or female, bass or tenor, soprano or contralto;

---

[477] McLean 1984.

in the latter whether a symphony orchestra, early music ensemble or some other combination of instruments, and very often the exact instruments employed; frequently the name of the composer, or even the precise work itself. How does one do this? By analysis, obviously, and by accurate and instantaneous perception of timbre, melodic intervals, characteristic rhythms, harmony, accompaniment, and a host of other elements, all perceptible, all accessible by analysis, and all except timbre capable of being written down in standard notation. Mantle Hood believed otherwise, stating:

> There must be enough information in that half second, based on parameters that are not those we normally consider as relevant in our analyses, and for which we have not developed adequate analytical tools.[478]

This he uses as justification for his "quantum theory of music", but the assumption that the parameters perceived in the half second are not the familiar ones is unjustified. The unaided human ear itself is an adequate analytic tool if one has the terminology to know what it is one is perceiving.

Cantometrics

Cantometrics is a comprehensive system of analysis developed by Alan Lomax (1915–2002) at Columbia University from 1961 onwards. Its objectives and the results of Lomax's use of the method will be discussed in a later section.

The method requires listening to recorded samples of music, and subjectively rating them on 3-13 point scales in each of 37 analytic categories, including many of those employed also in standard analysis. An advantage of the method is that it provides a means of rating aspects of "manner of singing" for which no precise measures were hitherto available. The problem with singing quality has been that terms such as tense, relaxed, nasal, hoarse, raspy, pulsating, pinch-voiced etc. acquire meaning only by example. One could play a piece of music and say "this is what I mean by 'pinched', or this is what I mean by 'raspy' ", but anyone not privy to the listening experience would have only a vague idea of what was meant. Moreover, someone else using the same term might mean something completely different by it. Lomax solved this problem by issuing training tapes for use by persons wishing to use his method, and by doing so has transformed "manner of singing" into a much less problematic category of analysis than it once was. Teachers of ethnomusicology who have made use of Lomax's training tapes by no means accept all of his parameters. I tried out the entire course for several years at Auckland university, keeping records of student responses, and found that several of the categories to which students had similar responses year by year were in need of refinement. Nettl has reported similar results,[479] and doubtless others have found the same. Questionable as some of Lomax's parameters may be, however, those relating to "manner of singing" are useful.

---

[478] Hood 2000:369.
[479] Nettl 1983:84.

Kolinski

Methods of analysis developed by Mieczyslaw Kolinski (1901–1981) must be considered here, if only to recommend mostly against them. The discussion is necessarily complex, and casual or general readers may prefer to omit this section.

Two systems of describing contour were devised by Kolinski. The first was his use of level formulae. This divides the melodic range of a song into a hundred units, and expresses the ratio between the initial note and the final note of a melody in terms of these units in order to indicate the general direction of melodic movement. For example, a formula 35°:22° shows an initial note 25 hundredths of the song's range above the lowest note and a concluding note 22 hundredths above the lowest note. The method was introduced by Kolinski in a short paper,[480] and exemplified for large bodies of songs a few years later.[481] It has been used by some other scholars, notably Merriam, but a weakness of the method is that initial notes are uncertain in many music systems and this will upset the calculated level. Moreover, no account is taken of the tonic, which is of obvious importance in contour analysis, and worse still the method gives misleading results for contours which the system is unable to reveal. For example, a tile contour beginning and starting at the same level with an initial rapid rise in pitch and subsequent slow falls would be regarded by most analysts as descending, but the method would represent it as level. The same is true of specialised contours such as "the Rise", which is neither rising nor falling.

A more elaborate system was put forward by Kolinski in a paper entitled "The Structure of Melodic Movement."[482] In this paper he used a highly specialised terminology of his own to describe melodic lines in terms of returning and progressing pendulums, up and down flexures, and others, in a manner so detailed as to amount almost to an alternative system of transcription. At the end of the paper he gives four examples in musical notation with detailed descriptions using his new system. It is a method that has not caught on, and is unlikely to provide insights into the nature of melodic movement or answers to practical problems involving contour.

In Western music, a familiar means of expressing tempo is in terms of beats per minute by means of M.M. (Maetzel Metronome) markings, which is useful only if there are clearly defined beats. Kolinski's solution, which applies to both metric and non-metric music, is to time the number of notes per minute. In his paper on the topic,[483] he provides a formula to derive notes per minute from the metronome figure, and gives a number of graphs which show clear differences between the average tempi of the songs of different ethnic groups and different song types. There is no doubt that this is a useful analytical tool for comparison, though more refined statistical techniques would greatly improve Kolinski's results. Essentially, his graphs are a series of normal distribution curves using grouped data. Statistical formulae could be applied to them to determine whether or not the observed differences between the means are significant.

---

[480] Kolinski 1957a.
[481] Kolinski 1965a.
[482] Kolinski 1965b.
[483] Kolinski 1959.

The idea of measuring notes per minute seems to have been hit upon independently of Kolinski by Dieter Christensen (1932–), in his case calculating the number of notes directly instead of doing so through the metronome figure.[484] This measure Christensen calls "inner tempo", distinguishing also "melodic tempo", which is his term for the number of changes of pitch per minute. The latter, however, is of little practical use because it takes no account of repetitions.

Better than either method is simply to count the number of syllables of text per minute. This can be done for any music for which a text is available, and has the advantage that no prior music transcription is needed. Applied to Maori music it yielded results equally as useful as "notes per minute" for statistical comparison of bodies of song.[485]

Kolinski's most ambitious system, claimed by him to be appropriate for all of the world's music, emerged from two influences brought to bear during his European training. The first was theories of consonance to which Kolinski was exposed while working for Hornbostel at the Berlin Phonogramm-Archiv, and the other was the European preoccupation with classification of folk song. In his paper "Classification of Tonal Structures",[486] Kolinski's declared aim is to discover universals in music structure, an aim doomed from the beginning to failure. He bases this system on his own individual theory of consonance, which he reported in two earlier papers. The first is his "Determinants of Tonal Construction in Tribal Music".[487] Here he introduces his terms "shading" and "tint", arrived at by visual analogy with the continuous transition from black to white through various shades of grey. He uses the word "shading" for the distance between notes low to high. Thus "shading" is Kolinski's term for pitch or frequency. "Tint" is his term for varying degrees of the quality inherent in octave identity. Thus "tint" is Kolinski's own term for consonance. Using this terminology, C^1 and $C\#^1$ have similar "shading" but different "tint", while C^1 and C^2 have different "shading" but identical "tint". In other words, C^1 and $C\#^1$ are close in pitch but are dissonant if they are sounded together, while C^1 and C^2 are an octave apart in pitch but are as consonant as it is possible to get when notes are sounded together. Kolinski's rule for consonance in this paper is "affinity of tints decreases with their increasing distance through the cycle of fifths."

Explaining this in a later paper, he begins by observing: "Among the intervals that are composed of two different tints, the fifth and its inversion, the fourth, stand out as the most consonant ones." [488] Now occurs the fundamental assumption upon which Kolinski bases his whole argument:

> Evidently the high degree of tint homogeneousness of the fifth and fourth is conditioned by the high degree of affinity between the two tints contained in these intervals. This means that two different tints have the greatest affinity when they follow each other in the cycle of fifths. For example F is most closely related to C, C to G, G to D and so forth. Consequently there is a second degree affinity between F and G as well as between C and D, a third degree affinity between C and A, etc. In other words the degree of affinity between two tints depends on their distance in the cycle of fifths; therefore the

---
[484] Christensen 1960.
[485] McLean 1965a (I):301-4.
[486] Kolinski 1961.
[487] Kolinski 1957b.
[488] Kolinski 1962:67.

degree of consonance of an interval depends on the distance in the cycle of fifths between the two tints of which the interval is composed.[489]

In fact, there is no reason to suppose that any of this is true. No evidence is offered. All we are given is unsupported assertion. The consequence of the theory is that the most consonant interval after the 5th is the 2nd, then the major 6th, which thus ranks before 3rds. For Kolinski this is an explanation for the use in some tribal musics of parallel seconds.

Abandoning Kolinski's own tabular summary for the moment, and working out consonance strictly on the criteria he has given, one finds that the M7 is four degrees more consonant than the m3, and the least consonant interval is the 4th, propositions with which no one would surely agree. But Kolinski does not depend for his view of the 4th on its position in the cycle of fifths, accepting it instead because it is the inverse of the 5th. On this basis, however, he should accept the M7 as the inverse of the M2 but does not do so. If he had, his argument in favour of the M2 would collapse, because it is not common for people to sing in parallel 7ths.

Unconvincing as Kolinski's theory of consonance may be, it was an essential basis for his later "classification of tonal structures" system. But this was not all.

The second postulate upon which this system depends is his proposition, which again there is no reason to accept:

> Since inter-relatedness of tints is symbolised by the cycle of fifths, it is the latter that has to serve as the principal means for a general typology and classification of tonal structures in tribal song.[490]

In this scheme melodies are classified according to the criteria:

> (1) How far through the cycle of fifths does one have to go to obtain all the notes in the composition?
>
> (2) How many notes in the resulting segment of the cycle of fifths are actually present in the specimen?
>
> (3) Which notes are they?[491]

To ensure uniformity, Kolinski provides a table of all possible segments of the cycle of fifths, comprising 12 tonal types divided into 348 tint complexes. To classify a melody, it is necessary only to transpose it into the key of C, write out the scale in the order of the cycle of fifths, and then look it up in the table. Thus, "Mary had a little lamb" becomes a No. 12 penta-type 4 tint complex. So impressive, and so easy!

---

[489] Kolinski 1962:67-68.
[490] Kolinski 1957b.
[491] Powers 1962:222.

Having carried out this exercise for a large number of songs, Kolinski finds pronounced similarities between the musical styles of totally unrelated peoples and concludes that such similarities are "apparently due to basic universal laws of musical creation."[492] The far more likely explanation is simply that Kolinski's system doesn't work.

It is a shame that Kolinski wasted so much of his life in such ways. A pernicious effect of Kolinski's eccentric, and supposedly universal but in practice mostly useless systems is that they have probably steered ethnomusicologists away from considering any other systems that might be more productive. I know of no one but myself, for example, who has made use of (or possibly even read) my own system of melodic interval analysis,[493] which was designed and has proven invaluable for music systems like the Maori and Tikopia ones of small range, few notes and readily identifiable tonic.

Linguistic approaches

Besides writing his highly influential book on Kaluli aesthetics, Steven Feld is recognised as an authority on linguistic applications to music. In an early article,[494] he debunks the use of linguistic models in ethnomusicology, and time has proven him to be largely right. The linguistic models central to Feld's arguments were Lévi Strauss structuralism, the transformational linguistics of Noam Chomsky, and semiotics. All three have been extremely seductive in their appeal, and all have continued to exert influence, along with other "models" that have since joined them. The crux of Feld's argument is that they are no more than analogies in terms of their application to music, and as such do not have explanatory power, much less "provide musicology with a mechanical and rigorous set of discovery procedures."[495]

Since Feld wrote his article, semiotics especially has developed as a highly specialised field of study with its own literature, but with little impact upon mainstream ethnomusicology. I have no experience of it beyond skimming through some of its literature, but from the little I have seen, I gain the impression that it is simply making use of different terminology to describe quite ordinary relationships within musical structures, and yields results in no way different from what one would expect from standard analysis, except for the different descriptive terms that are employed. If this is a fair statement, then there would be little point in abandoning the more familiar standard methodology in favour of the new one.

This is not to say that insights from linguistics are useless to ethnomusicology. On the contrary, it is crucial to problems involving text/music relationships.

TEXT/MUSIC RELATIONSHIPS

Blacking's attention to speech-tone in his *Venda Children's Songs* has been paralleled many times before and since by researchers from other areas, with varying results. An example from Oceania is a paper by Pugh-Kitingen in which she discusses articulation of words in the jew's

---

[492] Kolinski 1961:72.
[493] McLean 1966.
[494] Feld 1974.
[495] Feld 1974:212.

harp music of Huli and neighbouring peoples of Papua New Guinea and, in the case of the Huli, on musical bows and panpipes.[496] In a later paper,[497] she examines relationships between melody and speech-tone in the music of the Huli, who, like Blacking's Venda people of South Africa, speak a tone language. In a careful analysis, she finds that speech-tone is preserved in terms of musical contour. Rising melodic figures represent low-rising speech-tone, while falling patterns usually indicate high-falling speech tone, and level progressions signify mid-level speech-tone.

A paper of my own [498] emerged from an important discovery made by the linguist Bruce Biggs.[499] Biggs noticed that the texts of a significant proportion of Maori waiata, as notated in the McLean and Orbell publication *Traditional Songs of the Maori*,[500] had a vowel-count of exactly eight in each half line of the notated song (counting short vowels as one and long vowels as two). In the Maori language, the distinction between long and short vowels has phonemic significance, just as speech-tone does in Huli and Venda. My concern was the same as that of Pugh-Kitingen and Blacking, in this case to find out the degree to which the long and short vowels in the Maori texts were conserved in the music. In "rule-of-eight" waiata, an almost exact correspondence was found between long vowels (the linguistically "marked" or significant feature) and musical long notes, though not between short vowels and short notes. This was shown to result from the use of a rhythmic model such that any rule-of-eight text can be sung to any rule-of-eight tune. A linguistic "spin-off" is that a short vowel count in a rule-of-eight line indicates that a long vowel has mistakenly been treated as short. The close correspondence between music and text provides in such cases a means of determining the correct pronunciation of obsolete names whose pronunciation is no longer known.

Using similar methods, Kevin Salisbury has discovered even closer associations between song texts and music structure in the Northern Cook Islands atoll of Pukapuka, where both short and long vowels are conserved in the music, and half lines in this case have a count of six. Even more remarkably, the most common Pukapukan chant style, the *mako*, exhibits linguistic conditioning of pitch close enough to enable a tune to be predicted with a high degree of reliability from its text alone.[501]

A not yet fully understood phenomenon, both on Pukapuka and on the Polynesian Outlier Islands of Bellona, Ontong Java and Tikopia is modification of vowel quality when texts are sung, usually from *a* to *o*, though on Tikopia vowel shifts from *e* to *i*, and *o* to *u*, as well as changes in the opposite direction also occur.[502]

Resolution of these and other problems of song/text relationship clearly require either linguistic expertise on the part of ethnomusicologists or collaboration between ethnomusicologists and linguists.

---

[496] Pugh-Kitingen 1982.
[497] Pugh-Kitingen 1984.
[498] McLean 1982; discussed also in McLean 1996: Ch.15.
[499] Biggs 1980.
[500] McLean & Orbell 1975.
[501] Salisbury 1983:146-64.
[502] Salisbury 1983:143; Hugo Zemp (pers.comm.); McLean 1991:33-6.

STATISTICS

It has always been a source of some bewilderment to me that formal statistics has been so little taken advantage of by ethnomusicologists. The sole paper routinely and reverentially cited on the subject, even on the possibility of it, is an early publication by Linton and Merriam.[503] Nettl reports a handful of other studies, but they are extremely thin on the ground.[504] One seriously wonders whether ethnomusicologists are either mostly innumerate, or feel that something so akin to mathematics is inappropriate for the humanities. Perhaps part of the reason is the move away from analysis in general and comparison of bodies of data, as statistics is at its best in such a role. Probably there have been more such applications than commonly realised, though they appear to be foreign to persons with musical rather than scientific training. My own PhD thesis was concerned largely with the statistical comparison of samples of Maori song by tribe and by song type. Measures of significance between statistical means revealed statistically significant differences in interval preference, melodic range and other parameters. The differences were subtle, and Maori music as a whole was found to be homogeneous within broad limits. As Linton and Merriam pointed out long ago, because music structure is quantifiable, such methods could profitably be applied to other styles. As well, a potentially very powerful technique is the use of statistical clustering to elucidate music areas. The only such attempts I know of are my own using hand-clustering methods for Oceania (discussed later), and by Lomax for his Cantometrics project.

MUSIC AND COMMUNICATION

By now it is substantially agreed by ethnomusicologists that music is not, as popularly supposed, a "universal language", though some of what may be called its "dialects" are mutually intelligible. The question that must now be asked, however, is whether in any real rather than figurative sense it is a language at all and, if so, what if anything it "communicates".

Fundamental to all discussions on the topic, though seldom acknowledged by anyone, are at least three assumptions: first that music is a form of utterance distinct from speech but related to it in some way; second that all human populations practice some form of it; and third that all forms of music share characteristics of some kind. All three assumptions take the form of generalisations that have been accepted as axiomatic without critical examination, and none can be relied upon as certain. Especially, without agreement upon what "music" is, discussion takes place on a very shaky foundation.

But this is not all. In a long article,[505] which I shall use as a basis for discussion, Doris Stockmann (1929–) has made a brave attempt to bring together literature bearing upon this issue. Early in her article, two further seemingly universal assumptions appear: namely that music is a form of "communication", and that it communicates "meaning" of some kind. If either of these propositions is true, and if music, like speech, is truly characteristic of all populations and in this sense "universal", then it ought to be possible to find out what music communicates by asking anyone at all, including oneself. It should be a particularly easy form of field work, without need

---

[503] Linton & Merriam 1956.
[504] Nettl 1983:125-7.
[505] Stockman 1991.

to travel beyond ones own immediate neighbourhood. One should be able to arrive at initial answers by simple introspection, and then, as everyone is supposed to possess a concept of music, the initial conclusions should be easy to test simply by asking other persons. A relatively small sampling of opinion should be sufficient for arriving at a consensus at least for the music of ones own culture, and the investigation could then be broadened to find out if the conclusions remain true cross-culturally. If, on the other hand, such an investigation fails to provide satisfactory answers, then one would have to conclude that one or more of the basic assumptions is not true, and the questions themselves may not be worth asking. Is this, then, the case?

Stockmann points to an "explosion" of relevant publications since the 1970s, from a diversity of subject areas within music studies such as "psychological, sociological, reception studies, pedagogical, anthropological, aesthetic, and semiotic", as well as non-musical ones of "information theory and communication research, philosophy, general semiotics and aesthetics, psychology, linguistics, and others", some of which she dismisses as unworthy of attention. "Negotiating the jungle" even of the credible remainder is seen as barely possible without serious shortcomings. Stockmann's solution is to add yet further complications to the mix, namely: "sociological interpretation, as well as some basic theory of music as process, structure, and function, on one side, and as concept, effect, and object of valuation, on the other", an approach seen by her to be epitomised by Charles Seeger in terms of "music as fact and value". Stockmann places considerable emphasis upon insights which she believes Seeger to have provided. But these seem rather to add yet another layer of obscurity, and Stockmann concedes the difficulty that remains in steering a path through the "thicket of fundamental problems".[506]

Let us return, then, to the most fundamental problems of all: namely those set out at the beginning of this section. Ignoring for the moment the first few, as well as the difficult problem of the nature of music itself, what is meant by "communication" and "meaning", and are these legitimate concepts to apply to music? First, if music communicates, what does it communicate?

Lay persons, when asked the loaded question of what music "communicates" are apt to say that it conveys emotion, an idea exploited by Steven Feld in his Kaluli book, and also alluded to by Mantle Hood in his essay "Music the Unknown". But, as Hood points out, responses to music vary too much from person to person, even within our own culture, and with regard to the same piece of music, for this to be tenable.[507]

Before going any further, let us try a little simple introspection by way of a thought experiment. As its subject, please consider the words and tune of "Twinkle, twinkle, little star." It is a nursery song known to nearly everyone in the Western world, so it should not be hard to bring it to mind. Mozart composed a set of variations on it. Lewis Carroll wrote a parody of the words. Doubtless the text is sung in more than one language. Please, reader, at this point, sing the song over in your head.

Twinkle, twinkle, little star
How I wonder what you are
Way above the world so high

---

[506] Stockman 1991:320.
[507] Hood 1963:285.

Like a diamond in the sky
Twinkle, twinkle, little star
How I wonder what you are

After singing the song through, please answer the following questions:
What did you perceive? Did the song convey any emotions? Did it remind you of anything else? Apart from the words, did it "mean" anything? If so, what? Do you think your responses were the same as all the other people who carried out the same experiment? If you are like most people, these questions will have been hard to answer.

I suggest that what you perceived was no more than a set of words with an associated tune, and the tune has a set of characteristics analysable in terms of intervallic, durational, formal and perhaps implied harmonic relationships in which the words are in one-to-one relationship with the tune. That's all. Any emotional response you may have had, or reminders of childhood, or anything else, are extra-musical, incidental, and not intrinsic to "Twinkle, twinkle, little star."

Now consider Lewis Carroll's version:

Twinkle, twinkle, little bat
How I wonder what you're at
Way above the world you fly
Like a teatray in the sky
Twinkle, twinkle, little bat
How I wonder what you're at

Now we have an element of humour. Does it make any difference to the song? With its new words, is the song "communicating" anything different? Clearly only the words have changed, and the rest of the song is the same. Do the new words have any relationship to the old? Yes, of course. What is the relationship? The new mirrrors the old. The rhyming pattern, duple word rhythms, and the formal structure of six lines, including repetition, are still present, and remain in one-to-one correspondence with the tune. Again, that's all. Lewis Carroll "understood" the tune as well as its relationship to the original words, or he could not have written his parody. Mozart was able to perceive not only the original relationships but a host of implied ones as well. What both he and Carroll understood, however, was not mysterious or ineffable, even if it is hard to express in words.

Is there any reason to believe that "Twinkle, twinkle" differs in any essential way from any other song, folk or otherwise? I would suggest not. All we are looking at is sets of musical and textual relationships, and the relationships can be explicated by analysis. Moreover, if this can be accepted as true, then anything else the song or tune may communicate is also dependent upon and a function of the same relationships.

But, you may protest, there's got to be more to it than this. If a Brahms quartet or a Kaluli song, depending upon cultural conditioning, can move a listener to tears, surely aesthetic response to music must reside in something more than relationships. I don't think so. Some relationships are simply more satisfying, or if extra-musical elements are involved, more evocative than others. The relationships are still intrinsic to the response.

All of this was made clear years ago by Leonard B. Meyer (1918–), in his book *Emotion and Meaning in Music*,[508] which, along with his later thought, has received less attention from ethnomusicologists than it deserves.

MUSIC STRUCTURE v. SOCIAL STRUCTURE

In 1964, when Alan P. Merriam published his book *The Anthropology of Music*, ethnomusicology was changed forever. Thenceforth music anthropology, or as Merriam defined it, "music in culture", or even as it was later renamed "music as culture", occupied half of the discipline, with music structure making up the other half, albeit still commanding most of the attention. Currently the pendulum has swung the other way with music structure by and large sidelined and neglected, to the detriment of ethnomusicology as a whole.

Merriam's famous feedback model of concept–behaviour–sound with sound in turn affecting concept created expectations. It was thought by most of Merriam's students that he himself would develop his model further, and resolve the problem of the relationship between music structure and music behaviour. They were agog when three years later Merriam's book on Flathead Indian music was published without addressing the issue.[509] Behaviour and structure occupied separate halves of the book. Was there, after all, no relationship between the two?

At about the same time, Alan Lomax was developing his Cantometrics project which sought to relate singing style and social structure by evaluating listening samples of music from throughout the world. Some not very exciting correlations emerged: for example that choral singing with a high degree of blend was characteristic of "cohesive" societies. But how else could it emerge? Plainly co-operation is required to achieve blend, and a desire for blend in the first place could be expected to result only in a venue of such co-operation. After years of effort, however, Lomax was unable to demonstrate any correlations at all between social structures and specifics of music structure such as melodic form, metrical structure and harmonic style, all of which, according to Lomax himself, failed to yield "orderly relationships".[510]

In the 1970s, John Blacking became prominent, especially as a result of his widely read and highly influential book *How Musical Is Man*[511] in which he strongly asserts a relationship between music structure and social structure, though, as in his *Venda Children's Songs*,[512] without offering convincing evidence for one. During the 1970s Blacking issued a challenge to ethnomusicologists to look for such relationships and document them. In the field of tribal music, where one might expect behavioural relationships to be most readily observable if they exist, a few minor papers resulted, but nothing emerged that was not either obvious or trivial or both, or in some cases explicable in terms of physical environment. In instrumental music, for example, available materials self-evidently govern the nature of the instruments that will be made and employed. (Thus, to state the obvious, bamboo flutes don't occur where bamboo doesn't grow,

---

[508] Meyer 1956. In this book, Meyer develops the idea that "meaning" in music depends upon expectations aroused initially in the listener by the structural conventions of the music, and the listener's response as these are progressively confirmed or denied and ultimately satisfied during the listening process.
[509] Merriam 1967.
[510] Lomax 1968:36.
[511] Blacking 1973.
[512] Blacking 1967.

and body percussion is favoured in areas such as Micronesia where there is a lack of materials with which to make percussion instruments.) Similarly, there is a self-evident relationship between motor behaviour and music structure, especially in instrumental music and in songs accompanying dance. The close relationship and synchronicity of dance movement with music structure is nicely illustrated by a story told by Maud Karpeles, who

> remembered with very great pleasure an occasion when a blind man in a village audience said to her, "you are a very fine dancer." Maud's comment that he could hardly be a judge of her dancing brought the reply, "but I heard your feet moving and your bells ringing." [513]

Another obvious example of behavioural relationship to music structure is in ensemble performance, where the spatial arrangement of performers may impact upon polyphony, or on leader /chorus interaction. But it is crucial also to be aware that the resulting music structures remain isolable for purposes of analysis.

In 1979, Anthony Seeger (1945–), a grandson of the famous Charles Seeger, published a paper about his field work with Suya Indians of Brazil in South America,[514] which has been widely hailed as proving a relationship between song structure and social structure. Nettl says unequivocally of this paper that it provides a model for the relationship of musical sound and music behaviour, "integrating approaches that earlier scholars such as Kolinski and Merriam had despaired of consolidating." [515]

But does it really? Nettl's evaluation is so sweeping, it is worth examining Seeger's paper in some detail:

The Suya are a small group of only 150 persons, speaking a language known as Northern Gê. Males perform ceremonies in a village plaza, surrounded by family residences from within which the performances are audible to the occupants. Married men live with their wives' families after a child is born. There are two moieties, each with its own residential house for males located at opposite ends of the plaza. Every male belongs to one of the two moieties. Membership depends on birth order in a family, with brothers who are adjacent in birth order belonging to opposite moieties. The ceremonies involve the moieties and the saying of the members' names.

Seeger begins his paper by distinguishing two Suya song types: *akia*, "individually sung or shouted songs in a high register"; and *ngere*, "unison songs performed in a low register" by groups of singers.[516] Later in the paper it emerges that *akia* are performed outdoors in the public venue of the village plaza by men to impress real and classificatory sisters who are within earshot in their houses, while *ngere* are performed indoors in the residential houses. More than one *akia* may be performed simultaneously so there is evidently an element of competition among men, each of whom is striving to be heard, by singing loudly in characteristically strained performing style. *Ngere* are performed co-operatively in more relaxed style by groups of singers

---

[513] Wachsmann 1976:11.
[514] Seeger 1979. The paper was followed close to a decade later by a book (Seeger 1987) on the same subject.
[515] Nettl 2002:220.
[516] Seeger 1979:374.

who are aiming for tonal blend. So far, then, there are clear differences between the two song types in terms both of song use and performance practice.

The essential core of Seeger's paper concerns a common formal structure shared by the two song types *akia* and *ngere*. In each case, the text falls into two sections: "first half" (*kradi*) and "second half" (*sindaw*), each subdivided into 1. "without substance", 2. "telling the name", and 3. "end". Subdivision 1. further divides into (a) "really without substance", and (b) "approaching the name". The revelation of the "name" is evidently the objective in all of the songs.

Now comes the dénouement towards which Seeger has been heading.

The dualism running through Suya society has to do with the directions east (*kaikwa kradi*) and west (*kaikwa (s)indaw*). One men's house, the home of one of the moieties, is at the eastern end of the plaza, and the other at the western end. The "first half" of each song is sung in front of the eastern men's house and the "second half" in front of the western one.

So here at last, it seems, is the long-sought proof of connection between music structure and social structure that Blacking had so conspicuously failed to provide. Not only are the two related in the Suya case, but even share the same names!

But wait. This is textual form Seeger is talking about, and wouldn't one expect musical form to follow the text, with a defined beginning, middle and end, as happens here? Moreover, "form", especially textual form, is just one element of music structure as such, and is the one most likely to be conceptualised and have its components named by singers, and on this account is the most likely to be correlated in some way with performance. Elements of Suya song structure other than form, such as melody and rhythm, have no associated Suya vocabulary that Seeger was able to discover and have no demonstrable relationship with social structure. As well, and perhaps more importantly, the assumption that Seeger proved the long-sought and elusive connection between structure and behaviour that Merriam and others failed to find rests on a confusion between the word "structure" in its narrow sense as connoting textual or musical "form" and its broader one as referring to the entire system of components that together make up a music style. Finally, the two song types described by Seeger could be glossed together as "moiety songs", as this is their sole purpose, so it cannot be a surprise to find named verses in them relating to the moieties.

Perspectives from Oceania

Of living scholars, the two who have done most to shift perceptions of ethnomusicology, and are most frequently cited as having done so, are Hugo Zemp (1937–) and Steven Feld (1949–), both as a result of research in Oceania. Zemp is renowned especially for his work with the 'Are'are people of Malaita in the Solomon Islands of Melanesia, and Feld for his writings about the Kaluli people of Papua New Guinea.

Zemp, who is a brilliant professional photographer as well as an ethnomusicologist, has produced stunning visual images and an outstanding 3-hour documentary movie about the relationship of ceremony with 'Are'are music,[517] providing detailed visual context.[518] He has also published information on 'Are'are music classification terminology, of which more will be said later.

Feld and the muni bird

A work which has been widely accepted as demonstrating relationship of social parameters with musical ones is Steven Feld's book on the Kaluli of Papua New Guinea.[519] In its findings it has remained a "one off", though frequently cited as proof of Blacking's assertions. In the words of Peter Manuel:

> The work of Steven Feld is often singled out as the most provocative and theoretically original in our field; his research on the Kaluli . . . illuminates in a brilliant and eloquent fashion how musical structure in a given society can iconically reflect social structure and religious and aesthetic values.[520]

Feld's approach is through metaphor. His central thesis is that the cry of a bird called the *muni*, stylised weeping at funerals, and songs called *gisalo* are metaphorically linked. Feld begins with a Kaluli myth in which a boy is denied food by his older sister, a situation of unbearable pathos for the Kaluli. In the myth the boy becomes a *muni* bird and flies away sobbing the *muni* cry. The *muni* cry is represented by a descending series of four notes. Women who weep use the same four notes. So do the songs of *gisalo*, a song type whose object is to move men to tears. According to Feld,[521] this three- or four-note melody "is used as a sound metaphor for sadness, expressing the sorrow of loss and abandonment". Birds are also the spirits of Kaluli dead, and bird voices "are voices of those who have gone to the treetops in spirit reflection".[522] "Bird words" are the origin of poetic convention, and the poems are the texts of the songs. Over and over again, in numerous ways, Feld makes the same points. He argues an elegant case and the cumulative impact is very strong. It is unfortunate that the case does not quite hold up under scrutiny.

The real cry of the *muni* bird is not in fact a series of four pitches as represented by the Kaluli, though one must accept that it reminds them of weeping. Moreover it turns out that all Kaluli song types contain the same descending intervals as the conventionalised bird-cry, including borrowed ones which the Kaluli do not associate either with weeping or the bird myth. The true starting point appears to be the common denominator of the Kaluli tonal system: namely, the anhemitonic pentatonic scale, which the Kaluli use for all of their musical utterances as well as stylised weeping and the cry of the *muni* bird. At this rather mundane level there is regrettably little need to postulate elaborate aural metaphors "mediated" by the *muni* bird.[523]

---

[517] *Musique 'Are'are*. 16mm., colour, magnetic sound. Produced by the Centre National de la Recherche Scientifique (SERDDAV.
[518] For some of Zemp's photographic work see Coppet and Zemp 1978.
[519] Feld 1982.
[520] Manuel 1995.
[521] Feld 1982:33.
[522] Feld 1982:28.
[523] In a 1984 paper, Feld applies his Kaluli experience specifically to the problem of "Sound Structure as Social Structure". Six "rubrics" of competence, form, performance, environment, theory, value and equality are examined

Pioneers of Ethnomusicology: Part V

Structural terminology

A means towards finding out whether there are social correlates of elements of music structure is to gather terms for the latter in the hope that these will throw light on the problem. The first to document such terminology in a systematic way for Oceania was Hugo Zemp. In the 1970s he issued a series of recordings of 'Are'are panpipe music from the Solomon Islands, and also published several papers about 'Are'are music terminology. In his " 'Are'are Classification of Musical Types and Instruments",[524] he demonstrated their use of the lexeme *'au* (bamboo) with qualifying terms to distinguish not only different kinds of musical instruments made of bamboo but also scales of notes, whether equiheptatonic or non-equiheptatonic, employed by the panpipes. In his "Aspects of 'Are'are Musical Theory",[525] Zemp shows that panpipe intervals are conceptualised by 'Are'are in terms of differences in length between the bamboo pipes played to produce the intervals. Terms also exist for the direction of melodic movement, melodic and rhythmic segmentation, ostinato, legato, cadential formulae, rhythmic unison, musical devices such as pulsation, polyphony in two, three and four parts, and canon. Zemp makes no claim that these concepts transfer from the instruments to 'Are'are vocal music and nor does he try to relate them to social structure. Rather, he provides ample support for an observation he cites from Herzog that "terminology and technical theory may well develop where there is an object or instrument on which an otherwise abstract system can be observed in visible operation".[526]

Feld's work is in considerable contrast to Zemp's more sober descriptive approach. Besides his *muni* bird paradigm, which has captured the imagination of ethnomusicologists, Feld elicited a number of Kaluli terms relating to music structure which once again he interprets in terms of metaphor. Whereas the 'Are'are terminology has to do with bamboo, the Kaluli relates to waterfalls.

According to Feld,[527] ". . . Kaluli terminology for intervals and melodic contours derive from waterfall terms." Kaluli melodies are all anhemitonic pentatonic and, from examples given by Feld, appear generally to be of tile or terrace contour. The main intervals in this tonal system are the descending M2 which Kaluli call *gese* and the descending m3, called *sa*. *Gese* in ordinary speech refers to descent of a plaintive nature as in weeping and the begging intonations of children's speech. *Sa* by itself means "waterfall". Waterfall terms are also used to designate melodic contour patterns of descent, level movement and ascent. Thus the term for ledge or the upper plane from which water drops is also the initial pitch from which a melody begins to descend; the term for descent of water into a pool is used also for a melodic descent to level contour; the term for an overflow of water from such a pool is also used for descent from the tonal centre by a m3 and back again. It is apparent that these terms apply within melodic units which the Kaluli

---

and, for each, metaphor is again seen as central. For competence the metaphor is halaido or 'hard". For form the metaphor is dulugu ganalan 'lift up over", the Kaluli term governing their characteristic interlocking, overlapping and alternating polyphony. On the main theme of his paper Feld's findings are essentially negative (one cannot predict the Kaluli music system from "their mode of production and techno-economic complexity" (p.405).) He concludes (p.406): "For any given society, everything that is socially salient will not necessarily be musically marked. But, for all societies, everything that is musically salient will undoubtedly be socially marked". One can agree with the first part of this proposition, but the second has not been demonstrated.

[524] Zemp 1978.
[525] Zemp 1979.
[526] Herzog 1945:232.
[527] Feld 1981:30.

conceptualise as such. There are no terms for the ascending M2 or for the larger ascending intervals of m3 and perfect 4th, even though these are frequent in Kaluli music. A common feature of 'Are'are and Kaluli is that both groups, using bamboo terminology in the one case and waterfall terms in the other, name and conceptualise those aspects of the system which are culturally meaningful or essential. Another common feature is that most of the specialist vocabulary is drawn from the general vocabulary of the language. Feld does not hesitate to call such usage "metaphor" or even to invest it with symbolic significance. One questions whether such usages necessarily retain force as metaphors. One can think of numerous examples in English where this is not the case. Few persons would think of the mouth of a jar as analogous to a physical mouth, or a head of cabbage to a real head. And 1 doubt whether many Western musicians conceptualise the term "interval" as meaning "intervening time and space" or think of "contour" as an "outline of coasts, mountains, etc." Likewise one wonders whether the Kaluli use of waterfall terminology for their most common musical contour is more or less metaphorical than our own terms "tile" or "terrace" for the same type of structure.

The use of general vocabulary in contexts with semantic specialisation extends well beyond the English language or the Kaluli, and maybe this is a genuine "universal". In Polynesia, for example, such usage is widespread for music, especially in relation to form. Thus in Tikopia the form of a song is likened to a tree. The first stanza of a dance song is called the *tafito* or 'base" of a song just as the *tafito* of a tree is the portion of the trunk closest to the ground; the second stanza is the *kupu* which also means stanza in a general sense; the third or last stanza is *safe* which is a word applying also to the fruit bunch of the banana.[528] Likewise, according to Kunst,[529] on Numfor Island in Irian Jaya a distinction is made between the beginning of a song or "head" and the remainder, the "trunk", and in the Trobriand Islands sacred formulae distinguish "foot" (as of a tree), "body" and "crown". One would expect that if more field workers were to apply the methods used so successfully by Zemp and Feld then more such terminology would be discovered. Both authors make the point that only by participant observation over a period of time was it possible to discover the vocabulary by listening to singers' spontaneous comments and the singers' verbal corrections of their own and the authors' mistakes. Feld's purposeful mistakes, for instance, were always greeted either with laughter or remarks like "the waterfall ledge is too long before the fall" (as interpreted by Feld, a "problem with an imbalanced phrase before the tonal center").[530]

The case for independence

Impressive as the foregoing revelations may be, however, they fall short of proving a necessary connection between concept, behaviour and music structure, much less a necessity to concentrate on "process" rather than "product". Meanwhile, it seems, the idea was taken aboard at UCLA and applied to Indonesian music by followers of Mantle Hood. Currently, a 100 level course for beginners is even offered on the subject as follows:

> Anthropology of Music: Intended for Ethnomusicology, Music History, and Anthropology majors. Cross-cultural examination of music in context of social behavior and how

---

[528] Firth 1936:285.
[529] Kunst 1967:105.
[530] Feld 1981:42.

musical patterns reflect patterns exhibited in other cultural systems, including economic, political, religious, and social structure.[531]

Intriguingly, but without providing detail, Ellingson claims the emergence of a "new paradigm" in which such a relationship is evidently now taken for granted:

> The independent status maintained for music by both the Berlin and American anthropological branches of the tradition encouraged the growth and integrity of a separate discipline of cross-cultural music studies; but it maintained an artificial separation between acoustical and cultural aspects of music that would break down only with the emergence of a new paradigm. This paradigm, which emphasized field research that related musical sounds to elements of culture such as history, ideology and the conceptual and theoretical systems of the culture being studied, is strongly associated with the tradition of research in Indonesian gamelan music deriving from the work of the Dutch ethnomusicologist Jaap Kunst (1891–1960). Its theoretical formulation emerged slowly over the later part of the century.[532]

Insofar as this "paradigm" has validity, it makes no difference to the essential independence of music and social structures, which performers themselves will often confirm. Music practitioners, in both so-called "high cultures" and tribal communities of course have their own concepts, and frequently, as shown above, have advanced terminologies as well, especially for instrumental music, concerning the structures of the music they perform. Of course ethno-music-ologists should (and now most often do) elicit such information in the course of their field work. Having done so, they will find that the structures identified in the ethnomusicologist's own analysis of the music (albeit using "Western" techniques of analysis) will correspond in whole or in part with the same structures as recognised by the performers. Thus the Maori "oro" or intoning note in waiata is the same as the European concept of tonal centre or tonic (without need to relate it metaphorically to thunder muttering on the horizon, which is one of the ordinary meanings of the term). Comparison of the two sets of terminologies, indigenous and ethnomusicological, helps to isolate "central" features of style as recognised and conceptualised by the performers from non-central ones, which are not acknowledged by the performers, but are none-theless equally characteristic of the music. It is a mistake to ignore the non-central features or to regard them as insignificant or unimportant on the grounds that they are not recognised or acknowledged by the performers. If analysis reveals such structures to be present, of course they are important, because, even though they may be unverbalised and carried subliminally rather than consciously by the performers, they may still be essential to the style.

More than 30 years after the publication of Merriam's Flathead book I followed essentially the same dual approach in my book *Weavers of Song* about Polynesian music and dance.[533] Behavioural topics like uses of music, learning and instruction , composition, and song ownership are treated separately from music structure, and for good reason. The evidence from Polynesia, and indeed from Oceania over-all, is that music structures are largely autonomous and diffuse from place to place regardless of social structure. A case in point is the mutual presence of anhemi-

---

[531] From UCLA Ethnomusicology Department web site.
[532] Ellingson 1992:131.
[533] McLean 1999.

tonic pentatonic tonal structures in the music of the Polynesian Outlier Tikopia, and in geographically adjacent but culturally and ethnically different Melanesian areas in the Solomon Islands. Everywhere, the music of a given area is most like that of its geographical neighbours. Plainly such styles are associated and did not emerge in the several places independently.

It is apparent that even if social structures are linked in some way to the musical ones in the donor area, the social structures do not always move with the music. Obviously there has to be social contact between the parties to the process. Beyond this there is no necessary relationship.

The surprise to me is that there has been so little recognition of this by now plainly obvious truth. Instead, despite the universal lack of evidence for the Blacking hypothesis, it has been enshrined in current orthodoxy and used to justify abandonment of structural analysis of music sound. According to the now dominant view, it is inappropriate or even unethical to analyse non-Western music in "Western" terms without regard to the alleged "holistic" nature of music as part and parcel of the social frame within which it occurs. The result, inevitably, is not a holistic analysis of music in all its manifold and interrelated aspects, but neglect of music structure altogether. The coin is tossed; the tail is lovingly pontificated upon; and the head is ignored.

I do not know what Merriam's attitude was to Blacking's work. I do know that if he had lived he would sooner or later have clashed with Blacking by demanding the evidence that Blacking consistently failed to provide. With his strong sense of mission and direction, Blacking, regrettably, did have a tendency to ignore matters that did not comply with his views. At an IFMC conference I attended in Honolulu in 1977, Blacking presented a paper that received a good deal of attention.[534] Later in the same conference I was scheduled to read my paper "Innovations in *waiata* style".[535] I told Blacking it contained information that seemed to run contrary to his own hypotheses and suggested he might like to attend. After the reading of my paper, Blacking rose from his seat, advanced down the aisle towards the podium with his hand outstretched towards me, exclaiming: "Mervyn, what a splendid paper!" This warm, generous and disarming reaction was highly gratifying to receive, but there was never a word said either then or later about the inconsistencies between his paper and mine. Much the same happened in a panel discussion at a conference we both attended a number of years later at the University of Western Australia. Blacking agreed with good humour to challenging of his views, but did not allow it to alter his convictions.

For all of Blacking's zeal and the very real contributions he has made to ethnomusicology, I think it is time to recognise that on this particular issue he was wrong, that the consequences of accepting his position have been inimical, and music structure, which has been one of the casualties, should now be reinstated as a legitimate avenue of study in its own right.

Let me make it clear that I am not advocating analysis of musical sound as the only way to examine music. One agrees fully with an early statement by Merriam:

---

[534] Blacking 1977.
[535] McLean 1977.

> To look at music as an object in itself without reference to its cultural background is thus to reify the results of behavior without a sure knowledge of how the object has been shaped.[536]

The point to be made is not that the study of music structure should be an exclusive activity, but that it be carried out in tandem with study of behavioural aspects, without assumptions of a necessary relationship, as exemplified by Merriam himself in his book on Flathead music.

If it is any comfort to the protagonists of what is now being called the "anthropological" view, music structure can contribute to the solution of problems such as those of culture contact that still concern anthropologists. My own book *Weavers of Song*, whose findings confirm ethnographic, archaeological, historical, linguistic and other evidence about Polynesian migrations, is a case in point.

I cannot refrain from concluding that in my view the entire issue has reached its present state unnecessarily: in the first place through undue extension of Merriam's model of concept–behaviour–sound, and in the second place by ignoring contrary evidence, including the independence of music structure in our own most familiar music. Why does no one look for "holistic" links between social structure and music structure for "Home on the range", a Beethoven quartet or the latest pop song, all of which are as much a product of behaviour as any form of ethnic music? The reason is that we know too much about them. We know that in these cases the sought-for connections do not exist. We look for them in other forms of music only because, as yet, we know less about them.

What then, is the lesson to be drawn from the above? Is music related to social structure or isn't it? The answer, quite plainly, is sometimes, but not always and, where a relationship does exist, in some respects but not all. In seeking for anything beyond this, ethnomusicologists have been deluding themselves, and the widespread perception that the problem of relationships has been solved by choosing to study music exclusively as "process" is simply wrong. The way to find out whether in any given case a relationship exists is the reverse of the currently approved one: namely, to carry out a systematic analysis of the music structure and then examine the results in light of the social parameters. Finally, if a relationship is to be found, it can be expected to lie with those elements of the music structure that are named and conceptualised by the performers, as these elements, by definition, are the "central" ones of the system (though not the sole or necessarily most important ones) and for this reason are more likely to relate to behavioural or social elements that are also named, conceptualised and thereby "central".

MUSIC SYSTEM ANALYSIS

As Constantin Brailoiu (1893–1958) pointed out many years ago, we are obliged to use the word 'system' "each time investigation discovers a coherent group of artistic procedures ruled by intelligible laws. Though they have never been codified and their bearers know nothing of them, these laws . . . often astonish us by their rigour. It falls to the folklorist to penetrate them and set them forth."[537]

---

[536] Merriam 1964b:181.
[537] Cited by Rougier 1984:xiii.

For "folklorist" in this passage, read "ethnomusicologist", which is what Brailoiu really was, and we have a prescription for effective investigation which for too long since Brailoiu's time has been neglected.

Generations of composition students in university music departments world wide have been taught the rules of traditional Western harmony and counterpoint, and how to write 5-part motets in the style of Palestrina, 3-part inventions in the style of Bach and, at the most advanced level, the art of Baroque fugal writing. These exercises are possible because the rules of the respective styles have long since been worked out by musicologists and can be taught from text books. In principle, the same could be done for any music system. With the aid of a handy rule book, a student could then compose a Maori waiata or a Swiss mountain song, or produce a passable imitation of bebop. Nobody has bothered, however, to formulate such rules, or even work out a method of analysis that would enable them to be discovered, and there is and has been, little interest in the topic of systems of music structure as such. Given the current flight from musical analysis of any kind it is unlikely that anyone will do so in the near future, though I am mildly surprised that no one trained in composition has thought to do so.

Even within the limits of the 12 semitones of the Western well-tempered scale, an almost infinite variety of melodic styles has emerged in world music. Add in other elements of style such as rhythm, form and polyphony, and the permutations and combinations become huge indeed. The public at large is learning to marvel at the offerings as more and more CDs of non-Western music, both "traditional" and syncretic are released. But ethnomusicologists are increasingly ignoring them as "music", concentrating instead on such matters as cognition, performance practice, iconicity, metaphor, and identity. Why? Whatever the social parameters, and whatever theoretical meta-systems may or may not underlie them all, the primary concern of ethnomusicologists should surely be musical sound, just as linguists are interested in language. The crux of the matter is that in the same way as grammar and syntax underpin spoken language and are not dependent on the behaviour of the speakers, so too there are rules, albeit, as Brailoiu knew, in most respects subliminal and unspoken, that underlie music. The evidence for this is all around us. It should be obvious that co-ordinated group singing and performance, as well as the transmission of musical compositions to others, whether sung or instrumental, can take place only if the performers are in agreement with each other on the rules. One of the main tasks of ethnomusicologists should be to find out what these rules are. The tools that have been devised so far to assist the process are not yet fully adequate. Analysis of melody, rhythm, form, polyphony, manner of singing, and other elements of music style, isolated and systematised by Hornbostel and others in the early 20th century, and supplemented more recently by Lomax; the introduction of the Hornbostel system into the United States by Herzog; and codification and transmission of this method by Nettl and others in ethnomusicology text books, served their purpose well for many years, and were productive of many insights, both in Europe and the United States, and elsewhere. But the test of analysis ought to be synthesis, and by the late 1960s it was already obvious to most graduate students of ethnomusicology, if not to their teachers, that the Hornbostel system of analysis did not reveal enough about music systems for this to be possible. In particular, it was unable to produce rules that would allow composition within the system analysed. In other words, it did not disclose "essential" elements of the music such as melodic syntax or the equivalent of the grammatical rules of speech. Attempts at universal systems of analysis such as those of Kolinski were not the answer either, and we still await, in particular, a satisfactory method of analysing rhythm. It is unfortunate that the key persons in charge of ethnomusicology in the 1960s were satisfied with the status quo. Alan Merriam, for example, whose opinions I respect on most issues, himself had used the Hornbostel system and even made use of Kolinski's methods in his analysis of Flathead music. My reaction to the inadequacies of existing methods of analysis was to try to devise better ones. Merriam, who was happy with the ethnographic insights in my PhD thesis on Maori music,[538] was not interested in the "New Method of Melodic Interval Analysis" exemplified in it.[539] "We have enough analytic systems already," he told me. "We don't need any more." Wrong. It's a shame that other ethnomusicologists mostly took an even more extreme view and abandoned structural analysis altogether. Deficient as the earlier methods of analysis may have been, this was an over-reaction.

The most effective way of solving any problem is to work from the bottom up, from the particular to the general, and from known to unknown rather than the other way round. In other words, start with the data at hand and see what emerges from it. Next, as another fundamental principle, if something should turn up that seems contrary to initial assumptions or hypotheses, or is hard to understand or describe in current terms, make no attempt to dismiss it or explain it away, but worry away at the problem until a solution emerges. Only in this way can progress be made. In my experience, all significant advances (or what some are fond of calling quantum leaps) occur from observing this principle. First is the realisation that there is a contradiction. Second comes the question "why?". Only later does the solution emerge, and new lines of enquiry begin.

The essential error of early systematic approaches, such as those of Kolinski, was devising a broad supposedly universal method and then applying it to specifics. What is needed is the very reverse. Start with the multiplicity of styles now manifesting themselves around the globe, analyse each in its own terms in order to get at its basics, and then merge the results into a broader framework, if this should prove feasible. Finally, if such a process seems too burdensome as an "add-on", then make room for it as a subdiscipline within current ethnomusicology, establish a journal dedicated to it, invite contributions, and get the analytic and comparative ball rolling again.

Stephen Blum has pointed out that in the early history of ethnomusicology the term "music system" meant different things to different people. In particular, the German term "musiksystem" and the French "système musical" had specialised meanings, and for later comparative musicologists the term "musical system" was synonymous with "tone systems",[540] which, in fact, are most amenable to such analysis. My use of the term applies to all aspects of music structure and not just the melodic ones. It does not, however, extend to behavioural and other parameters that may or may not also be involved, except insofar as these assist analysis. If a performer plucks a string, all that matters in terms of structural analysis is the resulting sound and its relation to other sounds in the same performance. How or why the performer plays the instrument is irrelevant to the structural analysis. Although in the broadest sense it is now customary to regard music sound and music behaviour as holistically related and indissoluble, and in this sense a "system", they are opposite sides of a coin. The older idea that ethnomusicology is a dual discipline embracing both anthropology and music was correct, and so was Alan P. Merriam's

---

[538] McLean 1965.
[539] McLean 1966.
[540] Blum 1991:10.

decision in his book on Flathead music[541] to treat the two halves of music sound and music behaviour separately, rather than try to merge them. To provide a full account of a music culture both sides of the coin must be addressed, as Merriam did in his book and I have done in my own work.[542] But a music culture is not the same thing as a music system, and the two should not be confused.

By system analysis, then, I mean analysis of music systems in terms of music sound or structure alone, without consideration of extra-musical parameters unless these are strictly and straightforwardly relevant. Let me emphasise once again that I do not advocate neglect of the latter. As Merriam made very clear in the 1960s, and is surely by now accepted by everyone, there can be no music sound without human behaviour of some kind to produce it. What is at issue is the relationship of the immediate behaviour of performers to the sound or, at further remove, elements of social structure that may or may not affect the behaviour that produces the sound.

A simple example from Maori music will illustrate the point. Waiata and pao are two named song types that serve different social needs. Waiata are performed by groups of singers at meetings as a kinaki or "relish" to mark the conclusion of formal speeches. In this context they serve a social function. They are carefully crafted compositions with poetic texts that are difficult to understand and can take a long time to learn. As indicated earlier, the formal structure is one of repeating strophes coincident with textual lines. At the end of each line the song leader performs a short solo that aids performance by allowing time for the other singers to breath and to recall the next line. Pao are performed by individuals, usually for entertainment, are ephemeral in nature, and the words may be improvised. The structure takes the form of short couplets that are easy to compose and remember and, because the entire couplet is sung in the first place by an individual, and is then repeated by the group, there are no leader solos. The relationship in each case between the purpose of the song, the manner of performance and the formal structure of the song is plain.

But there needs to be a recognition that there is a hierarchy of relevance in terms of interaction between the musical or structural and the extra-musical or behavioural. When, for example, I worked with Raymond Firth on my analysis of Tikopia music,[543] our correspondence extended over the entire three years the work took to complete, during which I raised questions with Firth, and he provided me with the necessary ethnography to answer them. The analysis was not done in isolation from the ethnography but in the context of it. In the Tikopia case, rhythm and metre have an obvious relationship with dance, accompanying instruments, and bodily behaviour such as handclapping and even waving fans. Somewhat less important but still relevant in terms of interaction are matters such as the disposition of leaders with regard to other members of a singing group. Of no relevance to behaviour at all, neither in Tikopia nor in the case of the Maori, are other no less important elements of structure such as the exact number of notes in a scale, melodic syntax, or the intimate and systematic relationship these have with interval structure.

The concern in music system analysis, then, just as it would be with a Beethoven sonata or a Shostakovich symphony, must be with the internal relationships of the music structure. It needs

---

[541] Merriam 1967.
[542] McLean 1996; Mclean 1999.
[543] McLean 1990b; McLean 1991.

to be understood that I am not speaking here of the kind of note by note, bar by bar, purely descriptive analysis of single pieces of music that every music student learns to do. At best this is "homework" that is no more than preliminary to the real work. In system analysis, "system" is the operative word, and the objective is to elicit the "rules" of the system by examining representative bodies of music. What does one "piece" within the system have in common with another? What distinguishes one genre within the repertoire from another? And ultimately, what are the rules that would allow the analyst to compose a credible piece of music within the system?

If analysis of this kind were to emerge as an approved activity in ethnomusicology, particularly if improvements on current methods can be devised, glittering further prospects will open up, and some of the dreams of the early comparative musicologists may yet be realised. Attempts to transfer linguistic techniques of analysis to music have so far proven largely unproductive. There is, however, a very useful general analogy (though it is only this) between the two domains of speech and music: William P. Malm (1928–) spoke often of the "languages" and "dialects" of music. Just as a speaker of German has a better chance of understanding Dutch than (say) a speaker of Hindi or Icelandic, so too will a practitioner of Maori music find familiarities in the music of related areas of Polynesia, because these contain common elements. What in each case is the nature of the relationship? In what ways are "dialects" of music related? What distinguishes the different musical "languages" from the dialects? If such studies were to eventuate, then the next step would be to try to isolate music "families", just as linguists distinguish language families or phyla. This, in turn, would relate to evidence from ethnography, ethnohistory, archaeology, physical anthropology, and other disciplines that seek to track migrations and relationships of human populations, albeit without uncovering the earlier sought, elusive and quite likely mythical "origins" of music. The Berlin comparativists made an attempt at it, flawed by untenable assumptions. Lomax tried to do it with his cross-cultural cantometrics project, a laudable attempt that failed because of inadequate sampling and other flaws. In neither case, however, was there much wrong with the objective. Ethnomusicologists now have the means to resume the search. albeit in different ways, and with the benefit of hindsight, where Lomax and the early comparativists left off.

Comparison

The current flight from the earlier concerns of ethnomusicology forms an integrated package within which transcription, analysis and comparison are all currently out of favour. The two former, however, have traditionally been engaged in not as activities worthwhile in their own right, as critics of them perhaps suppose, but as a means to an end. Transcription is an essential preliminary to analysis, and analysis is a necessary first step towards comparison. Abandon one, and the others follow.

A likely initial reason for the demise of comparison was the change of name to ethnomusicology from "comparative musicology" in the 1950s. But the change was not made because of any idea that there was something the matter with comparison. The principal reason advanced in favour of the new name at the time was not that comparison was inappropriate but that everyone was doing it, and ethnomusicologists were no more engaged in it than anyone else. This was in itself untrue, but is a far from good reason not to compare at all.

In recent decades, a perception has clearly grown that comparison is not only "old fashioned" but also in some sense unacceptable or even indefensible. One reason may be scorn for "armchair" ethnomusicology in favour of personal field work, which has become standard. But few scholars are likely to gain first-hand experience in more than a handful of field areas in a lifetime, especially as sustained residence is a common requirement, so to restrict researchers to their own back yards forever is unrealistic. In any case, why publish ones work if it is only going to be read by people in the same small field area?

The reason most often advanced against comparison is one that has persisted now for at least 40 years since Mantle Hood aired the idea in his article "Music the Unknown": that it is "too soon" to begin comparison, because not enough is known about individual music systems for comparison of them to be possible or worthwhile.[544] The idea has probably grown in force as the number of areas about which at least something is known has multiplied. More and more about less and less has become the rule as ethnomusicologists retreat into ever-smaller niches. Alan P. Merriam, however, was fond of telling his students and colleagues "it is never too soon to compare". Nor was this a mere casual belief, unsupported by evidence. In what may well have been the last article he ever wrote, published posthumously in a festschrift for Mieczyslaw Kolinski,[545] he argues both the validity of comparison and the continuing necessity for it in ethnomusicology, characterising objections to it as "either half-truths or simply vague statements of the views of their proponents."[546] In these judgements, as in his ancillary arguments in the same article in defence of structural analysis, I believe Merriam was absolutely right. The components of individual music systems, which critics of comparison have assumed to be wholly culture-bound, are less unique than people think they are and, as globalisation impacts more and more on everyone, the ways in which the many systems of the world interact with each other, and have done so in the past, become an ever more cogent, pressing, and fruitful line of enquiry.

What other reasons might there be for the current failure to compare?

One possibility, which I hope is not true, was advanced by Alexander Ringer in an article favouring a return to comparison. He suggested that comparison has become unpopular because of a now prevailing egalitarianism which, by tending at times "to confuse equality with sameness",[547] perceives differences of any kind as ideologically unacceptable. If ethnomusicologists have fallen into this trap and are really turning a blind eye to differences which in many cases are among the wonders of the world and deserve acclamation rather than censure, then this is simply insane, besides being in the interests of no one.

Three other reasons can be isolated in explanation of the current attitude to comparison. The first is that most early comparative musicology was based on now long-discredited theories related to Kulturkreise and evolutionary ideas about the origin of music, as exemplified particularly in the work of scholars such as Marius Schneider and Curt Sachs. No one wants to be tainted with such a brush, and there is irrational distaste for the whole idea of comparison as a result. Regrettably, too, the literature is full of misguided attempts at comparison which disre-

---

[544] Hood 1963:233.
[545] Merriam 1982.
[546] Merriam 1982:174.
[547] Ringer 1991:187.

gard the principle of not comparing like with unlike, and this too would have helped to get the process into disrepute.

The most recent development contributing to abandonment of comparison can be laid at the door of John Blacking. Elsewhere in the present book I argue against his assertions that music structure is indissolubly bound up with social structure to the point that the one is a "reflection" of the other. A corollary of this idea is Blacking's belief that apparently similar musical "surface" structures are non-comparable if their "meaning" is different because of differences in the underlying non-musical "deep" structures which allegedly give them rise. Thus, says Blacking:

> Cross-cultural comparisons of different musical styles cannot be made until we know what we are comparing: if similar surface structures have been generated by entirely different processes, they cannot be compared simply because they *sound* alike.[548]

The operative word here, it must be pointed out, is "if", and if, as I have suggested, Blacking's ideas about the relationship of social structure and music structure are wrong, then so is his objection to comparison.

The third main reason against comparison, quite simply, is that like transcription and analysis, it is not easy to do. If it is to be engaged in, then the scholar's knowledge and interest in the areas he or she is comparing must be all-embracing and close to encyclopaedic. Few scholars are willing to invest enough time for credible comparison to be feasible, and are perhaps over-willing on this account to condemn the process itself. The problem of comparison, however, is something the discipline must confront and overcome. Perhaps part of the answer lies in collaborative projects, such as those that for more than 40 years have occupied anthropologists, linguists, historians and others at the University of Auckland, the University of Hawai'i and the Australian National University in the field of Pacific studies. Technological and other aids are also now so much better than they used to be that such collaboration need no longer be local. I can point to personal experience in the value of such research. My work on Polynesian music was immensely aided by the proximity of colleagues in related fields at Auckland university; my work with Margaret Orbell on traditional Maori waiata has resulted in significant breakthroughs as a result of our complementary skills; and my collaboration with Raymond Firth on Tikopia music over a period of three years, albeit mostly by airmail correspondence between London and Auckland, also yielded useful results. How much easier it would have been by e-mail!

In summary, none of the reasons for abandoning comparison as an objective of ethnomusicology stands up to scrutiny. It is time to compare again.

---

[548] Blacking 1971:108.

MUSIC AREAS

A detailed account of studies of style distribution, or what Nettl has called "musical geography", is unnecessary here. Nettl has supplied one in his book *The Study of Ethnomusicology*, under the heading "The Singing Map",[549] comprehensively covering most aspects of the subject, though without offering solutions to problems which he identifies.

There have been just three attempts at delineating music areas of non-Western styles which I would regard as successful: one by Bruno Nettl for North America,[550] and two of my own for Oceania.[551] An attempt by Merriam to draw up music areas for Africa[552] was less successful than the others, because it did no more than plot the incidence of African western traits on the one hand and Arabic northern traits on the other in each of the standard ethnographic areas. Predictably, all that emerged was a gradient of northern traits from north to south and of western ones from west to east.

Nettl's effort for North America was preceded by two others by Herzog and Roberts respectively,[553] each of whom contributed interim solutions, but it was Nettl who completed the process. In his later publications Nettl has tended to throw cold water on his own early effort, but he should have stuck to his guns. His study was, in fact, brilliantly done, resulting in the emergence of six stylistic areas for the continent. So long as it is understood that no trait is unique to particular areas and that areas are distinguished rather by constellations of dominant traits, the approach is seen to work extremely well. A simple statistical technique developed by Harold Driver of Indiana University that I later applied to Nettl's results as a pilot study resulted in a flow chart that can be followed to identify styles by simple listening (see next page).

But the method can also be a powerful one for identifying historical movements of styles. The same clustering technique, when applied to Oceanic music in my own study,[554] identified Samoa in Western Polynesia as the area from which Eastern Polynesia was most likely settled. Today, some 20 years after the publication of this paper, archaeologists are agreed that Samoa was indeed the jumping-off point for the peoples of Eastern Polynesia, who began their migrations almost 2000 years ago.

---

[549] Nettl 1983:Ch.16.
[550] Nettl 1954.
[551] McLean 1979; McLean 1994.
[552] Merriam 1962:76-80.
[553] Herzog 1930; Roberts 1936.
[554] McLean 1974.

FLOW CHART: MUSIC AREAS: NTH AMERICAN INDIAN

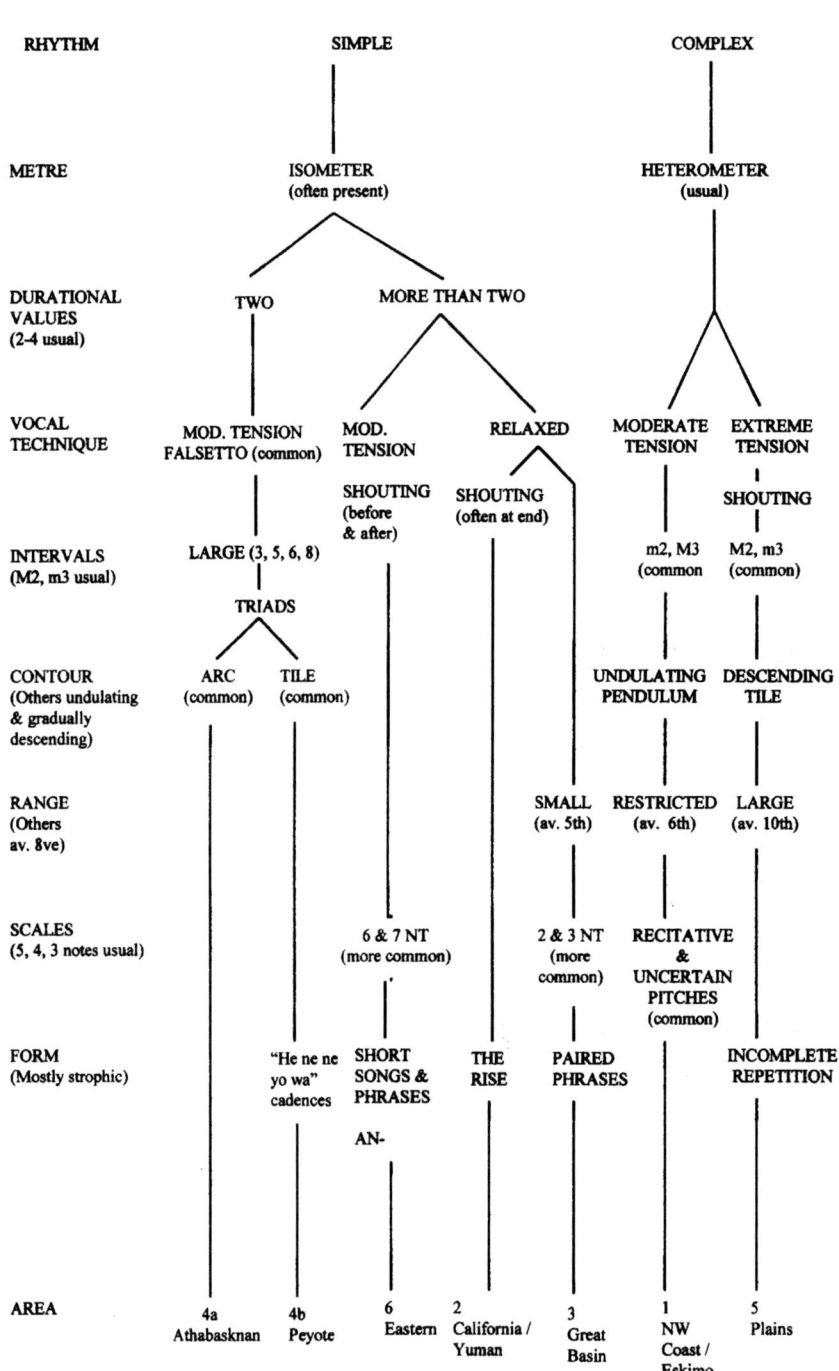

Apart from the benefits of contributing to anthropology, such results have profound implications for ethnomusicology itself, by reaffirming the reality of continuity and the stability of traits as complementary to change, and justifying efforts to track styles over time. My approach in the above paper, which avoids some of the problems identified by Nettl, was to define the term "music area" as "a geographical region unified in terms of clusters of co-occurring musical traits which are either absent in other areas or are associated in them with different traits." The possibility both of borrowing from adjacent areas and historical connection with more remote ones was assumed; and areas were worked out strictly in accordance with shared traits as these emerged from the data, avoiding bias which would have been introduced by using established culture areas as a starting point.[555]

The hand-clustering method I employed for the Oceania study is difficult to apply to large bodies of data, though a computer programme could probably be developed that would do the same job more readily. The method I would now recommend instead is an extremely simple one I developed for a study of musical instrument diffusion in New Guinea. It is fully reported in a monograph available from the Institute of Papua New Guinea Studies.[556] Again, results were extremely productive; as well as consistent, I am told, with later linguistic findings; and the method itself is probably capable of adaptation for use with standard computer graphics programmes capable of "layering".

Diffusion

Two points must be made at the outset which should be unnecessary. The first is that "diffusion" is not the same as "diffusionism". The second is that although diffusionism (or as it was known in German, Kulturkreise) has been thoroughly discredited as a theoretical system, the ideas encapsulated in it were not wholly mistaken and, with appropriate correctives and safeguards, some remain useful. An early critic of diffusionism was George Herzog, who made a huge and universally acknowledged contribution to ethnomusicology by demonstrating the necessity of anthropological method. His work was seen by most as a departure from the Berlin School of Hornbostel with its emphasis on diffusionism as a method. But when scholars followed Herzog's lead by rejecting diffusionism, the still viable techniques associated with it were thrown out as well. In the minds of many, diffusionism was confused with diffusion, and diffusion studies largely disappeared from consideration. Herzog himself made no such mistake. In his paper on the diffusion of the Ghost Dance he demonstrated the reality of diffusion in North America.[557] And Willard Rhodes's well-known paper on the diffusion of the Peyote cult, together with David McAllester's comprehensive monograph on the same subject, provides an even more compelling object lesson.[558] Plotting the data provided by McAllester on to a map (and what a pity McAllester did not do this himself) reveals a classic ripples in the pond demonstration of diffusion at work.

---

[555] McLean 1979:717-8.
[556] McLean 1994.
[557] Herzog 1935a.
[558] Rhodes 1958; McAllester 1949.

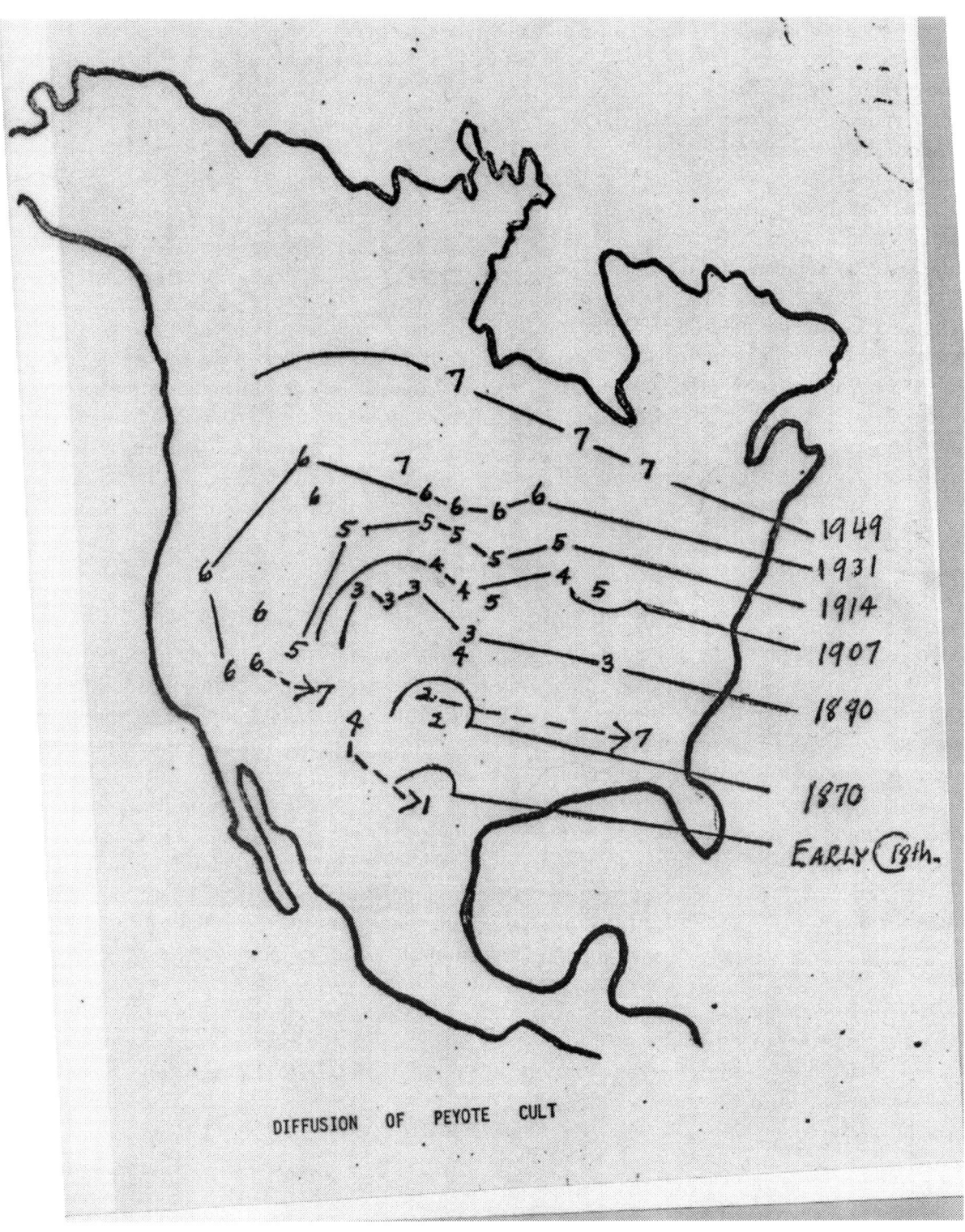

When I later wrote my monograph about the diffusion of musical instruments in New Guinea, and this was scheduled for discussion by the European Seminar in Ethnomusicology, I feared that as I would not be present to offer correctives I might be regarded as a diffusionist. In the event, I was told, the work was respectfully received. And later I was relieved to read in a favourable review of the book by Jeremy Montagu his sentence: "The old ideas of *Kulturkreise* are well and truly dead, but if they were not, this book would certainly kill them off".[559]

CANTOMETRICS

Among the unsuccessful efforts at establishing music areas, I rank most of the results of Alan Lomax's Cantometrics study, as reported in his book *Folk Song Style and Culture*.[560] The object of the study was to map song styles on a world-wide basis and to discover relationships between the components of singing style and cultural variables such as subsistence activities and "social solidarity." As Lomax himself put it, once culture areas had been determined: "We hoped to show that each pattern of sung communication sympbolized the dominant patterns of social structure and communication style in that large area."[561]

Although hailed initially as a landmark in ethnomusicology and as a "milestone in comparative research",[562] Lomax's methodology and results have been severely criticised by ethnomusicologists, if not always justifiably. The present book, however, is not the place for a detailed critique. Two reviews of Lomax's book are especially recommended for further reading: one by Hewitt Pantaleoni in the *Yearbook of the International Folk Music Council*,[563] and the other a review essay of my own, which seems not to have been much noticed, published in the *Journal of the Polynesian Society*.[564] In these reviews, Lomax's results are seen to be deeply flawed both in concept and execution as well as the results obtained. As indicated earlier, his measures of manner of singing and vocal timbre are useful and worth adopting, and the book must be recognised as a major contribution to cross-cultural research. Among its shortcomings, however, are inadequate sampling techniques, extreme subjectivity of rating criteria, unacceptable assumptions implicit in the use of evolutionary scales, lack of rigour in interpreting evidence, and unwarranted historical inferences.[565] Worse still, the widely recognised deficiencies of the book have helped to bring unjustified calumny upon comparison in general.

UNIVERSALS

After an inconclusive start in the 19th century, one thing upon which most ethnomusicologists were probably agreed until about the 1970s is that music is most emphatically not a "universal language" except in the limited sense that no human population is known that does not have some form of it, just as there is none that does not have spoken language. By this time, the musical languages of the world had been shown to be too diverse to support any notion of "universals". But then, as always, the pendulum swung, and questions about universals were again

---

[559] Montagu 1997:253.
[560] Lomax 1968.
[561] Lomax 1968:x.
[562] Driver & Downey 1970.
[563] Pantaleoni 1972.
[564] McLean 1973.
[565] McLean 1973:422.

being asked. For example, by analogy with then current linguistic theory, promulgated by Noam Chomsky, could apparently different musics, as asked by Blacking,[566] have "deep structure" in common? Alternatively, can anything whatsoever be isolated in the surface structures of known forms of music that all of them have in common? The answer, despite the considerable renewed scrutiny, appears to be simply no. To start with there is no agreed definition of what is meant by "music". A common definition of music is that it is "structured sound", but so is language, so this gets us nowhere. And other definitions can just as readily be shot down. Music takes too many forms for a definition that fits every known kind to be feasible except by cataloguing the differences. About all one can say with reasonable confidence is that music involves sound, is performed by humans, and is distinguishable from speech. Another problem is that even if one could find common features in all known musics, a single exception in an as yet unstudied form of music could invalidate the conclusion at some future time. Having examined the problem in a 1983 book, the best Nettl can suggest is that the closest it is possible to come to universals is to narrow the search to what "most" rather than "all" forms of music have in common.[567] But by definition such features would not be universals.

A remote possibility is that ethnomusicologists have been looking for universals in the wrong places, and music universals, if they exist, are to be found in the domain of cognitive psychology. If so, then perhaps some day physiologists or behavioural psychologists will give us the answers, as hoped for by the 1997 Florence conference earlier referred to, where the thorny question of "what is music" assumed the same significance for "universals" as it does for "origins". The literature on the subject of universals is now extensive but is as inconclusive as ever, and the reader must excuse me for not reviewing it here. I must confess that I have no personal enthusiasm for the topic, and my own judgement is that it is probably another subject, along with "origins of music" and other unachievable objects of enquiry, that the books can reasonably be closed upon.[568] I find myself most in sympathy with the position taken by George List,[569] beginning with his assessment of Seeger, and his admission that as far as Seeger was concerned, he rarely understood what Seeger's position was. On the matter of universals, List's conclusion was that the most universal characteristic of music was its non-universality, a perception as true of music in our own society as any other. As always, List was calling a spade a spade, and all praise to him for doing so.

Product and process

Encapsulated in the phrase "product and process" are the two main streams of influence that have driven ethnomusicology in the United States: Kunst–Seeger–Hood and Boas–Herzog–Merriam, culminating with the celebrated UCLA v. Indiana split of the 1960s, and resulting ultimately in an apparent triumph of the putatively anthropological over the supposedly musicological, though neither is what it seems or can be accepted at face value. If I can be forgiven a

---

[566] Blacking 1971.
[567] Nettl 1983:36-43.
[568] A sampling of writings on universals includes Meyer 1960; Kolinski 1967; *Ethnomusicology* vol. 15, no. 3 (1971), containing contributions from David McAllester, Klaus Wachsmann, Charles Seeger, and George List; *The World of Music* vol. 19, no.1-2 (1973) in a special issue with contributions from John Blacking, Frank Harrison, Mantle Hood, Gertrude Kurath, Alan Lomax, Jean-Jacques Nattiez, Bruno Nettl, and Trân Van Khê; and Harwood 1976.
[569] List 1971.

little rhetoric, the resultant entity is all-pervasive: rather like a giant two-headed octopus that sprawls over the discipline, extending its tentacles into every corner, squirting ink in all directions, and thoroughly obscuring the waters. The ramifications are too numerous and too complex to be treated adequately here, and no doubt will take decades to resolve. I can offer only a few random thoughts.

REPERTOIRE

Associated with the current shift of emphasis in ethnomusicology towards "process" rather than "product" there appears to be a widespread perception that Western emphasis upon music as "pieces" is inappropriate for other kinds of music, and that "pieces" are no more than temporary stepping stones at specific points in time, with no real validity beyond this.

According to Nettl:

> . . . both in America and Europe, the 1980s were a time in which ethnomusicologists . . . definitively changed from looking at music as a group of products, artifacts, or pieces, to seeing musical culture as constantly a process.[570]

The operative word here is "constantly", with its implied denial of any kind of stability. Such a view of music, however, is both an over-generalisation and a product of areal interests focusing predominantly on non-Western art musics involving improvisation. The criticism might have been more aptly expressed in terms of Western preoccupation with "master works" in the classical repertoire, rather than pieces as such. An Indian raga, Indonesian patet, Iranian dastgah or Iraqi taqsim might well be best considered as process. But "pieces" assuredly exist outside of Western repertoire, and demand consideration as such, especially in areas of folk and tribal music where "pieces" may endure for generations, subject to change as may be, but without losing their identity. As often said, change is indeed a constant, but so is stability, and both can co-exist in the same "piece". A good example is provided by the New Zealand Maori.

More than 150 years ago, New Zealand's governor Sir George Grey (1812–1898) (photo left) published the first anthology containing texts of classic Maori songs (many of which are still being sung) of the genre known as waiata.[571] Recent such anthologies, with words and music, have been published by the present writer in association with Margaret Orbell.[572] Each waiata is a "piece", precisely in the Western sense, though owing nothing to it. Each such "piece" has its own tune, known to singers from disparate areas who come together in ad hoc groups from time to time to perform the songs; each has an acknowledged composer (albeit sometimes notional); each is referred to by title or by the first line of its text; and each is supposed to be performed the same way at each presentation, just as a Western "piece" would be. It is no less

---

[570] Nettl 2002:204.
[571] Grey 1851.
[572] McLean & Orbell 2004: Orbell & McLean 2002.

a "piece" than a Mozart symphony or a rendition of "She'll be comin' round the mountain" at a square dance (both of which are also subject to change). The same is true throughout Polynesia, as witness the most recent example of an anthology of such pieces in Raymond Firth's book *Tikopia Songs*.[573] In this sense, then, process simply doesn't have primacy over product in Polynesia. Nor can it be supposed that Polynesia is unique in this respect. If ethnomusicologists wish to deal with realities of repertoire, it is time to resurrect the idea of the "piece".

MECHANISMS OF CHANGE

Here is a topic that can only be considered with due regard to music structure. For this reason it is perhaps less popular than it used to be because it requires recourse to music analysis. The topic has been addressed in a special issue of the journal *World of Music* (vol.28 no.1 (1986)), in articles by Béhague, Blacking, Kubik, McLean, Nettl and Shiloah. In my own article, building upon the work of Nettl and others concerning centrality, compatibility and other aspects of change, I believe I have "cracked" the problem of acculturative change in music, distinguishing and naming six different forms of it and illustrating each diagramatically and with examples from Oceania. The six forms of change identified in the article are Fusion, Transfer, Modification, Independence, Abandonment, and Revival, of which the first, Fusion, is my own alternative term for the process known in much of the literature as "syncretism". I prefer not to use the latter term because of a misapprehension on the part of too many writers that it is a technical term for change in general rather than a specific form of it. The next step could well be comparative follow-up from other areas of the world, documenting and discussing each type of change further in terms of the McLean typology to confirm whether or not it is useful as a general tool. The following is the essential information from the article:

> The typology (see Fig.1) develops and systematises earlier published formulations.[574] Except for nos. 4 and 6 the responses illustrated are all examples of acculturation or, to use Kartomi's term "transculturation".[575] Essential concepts for understanding the typology are "compatibility" or "degree of significant similarity",[576] and "centrality" or those elements of a music system which are essential to it "as indicated by their pervasiveness in a repertory, the degree to which members of a society accord them primacy (and) . . . their tenacity in times of change".[577] A four-fold classification emerges (see Figs.1 & 2):
>
> *Central/compatible*
>
> Easiest to understand is "merging", "blending" or, as it has long been known, "syncretism"; the present writer's term is FUSION. It occurs "when the two musical systems in a state of confrontation have compatible central traits".[578] An excellent Oceanic example, as striking and as clear as the better known Afro-American, is that of Tonga [which has assimilated European music into the traditional system because of a mutual presence of polyphony.].

---

[573] Firth with McLean 1990.
[574] See especially Nettl 1978b and Kartomi 1981.
[575] Kartomi 1981:233.
[576] Nettl 1978b:125.
[577] Nettl 1978b:126.
[578] Nettl 1978b:134.

Issues

	COMPATIBLE	NON-COMPATIBLE
CENTRAL	1. FUSION	2. TRANSFER
NON-CENTRAL	3. MODIFICATION	4. INDEPENDENCE (a) Rejection (b) Coexistence 5. ABANDONMENT (a) Displacement (b) Diminution (c) Substitution 6. REVIVAL

Figure 1: Types of response

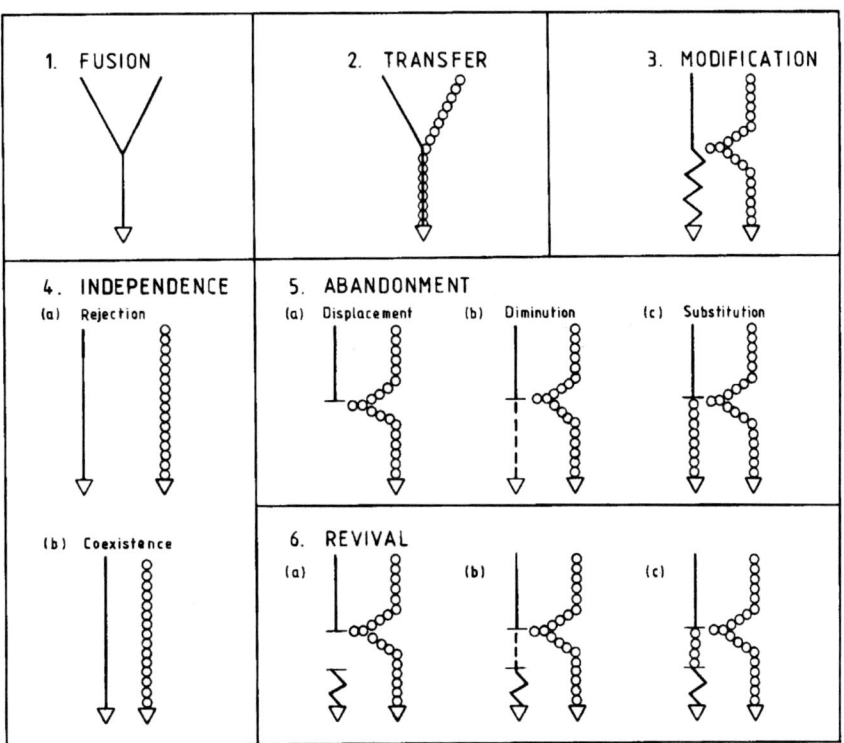

Figure 2: Classification

Central/non-compatible

TRANSFER is the introduction of a completely new central element such as harmony into a system which did not have it before. Because the intrusive element is non-compatible the only effect upon the borrowing system is accretion. Because the new element is also central it cannot fail to be noticed. In common with fusion, transfer can accordingly take place only if the element involved is both perceived and knowingly adopted by the receiving culture. A possible Oceanic example is the Tahitian *himene* [now confirmed to have emerged from missionary introduction of fuging hymn tunes and adoption of the principle by Tahitians].[579]

Non-central/compatible

MODIFICATION is difficult to distinguish in practice from transfer. The essential difference is that central features of the host system are retained and intrusive elements affect only those features which are not perceived as core or essential by the borrowing culture. Nettl refers to this process as "modernization".[580] Because modification affects only non-central elements it may occur without the recipients being aware that change has been introduced. A contemporary example is unknowing imposition of European scales and meter when young and middle-aged Maori attempt to learn traditional waiata.[581]

Non-central/non-compatible

When two systems are unable to interact the only possible relationships are either independence from each other or abandonment of the one in favour of the other. INDEPENDENCE takes two forms. The most radical is REJECTION, illustrated nicely by the case of Pukapuka [where missionaries laboured for 90 years before succeeding in teaching European hymn tunes]. COEXISTENCE occurs when the practitioners of one musical system become bimusical in another. Thus many Maori are able to sing comfortably both traditional waiata (which until recently has maintained its separate system) and Action Song (whose melodies are European). DIMINUTION refers to impoverishment of repertoire. It could be characterised as song loss in progress. SUBSTITUTION occurs when a new form assumes the function of an old one. Finally REVIVAL is a possible aftermath of displacement, diminution or substitution. It cannot follow fusion, transfer or modification because these entail irreversible changes to some or all of the earlier unmodified tradition. Revival always follows some form of break in continuity and for this reason is unlikely to replicate the original style exactly. Modification rather than transfer or fusion will be involved because the new elements must not threaten the revived system, as such must be of an unconscious nature, and are therefore necessarily non-central.[582]

---

[579] McLean 1999:33-46.
[580] Nettl 1978b:134.
[581] McLean 1984:33-4.
[582] McLean 1986:37-41.

THE ROLE OF THE SUBLIMINAL

In several of John Blacking's lectures and papers he refers in passing to "decision-making" as part and parcel both of composition and the process of oral transmission. A discussion of his position appears in his 1977 paper "Some Problems of Theory and Method in the Study of Music Change", where he devotes most of the final section of his paper to the topic. It was this issue that I saw to be in conflict with my own reporting of innovations in Maori waiata at the same conference. Essential to my paper was a finding that radical changes had taken place in the music structure of waiata, at the hands of neophyte singers, of which the singers themselves were not aware. Blacking's stance was that music change is a result of decision-making by singers which, if true, would rule out changes except by deliberate conscious choice.

Blacking begins the final section of his paper with apparently unequivocal assertions: (a) that "musical change is brought about by decisions made by individuals about music-making and music on the basis of their experiences of music and attitudes to it in different social contexts," and (b) "Melody is a product of human decisions about the selection and use of acoustic and physiological elements . . ."[583] My response to this would have been "sometimes, and sometimes not."

Having assumed that change is a result of decision-making, Blacking goes on to speculate how the analyst can find out "precisely when and how the crucial decisions were made."[584] No precise answers emerge. Historical study is seen by Blacking to distort the past, and a year or two of field work is regarded as insufficient to provide answers in the present.

In terms of hard evidence for his idea, it has to be said that Blacking, as in most of his writing, is difficult to pin down. The paper is highly discursive; terms are inadequately defined and set out; and Blacking keeps shifting his ground and raising multiple side issues in the course of the writing. Some of his conclusions are acceptable, though not always for the reasons stated. But on the face of it, most of the rest must be rejected if the initial assumptions, as stated above, are either wrong or not necessarily or always true. It is a position that can be salvaged untidily by maintaining either that a music system is not always a music system, or that change is sometimes not change. After examining and rejecting some reported examples of musical change as examples of innovation within a system rather than real change,[585] Blacking opts for the latter:

> 1 hope that it is now clear why 1 consider that most changes of repertory, many examples of changes of style, and even cases of acculturation, may not be significant as musical change.[586]

In other words he has adopted a narrow view such that changes resulting from decision-making are regarded as "significant" and on this account qualify as "musical change" but other changes to music do not.

---

[583] Blacking 1977:12
[584] Blacking 1977:13.
[585] Blacking 1977:15.
[586] Blacking 1977:18.

It turns out that Blacking is well aware of the reality that some changes to music occur without explicit recognition by the performers. His list of circumstances in which change can occur is headed by:

> 1. An audible change in the norms of performance that is not recognised as such by performers and audience, and is not merely a variation or a new item in an established style, or a new style in a tradition that incorporates stylistic variation.[587]

and

> 2. An audible change in the norms of performance that is not categorised as such by performers and audience, and is not classed as an exceptional variation, but is considered significant by an external observer, chiefly as a result of objective measurement.[588]

It is the latter type of change, of course, that I was reporting and would maintain to be just as significant as the kinds of change that Blacking was willing to recognise and chose to concentrate upon.

In the foregoing section on mechanisms of change, a distinction is made between "Central" and "Non-Central" elements of a music system. Central elements are those that are explicitly recognised, and often named, by the practitioners of the system. Non-central elements are those that are equally part of the system but are not recognised or acknowledged by the practitioners. There is no implication, as some ethnomusicologists seem to assume, that non-central elements are non-essential. It would appear that Blacking chose to focus only on central elements of styles, and for these any changes which might ensue would indeed be a matter of choice and conscious decision-making. What Blacking neglected to do was to take into account that non-central elements are also essential elements of music systems. The nature of non-central components can sometimes be a surprise to an ethnomusicologist. For example, in the Maori case, scales are non-central because there is no Maori word for them and no Maori concept of them. The same is true of specific rhythms, metre, form, and most other elements of music structure which emerge not from asking singers about them, but only as a result of analysing the sung product. They are none-the-less vital to the system, taking the form of non-conceptualised and unverbalised rules to which the singers conform without being aware of doing so, just as a speaker of English, for example, may be blissfully unaware of the grammatical and syntactical rules of the language upon which most of its speakers, as a condition of being able to communicate at all, nevertheless agree. Thus, just as speakers of a language can talk to each other without knowing the rules of their language, so too practitioners of a music system can sing or play musical instruments in a manner intelligible to other practitioners of the same system.

MERRIAM'S FEEDBACK MODEL

One great merit of Merriam's book *The Anthropology of Music* (1964) is that for each and every topic relating to music behaviour which he isolated, he provided a rational structure of discourse, and example after example illustrating his points from different areas of the world.

---

[587] Blacking 1977:19.
[588] Blacking 1977:20.

Effectively, by providing such categories, he did for music ethnography what analysts of the end product had for years been doing for music structure. With Merriam's work as a guide it was now possible to provide a tidy music ethnography of any area, under uniform readily understandable headings (see Appendix). Effectively, he supplied the anthropology half of the entire discipline of ethnomusicology as it was henceforth to develop, and also henceforth obliged ethnomusicologists to gain at least a nodding acquaintance with the methods and insights that anthropology was able to provide. The present writer, for one, travelled from the other side of the world as a post-doctoral fellow to sit at Merriam's feet for a while at Indiana University and absorb more of what he had to offer. For many, however, becoming an anthropologist as well as a musician was perhaps too tall an order. It was probably inevitable that some of Merriam's teaching would be poorly understood, or misapplied, especially after his death in 1980, when he was no longer with us to provide correctives. His feedback model of concept–behaviour–sound is very much a case in point, having been taken to mean that music sound cannot be understood at all without involvement of the other elements of the "model", and consideration of these involves everything else that was discussed by Merriam in his book. Thought of in this way, music is so tightly intertwined with culture that it can only be considered essentially *as* culture, and culture in all of its aspects must in some way be related to music. This, I believe, is mistaken, and I doubt if Merriam would insist upon it either if he were able to continue the debate. I think, indeed, that he would be appalled to find that on account of his theory, so-called "process" is now given primacy over "product", and the latter is now too often dismissed as irrelevant. Merriam, in fact, knew perfectly well that an all-embracing view of his model could not be applied in a practical way to guide investigation of music, as otherwise he would not have separated music structure and music behaviour in his own later book on Flathead music.[589] It seems to me that the three-part Merriam model has limited application only. The idea of feedback within culture goes back to Boas, and would have been very much still in the air when Merriam was a student under Herskovits. As a process it operates on elements of culture but not the entire panoply. In the case of music, it is relevant to the process of oral transmission and little else. Someone composes a song and others learn it. Having learnt it, they engage in behaviour by performing it. In their heads they have a concept of the song which probably already differs from that of the composer. Their concept of the song guides their future performances of it. As a result of these performances, still others learn the song and gain a yet different concept of it which in turn shapes their subsequent performances. And so round and round we go: concept to behaviour to product and back again through concept and behaviour to a perhaps slightly changed product. That, however, is all. Too much has been made of the idea.

ANTHROPOLOGY v. MUSIC

To conclude this portion of the book, it is now time to pull a few threads together. When I was at Indiana University as a visiting fellow in 1966, there was some disagreement as to whether it was possible for a student to become an ethnomusicologist without formal training in music. Some tried to do so, though I doubt if many succeeded. On the other side of the fence were students of music who eschewed anthropology, thrived, and have since become influential in the profession. There is room for and plenty of evidence of useful and successful studies that ignore one or other of these components of what is accepted as ethnomusicology. I would maintain, however, that a complete study of any music culture requires attention to both. In my own

---

[589] Merriam 1967.

teaching I accepted students from within both anthropology and music, advising them that, although there was no formal requirement to do so, music students had better learn something about anthropology, and anthropology students could not expect to advance professionally in ethnomusicology without a knowledge of music. In practice, it is easier for music students to "pick up" enough knowledge of anthropology than it is for an anthropology student to learn enough music. In my view, a "complete" ethnomusicologist, among whom I number ethnomusicologists such as Devid McAllester (1916–) and Bruno Nettl (1930–), should have equal competence in both.

It had taken approximately a decade for the Hood/Merriam stand-off to reach its peak. By about 1970, there was acceptance among most scholars that ethnomusicology had become a divided discipline, with a fundamental distinction between the approaches of scholars trained in music, as exemplified at that time by the programmes at UCLA under the direction of Mantle Hood, and those who followed Merriam after his publication of *The Anthropology of Music* in 1964. The schism appears now to have healed over the years to the extent that most scholars agree that ethnomusicology embraces both music and anthropology, with key ideas drawn from both (together with a substantial and increasing leavening from other disciplines such as cognitive psychology). The trend, indeed, seems to have lurched towards lip service to anthropology, not always soundly based or well understood, and a notion that the earlier specifically musical approaches (especially those involving transcription and analysis) are no longer acceptable. Who then is driving this movement, and from whence do they come? Surprisingly, it seems, not from within anthropology. Most persons espousing the new orthodoxy appear to be musically trained, but have turned away from their own most familiar territory in favour of what must seem new and more exciting vistas.

The flight from transcription and analysis appears also to be associated with and driven by ethnomusicologists whose areal affiliations are primarily with non-Western, especially Oriental, art musics. The latter orientation, indeed, seems to be crucial. It is a truism that music-trained ethnomusicologists, whose initial interests and instruction has been with Western art music, gravitate towards non-Western art music, whereas those trained in anthropology with its focus on tribal cultures move naturally into tribal musics. This is a pity, because it is from music graduates, or at any rate persons competent to read and write music, that a renewal of interest in the structure of tribal music can be expected to come. So long as such persons are willing to broaden their horizons to include some competence in anthropology, this may enable them to avoid a further problem that has come to the fore in recent years, namely a perceived necessity for tutelage – rather like attending master classes at a conservatory – from practitioners of the culture to be studied.

Especially among music school scholars whose focus is upon non-Western art music, there is plainly now a perception that "insider" research has greater validity than outsider, and the key to understanding such music lies with the insiders rather than the application of "Western" methods which are seen as presumptuous at best and "colonialist" or even racist at worst. This too probably accounts for a considerable focus on "ethical" issues, which has been a preoccupation at least since the 1980s. It also drives performance studies as a natural progression from conservatory-based instruction in Western music to an application of the same methods to non-Western music. Because such scholars are familiar primarily with their own areal and other interests, talk mostly to people with similar interests, and perpetuate both their interests and judgements in the courses they teach, their attitudes to such fundamental issues as transcription and analysis are inevitably coloured by their own experience and are not necessarily relevant to the world at large.

The problems have steadily escalated and become entrenched over a period of 30 years after the International Folk Music Council (later International Council for Traditional Music) moved its administration from Europe to North America in 1969, changing orientation and becoming effectively more Anerican, like its sister organisation, the Society for Ethnomusicology. It is true that both organisations are international, and ethnomusicologists who live outside of the USA are mostly members of one or both organisations. However, as rank and file members, they have had little voice. The ICTM has come closest to providing one with its policy of holding conferences in different parts of the world each year, appointment of liaison officers in numerous countries, and its many long-standing national committees and study groups. But with the move away from Europe where study groups had more frequent opportunities to meet, most became less active than they once were. With members so dispersed, it is hard to see how matters could be any different. The Oceania study group, for example, meets of necessity only as an informal adjunct of annual conferences or other events to provide a get-together for whoever happens to be present. By and large, the international members of both the SEM and the ICTM work quietly away on their own, publishing work from time to time that few outside their own immediate circle even notice. The most conspicuous activity in ethnomusicology has unquestionably until now taken place in the United States. With no disrespect intended, in terms of focus and issues confronting the discipline as a whole, the United States tail has been wagging the world dog.

Some encouraging developments have taken place recently that may help counter this trend. One was the 37th World Conference of the ICTM, held in China in 2004, focussing attention on this huge and neglected area. Others were announcements that in 2006 the ICTM Secretariat will move to Canberra, Australia, and a decision by the Society for Ethnomusicology to hold its 2006 conference in Honolulu, Hawai'i. One hopes that the latter events signal **increased awareness of Oceania**, which currently is one of the last ethnomusicological frontiers in the world.

What, then, of the music/anthropology split which caused so much concern in the 1960s? What has the outcome been? Has there been an effective merger? I think, on the contrary, there is a case for claiming that the least important and least productive elements have survived from both camps and now predominate.

There has been a huge shift from the descriptive to the theoretical, from the "what" and "where" to the "how" and "why": not in terms of empirical reality, but in terms of abstract "models" and theoretical constructs. When I was a post-doctoral fellow at Indiana University in 1966–67, I was of the right age and career status to move readily within the social circles of both graduate students and faculty. In discussions with student friends, there was a tendency, common enough for me to think of it as "American", for them to talk in terms of abstractions. Theoretical ideas became reified and assumed life of their own. One abstraction could then be discussed in terms of another while the speaker's feet never touched the ground. To an extent, this has always been true, and there is a certain tradition of it, as exemplified by Charles Seeger, who was highly influential in this regard. Nowadays, however, the theory tends increasingly to draw upon concepts from anthropology, which has always had a prominent theoretical orientation of its own. The two have reinforced each other, creating a world of theory that, in my view, is increasingly divorced from reality. The theory now drives the research instead of the other way round. My own strongly held view and appeal to ethnomusicologists is that real progress is unlikely so long as "models" determine what will or will not be studied when an ethnomusicologist begins work in the field. The tried and true method is to gather data first, in all its complexity, and let the theory come later.

Aftermath

UCLA v. INDIANA

In preceding pages, there is discussion of the 1960s difference in approach between the followers of Mantle Hood at UCLA and Alan P. Merriam at Indiana University which split ethnomusicology into supposedly "musicological" and "anthropological" camps. What, then, has been the outcome? Nominally, the two streams have now converged. With the untimely death of Alan P. Merriam in the Polish aircrash of 1980, and the almost universal adoption of performance-based studies in ethnomusicology programmes throughout the United States, ideas that originated within Hood's former Institute of Ethnomusicology at UCLA have become entrenched and have gone virtually unchallenged. On the other hand, nearly everyone now gives at least lip service to the principles espoused by Merriam, and most teaching programmes profess to implement them, though not necessarily in a form that would have been accepted by Merriam.The most fully rounded approaches to ethnomusicology, in my view, have come from outside the former orbit of both Indiana and UCLA, at the hands of persons trained in both anthropology and music. The discipline has nevertheless moved further than ever away from any possibility of unification, as hoped for by Merriam, and later by Blacking, as ethnomusicology adopts new areas of study such as popular music, and takes aboard approaches that were formerly foreign to it.

POPULAR MUSIC

A question that must be asked is why there is now such a shift towards studies of popular music, and what its role is likely to be within the discipline.

According to Nettl, the movement started at the University of Illinois on the initiative of Charles Hamm (1925–). When Nettl was president of the SEM in 1970 and Hamm president of the AMS, they arranged for a joint session of the two societies in 1971 at which popular music was a feature for the first time. It was evidently not a success, yet in the 1990s the SEM and other societies were regularly receiving large numbers of paper abstracts on popular musics.[590] So what changed?

One reason for the current swing to popular music is simply that, like Mount Everest, it is there, and very little scholarly attention was directed towards it in the past. Musicologists whose allegiance is primarily to Western art music ignored it, and ethnomusicologists, who are less likely than their musicological colleagues to make value judgements, moved into the gap. Academic

---

[590] Nettl 2002:159.

respectability for the subject can be said to have come in 1981 when a journal began publication that was specifically devoted to it. For popular music to be fully embraced by ethnomusicology will, however, require some further stretching of definitions. There is nothing particularly "ethnic" about Western popular music and, except for folk music, ethnomusicologists have traditionally studied cultures other than their own. For my part, I would like to see research on popular music not so much in terms of analysis of style and genres and the dynamics of performance groups, as the impact it is having on world populations at large. In the form of what used to be called "musak", it is now inescapable not only in every public space and most private or public gatherings, but also on radio, television and film as an increasingly obtrusive "background" to advertising, documentaries, movies, and news presentations. It has become so much a part of Western daily life that most people are now uncomfortable without it, and supply their own by way of radio, CD, DVD and other technology if it is otherwise unavailable to them. In terms of its sheer scale this is an amazing phenomenon yet, because it is so familiar, it is taken for granted. What is it doing to people? How does it affect their behaviour? These and other questions are surely worthy of scholarly attention.

MODELS

For more than 40 years, American ethnomusicology has had a quite extraordinary obsession with "models", about which I have been extremely critical in earlier pages of this book. Much as I admire most of Merriam's work, this may be one of his least desirable legacies because of his almost too well-known "model" of concept–behaviour–sound. As we have seen, Rice tried to improve Merriam's model; Herndon and Gourlay suggested "models" of their own; and numerous others have followed suit, considering music not in terms of empirical reality, but at one or more removes as part of a "model". Much of the theoretical work that now fills the pages of the journals concerns the merits of this or that model compared with other models. Meanwhile, again as emphasised in preceding pages, one of the most pernicious outcomes of the application (or more accurately misapplication) of Merriam's model is that it has led to the "sound" component of the model effectively becoming lopped off in favour of the remainder, because analysis of "mere sound" is supposed to obscure the reality of whatever it is that lies behind it. Ethnomusicologists perhaps need to be reminded that "models" themselves are not real.

LEAPS OF LOGIC

Speaking of rationalism in philosophy, which is often attributed solely to the 17th century, the British philosopher Bertrand Russell once said:

> Rationalism and anti-rationalism have existed side by side since the beginning of Greek civilisation, and each, when it had seemed likely to become completely dominant, has always led, by reaction, to a new outburst of its opposite.[591]

The same is true within ethnomusicology, and the flirtation with anti-rationalism, which began in the 1970s, is overdue for another U-turn. As Hegel is reputed to have said, to limit reason by reasoning is like trying to swim without entering the water. If reason is not to be trusted, then there is no reason to consider reasons for rejecting it. Reason may be an imperfect tool, but it is

---

[591] From Russell *In Praise of Idleness* (1935), cited by Denon 1952:205-6.

the only one we have. Without it, we are thrown back on faith, which appears largely to have driven John Blacking, and of which the best definition I know is that of St Paul. Though beautifully expressed in the King James version of the bible, and framed with the best of positive intentions, it is itself an indictment and runs: "Faith is the substance of things hoped for, the evidence of things not seen." Wishful thinking has too often clouded our discipline, and there is no place for it.

SPLIT BRAINS

Drawing upon multiple sources as it does, one has wondered whether some of the new orthodoxy in ethnomusicology is underpinned by and gains impetus and credibility from popular misunderstanding of "split brain" research, the left hemisphere of the brain supposedly concerned exclusively with speech and logic and the right with spatial and musical perception and intuition. Commonly accepted notions about it are epitomised in a paper by Baumann as "verbal vs. non-verbal, temporal vs. spatial, analytical vs. synthetic, and "rational vs. intuitive".[592] If this is accepted uncritically, the hemispheres are conceptualised as alternative to each other, and the so-called "musical" hemisphere is given primacy, then of course it becomes unacceptable to analyse music, exercise rational judgement concerning it, or even talk about it. Consider too the associative power of words and dichotomies, so effectively exploited in a subliminal way by the advertising industry. Left and right is one pairing, right and wrong is another. Confuse the two and we get the classic left and sinister, together with left and wrong, rational and wrong, analytical and wrong, verbal and wrong. Don't argue with me, you're being rational and verbal!

Later in his article, in a series of quotations from various writers, and in a manner strongly reminiscent of Lévi-Strauss structuralism,[593] which has plainly converged as one of the components of current thinking, Baumann makes the above connection and supposition explicit, investing them also with issues of gender and a "holistic" view of ethnomusicology:

> Left and right hemispheres are more than empirical experiences . . . The male dominance of fragmentation and splitting has risen above the female (non-dominant) unification."

> "The non-dominant hemisphere can process information in a holographic (holistically transforming) way."

> "The change in paradigm towards a holistic world view marks a turning point where the goal becomes a new consciousness that rehabilitates both holistically functioning hemispheres in their balanced complementarity."

> "The rational way begins to cross over that of mystical intuition"

> ". . . society has persistently promoted the approaches which the Chinese designate as Yang [male] and has neglected the complementary values and approaches of Yin [fe-

---

[592] Baumann 1992:128.
[593] For which Edmund Leach's book on Lévi-Strauss (1970) is an effective corrective and antidote.

male] . . . analysis to synthesis, rational knowledge to intuitive wisdom, science to religion, competition to co-operation, expansion and exploitation to preservation etc.".[594]

These two polarities are next seen, again in structuralist terms, as a "third way that endeavours to mediate between them", named as "The Path of Listening," in effect a "third ear" comparable with the mystic "third eye" of cosmic consciousness.

We now enter into speculation about where the conscious mind might be located, if not in the two hemispheres; "morphic fields" which cannot be explained in terms of matter; "morphic resonance" of such fields; and "collective memory" resulting from morphic resonance, residing outside the brain. This paradigm we are told:

> opens new models of explanation for those musical phenomena connected to a special kind of perception. Mythical narrations about music as revealed to men, reports of how melodies were given to mankind by gods or animals, altogether the inspiration theories of composers, mediators, trance dancers, of all forms of listening -- all these phenomena could suddenly be interpreted in the light of morphic fields.[595]

This, I believe, is quite enough space to have devoted to the topic. "Reductionist" and "objectivist" I may be, not to mention positivist and a few other "ist"s, as well as male and dominated by the left hemisphere of my brain, but I don't buy a word of it. I hope ethnomusicologists at large will not do so either. For an entirely convincing explanation of the North American Indian Vision Quest alluded to in the above paragraph, in which songs are revealed by totem spirits, based on empirical evidence without recourse to concepts such as morphic fields or collective memory, see Alan P. Merriam's classic article on the subject in the journal *Ethnomusicology*.[596]

Postlude

Senior citizen as I now am, and no longer working at the coalface, it may seem to some readers that the present attempt to revisit the past is motivated by nostalgia. The German saying: "Das waar ein maal, und komt nicht wieder": (loosely: "those were the days and they'll never return") may be thought to apply. Neither half of the saying, however, is fully applicable. The early days of ethnomusicology, to the extent that they coincided with my own tenure within them, were certainly exciting and full of debate. There was a strong sense that new paths were being laid down, we were on the forefront of a new discipline, intellectual progress was being made, the latest issues of the key journals were eagerly awaited, the field was small enough for everyone to have some interest in others' work, and there was some degree of evangelistic fervour abroad. The euphoria, and the sense of mission, have now, I believe, largely gone. Ethnomusicologists are currently less at the crossroads than lost in the wilderness. New initiatives which emerged in the 70s and 80s, and are now dominant, have not fulfilled their promise, and are contributing to the current disillusion. But the past was not perfect either. It might be sensible to think of it in terms of epochs and the persons within each who wielded the most influence. At the top of the

---

[594] Baumann 1992:133-4.
[595] Baumann 1992:138.
[596] Merriam 1965. See also Shermer 2005 for a sceptic's view of "morphic fields".

heap in the 1950s when I began my own work, and very much "king of the castle", stood the towering figure of Curt Sachs, whose books were obligatory reading for students at this time, but whose theoretical foundation to the last was with outmoded concepts such as cultural strata and the contemporary ancestor espoused by the Berlin School of comparative musicology and its offshoots. The turning point possibly came in 1957 with volume 1 of the *"New" Oxford History of Music*,[597] which began with an article on "Primitive Music" by another stalwart of the Berlin School, Marius Schneider.[598] It exemplified all the deficiencies of the then prevailing evolutionist view of music as having developed from a primitive past whose remnants could be studied in the tribal musics of today. It provoked a counter-reaction, albeit a largely unspoken one. In the 1960s I discovered that I was not alone in rejecting this deeply flawed approach, and almost everyone then active in ethnomusicology had likewise turned their backs on it, without even feeling a need to say so. In light of the new thinking, the eclipse of evolutionism was so total as to be taken simply for granted.

For persons such as myself, interested in tribal music or, as it was then called "primitive music", a breath of sanity was injected at about the same time as Schneider's article by the publication in 1956 of Bruno Nettl's text-book *Music in Primitive Culture*.[599] Along with his later book, *Theory and Method in Ethnomusicology*,[600] it guided subsequent generations of students into more productive paths than had been the case hitherto.

Despite the presence of burgeoning ethnomusicology programmes such as those of Nettl at Illinois, Malm at Michigan, McAllester at Wesleyan, and Garfias at Washington, the 1960s and 1970s were unquestionably dominated by ideas associated with Mantle Hood at UCLA and Alan Merriam at Indiana University: Hood with his concept of bi-musicality and pedagogy of performance-based ethnomusicology; Merriam with his seminal work *The Anthropology of Music*,[601] and his concept of ethnomusicology as the study of music in culture, which henceforth required music behaviour to be treated as seriously as music sound.

With Merriam's tragic death in a plane crash in 1980, the anthropological cohorts were taken over with missionary zeal by John Blacking, whose own death 10 years later brought this era to an end also. Meanwhile, the legacy of Hood did not go away. Performance of ethnic music has become by now an accepted, and even obligatory, form of instruction in numerous music schools throughout the United States and the rest of the world.

If ethnomusicology was ever close to being a single entity or unified discipline, it is no longer so. Since the days of the Hood/Merriam split, the process of fission has gone much further. Ethnomusicology and its predecessor comparative musicology has always been a cross-disciplinary area of scholarship, drawing ideas from diverse fields including acoustics, history, linguistics, psychology, philosophy and many others besides the primary disciplinary areas of musicology, folklore and anthropology. But the process has gone too far. Especially in America, ethnomusicology now lies shattered in a myriad of pieces; the king's horses and king's men are mostly riding in different directions; and no one seems concerned to put Humpty Dumpty together

---

[597] Wellesz 1957.
[598] Schneider 1957.
[599] Nettl 1956.
[600] Nettl:1964.
[601] Merriam 1964.

again. Part of the problem is that there isn't a king (or queen) and, with all due respect to Merriam and Hood, and later Blacking, there never was one. No single school of ethnomusicology has emerged, and none seems likely or even possible. But the greatest problem of all may be a quite practical and potentially remediable one: namely, the requirement of most American academic institutions to demand some kind of theoretical orientation for dissertations. In ethnomusicology, the trend is encouraged and in part driven by notions of "insider" priority that have left ethnomusicologists on the sidelines, and forced them to stake out a claim to territory less likely to be challenged. In this environment, merely describing the nature of a music system no longer qualifies as a legitimate aim unless it can be fitted into a theoretical framework and becomes grist to the theoretical mills. As a result, American ethnomusicology is now awash with theory that becomes ever more esoteric, moves ever further from its sources, and argument as often as not turns on how one abstraction relates to another.

Much of the current theorising makes use of ideas taken over from anthropology, which likewise is moving further from its roots. But ironically this is mostly being done not by students trained in anthropology, or competent in both music and anthropology, but from music departments. How times have changed!

In terms of what they say they do and, in practice, what one assumes they in fact do, the curricula of the major US programmes in ethnomsicology are revealing. Most have a strong commitment to performance-based teaching. Surprisingly to me, most programmes still teach transcription and analysis, even though these are absent from most currently published work. What's going on? Apart from the basics, which most departments still aspire to teach, there is strong emphasis upon interdisciplinary approaches, especially in terms of cognitive psychology, semiotics and anthropological linguistics generally, and theoretically oriented methodology. On top of this is a strong overlay of iconoclasm, resulting in the rejection of most earlier work, and an expectation on the part of students that the way to academic success is to present ones work in terms of theory rather than "mere description". There are two problems with this. The first is that it diverts attention from still viable concerns of early ethnomusicology that have never been resolved and are worthy of resurrection. The second is that most world music has not yet been adequately described and, to this extent, theory is both premature and non-productive.

In the final chapter of his book *Encounters in Ethnomusicology*,[602] Bruno Nettl eulogises present-day American ethnomusicology as a splendid example of team work on all levels: a vast network of scholars working on the "buddy" system, all known to each other, helping each other to get jobs, and operating what sounds very much like a highly incestuous closed shop. If this is an accurate picture, the problems now besetting American ethnomusicology may be irremediable, because the flaws in the system are entrenched and endemic, in which case the only remedy would be an entirely unlikely restructuring of the whole.

A case could be made for splitting off the theorists from the mainstream of ethnomusicology as it is so unpalatable to them, and establishing their own discipline and journal, leaving others to get along with what many would regard as the real work. But there are now far too many theorists for this to be practicable. In America they *are* the mainstream. The establishment of the European Seminar in Ethnomusicology as a rival organisation to the ICTM, after this moved to

---
[602] Nettl 2002.

America, perhaps signals dissatisfaction with the current situation from this quarter, and a recognition that radical reform is now needed. One hopes, however, there is no need for such a drastic solution. In order to strike a more equitable balance, a niche needs to be opened up for the benefit of persons who wish to use methods and pursue goals that are different from the currently approved ones. I have maintained for many years, and I say it again now, that the problem could be resolved if graduate schools could only be persuaded that a straightforward music ethnography of areas as yet unstudied is appropriate as a topic for a PhD dissertation. The student, in other words, would follow the time-honoured and still desirable imperative of undertaking field work among the practitioners of the style to be studied, wherever that may be, with no preset agenda of what must be found, immerse him- or herself in it, study it in depth from every conceivable perspective, and then write about it, released from the obligation to define a problem, devise hypotheses, test the hypotheses, and ultimately spawn yet another theory. This stance is the same as that of Franz Boas who was one of the first to advocate in-depth research of cultures. It is also consistent with Blacking's view of PhD research: "At this stage in the development of ethnomusicology," he said, "there cannot be too much fuss about fancy theories. Rather, we should be concerned with the publication of what is often rapidly disappearing ethnographic data." [603]

There are many hundreds, if not thousands, of music cultures that have never received such treatment; there are others now in need of revisiting and re-study in order better to understand the processes of change; and there are entire music cultures and systems that have never been described or analysed at all. Finally, once a student has had some exposure to a music system "on the ground" by going through the necessary baptism in the field, work can start on transcription, analysis and comparison of archival recordings from the same and related cultures, again to assist both an understanding of the styles themselves and to document them fully for the future. Is the end-product of music-making really so unimportant? Aren't people curious about *music* any more? Are the present-day antecedents of future styles of no interest? It is work crying out to be done. Why not do it?

---

[603] Howard 1991:68.

CHRONOLOGY

1271–95: Marco Polo journeys to China, establishing an overland trade route to Europe, and stimulating interest in the Orient.

1338–1450: Hundred Years War between England and France.

1347–49: Black Death decimates Europe. Further outbreaks occur in 1350, 1361, 1374, and again in the 1460s and 1470s.

15th and 16th centuries: Portuguese and Spanish navigators open up sea routes to Africa, the Far East and the New World.

c.1450: Johannes Gutenberg invents the printing press. Exploration aided by printing of charts and navigational tables. Books no longer the monopoly of the church.

1465: First printed music appears in Europe.

1476: Caxton's printing press set up at Westminster.

1500s: Printed broadside ballads become popular in England.

1562: Britain begins slave trade in Africa.

1577–80: Sir Francis Drake circumnavigates the globe, beginning an era of British sea supremacy.

1582: Jesuit missionaries begin mission work in China.

1585: Foundation of Oxford University Press.

1600: Foundation of British East India Company, leading eventually to a huge trade empire and the creation of British India.

1602: Establishment of the Dutch East India Company in Indonesia.

1608: Hans Lippershey tries to patent an optical refracting telescope, and the following year Galileo Galilei builds one.

1618–48: Thirty Years War in central Europe.

1687: Publication of Isaac Newton's *Principia* . Newtonian physics remains fundamental in the development of science until the advent of Einstein in the 20th century.

1700–1800: Industrial Revolution gets rapidly underway in England with introduction of steam power and improved textile machinery. Newcomen steam engine (1712); flying shuttle (1733); spinning jenny (1764); spinning mule (1779); Cartwright power loom (1787); cotton gin (1793).

1709: Bartolommeo Cristofori (1655–1732), curator of musical instruments for the Medici family in Italy, invents his *gravicembalo col piano e forte*, the precursor of the modern piano.

1711: John Shaw invents the tuning fork.

1735: French Jesuit Jean-Baptiste Du Halde publishes information about Chinese music.

1756–63: Seven Years War in Europe.

1756–57: Industrial exhibitions are held in England, sponsored by the Society of Arts. From now onwards, especially throughout the 19th and early 20th centuries, hundreds of international exhibitions are mounted in various parts of the world, often including musical instruments and music performances.

1759: British Museum opens to the public.

1761: Marine chronometer developed by John Harrison.

1763: Treaty of Paris cedes India to Britain.

1766–69: Bougainville's voyage to the South Seas a sensation after his return to France. Nose flutes and other wonders described.

1767: Jean Jacque Rousseau publishes his *Dictionnaire de la musique* containing examples of world music.

1768–80: Captain James Cook's three voyages round the world gather scientific evidence from Pacific islands, including descriptions of music, and bring back musical instruments and other artefacts, now housed in the British Museum.

1772: Joshua Steele accurately measures the pitches of two Tongan panpipes and a Tahitian nose flute supplied to him from Cook's second expedition by Furneaux and Banks.

1775: James Watt introduces a more efficient steam engine.

1775–83: American War of Independence.

1776–89: Charles Burney publishes his *A General History of Music*, becoming the pre-eminent music historian in English of the 18th century. Unlike his contemporary Jean Jacque Rousseau, he is scornful of any music other than the cultivated music of his own era.

1779: Jesuit priest Father Jean Joseph Amiot publishes monograph on Chinese music.

1780: J.B. de La Borde publishes his *Essai sur la Musique Ancienne et Moderne*, with sections on non-Western music.

1784: Foundation of the Paris Conservatoire under the name École royale de chant et de déclamation.

1784: Foundation in Calcutta of the Asiatick Society of Bengal by Sir William Jones, who becomes its first president as well as a contributor to its journal.

1789–93: French Revolution.

1791: Metric system formulated in France. Provides basis for all future scientific measurement, including Ellis's cents system the following century.

1792: Publication of Sir William Jones's study "On the Musical Modes of the Hindoos."

1799: Publication of Mungo Park's *Travels in the Interior of Africa* stimulates widespread interest in the African continent.

1800: Establishment of Library of Congress in America.

1800–50: Conservatories of music proliferate in Europe, among them Prague (1811), Brussels (1813), Vienna (1817), Geneva (1835), Leipzig (1843), Cologne (1845), Munich (1846), and Berlin (1850).

1801: Robert Trevithick demonstrates a steam locomotive.

1803–15: Napoleonic Wars.

1814: J.N. Maelzel invents the metronome in Vienna.

1815: Humphry Davy invents the miners' safety lamp.

1822: Publication by Davies Gilbert of his collection *Some Ancient English Carols*, with tunes.

1830: George Stephenson begins rail service between Liverpool and London.

1830: Publication by William C. Stafford of *A History of Music*, including extensive treatment of non-Western music.

1831–36: Charles Darwin's voyage as naturalist on board the research vessel *Beagle* yields information leading to his theories of natural selection and human evolution.

1835: Samuel Morse develops the morse code.

1838–42: United States Exploring Expedition of five ships and crews under the command of Charles Wilkes to the South Seas gathers scientific and ethnographic information including descriptions of music.

1839: Louis-Jacques-Mandé Daguerre perfects his Daguerrotype photographic process. The French government acquires the patent and announces the invention as a gift "Free to the World."

1840: Treaty of Waitangi between Maori and the British Crown in New Zealand safeguards native rights while allowing colonisation.

1843: Samuel Morse builds the first long-distance electric telegraph line.

1843: John Broadwood publishes anonymously a collection of English folk songs, the first "from the mouths of the people".

1844: J. Adrien de La Fage opublishes a history of music and dance with extensive reference to non-Western music.

1850: Museum of Ethnology established in Hamburg, Germany.

1851: Great Exhibition, Hyde Park, London, held in specially constructed "Crystal Palace", designed by Sir Joseph Paxton, as a showcase for British and colonial science and industry. Over 13,000 exhibits displayed and viewed by over 6,200,000 visitors to the exhibition.

1851: A.H. Pitt-Rivers arranges technological exhibits at University Museum of Oxford.

1851: Sir George Grey, Governor of New Zealand, publishes first anthology of traditional Maori song texts.

1853: Japan opened to foreigners and Western trade by Commodore Matthew Perry.

1854–56: Crimean War.

1854: British philosopher Herbert Spencer publishes an essay on "The Origins of Music."

1855: Publication of James A. Davies's, "On the Native Songs of New Zealand."

1857: Transatlantic cable completed.

1859: Publication of Charles Darwin's *On the Origin of Species*. Under the influence of Darwin and his contemporary Herbert Spencer, evolution laater becomes a preoccupation of European comparative musicologists.

1859: First tunnels under the Thames river in London.

1861–65: American Civil War.

1862: French begin to colonise Vietnam.

1862 & 1867: Japanese art shown at exhibitions in London and Paris. Kimonos and fans became fashion accessories.

1862–82: Five volumes published of *Geschichte der Musik* by August Wilhelm Ambros, volume 1 of which deals with the music of China, India, Arabia and Greece.

1863: Henri Fourneaux introduces the player piano.

1866: Peabody Museum of Archaeology and Ethnology established at Harvard University.

1869: Suez Canal opened.

1869: First US transcontinental railroad completed.

1869–76: Publication of Françoise Joseph Fétis's unfinished attempt at a universal history of music, *Histoire génerale de la musique*. Volume 2 is devoted to music of the Arabs, Moors, Hindus, Persians and Turks.

1871: Charles Darwin publishes his *Descent of Man* in which he offers the so-called "Darwinian hypothesis" about the origin of music.

1872: Trinity College of Music established in London.

1873: Royal College of Music established in London.

1873: Foundation of the Museum für Völkerkunde, Berlin.

1874–78: Remington & Sons market the first typewriter.

1876: Alexander Graham Bell makes the first telephone call.

1876: Queen Victoria becomes Empress of India.

1877: Invention of the phonograph by Thomas Alva Edison.

1878–89: First edition of *Grove's Dictionary of Music and Musicians*. 4 vols, planned and edited by Sir George Grove.

1879: Thomas Alva Edison perfects a practical incandescent light bulb.

1879: Anglo-French control of Egypt.

1880–1922: Victor Mahillon publishes his monumental catalogue of the musical instruments of the Royal Conservatory, Brussels.

1882: Theodore Baker's doctoral thesis on the music of the North American Indians is published in Leipzig.

1882: Members of the Bella Coola Indian tribe of British Columbia on exhibit at Ethnologischen Abtheilung der Koniglichen Museen (Royal Ethnographic Museum), Berlin.

1883: Francis Child publishes the first volume of his anthology *The English and Scottish Popular Ballads* (1883–98).

1884: Foundation of Pitt-Rivers Museum, Oxford.

1884: Internation Health Exhibition, London. Lectures on Chinese music are delivered by J.A. Van Aalst. A book on Chinese music published by him in the same year was probably written for distribution at the exhibition.

1884: Publication by A.J. Ellis of his "Tonometrical Observations on some Existing Non-harmonic Scales" draws attention to exotic tuning systems.

1885: Canadian-Pacific Railway completed.

1885: Guido Adler defines Vergleichende Musikwissenschaft, or Comparative Musicology, thereby launching the discipline. His article is in the first issue of the periodical *Vierteljahrschrift für Musikwissenschaft*, which also contains other articles relevant to the new subject.

1885: International Exhibition of Inventions and Music, London, England. Alfred James Hipkins is a member of the organising committee. Victor Mahillon contributes instruments to its Loan Collection.

1886: Monograph by Carl Stumpf on music of Bella Coola Indians of British Columbia who visited Berlin in 1882.

1886: Karl Benz is granted a patent in Germany for a gasoline-powered automobile, generally acknowledged to be the world's first.

1887: Emile Berliner patents phonographic disc.

1888: George Eastman patents Kodak hand camera.

1889: First field recording on Edison phonograph of American Indian music, and of any non-Western music, by Jesse Walter Fewkes.

1890: London underground railway network begun.

1891: Fewkes's North American recordings transcribed and published by Benjamin Ives Gilman.

1891: English army officer Charles Russell Day publishes *The Music and Musical Instruments of Southern India and the Deccan*.

1893: Alice Cunningham Fletcher, Francis La Flesche and John Comfort Fillmore jointly oublish a monograph on Omaha music.

1893: Columbian Exposition, Chicago, provides opportunity for recordings at living ethnological displays. Benjamin Ives Gilman records performances at Javanese, Samoan, and Kwakiutl villages.[604]

1895: Incorporation of the Berliner Gramophone Company.

1896: Franz Boas begins to lecture at Columbia University, becoming its first professor of anthropology in 1899, remaining in the post for 37 years, and initiating an American School of anthropology.

1897–1902: Franz Boas records Kwakiutl music during a North Pacific Expedition to British Columbia.

1898: Spanish-American War.

1898: Folk Song Society founded in England, becoming focus for collectors such as Cecil Sharp, Ralph Vaughan Williams, George Butterworth, Anne Gilchrist, and others.

1898–99: Cambridge Anthropological Expedition to Torres Straits and Sarawak. As an outcome of his expedition experience, Charles Myers later publishes significant studies of the music (1912 & 1913–14).

1899: Establishment of Phonogrammarchiv der Österreichischen Akademie der Wissenschaften in Vienna. Recordings from round the world are accessioned.

1899–1902: Boer War.

By the end of the century the British Empire is at its height. Much of the world now in the hands of European colonial powers.

1900: International Exposition Universelle held in Paris, France, with 76,000 exhibitors and more than 50 million visitors. The Eiffel Tower is a landmark feature.

1900: Eastman Kodak introduces the box Brownie camera, making photography accessible to all.

1900: Carl Stumpf and Otto Abraham record a Siamese theatre ensemble on wax cylinder in Berlin, and Stumpf establishes the Berlin Phonogramm-Archiv.

---

[604] Myers 1993:24.

1901: Death of Queen Victoria ushers in the Edwardian era in England.

1901: Guglielmo Marconi sends the first transatlantic radio signal between England and Canada.

1903: Wright brothers make a controlled powered flight at Kittyhawk in a heavier-than-air aircraft.

1904–09: Cecil Sharp publishes his *Folk Songs from Somerset.*

1905: Einstein's Special Theory of Relativity.

1905: Erich von Hornbostel appointed director of the Berlin-Phongramm-Archiv, which becomes a nucleus for comparative musicology.

1905: Béla Bartók and Zoltán Kodály set off on the first of many expeditions to collect traditional Hungarian folk music.

1907: Frances Densmore begins 50 years as Collaborator of the Bureau of American Ethnology, which ultimately publishes 13 monographs by her on Amerindian music.

1907: Publication of Cecil Sharp's *English Folk Song: Some Conclusions.* Principles espoused in it later guide the International Folk Music Council throughout its early history.

1908: Model "T" Ford begins production.

1908: First double-sided 78 rpm discs introduced by Columbia Records.

1910: John Lomax begins to record American cowboy music.

1911: English Folk Dance Society founded by Cecil Sharp.

1914: Panama Canal completed.

1914: Publication of *The Music of Hindostan* by A.H. Fox Strangways.

1914: Curt Sachs and Erich von Hornbostel publish their jointly devised system for classifying musical instruments.

1914–18: First World War. Break-up of Cecil Sharp's group of folk song enthusiasts because of call-up for active service. Recruitment of Maud Karpeles as Sharp's assistant in the Appalachians (1916–18). Bartók forced to abandon field work in Hungary. Disruption of scholarly activity everywhere.

1915: Einstein's General Theory of Relativity.

1917: First jazz records.

1920: League of Nations established.

1920–21: Helen Roberts in Jamaica.

1922: Foundation of British Broadcasting Corporation (BBC) in England.

1922: Major General George O. Squier patents Muzak system in the USA and forms a company that become Musak Corporation in 1934.

1922: Formation of USSR.

1923–24: Helen Roberts in Hawai'i.

1924: Death of Cecil Sharp.

1925: George Herzog moves from Berlin to New York to study anthropology under Franz Boas at Columbia University. His reconciliation of the methods of Hornbostel with those of Boas proves crucial to the development of ethnomusicology in the United States.

1927: Western Electric licenses motion picture industry to introduce "talkie" movies using its system of 16-inch acetate-coated 33 1/3 rpm discs to synchronise the sound.

1927: Al Jolson's "Jazz Singer", the first "talkie" movie.

1928: Major film companies Paramount, MGM, and others sign with AT&T to produce movies with sound on film.

1928: Archive of American Folk Song (later Archive of Folk Song) established as a section within the Music Division of the American Library of Congress.

1928: Foundation of Museum für Völkerkunde in Vienna.

1928: Milton Metfessel develops phonophotography, leading ultimately to machine transcription of music.

1929–35: The Great Depression. As a result of it, Jaap Kunst loses his government job in Indonesia in 1934 and returns to the Netherlands.

1930s: Rise of Nazi-ism in Germany. In 1933 Hitler becomes Chancellor. Expulsion of jews, break-up of Hornbostel's Berlin school and resulting diaspora, enriches ethnomusicology elsewhere.

1930–34: Jaap Kunst, employed as a Dutch colonial civil servant in Indonesia. Begins his acquaintance with the music.

1930: Cornell University becomes the first in the United States to establish a chair in musicology.

1930s & 40s: 16-inch acetate-coated 33 1/3 rpm discs, originally developed for "talkie" movies, extensively used by radio stations for recording programmes and for transcription exchange services, and by the military for recording soldiers' messages during World War II. Though cumbersome, the system was used also for field recording, supplanting wax cylinders. It continued as a mainstay of the broadcasting industry until the early 1950s until replaced by tape recording.

1931–34: Arnold Bake begins extensive field work in India and Nepal.

1931: Empire State Building opens with music piped into its elevators. "Elevator music" henceforth becomes a vogue.

1932: John and Alan Lomax begin recording American folk song for the Library of Congress, ultimately collecting more than 3000 records, the largest collection in the Archive of Folk Song.

1932: Merger of English Folk Song Society and English Folk Dance Society to form English Folk Song and Dance Society under Douglas Kennedy.

1933–34: Chicago World's Fair proclaims "A Century of Progress".

1934: Musak Corporation is founded. Piped music subsequently spreads world wide.

1934: Beginning of apartheid in South Africa.

1935: Death of Erich von Hornbostel at Cambridge, England.

1935: Ludwig Blattner (d. 1935) invents the Blattnerphone, a primitive form of electromagnetic tape recorder using steel tape.

1936: Helen Roberts loses her job at Yale University, as a result of which she retires, never returning to the study of music.

1937: Sir Frank Whittle invents the jet engine.

1937: Curt Sachs appointed professor of music at New York University.

1938: Publication by Carl Seashore of his ground-breaking book *Psychology of Music*, using the technique of phonophotography to answer questions about music perception that did not become prominent in ethnomusicology until the advent of machine transcription in the 1950s.

1939–45: World War II. Opportunities for communication among scholars diminish. Social upheaval world wide, but significant war-driven advances in technology.

1940: Béla Bartók moves from Hungary to the United States.

1940: Library of Congress establishes a Recording Laboratory with its own staff.

1940–52: Willard Rhodes makes notable recordings on disc and tape of North American Indian music, visiting over 50 tribes and publishing a series of 10 edited LPs under auspices of the Library of Congress.

1943: Curt Sachs publishes his influential book *The Rise of Music in the Ancient World*.

1944: First official public announcement of Frank Whittle's development of the jet engine, and a jet-engined Gloster Meteor aircraft flies in combat.

1944: Wire recorders are introduced commercially in the United States.

1944: First printing of *Harvard Dictionary of Music* edited by Willi Apel. Includes articles on primitive music and comparative musicology, as well as Arabian, Hindu, Japanese and other non-Western musics.

1945: Atom bombs dropped on Hiroshima and Nagasaki bring World War II to an end.

1945: United Nations established.

1946: Formation of the Galpin Society in England.

1947: Indian independence. Partition of India and Pakistan. From now onwards, Britain progressively divests itself of all former colonies, and other European powers eventually follow.

1947: Formation of International Folk Music Council (IFMC) by Maud Karpeles and others in London, with composer and folk song collector Ralph Vaughan Williams as first president.

1948: Inaugural annual conference of the International Folk Music Council held in Basle, Switzerland.

1948: Kurt Reinhard begins 20 years as director of the Berlin Phonogram-Archiv, devoting himself to rebuilding it after World War II.

1948: Archives of Traditional Music founded at Indiana University by George Herzog.

1948: Folkways Records founded by Moses Asch. By the time of his death in 1986 he has issued over 2000 albums.

1948: Ampex introduces audio tape recorder.

1948: Microgroove 33 1/3 vinyl LP disc introduced.

1948: Bell Laboratories announce invention of the transistor.

1949: Scientists led by Willard Libby develop carbon dating.

1949: China becomes communist.

1949: First issue of *Journal of the International Folk Music Council.*

1950s: McCarthyism creates anti-Communist climate of fear in America. Academic freedom is profoundly affected.

1950–53: Korean War.

1950: International Folk Music Council holds it 3rd annual meeting at Indiana University, Bloomington, Indiana, USA.

1950: The term "ethno-musicology" (initially with a hyphen) is coined by Jaap Kunst.

1951: First commercially available computer, UNIVAC.

1951: Stefan Kudelski in Switzerland builds the first Nagra portable, self-contained tape recorder. Later Nagra recorders become the ultimate standard for field recording.

1951: Charles Seeger announces his "Instantaneous Music Notator."

1952: David McAllester, Alan P. Merriam, Willard Rhodes and Charles Seeger meet and agree to promote contact among students and scholars of ethnomusicology.

1952–57: Under direction of Peter Kennedy, BBC carries out systematic field recording of folk song throughout the British Isles.

1953: Launching of *Ethnomusicology Newsletter* under the editorship of Alan P. Merriam.

1954: Foundation of Colloques de Wégimont by Paul Collaer.

1954: Hugh Tracey establishes International Library of African Music. Ultimately publishes over 250 LP records in "Sound of Africa" series.

1955: Columbia Records issues an 18-volume set of recordings, compiled by Alan Lomax, entitled the Columbia World Library of Folk and Primitive Music.

1955: Establishment in London of the British Institute of Recorded Sound under the direction of Patrick Saul (1913–1999). It becomes a department of the British Library and changes its name to National Sound Archive in 1983. By the year 2000 it holds almost a million discs and 130,000 tapes of recordings from all over the world.

1955: Establishment of the Society for Ethnomusicology in America, with Willard Rhodes as first president.

1956: The Space Age begins with the successful launching of the world's first artificial satellite, Sputnik I, by the Soviet Union.

1956: Inaugural meeting of the Society for Ethnomusicology held in Philadelphia, USA.

1956: Publication of Bruno Nettl's text book *Music in Primitive Culture*.

1956: First commercial video tape recorder introduced by Ampex.

1957: Publication of *New Oxford History of Music*, volume 1, *Ancient and Oriental Music*, with chapters by Schneider, Picken, Bake, and Farmer.

1958: *Ethnomusicology* journal launched as successor to *Ethnomusicology Newsletter*.

1958: Mantle Hood begins a gamelan performance programme at UCLA, the first of more than 100 ultimately to be established in the USA.

1958: In the first of two books, *The Idiom of the People*, followed by his second book, *The Everlasting Circle* in 1960, James Reeves raises the ire of English folk song purists by revealing a *lingua franca* of sexual innuendo in the seemingly innocent song texts.

1958: Karl Dahlback publishes a book *New Methods in Vocal Folk Music Research*, describing the results of machine transcription of music in Norway.

1958: Charles Seeger publishes his paper "Prescriptive and Descriptive Music Writing," including some results of melographic studies with the Seeger melograph.

1958: Integrated circuit conceived by Texas Instruments.

1959: Jaap Kunst publishes his general bibliography *Ethnomusicology*, with a supplement in 1960.

1959: First commercial Xerox copier.

1960s: Period of expansion of universities as post-war birth-bulge reaches tertiary level. Eighteen new universities created in Britain alone between 1961 and 1966.

1960: Institute of Ethnomusicology established at UCLA by Mantle Hood.

1960: Alan P. Merriam defines ethnomusicology as "the study of music in culture", and Mantle Hood introduces his concept of "bi-musicality".

1961–73: Vietnam War. As the war escalates, graduate studies are disrupted as students either join the conflict or flee to Canada to escape the draft.

1961: Berlin Wall erected.

1961: IBM introduces "Selectric" electric typewriter.

1961: Caedmon Records begin issue of classic 10-volume set of LP records edited by Alan Lomax and Peter Kennedy, *Folk Songs of Britain*, later reissued (1968–71) by Topic Records.

1961: Unesco Collection of Traditional Music on LP launched by Alain Daniélou. Over 100 LPs produced in separate series: An Anthology of African Music, A Musical Anthology of the Orient, Musical Atlas, and Musical Sources.

1962: Alan Lomax begins Cantometrics project at Columbia University.

1962: Philips introduces the "Compact Cassette" audio recorder. As production increases and cheap recorders become available, indigenous peoples are released from dependence on ethnomusicologists and henceforth have the means to make their own recordings.

1962: First telecommunications satellite, "Telstar", in orbit.

1963: Flights begin with Boeing's first commercial jet airliner, the 727.

1963: International Institute for Comparative Music Studies and Documentation founded in Berlin under direction of Alain Daniélou.

1963: Maud Karpeles retires as Honorary Secretary of the International Folk Music Council and is appointed Honorary President.

1963: In a book co-written with Harrison and Palisca, Mantle Hood publishes "Music the Unknown", setting out his views on "bi-musicality" and other issues.

1964: Publication of Alan P. Merriam's *The Anthropology of Music*. This book and Hood's article the previous year mark the beginning of a rivalry between the approaches of Hood at UCLA and Merriam at the University of Indiana.

1964: Bruno Nettl publishes his text book *Theory and Method in Ethnomusicology*.

1964: Establishment of the Australian Institute of Aboriginal Studies (AIAS) in Canberra, Australia. Aboriginal music research is among its activities. In 1989 it changes its name to Australian Institute of Aboriginal and Torres Strait Islander Studies (AIATSIS).

1965: In a History of Music series by Prentice-Hall, Bruno Nettl publishes an elementary text book, *Folk and Traditional Music of the Western Continents*. A matching volume covering the rest of the world follows two years later from William P. Malm.

1966–75: Publication of *Annual Bibliography of European Ethnomusicology* (Bratislava), with a cumulative index of the ten volumes in 1981.

1966: Cultural revolution in China.

1967: IFMC moves secretariat temporarily to Denmark.

1967: In the Prentice-Hall History of Music series, William P. Malm publishes *Music Cultures of the Pacific, the Near East, and Asia*.

1967: Boeing introduces its 737 aircraft.

1967: Society for Ethnomusicology obliged to reintroduce a newsletter, re-named *SEM Newsletter*, in addition to its journal in order to keep members informed of increasing activities.

1967: Publication begins of RILM Abstracts of music literature by Répertoire International de Littérature Musicale, New York under the sponsorship of The International Musicological Society, the International Association of Music Libraries, and the American Council of Learned Societies. It is a multi-language classified bibliography with abstracts, aiming at total coverage of all scholarly books, articles, reviews and other publications on music, including ethnomusicology.

1968; Dieter Christensen succeeds Kurt Reinhard as director of the Berlin Phonogramm-Archiv.

1968: Alan Lomax publishes *Folk Song Style and Culture*, reporting the results of his Cantometrics programme.

1968: Ten years after the introduction of Indonesian gamelan performance at UCLA, performance groups in the United States universities have proliferated to include instruction in music of India, Persia, Japan, Mexico, Africa, Native America and others.

1969: IFMC moves secretariat to Queens University, Kingston, Ontario, Canada, with Graham George as Executive Secretary, and replaces its Journal with a Yearbook.

1969: Under the auspices of Unesco and the International Music Council, and with the support of numerous other international bodies, Barry S. Brook (1918–1997) initiates a project, Music in the Life of Man (MLM), later The Universe of Music: A History (UMH), for a history of world music to be written from indigenous perspectives. Conferences are held in different parts of the world, and a massive scholarly effort ensues, but the project founders when funds run out, with the death of Brook, and when the project is overtaken by a rival commercial publication, the similarly conceived 10-volume *Garland Encyclopaedia of World Music* (1997–2002).

1969: Neil Armstrong becomes the first man on the moon.

1969: First flight of Boeing's Jumbo Jet, the 747.

1969: Forerunner of internet, ARPANET, set up by US government for scientific communication.

1969: Apartheid regime of South Africa expels John Blacking, resulting in the ultimate establishment of his influential ethnomusicology programme at Queen's University, Belfast.

1970s: Travel by air becomes common. International meetings of scholars facilitated.

1970: Sony introduces the U-Matic videotape recorder.

1970: Archive of Maori and Pacific Music founded at University of Auckland by Mervyn McLean. Begins innovative free dubbing service to supply cassette recordings for Maori waiata schools.

1971: Publication of Mantle Hood's book *The Ethnomusicologist*.

1972: Dieter Christensen succeeded as director of the Berlin Phonogramm-Archiv by Atur Simon.

1972: Lexitron introduces first word-processing system.

1973: Oil embargo by Opec creates "oil shock" and forces economic adjustments world wide.

1973: Publication of John Blacking's *How Musical Is Man?*

1974: Hood's Institute of Ethnomusicology disestablished at UCLA and ethnomusicology becomes a responsibility of the Music Department.

1976: Death in London of the IFMC/ITCM co-founder, Maud Karpeles.

1977: Paul Allen and Bill Gates found Microsoft.

1979: Under the auspices of the Chinese Ministry of Culture and the Chinese Musicians' Association a massive folk song collection is begun in China. It results in the publication of an immense anthology of more than 300 volumes, containing folk music from all over China.

1980s: Rise of market economics and globalisation. In Britain it becomes known as Thatcherism after Prime Minister Margaret Thatcher, who implements it; in the United States it is called Reaganomics after President Ronald Reagan; and in New Zealand, it is named Rogernomics after Roger Douglas who became Finance Minister in 1984.

1980s: From this decade onwards, world music proliferates on LP and CD, and numerous new labels emerge.

1980: Death of Alan P. Merriam in an aircrash. His Anthropology Department programme of ethnomusicology comes to an end at Indiana University and ethnomusicology there moves primarily to the Department of Folklore.

1980: Silver Jubilee meeting of Society for Ethnomusicology at Indiana University. Death of Merriam casts a shadow over events.

1980: Publication of *The New Grove Dictionary of Music and Musicians*, edited by Stanley Sadie. Includes much expanded coverage of non-Western music.

1981: Phillips introduces the Compact Disc (CD).

1981: IBM PC introduced.

1981: IFMC moves secretariat to Columbia University, New York, USA. At the initiative of its new secretary-general, Dieter Christensen, formalises its increasingly broader scope with a change of name to International Council for Traditional Music (ICTM), and a corresponding change of title for its yearbook to *Yearbook for Traditional Music*.

1981: European Seminar in Ethnomusicology (ESEM) founded in Belfast by John Blacking, filling gap left by the departure from Europe of the IFMC.

1982: Steven Feld publishes an innovative ethnography, *Sound and Sentiment*, about weeping, poetics and song of the Kaluli of Papua New Guinea.

1983: European Seminar in Ethnomusicology holds its inaugural meeting in Cologne, meeting next in Belfast (1985), and thereafter annually in various European centres.

1984: Publication of *The New Grove Dictionary of Musical Instruments*, edited by Stanley Sadie. Includes many articles on non-Western instruments, including over 180 new entries on Oceanic instruments, not mentioned in the 1980 New Grove.

1985: Microsoft develops "Windows" operating system for the IBM PC.

1986: Publication of *The New Harvard Dictionary of Music*, edited by Don Randel. Compared with earlier editions, the coverage of non-Western and popular music and of musical instruments of all cultures is much enlarged.

1987: International Council for Traditional Music (formerly International Folk Music Council) celebrates its 40th year.

1988: Ethnomusicology at UCLA restored to full department status.

1989: Fall of the Berlin Wall.

1990: Old collection of the Berlin Phonogramm-Archiv, long thought lost after the war, restored to its original home from East Germany.

1990: Death of John Blacking.

1991– : Rise of the internet after invention of the World Wide Web. Access to library catalogues and other research aids, as well as communication with colleagues world-wide by means of e-mail revolutionises scholarship.

1991: Gulf War.

1991: Break-up of the Soviet Union.

1991: Department of Ethnomusicology at UCLA establishes full undergraduate curriculum, becoming the largest provider of ethnomusicology instruction in the USA.

1997: 50th anniversary of the foundation of the International Folk Music Council.

1997–2002: Publication of 10-volume *The Garland Encyclopedia of World Music*.

1999: The world's oldest sound archive, the Vienna Phonogrammarchiv, celebrates its 100th anniversary.

2000: By the end of the century decolonisation almost complete throughout the world, with most former colonies now independent. A new kind of colonialism replaces it as American economic influence through globalisation becomes dominant. New problems emerge for ethnomusicologists as field work becomes difficult for outside researchers in former colonies.

2000: Berlin Phonogramm-Archiv 100 years old.

2001: ICTM moves secretariat to UCLA, Los Angeles, USA, with Anthony Seeger as Secretary-General.

2003: Iraq War.

2005: United Nations marks the 60th anniversary of the signing of its charter.

2005: Death of Mantle Hood.

2005: Society for Ethnomusicology celebrates its 50th jubilee.

2006: ICTM moves secretariat to Australian National University, Canberra, under new Secretary-General Stephen Wild.

REFERENCES

Abbreviations

ANB = Garraty &Carnes 1999 (American National Biography)

Anth = Anthropology Biography Web

Baker = Baker 1984

BRC = Biography Resource Center. Gale Group on-line database (2005). Includes entries from:
(A) *Baker's Biographical Dictionary of Music* (2001)
(B) *Contemporary Authors Online* (2004)
(C) *Dictionary of Americcan Biography* (1928–36)
(D) *Encyclopedia of World Biography* (1998)

Bull ICTM= *Bulletin of the International Council for Traditional Music* (1981–)

DBE = *Deutsche biographische Enzyklopädie*

E-Brit = Encyclopædia Britannica Online.

Eth = Biographical Notes section, *Ethnomusicology* (Journal of the Society for Ethnomusicology) (1957–)

Everyman = *Everyman's Encylopaedia in Twelve Volumes*. 3rd edition. London: Dent (1949–50).

LSE = London School of Economics

NDB = *Neue deutsche Biographie*

New Grove = The New Grove Dictionary of Music and Musicians, on line edition. Oxford University Press (2003–05)

Notes and Queries = Royal Anthropological Institute of Great Britain and Ireland, 1951.

ODNB = Oxford Dictionary of National Biography, on line edition. Oxford University Press (2004–05)

Vir.Lab = The Virtual Laboratory

WWW = *Who Was Who*

WWWA = *Who Was Who in America*

Readers are reminded that web pages are ephemeral and subject to change. Some of the web addresses cited below may no longer be active.

ABRAHAM, Otto and Erich M. von HORNBOSTEL, 1902–03. "Studien über das Tonsystem und die Musik der Japaner." *Sammelbände der internationalen Musikgesellschaft*, 4:302-60.

ABRAHAM, Otto and Erich M. von HORNBOSTEL, 1903–04. "Phonographierte indische Melodien." *Sammelbände der internationalen Musikgesellschaft*, 5:348-401.

ABRAHAM, Otto and Erich M. von HORNBOSTEL, 1904. "Phonographierte türkische Melodien." *Zeitschrift für Ethnologie*, 36:203-31.

ABRAHAM Otto and Erich M. von HORNBOSTEL, 1906. "Phonographierte Indianermelodien aus Britisch-Columbia," in B. Lanfer (ed.), *Boas Anniversary Volume*. New York: Stechert, pp. 447-74.

ABRAHAM, Otto and Erich M. von HORNBOSTEL, 1909–10. "Vorschläge für die Transkription exotischer Melodien." *Sammelbände der internationalen Musikgesellschaft*, 11:1-25. [For an English translation see next]

ABRAHAM, Otto and Erich M. von HORNBOSTEL, 1994. "Suggested Methods for the Transcription of Exotic Music," translated by George and Eve List. *Ethnomusicology*, 38(3):425-56.

ADLER, Guido, 1885. "Umfang, Methode und Ziel der Musikwissenschaft." *Vierteljahrschrift für Musikwissenschaft*, 1:5-20.

ADLER, Guido, 1935. *Wollen und Wirken : aus dem Leben eines Musikhistorikers*. Wien: Universal-Edition.

AGAWU, Kofi, 1997. "Review Article: John Blacking and the Study of African Music." *Africa*, 67(3):491-9.

AIATSIS (Australian Institute of Aboriginal and Torres Strait Islander Studies), 2005. "Biographical Note: Alice Marshall Moyle," in MS2501 Alice Moyle Collection. Web page: http://www.aiatsis.gov.au/lbry/ms/finding_aid/MS3501.htm

ALEXANDER, Hartley B., 1933. "Francis La Flesche."*American Anthropologist*, 35(3):328-31.

ALLEN, Warren Dwight, 1962. *Philosophies of Music History*. New York: Dover (First published 1939).

ALVEY, R. Gerald, 1973. "Phillips Barry and Anglo-American Folksong Scholarship." *Journal of the Folklore Institute*, 10:67-95.

AMBROS, August Wilhelm, 1862–82. *Geschichte der Musik*. 5 vols. Breslau: Leuckart.

AMERICAN PHILOSOPHICAL SOCIETY, 2004. Fanz Boas Collections. Web page: http://www.amphilsoc.org/library/mole/b/boas.htm

AMIOT, Jean Joseph, 1779. *Mémoire sur la musique des Chinois, tant anciens que modernes.* Paris.

ANDERSON, Douglas D., 1996–2003. "Davies Gilbert," in The Hymns and Carols of hristmas. Web page: http://www.hymnsandcarolsofchristmas.com/Hymns_and_Carols/Biographies/davies_gilbert.htm

ANDERSON, Robert, 2003. "Hickmann, Hans." New Grove.

ANDREWS UNIVERSITY, 2004. Franz Boas (1858-1942). Web page: http://www.andrews.edu/MDLG/german/german-american/notable/B/boas_franz/boas-e.html

ANING, B.A., 1967. *An Annotated Bibliography of Music and Dance in English-speaking Africa.* Legon: University of Ghana.

ANON, 1912. "Mr. Cecil Sharp." *The Musical Times*, 53(836):639-43.

ANON, 2003a. The History of the Edison Cylinder Phonograph. Web page: http://memory.loc.gov/ammem/edhtml/edcyldr.html

ANON, 2003b. Alain Danielou (1907–1994). Web page: http://www.alaindanielou.org/anglais/biographie/biographie.htm

ANON, 2004. "In Memoriam [Sibyl Marcuse]." *Newsletter of the Yale University Collection of Musical Instruments*, 27:3.

ANON, 2005. The History of Bolton Choral Union. Web page: http://www.boltonchoral.org.uk/history.htm

ANTHROPOLOGY BIOGRAPHY WEB. Web page: http://emuseum.mnsu.edu/information/biography/

APEL, Willi, 1956. *Harvard Dictionary of Music.* Cambridge, Mass.: Harvard University Press.

ARETZ, Isabel, 1966a. "Carlos Vega, 1898–1966." *Ethnomusicology*, 10(3):318-21.

ARETZ, Isabel, 1966b. "Obituary: Carlos Vega." *Journal of the International Folk Music Council*, 18:81-2.

ARTHUR, Dave, 1993. "A.L. Lloyd 1908–82: An Interim Bibliography," in Georgina Boyes, *The Imagined Village: Culture, Ideology, and the English Folk Revival.* Manchester University Press, pp. 165-77.

ARTHUR, Dave, 2003. "Lloyd, A(lbert) L(ancaster)." New Grove.

ATKINSON, David, 2001. "Resources in the Vaughan Williams Memorial Library: The Maud Karpeles Manuscript Collection." *Folk Music Journal*, 8 (1):90-101.

AUBERT, Laurent, 1985. "La quête de l'intemporel. Constantin Brailoiu et les Archives internationales de musique populaire." *Bulletin annuel du Musée d'ethnographie* (Genève: Musée d'ethnographie), 27:39-64.

AUSTRALIAN MUSIC CENTRE, 2005. Trevor Jones. Web page: http://www.amcoz.com.au/comp/j/tjones.htm

BAILEY, Rona and Herbert ROTH, 1967. *Shanties By the Way*. Christchurch: Whitcombe & Tombs.

BAILY, John, 1990. "John Blacking and his Place in Ethnomusicology." *Yearbook for Traditional Music*, 22:xii-xxi.

BAILY, John, 2003. "Blacking, John (Arthur Randoll)." New Grove.

BAKE, Arnold, 1957. "IV. Indian Music," in Wellesz 1957:195-227.

BAKER, Anne Pimlott, 2004. "Hipkins, Alfred James (1826–1903)." ODNB.

BAKER, Theodore, 1882. *Ueber die Musik der nordamerikanischen Wilden*. Leipzig: Breitkopf & Hartel.

BAKER, Theodore, 1984. *Baker's Biographical Dictionary of Musicians*. 7th edition. Revised by Nicolas Slonimsky. New York: Schirmer Books; London: Collier Macmillan (First published 1900).

BALFOUR, Henry, 1899. *The Natural History of the Musical Bow*. Oxford: Clarendon Press.

BARING-GOULD, Sabine, 1895–?. *English Minstrelsie; A National Monument of English Song with Notes and Historical Introductions*. 8 vols. Edinburgh: T.C. & E.C. Jack.

BARING-GOULD, Sabine, 1909. *Cornish Characters and Strange Events*. London & New York: John Lane.

BARNETT, Elise B., 1970. "Special Bibliography: Art Music of India." *Ethnomusicology*, 14(2):278-312.

BARNETT, James H., 1959. "Edwin Grant Burrows 1891–1958." *American Anthropologist*, 61:97-8.

BARRETT, William Alexander, 1891. *English Folk Songs*. London: Novello.

BARRY, Phillips et al., 1929. *British Ballads from Maine*. New Haven: Yale University Press and London: Oxford University Press.

BARTLETT, F.C., 2004. "Myers, Charles Samuel (1873–1946)." ODNB.

BARTÓK, Béla, 1931. *The Hungarian Folk Song*. London: Oxford University Press.

BARTÓK, Béla (ed.), 1959. *Slovenské l'udové piesne: Slovakian Folk Songs*, vol.1. Bratislava: Slovenska Akademia Vied.

BARTÓK, Béla and Albert B. LORD, 1951. *Serbo-Croatian Folk Songs; Texts and Transcriptions of Seventy-five Folk Songs from the Milman Parry Collection and a Morphology of Serbo-Croatian Folk Melodies*. New York: Columbia University Press.

BARWICK, Linda M. 1995. "Catherine Ellis: Career History and List of Publications, Papers and Reports," in L. Barwick et al. (eds.), *The Essence of Singing and the Substance of Song: Recent Responses to the Aboriginal Performing Arts and Other Essays in Honour of Catherine Ellis*. Oceania Monograph 46. Sydney: University of Sydney, pp. 209-22.

BARWICK, Linda M., 1996. "Catherine Ellis 1935-1996." *Yearbook for Traditional Music*, 28:ix-xi.

BASCOM, William, 1972. "In Memoriam: Richard Alan Waterman (1914–1971)." *Yearbook of the International Folk Music Council*, 4:146-51.

BAUMANN, Max Peter, 1992. "The Ear as Organ of Cognition: Prologomenon to the Anthropology of Listening," in Baumann et. al. 1992:123-41.

BAUMANN, Max Peter, 1998. Bibliographie Transkription und analyse. Web page: Universität Bamberg
http://www.uni-bamberg.de/~ba2fm3/bibl_transkript.htm

BAUMANN, Max Peter, A. SIMON, and U. WEGNER (eds.), 1992. *European Studies in Ethnomusicology: Historical Developments and Recent Trends*. Wilhelmshaven: Florian Noetzel Verlag.

BAYARD, Samuel, 1944. *Hill Country Tunes: Instrumental Folk Music of Southwestern Pennsylvania*. Philadelphia: American Folklore Society.

BAYARD, Samuel, 1950. "Prolegomena to a Study of the Principal Melodic Families of British-American Folksong." *Journal of American Folklore*, 63(247):1-44. [Reprinted in McAllester 1971:65-109.]

BAYARD, Samuel, 1982. *Dance to the Fiddle, March to the Fife: Instrumental Folk Tunes in Pennsylvania*. University Park : Pennsylvania State University Press.

BECKER, Heinz and Reinhard GERLACH (eds.), 1970. *Speculum musicae artis. Festgabe für Heinrich Husmann zum 60. Geburtstag am 16. Dez 1968*. München: Fink.

BECKWITH, John and Gage AVERILL, 2003. "Kolinski, Mieczyslaw." New Grove.

BÉHAGUE, Gerard, 2003. "Ramón y Rivera, Luis Felipe." New Grove.

BÉHAGUE, Gerard, 2004a. " Aretz (de Ramón y Rivera), Isabel." New Grove.

BÉHAGUE, Gerard, 2004b. "Vega, Carlos." New Grove.

BERGSAGEL, John and Henrik KARLSSON, 2003. "Emsheimer, Ernst." New Grove.

BIGGS, Bruce, 1980. "Traditional Maori Song Texts and the 'Rule of Eight'." *Panui* (Auckland), 3:48-50.

BLACKING, John, 1967. *Venda Children's Songs*. Johannesburg: Witwatersfand University Press.

BLACKING, John, 1970. "Tonal Organization in the Music of Two Venda Initiation Schools." *Ethnomusicology*, 14(1):1-54.

BLACKING, John, 1971. "Deep and Surface Structures in Venda Music." *Yearbook of the International Folk Music Council*, 3:91-108.

BLACKING, John, 1973. *How Musical Is Man?* Washington: University of Washington Press.

BLACKING, John, 1977a. "Some Problems of Theory and Method in the Study of Music Change." *Yearbook of the International Folk Music Council*, 9:1-26.

BLACKING, John, 1977b. "Can Musical Universals be Heard?" *The World of Music* (Berlin), 19(1/2):14-29.

BLACKING, John, 1987. *A Commonsense View of All Music: Reflections on Percy Grainger's Contribution to Ethnomusicology and Music Education*. Cambridge: Cambridge University Press.

BLAUSTEIN, Richard, 1997. "Obituary: Samuel Preston Bayard (1908–1997): An Appreciation. *Journal of American Folklore*, 110 (438):415-7.

BLOM, Eric, 1948a. "Bartók, Béla," in H.C. Colles (ed.) 1948(1):232-5.

BLOM, Eric, 1948b. "Kodály, Zoltán," in H.C. Colles (ed.) 1948(3):41.

BLOM, Eric (ed.), 1954. *Grove's Dictionary of Music and Musicians*. 5th edition. London: Macmillan.

BLUM, Stephen, 1991. "European Musical Terminology and the Music of Africa," in Nettl & Bohlman 1991:3-36.

BLUM, Stephen, 1992. "Chapter VII: Analysis of Music Style," in Myers 1992:165-218.

BLUM, Stephen, P.V. BOHLMAN and D.M. NEUMAN (eds.), 1991. *Ethnomusicology and Modern Music History: Festschrift Bruno Nettl*. Urbana: University of Illinois.

BLUME, Friedrich (ed.), 1949–68. *Die Musik in Geschichte und Gegenwart*. 14 vols. Kassel: Bärenreiter.

BOHLMAN, Philip, 2003. "Nettl, Bruno." New Grove.

BÖLSCHE, Wilhelm, 1906. *Haeckel, His Life and Work*. London: Fisher Unwin.

BOR, Joep, 1988. "The Rise of Ethnomusicology: Sources on Indian Music c.1780–1890." *Yearbook for Traditional Muaic*, 20:51-73.

BORDEN, Charles E., 2001. "Halpern (b Ruhdörfer), Ida," in Encyclopedia of Music in Canada. Web page:
http://www.nlc-bnc.ca/music/17/m17-118-e.php?uid=5796&uidc=ID

BOSE, Fritz, 1934. "Die Musik der Uitoto." *Zeitschrift für vergleichende Musikwissenschaft*, 2:1-40 and appendix.

BOSE, Fritz, 1953. *Musikalische Völkerkunde*. Freiburg: Aflantis Verlag.

BOSE, Fritz, 1961. Review of Bartók 1959. *Ethnomusicology*, 5(1):62-3.

BOYES, Georgina, 2003a. "Karpeles, Maud Pauline." New Grove.

BOYES, Georgina, 2003b. "Gilchrist, Anne Geddes." New Grove

BRACKEN, Thomas, 1890. *Musings in Maoriland / With an Historical Sketch by Sir Robert Stout ,K.C.M.G. and Preface by Sir George Grey, K.C.B*. Dunedin, Wellington & Sydney: Keirle.

BRITISH LIGHT INFANTRY REGIMENTS, 2003. Officers who died in the Boer War 1899–1902. Web page:
http://www.lightinfantry.org.uk/regiments/Ox%20&%20Bucks%20LI/other/boerofficers.htm

BRONSON, Bertrand, 1959–72. *The Traditional Tunes of the Child Ballads* . 4 vols. Princeton, N.J.: Princeton University Press.

BRONSON, Bertrand, 1969a. *The Ballad As Song*. Berkeley: University of California Press.

BRONSON, Bertrand, 1969b. "Ch. 15 Folk-Song in the United States," in Bronson 1969a:243:56.

BROADWOOD, Lucy E. and J.A. FULLER-MAITLAND, 1893. *English Country Songs*. London: Cramer et al.

[BROADWOOD, Rev John], 1843. *Old English Songs, As Now Sung By the Peasantry of the Weald...* London: Balls & Co.

BROWN, Howard, 2003. "Sachs, Curt." New Grove.

BROWN, John, 1763. *A Dissertation on the Rise, Union, and Power... of Poetry and Music...* London: Davis & Reymers.

BRYER, Valerie, 1965. *Professor Percival Robson Kirby M.A., D.Litt., F.R.C.M. Head of the Department of Music, University of the Witwatersrand 1921–1954: A Bibliography of his Works*. Johannesburg: Johannesburg Public Library.

BÜCHER, Karl, 1909. *Arbeit und Rhythmus*. Leipzig & Berlin: Teubner.

BURNEY, Charles, 1776–89. *A General History of Music from the Earliest Ages to the Present Period*. 4 vols. London: The author.

BURROWS, Edwin G., 1933. *Native Music of the Tuamotus*. Honolulu: BP Bishop Museum Bulletin, 109.

BURROWS, Edwin G., 1936. *Ethnology of Futuna*. Honolulu: BP Bishop Museum Bulletin, 138.

BURROWS, Edwin G., 1937. *Ethnology of Uvea*. Honolulu: BP Bishop Museum Bulletin, 145.

BURROWS, Edwin G., 1938. *Western Polynesia: A Study in Cultural Differentiation*. Goteborg: Etnologiska Studier, no.7
[Reprinted c.1970, Dunedin (NZ), University Book Shop]

BURROWS, Edwin G., 1945. *Songs of Uvea and Futuna*. Honolulu: BP Bishop Museum Bulletin, 183.

BYRNE, David, 1999. "I Hate World Music." *New York Times*, October 3.

BYRON, Reginald (ed.), 1995. *Music, Culture, & Experience: Selected Papers of John Blacking*. Chicago & London: University of Chicago Press.

BYRON, Reginald, 2004. "Blacking, John Anthony Randoll (1928–1990)." ODNB.

CAMPBELL, Joseph, 1974. *The Masks of God: Creative Mythology*. London: Souvenir Press.

CAPWELL, Charles, 1991. "Marginality and Musicology in Nineteenth Century Calcutta: The Case of Sourindro Mohun Tagore," in Nettl & Bohlman 1991:228-43.

CARD, Caroline, 1981. "Preface," in Card & Rahkonen 1981a:ix-xiv.

CARD, Caroline and Carl RAHKONEN, 1981a. *Discourse in Ethnomusicology II: A Tribute to Alan P. Merriam*. Bloomington, Indiana: Ethnomusicology Publications Group.

CARD, Caroline and Carl RAHKONEN, 1981b."The Works of Alan P. Merriam," in Card and Bahkonen 1981a:237-66.

CARD, Caroline and Carl RAHKONEN, 1982. "Alan P. Merriam: Bibliography and Discography." *Ethnomusicology*, 26:107-20.

CARONI MUSIC, 2004. Luis Felipe Ramón y Rivera. Web page: http://www.caronimusic.com/pagesAnglais/Ramon.php?idsession=12001095742266&pagec=0

CARRUTHERS, Sir Joseph, 1930. *Captain James Cook, R.N.: One Hundred and Fifty Years After*. London: Murray.

CAVANAGH, Beverley, 1972. "Annotated Bibliography: Eskimo Music." *Ethnomusicology*, 16(3):479-87.

CAVANAGH, Beverley, 1981. "In Memoriam: Mieczyslaw Kolinski." *Ethnomusicology*, 25(2):285-6.

CHASE, Gilbert, 1979. "An Exagmination Round His Factification for Incamination of Work in Progress: (Review Essay and Reminiscence)." *Yearbook of the International Folk Music Council*, 11:138-44.
[Review of Seeger 1977.]

CHEYRONNAUD, Jacques, 1990. "Une vie consacrée à l'ethnomusicologie Claudie Marcel-Dubois (1913–1989)." *Cahiers de musiques traditionnelles*, 3:173-85.

CHILD, Francis, 1883–98. *The English and Scottish Popular Ballads*. 5 vols. Boston & New York: Houghton, Mifflin.

CHRISTENSEN, Dieter, 1960. "Inner Tempo and Melodic Tempo." *Ethnomusicology*, 4(1);9-14.

CHRISTENSEN, Dieter, 1980. "Obituary: Kurt Reinhard 1914–1979." *Ethnomusicology*, 24(1):v-vi.

CHRISTENSEN, Dieter, 1983. "In Memoriam: George Herzog 1901–1983." *Bulletin of the International Folk Music Council*, 63:2

CHRISTENSEN, Dieter, 1984. "In Memoriam: Klaus P. Wachsmann." *Yearbook for Traditional Music*, 16:xii-xiii.

CHRISTENSEN, Dieter, 1991. "Erich M. von Hornbostel, Carl Stumpf, and the Institutionalization of Comparative Musicology," in Nettl & Bohlman 1991:201-09.

CHRISTENSEN, Dieter and Gerd KOCH, 1964. *Die Musik der Ellice Inseln*. Berlin: Museum für Völkerkunde.

COLE, Douglas, 1999. *Franz Boas: The Early Years, 1858–1906*. Seattle: University of Washington Press.

COLLES, H.C. (ed.), 1948. *Grove's Dictionary of Music and Musicians*. 4th edition. 6 vols. London: Macmillan.

COLLES, H.C., 1948a. "Fox Stranoways, Arthur Henry," in H.C. Colles (ed.) 1948(2):290.

COLLES, H.C., 1948b, "Galpin, Rev Francis William," in H.C. Colles (ed.) 1948(2):344-5.

COLLES, H.C. and Frank HOWES, 2003. "Fox Strangways, A(rthur) H(enry)." New Grove.

CONDLIFFE, J.B., 1971. *Te Rangi Hiroa: The Life of Sir Peter Buck*. Christchurch: Whitcombe & Tombs.

COOPER, Martin, 2003. "Howes, Frank (Stewart)." New Grove.

COPPET, Daniel de and Hugo ZEMP, 1978. *'Are'are: Un peuple mélanésien et sa musique*. [Paris]: Éditions du Seuil.

CORBETT, Julian, 1928. *Sir Francis Drake*. London: Macmillan.

COWL, Carl and Sheila M. CRAIK, 1999. *Henry George Farmer: A Bibliography*. Glasgow: Glasgow University Library.

GRAGG, Larry, 2004. "Steele, Joshua (c.1700–1796)." ODNB.

CROSSLEY-HOLLAND, Peter (ed.), 1968. *Proceedings of the Centennial Workshop on Ethnomusicology*. Victoria, BC: Government of the Province of British Columbia.

CROSSLEY-HOLLAND, Peter (ed.), 1978. *Proceedings of the Centennial Workshop on Ethnomusicology: Volume 2 The Complete Discussions*. Victoria, BC: Government of the Province of British Columbia.

CURTIS, Natalie, 1918–19. *Hampton Series Negro Folk-songs*. 4 vols. New York: Schirmer.

CURTIS, Natalie, 1920. *Songs and Tales from the Dark Continent*. New York: Schirmer.

CURTIS, Natalie, 1968. *The Indians' Book: Songs and Legends of the American Indians*. New York: Dover (First published 1907).

DAHLBACK, Karl, 1958. *New Methods of Vocal Folk Music Research*. Oslo: Oslo University Press.

DANCKERT, Werner, 1939. *Das europäische Volkslied*. Berlin: Hahnefeld.

DANIÉLOU, Alain, 1968. *The Rāga-s of Northern Indian Music*. London: Barrie & Rockliff.

DARBELLAY, Etienne and Dorothea BAUMANN, 2003. "Estreicher, Zygmunt." New Grove.

DARWIN, Charles, 1859. *On the Origin of Species*. London: Murray.

DARWIN, Charles, 1871. *The Descent of Man*. New York: Appleton.

DARWIN, Charles, 1902. *The Origin of Species*. London: Murray. Reprint of 6th edition.

DARWIN, Erasmus, 1794–96. *Zoonomia, or, The Laws of Organic Life*. 2 vols. Dublin: Byrne & Jones.

DAVIES, James A., 1855. "On the Native Songs of New Zealand." Appendix in Sir George Grey, *Polynesian Mythology*. London: Murray, pp.313-33.

DAY, Charles Russell, 1891a. *The Music and Musical Instruments of Southern India and the Deccan*. London & New York: Novello, Ewer.

DAY, Charles Russell, 1891b. *A Descriptive Catalogue Of The Musical Instruments Recently Exhibited At The Royal Military Exhibition, London 1890*. London: Eyre & Spottiswoode.

DEAN-SMITH, Margaret, 1954. *A Guide to English Folk Song Collections*. Liverpool: University Press of Liverpool.

DEAN-SMITH, Margaret, 1957–58. "The Work of Anne Geddes Gilchrist, OBE, FSA, 1863–1954."*Proceedings of the Royal Musical Association*, 84:43-53.

DE HEN, Ferdinand J., 1980. "In Memoriam: Paul Collaer (1891–1989)." *Ethnomusicology*, 34(3):423-4.

DE LERMA, Dominique-Rene, 1981. *Bibliography of Black Music*. 4 vols. Westport, CT: Greenwood Press.

DENON, Lester D. (ed.), 1952. *Bertrand Russell's Dictionary of Mind, Matter and Morals*. New York: Philosphical Library.

DENSMORE, Frances, 1910–13. *Chippewa Music*. 2 vols. Washington: Government Printer.

Deutsche biographische Enzyklopädie (DBE). 12 vols. in 14, 1995–2000. München ; New Providence: Saur.

DeVALE, Sue Carole, 1985. " 'Intrusions': A Remembrance of Klaus Wachsmann (1907–1984)." *Ethnomuicology*, 29 (2):272-82.

DeVALE, Sue Carole, 2003a. "Boas, Franz." New Grove.

DeVALE, Sue Carole, 2003b. "Fewkes, Jesse Walter." New Grove.

DeVALE, Sue Carole, 2003c. "Fillmore, John Comfort." New Grove.

DeVALE, Sue Carole, 2003d. "Fletcher, Alice Cunningham." New Grove.

DeVALE, Sue Carole, 2003e. "Gilman, Benjamin Ives." New Grove.

DIAMOND CAVANAGH, Beverley A., 2001. "Kolinski, Mieczyslaw," in Encyclopedia of Music in Canada. Web page: http://www.nlc-bnc.ca/music/17/m17-214-e.html

DICKSON, W.K.-L. and Antonia DICKSON, 1894. *The Life and Inventions of Thomas Alva Edison*. London: Chatto & Windus.

DRECHSLER, Wolfgang and Rainer KATTEL, 1997. "Karl Bücher in Dorpat." *Trames* (Tartu University), 1(4):322-68.

DRIVER, Harold and James C. DOWNEY, 1970. Reviews of Lomax 1968. *Ethnomusicology*, 14(1):57-62 & 63-7.

DUCROS, Louis, n.d. *J.-J. Rousseau*. Collections des Classiques Populaires. Paris: Société Française d'Imprimerie et de Librairie (Ancienne Maison Lecène, Oudin et Cie).

DU HALDE, Jean-Baptiste, 1735. *Description géograpique, historique, chronologique, politique et physique de l'empire de la Chine et de la Tartarie chinoise*. Paris.

DUNAWAY, David K., 1980. "Charles Seeger and Cari Sands: The Composers' Collective Years." *Etbnomusicology*, 24(2):159-68.

DURAN, Lucy, 1982. "A.L. Lloyd—A Tribute." *Yearbook for Traditionsl Music*, 14:xiii-xv.

DURAN, Lucy, 2003. "Tracey, Hugh (Travers)." New Grove.

EGGEBRECHT, Hans Heinrich, 2003a. "Reinhard, Kurt." New Grove.

EGGEBRECHT, Hans Heinrich, 2003b. "Wiora, Walter." New Grove.

EGGEBRECHT, Hans Heinrich, David HILEY, and Pamela M. POTTER, 2003. "Husmann, Heinrich." New Grove.

EGGEBRECHT, Hans Heinrich and Pamela M. POTTER, 2003. "Bose, Fritz." New Grove.

EHRLICH, Cyril, 2003. "Hipkins, Alfred (James)." New Grove.

ELKIN, A.P. and Trevor A. JONES, c.1957. *Arnhem Land Music, North Australia*. Oceania Monograph No. 9. Sydney: University of Sydney.

ELLINGSON, Ter, 1992. "Chapter V Transcription," in Myers 1992:110-52.

ELLIS, Alexander J., 1884. "Tonometrical Observations on Some Existing Non-harmonic Scales." *Proceedings of the Royal Society of London*, 37:368-85.

ELLIS, Alexander J., 1885. "On the Musical Scales of Various Nations." *Journal of the Society of Arts*, 33:485-527.

ELLIS, Catherine, 1964. *Aboriginal Music Making: A Study of Central Australian Music*. Adelaide: Libraries Board of South Australia.

ELLIS, Catherine, 1965. "Pre-Instrumental Scales." *Ethnomusicology*, 9:126-37.

ENGLAND, Nicholas et al., 1964. "Symposium on Transcription and Analysis." *Ethnomusicology*, 8(3):233-77.

EÖSZE, László, Mícheál HOULAHAN and Philip TACKA, 2003. "Kodály, Zoltán." New Grove,

ERDELY, Stephen, 1962. "Classification of Hungarian Folk songs." *The Folklore and Folk Music Archivist* (Bloomington), 5(3):1-2; 5(4):2.

ERDELY, Stephen, 1965. *Methods and Principles of Hungarian Ethnomusicology*. Bloomington: Indiana University.

ESCOFFIER, Jeffrey, 2002. McPhee, Colin (1900–1964). Web page: http://www.glbtq.com/arts/mcphee_c.html

FALCK, Robert, and Timothy RICE (eds.), 1982. *Cross Cultural Perspectives on Music*. Toronto: University of Toronto Press.

FARMER, Henry George, 1957a. "VThe Music of Ancient Mesopotamia," in Wellesz 1957:228-54.

FARMER, Henry George, 1957b. "VI The Music of Ancient Egypt," in Wellesz 1957:255-82.

FARMER, Henry George, 1957c. "XI The Music of Islam," in Wellesz 1957:421-77.

FELD, Steven, 1974. "Linguistic Models in Ethnomusicology." *Ethnomusicology*, 18(2):197-217.

FELD, Steven, 1981. "Flow Like a Waterfall: The Metaphors of Kaluli Musical Theory." *Yearbook for Traditional Music*, 13:22-47.

FELD, Steven, 1982. *Sound and Sentiment: Birds, Weeping, Poetics, and Song in Kaluli Expression*. Philadelphia: University of Pennsylvania Press.

FELD, Steven, 1984. "Sound Structure as Social Structure." *Ethnomusicology*, 28(3):383-409.

FELD, Steven, 1994. "From Ethnomusicology to Echo-Muse-Ecology: Reading R. Murray Schafer in the Papua New Guinea Rainforest." *The Soundscape Newsletter*, Number 08, June 1994. Web page: Echo Muse Ecology http://www.earthear.com/sscape/echomuseecology.html

FÉTIS, Françoise Joseph, 1869–76. *Histoire génerale de la musique*. Paris: Frères.

FIELD, Christopher, 1997. "John Donaldson and 19th-century Acoustics Teaching in the University of Edinburgh." *Proceedings of the Institute of Acoustics*, 19(5):509-20.

FIFIELD, Christopher, 2003. "Bülow, Hans." New Grove.

FILLMORE, John Comfort, n.d. "Preliminary Report on Kwakiutl Songs" and songs (transcribed in notation from Boas' wax cylinder recordings. Item 8.7 pp.143-158," in Peabody Museum Director Records - Frederic W. Putnam (1839–1915), 1870–1923: A Finding Aid. Harvard: Peabody Museum Archives. Web page (1999): http://oasis.harvard.edu/html/pea00005.html

FILLMORE, John Comfort, 1888. "The Harmonic Structure of Indian Music." *American Anthropologist*, 1:297-318.

FILLMORE, John Comfort, 1895. "What Do Indians Mean to Do When They Sing . . .? *Journal of American Folklore*, 8:139-41.

FIRTH, Raymond, 1936. *We the Tikopia*. London, Allen & Unwin.

FIRTH, Raymond with Mervyn McLEAN, 1990. *Tikopia Songs*. London: Cambridge University Press.

FLETCHER, Alice Cunningham, Francis LA FLESCHE and John Comfort FILLMORE, 1893. *A Study of Omaha Indian Music*. Cambridge, MA: Peabody Museum of American Archæology and Ethnology.

FLETCHER, Alice Cunningham and Francis LA FLESCHE, 1911. "The Omaha Tribe." *Annual Report of the Bureau of American Ethnology 1905–1906*, 27:7-672.

FOLLOWS, Stephen, 2005. "Holland, Peter Charles Crossley- (1916–2001)." ODNB

FOX STRANGWAYS, A.H., 1933. *Cecil Sharp By A.H. Fox Strangways, in Collaboration with Maud Karpeles*. London: Oxford University Press.

FRANCMANIS, John, 1999. 'Introduction,' in "Frank Kidson: His 'Grove' Contributions." *Musical Traditions* Article MT039. Web page:
http://www.mustrad.org.uk/articles/kidson.htm

FRISBIE, Charlotte J., 1989. "Helen Heffron Roberts (1888–1985): A Tribute." *Ethnomusicology*, 33(1):97-111.

FRISBIE, Charlotte J., 1991. "Women and the Society for Ethnomusicology: Roles and Contributions from Foundation Through Incorporation (1952/53–1961)," in Nettl and Bohlman 1991:244-65.

FULLER-MAITLAND, J.A., 1932. *A Door-keeper of Music*. London: Murray.

FULLER-MAITLAND, J.A., 1948. "Day, Major Charles Russell," in H.C. Colles (ed.) 1948(2):25-6.

FULLER-MAITLAND, J.A. et al., 2003. "Wallaschek, Richard." New Grove. [Some dates also obtained from the original article in Grove 4th edit. (1948), omitted in the revised article].

GALLUSSER, Werner, 2003. "Ellis [née Caughie], Catherine J(oan)." New Grove.

GALLUSSER, Werner, 2004. "Jones, T(revor) A(lan)." New Grove.

GARRATY, John A. and Mark C. CARNES (eds.), 1999. *American National Biography*. 24 vols. New York: Oxford University Press.

GASKIN, L.J. P., 1965. *A Select Bibliography of Music in Africa*. London: International African Institute.

GEIRINGER, Karl, 1948. "Sachs, Curt," in H.C. Colles (ed.) 1948 (Supp):557-8.

GERSON-KIWI, Edith, 1937. *Studien zur Geschichte des italienischen Liedmadrigals im XVI. Jahrhundert: Satzlehre und Genealogie der Kanzonetten*. Würzburg: Triltsch.

GERSON-KIWI, Edith, 1973–74. "Two Anniversaries: Two Pioneers in Jewish Ethnomusicology." *Orbis musicae*, 2:17-28.

GERSON-KIWI, Edith, 1974. "Robert Lachmann: His Achievement and his Legacy." *Yuval*, 3:100-08.

GERSON-KIWI, Edith, 1980. *Migrations and Mutations of the Music in East and West: Selected Writings*. Tel-Aviv: Tel Aviv University, Faculty of Visual and Performing Arts, Department of Musicology.

GERSON-KIWI, Edith, 2003. " Lachmann, Robert." New Grove.

GERSON-KIWI, Edith and Israel J. KATZ, 2003. "Idelsohn, Abraham Zevi." New Grove.

GILBERT, Davies, 1822. *Some Ancient Christmas Carols with the Tunes to Which they were Formerly Sung*. London: Nichols (printer).

GILLIES, Malcolm, 2003. "Bartók, Béla." New Grove.

GILLIS, Frank, 1958. Letter to the Editor: [Bibliography of Frances Densmore: Additions and Errata]. *Ethnomusicology*, 2(3):131-2.

GILLIS, Frank, 1969. "Special Bibliography: Willard Rhodes." *Ethnomusicology*, 13(2):305-08.

GILLIS, Frank, 1980. "Alan P. Merriam (1923–1980)." *Ethnomusicology*, 24(3):v-vii.

GILLIS, Frank, Fritz BOSE and James ELROD, 1969. "[Obituary]:Hans R.H. Hickmann with Supplementary Bibliography." *Ethnomusicology*, 13(2):316-9.

GILLIS, Frank and Alan P. MERRIAM, 1973. "Richard Alan Waterman: Bibliography and Discography 1941–1971," in Merriam 1973:89-94.

GILMAN, Benjamin Ives, 1891. "Zuni Melodies." *Journal of American Ethnology and Archaeology*, 1:63-91.

GILMAN, Benjamin Ives, 1908. "Hopi Songs." *Journal of American Ethnology and Archaeology*, 5: [whole issue].

GIURIATI, Giovanni, 2005. "Hood, Ki Mantle." New Grove.

GLASGOW UNIVERSITY LIBRARY, 2003. Manuscripts Catalogue - Name Details "Henry George Farmer." Web page:
http://special.lib.gla.ac.uk/manuscripts/search/detailp.cfm?NID=2277&DID=&AID=4627

GOLDSTEIN, Kenneth, S., 1964. *A Guide for Field Workers in Folklore*. Hatboro, Penn.: Folklore Associates.

GOURLAY, Kenneth A., 1978. "Towards a Reassesment of the Ethnomusicologist's Role in Research." *Ethnomusicology*, 22(1):1-35.

GRAEBE, Martin, 2000. Sabine Baring-Gould and the Folk Songs of South-west England. Web page: Sabine Baring Gould http://www.btinternet.com/~greenjack/
GRAF, Walter, 1950. *Die musikwissenschaftlichen Phonogramme Rudolf Pöchs von der Nordküste Neuguineas*. Wien: Rohrer.

GRAF, Walter (ed.), 1954. *Robert Lach: Persönlichkeit und Werk: zum 80. Geburtstag*. Wien: Musikwissenschaftliches Institut.

GRAF, Walter, 1958. "Memorial to Robert Lach." *Ethnomusicology*, 3(3):130-1.

GRAF, Walter, 1962. "The PhonogrammArchiv der Osterreichischen Akademie der Wissenschaften in Vienna." *The Folklore and Folk Music Archivist* (Bloomington), 4(4):1-2.

GRAY, John, 1991. *African Music: A Bibliographical Guide to the Traditional, Popular, Art, and Liturgical Musics of Sub-Saharan Africa*. Westport, CT: Greenwood.

GREENSTREET, William John, 1927. *Isaac Newton, 1642–1727*. London: Bell.

GREER, Taylor Aitken, 1998. *A Question of Balance: Charles Seeger's Philosophy of Music*. Berkeley, Los Angeles & London: University of California Press.

GREGORY, David E., 1997. "A.L. Lloyd and the English Folk Song Revival, 1934–44." *Canadian Journal for Traditional Music*. Web page: http://cjtm.icaap.org/content/25/v25art2.html

GREGORY, Mark, 1970. "A.L. Lloyd: Folklore and Australia." *Overland Magazine*. Web page: Australian Folk Songs http://www.crixa.com/muse/songnet/reviews/lloyd/

GREY, Sir George, 1851. *Ko nga Moteatea, me nga Hakirara o nga Maori*. Wellington: Stokes.

GUÉDON, Marie Françoise, 1972. "Canadian Indian Ethnomusicology: Selected Bibliography and Discography." *Ethnomusicology*, 16(3):465-78.

GÜNTHER, Robert A., 1969. "Special Bibliography: Marius Schneider." *Ethnomusicology*, 13(3):518-26.

GÜNTHER, Robert A., 2003."Schneider, Marius." New Grove.

HAASE, Gesine, 1977. *Studien zur Musik im Santa Cruz-Archipel*. Hamburg: Wagner.

HADDON, A.C., 1940. "Henry Balfour 1863–1939." *Obiturary Notices of Fellows of the Royal Society*, 3(8):108-15.

HALPERN, Ida, 1976. "Aural History and Ethnomusicology." *Canadian Journal for Traditional Music*. (Reprinted from *Sound Heritage*, Vol. IV, No. 1)
Web page: http://cjtm.icaap.org/content/4/v4art9.html

HAMMOND, L. Davis (ed.), 1970. *News from New Cythera: Report of Bougainville's Voyage 1776–1769*. Minneapolis: University of Minnesota Press.

HAMY, Alfred, 1893. *Galerie illustree de la Campagnie de Jesus*. 8 vols. Paris: The author.

HARICH-SCHNEIDER, Eta, 1973. *A History of Japanese Music*. London: Oxford University Press.

HARRISON, Frank, 1973. *Time, Place and Music*. Amsterdam: Knuf.

HARRISON, Frank, 1977. "Universals in Music: Towards a Methodology of Comparative Research." *The World of Music (Berlin)*, 19(1/2):30-42.

HARRISON, Frank, Mantle HOOD and Claude V. PALISCA, 1963. *Musicology*. Englewood Cliffs: Prentice-Hall.

HARVARD ARCHIVES, 2005. Biographical file for Phillips Barry (call no. HUG 300) and undergraduate record card for Phillips Barry (call no. UA III.15.75.10).

HARVARD UNIVERSITY, 1925. *Harvard College Class of 1900*. Twenty-fifth Anniversary Report. Report VI. Privately printed for the class by the University Press.

HARVARD UNIVERSITY, 1930. *Quinquennial Catalogue of the Officers and Graduates 1636-1930*. Cambridge, MA: Harvard University Press.

HARVARD UNIVERSITY, 1940. *Harvard College Class of 1900*. Secretary's Ninth Report. Privately printed for the class by the Crimson Printing Company, Cambridge Mass.

HARWOOD, Dane L., 1976. "Universals in Music: A Perspective from Cognitive Psychology." *Ethnomusicology*, 20(3):521-33.

HAWKINS, Sir John, 1776. *A General History of the Science and Practice of Music*. 4 vols. London: Payne.

HAYDON, Glen, 1941. *Introduction to Musicology*. Chapel Hill: University of North Carolina Press.

HEANEY, Michael, 2004a. "Karpeles, Maud Pauline (1885–1976)." ODNB.

HEANEY, Michael, 2004b. "Sharp, Cecil James (1859–1924)." ODNB.

HEDIN, Sven, Henning HASLUND-CHRISTENSEN, K. GRØNBECH and Ernst EMSHEIMER, 1943. *The Music of the Mongols Part 1: Eastern Mongolia: Reports from the Scientific Expedition to the North-Western Provinces of China under the Leadership of Dr. Sven Hedin-The Sino-Swedish Expedition*. Publication 21. VIII. Ethnography 4. Stockholm: Thule.

HEINS, Ernst, 1994. "Jaap Kunst and the Rise of Ethnomusicology," in Heins et al. 1994:13-23.

HEINS, Ernst, Elizabeth DEN OTTER and Felix VAN LAMSWEERDE (comps.), 1994. *Jaap Kunst: Indonesian Music and Dance*. Amsterdam: Royal Tropical Institute.

HERNDON, Marcia, 1974. "Analysis: The Herding of Sacred Cows?" *Ethnomusicology*, 18(2):219-62.

HERNDON, Marcia and Norma McLEOD, 1983. *Field Manual for Ethnomusicology*. Norwood: Norwood Editions.

HERSKOVITS, Melville, 1948. *Man and His Works: The Science of Cultural Anthropology*. New York: Knopf.

HERSKOVITS, Melville, 1953. *Cultural Anthropology*. New York: Knopf.

HERSKOVITS LIBRARY, 2001. Web page:
http://www.library.northwestern.edu/africana/herskovits.html

HERZOG, George, 1928. "The Yuman Musical Style." *Journal of American Folklore*, 41:183-231.

HERZOG, George, 1930. "Musical Styles in North America." *Proceedings of the 23rd International Congress of Americanists* (New York), pp.455-8.

HERZOG, George, 1934. "Speech-Melody and Primitive Music." *Musical Quarterly*, 20:452-66.

HERZOG, George, 1935a. "Plains Ghost Dance and Great Basin Music." *American Anthropologist*, 37:403-19.
[Reprinted in McAllester 1971:116-31.]

HERZOG, George, 1935b. "Special Song Types in North American Indian Music." *Zeitschrift für vergleichende Musikwissenschaft*, 3(1-2):23-33.

HERZOG, George,1936. "A Comparison of Pueblo and Pima Musical Styles." *Journal of American Folklore*, 49:283-417.

HERZOG, George, 1938a. "Music in the Thinking of the American Indian." *Peabody Bulletin* (May 1938):1-5.

HERZOG, George, 1938b. "Phillips Barry." *Journal of American Folklore*, 51:439-41.

HERZOG, George, 1945. "Drum-Signaling in a West-African Tribe." *Word*, 1:217-38.

HERZOG, George, 1950. "Song," in M. Leach (ed.), *Funk and Wagnall's Standard Dictionary of Folklore,Mythology, and Legend*. New York: Funk & Wagnall, vol. 2, pp. 1032-50.

HIPKINS, Alfred J., 1888. *Musical Instruments: Historic, Rare and Unique*. Edinburgh: Black.

HIPKINS, Alfred J., 1948. "Mahillon, a Belgian family," in H.C. Colles (ed.) 1948(3):291.

HIPKINS, Alfred J. and Edward DENT, 1948. "Ellis (formerly Sharpe), Alexander, John," in H.C. Colles (ed.) 1948(2):158.

HITCHCOCK, H. Wiley, 2003. "Baker, Theodore." New Grove.

HOFFMANN-ERBRECHT, Lothar and Pamela M. POTTER, 2003. "Wolf, Johannes." New Grove.

HOLMES, Lowell D., 1965. *Anthropology: An Introduction.* New York: Ronald Press.

HOOD, Mantle, 1960. "The Challenge of Bi-Musicality." *Ethnomusicology*, 4(2):55-99.

HOOD, Mantle, 1963a. "Music the Unknown," in Harrrison, Hood and Palisca 1963:215-326.

HOOD, Mantle, 1963b. "Musical Significance." *Ethnomusicology*, 7(3):187-92.

HOOD, Mantle, 1971. *The Ethnomusicologist.* New York: McGraw-Hill.

HOOD, Mantle, 1977. "Universal Attributes of Music." *The World of Music*, 19(1/2):63-75.

HOOD, Mantle, 1979. "Reminiscent of Charles Seeger." *Yearbook of the International Folk Music Council*, 11:76-9.

HOOD, Mantle, 1998. "The Musical River of Change and Innovation." *Oideion: Performing Arts Online 2.* Web page: http://iias.leidenuniv.nl/oideion/issues/issue2/articles/hood/frame-o.html.

HOOD, Mantle, 2000. "Ethnomusicology's Bronze Age in Y2K." *Ethnomusicology*, 44(3):365-75.

HOOD, Mantle, 2003. "Kunst, Jaap [Jakob]." New Grove.

HOOD Mantle and Harold C. FLEMING, 1966. Review of Jones 1964. *Ethnomusicology*, 10(2):214-8.

HOPKINS, Pandora, 1977. "The Homology of Music and Myth: Views of Lévi-Strauss on Musical Structure." *Ethnomusicology*, 21(2):247-61.

HOUGH, Walter, 1923. "Alice Cunningham Fletcher." *American Anthropologist*, 25:254-8.

HOUGH, Walter, 1932. *Biographical Memoir of Jesse Walter Fewkes, 1850–1930.* Biographical Memoirs, vol. XV-Ninth Memoir. Washington, The National Academy of Sciences, pp.[259]-83.

HOWARD, Keith, 1991. "John Blacking: An Interview Conducted and Edited by Keith Howard." *Ethnomusicology*, 35(1):55-76.

HOWES, Frank, 1948. "Gilchrist, Anne Geddes, " in H.C. Colles (ed.) 1948 (Supp):239-40.

HOWES. Frank, 1967. "In Memoriam: Zoltán Kodály 1882–1967." *Musical Times*, (May 1967). Web page: The Musical Times.
http://www.musicaltimes.co.uk/archive/obits/196705kodaly.html

HOWES, Frank, 1969a. *Folk Music of Britain – and Beyond* . London: Methuen.

HOWES, Frank, 1969b. "A.H. Fox Strangways." *Music and Letters*, 50:9-14.

HOWES, Frank, 2003. "Sharp, Cecil (James)." New Grove.

HUGHES, H. Stuart, 1964. *History as Art and as Science: Twin Vistas on the Past*. University of Chicago Press.

HUSMANN, Heinrich, 1951. *Fünf- und siebenstellige Centstafeln zur Berechnung musikalischer Intervalle*. Leiden:Brill.

HUSMANN, Heinrich, 1956. "Antike und Orient in ihrer Bedeutung für die europäische Musik." *Gesellschaft für Musikforschung, Kongressbericht* (Hamburg), 1956:24-32.

HUSMANN, Heinrich, 1961. *Grundlagen der antiken und orientalischen Musikkultur*. Berlin: de Gruyter.

HUXLEY, Thomas H., 1893. "Chapter 10: Obituary (1888)," in *Collected Essays*, Vol.2: *Darwiniana*. London: Macmillan.

HUXLEY, Leonard, 1903. *Life and Letters of Thomas Henry Huxley*. 3vols. London : Macmillan.

IDELSOHN, Abraham Zevi (comp.), 1914–32. *Hebräisch-orientalischer Melodienschatz*. 10 vols. Leipzig: Breitkopf & Härtel.
[For English edition see Idelsohn 1973.]

IDELSOHN, Abraham Zevi (comp.), 1973. *Thesaurus of Hebrew Oriental Melodies*. 10 vols. in 4, [New York]: Ktav Publishing House. (First published 1914–32.)

INDIANA UNIVERSITY, 2000. History of The Archives of Traditional Music. Web page: http://www.indiana.edu/~libarchm/history.html

INTERNATIONAL MUSIC COUNCIL, 1952. *Notation of Folk Music. Recommendations of the Committee of Experts, Convened by the International Archives of Folk Music*. Paris: Unesco.

IVENS, Walter G., 1930. *The Island Builders of the Pacific*. London: Seeley Service.

IZIKOWITZ, Karl Gustav, 1934. *Musical Instruments of the South American Indians*. Göteborg: Elanders Boktryckeri Aktiebolag (Republished S.R. Publishers 1970).

JAIRAZBHOY, Nazir, 1971. *The Rags of North Indian Music: Their Structure and Evolution.* London: Faber & Faber.

JAIRAZBHOY, Nazir, 1983. "Essays in Honor of Peter Crossley-Holland on His Sixty-fifth Birthday: Introduction." *Selected Reports in Ethnomusicology*, 4:ix-xii.

JAIRAZBHOY, Nazir, 1990. "The Beginnings of Organology and Ethnomusicology in the West: V. Mahillon, A. Ellis and S.M. Tagore." *Selected Reports in Ethnomusicology*, 8:67-80.

JAIRAZBHOY, Nazir, 1991. "The First Restudy of Arnold Bake's Fieldwork in India," in Nettl and Bohlman 1991:210-27.

JAIRAZBHOY, Nazir, 1993. "Chapter IX South Asia,"in Myers 1993:274-99.

JAIRAZBHOY, Nazir, 2003. "Baké, Arnold Adriaan." New Grove.

JAIRAZHBOY N.A. and A.W. STONE, 1963. "Intonation in Present-Day North Indian Classical Music." *Bulletin of the School of Oriental and African Music*, 26:119-32.

JESUIT FAMILY ALBUM, 2003. Joseph M. Amiot. Web page: http://www.faculty.fairfield.edu/jmac/jp/jpabe.htm

JOHNSON, Allen and Dumas MALONE (eds.), [1946]. *Dictionary of American Biography.* 11 vols. New York : Scribner.

JONES, A.M., 1959. *Studies in African Music.* 2 vols. London: Oxford University Press.

JONES, A.M., 1964. *Africa and Indonesia: The Evidence of the Xylophone and Other Musical and Cultural Factors.* Leiden: Brill.

JONES, A.M., 1977. "In Memoriam: Hugh Travers Tracey (1903–1977)." *Yearbook of the International Folk Music Council*, 9:96-9.

JONES, Stephen, 2003. "Reading Between the Lines: Reflections on the Massive Anthology of Folk Music of the Chinese Peoples." *Ethnomusicology*, 47 (3):287-337.

JONES, Sir William, 1792. "On the Musical Modes of the Hindoos." *Asiatick Researches*, 3:55-87; republished in E. Rosenthal, *The Story of Indian Music and its Instruments.* London (1928), pp.157-204.

KANAZAWA, Masakata, 2003. "Kishibe, Shigeo." New Grove.

KARPELES, Maud. 1944. Review of Lloyd 1944. *Journal of the English Folk Dance and Song Society*, 4(5):207-8.

KARPELES, Maud (ed.), 1958. *The Collecting of Folk Music and Other Ethnomusicological Material: A Manual for Field Workers*. London: International Folk Music Council and Royal Anthropological Institute.

KARPELES, Maud (ed.), 1966. *English Folk-songs from the Southern Appalations Collected by Cecil Sharp*. London: Oxford University Press.

KARPELES, Maud, 1967. *Cecil Sharp: His Life and Work*. Chicago: University of Chicago Press.

KARPELES, Maud, 1973. *An Introduction to English Folk Song*. London: Oxford University Press.

KARPELES, Maud, 1974. "In Memoriam: Frank Howes (1889 [sic]–1974." *Yearbook of the International Folk Music Council*, 6:9.

KARTOMI, Margaret, 1981. "The Processes and Results of Musical Culture Contact: A Discussion of Terminology and Concepts." *Ethnomusicology*, 25(2):227-49.

KARTOMI, Margaret, 1997. "Catherine Ellis (1935–1996)." *Musicology Australia*, 20:2-3.

KASILAG, Lucrecia, 2003. " Maceda, José." New Grove.

KASSLER, Jamie C., 2003. "Steele, Joshua." New Grove.KATZ, Israel J., 1970. "Marius Barbeau 1883–1969." *Ethnomusicology*, 14(1):129-42.

KATZ, Israel J., 1975–76. "Abraham Zevi Idelsohn (1882–1938): A Bibliography of his Collected Writings." *Musica Judaica*, 1:1-32.

KATZ, Israel J., 1988. "Eric Werner (1901–1988): A Bibliography of his Collected Writings." *Musica Judaica*, 10:1-36.

KATZ, Israel J., 1989. "In Memoriam: Eric Werner (1901–1988)." *Ethnomusicology*, 33:113-9.

KATZ, Israel J., 2003a. " Abraham, Otto." New Grove.

KATZ, Israel J., 2003b. "Barbeau, (Charles) Marius." New Grove.

KATZ, Israel J., 2003c. "Farmer, Henry George." New Grove.

KATZ, Israel J., 2003d. "Gerson-Kiwi, (Esther) Edith." New Grove.

KATZ, Israel J., 2003e. "Herzog, George." New Grove.

KATZ, Israel J., 2003f. "Hornbostel, Erich M(oritz) von." New Grove.

KATZ, Israel J., 2003g. "Sendrey [Szendrei], Alfred [Aladar]." New Grove.

KATZ, Israel J., 2003h. "Werner, Eric." New Grove.

KATZ, Israel J. and Pamela M. POTTER, 2003. "Danckert, Werner." New Grove.

KATZ, Ruth, 2003. *The Lachmann Problem: An Unsung Chapter in Comparative Musicology.* Jerusalem: Hebrew University Magnes Press.

KAUFMANN, Walter, 1967. *Musical Notations of the Orient.* Bloomington: Indiana University Press.

KAUFMANN, Walter, 1968. *The Ragas of North India.* Bloomington: Indiana University Press.

KAUFMANN, Walter, 1976. *The Ragas of South India.* Bloomington: Indiana University Press.

KIDSON, Frank, 1891. *Traditional Tunes: A Collection of Ballad Airs, Chiefly Obtained in Yorkshire and the South of Scotland; Together with their Appropriate Words from Broadsides and from Oral Tradition.* Oxford: Taphouse.

KIRBY, Percival, 1968. *The Musical Instruments of the Native Races of South Africa.* Johannesburg: Witwatersrand University Press (First published 1934).

KISHIBE, Shigeo, 1984. *The Traditional Music of Japan.* 2nd edition. Tokyo: Japan Foundation (First published 1966).

KISHIBE, Shigeo, 2005. *Tôdai ongaku no rekishiteki kenkyû, Gakusei-hen* (A Historical Study of the Music of the Tang Dynasty). Ôsaka: Izumi Shoin. (First published 1960).

KODÁLY, Zoltán, 1960. *Folk Music of Hungary.* London: Barrie & Rockcliff.

KOLINSKI, Mieczyslaw, 1936. "Suriname Music," in Melville and Frances Herskovits (eds.), *Suriname Folk-lore.* New York: Columbia University Press.

KOLINSKI, Mieczyslaw, 1957a. "Ethnomusicology: Its Problems and Methods." *Ethnomusicology Newsletter,* 10:1-7.

KOLINSKI, Mieczyslaw, 1957b. "Determinants of Tonal Construction in Tribal Music." *Musical Quarterly,* 43:50-6.

KOLINSKI, Mieczyslaw, 1959. "The Evaluation of Tempo." *Ethnomusicology,* 3(2):45-57.

KOLINSKI, Mieczyslaw, 1961. "Classification of Tonal Structures." *Studies in Ethnomusicology,* vol.1 (New York: Folkways), pp.38-76.

KOLINSKI, Mieczyslaw, 1962. "Consonance and Dissonance." *Ethnomusicology,* 6(2):66-74.

KOLINSKI, Mieczyslaw, 1965a. "The General Direction of Melodic Movement." *Ethnomusicology,* 9:240-64.

KOLINSKI, Mieczyslaw, 1965b. "The Structure of Melodic Movement: A New Method of Analysis." Revised version, in Mieczyslaw Kolinski (ed.), *Studies in Ethnomusicology*, vol 2 (New York: Oak Publications), pp.95-120.

KOLINSKI, Mieczyslaw,1967. "Recent Trends in Ethnomusicology." *Ethnomusicology*, 11(1):1-24.

KORSON, Rae, 1959. "The Archive of Folk Song in the Library of Congress." *The Folklore and Folk Music Archivist* (Bloomington), 2 (1):1-2; 2(2):1-2.

KORSON, Rae and Joseph C. HICKERSON, 1969. "The Willard Rhodes Collection of American Indian Music in the Archive of Folk Song." *Ethnomusicology*, 13(2):296-304.

KRADER, Barbara, 1956. "[Bibliography of] George Herzog." *Ethnomusicology*, 1 (6):11-20; 1(8):10.

KRADER, Barbara, 1958. "Bibliography: André Schaeffner." *Ethnomusicology*, 2(1):27-34.

KRADER, Barbara, 1967. "Kodály, Zoltán 16 December 1882 - 6 March 1967." *Ethnomusicology*, 11(3):386.

KRADER, Barbara, 2003. "Roberts, Helen (Heffron)." New Grove.

KUNST, Jaap, 1939. *Music in Nias*. Leiden: Brill.

KUNST, Jaap, 1942. *Music in Flores*. Leiden: Brill.

KUNST, Jaap, 1959a. *Ethnomusicology*. 3rd edition. The Hague: Nijhoff.

KUNST, Jaap, 1959b. "Memorial to Curt Sachs." *Ethnomusicology*, 3(2):71-4.

KUNST, Jaap, 1960. *Supplement to the Third Edition of Ethnomusicology*. The Hague: Nijhoff.

KUNST, Jaap, 1967. *Music in New Guinea: Three Studies*. S'Gravenhage: Nijhoff.

KUNST, Jaap, 1968. *Hindu-Javanese Musical Instruments*. The Hague: Nijhoff.

KUNST, Jaap, 1973. *Music in Java*. 2 vols. 3rd enlarged edition. The Hague: Nijhoff (First published in Dutch, 1934).

KUO-HUANG, Han, 1988. "J.A. Van Aalst and his Chinese Music." *Asian Music*, 19(2):127-30.

KURATH, Gertrude, 1958. "Memorial to Frances Densmore." *Ethnomusicology*, 2(2):70-1.

KURATH, Gertrude, 1960. "Panorama of Dance Ethnology". *Current Anthropology*, 1:233-54.

LA BORDE, J.B. de, 1780. *Esssai sur la musique anciennne et modern*, vol. 1. Paris: Pierres.

LA FAGE, J. Adrien de, 1844. *Histoire génerale de la musique et de la danse*, vol.1. Paris: Au Comptoir.

LA FLESCHE, Francis, 1900. "An Indian Allotment." *The Independent* (New York), 52 (no. 2710):2686-8.

LA FLESCHE, Francis, 1921. "The Osage Tribe: Rite of the Chiefs; Sayings of the Ancient Men," in *Thirty-sixth Annual Report of the Bureau of American Ethnology to the Secretary of the Smithsonian Institution, 1914–15*, pp. 37-597, pls. 1-23, figs. 1-15.

LA FLESCHE, Francis, 1925. "The Osage Tribe: The Rite of Vigil," in *Thirty-ninth Annual Report of the Bureau of American Ethnology to the Secretary of the Smithsonian Institution, 1917–18*, pp. 31-630, pls. 1-17, figs. 1-4.

LA FLESCHE, Francis, 1928. "The Osage Tribe: Two Versions of the Child-naming Rite," in *Forty-third Annual Report of the Bureau of American Ethnology to the Secretary of the Smithsonian Institution, 1925–26*, pp. 23-164, pls. 1-12, figs. 1-8.

LA FLESCHE, Francis, 1930. "The Osage Tribe: Rite of the Wa-xo'-be," in *Forty-fifth Annual Report of the Bureau of American Ethnology to the Secretary of the Smithsonian Institution, 1927–28*, pp. 523-833, pls. 14-29, figs. 46-47 [figure numbers duplicated].

LA RUE, Hélène, 2004. "Balfour, Henry (1863–1939)." ODNB.

LAFITAU, Père 1724. *Moeurs des sauvages ameriquains*. Paris: Saugrain.

LAMARCK, Jean-Baptiste, 1801 .*Système des animaux sans vertèbres*. Paris: Deterville.

LANDRY, Renée and Denise MÉNARD, 2001. "Barbeau, (Charles) Marius." Encyclopedia of Music in Canada. Web page: http://www.nlc-bnc.ca/music/17/m17-214-e.html

LANFER, Berthold (ed.), 1906. *Boas Anniversary Volume: Anthropological Papers Written in Honor of Franz Boas, Professor of Anthropology in Columbia University, Presented to Him on the Twenty-fifth Anniversary of his Doctorate, Ninth of August, Nineteen hundred and six*. New York: Stechert.

LEACH, Edmund, 1970. *Lévi-Strauss*. London: Fontana/Collins.

LEE, Dorothy Sara and Maria LA VIGNA (eds.), 1985. Record Notes. Omaha Indian Music: Historical Recordings from the Fletcher/La Flesche Collection. Washington, D.C.: Library of Congress.
[From web site: Omaha Indian Music Album Booklet
http://memory.loc.gov/ammem/omhhtml/omhoim2.html#acf]

LEMS-DWORKIN, Carol, 1991. *African Music: A Pan-African Annotated Bibliography.* New York: Zell.

LEVY, Mark, 1982. *Intonation in North Indian Music: A Select Comparison of Theories with Contemporary Practice.* New Delhi: Biblia Impex Private Limited.

LIBRARY OF CONGRESS, 1996. Willard Rhodes Collection. Web page: http://www.loc.gov/spcoll/198.html

LIEBERMAN, Fredric, 1979. *Chinese Music: An Annotated Bibliography.* 2nd edition. New York: Garland.

LIEBERMAN, Fredric, 1987. "In Memoriam: Ida Halpern (1910–1987)." *Ethnomusicology,* 31(3):537-8.

LIEBERMAN, Fredric, 2003. "Amiot, (Jean) Joseph (Marie)." New Grove.

LINDLEY, Mark, 1984. "Temperaments," in Sadie 1984 (3):540-55.

LING, Jan, 1990. "In Memoriam: Ernst Emsheimer." *Ethnomusicology,* 34(3):435-8.

LINTON, C. Freeman and Alan P. MERRIAM, 1956. "Statistical Classification in Anthropology: An Application to Ethnomusicology." *American Anthropologist,* 58:464-72. [Reprinted in McAllester 1971:56-64.]

LIST, George, 1963. "The Musical Significance of Transcription." *Ethnomusicology,* 7(3):193-6.

LIST, George, 1971. "On the Non-universality of Music Perspectives." *Ethnomusicology,* 15(3):399-402.

LIST, George, 1974. "The Reliability of Transcription." *Ethnomusicology,* 18(3):353-78.

LLOYD, A.L., 1944. *The Singing Englishman: An Introduction to Folksong.* London: Workers' Music Association.

LLOYD, A.L., 1967. *Folk Song in England.* London: Lawrence & Wishart.

LLOYD, A.L. (ed.), 1984. *Problems of Ethnomusicology: Constantin Brailoiu.* Cambridge: Cambridge University Press.

LOMAX, Alan, 1968. *Folk Song Style and Culture.* Washington: American Associates for the Advancement of Science.

LOMAX, Alan, 1977. "Universals in Song." *The World of Music (Berlin),* 19(1/2):117-41.

LOMAX, John A. and Alan LOMAX, 1934. *American Ballads and Folk Songs*. New York: Macmillan.

LONDON SCHOOL OF ECONOMICS, 2003. LSE Achives: Guide to Holdings: Anthropology. Web page: http://www.lse.ac.uk/library/archive/gutoho/anthropology.htm

LONERGAN, D., 1994. "Alan Lomax: An Essay and Bibliography." *Music Reference Services Quarterly*, 3(2):3-16.

LOTZ, Rainer E., 2003. The First Time of Recording outside Siam in Berlin Germany in 1900. Web page: http://waxcylinder.com/rainer.html

MACEDA, José, 1981. *A Manual of a Field Music Research with Special Reference to Southeast Asia*. Quezon City: University of the Philippines.

MacMAHON, M.K.C., 2004. "Ellis, Alexander John (1814–1890)." ODNB.

MAHILLON, Victor, 1880–1922. *Catalog descriptif et analytique du Musée instrumental du Conservatoire Royal de Bruxelles*. Ghent: Hoste.

MALM, William P., 1967. *Music Cultures of the Pacific, the Near East, and Asia*. Englewood Cliffs: Prentice-Hall.

MALTHUS, Thomas, 1798. *An Essay on the Principle of Population*. London: Johnson.

MANILA TIMES, 2004. "[Obituary] Maceda, National Artist for Music, 87." *Manila Times*, Friday, May 07, 2004.

MANUEL, Peter, 1995. "New Perspectives in American Ethnomusicology." *Revista Transcultural de Música (Transcultural Music Review)*, v1.

MARCUSE, Sibyl, 1964. *Musical Instruments: A Comprehensive Dictionary*. New York: Doubleday.

MARCUSE, Sibyl, 1975. *A Survey of Musical Instruments*. London: David & Charles.

MARR, R. and Maud KARPELES, 1964. "Obituary: Arnold A. Bake." *Journal of the International Folk Music Council*, 16:110-11.

MAULTSBY, Portia K., 1975. "Selective Bibliography: U.S. Black Music." *Ethnomusicology*, 19(3):421-9.

McALLESTER, David P., 1949. *Peyote Music*. Viking Fund Publications in Anthropology Number Thirteen. New York: Johnson Reprint Corporation.

McALLESTER, David P., 1954. *Enemy Way Music*. Reports of the Rimrock Project. Values Series, No. 3. Cambridge, Mass: The Museum.

McALLESTER, David P., 1959. "Memorial to Edwin Grant Burrows." *Ethnomusicology*, 3(1):14-17.

McALLESTER, David P., 1971a. *Readings in Ethnomusicology*. New York: Johnson Reprint Corporation.

McALLESTER, David P., 1971b. "Some Thoughts on Universals in World Music." *Ethnomusicology*, 15(3):379-80.

McALLESTER, David P., 1985. "In Memoriam: George Herzog (1901–1984)." *Ethnomusicology*, 29(1):86-7.

McALLESTER, David P., 1993. "Obituary: Willard Rhodes (1901–1992)." *Ethnomusicology*, 37(2):251-62.

McLEAN, Mervyn, 1961. "Oral Transmission in Maori Music." *Journal of the International Folk Music Council*, 13:59-62.

McLEAN, Mervyn, 1965a. Maori Chant: A Study in Ethnomusicology. PhD thesis. 2 vols. University of Otago, NZ.

McLEAN, Mervyn, 1965b. "Song Loss and Social Context Amongst the N.Z. Maori." *Ethnomusicology*, 9 (3):296-304.

McLEAN, Mervyn, 1966. "A New Method of Melodic Interval Analysis." *Ethnomusicology*, 10(2):174-90.

McLEAN, Mervyn, 1969. "Song Types of the New Zealand Maori." *Studies in Music* (Perth), 3:53-69.

McLEAN, Mervyn, 1973. "Review article: *Folk Song Style and Culture* by Alan Lomax." *Journal of the Polynesian Society*, 82(4):415-22.

McLEAN, Mervyn, 1977a. "Innovations in *Waiata* Style." *Yearbook of the International Folk Music Council*, 9:27-37.

McLEAN, Mervyn, 1977b. "New Zealand Archives: XI. The Archive of Maori and Pacific Music." *Archifacts* (Wellington), n.s. No. 2:26-30.

McLEAN, Mervyn, 1978. "New Zealand Archives: XIII. Maori Resources in the Archive of Maori and Pacific Music." *Archifacts* (Wellington), n.s. Nos. 4 & 5:82-9.

McLEAN, Mervyn, 1979. "Towards the Differentiation of Music Areas in Oceania." *Anthropos*, 74:717-36.

McLEAN, Mervyn, 1982. "The 'Rule of Eight' and Text/Music Relationships in Traditional Maori Waiata." *Anthropological Linguistics*, 24(3):280-300.

McLEAN, Mervyn, 1983. *Catalogue of Maori Purposes Fund Board Recordings Recorded by W.T. Ngata 1953–58. MPFB 1–120.* Auckland: Archive of Maori and Pacific Music.

McLEAN, Mervyn, 1984. "PreservingWorld Musics: Perspectivesfrorn NewZealand and Oceania." *Studies inMusic* (Perth), 17:23-37.
[Reprinted in Shelemay 1990:359-73.]

McLEAN, Mervyn, 1985. Review of *Problems of Ethnomusicology* by Constantin Brailoiu. *American Ethnologist*, 12(4):808-9.

McLEAN, Mervyn, 1986. "Towards a Typology of Musical Change: Missionaries and Adjustive Response in Oceania." *World of Music* (Berlin), 28(1):29-43.

McLEAN, Mervyn, 1990a. "The Archive of Maori and Pacific Music: Twenty Years On." *Archifacts* (Wellington), April: 40-4.

McLEAN, Mervyn, 1990b. "The Structure of Tikopia Music," in Firth with McLean 1990:107-24.
[Shortened version of McLean 1991a].

McLEAN, Mervyn, 1991a. *The Structure of Tikopia Music.* Occasional Papers in Pacific Ethnomusicology No.1. Auckland, Archive of Maori and Pacific Music.

McLEAN, Mervyn, 1991b. *Catalogue of Radio New Zealand Recordings of Maori Events 1938–1950 RNZ 1–60.* Auckland: Archive of Maori and Pacific Music.

McLEAN, Mervyn, 1994. *Diffusion of Musical Instruments and Their Relation to Language Migrations in New Guinea.* Kulele: Occasional Papers on Pacific Music and Dance, 1. Boroko: Cultural Studies Division, National Research Institute.

McLEAN, Mervyn, 1995. *An Annotated Bibliography of Oceanic Music and Dance.* Revised and enlarged 2nd edition. Warren, MI: Harmonie Park Press.

McLEAN, Mervyn, 1996. *Maori Music.* Auckland; Auckland University Press.

McLEAN, Mervyn, 1999. *Weavers of Song: Polynesian Music and Dance.* Auckland: Auckland University Press.

McLEAN, Mervyn, 2004. *To Tatau Waka: In Search of Maori Music.* Auckland: Auckland University Press.

McLEAN, Mervyn and Jeny CURNOW, 1992a. *Catalogue of McLean Collection Recordings of Traditional Maori Songs 1958–1979 McL 1–1283.* Auckland: Archive of Maori and Pacific Music.

McLEAN, Mervyn and Jeny CURNOW, 1992b. *Catalogue of Museum of New Zealand Recordings of Traditional Maori Songs 1919–c.1935*. Auckland: Archive of Maori and Pacific Music.

McLEAN, Mervyn and Margaret ORBELL, 2004. *Traditional Songs of the Maori*. 3rd edition, with CDs. Auckland: Auckland University Press (First published 1975).

McLEOD, Norma, 1957. The Social Context of Music in a Polynisian Community. MA thesis, London School of Economics, London.

McNUTT, James C., 1984. "John Comfort Fillmore: A Student of Indian Music Reconsidered." *American Music*, 2(1):61-70.

McPHEE, Colin, 1946. *A House in Bali*. New York: Day.

McPHEE, Colin, 1966. *Music in Bali*. New Haven: Yale University Press.

McVEAGH, Diana, 2004. "Howes, Frank Stewart (1891–1974)." ODNB.

MELVILLE, Annette, 1980. "Peabody Museum Collection," in Special Collections in the Library of Congress. Web page: http://www.loc.gov/spcoll/181.html

MERRIAM, Alan P., 1954a. *A Bibliography of Jazz*. Philadephia: The American Folklore Society.

MERRIAM, Alan P. (ed.), 1954b. "[Bibliography of] Erich Moritz von Hornbostel." *Ethnomusicology*, 1(2):8-15; 1(3):7.

MERRIAM, Alan P. (ed.), 1956–57. "[Bibliography of] Frances Densmore." *Ethnomusicology*, 1(7):14-29; 1(10):15.

MERRIAM, Alan P. (ed.), 1958. "[Bibliography of Frances Densmore: Errata and Additions." *Ethnomusicology*, 2(1):26.

MERRIAM, Alan P., 1960. "Ethnomusicology: Discussion and Definition of the Field." *Ethnomusicology*, 4(3):107-14.

MERRIAM, Alan P., 1962. "African Music," in William Bascom and Melville J. Herskovits (eds.), *Continuity and Change in African Cultures*. Chicago: University of Chicago Press, pp.49-86.

MERRIAM, Alan P., 1963. "Melville Herskovits 1895–1963." *Ethnomusicology*, 7(2):79-82.

MERRIAM, Alan P., 1964a. *The Anthropology of Music*. Northwestern University Press.

MERRIAM, Alan P., 1964b. Review of Hood "Music the Unknown," in Harrison, Hood and Palisca 1963. *Ethnomusicology*, 8(2):179-85.

MERRIAM, Alan P., 1965. "The Importance of Song in the Flathead Indian Vision Quest." *Ethnomusicology*, 9(2):91-9.

MERRIAM, Alan P., 1967. *Ethnomusicology of the Flathead Indians*. Chicago: Aldine.

MERRIAM, Alan P., 1973. "Richard Alan Waterman 1914–1971." *Ethnomusicology*, 17(1):72-94.

MERRIAM, Alan P., 1977. "Definitions of 'Comparative Musicology', and 'Ethnomusicology': An Historical-Theoretical Perspective." *Ethnomusicology*, 21(2):189-204.

MERRIAM, Alan P., 1982. "On Objections to Comparison in Ethnomusicology," in Falck & Rice 1982:174-89.

METFESSEL, Milton, 1928. *Phonophotography in Folk Music*. Chapel Hill: University of Carolina Press.

MEYER, Leanard B., 1956. *Emotion and Meaning in Music*. Chicago & London: University of Chicago Press.

MEYER, Leonard B., 1960. "Universalism and Relativism in the Study of Ethnic Music." *Ethnomusicology*, 4(2):49-54.
[Reprinted in McAllester 1971:269-76.]

MIKAEL, 2002. The Founding of Universities. Web page: http://130.238.50.3/ilmh/Ren/bibl-TIMELINE-univ.htm

MILLER, Geoffrey F., 2000. "Evolution of Human Music Through Sexual Selection," in N.L. Wallin et al. 2000:329-60.

MILLER, Hugh, 1964. "A Data Check-list for the Study of Ethnic Dance." *Ethnomusicology*, 8(1):55-7.

MINNESOTA HISTORICAL SOCIETY, 2002. Minnesota Author Biographies Project: Francis Densmore Biographical Notes. Web page: http://people.mnhs.org/authors/biog_detail.cfm?PersonID=Dens195

MOCKLER-FERRYMAN, A.F. (ed.), 1901. *The Oxfordshire Light Infantry in South Africa: A Narrative of the Boer War*. London: Eyre & Spottiswoode.

MONTAGU, Jeremy, 1997. Review of McLean 1994. *Galpin Society Journal*, 50:252-3.

MORGAN, Paula, 2003. "Crossley-Holland, Peter." New Grove.

MORGAN, Paula and Sue Carole DeVALE, 2003. "Wachsmann, Klaus P(hilipp)." New Grove.

MORGAN, Paula and Bruno NETTL, 2003. "Merriam, Alan P(arkhurst)." New Grove.

MOYLE, Alice M., 1971. "Source Materials: Aboriginal Music of Australia and New Guinea." *Ethnomusicology*, 15(1):81-9.

MOYLE, Richard, 1979. *Songs of the Pintupi*. Canberra: Australian Institute of Aboriginal Studies.

MOYLE, Richard, 1986. *Alyawara Music*. Canberra: Australian Institute of Aboriginal Studies.

MUSEUM OF FINE ARTS, 2003. MFA Collections: Musical Instruments. Web page: http://www.mfa.org/artemis/collections/mi.htm

MYERS, Charles S., 1911. "Music of the Veddas," in Charles G. and Brenda Seligman, *The Veddas*. Cambridge: Cambridge University Press.

MYERS, Charles S., 1912. "Music." Chapter 12 in Alfred C. Haddon (ed.), *Reports of the Cambridge Anthropological Expedition to Torres Straits*, vol. 4. Cambridge: Cambridge University Press.

MYERS, Charles S., 1913–14. "A Study of Sarawak Music." *Sammelbände der InternationalenMusikgesellschaft*, 15:206ff.

MYERS, Charles S., 1936. "Charles Samuel Myers," in Carl Murchison (ed.), *A History of Psychology in Autobiography*. New York: Russell & Russell, vol. III, pp.215-30.

MYERS, Helen (ed.), 1992. *Ethnomusicology: An Introduction*. London: Macmillan.

MYERS, Helen, 1993. *Ethnomusiclology: Historical and Regional Studies*. London: Macmillan.

NADEL, Siegfried F., 1930. "The Origin of Music." *Music Quarterly*, 16:531-8. [Reprinted in McAllester 1971:277-89.]

NADEL, Siegried F., 1931. *Ferruccio Busoni 1866–1924*. Leipzig: Breitkopf & Härtel.

NATTIEZ, Jean-Jacques, 1977, "Under What Conditions Can One Speak of the Universals of Music?" *The World of Music* (Berlin), 19(1/2):92-116.

NELSON, Lesley, 2003. Francis J. Child Ballads. Web page: http://www.contemplator.com/history/childbio.html

NELSON, Steven G. (comp.), 2003. *Annotated Bibliography of the Major Publications of Dr. Kishibe Shigeo: In Celebration of His Ninetieth Birthday*. Tokyo: Kishibe Shigeo Hakushi Sotsuju Kinen Jigyo Iinkai (Committee for the Commemoration of the Ninetieth Birthday of Dr. Kishibe Shigeo).

NETTL, Bruno, 1954. *North American Indian Musical Styles*. Philadelphia: American Folklore Society.

NETTL, Bruno, 1956. *Music in Primitive Culture*. Cambridge, Mass.: Harvard University Press.

NETTL, Bruno, 1964. *Theory and Method in Ethnomusicology*. New York: Free Press of Glencoe.

NETTL, Bruno, 1965. *Folk and Traditional Music of the Western Continents*. Englewood Cliffs: Prentice-Hall.

NETTL, Bruno, 1967. *Reference Materials in Ethnomusicology: A Bibliographic Essay*. 2nd. edition. Detroit: Information Coordinators (First published 1961).

NETTL, Bruno, 1977. "On the Question of Universals." *The World of Music* (Berlin), 19(1/2):2-13.

NETTL, Bruno (ed.), 1978a. *Eight Urban Musical Cultures.* Urbana: Univeristy of Illinois Press.

NETTL, Bruno, 1978b. "Some Aspects of the History of World Music in the Twentieth Century: Questions, Problems, and Concepts." *Ethnomusicology*, 22(l):123-36.

NETTL, Bruno, 1981. "George Herzog: An 80th Birthday Appreciation." *Ethnomusicology*, 25(3):499-500.

NETTL, Bruno, 1983. *The Study of Ethnomusicology: Twenty-nine Issues and Concepts*. Urbana: University of Illinois Press.

NETTL, Bruno, 1988. "The IFMC/ICTM and the Development of Ethnomusicology in the United States." *Yearbook for Traditional Music*, 20:19-25.

NETTL, Bruno, 1989. *Blackfoot Musical Thought.* Kent, Ohio: Kent State University Press.

NETTL, Bruno, 1991. "The Dual Nature of Ethnomusicology in North America: The Contribution of Charles Seeger and George Herzog," in Nettl and Bohlman 1991:266-76.

NETTL, Bruno, 1992.*The Radif of Persian Music.* 2nd edition. Champaign, Il: Elephant & Cat.

NETTL, Bruno, 1995a. "The Seminal Eighties: A North American Perspective of the Beginnings of Musicology and Ethnomusicology." *Revista Transcultural de Música (Transcultural Music Review)*, v1.

NETTL, Bruno, 1995b. *Heartland Excursions: Ethnomusicological: Reflections on Schools of Music*. Urbana: University of Illinois Press.

NETTL, Bruno, 1998. Bruno Nettl. Web page: http://www.anthro.uiuc.edu/faculty/nettl/

NETTL, Bruno, 2002. *Encounters in Ethnomusicology: A Memoir*. Detroit Monographs in Musicology/Studies in Music, No. 36. Warren, Michigan: Harmonie Park Press.

NETTL, Bruno, 2003. "Waterman, Richard Alan." New Grove.

NETTL, Bruno and Philip BOHLMAN (eds.), 1991. *Comparative Musicology and Anthropology of Music: Essays in the History of Ethnomusicology*. Chicago: University of Chicago Press.

Neue deutsche Biographie / herausgegeben von der Historischen Kommission bei der Bayerischen Akademie der Wissenschaften, c.1953–c.2001. Berlin: Duncker & Humblot.

NEUMANN, K.L., 1965. "Special Bibliography: Hans Hickmann." *Ethnomusicology*, 9(1):45-53.

NEWTON, Isaac, 1686. *Principia Philosophiæ Naturalis Principia Mathematica*. Londini: Streater.

NICHOLLS, David, 1990. *American Experimental Music: 1890–1940*. Cambridge: Cambridge University Press.

NICHOLS, Frances S., [1919]. *Biography and Bibliography of Jesse Walter Fewkes*. [Washington].

NOBLITT, T. (ed.), 1981. *Music East and West: Essays in Honor of Walter Kaufmann*. New York: Pendragon Press.

OJA, Carol J., 2003. "McPhee, Colin (Carhart)." New Grove.

OJA, Carol J., 2004. *Colin McPhee: Composer in Two Worlds*. Urbana & Chicago: University of Illinois Press.

ONIONS, G.T. (ed.), 1959. *Shorter Oxford English Dictionary*. 2 vols. 3rd edition (with corrections). Oxford: Clarendon Press.

ORBELL, Margaret and Mervyn McLEAN, 2002. *Songs of a Kaumātua*. Auckland: Auckland University Press.

PACKARD, Alpheus S., 1901. *Lamarck, the Founder of Evolution: His Life and Work*. New York etc.: Longmans, Green.

PANTALEONI, Hewitt, 1972. Review of Lomax 1968. *Yearbook of the International Folk Music Council*, 4:158-61.

PEARSON, Hesketh, 1930. *Doctor Darwin*. London & Toronto: Dent.

PENNSYLVANIA STATE UNIVERSITY, 1997. Intercom On Line Volume 26, Issue 18. Web page: http://www.psu.edu/ur/archives/intercom_1997/Jan30/CURRENT/news4.html

PERLIS, Vivian, 1995. Review of Pescatello 1992. *Ethnomusicology*, 39(2):290-2.

PESCATELLO, Ann M., 1992. *Charles Seeger: A Life in American Music*. Pittsburgh, PA: University of Pittsburgh Press.

PESCATELLO, Ann M., 2003. "Seeger (1) Charles (Louis) Seeger." New Grove.

PIGGOTT, Sir Francis, 1893. *The Music and Musical Instruments of Japan*. London: Batsford.

PLATT, Peter and Ian WOODFIELD, 2003. "Jones, Sir William (ii)." New Grove.

PORTER, James, 1995. "New Perspectives in Ethnomusicology: A Critical Survey." *Revista Transcultural de Música (Transcultural Music Review)*, v1.

PORTER, James, 2001. "Peter Crossley-Holland (January 28, 1916–April 27, 2001." *SEM Newsletter*, 35(4):17.

PORTER, James, 2002. "The Distant Isles: The Scholarship and Music of Peter Crossley-Holland (1916–2001)." *Ethnomusicology*, 46(2):323-9.

PORTER, James, 2003a. "Barry, Phillips." New Grove.

PORTER, James, 2003b. "Bayard, Samuel Preston." New Grove.

PORTER, James, 2003c. "Bronson, Bertrand Harris." New Grove.

PORTER, James and Timothy RICE et al. (eds.), 1997–2002. *The Garland Encyclopedia of World Music*. 10 vols. New York: Garland.

POST, Jennifer, 2004. *Ethnomusicology: A Research and Information Guide*. New York & London: Routledge.

POST, Jennifer, Mary Russell BUCKNUM and Laurel SERCOMBE, 1994. *A Manual for Documentation, Fieldwork, and Preservation for Ethnomusicologogists*. Bloomington: The Society of Ethnomusicology.

POTTER, Pamela M., 2003. "Lach, Robert." New Grove.

POWELL, Jim, 1995. "Herbert Spencer: Liberty and Unlimited Human Progress." *The Freeman*, Vol. 45, No. 4.

POWERS, Harold S., 1962. Review of Kolinski 1961. *Ethnomusicology*, 6(3):220-8.

PRAETORIUS, Michael, 1619. *Syntagma musicum ex veterum & recentorium ecclesiasticorum autorum lectione. . . Tomus secundus: De Organographia*. Wolfenbüttel: Holwein.

PRESCOTT, William Hickling, 1843. *History of the Conquest of Mexico*. 3 vols. London: Bentley.

PROKOP, Manfred, 2003. Biographical Dictionary of Austrians in Canada. Web page: http://www.arts.ualberta.ca/CCAuCES/dictionary/start.htm

PUGH-KITINGAN, Jaqueline, 1982. "Language Communication and Instrumental Music in Papua New Guinea: Comments on the Huli and Samberigi Cases." *Musicology* (Melbourne), 7:104-79.

PUGH-KITINGAN, Jaqueline, 1984. "Speech-tone Realisation in Huli Music," in Jamie C. Kassler and Uill Stubington (eds.), *Problems and Solutions: Occasional Essays in Musicology Presented to Alice M. Moyle*. Sydney: Hale & Iremonger, pp.95-120.

RAHKONEN, Carl, 1985. "In Memoriam Walter Kaufmann (1907–1984)." *Ethnomusicology*, 29(1):88-9.

RAHKONEN, Carl, 1998. "Special Bibliography: Natalie Curtis (1875–1921)." *Ethnomusicology*, 42(3):511-22.

RAHKONEN, Carl, 2003. The Real Song Catchers: American Women Pioneers of Ethnomusicology. A paper presented at the Music Library Association, Women's Music Round Table, Austin, Texas, February 14, 2003. Web page: http://www.people.iup.edu/rahkonen/WP/real_song_catchers.htm

RAINBOW, Bernarr, 2003. "Baring-Gould, Sabine." New Grove.

RANDEL, Don (ed.), 1986. *The New Harvard Dictionary of Music*. Cambridge, Mass.: Belknap Press.

RANDEL, Don (ed.), 2003. *The Harvard Dictionary of Music*. 4th edition. Cambridge, Mass.: Belknap Press.

READE, William Winwood, 1876. *The Martyrdom of Man*. New York: Somerby.

REESE, Gustave, 1949. *Music in the Middle Ages*. New York: Norton.

REEVES, James, 1958. *The Idiom of the People*. London: Mercury Books.

REEVES, James, 1960. *The Everlasting Circle*. London: Heinemann.

REINHARD, Kurt, 1962. "The Berlin Phonogramm-Archiv." *The Folklore and Folk Music Archivist* (Bloomington), 5(2):1-4.
[Reprinted in McAllester 1971:17-23.]

RHODES, Willard, 1958. "A Study of Music Diffusion Based on the Wandering of the Opening Peyote Song." *Journal of the International Folk Music Council*, 10:42-9.
[Reprinted in McAllester 1971:132-41.]

RHODES, Willard, 1977. "Memorial Obituary: Maud Karpeles, 1885–1976." Ethnomusicology, 21(2):283-8.

RHODES, Willard, 1979. "Charles Seeger (1886–1979)." *Ethnomusicology*, 23(2):177-8.

RHODES, Willard, 2003. "Densmore, Frances." New Grove.

RICE, Timothy, 1987. "Toward a Remodeling of Ethnomusicology." *Ethnomusicology*, 31(3):469-88, with responses and a reply, pp.489-516.

ROHDE, Joy Elizabeth, 2000. Register to the Papers of Alice Cunningham Fletcher and Francis La Flesche. Washington, DC.: Smithsonian Institution. [Includes biographical chronologies]. Web page: http://www.nmnh.si.edu/naa/fa/fletcher_la_flesche.htm#chronology1

RINGER, Alexander, 1969. "Editor's Introduction." *Yearbook of the International Folk Music Council*, 1:3-7.

RINGER, Alexander, 1991. "One World or None?: Untimely Reflections on a Timely Musicological Question," in Nettl and Bohlman 1991:187-98.

ROBERTS, Helen H., 1926. *Ancient Hawaiian Music*. Honolulu: B.P. Bishop Museum Bulletin, 19.

ROBERTS, Helen H., 1936. *Musical Areas in Aboriginal North America*. Publications in Anthropology, 12. New Haven: Yale University Press.

ROBERTS, Helen H., 1967. "Special Bibliography: Helen Heffron Roberts." *Ethnomusicology*, 11(2):228-33.

ROHNER, Ronald P. (ed.), 1969. *The Ethnography of Franz Boas*. Chicago: University of Chicago Press..

ROUGET, Gilbert, 1981. "In Memoriam: André Schaeffner (1895–1980)." *Ethnomusicology*, 25(1):99-101.

ROUGET, Gilbert, 1984. "Preface," in Brailoiu 1984:vii-xviii.

ROUGET, Gilbert, 2003. "Brailoiu, Constantin." New Grove.

ROUNDER RECORDS, 2003. The Alan Lomax Collection. Web page: http://www.rounder.com/series/lomax_alan/timeline.htm

ROUSSEAU, Jean Jacque, 1767. *Dictionnaire de la musique*. Paris.

ROUTLEDGE, Robert, 1898. *Discoveries and Inventions of the Nineteenth Century*. 12th edition. London: Routledge.

ROW, Peter, 1984. Review of Levy 1982. *Ethnomusicology*, 28(1):154-6.

ROYAL ANTHROPOLOGICAL INSTITUTE OF GREAT BRITAIN AND IRELAND, 1951. *Notes and Queries on Anthropology*. 6th edition. London: Routledge & Kegan Paul.

ROYAL SOCIETY, 2003. List of Fellows of the Royal Society 1660–2003. Web page: http://www.royalsoc.ac.uk/library/fell_list.htm

RSA ARCHIVE, 2003. Web page catalogue: http://www.rsa.org.uk/rsa/archive.asp

RUSSELL, Bertrand, 1946. *A History of Western Philosophy*. London: Allen & Unwin.

RYAN, Robin, 1997. "The Published Works of Catherine Ellis." *Musicology Australia*, 20:4-5

SACHS, Curt, 1913. *Reallexikon der Musikinstrumente*. Berlin: Bard.

SACHS, Curt, 1914. *Die Musikinstrumente Indiens und Indonesiens*. Berlin & Leipzig: de Gruyter.

SACHS, Curt, 1920. *Handbuch der Musikinstrumentenkunde*. Leipzig: Breitkopf & Härtel.

SACHS, Curt, 1937. *World History of the Dance*. New York: Norton.

SACHS, Curt, 1940. *The History of Musical Instruments*. New York: Norton.

SACHS, Curt, 1943. *The Rise of Music in the Ancient World, East and West*. New York: Norton.

SACHS, Curt, 1953. *Rhythm and Tempo: A Study in Music History*. New York: Norton.

SACHS, Curt, 1956. *A Short History of World Music*. Rev. second edtion. London: Dobson.

SACHS, Curt, 1961. *The Wellsprings of Music: An Introduction to Ethnomusicology*. The Hague: Nijhoff.

SACHS, Curt and E.M. von HORNBOSTEL, 1914. "Systematik der Musikinstrumente." *Zeitschrift für Ethnologie*, 46:553-90.

SADIE, Stanley (ed.), 1980. *The New Grove Dictionary of Music and Musicians*. 20 vols. London: Macmillan.

SADIE, Stanley (ed.), 1984. *The New Grove Dictionary of Musical Instruments*. 3 vols. London: Macmillan.

SALAT, Jana, 2004. "Nadel, Siegfried Ferdinand Stephan (1903–1956)." ODNB.

SALISBURY, Kevin, 1983. Pukapukan People and Their Music. MA thesis in music. University of Auckland.

SALTER, Lionel, 2003. "Harich-Schneider, Eta." New Grove.

SASLAW, Janna, 2003. "Hauptmann, Moritz." New Grove.

SCHMIDL, Carlo, 1926–38. *Dizionario universale dei musicisti*. 2 vols. and supplement. Milan: Sonzogno.

SCHNEIDER, Marius, 1957. " I. Primitive Music," in Wellesz 1957:1-82.

SCHNEIDER, Marius, 1969. *Geschichte der Mehrstimmigkeit*. Tutzing: Schneider (First published 1934).

SCHOLES, Percy A., 1953. *The Life and Activities of Sir John Hawkins, Musician, Magistrate, and Friend of Johnson*. London: Oxford University Press.

SCHOLES, Percy A., 1972a. *The Oxford Companion to Music*. 10th edition. London: Oxford University Press.

SCHOLES, Percy A., 1972b. "The Problem of 'Touch' as Related to Tone Quality," in Scholes 1972a:803-4.

SCHOTT, Howard, 2003a. "In Memoriam—Sibyl Marcuse (Februay 13, 1911–March 5 2003)." *Newsletter of the American Musical Instrument Society*, 32 (3):15-16.

SCHOTT, Howard, 2003b. "Marcuse, Sibyl." New Grove.

SCHÜLLER, Dietrich et al. (eds.), 2000. Series 3: Papua New Guinea (1904-1909): The collections of Rudolf Pöch, Wilhelm Schmidt, and Josef Winthuis. 5 CDs, 1 CD-ROM, and Booklet. . Wien: Verlag der Österreichischen Akademie der Wissenschaften.

SCHUURSMA, Ann Briegleb, 1991. *Ethnomusicology Research: A Select Annotated Bibliography*. New York: Garland.

SEASHORE, Carl E., 1938. *Psychology of Music*. New York: McGraw-Hill.

SEEGER, Anthony, 1979. "What Can We Learn When They Sing?: Vocal Genres of the Suya Indians of Central Brazil." *Ethnomusicology*, 23(3):373-94.

SEEGER, Anthony, 1992. "Chapter IV Ethnography of Music," in Myers 1992:88-109.

SEEGER, Anthony, 1987. *Why Suya Sing: A Musical Anthropology of an Amazonian People*. Cambridge: Cambridge University Press.

SEEGER, Charles, 1930. "On Dissonant Counterpoint." *Modern Music*, 7(4):25-31.

SEEGER, Charles, 1951. "An Instantaneous Music Notator." *Journal of the International Folk Music Council*, 3:103-6.

SEEGER, Charles, 1958. "Prescriptive and Descriptive Music Writing." *Musical Quarterly*, 44:184-95.
[Reprinted in McAllester 1971:24-34.]

SEEGER, Charles, 1970. "Toward a Unitary Field Theory for Musicology." *Selected Reports*, 1(3):171-210.

SEEGER, Charles, 1971. "Reflections upon a Given Topic: Music in Universal Perspective." *Ethnomusicology*, 15(3):385-98.

SEEGER, Charles, 1977. *Studies in Musicology: 1935–1975*. Berkeley & Los Angeles: University of California Press.

SEEGER, Charles and Bonnie WADE (eds.), 1977. *Essays for a Humanist: An Offering to Klaus Wachsmann*. New York: Town House Press.

SENDREY, Alfred, 1951. *Bibliography of Jewish Music*. New York: Columbia University Press.

SENDREY, Alfred, 1969. *Music in Ancient Israel*. New York: Philosophical Library.

SENDREY, Alfred, 1970. *The Music of the Jews in the Diaspora (up to 1800): A Contribution to the Social and Cultural History of the Jews*. New York: Yoseloff.

SENDREY, Alfred, 1974. *Music in the Social and Religious Life of Antiquity*. Rutherford, NJ: Fairleigh Dickinson University.

SHARP, Cecil, 1904–09. *Folk Songs from Somerset: Gathered and Edited with Pianoforte Accompaniment*. London: Simpkin.

SHARP, Cecil, 1907. *English Folk Song: Some Conclusions*. London: Simpkin.

SHARP, Cecil, 1907–13. *The Morris Book*. London: Novello.

SHAY, Frank, 1932. *Incredible Pizarro - Conqueror of Peru*. New York: Mohawk Press.

SHELEMAY, Kay Kaufman (ed.), 1990. *The Garland Library of Readings in Ethnomusicology, Volume 1: History, Definitions, and Scope of Ethnomusicology*. New York & London: Garland.

SHERMER, Michael, 2005. " Rupert's Resonance." *Scientific American*, 293(5):38.

SIMON Artur (ed.), 2000. *Das Berliner Phonogramm-Archiv 1900–2000. Sammlungen der traditionellen Musik der Welt. / The Berlin Phonogramm-Archiv 1900–2000. Collections of Traditional Music of the World*. Berlin: VWB - Verlag für Wissenschaft und Bildung.

SIMPSON, George Eaton, 1973. *Melville J. Herskovits*. New York: Columbia University Press.

SLOCOMBE, Marie, 1964. "The BBC Folk Music Collection." *The Folklore and Folk Music Archivist* (Bloomington), 7(1):2-13.

SMITHSONIAN INSTITUTION, 1998. Jesse Walter Fewkes 1850–1930. Web page: http://www.mnh.si.edu/anthro/laexped/fewkessns.htm

SOCIETY FOR ETHNOMUSICOLOGY, 2003. About the Society for Ethnomusicology. Web page: http://www.ethnomusicology.org/aboutsem/mission.html

SONG, Bang Song, 1971. *An Annotated Bibliography of Korean Music*. Providence, RI: Brown University.

SORRENSON, M.P.K., 1986–88 (ed.). *Na To Hoa Aroha: From Your Dear Friend:The Correspondence between Sir Apirana Ngata and Sir Peter Buck, 1925–50*. 3 vols. Auckland: Auckland University Press.

SPIESSENS, Godelieve and Sylvie JANSSENS, 2003. "Collaer, Paul." New Grove.

SPIETH-WEISSENBACHER, Christiane, 2003. "Marcel-Dubois, Claudie." New Grove.

SPIETH-WEISSENBACHER, Christiane and Jean GRIBENSKI, 2003a. "Daniélou, Alain." New Grove.

SPIETH-WEISSENBACHER, Christiane and Jean GRIBENSKI, 2003b. "Schaeffner, André." New Grove.

SPENCER, Herbert, 1851. *Social Statics: or, The Conditions Essential to Human Happiness Specified and the First of Them Developed*. London: Chapman.

SPENCER, Herbert, 1854. "On the Origins of Music," in *Illustrations of Universal Progress: A Series of Discussions*.

SPENCER, Herbert, 1857. "Progress: Its Law and Causes." *The Westminster Review*, 67:445-447, 451, 454-6, 464-5.

SPENCER, Herbert, 1904. *An Autobiography*. 2 vols. London: Williams & Norgate.

SPENCER, Herbert, 1911. *Essays in Education*. Everyman's Library No. 504. London: Dent.

STAFFORD, William C., 1830. *A History of Music*. Edinburgh: Constable.

STANNER, W.F.H., 1956. "Siegfried Frederick Nadel 1903–1956." *Oceania*, 27(1):1-11.

STEELE, Joshua, 1775a. "Account of a Musical Instrument Which Was Brought by Captain Fourneaux from the Isle of Amsterdam in the South Seas to London in the Year 1774." *Philosophical Transactions of the Royal Society of London*, 65:67-71.

STEELE, Joshua, 1775b. "Remarks on a Larger System of Reed Pipes from the Isle of Amsterdam, with Some Observatons on the Nose Flute of Otaheiti." *Philosophical Transactions of the Royal Society of London*, 65:72-8.

STEPHEN, Leslie and Sidney LEE (eds.), 1908–09. *The Dictionary of National Biography*. 22 vols. London: Smith, Elder.

STEVENSON, Robert, 1968. *Music in Aztec and Inca Territories*. Berkeley & Los Angeles: University of California Press.

STEVENSON, Robert, 1994. "Luis Felipe Ramón y Rivera (1913–1993)." *Inter-American Music Review*, 14(1):163-4.

STEVENSON, Robert, 2006. "Isabel Aretz (1908-2005)." *Ethnomusicology Newsletter*, 40(1):31.

STOCKMANN, Doris, 1991. "Interdisciplinary Approaches to the Study of Musical Communication Structures," in Nettl and Bohlman 1991:318-41.

STUBINGTON, Jill, 1984. "Alice M. Moyle: An Australian Voice," in Jamie C. Kassler and Jill Stubington (eds.), *Problems & Solutions : Occasional Essays in Musicology Presented to Alice M. Moyle*. Sydney: Hale & Iremonger, pp.358-81.

STUMPF, Carl, 1883–90. *Tonpsychologie*. 2 vols. Leipzig: Hirzel.

STUMPF, Carl, 1886a. "Lieder der Bellakula Indianer." *Vierteljahrschrift für Musikwissenschaft*, 2:405-26.

STUMPF, Carl, 1886b. Review of Ellis 1885. *Vierteljahrschrift für Musikwissenschaft*, 2:511-24.

STUMPF, Carl, 1887. "Mongolische Gesänge." *Vierteljahrschrift für Musikwissenschaft*, 3:297-304.

STUMPF, Carl, 1892. "Phonographierte Indianermelodien." *Vierteljahrschrift für Musikwissenschaft*, 8:127-44.

SUCHOFF, Benjamin (ed.), 1992. *Béla Bartók Essays*. Lincoln: University of Nebraska Press (First published 1976).

SUCHOFF, Benjamin (ed. & transl.), 1997. *Béla Bartók Studies in Ethnomusicology*. Lincoln: University of Nebraska Press.

SUNDARAM, V., 1986. "Ambassador Between the East and West." *The Hindu*, Sunday, July 27, 1986. Web page: http://www.iisc.ernet.in/ssangha/archives/articles/jones.html

SUPPAN, Wolfgang, 1971. "Werner Danckert 1900–1970." *Ethnomusicology*, 15(1):94-9.

SWEET, William, 2001. "Herbert Spencer (1820–1903)," in The Internet Encyclopedia of Philosophy. Web page: http://www.utm.edu/research/iep/s/spencer.htm

TAGORE, Sourindro Mohun, 1875. *Yantra Kosha: or a Trewsury of the Musical Instruments of Ancient and Modern India and Various Other Countries*. Calcutta: Ghose.

TAGORE, Sourindro Mohun, 1882. *Hindu Music from Various Authors*. Calcutta: Bose.

TAGORE, Sourindro Mohun, 1894. *The Musical Scales of the Hindus with Remarks on the Applicability of Harmony to Hindu Music*. Calcutta: Bose.

TAGORE, Sourindro Mohun, 1896. *Universal History of Music: Compiled from Diverse Sources*. Calcutta.

TALLIÁN, Tibor, 2003. "Kodály, Zoltán." New Grove.

TEIGNMOUTH, Baron John Shore, 1806. *Memoirs of the Life, Writings and Correspondence of Sir William Jones*. 2nd edition. London: Hatchard.

The Living Composers Project, 2004. Web page: http://composers21.com/compdocs/macedaj.htm

The Virtual Laboratory, 2003. Max Planck Institute for the History of Science. Web page: http://vlp.mpiwg-berlin.mpg.de/index.html

THIEME, Darius L., 1964. *African Music; A Briefly Annotated Bibliography*. Washington: Library of Congress Music Division.

THIEME, Darius L., 2003. "(2) Alan Lomax." New Grove.

THIÉRY, Maurice, n.d. *Bougainville, soldat et marin*. Paris: Roger.

THOMAS, W.R. and J.J.K. RHODES, 2003. "Ellis [Sharpe], Alexander J(ohn)." New Grove.

THOMPSON, Herbert et al., 2003. "Kidson, Frank." New Grove.

THOMPSON, Oscar (ed.), 1964. *International Cyclopedia of Music and Musicians*. 9th edition. London: Dent.

TRACEY, Hugh T., 1961. "The International Library of African Music." *The Folklore and Folk Music Archivist* (Bloomington), 4(2):1-3.

TRACEY, Hugh T., 1969. *Codification of African Music and Textbook Project: A Primer of Practical Suggestions for Field Research*. Roodeport: International Library of African Music.

TRACEY, Hugh T., 1970. *Chopi Musicians: Their Music, Poetry and Instruments*. London: Oxford University Press (First published 1948).

TRÂN VAN KHÊ, 1977. "Is the Pentatonic Universal? A Few Reflectionson Pentatonism." *The World of Music* (Berlin), 19(1/2):76-91.

TRASOFF, David, 2003. "Tagore, Sir Sourindro Mohun." New Grove.

TRIMILLOS, Ricardo, 2005. "In Memoriam: José Maceda (1917–2004)." *Ethnomusicology Newsletter*, 39(1):14-16.

TSUGE, Gen'ichi, 1986. *Japanese Music: An Annotated Bibliography*. New York: Garland.

TSUKADA, Kenichi, 2005. "Obituary: Dr. Shigeo Kishibe." *Bulletin of the International Council for Traditional Music*, 106:59-60.

TURK, Ivan, 2003. Neanderthal Flute. Web page: Republic of Slovenia: Slovensko Government Public Relations and Media Office.
http://www.uvi.si/eng/slovenia/background-information/neanderthal-flute/

TYRRELL, John, 2003. "Kirby, Percival (Robson)." New Grove.

UCLA ASIA INSTITUTE, 2002. Mantle Hood receives USINDO Award. Web page:
http://international.ucla.edu/asia/article.asp?parentid=2097

UCLA ETHNOMUSICOLOGY ARCHIVE, 2003a. Baké, Arnold. Web page:
http://www.ethnomusic.ucla.edu/Archive/biobake.htm

UCLA ETHNOMUSICOLOGY ARCHIVE, 2003b. McPhee, Colin. Web page:
http://www.ethnomusic.ucla.edu/Archive/biomcphee.htm

UCLA ETHNOMUSICOLOGY ARCHIVE, 2003c. Rhodes, Willard. Web page:
http://www.ethnomusic.ucla.edu/Archive/biorhodes.htm

UCLA ETHNOMUSICOLOGY ARCHIVE, 2003d. Wachsmann, Klaus. Web page:
http://www.ethnomusic.ucla.edu/Archive/biowachsmann.htm

UCLA ETHNOMUSICOLOGY ARCHIVE, 2004. Maceda, Jose (1917–2004). Web page:
http://www.ethnomusic.ucla.edu/Archive/biomaceda.htm

UNIVERSITÄTSBIBLIOTHEK FREIBURG, 2001. Nachlass Werner Danckert. Web page:
http://www.ub.uni-freiburg.de/sls/danckert.html

UNIVERSITY OF CALIFORNIA, 2003. University of California: In Memoriam, 1986: Bertrand H. Bronson, English: Berkeley. Web page:
http://dynaweb.oac.cdlib.org:8088/dynaweb/uchist/public/inmemoriam/inmemoriam1986/@Generic__BookTextView/856

UNIVERSITY OF CAPETOWN, 2003. The Percival R. Kirby Collection. Web page:
http://web.uct.ac.za/depts/sacm/kirby.htm

UNIVERSITY OF LONDON LIBRARY, 2003a. Arnold Adrian Baké. Web page: http://www.aim25.ac.uk/cgi-bin/search2?coll_id=159&inst_id=19

UNIVERSITY OF LONDON LIBRARY, 2003b. HIPKINS, Alfred James (1826-1903). Web page: http://www.aim25.ac.uk/cgi-bin/search2?coll_id=1976&inst_id=14

VAN AALST, J.A., 1884. *Chinese Music*. Special Series Number 6. Maritime Customs. Shanghai: Statistical Department, Imperial Inspectorate General.

VANSINA, Jan, 1973. *Oral Tradition: A Study in Historical Methodology*. Harmondsworth: Penguin Books.

VAUGHAN WILLIAMS, Ralph, 1963. *National Music and Other Essays*. London: Oxford University Press (First published 1934).

VAUGHAN WILLIAMS, Ralph and A.L. LLOYD, 1959. *The Penguin Book of English Folk Songs*. Harmondsworth: Penguin Books.

VILLOTEAU, Guillaume-Andre, 1809. *Description de l'egypte, ou Recueil des observations et des recherches qui ont faites en egypte pendant l'expedition de l'arme Francaise. I. Antiquites Tome premier*. Paris: Imprimerie imperiale.

WACHSMANN, Klaus P., 1971. "Universal Perspectives in Music." *Ethnomusicology*, 15(3):381-4.

WACHSMANN, Klaus P., 1976. "In Memoriam: Maud Karpeles (1885–1976)." *Yearbook of the International Folk Music Council*, 8:9-11.

WACHSMANN, Klaus P., et al. (eds.), 1976. *Hornbostel Opera Omnia*. The Hague: Nijhoff.

WALCOTT, Ronald, 1981. "Francis La Flesche: American Indian Scholar." *Folklife Center News*, 4(1):1, 10-11. Web page: http://memory.loc.gov/ammem/omhhtml/omhfcn1.html

WALLASCHEK, Richard, 1893. *Primitive Music*. London: Longmans, Green.

WALLIN, Nils L., Björn MERKER and Steven BROWN (eds.), 2000. *The Origins of Music*. Cambridge: MIT Press.

WATERHOUSE, William, 2003. "Mahillon, Victor-Charles." New Grove.

WATERMAN, Richard, 1952. "African Influence on the Music of the Americas, " in Sol Tax (ed.), *Acculturation in the Americas*. Chicago: University of Chicago Press, vol. 2, pp.207-18.

WATERMAN, Richard, 1947–51. "Bibliography of Asiatic Musics." *Notes*, v (1947–48), 21-35, 178-86, 354-62, 549-62; vi (1948–49), 122-36, 281-96, 419-36, 570-83; vii (1949–50), 84-98, 265-79, 415-23, 613-21; viii (1950–51), 100-18, 322-9.

WEBER, William, 2003. "Conservatories, §III: 1790–1945." New Grove.

WELLEK, Albert et al,, 2003. "Stumpf, (Friedrich) Carl." New Grove.

WELLESZ Egon (ed.), 1957. *The New Oxford History of Music*, Vol. 1: *Ancient and Oriental Music*. London: Oxford University Press.

WERNER, Eric, 1957. "VIII, The Music of Post-biblical Judaism," in Wellesz 1957:313-5.

WERNER, Eric, 1970. *The sacred Bridge; Liturgical Parallels in Synagogue and Early Church*. New York: Schocken Books.

WESLEY-SMITH, Peter, 2004. "Piggott, Sir Francis Taylor (1852–1925)." ODNB
WHITEHEAD, Alfred and Bertrand RUSSELL, 1910. *Principia Mathematica*. Cambridge: Cambridge University Press.

Who Was Who: A Companion to Who's Who, Containing the Biographies of Those Who Died. Vol. 1, 1897–1915; Vol. II, 1916–1928; Vol. III, 1929–1940; Vol.IV, 1941–1950. London: Black.

Who Was Who in America : A Companion Biographical References Work to Who's Who in America, 1943. Chicago : Marquis.

WILD, Stephen, Bruno NETTL, Caroline CARD and Carl RAHKONEN, 1982. "In Memoriam: Alan P. Merriam (1923–1980)." *Ethnomusicology*, 26(1):91-120.

WILGUS, D.K., 1959. *Anglo-American Folksong Scholarship*. New Bruswick: Rutgers University Press.

WILLARD, N. Augustus, 1834. *A Treatise on the Music of Hindoostan*. Calcutta: Baptist Mission Press

WILLIAM AND GAYLE COOK MUSIC LIBRARY, 1997–98. Walter Kaufmann Archive : Biography. Web page: http://www.music.indiana.edu/collections/kaufmann/biograph.html

WILLIAMSON, Rosemary, 2003. "Galpin, Francis William." New Grove.

WILSON, Steuart, 2004. "Strangways, Arthur Henry Fox (1859–1948)." ODNB.

WIORA, Walter, 1967. *The Four Ages of Music*. New York: Norton.

WOLZ, Lyn, 2005. "Resources in the Vaughan Williams Memorial Library: The Anne G Gilchrist Manuscript Collection." *Folk Music Journal*, 8 (5):619-21.

YOUNG, Robert M., 1967. "Herbert Spencer and 'Inevitable' Progress." *Actes du XIe Congrès International d'Histoire des Sciences* (Warsaw), 2:273-78.

YUNG, Bell and Helen REES (eds.), 1999. *Understanding Charles Seeger, Pioneer in American Musicology*. Urbana & Chicago: University of Illinois Press.

ZEMP, Hugo, 1972. "Instruments de musique de Malaita II." *Journal de la Soceété des océanistes*, 28/34:7-48.

ZEMP, Hugo, 1978. " 'Are'are Classification of Musical Types and Instruments." *Ethhnomusicology*, 22(1):37-67.

ZEMP, Hugo, 1979. "Aspects of 'Are'are Musical Theory." *Ethnomusicology*, 23(1):6-48.

APPENDIX

A FIELD QUESTIONNAIRE

In recent years, ethnomusicological field work, if undertaken at all, has tended to be "problem oriented". The ethnomusicologist enters the field with an already formulated question or hypothesis to be tested, and develops his or her own methods in order to find the answers. The old idea of systematically gathering as much information about as many aspects as possible of the music and its cultural context has become passé. Particularist methods have their uses and have been productive of interesting and even valuable results but, especially in areas that have not had the benefit of prior study, the results have too often been obtained at the expense of an understanding of the music as a whole, as well as heading off any prospect of comparison with musics elsewhere. It can be argued, indeed, that in an as yet unstudied field area, the ethnomusicologist has a duty to be as comprehensive as possible, and it is such work that the present questionnaire is designed to assist.

The questionnaire draws freely on previously published guides such as those of Nettl (1964),[605] Notes and Queries (1951), and Karpeles (1958). It differs from them, however, in systematising the questions under well-defined headings representative of the main subjects of interest to music ethnographers. These headings are mostly derived from Alan P. Merriam's book *The Anthropology of Music* (1964). Some topics such as the functions of music in a culture cannot be elicited by questionnaire and here reference can best be made to Merriam's book.

The questionnaire headings are song types, composition, ownership of music, the musician, learning and instruction, performance, musical values and concepts, and musical instruments. Readers interested in dance are referred to Kurath (1960) and Miller (1964).

Under the heading "song types" appear questions concerned with the uses of music. Generally each song type can be shown to serve specific economic, social, political or religious needs.

Details of "composition" of interest to ethnomusicologists include sources of music, kinds of composer, and techniques of composition. Music is not always recognised as originating with individuals. Sometimes composition is carried out by groups rather than by individuals; sometimes the origin of music is attributed to the supernatural, as in the Plains Indian Vision Quest; or the song may be dreamed. Another, and sometimes the only recognised means of acquiring songs is by borrowing from an outside source. Of kinds of composer, distinctions may be made between specialist and casual composers. Techniques of composition include re-working or adapting an old song, and improvisation, as well as the straightforward creation of new material to which prior thought has been given.

Ownership of music may be by individual, family, tribe, village or other social unit, or there may be little concern with ownership. An important topic is the exact mechanism of transfer of ownership should this occur.

---

[605] Nettl 1964:73-7.

Under the heading of "the musician" can be found questions relating to attitudes towards musicians, the status of musicians, specialisation, and professionalism.

Useful information about "learning and instruction" will include details about formal or informal training of individuals or groups, of incidental learning, of motivation and, if applicable, of rehearsal techniques.

Under "performance" is subsumed such headings as concern for accuracy, restrictions or proscriptions, performance terminology, singing faults and standards of performance, leadership and the qualities expected of a good singer or leader, sex and age specialisation, questions relating to musical talent, gesture. posture and stance, the optimum size of a performing group, and voice quality.

"Musical values and concepts" is a topic beset with problems. Not the least of the practical difficulties is the near impossibility of expecting informants to be articulate about matters to which they have given no previous thought. Although this is potentially one of the most interesting subjects in ethno-music, detailed attention to it is probably best avoided in a general survey. Consequently, only a few questions have been provided. McAllester (1954) is the best-known study on musical values. Merriam discusses McAllester's work . briefly,[606] and Nettl reproduces a questionnaire compiled by McAllester for his study, which is largely devoted to determining Navaho attitudes to music.[607]

"Musical instruments" is the final category in the present questionnaire, and here questions are grouped under the sub-headings description of instrument, use, construction, and playing method.

Regarding use of the questionnaire, it will hardly be necessary to remind field workers that informants quickly tire of being asked one question after another. It is hoped that the questionnaire will not be used exclusively in this way but will serve rather as a guide to the kinds of information to be sought. Sessions with the questionnaire should be kept short, plainly irrelevant questions or those upon which information has already been volunteered should be omitted, and as many questions as possible should be answered by observation rather than by relying entirely on informants. Finally, an effort has been made to avoid leading questions in the questionnaire but where this is unavoidable, more general questions have been listed first. The reader is urged to elicit as much information as possible from these more general questions before going on to the specific ones.

THE QUESTIONNAIRE

SONG TYPES

1. What types (kinds) of music are there? (Give examples of known types).
2. What are they used for? When and where are they performed?

---

[606] Merriam 1964:248-9.
[607] Nettl 1964:78-81.

3. Can they be used on other occasions?
4. Do they sound different from each other?
5. Are any sung just for amusement?
6. Are there songs sung only at certain times of the day?. year?, on special occasions?, in particular places?
7. Are there occasions upon which a set number of songs must be performed? Are they performed in a set order?
8. Are there abusive songs, boasting songs, canoe songs, children's songs, dancee songs, farewell songs, game songs, genealogical songs, greeting songs, hauling songs, historical songs, incantations, laments, love songs, lullabies, marriage songs, narrative songs, paddling songs, praise songs, recreational songs, sacred songs, secret songs, taunting songs, war songs, watch songs, work songs, others? Give names.
9. Do any of the song types have accompanying musical instruments?
10. Are they sung solo or by groups?
11. Which song types are the oldest?

COMPOSITION

12. Where do songs come from? Are there any legends or traditions about the origin of music or of musical instruments?
13. Are songs ever dreamed?
14. Are songs made up by individuals? If so, are the names of the composers remembered?
15. Are songs ever made up by groups of people?, or more than one person?
16. Do any songs come from other islands (places)?
17. Can anyone make up songs?
18. Are some people specially good at making up songs?
19. If so, do they make up songs for other people?
20. Is anyone ever paid for making up a song?
21. How are songs composed?
22. Are old songs ever changed to make new ones?
23. How long does it take to make up a song?
24. Are text and tune composed together or separately?
25. Are new songs still being composed?
26. If so, do they sound like the old ones or are they different?

OWNERSHIP OF MUSIC

27. Are there songs which may be sung only by particular people?
28. Who is allowed to learn songs?
29. Are songs owned?
30. If so, are they owned by persons?, families?, tribes?, villages?
31. Can anyone own a song?
32. How does a person prove he owns a song?
33. Can songs be inherited?
34. Can songs be bought?, exchanged?, traded for goods?

THE MUSICIAN

35. Can everybody sing or play an instrument? Do all people know songs (and/or play instruments?
36. If not, can anyone become a musician?
37. Are some people more likely to become good musicians than others? What qualifies a person as a musician?
38. Does anyone get paid or given gifts for performing or composing music?
39. Would it be possible to do without musicians?
40. What do other people think of musicians?
41. Do musicians behave differently from other people?

LEARNING AND INSTRUCTION

42. How do people learn songs? How did you learn your songs?
43. Did someone teach you?
44. Were you taught alone or were others taught with you?
45. Were there special schools or special meetings for learning songs?
46. If so, how often did they meet and for how long?
47. Could anyone go or only special people?
48. What methods of instruction were used?
49. Did you ever just pick up songs by listening to them?
50. If so. where did you learn these songs?
51. How old were you when you began to learn songs?
52. Whose idea was it for you to learn songs?
53. Are songs practised? When? Where?
54. What methods are used?
55. What happens when people make mistakes in learning songs?
56. Were you given anything for learning songs?
57. Were you scolded or punished if you did not learn?
58. Are some kinds of song easier to learn than others?
59. Are you teaching songs to anyone?
60. How do you teach them?
61. How long does it take to learn a song?

PERFORMANCE

62. Should songs be sung the same way each time they are performed, or can they be changed?
63. Are songs sung the same way now as they used to be?
64. What is your word for singing?, dancing?, playing an instrument?
65. Is there any time when you are not supposed to sing?, or dance?. or play musical instruments?
66. Are some people recognised as better performers than others?
67. If so, how do they become better? Are they born better? Do they have more opportunity? Do they work harder?
68. How can you tell a good singer from a bad singer? (i.e. What qualities must a good singer have?)

69. Are there mistakes which should be avoided when you are singing? What are they?
70. Do mistakes matter very much?
71. What happens to a performer who makes mistakes?
72. Do any songs need a leader?
73. What does the leader do?
74. What qualities should a good leader have?
75. Do women lead as well as men?
76. Does the leader ever sing by himself or herself?
77. Do any songs have actions?
78. Are there songs for men only?
79. Are there songs for women only?
80. Are there songs for children only?
81. Are there songs for old people only?
82. How many people should there be in a performing group?, singing group?, instrumental group?
83. Are there different ways of making the voice sound in singing?

MUSICAL VALUES AND CONCEPTS (additional to above)

84. Is there a word for music?
85. What makes music different from noise?
86. What is music for?
87. Is there good and bad music? How can you tell one from the other?
88. Is there a way of telling old music from new music? Is one better than the other?
89. How important is music? Could ;o u do without it?
90. Are there words for describing music? (structure) high/low, soft/loud.

MUSICAL INSTRUMENTS

Description

91. What musical instruments are there?
92. What are they called?
93. What do they look like?
94. Do other islands (places) have similar instruments? What are their names?
95. Is it known where the instruments came from?

Use

96. When and where is the instrument used?
97. Who may play the instrument?
98. Who may bear the instrument?
99. Is there a set number of pieces for the instruments?
100. Is new music made up for the instruments?
101. Do people improvise on the instrument?
102. Is the instrument played by itself? (solo), with other instruments?, with others of its kind?, with singing? with dancing?

103. (For drums) Is there a way of saying the rhythms?

Construction

104. How is the instrument made? Materials? Construction techniques? Decoration? Rituals involved?
105. Who makes the instrument? Just anyone?, or special people?
106. How do people learn to make the instrument?
107. Is the maker of an instrument paid for his work?
108. Who owns the finished instrument?
109. How long will it last?
110. Is an old instrument better than a new one? Why?

Playing method

111. How is the instrument played?
112. Are there different ways of playing it?
113. How can you tell when an instrument is well played?

ACKNOWLEDGEMENTS

Assistance with information about individuals and/or with finding photographs of them is gratefully acknowledged from:

Laurent Aubert
Brenno Boccadoro
Ton Bruins
Alan Costall
Mark R. Dickerson
Robert Falck
Don Fleming
John Francmanis
Charlotte J. Frisbie
Irene Ferguson
Brian Galpin
Holly Gardinier
Florence Hayes
Luke Hambley
Israel J. Katz
Fredric Lieberman
Suzanne M. Lodato
Maureen Melton
Jeremy Montagu
Steven Nelson
Michael Nixon
Karen Olsen
Carol Oja
Peter Petersen
Karin Pettersson
Carl Rahkonen
Bruce Rosenstock
Edwin Seroussi
Andrew Tracey
László Vikárius
Jane Waller
Helene C. Williams

Thanks is extended also to the many libraries, archives and other institutions whose staff responded to requests for information, and to individuals who, though unable to help directly, provided contacts. Photographs are acknowledged separately in the Illustration Credits (see next).

ILLUSTRATION CREDITS

Because of ownership and copyright requirements, approval must be sought from the donors before any re-use is made of photographs contributed for the present book.

A few consents have been received from publishers in respect of photographs for which the publisher has been unable to trace or contact the photographer. In such cases the publisher concerned will be pleased to rectify any errors or omissions at the earliest opportunity.

It is regretted that photos of some individuals could either not be found or, for copyright or other reasons, could not be included.

The writer extends his heartfelt and most grateful thanks to the many institutions and individuals named below who provided courtesy photos. Full details of published sources of photographs can be found in the References.

Biographies

Amiot: Hamy 1893:vol.1, courtesy Father Joseph MacDonnell
Bake: Kunst 1959a:222 with kind permission of Springer Science and Business Media
Balfour: Kunst1959a:219 with kind permission of Springer Science and Business Media
Barbeau: Canadian Museum of Civilization, negative no. J4992, courtesy Canadian Museum of Civilization
Barry: Harvard University 1925, courtesy Harvard University Archives.
Bartók: Courtesy Bartók Archives, Institute for Musicology of the Hungarian Academy of Sciences
Bayard: Courtesy Richard Blaustein
Blacking: Blacking 1973: cover photo by permission University of Washington Press
Boas: Lanfer 1906:frontispiece
Bose: Courtesy Technical University, Berlin
Brailoiu: Photo: Willi Pragher, Geneva, 1953; courtesy Archives Internationales de Musique Populaire (AIMP), Geneva
Bronson: Bancroft Library, University of California, Berkeley
Burrows: Courtesy Nani Burrows Ball
Child: Courtesy Harvard University Archives
Collaer: Courtesy Koninklijke Bibliotheek van België
Crossley-Holland: Courtesy Barbara Racy
Curtis: Courtesy Alfred R. Bredenberg, Natalie Curtis Burlin Center for American Culture Studies
Daniélou: Courtesy Jacques Cloarec
Day: Mockler-Ferryman 1901:283
Densmore: Courtesy Oberlin College Archives, Oberlin, Ohio
Ellis, Alexander: Courtesy University of Amsterdam
Ellis, Catherine: Courtesy Elder School of Music, University of Adelaide
Emsheimer: Courtesy Jan Ling
Estreicher: Courtesy Anne Estreicher

Farmer: Glasgow University Library, Department of Special Collections
Fewkes: Nichols [1919]: frontispiece
Fillmore: Courtesy Pomona College Archives, Honnolk/Mudd Special Collections, The Libraries of the Claremont Colleges, Claremont, California
Fletcher: Hough 1923:opp.254
Fox Strangways: Howes 1969b:frontispiece by permission Oxford University Press, Department of Journals
Galpin: Courtesy The Galpin family
Gerson-Kiwi: Courtesy National Sound Archives, Hebrew University, Jerusalem
Graf: Courtesy Austrian Academy of Sciences Archives Portraitsammlung
Halpern: *Fugue* (Toronto), 2(4):14 (1977) by permission Diane Watts (editor) and Jurgen Gothe (author)
Harich-Schneider: Harich-Scheider 1978:opp.240
Herskovits: Courtesy Northwestern University Archives
Herzog: Courtesy Indiana University Archives
Hickmann: Kunst 1959a:224 with kind permission of Springer Science and Business Media and University of Amsterdam
Hornbostel: Simon 2000:29, fig.2 by permission Berlin Phonogramm-Archiv. Photo: Familie Brinkgreve-Kunst
Howes: Courtesy Hugh Howes
Husmann: Becker & Gerlach 1970:frontispiece by permission Heinz Becker
Idelsohn: Courtesy American Jewish Archives, Cincinnati, Ohio
Izikowitz: Frontispiece *Ethnos* v.40 (1975) by permission Museum of World Culture, Gothenburg, Sweden
Jones, Father A.M.: Courtesy University of Amsterdam
Jones, Trevor: Courtesy Trevor Jones
Jones, Sir William: Teignmouth 1806
Karpeles: Courtesy Memorial University of Newfoundland. Photo Carole Henderson Carpenter MUNFLA 79-771/P8943)
Kaufmann: Courtesy William & Gayle Cook Music Library, Indiana University
Kidson: Baring Gould 1895(7):xiii
Kirby: Kunst 1959a:222 with kind permission of Springer Science and Business Media and University of Amsterdam
Kishibe: Courtesy TAKEI Kôichi
Kittredge: Courtesy Harvard University Archives
Kodály: Courtesy International Kodály Society
Kolinski: Falck & Rice 1982:frontispiece, with permission.
Kunst: Courtesy KIT Troppenmuseum, Amsterdam
La Flesche: La Flesche 1900:2687 by permission University of Virginia Electronic Text Center.
Lach: Courtesy Archiv der Universität Wien Bildarchiv
Lachmann: Courtesy National Sound Archives, Hebrew University, Jerusalem
Lloyd: Courtesy Bruce and Ken Olsen
Lomax: Photo by Peter McClanahan, courtesy The Alan Lomax Archive
Maceda: Courtesy Center for Ethnomusicology, University of the Philippines, Diliman
Mahillon: Courtesy Musées Royaux, Brussels
Marcel-Dubois: Courtesy Jacques Cheyronnaud and Marie-Marguerite Pichonnet-Andral. Photo: Thérèse Le Brat, 1946.

Marcuse: Courtesy Yale University Collection of Musicsl Instruments
McPhee: Courtesy Carol J. Oja
Merriam: Courtesy Indiana University Archives
Moyle: Courtesy Jill Stubington
Myers: Courtesy British Psychological Society
Nadel: Courtesy Australian National University
Nettl: Courtesy Bruno Nettl
Reinhard: Simon 2000:35, fig.4 by permission Berlin Phonogramm-Archiv. Photo: Dietrich Graf 1975
Rhodes: Courtesy David P. McAllester
Roberts: Courtesy Jane Broman Brown and Charlotte J. Frisbie
Sachs: Courtesy University of Amsterdam
Schaeffner: Courtesy André Schaeffner Collection, Paul Sacher Foundation, Basel, Switzerland
Schneider: : Simon 2000:31, fig.3 by permission Berlin Phonogramm-Archiv. Photo: Robert Günther 1965
Seeger: Courtesy Ann M. Pescatello.
Sendrey: Courtesy Israel J. Katz
Sharp: Fox Strangways 1933: Pl.V
Stumpf: Simon 2000:27, fig.1 by permission Berlin Phonogramm-Archiv
Tagore: Courtesy R.P. Gupta, Calcutta, and Charles Capwell
Tracey: Courtesy International Library of African Music and Rhodes University
Vega: Courtesy Folklore del Note Argentino
Wachsmann: Seeger & Wade 1977:frontispiece by permission Bonnie Wade. Photo: Erika Wachsmann
Waterman: Kunst 1960:25 with kind permission of Springer Science and Business Media.
Werner: Courtesy Israel J. Katz
Wiora: Courtesy Department of Musicology, University of Saarbrücken

Other

Adler: Adler 1935
Baring Gould: Baring Gould 1895(7):frontispiece
Bougainville: Thiéry n.d.:frontispiece
Bücher: Courtesy Bernardo Díaz Nosty, Universidad de Málaga - España
Burney: Burney 1927:frontispiece
Chrysander: Courtesy Inge Wolf
Cook: Carruthers 1930:frontispiece
Cortés: Prescott 1843(II):frontispiece
Darwin, Charles: Darwin 1902:frontispiece
Darwin, Erasmus: Pearson 1930:opp.200
Donaldson: Detail from portrait by William Smellie Watson, RSA. Courtesy Talbot Rice Gallery, University of Edinburgh
Drake: Corbett 1928:frontispiece
Edison: Dickson & Dickson 1894:frontispiece (detail)
Fétis: Courtesy Sjaak Rontberg
Founders of the SEM: The William P. Malm Photography Collection, courtesy William P. Malm

Fuller-Maitland: Fuller-Maitland 1932:frontispiece
Gilbert: Mezzotint by Samuel Cousins ARA, after a picture by Henry Howard RA. Baring-Gould 1909, courtesy Cornish Studies Library
Grainger: Courtesy The Grainger Society
Grey: Bracken 1890:opp.312
Haekel: Bölsher 1906:292 detail
Hawkins: Scholes 1953:frontispiece by permission Oxford University Press
Helmholtz: Routledge 1898:374
Huxley: Huxley 1903(3):frontispiece
Lamarck: Packard 1901:opp.189
Newton: Greenstreet 1927:frontispiece
Pizarro: Shay 1932
Riemann: Courtesy web-helper.net
Seashore: Courtesy Kent Photo Collection, University Archives, Department of Special Collections, University of Iowa Libraries, Iowa City, Iowa
Spencer: Spencer 1904(2):frontispiece
Spitta: Universitätsbibliothek der Humboldt-Universität zu Berlin
Vaughan Williams: Courtesy Ursula Vaughan Williams and EFDSS
Wolf: Universitätsbibliothek der Humboldt-Universität zu Berlin

INDEX OF SUBJECTS

This index is limited to major topics only. For context see Table of Contents.

Aesthetics 292
Analysis 70, 290-314
    Cantometrics 194, 293, 303, 321
    Kolinski 294-7
    Linguistic approaches 297
    Standard 292-3
    System 310-4
Anthropology v. music 329-21
    See also UCLA/Indiana divide
Archiving 264
Areas, music 317-9
Armchair ethnomusicology 266-7
Austro-German schools 39-51
    Berlin school 39-42, 248
    Vienna school 42, 249
Authenticity 258-60
Berlin Phonogram-Archiv 39-41
Bibliography 267-8
Bi-musicalility 63-4, 262-4
Biographies (A–Z) 91-245
Cantometics *See* Analysis
Cataloguing 265-6
Change, mechanisms of 324-6
Chronology 339-56
Classification 265-6
Communication, music and 299-302
Comparative musicology
    Methods of 43-51
    Schools of: *See* Austro-German Schools
Comparison 71, 314-6
Culture, music in 65-6
Diffusion 319-20
Disciplines, other 15, 71, 95
Early work, attitudes to 69
Eighties, seminal 37-9
Ethnomusicology
    American school 52-9, 251
    Antecedents 30-2
    Definition 12-16, 61
    Middle years in America 61-7
    New directions 67-76
Evolution 25-8

Feedback model, Merriam 68, 302, 328-9
Field questionnaire 405-10
Field work 255-64
History, role of 10-11
Holistic approach 72-4
Insider/outsider relations 255-8
Instruction 261-2
    See also Bi-musicality
Intellectual ancestry charts 247-51
    Chart 1: Berlin School 249
    Chart 2: Vienna School 250
    Chart 3: American School 251
International societies 59-61, 331
Intonation 278-83
Models 70, 297, 333
Nationalism 20-1
Notation: *See* Transcription
Observer, role of 260-1
Organology 32-3
Origins, quest for 45-50
    Darwinian hypothesis 47-8
    Other theories of origin 49-50
Paradigms, past and present 76-9
Perception, limits of 287-8
Popular music 332-3
Product and process 70, 322-32
Progress, idea of 29-30
Repertoire 323-4
Representation, crisis of 71
Schools of music 33-5
Science, rise of 21-4
Social correlates of music 48, 194, 302-10
    See also Holistic approach
Statistics 299
Subliminal, role of 327-8
Subject divisions 79-90
    Folk music 81-7
    Oriental music 88
    Tribal music 89
Text/music relationships 297-8
Theory-building 70-1
    See also Models
Transcription 268-89
    Composite 277-8
    Conceptual 273-5
    Machine 283-8
    Prescriptive v. descriptive 270-3

Transcription (contin.)
 Reliability of 289
UCLA/Indiana divide 63, 322, 332
Universals 3213
World view 19-20

INDEX OF PERSONS

Numbers in italics at the ends of entries refer to illustrations

Abraham, Otto 39, 41, 97, 98, 165, 249, 345
Adler, Guido 36, 37, 95, 96, 137, 152, 188, 209, 244, 250, 344, *36*
Allen, Warren Dwight 22-3, 32
Ambros, August Wilhelm 31, 343
Amiot, Jean Joseph Marie 30, 31, 88, 96, 97, 99, 340, *99*
Andersen, Johannes 263 ftnt 356
Aretz, Isabel 10, 87, 96, 100
Asch, Moses 349

Baermann, Carl 132
Bake, Arnold Adriaan 35, 88, 94, 101-2, 261, 348, *101*
Baker, Theodore 34, 38, 52, 96, 103, 251, 344
Baldwin Spencer, Walter 207
Balfour, Henry 32, 96, 97, 104-05, *104*
Banks, Joseph 229
Barbeau, Marius 59, 87, 89, 96, 106-7, *106*
Baring Gould, Sabine 84, *80*
Barrett, William Alexander 84
Barry, Phillips 87, 96, 97, 108, 119, *108*
Bartók, Béla 10, 20, 109-11, 251, 260, 265-6, 267, 272, 346, 348, *109*
Baumann, Max Peter 290, 334-5
Bayard, Samuel Preston 59, 87, 96, 112, 266, *112*
Becking, Gustav 128, 176
Benedict, Ruth 54, 116
Bennett, Sir William Sterndale 145
Bentham, Jeremy 10
Bentley, J.M. 149
Berndt, Ronald & Catherine 171
Biggs, Bruce 298
Blacking, John 12, 15, 48, 61, 67, 68, 72-5, 85, 89, 93, 94, 96, 113-4, 222, 251, 263, 292, 297, 298, 302, 303, 305, 309, 316, 322, 324, 327-8, 332, 334, 336, 338, 333, 353, 354, 355, *113*
Blaustein, Richard 112
Blum, Stephen 68, 312

Boas, Franz 54, 55, 65, 67, 73, 96, 97, 115-6, 122, 142, 156, 158, 159, 184, 218, 251, 322, 329, 338, 345, 347, *115*
Bor, Joep 31
Bose, Fritz 41, 42, 95, 96, 97, 117, 248, 249, 265, *117*
Bougainville, Louis de 20, 340, *18*
Boulanger, Nadia 216
Brailoiu, Constaine 96, 118, 124, 222, 310, *118*
Brentano, Franz 232, 249
Broadwood, John 82-4, 342
Broadwood, Lucy 82, 84, 86
Bronson, Bertrand 59, 87, 87 ftnt 217, 96, 109, 119-20, *119*
Brook, Barry 255, 257, 353
Brown, John 51
Bücher, Karl 49, *49*
Buck, Peter (See Hiroa, Te Rangi)
Bülow, Hans (Guido) Freiherr von 262
Burney, Charles 23, 30, 340, *23*
Burrows, Edwin Grant 90, 96, 121-2, 251, *121*
Busoni, Ferruccio 210, 244
Butterworth, George 85, 345
Byrne, David 14

Campbell, Olive Dame 11
Carnegie, Andrew 28
Carroll, Lewis 300
Chase, Gilbert 57, 68
Child, Francis James 87, 123, 181, 344, *123*
Chomsky, Noam 76, 297, 322
Christensen, Dieter 61 ftnt 151, 266, 295, 353, 354, 355
Chrysander, Friedrich 37, *36*
Collaer, Paul 94, 96, 124, 346, *124*
Colquhoun, Neil 87 ftnt 217
Cook, James 19, 20, *18*
Copland, Aaron 200
Cortés, Hernándo 19, *18*
Cortot, Alfred 196, 216, 223

Cowell, Henry 56, 200
Creighton, Helen 87
Cristofori, Bartolomeo 34, 336
Crossley-Holland, Peter 88, 95, 96, 97, 125-6, *125*
Curtis, Natalie 53, 94, 96, 127, *127*

Dahlback, Karl 283, 351
Danckert, Werner 35, 96, 97, 128
Daniélou, Alain 88, 96, 129-30, 261, 352, *129*
Dart, Thurston 171
Darwin, Charles 24-5, 27, 28, 46-8, 50, 76, 341, 342, 343, *24*
Darwin, Erasmus 25, *26*
Davids, Thomas Rhys 240
Davies, James A. 280, 281, 343
Day, Charles Russell 131, 261, 345, *131*
Dean-Smith, Margaret 82
Densmore, Frances 52, 53, 58, 94, 96, 132-3, 267, 346, *132*
Donaldson, John 92, 93, 134, 249, 251, *93*
Dósa, Lidi 110
Drake, Sir Francis 19, 339, *18*
Driver, Harold 317
Du Halde, Jean-Baptiste 30, 340

Eckstorm, Fannie 109
Edison, Thomas Alva 37, 38, 39, 52, 343, *36*
Einstein, Albert 58, 59, 335
Elkin, A.P. 171, 266
Ellingson, Ter 270, 273-5
Ellis, Alexaner John 38, 39, 62, 67, 92, 93, 96, 97, 134-5, 162, 165, 230, 233, 249, 251, 278, 279, 280, 281, 341, 344, *134*
Ellis, Catherine 90, 95, 136, 266, 280, *136*
Emory, Kenneth 122
Emsheimer, Ernst 88, 96, 137, 250, *137*
Erdely, Stephen 265
Estreicher, Zygmunt 89, 96, 138, *138*

Farmer, Henry George 35, 88, 95, 96, 139-40, 351, *139*
Feld, Steven 261, 291-2, 297, 300, 304-7, 355
Fétis, Françoise Joseph 31, 197, *31*

Fewkes, Jesse Walter 39, 52, 96, 97, 141, 219, 231, 267, 344, *141*
Fillmore, John Comfort 34, 53, 96, 97, 142, 143, 279, 345, *142*
Firth, Raymond 72, 251, 266, 269, 280, 281, 313, 316, 324
Fleming, Harold C. 170
Fletcher, Alice Cunningham 52, 53, 96, 142, 143, 267, 345, *143*
Fortes, Meyer 72, 251
Fox Strangways, Arthur Henry 88, 96, 144, 261, 346, *144*
Franke, Kuno 108
Friedheim, Arthur 200
Fuller-Maitland, J.A. 84, 96, 177, *80*
Furneaux, Tobias 229

Galpin, Francis William 32, 95, 96, 145-6, *145*
Garfias, Robert 289, 336
George, Graham 61 ftnt 151, 353
Gerson-Kiwi, Edith 35, 88, 95, 96, 147-8, 189, 250, *147*
Gilbert, Davies 82, 341, *80*
Gilchrist, Anne 86, 96, 97, 149-50. 345
Gillis, Frank 159, 203
Gilman, Benjamin Ives 39, 52, 96, 97, 141, 151, 231, 249, 251
Glosson, Ernest 197 ftnt 305
Godowski, Leopold 132
Goossens, Sir Eugene 171
Gourlay, Kenneth 68, 260, 333
Graf, Walter 42, 96, 152, 250, 264, *152*
Grainger, Percy 85, 267, *80*
Grey, Sir George 323, 342, *323*
Gurlitt, Wilibald 137, 250
Gurney, Edmund 37
Guthrie, Woody 87

Haase, Gesine 266
Haddon, Alfred Cort 207
Haeckel, Ernst 25, *26*
Halpern, Ida 42, 89, 96, 153-4, 250, *153*
Hamm, Charles 332
Hanslick, Eduard 96, 250
Harich-Schneider, Eta 88, 94, 95, 96, 97, 155, *155*

Harrison, Frank 30
Hart, Sir Robert 236
Hauptmann, Moritz 34, 52, 251
Hawkins, Sir John 23, *23*
Helmholtz, Hermann 92, 93, 134, *93*
Herndon, Marcia 68, 70, 291, 333
Herskovits, Melville 156-57, 251, *156*
Herzog, George 41, 53, 54-5, 57, 59, 96, 109, 122, 158-9, 165, 249, 251, 292, 306, 311, 317, 319, 322, 347, 349, *158*
Hickmann, Hans 42, 88, 96, 160, 165, 249, *160*
Hipkins, Alfred James 96, 135, 161, 249, 251, 344
Hiroa, Te Rangi 121, 122, 251
Holst, Gustav 228
Hood, Mantle 9, 32, 58, 62, 63-5, 66, 67, 68, 69, 81, 85, 88, 96, 163-64, 170, 187, 201, 251, 255, 262, 263, 269, 283, 284, 285, 286-7, 288, 289, 293, 300, 307, 315, 322, 330, 332, 336, 351, 352, 354, 356
Hornbostel, Erich von 33, 38, 39, 41, 44, 53, 54, 95, 96, 97, 98, 109, 117, 158, 160, 165, 167, 184, 187, 207, 210, 221, 223, 232, 233, 238, 239, 245, 246, 249, 251, 255, 269, 279, 282, 292, 295, 311, 319, 345, 347, 348, *164*
Howard, Keith 263
Howells, Herbert 171
Howes, Frank 165, *165*
Hughes, H. Stuart 275
Hughes, Kino 278
Husmann, Heinrich 35, 42, 96, 165, 167, 215, 218, 248, 249, 279, *166*
Huxley, Thomas Henry 25, 28, *26*

Idelsohn, Abraham 35, 88, 96, 148, 168, *168*
Ireland, John 125
Ives, Burl 87
Izikowitz, Karl-Gustav 33, 169, *169*

Jairazbhoy, Nazir 95, 102, 259, 281, 291
Jones, Father Arthur Morris 89, 97, 170, *170*
Jones, Trevor 10, 90, 95, 96,, 136, 171-2, 266, *171*

Jones, Sir William 30, 31, 88, 96, 173, 261, 281, 341, *173*

Karpeles, Maud 10-11, 12, 59, 69, 86, 96, 144, 166, 174-5, 192, 227, 228, 258, 259, 203, 346, 349, 352, 364, *174*
Kartomi, Margaret 324
Katz, Israel J. 147
Katz, Ruth 189
Kaufmann, Walter 42, 88, 96, 176, 250, *176*
Kennedy, Douglas 348
Kennedy, Peter 350, 353
Kidson, Frank 84, 85, 149, 177, *177*
Kirby, Percival 89, 95, 96, 178, *178*
Kishibe, Shigeo 88, 179-80, *179*
Kittredge, George Lyman 87, 96, 108, 109, 181, *181*
Koch, Gerd 266
Kodály, Zoltán 10, 21, 60, 82, 94, 95, 96, 110, 158, 182-4, 260, 346, *182*
Kolinski, Mieczyslaw 41, 60, 68, 70, 94, 96, 97, 157, 165, 184-5, 232, 250, 269, 289, 294-7, 303, 311, 311, *184*
Korson, Rae 262
Krader, Barbara 59
Kroeber, Alfred 16
Kudelski, Stefan 350
Kunst, Jaap 33, 38, 45, 49, 61-2, 63, 64, 67, 81, 88, 90, 94, 95, 96, 186-7, 251, 267, 268, 272, 273, 279, 284, 285, 286, 307, 308, 322, 347, 350, 351, *186*
Kurath, Gertrude 59

La Borde, J.B. de 31, 341
La Fage, J. Adrien de 31, 342
La Flesche, Francis 53, 96, 142, 143, 188, 345, *188*
Lach, Robert 38, 42, 95, 152, 154, 189, 209, 240, 244, 250, *189*
Lachmann, Robert 42, 88, 96, 147, 148, 165, 190, 248, 249, *190*
Lafitau, Père 51
Lamarck, Jean-Baptiste 25, 27, 28, 47, *26*
Landowska, Wanda 147, 155
Lang, Paul Henry 196
Lasso, Orlando de 30
Leach, Edmund 334 ftnt 593

Lévi-Strauss, Claude 76, 334
Levy, Mark 281 ftnt 433
Lieberman, Fredric 99
List, George 159, 264, 286, 289, 322
Liszt, Franz 34
Lloyd, A.L. 86, 118, 191-2, *191*
Lomax, Alan 48, 52, 59, 67, 87, 96, 97, 193-4, 277, 293, 299, 302, 311, 314, 321, 348, 350, 352, 353, *193*
Lomax, John Avery 346, 348
Lord, Albert B. 111, 267
Lotze, Rudolf 232, 249
Lowinsky, Edward E. 196
Lussy, Mathis 37

Maceda, José 88, 94, 96, 195-6, *195*
MacMillan, Ernest 107
Mahillon, Charles 197
Mahillon, Victor-Charles 31, 33, 197, 233, 339, 340, *197*
Malinowski, Bronislaw 72, 209, 242, 251, 255
Malm, William P. 9, 60, 314, 336, 352
Malthus, Thomas 47
Manuel, Peter 68, 69-71, 291, 305
Marcel-Dubois, Claudie 96, 97, 124, 198, *198*
Marcuse, Sibyl 199, *199*
Marx, Karl 191, 240
McAllester, David P. 15, 59, 60, 159, 319, 330, 336, 350, 406, *60*
McLeod, Norma 266, 280, 281
McPhee, Colin 88, 94, 96, 200-0`, *200*
Mead, Margaret 116
Menuhin, Yehudi 130, 282
Merriam, Alan P. 2, 12, 15, 43, 44, 45, 46, 54, 59, 60, 62, 64, 65-6, 67, 68, 69, 71, 72, 73, 74, 75, 76, 81, 85, 89, 93, 95, 96, 157, 202-3, 243, 251, 263, 267, 285, 286, 287, 291, 294, 299, 302, 303, 304, 308, 309, 310, 312, 313, 315, 317, 322, 328-9, 330, 332, 333, 335, 337, 350, 351, 352, 354, *60*, *202*
Metfessel, Milton 283, 288, 347
Meyer, Leonard B. 302
Miller, Geoffrey 47
Mittwoch, Eugen 189
Montagu, Jeremy 321

Morton, Leslie 191
Moyle, Alice 90, 136, 204-5, 266, *204*
Moyle, Richard 229, 281
Myers, Charles 90, 95, 96, 97, 206-8, 345, *206*
Myers, Helen 12, 81, 290

Nadel, Siegfried F. 42, 45, 47, 50, 96, 97, 209-10, *209*
Nettl, Bruno 9, 10, 14, 15, 30, 37, 43, 45, 46, 47, 49, 55, 57, 59, 64, 68, 92, 83, 96, 128, 211-12, 242, 260, 267, 268, 292, 293, 299, 303, 311, 317, 319, 322, 323, 324, 326, 330, 332, 336, 337, 351, 352, *211*
Nettl, Paul 176, 212, 251
Newton, Sir Isaac 21, 22, 27, 58, 339, *22*
Nketia, J.H. Kwabena 255

Orbell, Margaret 258, 278, 298, 316, 323

Paine, John K. 132
Pantaleoni, Hewitt 321
Parry, Milman 111
Paul, Oscar 34, 52, 103, 176, 251
Peel, J.D.Y. 28
Perlis, Vivian 57
Petri, Egon 158
Picken, Laurence 9, 35, 62, 95, 351
Piggott, Sir Francis Taylor 88, 96, 213
Pitt-Rivers, A.H. 20, 342
Pizarro, Franciso 19, *18*
Pöch, Rudolf 42
Polo, Marco 19, 339
Porter, James 68, 69-71, 73, 126
Post, Jennifer 268
Praetorius, Michael 32
Prime, Dalvanius 14
Pugh-Kitingan, Jaqueline 297-8
Putnam, Frederic W. 143

Ramón y Rivera, Luis Felipe 10, 87, 96, 97, 100, 214
Randel, Don 355
Reade, Winwood 30 ftnt 36
Reinhard, Kurt 35, 89, 96, 215, 249, 264, 349, 353, *215*

Rhodes, Wllard 59, 60, 89, 96, 106, 216-7, 289, 319, 349, 350, *60, 216*
Rice, Timothy 68-9, 333
Richter, Ernst Friedrich 52
Riemann, Hugo 34, 35, 249, 250, *34*
Ringer, Alexander 258-9, 315
Rivers, William Halse 207
Roberts, Helen Heffron 52, 53-4, 90, 94, 96, 122, 218-9, 251, 269, 317, 347, 348, *218*
Rouget, Gilbert 124
Rousseau, Jean Jacque 30, 47, 231, 340
Rubbra, Edmund 125
Rubinstein, Anton 34
Russell, Bertrand 21, 27, 57, 58, 333
Russell, Sir Charles 213

Sachs, Curt 33, 35, 39, 41, 42, 44, 45, 47, 50, 56, 62, 69, 95, 96, 117, 161, 165, 176, 184, 198, 220-1, 222, 223, 234, 238, 239, 244, 245, 248, 249, 251, 316, 335-6, 346, 348, 349, *220*
Sadie, Stanley 354, 345
Salisbury, Kevin 298
Sanderson, Rev. J.T. 227
Sandwich, Lord 30
Sapir, Edward 107, 116, 122, 219
Saul, Patrick 350
Schaeffner, André 89, 96, 97, 113, 198, 220, 222, *222*
Scheibe, Johann 45
Schmidt, Wilhelm 49
Schneider, Marius 41, 42, 45, 50, 96, 97, 124, 165, 223, 249, 316, 336, 351, *223*
Scholes, Percy 262
Schreker, Franz 176
Schumann, Clara 34, 116
Schünemann, Georg 39
Schursma, Ann 268
Seashore, Carl 282-3, 287, 288, 342, *279*
Seeger, Anthony 60 ftnt 150, 240, 303-4, 356
Seeger, Charles 54, 56-9, 60, 63, 64, 68, 72, 93, 96, 224-5, 251, 269, 270-1, 279, 283-4, 286, 287, 288, 300, 322, 331, 350, 351, *60, 224*
Seligman, Charles G. 209
Sendrey, Alfred 33, 35, 88, 96, 97, 226, *226*

Shankar, Ravi 130
Sharp, Cecil 11, 12, 48, 69, 84-5, 86, 96, 97, 109, 144, 174, 175, 177, 227-8, 259, 260, 262, 270, 272, 345, 346, 347, *227*
Simon, Artur 42 ftnt 70, 354
Slocombe, Marie 264
Smitz, Robert 196
Smyth, Mary W. 109
Spencer, Herbert 25, 27-30, 37, 43, 47, 48, 49, 342, *28*
Spitta, Philipp 37, 249, *36*
Stafford, William C. 31, 341
Stanford, Sir Charles 145
Steele, Joshua 229, 340
Stockmann, Doris 299-30
Strehlow, T.G.H. 136, 266
Stumpf, Carl 37, 39, 41, 42, 49, 95, 96, 97, 98, 117, 165, 189, 207, 230-3, 248, 249, 251, 264, 279, 282, 344, 345, *230*
Sully, James 37, 240, 250
Suppan, Wolfgang 128

Tagore, Rabindranath 101, 144
Tagore, Sourindro Mohun 31, 88, 197, 233-4, 281, *233*
Terry, Charles Sanford 178
Thompson, Stith 59
Tibbles, Thomas H. 190
Toch, Ernst 163
Tracey, Hugh Travers 89, 113, 235, 264, 350, *235*
Trân Van Khê 255
Tuki, Ishmael 266

Van Aalst, J.A. 88, 95, 96, 236, 344
Vaughan Williams, Ralph 20, 60, 85, 175, 192, 228, 272, 345, 349, *80*
Vega, Carlos 87, 95, 96, 100, 214, 237, *237*
Vikárius, László 111
Villoteau, G-A. 31
Voit, Paula 110

Wachsmann, Klaus 68, 89, 96, 165, 238-9, 249, *238*
Wagner, Richard 49
Wallaschek, Richard 42, 95, 96, 97, 188, 240-1, 250

Waterman, Richard A 59, 65, 89, 93, 94, 95, 96, 242-3, 251, 267, *242*
Wellesz, Egon 223 ftnt 323
Werner, Eric 88, 95, 96, 97, 244, *244*
Whitehead, Alfred 58
Wiener, Leo 108
Wild, Stephen 67, 356
Wilgus, D.K. 265
Willard, N.A. 31
Wiora, Walter 42, 96, 165, 245, 249, *245*
Wissler, Clark 122, 251
Wolf, Johannes 35, 39, 167, 189, 223, 244, 248, 249, *40*

Zemp, Hugo 282, 304, 306, 307

CPSIA information can be obtained at www.ICGtesting.com
Printed in the USA
LVOW022206281211

261405LV00001B/33/A